Crime Collection

CRIME COLLECTION

THE BUCK TAYLOR NOVELS:

CRIME INTERRUPTED

CRIME DELAYED

CRIME UNSOLVED

BY

CHUCK MORGAN

Contents

PART I

Buck Taylor Book I

Crime Interrupted

A BUCK TAYLOR NOVEL

BY

CHUCK MORGAN

Chapter One

Buck Taylor climbed over the parapet and in a crouch run, made his way to the front wall and knelt next to La Plata County Narcotics Office Terry Rubin. It was 5 AM on a hot July morning but the night air still had that little bit of coolness that comes from being in the mountains at 6,500 feet. Terry had located a great surveillance location on the roof of Guy's Auto Body Shop on Girard Street directly across the street from Colorado Overland Transportation.

Colorado Overland Transportation was a small trucking and distribution company located in Durango, Colorado and for the last couple days had been the subject of a huge surveillance net that had been dropped over it thanks to Buck and a host of local and federal law enforcement agencies. This had not been an easy task, coordinating all these varied elements in a relatively small mountain community without raising the suspicions of the locals. So far Buck was confident they had pulled it off.

Buck Taylor was 6 foot-tall and weighed in at 185 lbs. Very little of it flab for a 58-year-old man. Buck's hair was salt and pepper, with what seemed like a lot more salt than pepper and he wore it slightly longer than was typically the fashion of the day. Buck was always pleased when he looked in the mirror, since other than getting older, he was in as good a shape as he had been when he played defensive linebacker for the Gunnison High School Cowboys, back what seemed like a long time ago. He still tried to jog 5 miles every day when he could, and he tried to ride his mountain bike every weekend, weather permitting. The bike was always hanging off the back of his state provided Jeep Grand Cherokee. Except for a couple sore knees, coming mostly from age, Buck was in good shape, which was important in his line of work.

Buck Taylor was an Investigative Agent for the Colorado Bureau of Investigation. He was currently assigned to the CBI field office in Grand Junction, Colorado, but he hadn't really been in the office much during the past year. Somehow, he had become the favorite "go to" guy for the Governor of Colorado, Richard J Kennedy, who was in fact one of "those" Kennedys. The Governor had been in office about a year and half and Buck had been instrumental in closing several high-profile investigations during that period, that made the Governor look good and as a result, when a situation came up that might get a little hairy, the Governor always asked to have Buck assigned.

And that was how Buck ended up on a garage rooftop at 5 AM on a hot July morning. A week ago, Buck was in Teller County, working with the Teller County Sheriff's Office on a multiple victim homicide. The case had stalled while they waited for the State Crime Lab in Pueblo to complete some DNA testing and with a little bit of down time, the first he had had in a while, Buck had been standing hip deep in the South Platte River in Eleven Mile Canyon playing a real nice 16" German Brown Trout when his phone signaled that it was time to stop.

Chapter Two

Fly fishing was one of the hobbies Buck had used during the past year to help him get through the loss of his wife of 35 years. If you ask Buck, he will tell you that he fell in love with Lucinda Torres the first day of their senior year in high school. Lucy, on the other hand, would always tell people that Buck stalked her all senior year before she finally gave in, mostly to shut her friends up, and agreed to go to the movies with him. She had always considered him just another jock, another football player who was too full of himself. What she found on that first date was a shy, unassuming gentleman, for lack of a better word, who it seemed, cared more about pleasing her than in bragging about his prowess on the football field. She would tell people it was love at first sight that had taken a year to accomplish. From that day forward, they were inseparable.

During senior year Buck had been approached by several college football scouts who wanted to sign him to play for their schools. Gunnison High School was a pretty small school back in 1978 and Buck and his family were amazed at how many schools had noticed him, but for Buck college just wasn't in the cards. Buck hated school and spent a lot of time getting himself out of trouble instead of getting an education. When he found something that interested him, he had no problem learning all he could about the subject, but regular school work just bored him. After several long heartfelt discussions, first with Lucinda and then with his parents, he had decided to join the Army after graduation. Surprisingly, no one was surprised.

Buck had spent four years after high school in the army and by the time his enlistment was up he had been promoted to First Sergeant. He had spent three years of his enlistment in the Military Police and had really taken to police work. That was when he decided to apply for a position with the Gunnison County Sheriff's Department. Since he was already well known in the county he had no trouble getting a position as a patrolman. He proposed to Lucy on the night he received the call that he had gotten the position. His career was now set, and his life was set, and he made the most of his time with the Gunnison County Sheriff's Office, eventually becoming the Under Sheriff in Charge of the Investigations Division and coming to the attention of the Colorado Bureau of Investigations.

Buck had worked with the CBI on several investigations inside the county and had earned the respect of the investigators he had worked with. As twilight started to fall on Buck's career and knowing that unless he wanted to go into politics and run for Sheriff, that he had reached the highest position in the Sheriff's office that he could obtain. He really loved his job, but when the offer came in from the CBI, he sat down with Lucy and had a long heart to heart talk. He had spent 17 years in the Sheriff's Office and always figured he would retire from that job. They had three children, two in high school and one not too far behind and he was a well-respected member of the community. Did he really have the right to disrupt all their lives and pick up and move to someplace else and start all over? The kids had friends, Lucy owned a small deli/ice cream parlor and they had a good life. He could stick it out for another 10 years and retire and they could travel and see the world like they had always planned. Twice he turned down the offer from CBI, although more and more he felt like he was trapped behind a desk instead of doing what he loved, which was investigating crime.

The final offer came directly from Tom Cole, the then Director of the CBI. Buck always remembered the day. The Denver Broncos had just lost another game, the third one in a row and his friends had all packed up and headed home when there was a knock at the front door. Now, anyone who lives in a small community knows that no one ever used the front door, and no one ever knocks. Who could this possibly be this late on a Sunday evening?

Buck answered the door and was taken aback to see the Director of the Colorado Bureau of Investigations standing on his front porch. The Director smiled and said, "Before you close the door in my face, please listen to my offer."

Buck invited him in and he and Lucy sat on the couch and listened as the Director laid out his plan. He was opening a new Branch office in Grand Junction that would house five agents and a small forensics unit. Buck could continue to live in Gunnison but would have to report into the office in Grand Junction twice a month, otherwise he would be free to work out of his house. No disruption in his life other than having to spend some time on the road as his investigations warranted. He would mostly work alone, but he would have the resources of all the branch offices at his disposal.

Before Buck could say a word, Lucinda said, "Buck, this is what you have been waiting for, a chance to be a real investigator again. You have to take this." That was one of the things that made him love Lucy every day. She always knew what he was thinking and she always understood what drove him. She had nailed it this time. Buck looked at the Director and replied, "Well I guess it's settled, looks like you have a new investigator on your team."

That was seventeen years ago and essentially what led Buck to be on this rooftop at 5 AM on a hot July morning.

Chapter Three

The sky was Colorado blue without a cloud in it and the fish had been biting furiously all morning long when Buck hooked in the big Brown Trout. After a good fight he felt the trout finally give in and he scooped it up in the net. What a beauty it was. The spots on the side of its body glowed in the noon day sun and Buck just held it in the net and admired it for a minute.

Buck loved fly fishing. He was a firm believer in the old adage that time spent fly fishing was not deducted from your life clock. In the year since Lucy's death he often wished he could have gotten her interested in fly fishing. He would have liked to have the extra time with her. He also relished the fact that when you are standing hip deep in the middle of a river you had to concentrate on fly fishing. Fly fishing isn't complicated, but it is complex, and it takes all your focus. When you are casting a tiny bug imitation to a big rising trout, you must be focused. And once focused, everything else just clears out of your mind. For a minute it is just you and the trout. All the other day to day stuff goes away.

He had just pulled his phone out of his wader pocket to take a picture when the phone lit up with an incoming call. It was his day off and he almost didn't answer it, but that was never a good career move when the Director of the Colorado Bureau of Investigations was calling. Buck hit the answer button.

"Hope I didn't get you in the middle of something important." Said the Director, Kevin Jackson, before Buck could even say hello.

"No sir, just doing a little fishing until we get the DNA back from the lab."

"Good" the Director replied. "I hate to interrupt a man while he's fishing, but this is important."

Buck listened carefully as the Director explained the situation. Since Buck was on hold in Teller County the Director wanted him to head down to Durango to meet with the La Plata County Sheriff. It seems the Sheriff and her team had come across a possible drug distribution network working out of a small Durango based shipping company and it could have possible Mexican Cartel links. The Sheriff was worried that this could morph into something big and she wasn't sure she had the budget or the manpower to run a full investigation. She was requesting help from the CBI. He could use his own judgment on whom to involve if the information checked out, but he wanted it played low key until that decision was made. No sense getting the locals all fired up about drug cartels moving into their small town until all the facts were in.

Buck hung up the phone, removed the trout from the net and held it in the water facing upstream to revive it and watched as it streaked back towards the pool he had pulled it from. The sight of trout streaking through the water never failed to mesmerize Buck. He gave a silent prayer of thanks to the "river gods" for allowing him the privilege to catch the fish he caught today and headed for his Jeep. He hung his wet waders on a hanger he had fashioned so they could dry while hanging in the car and he broke down his four-piece 5 weight Orvis Clearwater fly rod and placed it back in its case. Finally finished stowing his gear, he took one last look at the river, got in his car and headed back down the dirt road he had followed in a couple hours ago. It had been a good day. Time to go to work.

Chapter Four

Durango, Colorado, population about 18,500 sits along the Animas River in southwest Colorado, not too far from the border with New Mexico. It is the county seat of La Plata County and the jumping off point for the Durango and Silverton Narrow Gauge Railroad. A dramatic train ride from the city of Durango to the City of Silverton, topping out at over 12,000 feet in elevation. Mostly a quiet mountain town until Fort Lewis College is in session and then the local police have their hands full with underage drinking and minor drug issues.

An outdoorsmen's paradise where hunting and fishing abound and the home of the Purgatory ski area. Lately more and more people called it the Durango Mountain Resort. I guess they don't like the idea of skiing in Purgatory although the locals still call it Purgatory, mostly out of a sense of history and probably to piss off the new comers who changed the name. By all accounts a perfect place to raise a family and live the good mountain life. Durango has all the amenities of a larger city in a self-contained small package. The kind of place where everyone knew everyone else and knew a lot about each other's business. Not the kind of place that a Mexican Drug Cartel would try to use as a base of operations.

First thing the following morning Buck met with the local Sheriff, Elizabeth Sinclair, and her Narcotics Officer, Terry Rubin. Liz, as she preferred to be called, was a seasoned twenty-year veteran of the Sheriff's Department who decided to run for the office when long time Sheriff Ed Maxwell decided to retire and go fishing in Florida. Liz had easily won the election since she ran unopposed and was now in her second term at the helm. She was smart, dedicated, the mother of two and grandmother of four and had been married to Ross for almost 30 years.

Buck had met Liz on several occasions and was extremely impressed with her knowledge and experience. He had never met Terry Rubin before and was surprised when the young man, probably in his early twenties, walked into the room. Of course, being Buck's age made pretty much everyone younger than him, but this young fella looked like he had just graduated from high school. He stood 5'9 and weighed about 150 lbs. soaking wet. He had a bald head and a small scruff of what you might call a beard on his chin. The most striking thing were the tattoos that completely covered both arms.

Buck grabbed a cup of coffee from the counter in the meeting room and introduced himself to Terry. After a little small talk, they all sat down at the conference table and settled in for a review of what they had so far.

"Buck" the Sheriff started. "Thanks for getting down here so quickly. I only spoke with Director Jackson yesterday morning."

"No problem, Liz. Happy to help."

The Sheriff smiled. "Terry, why don't you take Buck through what we have so far."

Terry pulled a pair of reading glasses from his pocket and opened the file he had in front of him.

"The information we received came to us last Wednesday from a local drug dealer and meth head I busted." Terry went on to explain that Carlos Montoya, AKA "Scratch" because he was constantly scratching at his arms until he was nothing but scabs, had been busted trying to sell thirty Oxycodone pills to a local high schooler and had been dumb enough to do it right in front of the kid's parents, who immediately called the Sheriff's Office. The family lived just outside the city limits which is how the Sheriff's Office got the call. Since Terry had had dealings with "Scratch" before, he knew exactly where to find him and arrested him in Fanto Park with the help of a Durango Police Department patrolman.

Buck held up his hand. "How screwed up is this guy and can you believe anything he has to say?"

Terry thought for a minute and replied, "In all the time he has been around, and this is not the first time he has tipped us to something going down, he has never lied to us."

"Keep going officer."

Terry now dug into his notes. "Right after we brought him in he told me he had something big to tell me if we could keep him from going up to the state penitentiary in Florence. He wanted to stay in Durango to serve whatever time he got. I told him I would see what I could do, but the info had to be good. Really good."

Terry went on the explain that "Scratch" had told him that he had gotten the drugs from a local company fronting for the Sonoma Cartel and that he had seen huge crates full of drugs in a warehouse right here in Durango and that they were planning to start shipping these drugs all over the western and southwestern US in the next week. He didn't know exactly when but soon. What also came out was that he wasn't supposed to have the drugs, but he had put a bunch of pills in his pocket for safe keeping while he watched the Mexican prisoners break the pills into small packages and hide them in kids toys.

Buck started to say something, but the Sheriff cut him off. "We are not sure what the Mexican prisoners is all about, but we think they may have a small labor force of illegals that they keep in the back of the warehouse, almost like prisoners. One of the clerks at the grocery store says that one of the employees of the shipping company came in the other day and bought a huge amount of food and water."

Chapter Five

Buck nodded, and Terry continued the briefing. Terry had set up a surveillance nest at his Brother in Law's auto body shop which was right across the street from the trucking company and with the help of two other deputies had been watching the company for the past couple nights. They noted several trucks coming in at very early hours in the morning and unloading several large crates. Colorado Overland Transportation was a small shipping company that had a decent amount of business, mostly local and regional shipping until last week. This week there are nine semi-trailers in the yard and about a dozen people loading the trailers. Seems like business had suddenly boomed for the small trucking company.

Everything up until the night before last looked like typical trucking business and we had no way to see what was in the crates. That all changed. At about four AM one of the laborers or prisoners, whatever you prefer, tried to make a break for the fence, which is always kept locked. As the deputy on surveillance watched, it looked like he threw something over the fence before he was tackled by two big goons and beat senseless. The two goons hauled him back inside and they closed the freight doors and locked the place down.

The deputy, hoping not to blow the surveillance, waited for

about an hour and then left his post to see if he could find what was thrown over the fence. At this point, Terry slid a box across the table to Buck. What Buck was looking at was what looked like a brand-new action figure in a sealed box. He opened the box, pulled out the figure and looked at it carefully.

"Pull off the head," said Terry.

Buck grabbed the head and with a slight twist pulled it off. He then turned the figure upside down and a pill fell out from inside. First just one, but the more he shook the figure the more pills fell out until he had a pile of about twenty pills lying on the table in front of him. To say he was surprised would be an understatement. Buck had seen a lot of weird things during his many years in law enforcement, but this was a new one.

The Sheriff got a very serious look on her face and said "Now you see why we called you guys. This could be huge. What do you think?"

Buck thought for a minute before answering. His mind had moved into what he called investigation mode and he was already running several scenarios around in his head. He took a long sip of his now cold coffee. "This could be a big problem." He looked at Terry. "Officer, you have done some good work here. We need to nail down the shipping schedule and I need to make a couple phone calls. Let's meet again at three o'clock. Is there an office I can use?"

Terry excused himself and Buck and the Sheriff walked back to an empty office just outside the bullpen. The Sheriff looked concerned. She had seen Buck move into Investigation mode and when it happened things moved quickly.

"How big a problem do you think we have?" She asked. Although she already knew this was serious.

"I think we have a big problem. If this is the Sonoma Cartel, then they have moved into the US a lot faster than anyone anticipated and that won't be good for anyone. We are going to have to move a bunch of people into town and keep this whole thing quiet as we can while we do it. Please keep the team that you have on this on a short leash until we get this worked out and let's keep observing the warehouse. We need to know if anything changes that might indicate the timeline is speeding up."

With that Buck walked into his temporary office and closed the door.

Chapter Six

Colorado Overland Transportation was a small company that suddenly had a great deal of business. The small trucking company was started 5 years ago by longtime friends Hector Vegas and Richard Dillon. This was their third attempt a starting a business together and the only one that seems to have grown legs and was still in operation. Hector's mom had died a few years back and had left him a small inheritance, about $45000, and after talking with his buddy Dick, they decided to buy a truck and become truck drivers.

Surprisingly, even to them, they found a little underdeveloped niche and concentrated on delivering goods to shops and businesses that operated along the Colorado-New Mexico border. Now a lot of this area was part of the Southern Ute reservation and as it turned out a lot of companies didn't like doing business in "Indian Land." That never bothered Hector and Dick. They had grown up in this area and knew how to make things work so that the money kept coming in. Within a couple years they had grown to four trucks and four drivers and had for the most part gotten off the road and into the office of the new warehouse they had leased.

Both men were married, Hector to his 3rd wife, and they

each had a couple kids. They each bought a nice middle-class house in Durango before the real estate boom hit and prices went through the roof. All in all, they looked like two guys who had finally found their little piece of the American dream. They had bank accounts, belonged to the PTO and the Elks Club and had even helped start the Downtown Business Association, which was great for them since the little mom and pop businesses in downtown Durango were their bread and butter. Every year at the holidays they contributed to the downtown holiday lighting display and their wives helped set up the annual Winter Festival. All outward appearances said these guys were fine upstanding members of the community. In the last ten years, they hadn't even gotten as much as a parking ticket.

There was nothing in their backgrounds that would have led anyone in law enforcement to look twice at these guys. At least that is what they had both been hoping for when the lure of big money came walking in their door one day a month back in the guise of Ernesto Salvatore. Ernesto pulled into the yard in a brand-new Mercedes AMC turbo, which immediately got the attention of their Office Manager Claire Ringsby. Ernesto walked into their office, confident as you please, and asked to speak to the owner. Claire, sensing something good, ran into the back and pulled Hector off the phone. Hector was the only owner in the office. Dick had gone to Mancos to deal with a problem client and wouldn't be back for a while.

Hector walked up front and extended his hand, "Hector Vegas, I'm one of the owners, how can I help you today?"

"Ernesto Salvatore, Attorney at Law. I represent a client who is looking to give a lot of business to a local trucking company and after doing a little research, believes you might fit the bill. Is there someplace we can talk privately?"

Hector led Ernesto back to his private office and closed the door after telling Claire he was not to be disturbed. Hector had seen "Slicks" before and he sized up Ernesto. Expensive shoes, expensive suit and a briefcase that probably cost as much as Hector's car. Definitely a "Slick", Hector thought to himself. But if his client could afford this mouthpiece then maybe they could be in for some big money. Hector decided to listen to what the lawyer had to say.

Hector sat down on the edge of his desk and pointed to the chair. Ernesto put his briefcase on the desk and sat in the visitor's chair and looked at Hector.

"Mr. Vegas," began the lawyer. "I am not here to blow smoke up your ass. My client is willing to invest heavily in your business and towards your continued success provided you are smart enough to see a great opportunity when it pops up in front of you. Once a month my client will be bringing in shipments of toys and other goods from Mexico and Central America. They will arrive by truck, be offloaded into your warehouse, redistributed in additional trucks that we will provide you with and the drivers to drive them. We will supply all the laborers to do the redistribution and cover all the costs for their upkeep and for this we will pay you and your partner one hundred thousand dollars a month each. All you need to do is make sure that this happens on schedule and that this whole operation is kept as quiet as possible."

Ernesto sat back in the chair and looked at Hector. Hector had heard a lot of stories in his day but this one was over the top. This guy just offered him and Dick one hundred grand each to basically do nothing except store some stuff and watch a schedule. What was the catch? And so he asked.

Ernesto didn't seem taken aback at all with the question. He explained that his client was a wealthy importer who was interested in expanding his import business into the Southwestern US and needed a discreet business partner to make this possible. He told him that his client had many competitors who would love to see him fail, thus the secrecy. Ernesto removed a laptop from his briefcase and open the cover turning it so that it was facing Hector. The screen was blank. He then looked directly into Hector's eyes.

"One thing you should know. This decision has already been made for you. You cannot reject this offer, all you can do is accept and follow the rules."

He pushed the enter button on the laptop and on the screen was his wife and youngest daughter in the kitchen of his house baking cookies. The picture was from inside his house. How could that be? Ernesto pushed the enter key again and the screen now switched to someplace in the desert. The screen showed a man kneeling on the ground with his hands tied behind his back. As Hector watched in horror another man walked up behind the kneeling man and with one swipe of a machete chopped off his head. Hector could not believe his eyes. Was this for real? It couldn't be, could it?

Ernesto closed the laptop and sat quietly, letting what Hector had just seen sink in. After a minute, Ernesto spoke. "That man was a Federal Police Officer assigned to a small town just south of the border. He had agreed to work for us and then had a sudden change of heart. We took care of the problem and that changed heart is no longer beating. Now we are not saying that the same thing could happen to you or your partner or your beautiful families. All you need to do is accept our money every month, keep your mouth shut and act like nothing is happening. If you can do that we will get along just fine."

With that Ernesto put away his laptop, removed two bank

account receipts for a bank in the Cayman Islands, each showing a deposit of one hundred thousand dollars and put his business card on the desk, closed his briefcase and stood up. Hector just sat there stunned. His mouth still hanging partly open, unable to speak.

"Tomorrow a construction crew will arrive to build some dormitory rooms in the back of the warehouse. In the next couple days, you will receive nine more slightly used semis and nine forty-foot trailers, all properly licensed, insured and registered. You will continue to operate as normal. Nothing changes. Someone will be in touch with you in a week or so with the first schedule. Do this right and you will be rich men and have access to all your wildest dreams. Mention this to anyone or damn up the schedule and you will live to regret your life. Have a nice day, Mr. Vegas."

With that Ernesto opened the door and walked out of the office, said a fond farewell to Claire, got in his car and drove away. Claire walked back to find Hector sitting at his desk looking dazed.

"Hector are you alright?" she asked sounding very concerned.

Hector looked at her and told her he was fine and that he didn't want to be disturbed until Dick got back. Claire left his office not certain what, if anything, had just happened.

Chapter Seven

Buck sat back in the chair in his temporary office. He had his fingertips together making a small steeple out of his hands and he had his eyes closed. Buck was not sleeping. What he was doing was organizing the investigation in his head. They had a lot of work to do in a minimal amount of time and he wasn't going to have a lot of time for organization once he started. The yellow pad on his desk sat empty.

Going to war against a local street gang was hard enough but going to war against a cartel, especially the Sonoma Cartel, was incredibly dangerous and Buck was going to be putting a lot of people in the crosshairs. This whole operation had to be done in secret and his entire team would have to have their identities protected. Cartels had notoriously long memories and even longer reach. No one will be safe.

Every federal law enforcement and intelligence agency had issued notices about the Sonoma Cartel during the past year. According to what Buck knew the Sonoma Cartel was a relatively young organization that had suddenly burst on the scene about two years ago. It was run by a major psychopath named Carlos Rojas. Rojas had been a minor player in the Los Angeles drug world when he was arrested and deported back to Mexico. He found a home with several of the cartels as his reputation for brutality grew. He became almost a legend. There was no one Rojas wouldn't kill for a price and it was said that sometimes he didn't need a price to kill. His signature was headless, limbless torsos, left on doorsteps, for all the world to see and to send a message that disloyalty would not be tolerated.

It wasn't long before Rojas got tired of working for someone else and he started turning on his overlords. He recruited a huge crew of psychopaths with the same penchant for violence he had and started taking out the leadership of the various cartels he had freelanced for, taking over territory and amassing a huge fortune in a very short time. It was estimated that he was personally worth over a hundred million dollars and his cartel had a bigger budget than a lot of third world countries.

The more Rojas moved forward, the more bodies piled up. He didn't care if you were a cop, a judge or a mom with three kids. If you crossed him, you were dead. It was a very simple plan. The Mexican government was powerless to stop him. The US government also feared that Rojas had his hand so far into the Mexican government that they would never be able to stop him.

Buck put his hands down and picked up his phone. Director Jackson answered on the second ring.

"How bad is it?" The Director asked.

"I think it's about as bad as it could get. The Sonoma Cartel has possibly moved into Durango."

There was silence on the other end of the phone. Buck just waited. "Are you absolutely certain? Up til now there has been no sign of them moving into the US. This will change the game significantly if you are right. Damn!! Do you have a plan?"

"I am working on that, but the problem is the timeline is real short."

Buck went on to give the Director as much of a briefing as he had been able to put together, explaining the need for secrecy, and laying out the bare basics of a plan. There were a lot of moving parts and when he was done the Director said, "Alright. It doesn't sound like we have enough evidence to get a search warrant, so we will need to put some assets in place who can get that. Do you think the Sheriff has enough to get a local judge to issue a wiretap warrant?"

"I think we can get that. Once we show the judge what we have, it should be enough to scare the shit out of him. That's usually a pretty good motivator."

"Ok", said the Director. "Start that ball rolling. I need to speak to the Attorney General and the Governor."

"Right. I was also going to call my local contacts at DEA, FBI and ICE. We are going to need all the help we can get." We are meeting again this afternoon at 3. I will send you a number so you can ring in. Later."

Chapter Eight

Buck hung up from the Director and speed dialed Hank Clancy. Hank was the Special Agent in Charge of the FBI's Denver Office. Buck had worked with Hank on several occasions and they seemed to hit it off. Hank was a hardnosed, by the book agent and Buck knew if he could convince Hank of what they had, he would have no trouble with the others he needed involved.

Hank answered his phone on the second ring. "I always hate it when your name pops up on my caller ID. It's never good. How the hell are you Buck?"

Doesn't anyone say hello anymore?

"If you hate it, then this is really going to make your day." Buck proceeded to tell Hank the overview of the situation. Like the Director, Hank didn't interrupt until Buck took a breath.

"Damn Buck" He seemed to be hearing those two words together a lot today. "This is our worst fear come true. Washington is going to go nuts. Are you certain of the connection'?

"As best we can. We have an iffy witness, surveillance video of a lot of activity in a tiny company and a doll full of drugs thrown over the fence by an illegal who we can't talk to because they probably either killed him already or beat him up pretty good. We will try to get a warrant to go electronic, but we are really on a short timeline here."

"Alright. Here is what we need to do," said Hank. "I need to call Washington and fill them in. I will talk to the US Attorney General and see if we can use a FISA warrant so we maintain secrecy all around. Talk to the rest of your local network and I will talk to you in a while. Do you have anything planned for strategizing yet?"

A FISA warrant is a secret document issued by the United States Foreign Intelligence Surveillance Court, which was authorized in 1978 by an act of Congress. Its primary function is to issue FISA Warrants authorizing secret electronic surveillance of suspected foreign spies operating inside the US borders. Due to increases in terrorism, the secret court had also, of late, been issuing warrants to surveil any bad actor, foreign or domestic, who posed an imminent threat to the people of the United States. The Sonoma Cartel certainly qualified.

"Yeah. Three o'clock in the Sheriff's conference room."

"Good," replied Hank. "I will try to get back to you before that. Damn. I really do hate when you call." Hank clicked off.

Buck wrote down the next name on his yellow pad and dialed the next number. Jessica Gonzales, DEA Agent in Charge of the Grand Junction field office, answered her phone.

"Buck Taylor. How the hell are you brother? It's been a long time."

"Hey, Jess. Good to hear your voice. You doing anything right now? I have a little problem and could use your help."

Jess replied. "I'm not going to like this am I, Buck?"

"No Jess. You're going to really hate it."

Once again Buck went through his briefing and once again he got the same response.

"Damn Buck, this is huge. We have been looking at these guys for months and thought they were contained in Mexico. This is gonna cause a shit storm."

Buck liked Jess. She didn't hold back on how she felt, and she had the mouth of a truck driver. When the shit hit the fan there was no better person to have covering your ass. She was a tough as they come and incredibly resourceful. And unlike a lot of her counterparts, she had no problem working with the locals. Sometimes it seemed like she almost enjoyed it.

Jess said. "Let me talk to some of my people and see if we can get some corroboration from the field. I can't believe they could get this set up this fast without there being some kind of chatter about it."

The conversation Buck had with Robert Townsend the local ICE Agent in Charge went pretty much the same way, but of course, Townsend's questions were more indicative of his position as lead enforcer of immigration laws.

"Buck, any idea how they were able to sneak a bunch of people into Durango without drawing attention to themselves? Seems like we may have a hole in our system."

"Right now, Bob, we are too early into this to know anything for certain. Hopefully, once we get a little deeper we can find the hole and plug it up."

"Okay. Let me get some people into play and I will get back to you in a couple hours. Thanks for reading me in on this Buck, much appreciated."

Buck sat back and checked his watch. Already past lunch time and he had about an hour and a half until he needed to meet with the Sheriff again. Time to grab a bite to eat.

Chapter Nine

Buck left the Sheriff's Department, hopped in his car, turned left out of the parking lot, turned left on US 550 and headed north. At 7th Street, he turned right until he got to Main Avenue, turned left and pulled into the first parking space he found. Just down the street was his lunch destination. The La Bon Cafe.

Buck didn't speak a lick of French but he knew one thing, the La Bon Cafe was neither La Bon whatever that meant or a cafe. What it was, was a 20-foot-wide hole in the wall, sitting between a local bookstore and a real estate office. Mostly it was a bar with about fifteen stools and six small tables along one wall. It was dark, musty and usually smelled like stale beer, amongst other fine cooking aromas. However, what it lost in atmosphere it made up for by having the best burgers in Durango.

Jimmy Palumbo looked up from where he was wiping the bar down after the lunch rush and blinked twice when he heard the front door open.

"Son of a gun, that looks just like Buck Taylor, in the flesh. But I must be dreaming cause he ain't been around in a couple years to visit his old pal Jimmy." Nobody says hello anymore.

"Jimmy is that you or is that your older, fatter brother? How the hell are you and how's it hanging?" Buck responded.

"Same as always." Jimmy replied, "About a foot long give or take." Jimmy laughed, he loved that line and he bellowed every time he used it, which thankfully wasn't often. Then Jimmy walked around the bar and gave Buck the biggest bear hug he'd had in years, or probably since the last time he saw Jimmy.

Jimmy Palumbo, now here was a real character. Jimmy was a bear of a man. Six feet six and two hundred seventy pounds and a good bit of it still muscle. He had gray hair tied up in a small ponytail and a neatly trimmed gray beard. He was dressed as always, jeans, T-shirt, that usually had a rude saying on it, but you usually couldn't read it because of the full apron he wore. Jimmy, with his girlfriend Loraine, were the proprietors, bartenders and as he liked to say, "head chefs of this fine establishment."

Jimmy was a transplant from Detroit by way of Southern California. At least that was the story most people heard. Although no one ever got the true story, it was told, mostly as legend, that Jimmy once rode with the Hell's Angels in Southern California and had to bug out when things got a little hot with the law. And he definitely looked the part. He had tattoos on every piece of visible skin and he had a very light scar on the side of his face, which was only visible when he shaved off his beard which hardly ever happened. However, Jimmy's appearance and his blood-stained apron made for quite a picture.

There was a soft side to Jimmy as well, which mostly only the locals got to see. Each year around the holidays, Jimmy would open his place and serve free food to the homeless and less fortunate. A charity event never happened in town that Jimmy wasn't a part of. And if anyone suffered an illness or a disaster, Jimmy was the first one in line to lend a hand, whatever it took. Deep under all that outside bravado was a simple man with a heart of gold.

Buck grabbed a seat at the bar and Jimmy threw a huge burger patty on the grill. Jimmy never asked you your order. If you were sitting at the bar or a table, you were there for a burger. That's all Jimmy sold. He didn't have chicken or salads and he definitely didn't have anything gluten-free or vegan. Jimmy was all meat and French fries. Sometimes this surprised the tourists but the locals all knew the program and at lunchtime, the bar was usually packed, and Jimmy would be standing behind the bar at the open grill, sweating, regaling folks with tall tales and cooking up a storm. Loraine, his longtime girlfriend, usually was at the register, taking in cash and handing out to go orders. They were quite a team.

Jimmy set a tall glass of Coke in front of Buck then turned back to the grill.

"Where's Loraine?" Buck asked.

Jimmy responded without turning from the grill. "Her momma had a heart attack about two weeks back and Loraine went back to Detroit for a while to take care of her since her brother is a worthless piece of shit. She's supposed to be back a week from Sunday." Jimmy flipped Buck's burger and sprinkled it with a little salt and pepper.

Jimmy looked over his shoulder and said. "We were sure sorry to hear about your wife. Ya doin ok?"

Buck's eyes got a little misty. Funny how a year had passed and that still happened sometimes when he thought of their time together. "Yeah, mostly good. Still hard to believe she's been gone almost a year now."

"Loraine was all broken up when we heard. She always liked

Lucy. We kept waiting to hear about a service, but no one knew anything. You keep it private?"

"It was supposed to be. Lucy didn't want a service. She wasn't much about religion and it was just like her to want to keep things low key. She never liked being the center of attention. We had agreed that I would scatter her ashes in the Gunnison River. There was a little spot with a handicapped fishing dock and she used to love to have me wheel her down there and we would just sit for hours and she would watch the birds. She really loved that spot."

Buck started to choke up a little. He took a sip of his Coke and composed his thoughts.

Jimmy said. "Hey, it's ok Buck, you don't need to relive it. Sorry man."

"No. It's ok. It gets easier each time I talk about it."

"I made plans with the kids to scatter the ashes early one Sunday morning. It was just supposed to be family. I should have known something was up. The park was never that busy on a Sunday morning. We all gathered on the dock, the kids and the grandkids and Lucy's brother and his family and her mom. Her dad had passed a couple years before and her other sister was out of the country. We all said a few words, and everyone got to sprinkle some of the ashes. When we finished and turned to head for the cars, we were stunned. There must have been three hundred people standing quietly behind us. I don't know how they all gathered so quietly. I guess word had gotten out that we were going to be there and everyone who knew her showed up. It was amazing. People had brought food and it turned into a huge picnic. Lucy would have loved it."

Jimmy handed Buck a handful of napkins and Buck wiped the tears from his face.

"Thanks for sharing, man. I can see that was hard." Jimmy

turned back to the grill and used the bar towel to wipe the tears from his eyes. It was quite a sight.

34

Chapter Ten

Turning from the grill, Jimmy walked over to where Buck was sitting and leaned in. "You on the job?" he said, almost in a whisper. Buck and Jimmy went back a long way and sometimes Jimmy had some useful information to share and Buck knew he could trust Jimmy to keep quiet.

Buck leaned in a little closer so that the four other customers still in the bar couldn't hear.

"Yeah. Working on something with the county. What have you heard about a large distribution network being set up in Durango?"

Jimmy turned back to the grill. "You want cheddar cheese?" Buck nodded yes. Jimmy came back to the table and set the plate down in front of Buck. The burger was a huge half-pound of some of the best beef Buck had ever tasted, topped with lettuce and tomato and a mile-high pile of golden-brown fries. It looked like it could feed a family of four. Buck dug in not realizing how hungry he had actually been.

Jimmy walked over to the register and checked out two of his last four customers and refilled the beer glasses for the other two and came back around the bar.

"Can't confirm anything, but Dick Dillon was in here a couple weeks ago, really pissed and drinking pretty hard. Kept putting his head in his hands and crying. Couple times he asked God to make sure his family didn't get killed and how if he ever got out of this he was going to kick the shit out of Hector and that he didn't want any part of it. Finally had to call his wife to come get him before he fell down and hurt himself."

"His wife say anything?" Buck asked.

"Just that he and Hector had a fight about a new business partner and Dick was scared. She didn't know why and I didn't want to push her. Was gonna mention it to the Chief next time I saw him but then this thing with Loraine's mom hit and I pretty much forgot about it. You think this might have something to do with what you are working?"

Buck knew that whatever he said to Jimmy would stay right here. Buck had first met Jimmy fifteen years ago during a homicide investigation. Buck was still new with CBI and he was working with his mentor, Phil Mitchell, a grizzled, seasoned veteran of forty years of police work and one of the best investigators Buck had ever worked with. One night he and Phil accompanied two Denver Homicide Detectives to interview a known drug dealer about his possible involvement in a recent murder. This was only going to be an interview and it should have been simple, but it went south in a big hurry. The guy they went to interview was waiting for the cops with a couple of his friends and had no plans to go back to prison.

As soon as they walked into the location and announced themselves, all hell broke loose. The two Denver narcotics detectives were both hit and seriously wounded, Buck dove for cover behind a desk but Phil wasn't that lucky. The first round went in just under his armpit, where his ballistic vest didn't cover. The second round hit him in the neck. The coroner would later say that either round would have killed him instantly. Buck was pinned down and returning fire when this mountain of a man who looked like one badass biker came charging in firing his weapon as he was going. At one point a bullet raked across his cheek leaving a deep bloody gash but he kept shooting.

By the time the cavalry arrived, the four bad guys were dead. Buck had been hit twice in the chest, but the vest had protected him. It still hurt like hell. The big guy who saved him hadn't been wearing a vest. He was lying against another desk, with blood dripping down the side of his face and three gunshot wounds in his chest and right arm. Buck had been putting pressure on his chest wound when the ambulance arrived. Every day since he thought about how Jimmy Palumbo's heartbeat kept getting weaker and weaker the harder he pressed to slow the flow of blood.

Jimmy was a ten-year veteran of the Denver Police Department and had been working undercover with the drug gang for the past two years. He wasn't even supposed to be at the location that night but had forgotten a gift for Loraine that he had left in the office. He had gone back for it and had just walked in the back door when he heard the detectives announce themselves at the front door and shooting started. He had no choice but to get involved.

Jimmy was in recovery for ten days and in rehab for ten months before he was told he could go back to work. The doctors said that if it wasn't for Buck, Jimmy would have probably bled out. Jimmy never forgot that. By the time rehab was over Loraine had convinced Jimmy that maybe a change of scenery was in order. Reluctantly Jimmy agreed but he never once looked back. Jimmy and Loraine ended up in Durango, after bouncing around Colorado for a few years, fell in love with the town and bought a small closed restaurant and bar.

Buck checked his watch and got off the stool. Even though Jimmy would never charge him a dime for the burger, Buck left a twenty on the bar. "Put that in the charity jar, ok?"

Jimmy nodded, and Buck headed out the door.

Chapter Eleven

Buck entered the front door of the Sheriff's Department and was buzzed through the security door, by the Deputy on duty. He walked back to his temporary office to gather his notes and headed for the conference room. He expected that for now, it would only be the Sheriff and Terry Rubin. He was surprised when he walked in and found his boss, Director Jackson, Hank Clancy, FBI and Jessica Gonzales, DEA sitting at the table. Before he could say anything, the Sheriff and Deputy Rubin walked in and closed the door.

Hank Clancy looked like a typical FBI agent and Buck liked to tease him that his underwear was probably government issue. Today he wore his typical FBI uniform. Dark suit, white shirt, striped tie and shiny black shoes. Hank hadn't always been a bureaucrat. In his long tenure with the bureau, he had been involved in some of its most high-profile cases.

Jessica Gonzales was one tough girl. Raised in Brooklyn, New York, she was the youngest DEA agent, male or female, ever, to be offered a position as an Agent in Charge. Buck had no idea how old she was and was afraid to ask. She had a thirteen-year-old son from a previous relationship and they lived with her mother. Jess was about five feet four, weighed about a buck twenty-five and was all muscle. She prided herself on her less than one percent body fat and worked out most days for two or three hours. She was also proficient in several different martial arts styles.

Today, her gray hair was short and spiked. She wore jeans, laced up boots and a black T-shirt that accentuated some impressive curves. It was rumored that she had several tattoos, but no one Buck knew had ever seen them. Her record at DEA was impeccable.

Kevin Jackson, the Director of the Colorado Bureau of Investigation was the youngest of the group. He had a stellar career with the Colorado Springs Police Department before being tapped for the top post at CBI. He was more bureaucrat than cop, having spent most of his career on the administrative side of things, but he was well respected in law enforcement and so far, Buck was impressed with him.

"I guess we all know each other so let's get started," said the Sheriff.

As Buck took his seat he said. "I'm surprised to see you guys here. What's going on?"

Hank Clancy was the first to respond. "We spoke with the Attorney General, the US Attorney for Colorado and the District Attorney for La Plata County. Pretty much burning up the phone lines from here to Washington. Everyone agrees this is bad news. The problem is we need more definitive proof that the Sonora Cartel is involved before we can really move. So, after talking with your Director, my Director and Jess's Director, and since this is still a local investigation, we are here strictly in an advisory capacity."

Buck looked confused and started to comment but was shut down by his boss.

"We are all on board with this for right now. Everyone understands the urgency but right now it's not federal. It is still a local matter. Now, in order for this to move forward, we are going to bend a few rules. I will let Hank continue."

Hank opened the folder that was sitting in front of him. He slipped a copy of a document across the table to the Sheriff and to Buck. Just then the conference room door opened and a Christine Brewer, the La Plata County District Attorney walked in and sat down in the empty chair next to Buck. Christine had been the District Attorney for the past twenty-two years and at sixty-four years old she was looking to retire in a year or two. She had graying blond hair and hazel eyes and carried probably twenty pounds more than she wanted on her five-foot-six frame. Buck had seen her in action in the courtroom during several of the cases he had worked in the area over the years and she was a formidable woman. She nodded to Buck as she sat down and removed a pair of reading glasses from her jacket pocket.

Hank spoke up. "First, we invited Christine here because, for the moment, she will be responsible for getting any warrants we need. Now for the good stuff. The document in front of you is a copy of the FISA warrant, I just received by secure fax, which will allow us to set up electronic surveillance on the location. Now since we are only here to advise, I need the lawyers in the room to cover their ears for a minute."

Christine Brewer laughed and made a feeble effort to cover her ears. Everyone at the table laughed.

Hank continued. "I have a "sneak and peek" team on the way down from Denver. They should be here by nine tonight. They will get as much eavesdropping equipment into the warehouse as they can. They are aware of the guards, but a lot of what they can do will happen right from here. They will tap phones, computers and basically anything they can find by doing various sweeps. They will also try to get a camera into the space. This team is very good. They will set up here at the Justice Center and monitor everything they get set up. If we can confirm electronically that the Sonoma Cartel is involved, directly, then the investigation will switch over to us. Buck, you will still be the lead agency. We will move from an advisory role to an assistance role."

Buck looked up from the warrant and looked at his boss. "This all makes sense, but I want it to be clear that this has been Deputy Rubin's case from the start and it will continue to be no matter what turn this thing takes. CBI is here by invitation from the Sheriff. She is the overall authority having jurisdiction on this. Clear?"

Everyone at the table nodded in agreement and Buck could see a small smile cross Terry Rubin's face.

"Now, so we can keep track of everyone. Your team will report to Terry here, and Terry will coordinate a couple Deputies to act as overwatch from across the street. We do not know how the bad guys are armed or even how many of them there really are, but I want some of our guys to back up your sneak team in case something happens."

No one made any objections, so Buck continued.

"Tomorrow morning Terry and I will re-interview his informant, "Scratch." I want to put my own eyes and ears on this guy. Terry can you get him over from the jail by eight AM?"

"Can do," Terry replied.

It was then that Buck looked at Jessica Gonzales. "Jess, what is the DEA bringing to the table?"

Chapter Twelve

Jess passed around a couple printed documents. "What you have in front of you is everything we have on some of the operators we believe might be behind setting up this distribution network. It's not much. We did find out that there has been a little chatter along the border about a big thing coming soon. Our guys failed to pick up on the importance and my boss is seriously pissed. Because of that, I have been ordered to put my resources, and any other resources we might need, at your disposal."

"Basically, my job is to save the DEA's collective ass. Because we have an unknown timeline I have also dispatched a DEA SWAT team. They will be staying at a hotel in Farmington, so as not to arouse suspicion and will be posing as a group of fishermen. One of our guys in New Mexico is a real-life river guide, so this works perfectly. We are also continuing to shake the bushes to see what we can find out."

Hank chimed in. "The FBI SWAT team will arrive tomorrow afternoon and will be staying at a small resort up near Wolf Creek Pass. Their cover is a small conference for a startup tech company. Their vehicle is being driven down as we speak and will be parked behind the Sheriff's office."

Buck smiled. "This sounds a little more like assisting than just advising." Sly smiles all around the table.

For the next hour or so, the group discussed rules of engagement, safety and what direction the investigation would head in. It was also agreed that the "sneak and peak" team would GPS tag all the trailers in the yard just in case they started to move as separate loads instead of as a group. There were still a lot of unknowns and this bothered everyone in the room.

Buck finally stood up and checked his watch. "Ok, except for Terry and his guys, let's call it a day and we will pick this up tomorrow morning at ten. That will give us time to maybe get some electronics in and talk to our snitch. Thanks everyone for your advice."

Everyone got up from the table and small conversations started throughout the room. Director Jackson approach Buck who was talking with Jess and the Sheriff. "Buck, a minute."

Buck led his boss down the hall to his temporary office and closed the door. Buck took the seat behind the desk and the Director one of the two chairs in front.

"This is going to get a whole lot bigger before we are done. Do you need me to send down some help?"

"No, sir. As you can see, in the next couple days I am going to have all the help I need. Hopefully, it will be enough. These are good people."

"That they are," agreed the Director. "I am heading back to Denver tonight. Keep me posted and if you need help, yell. I will send down the Cavalry."

The Director stood up, shook Buck's hand and walked out the door. Buck sat back for a minute and just shut down. A lot had happened since he had arrived in town a little over eight hours ago.

He hoped it would be enough. He had glanced at the info packet Jess had put together. If any of these were the guys involved, they were some scary dudes. Buck stood up, turned off the light and walked out the door. Tomorrow was going to be a long day.

Chapter Thirteen

"Are you out of your damn mind!"!

Hector had never seen Dick this pissed off. Dick turned around and slammed Hector's door. It made the whole building shake.

"You let a supposed cartel guy just walk in here and take over everything we have done here. Have you lost your damn mind?"

"Dick, he never gave me a chance, there was no discussion, I swear I wouldn't have done it, but he had a live feed of my wife and daughter from MY house. What the hell was I supposed to do?"

"You should have grabbed this guy by his neck and thrown his ass out the door. That's what I would have done."

"Dick…keep your voice down. They may have tapped our office like they did our houses."

"Don't tell me to keep my voice down. If you assholes are listening, then hear this. Go the fuck to hell. We ain't doing this, so shove your money up your ass. There now let's see how they react. God damn, Hector."

"Dick come on, man. We are talking about our families here. They cut off a guy's head while I watched. Scared me shitless'.

"Probably some Hollywood bullshit special effects and you fell for it. What a damn idiot."

"Come on Dick, this is serious. You weren't here. You didn't talk to this guy. We have to do this."

Dick turned the doorknob and swung open the door, which banged hard as it hit the filing cabinet behind the door. Dick walked out.

"Where ya going? Come on Dick. We need figure this out. Dick come on."

Hector sat down in his chair. His whole body was shaking. He was scared of the cartel guys, but he might have just lost his best friend and put his family in jeopardy. Claire Ringsby stood in the doorway.

"You guys ok?" She asked.

"Not even close. I did something really stupid, but I had no choice." He put his head in his hands. "I had no choice."

Claire looked at Hector sobbing and didn't know what to do. She closed the door and walked back to her desk. Dick was behind her desk on the radio dispatching one of their regular drivers to pick up an order in Ignacio and bring it back to the warehouse. It was bound for Salt Lake City. No matter what that idiot Hector had done, Dick still had a business to run and he wasn't going down without a fight. He put down the radio, smiled a stupid little smile at Claire and told her to close up the office and take the rest of the day off. Then he walked out the front door, got in his truck and left. Claire knew exactly where he was going. Dick was heading straight for the nearest bar. She had no idea what was going on, but she was very concerned.

Dick parked outside the LaBon Cafe and tried to control the shaking in his hands. He really needed a drink but once he started he wasn't sure he'd be able to stop. He had promised his wife that he would cut back on his drinking, but this was something different and he had no idea what to do. He shut off the engine, climbed out and headed inside.

There were only a couple locals sitting at the bar, so he headed for a stool down the end, away from everyone. Said hey to the guys as he walked by, grabbed a seat and said hey to Jimmy. Dick ordered a beer and a double shot of tequila. Downed the tequila and ordered another. Took a sip of beer and just stared at the wall. Jimmy had seen people like this before and wisely decided not to ask if he was OK. It would either pass with a few drinks or he would eventually fall down. The drunker Dick got, the louder he got. Jimmy and the other fellas in the bar just let him rant. Dick was a shitty drunk and everyone knew it. Eventually, Jimmy started watering down his drinks and stopped taking his money off the bar. Jimmy called Dick's wife to come get him. The last thing he said before he passed out and fell asleep at the bar was,

"That damn Hector. If they don't kill him I might."

The guys at the bar helped load Dick into the front seat of his wife's car and then went back inside to finish their drinks. Jimmy had heard enough of what Dick was saying to get the feeling that something bad was going on with the business. He decided to mention it to the Chief of Police next time he saw him.

Chapter Fourteen

The FBI "sneak and peek" team pulled their white panel van into the parking lot behind the Sheriff's office just after eleven PM. Locking up, they headed inside and after identifying themselves, were buzzed in and directed back to the conference room where Terry Rubin and two deputies were waiting. The three FBI agents didn't offer up a lot. Shook hands all around and introduced themselves as Josh, tall, thin, thirty something with longish wavy brown hair and a small bit of fuzz just below his lip; Randall, a little older, average size with short neat hair, which made him look more like an FBI agent in the classic sense; and Toby, average height, medium brown complexion, bald head and wary eyes, that seemed to take in everything around him at once. Terry introduced himself and his 2 Deputies, Carl Peters and Katy Wilson.

Introductions complete, they got right to business. Terry had been able to get the construction drawings for the warehouse from the Durango Building Department and he spread them out on the table. At this point Josh took over and opened them quickly to the electrical pages. Toby started following electrical, fire and burglar alarm circuits with his finger, making notes on his laptop as they went. Since most of what they were saying sounded foreign to the

Deputies, tech speak, modulators and transducers and other techy stuff, the Deputies just sat back and let them work.

While Josh and Toby worked over the plans, Randall started setting up a couple laptops and a few other pieces of equipment that the deputies had never seen before. In response to the interested looks from the deputies, Randall told them that if he explained it to them, he would have to kill them. Nervous chuckles all around.

By one AM, it looked like the S & P team was ready. They gathered everyone around the table and Josh gave them a rundown of what they hoped to accomplish. Randall, it seemed, was the computer guru and he would remain in the conference room and would monitor the taps as the others installed them. They were hoping to pick up the phone and radio networks. This would entail accessing the electrical and security panels that according to the plans were mounted on the wall at the back of the building. Outside the space. They would be using the existing building circuitry to create a net inside the space, basically turning the entire building into one big phone and voice tap. Anything said inside the space or transmitted by any cell phone or land line would be engulfed by the net and would be transmitted instantly back to Randall's computers. This was super high tech and the nice thing about it was that even if the bad guys swept the building for listening devices, they wouldn't find any.

At the same time Randall would be attempting to locate any computers connected to WIFI. He would be using what he called a sniffer program to filter out computers from all around the area and attempt to isolate the ones that were active inside the building. Terry was amazed with what he was being told, but he also imagined what this stuff could do in the wrong hands. Scary. If Randall could locate the computers, he would hack into their systems, download their files and activate their cameras. Piece of cake.

They had also been instructed to install GPS trackers on each trailer. These were tiny little magnetic boxes about the size of a cigarette lighter. They would remain turned off so as not to be detected. Once they were alerted to a trailer moving, they would send a signal to the box and activate the tracker.

Lastly, they would try to access the roof, if possible, and attempt to drop a couple cameras down the HVAC, heating ventilation and air conditioning ductwork, until they reached a diffuser that they might be able to drop into. Josh showed the deputies the cameras. Unreal. They were smaller than a pencil eraser but when Randall brought one up on the computer screen, the picture in Hi Def, was amazing. This would be the hardest part since the roof would probably make noise once someone stepped foot on it. If that failed, they would try to find another access point to follow.

The one piece they forgot to mention was that while all this was happening, the NSA had tasked a satellite to ping the building and they were now in the process of isolating any satellite transmission that might be coming from inside the building. This included SAT phones and laptops not connected to WIFI. They would piggy back a coded signature on each line they discovered, that they could then use to track the signal back to the other end. They would be able to do this no matter what kind of encryption the bad guys were using. This was technology so sophisticated that there were only a handful of people in the country that even knew it existed.

The S & P team gathered up their equipment and headed for the van. Terry and his two Deputies geared up and headed for Terry's unmarked unit. The two Deputies, both dressed completely in black from head to toe, would position themselves at either end of the fence surrounding the truck yard since most of the activity would take place at the back of the building. Terry would take up his overwatch position on the roof of the auto body shop.

Chapter Fifteen

Terry did a final comm and sitrep check of the team and then gave the all clear. The S & P team, fully armed and dressed all in black looked like a couple ninjas as they raced across the parking lot behind the truck yard. This was where they would be the most exposed and everyone was on high alert. Once at the corner of the fence they pulled out an electric wrench and removed several of the bolts that tied the two fence corners together.

Opening a space large enough to squeeze through, they cleared the fence and knelt as low as they could and listened. Not hearing or seeing any movement, they raced across the grass and positioned themselves flat against the wall at the electrical panels. It only took a couple seconds to pick the lock on the electrical panel and the security system panel. Now Josh went to work with a bunch of wires and alligator clips and a monitor as he checked each circuit until he found the one he was looking for. He then removed a small black box from inside his jumpsuit, attached the wires and slid the box down into a space below the breakers where it wouldn't be seen.

At the same time, Toby was doing the same search on the security panel. At one point he tapped Josh on the arm and pointed to something in the box. Josh nodded, and Toby proceeded to attach a similar black box to the security panel. After about five minutes of activity, Josh tapped his finger on the microphone resting just under his chin.

"We are connected to the security and building electrical. Go ahead and run a diagnostic and make sure we have a good connection."

Back at the office, Randall started running his fingers over his keyboard, like a machine. Then he would wait, check a bunch of random numbers and move on to the next test.

"We are good. Reading five by five on those lines."

Josh began working on the cable box, which fed the WIFI signal to the building while Toby got out the tiny cameras and headed down to the roof ladder, that was conveniently located on the side of the building. While Josh was disconnecting the cable from the cable TV provider and connecting in a signal interceptor, Toby made a leap off the ground and was able to catch the bottom rung of the roof ladder located about eight feet off the ground. He hung there for just a second and then raced up the ladder and stepped over the low parapet wall.

Just then Terry sounded the alert. "Guys, movement at the front door. I've got one bad guy with a pistol coming out the front door. He's looking around in the air like he's checking the weather or something. Hold tight."

Everyone froze. A minute later Terry announced the all clear.

"I bet he was watching something on cable when I disconnected the antennae. He was probably checking to see if it was windy or something, which might have caused him to lose his signal," suggested Josh. "We are almost done here."

Meanwhile, on the roof, Toby had found a conduit outside one of the air conditioner unit, with some loose roofing sealant around it and had fed a camera down along it and was now watching the picture on his phone to make sure he could get a good view of the space. The camera suddenly popped out into the open and he had a view of the main garage space. He slowly twisted the camera cord looking for the best view and was stunned when the view picked up a wall of fenced off cells. There were 3 or 4 people sleeping in each cell. It looked like a prison. He counted eight such cells as he rotated the camera. Tapping the mike on the side of his head he asked Randall to check the camera feed. Randall responded that he had a good picture. Toby would have liked to get one more camera in the space, but he had already overshot the time they had allotted so he climbed back down the ladder and rejoined Josh.

They now headed around the front of the building, checked with Terry to make sure it was all clear and then ran along the row of trailers attaching a GPS tracker up under each trailer frame. Together they raced back to the corner of the fence and re-secured the chain link.

Josh reported that they were finished, and everyone headed back to their vehicles and returned to the office. Now they would just have to wait and see what the electronics revealed.

Chapter Sixteen

The morning following the visit by the attorney, a construction crew from a company Hector had never heard of showed up and starting loading materials from their truck into the loading dock. It seemed to Hector that they were unloading a lot of chain link fencing. He had no idea what they were planning.

The first thing the crew did was to start building a 2 X 4 wall separating four of the loading docks from the other two. They were efficient as hell and within 3 hours they had completely separated the two sections of the dock including installing a large man door with a very sophisticated electronic lock. They then turned their attention to the fencing and posts they had brought in and for the next 6 hours all anyone could hear was the drilling of concrete.

Claire tried to ask Hector what was going on but all she got from him was a shake of his head. Hector looked very uneasy, especially when he tried to ask the contractor what they were planning, and the lead worker refused to even answer him.

Dick arrived right in the middle of all the noise and walked right back out, not saying a word to anyone. He did not look pleased. Claire still had work to do so she contacted her drivers, answered calls from clients and continued arranging pickup and delivery schedules.

Hector was no help and she just decided to stay out of whatever was going on. She liked her job, but she had been looking for a job when she found this one, so she wasn't too worried. At least not yet.

By midnight the construction crew was finished with whatever they were building on the other side of the new wall and disappeared as quickly as they had arrived. Hector had left long before the contractors finished and Claire left at six PM just like every night. Once the contractors left, everything seemed to return to normal, but that was far from the case.

When Claire arrived for work the next morning, Dick was already in the office and was in the process of brewing a pot of coffee. He offered her a cup and then poured one for himself.

"What do you think is going on, on the other side of the wall?" he asked her.

"I have no idea", she replied. "I hoped you would know. What's going on, Dick?"

"I'd rather not tell you at this point. Right now, nothing makes sense." With that, Dick turned and headed towards his office and closed the door. End of discussion.

Hector arrived at his usual time, walked into the office said "Mornin", poured himself a cup of coffee and headed for his office. Claire thought to herself that this does not look good. Maybe it was time to look for another job.

Just as Claire was getting ready to head out the door for lunch a car pulled into the parking lot and parked in the "Visitors" space in front of the office door. Two men, a tall blond and a shorter Latino with a thick mustache got out of the car and walked in the door. Claire had never encountered anyone that she thought was menacing and she wasn't even sure she would recognize it if she did see it, but when these two approached the counter, she knew exactly what menacing meant and here it was looking over the counter at her.

"Help you gentlemen?" she inquired. It was obvious from their appearances that they were very well muscled and barely fit the suit jackets they were wearing.

"Tell Hector and Dick we are here to see them." Blondy smiled a sinister smile that sent a chill up Claire's back.

"Do you have an appointment?"

Mustache kind of sneered at her through two broken front teeth and said, "Never mind. We will find them ourselves." With that, they turned and walked down the hall toward Dick and Hector's offices. Claire thought better of trying to stop them, so she got up from her desk, walked out the door and headed to her car. Lunch was waiting, somewhere, anywhere. She really didn't care. She just wanted out of the office.

Chapter Seventeen

Mustache pushed open Hector's office door and Hector almost pissed in his pants. He jumped up out of his chair, but Mustache held up his palm to indicate stop and then pointed towards the chair. Hector sat back down. Mustache stepped aside, and Dick walked in, or more like was pushed in, followed by Blondy. Dick was not so subtlety pointed toward one of the visitor chairs. Blondy took the other chair and Moustache stood in the doorway. This was intimidating, and Hector just looked at Dick who was looking at Moustache.

"Good afternoon gentlemen." Said Blondy. Blondy had a southern accent but it wasn't a smooth silky southern accent. His was harsh and sounded like he came from a very rural environment.

"We represent your new business partners and want to welcome you to our business family. We will be overseeing the operation in the space next door. We only have a few simple rules. One, stay out of our space. Two, don't ask questions and three, do not talk to anyone about our new business arrangement. If you can follow those simple rules, then we will get along fine, and we will all get rich. If you violate any one of those rules, then we will get rich and you and your family will get dead."

Blondy paused for dramatic effect and Dick squirmed uneasily in his chair. Hector just looked scared.

Blondy continued, "Now our employer wants this little venture to be a success and we will do whatever it takes to make it a success. We can do that without you if necessary, but we would prefer to keep everything looking as normal as possible, so let's all just agree right now to get along."

Hector nodded in agreement. Dick, on the other hand, started to speak up. Before Dick knew what was happening, he was lying on the floor next to the chair he had been sitting in moments ago. The stunned look on his face and the bright red mark on his cheek said it all.

Blondy merely turned sideways in his chair and looked at Dick sitting on the floor. He glanced over his shoulder at Mustache, who just smiled that sinister smile. Blondy leaned forward.

"I guess I forgot to mention rule number four. Never try to voice your opinion to us. We don't care what you think or what you have to say. Now that was just an open hand slap. Next time I will break something. And by the way, my boss told me to make sure I tell you that if you ever tell him to shove his money up his ass again, we are going to have a serious problem and your family will not like the outcome. Understood?"

Hector looked at Dick and Dick looked at Blondy and they both shook their heads in agreement.

"Excellent." Blondy continued with a sneer on his face. "See, we are getting along already. This is going to be fun. So, you just keep running your operation and doing what you do, and we will take care of the rest."

With that Blondy got up from his chair and he and Mustache headed for the door.

Hector looked at Dick and said, "See I told you they had this place bugged."

Dick looked at Hector and didn't say a word, just headed back to his office rubbing his cheek. He never even saw Blondy move his hand, but it sure hurt like hell. He hadn't been hit like that since his old man beat him when he was a senior in high school and he had backtalked his mother. Inside he was steaming. He didn't know what he would need to do to take care of these guys, but he was starting to get mad and when he got mad he was unpredictable.

Chapter Eighteen

Buck and Terry sat across the table from "Scratch" in interview room one. Outside the window of the interview room stood Sheriff Sinclair, Christine Brewer, the District Attorney, and Jess Gonzales from the DEA. Scratch was coming down off the high he was on when Terry arrested him and squirmed in his seat. Buck offered him a cup of coffee or something to drink and then asked Terry to remove the handcuffs. Scratch rubbed his wrists and looked at Buck nervously.

Scratch, my name is Buck Taylor and I am an agent with the Colorado Bureau of Investigation and I would like to hear the story you told Deputy Terry, here. Can you repeat it for me?"

Scratch started scratching at the scabs on his right arm and looked around the room like he was trying to find the story is his drug addled mind. Finally, it looked like his brain engaged and he began telling Buck a story.

"Dem Mexicans have taken over Hector's place and they scarin the shit out a people. They got them kids all locked up in cages like it's the damn zoo and they only let them out to do they drug sorten and packin." His mind started to drift. "Some dem little chickitas are pretty sweet lookin, but I never touch any of them. Ain't lookin for no trouble with the blond boss. He wackier than a crazy old coot and meaner an a snake." Scratch stared at the ceiling.

"And you have seen these people in the cages yourself?" Buck asked.

"Sho have," replied Scratch. His brain engaged again. "I was over they heppin load one of the truck for Hector. He gives me a couple bucks to load trucks sometimes. I asked him what was behind the new wall, but he wouldn't say so, when he wasn't lookin and the blond guy came out the door I snuck in to get a peek. The kids was all stuffin pills in toys and putting em back in boxes like dey was new." He stopped again and just stared. Terry asked him if he was OK. Click, brain engaged. "I didn't steal no drugs. Dem pills was just lyin on the table and I was gonna go talk to one dem sweet chickitas, but then the Boss come back in the door and I grabbed a handful of pills en high tailed it for the back door. That was when I seen dem cages." Click, brain disengaged.

Buck looked at Terry, who tapped on Scratch's hand. That seemed to bring him back. Click, brain engaged.

"Did you ask Hector what was going on after you took the pills?"

"Nope. Ain't been back there. Scared Blondy might get me. Figured I'd sell dem pills and maybe go to Ignacio and party. Ain't been to Ignacio in a while. Knew this girl there once. Might look her up and...."

"Scratch focus," Buck raised his voice a notch or two. "Who else might know about the drugs, anyone you know?"

Scratche's brain was rapidly heading south. He looked at the ceiling again. Buck was about to give up.

"Claire probably knows. She knows everything. She always

been nice to me. Gives me money when I got no drugs to sell so I can eat. She not happy now." Click, Brain disengaged for the last time.

Buck got up and the Sheriff buzzed the door to let him out while Terry put the handcuffs back on Scratch and turned him over to one of the jail deputies.

Jess looked at Buck. "Guy sure has a way with words. Wonder how many pills he sampled. Should make a great witness."

Buck looked at Sheriff Sinclair. "Who is this Claire he mentioned. She real or imaginary?"

"Oh, she's real. She's the Office Manager. We go to the same church, but I haven't seen her much lately. You think she could help?"

"Let's get her address and see what she has to say. It's risky. If she is part of this, we could blow the whole case. I think we should also talk to some of their regular drivers. They may not be in on the deal and might be a good source."

Terry said he would get Claire's address and track down one or two of the local drivers.

Christine Brewer didn't look happy. "Buck, we don't have a lot to go on. This "witness" is pretty much worthless. If we don't get something back from the electronics, we may not have a case. Let me know if you need anything. I need to get to court." She left the office with a worried look on her face.

Jess chimed in. "She's right. We have our necks out a long way on this and we may not have anything to go on."

"Look, Jess," said Buck. "We all know something big is going on. Maybe we need to shake the bushes a little. I'm thinking we should try to talk to this Hector and Dick, someplace away from their warehouse. Maybe we can get something from them or at least push them to make a move. I have it on good authority that Dick has been talking in his beer and he doesn't sound like someone making a big score. More the opposite."

"Ok," Jess said. "But let's do this soon. We have a shit load of resources sitting on their asses." Jess headed out the door.

Sheriff Sinclair looked at Terry and Buck. "She's right. If we needed a warrant with what we have, we wouldn't get one. I'll talk to the sneak and peek team in a little bit and see what they have. In the meantime, why don't you to go talk to Claire Ringsby. The Sheriff left the room.

Chapter Nineteen

The first two delivery trucks arrived after midnight a couple nights after the construction crew completed their work and pulled up to the loading dock doors. Blondy and Mustache opened the loading dock door, and with the help of the three guards who had arrived the day before, silently and quickly offloaded the workers they had smuggled in from Mexico to sort and package the drugs. When he opened the back door of the first trailer he was met by a sea of young scared faces. Thirty in all.

The young people, mostly girls except for 10 young men had all been kidnapped by the cartel. The cartel had put out the word in the neighboring towns that they were looking for young laborers to work in the fields harvesting crops. When the young people showed up seeking those jobs they were immediately grabbed up and locked away in a warehouse in the middle of the desert. Their phones and other electronic devices were taken from them and their contact with the outside world was extinguished.

Over the next couple weeks, the young people had been drugged and abused. They were tortured until their will to escape had completely disappeared. Some of the young girls had been repeatedly raped. Even though their families had looked for them and had contacted the local authorities, no sign of the group was ever found. The cartel had done a thorough job of making these folks disappear without a trace.

Now, here they were in a foreign place in the middle of the night being herded into cages like animals. They had no idea of the date or the time or where they were, and they had no idea if they would still be alive tomorrow morning. Violence was their only reward for working sometime eighteen-hour days, with just enough food to sustain them.

The ride in the back of the hot stuffy trailer had taken 12 hours. The guards had come in just as they were finishing the meal of empty tortillas and a bottle of water and hustled them into a couple smaller panel trucks. The trucks had no windows, so again, no reference of where they were. Two hours later they arrived at a larger warehouse. This time they were given a bottle of water each and a couple rice cakes and put in the back of the trailer. Inside, the trailer was filled with metal cots with mattresses so thin you could almost see through them and some boxes filled with clothes. They were told to sit down and be quiet or they would be beaten, or worse.

It was a long hot drive and at one point they had stopped for a few minutes. They all thought they might have a chance to get out and stretch their legs or use a restroom instead of the two buckets that had been left with them, but that didn't happen. A few minutes later they were back on the road and they settled in for whatever awaited them.

During the long ride, several of the young people got sick from the heat and the movement of the trailer and after a few hours in the heat and stuffiness of the trailer, the space became almost unbearable due to the smell. The longer they went the hotter and more putrid it got.

The trailer finally came to a stop and when the doors were opened they drank in the fresh air. Then they saw Mustache and Blondy and all their fears returned. Blondy at least had a little bit of a compassionate side. Mustache was just brutal and he seemed to really enjoy it. Back at the first place they stayed Moustache never thought twice about picking out one of the prettier girls and taking her back to his office. The others would hear the screams of anguish coming from the office but there was nothing they could do but try to console that person when she returned.

Mustache also liked the young men, but not for sexual pleasure. He seemed to enjoy using them as punching bags and if Moustache wasn't satisfied by the young girl he took to his office he always found a young man to take it out on. Blondy would just watch and smile that sadistic smile.

It had taken a couple weeks but Mustache and Blondy and their helpers managed to break the spirits of everyone in the group. Eventually, there were no more tears, only the sad acceptance that this was to be their lives and that maybe someday they would be freed. They no longer thought about family or friends. They only cared about making it through another day alive and getting their next pill. Although the reality was that many of them would have preferred to be dead than to live like this.

Chapter Twenty

The young folks had no idea where they were, but they knew they were not near home anymore. The air seemed thinner and was a little cooler which was very much appreciated after the torturous trip they had just endured. The new space looked fresh and clean and did not smell of human waste and excrement like the old place did. Mustache gathered them around at the entrance to the cage and told them in Spanish that this would be their new home for a while and if they performed their tasks without any problems they would be released soon to return to their families. Many of these kids had grown up on the streets and had no recollection of families.

He continued on, telling them that they could use the restroom that was contained within the cage area and when they weren't working they were to remain in their cages. If they broke any of the rules punishment would be swift and painful. They were not to go outside the loading dock door without a guard and they were not to go through the door that was at the other end of the warehouse. Most importantly, if they were told to be quiet, they were to do exactly that, or they would be dealt with severely.

He gave them ten minutes to use the restroom and then they were to start removing the furniture and clothing from the trailer and setting up their cages. Once the trailer was empty and the cages set up, they were to start unloading the other trailer. They would have to hurry if they wanted to get any sleep, but work would start bright and early the next morning.

The young folks worked quickly, removing the crates from the back of the second truck. The idea of getting some sleep was on all their minds. Once the crates were all arranged in the middle of the floor, Blondy gave them permission to get a few hours sleep. They all headed off to the cages, except for Maria. Mustache had personally broken Maria and he enjoyed her a lot. She was spunky and had some spirit and the fact that she was only sixteen didn't concern him in the least. He grabbed her by the arm and pulled her toward the guard's office.

Blondy looked over and said. "Hey man. Why don't you let her get some sleep? She has to work in the morning."

Mustache looked over at him and smiled that toothless smile. "Damn you bro. She is going to work now." He laughed a wicked little laugh and slammed the door. Mustache was not quiet in the pursuit of his pleasures and the guards finally went and stood outside so they didn't have to hear what was going on.

Blondy actually hated the little cretin but he was a favorite of the boss and Blondy was getting paid good money for this gig, so he just walked away. After a while, the noise level dropped and Blondy and three of the guards headed to the little motel they were staying at about 10 miles outside of town on the way to Mancos. Mustache and the other two guards would take the first night's watch, at least what was left of it.

The young folks were roused from what little sleep they had been able to get. They were given a few minutes to wash up and use the restroom and then they assembled for breakfast. Mustache had a couple of the girls prepare breakfast in the new kitchen area that was installed next to the cages. It wasn't much: just a refrigerator, stove and some shelves and a counter. The young folks didn't care, for the first time in a long time they had a decent meal. The girls had cooked scrambled eggs and beans and that was piled on tortillas. This was almost like heaven if heaven were a prison. There was even coffee for those who wanted it.

Blondy returned just as breakfast was wrapping up and gave them their orders in Spanish. They were told to get the work tables set up that they had unloaded from the truck and to start sorting the pills into piles, just like they had been shown to do at their last place. The toys for the second part of the job would arrive by the end of the day and then they could start the assembly process. They knew they would be watched very carefully and taking pills off the table would result in a severe beating.

And this is how their day would go until the next truck arrived. They would be fed a second meal towards the end of the day and then locked in their cages for the night. This is how every day would go with only the hope of being released.

Chapter Twenty-One

Buck grabbed a bottle of Coke from the cooler in the lunchroom and went looking for Terry Rubin. He knew Terry had a long night with the "sneak and peek" so he wasn't sure if he was in yet. He found Terry sitting at his desk. Terry had his feet up and a cup of coffee in his hand. He looked so contemplative that Buck almost hated to disturb him.

"Morning," said Buck. "Were you able to get any sleep last night?"

"Yeah, a little," replied Terry. He put his feet on the floor and sat up, setting his coffee down on the desk. "Those guys were really amazing last night. They were quick, quiet and efficient as hell. They told me they thought they had everything they needed. They are monitoring from the conference room."

Buck looked at the mess of files on Terry's desk and wondered to himself how this young guy got anything accomplished with such a disorganized manner. Buck had always been meticulous in how he kept the files from an investigation and even last night he had spent several hours in his hotel room assembling his investigation notebook. This would eventually be the work product that would put Carlos Rojas and his cartel away for life.

"Were you able to get Claire Ringsby's address?" Buck asked.

"Right here," replied Terry. "She lives in a rental half way down East 4th Avenue, between East 4th and East 5th Streets. You want me to come along?" Terry handed Buck a slip of paper with the address written on it.

"No, I have this. What I would like you to do is track down one of the drivers we talked about and see if we can get someone to talk out of school."

Buck turned and headed towards the door but was stopped just as he got there by Sheriff Sinclair. "Oh, Buck. Glad I caught you. The "sneak and peek" team has started downloading computer files and they have already recorded a couple sat phone conversations. The FBI sent two computer analysts down this morning to help decipher the computer stuff. A lot of it is encrypted. NSA is attempting to break the encryption. Should have something we can look at in a couple hours."

"That's great," replied Buck. Text me when they have it together. I am heading out to see if I can find Claire Ringsby and then I might see if I can find either Dick or Hector and have a conversation."

"Ok," said the Sheriff. "You want any backup?"

"No. Hopefully this is just a conversation. By the way, I asked Terry Rubin to track down one of the drivers and see if we get anything with that approach. See you later." Buck walked out the back door and headed for his car.

Leaving the Sheriff's office parking lot, he headed back out to US 550 and headed north. At College Drive, he turned right until he got to East 4th Avenue and headed south past East 5th Street and found the address Terry had given him in the middle of the block on the right side. It was a small well-kept little ranch with a cute front porch and a separate garage that sat behind the house. A row of roses was in full bloom along a small picket fence that fronted the sidewalk. Buck turned off the engine and sat for a minute, contemplating his approach. He hoped this was not a huge mistake. He had a sense from his conversation with the snitch, if the snitch could be believed, that the two owners and the Office Manager might not be willing participants in this whole thing. If he was wrong, then his visit to Claire Ringsby was going to be a colossal mistake. He decided to just be straight up front with her and see where it went.

He opened the car door and stepped out realizing too late that it would be obvious to anyone who might be watching Claire's house that he was a cop. His badge was clipped to his belt and he carried a two-tone Kimber 45 caliber Ultra Carry pistol in a DiSantos brown leather holster in his waistband. Since this was July, he didn't have a coat or vest on to conceal the gun, so he decided, to hell with it, he would have to take a chance that she was not being watched.

He crossed the street and pushed open the little white picket gate and walked up the front walk. As he approached the porch he noticed that the door was open. He slowed his pace and unsnapped the thumb break on his holster and rested his right hand on his gun. He walked up the steps to the porch and looked through the open front door. Stepping across the threshold he called out.

"Claire Ringsby." He waited but received no response. "Ms. Ringsby, my name is Buck Taylor and I am with the Colorado Bureau of Investigation. Are you in there?"

Just then a little old lady stuck her head out of a door halfway down the hall. She looked a little nervous.

"Can I help you young man?" she said.

Buck smiled. He hadn't been a young man in a long time.

"Yes, Ma'am. I am looking for Claire Ringsby. Is that you by chance?"

"Heavens no," replied the little old lady. "I'm Martha Davidson. I own this house. What do you want with Claire if I might ask?"

"Ma'am. My name is Buck Taylor and I am an investigator with the Colorado Bureau of Investigation and I was told that Claire Ringsby was living here."

Mrs. Davidson stepped out of what Buck assumed was a bathroom and pulled off a pair of pink rubber gloves. She approached the front door and asked if Buck had any ID. Buck pointed to his badge on his belt and pulled his cred pack from his back pocket, opened it and showed her his CBI ID card.

"Sorry officer. My late husband told me to never be too careful. He was an accountant. A very meticulous man, but it paid off because he left me in good shape after he passed."

Buck smiled as he put away his ID. "Does Claire still live here?"

Mrs. Davidson replied. "She did until yesterday. Got a voicemail from her yesterday morning saying she was leaving town and I shouldn't worry about the security deposit because she was in a hurry. Came over here this morning to talk to her but she was already gone. Left everything here except her clothes from the looks of it. Don't know what I am going to do with all her furniture. Guess I can rent it out as "Furnished." Fifteen years she lived here, and she didn't even leave a forwarding address. Tried her phone but it went straight to voicemail. I hate talking on those things so I didn't leave a message."

"Ma'am. Would you mind if I came in and looked around?"

"Don't you need some kind of warrant or something to do that, officer?"

"No Ma'am. As long as I have your permission, it's ok."

Mrs. Davidson thought about it for a minute and said. "Well, I guess it's ok, you being a cop and all. Come on in."

Chapter Twenty-Two

Buck stepped into the entry foyer which was not much bigger than a coat closet. The house was set up like a typical old 4 square house. A living room and small kitchen on one side and a small dining room, a bathroom and one bedroom on the other side of a narrow hallway. Someone over the years had added a second bedroom in an addition off the back of the house. Buck noticed that the house was nicely painted, had beautiful woodwork built-ins, moldings and awesome dark stained hardwood floors. All in all, a very nice little house. Mrs. Davidson went back to cleaning.

Buck walked into each room and scanned them with the eye of a seasoned investigator. Looking for anything that seemed out of place or amiss. He had no idea what if anything he was looking for but he would know it if he found it. He didn't find it in the living room or in the kitchen. The dining room was set up with a table and four chairs and a small cupboard that contained a set of dinnerware and glasses. He found nothing of interest in the drawers in the cupboard.

Mrs. Davidson was still working in the bathroom, so he just glanced in as he walked by. Didn't see anything of interest and walked into the bedroom. The first thing he noticed was that the bed was made. If Claire Ringsby had been taken against her will, he doubted the bad guys would let her make the bed first. The closets and drawers in the dresser were all empty as well.

Buck headed for the back bedroom which it appeared Claire had used as an office and workout room. There was a small desk. No computer. A yoga mat was lying on the floor and a couple small five-pound weights sat next to it. Not much to see. As he was stepping out of the bedroom a thought occurred to him and he stepped over to the bathroom door.

"Mrs. Davidson. Did you find any trash in any of the trash cans when you got here this morning?"

Mrs. Davidson stopped cleaning the toilet and looked up. "There was trash in the kitchen can and in the back bedroom by the desk. Not much. I threw it in the cans out back by the garage."

"Thank you, Ma'am." Buck turned to head out the back door towards the garage.

Mrs. Davidson stood at the back door as he went and said, "You know, officer. If you're not doing anything later, there's a dance at the Grange Hall tonight. Might be fun."

"Thanks for the offer Ma'am but I have a lot to do." Buck continued along the walkway.

"You might find my expertise enjoyable." Mrs. Davidson said with a sly and slightly naughty smile. Buck waved his hand over his head and opened the garage door. The trash cans were lined up along the back wall of the garage. Other than those, the rest of the garage was totally empty. Who lives like this, thought Buck, thinking back to his own garage in Gunnison that was probably a mess right now.

Buck opened the first trash can and found it empty. The second one contained a small bag of trash. Buck turned the lid upside down, placed it on the floor and dumped the bag's contents onto the overturned lid. It was mostly paper stuff: tissues, napkins, an empty McDonald's bag and a drink cup. He almost missed the small slip of paper that was stuck to the wet side of the cup. He could barely make out the words, but it looked like it said United, with today's date, the number 275 and the time of 5:50 PM.

Claire Ringsby was running.

Buck pulled out his cell phone and called the Sheriff.

The Sheriff answered on the first ring. "Buck, I was just getting ready to call you. We have a body."

Buck stopped short. "What? A body? Where?"

"About 20 miles north of town in a culvert. Couple hikers found it."

"Ok," Buck replied. "I am on my way. You got forensics on the way?"

"Forensics just got here. What did you need?" the Sheriff asked.

'Oh, right. Can you get one of your people to write up a Material Witness warrant for Claire Ringsby and get a judge to sign it? She's in the wind and I think she is catching a flight today, but I don't know from where."

"Done. Get here soon as you can. Straight up 550. You can't miss us."

Buck headed out the driveway, mostly to avoid Mrs. Davidson, taking the little slip of paper with him. As he got in his car he dialed the Director's cell phone.

"Buck. I hear you have a body. Is it related to the drug thing?" No one still ever says, hello. Word also travels way too fast sometimes.

"Don't know yet sir, I am on my way. I need a little help, sir." Buck explained the scrap of paper he found at Claire Ringsby's house and that the Sheriff was putting together a witness warrant. He then asked the Director if he could get someone to contact the airline or TSA or whomever, and see where that flight was leaving from. It could be Denver, it could be Albuquerque or hell, it could even be Salt Lake City or Phoenix. If Claire left last night she could have reached any of those places by now.

The Director told him he would take care of it and he would call him back as soon as he knew. He told Buck to let him know what he found at the body site. The Director hung up. Seems like no one says goodbye anymore either. Buck disconnected, did a three-point turn in the street, headed back up to College Avenue, jumped on 550 and headed north. Once clear of the city he flipped on the blue and red flashers that were buried in the car's grill and dropped the hammer.

Chapter Twenty-Three

Dick Dillon wasn't sure what he was going to do. If this was all for real then he was going to get paid a lot of money to keep his mouth shut about what was going on at the trucking company. He hated the idea that someone could just waltz in and take over a business that he and Hector had worked so hard to develop. He hated, even more, the idea that they were somehow working for a Mexican cartel. He feared for his family and he feared for his workers, especially Claire Ringsby. She had been with the company since the beginning. She took a chance right from the start that she might not get paid or paid on time since starting a trucking company was not an easy deal.

Over the years Dick had always tried to help Claire out if she needed help. Money, time off. He did what he could. She was awesome at her job and kept the company humming like a well-oiled machine. She never missed a day of work. Never complained about the hours or the job and she got along great with the clients and the drivers. She was great to have around. Now she was right in the middle of their mess and it wasn't fair.

Dick picked up the note that Hector had given him with his offshore bank account number on it, picked up the phone and dialed the bank. He had no idea where the bank was, but it really didn't matter. After he identified himself, the person he spoke with helped him set up the new account and transfer the money he wanted moved over. He had never dealt with that kind of money and was a little nervous, but the person on the other end of the phone made it all seamless. He hung up and for the first time in a couple weeks felt good about himself.

Whatever he decided to do was one thing, but he had an obligation to Claire as well. She didn't ask for any of this and he was worried for her safety. He had walked into her office one day and caught Moustache leering at her and it bothered him a lot. He finally made a decision and he got up and headed toward Claire's office. When he got to her desk he put his finger up to his lips to signal her to be quiet and then pointed towards the front door. He wanted her to follow him.

Once outside, Dick looked around to make sure no one was watching. He moved closer to Claire.

"I have a bad feeling about everything that is going on around here and think you should make plans to get out of town before something happens."

Claire looked at him confused. "Are we in danger?"

Dick and Hector had never told Claire the whole story of what was going on, but she had a pretty good idea that what was going on wasn't good and was probably illegal in some way. She had already considered leaving. She liked her job and she liked working for Dick and Hector, but her imagination had started to run away on her. And she really didn't like Blondy or his friend.

She started to object. "Dick, my life is here. I can't just…"

"Look I am worried about what's going to happen once these guys decide they don't need us around. I am working on a plan for my family and I want to help you get out. I want you to book a flight out of Denver for as soon as you can get there. Maybe go visit the family in Vermont. That would be good. Clear out of your house and just go."

"Dick. I can't afford to just walk away from everything in my life."

Dick replied. "I took care of that for you. I set up an account in an offshore bank and transferred fifty grand into an account in your name."

He handed her a slip of paper with an account number written on it and the name of the bank. Claire was stunned.

"I can't take your money," she said.

"Yes, you can. Its money from them and I don't care about it. Take it and run. These guys have a long reach so keep a low profile. Finish out the day so no one is the wiser and then make your arrangements and go. Don't tell anyone where you are going. You're a nice lady Claire, and I have enjoyed working with you these many years, but I don't want to see you again after today. Stay safe."

Before she could respond, Dick headed for his car, hopped in and pulled out of the lot. Claire's life had just taken a strange turn and she was more scared now than she was before. She headed back inside to try to finish her day. Her life was about to change in ways she couldn't even imagine.

Chapter Twenty-Four

Terry Rubin and Deputy Danny Silvio left the Sheriff's Office parking lot and headed for 550. Turning north, they made a right at East 15th St, which turned into Florida Road and eventually turned left onto Folsom Place, which led them to the parking lot at Folsom Park. Terry had asked Danny to change out of his uniform so they would not attract attention when they went to see Franky Fortuna.

Danny and Franky were high school friends and had stayed in touch over the years. It was Danny's call to Franky's house that led the two Deputies to Folsom Park. Franky was one of the four regular drivers that worked for Colorado Overland Transportation. According to his wife, today was his day off so he had taken their son over to the park to practice batting and catching. Franky's son was in his first year of Little League and they tried to practice whenever they could.

Terry parked the car and the Deputies scanned the park, finally, Danny pointed to the baseball diamond. The Deputies were hoping they wouldn't spook Franky, but they still decided to approach together.

Walking across the grass toward home plate, Danny called out. "Hey, Franky." And gave a little wave. Franky turned and placing his hand over his eyes to block some of the sun, he stared to see who was calling him. Recognizing Danny, he waved back. He didn't recognize the guy he was with.

Franky told his son to hold the ball for a minute and walked toward the two men.

"Yo Danny. What's up?" he asked.

Danny and Terry closed the gap and Danny and Franky shook hands.

"Franky, this is Terry Rubin. We work together. Terry was wondering if he could ask you a couple questions?" Danny said.

Franky looked a little leery. "Sure. What's this about?"

Terry hadn't really come up with a game plan on the way over to the park, so he decided to just play it straight and gauge Franky's reaction.

"Franky, we have been hearing stories about some strange things going on over at Colorado Overland and I am trying to see what's real and what's not."

Franky looked a little puzzled at first and then a look of concern came over his face. He tried to fake his way through it.

"I'm not sure what you're talkin about. I just drive for them. Don't have anything to do with the business."

Terry wasn't biting. "Look, Franky, we can keep this really friendly so as not to concern your son or we can slap the cuffs on you and haul your ass down to the office and do this more formally. I'm willing to take this in whatever direction you want to go, but if you lie to me again, we are going to have a problem."

Franky glanced over his shoulder at his son standing at home plate. He gave him a little wave to show him everything was OK and turned back towards Terry.

"Look," he said. "I don't want to see anything happen to my

family. They got everybody at the shop scared. You got to keep me out of this."

Danny said. "I'm gonna leave you to it. I'll be over by your son. Take your time. We'll be OK for a few minutes."

"Ok Franky," said Terry. "We will do all we can to keep you out of this. At this point, we are just having a friendly conversation in a park. Don't make me regret this."

Franky could see that Terry was serious, so he decided it was in his best interest to be as straight as possible.

"We don't really know what's go on, me and the other drivers. Suddenly, this past month, they blocked off two-thirds of the warehouse and we are not allowed in that space. We have been handling our regular deliveries but there are nine more trucks and nine trailers in the yard. Our business has been good but not that good. That's a big investment."

Terry let him continue.

"We can hear people working next door, but we never see anybody and since we are on the road we are kind of out of the loop."

"I heard from someone that the bosses went after each other a couple weeks back. No one knows why but the rumor is they have a new partner. Big money and a lot of business. One of the other drivers said that he tried to ask one of the new loaders what was going on and a big blond guy came out and told him to mind his damn business."

"Any talk about drugs or illegals being in the place?" Terry asked.

"Nah. Nothing like that but I can tell from talking to Claire, the office lady, that she seems to be kind of scared all the time. What's going on?"

Terry explained. "Right now, we are just looking into some

stories we've heard, so we are not sure what's going on. Any indication that any of the other regular drivers are working with this new partner?"

"I doubt it. Everyone I spoke to seemed just as concerned as me. We just wondering if we gonna have a paycheck next month."

Terry thought for a minute and said. "If you hear anything new, you give Danny a call and he will get your message to me, ok? And don't let anyone know we were talking."

Franky asked. "This all sounds pretty serious. We are all a little scared but are we in danger? I got a family, man."

"Just be cool. You will be alright. You see a problem, you reach out right away. Ok?"

Terry waved at Danny, who handed the ball back to Franky's son and headed over to Terry. As he passed Franky, he said. "Hey man, you need anything give me a call. You and Terry cool?"

"Yeah, I think we are good. Thanks."

Danny caught up to Terry and was just about to ask if he got what he needed when Terry's phone rang.

"Terry," he said as he listened to the caller.

"Ok. Let the boss know we are on the way."

Terry hung up and looked at Danny. "Looks like we got a body up by Cascade Creek. We need to head that way."

Terry and Danny jogged to Terry's car. Hopped in. Terry hit the flashers and headed out the park, back down Florida Road and turned right onto 550. Once on the highway, he hit the gas.

Chapter Twenty-Five

Buck spotted the flashing lights farther up the hill, just as he passed the entrance into the Purgatory ski area. As he approached the scene, he had to pull past the turn for County 591, because the road was full of emergency vehicles. He pulled over on the side of the road. Just as he was about to get out of the car his phone rang.

Buck checked the caller ID and answered the call.

"Yes, sir?" he asked.

"Have you gotten to the body scene yet?" asked Director Jackson.

"Just pulling up now."

"Good," replied the Director. I just got off the phone with our tech guys. United Flight 275 leaves DIA at 5:50 tonight. We checked the passenger list. Don't ask me how. There is a Claire Ringsby traveling tonight to LaGuardia Airport in New York City. Do you have the witness warrant yet?"

"I will check with the Sheriff as soon as I can find her. Do we have someone who can intercept her at the airport?"

"I do. I have Tracy and Doonen en route to the airport now. They will hook up with Denver Police once they get there and then go grab her before she gets on the plane. I was going to have them handle the interview at the airport to save time. Anything specific you want to know? I have already briefed them about what you have going on."

"Thanks, boss. They should be able to handle this without me. I see the Sheriff up ahead. I will call you right back."

Buck disconnected the call and as he went to put his phone back in his pocket it rang again. This time it was Terry Rubin. "Buck, did you get the word that we have a body?"

"Yeah," replied Buck. "I just got to the site. Where are you?"

"Just passing Purgatory. We can see the lights."

"Good," Buck replied. "I need to find the Sheriff. Let's talk when you get here."

Buck disconnected his phone and put it away as he headed towards the yellow crime tape. As he got to the tape he presented his ID to the Deputy who was responsible for logging in all the people on the scene. He let Buck pass under the tape.

Buck walked up to the Sheriff who was standing just at the top of the ravine talking to two guys in plain clothes. As he approached, the Sheriff stopped talking.

"Hi Buck," she said. "Buck, these are my two homicide guys, Detectives Quinn and Romero. Guys, this is Buck Taylor, CBI."

Buck looked at the two homicide detectives. They looked like homicide detectives you would find in any law enforcement office in the country. He had worked with dozens of guys over the years who looked just like them. Quinn was probably Buck's age and was most likely the lead. He was about five-ten, two hundred and forty pounds, with a gut that hung over his belt from too many well-cooked meals. He wore a light gray suit with a wide tie. He had the knot pulled down a couple inches and his top button was unbuttoned. Buck figured his shirt collar had probably gotten a little too tight to keep buttoned. What little hair he still had was plastered to his head from the heat.

Romero was Hispanic and quite a bit younger than Quinn. He wore blue jeans and a short sleeve button down shirt with the top two buttons open. He had a thick mustache and curly black hair. His dark eyes didn't stop moving during the entire introduction like he was constantly looking for something. Buck figured he had good observations skills. In his hand, he held an HP tablet and was entering information as he was introduced. Buck shook hands with both men. Quinn's handshake was strong but damp. Romero's was firm and dry.

The Sheriff looked at Quinn. "Please fill Buck in on what we have so far."

He was about to start when Terry Rubin and Danny Silvio crossed under the crime scene tape and signed in with the deputy with the clipboard. Then walked over to where Buck, the Sheriff and the two detectives stood. Buck held up his hand to Quinn, signaling him to wait just a second.

As they arrived the detectives exchanged pleasantries with Terry and Danny. The formalities over, Buck asked Quinn to start. Quinn started the debrief with a strong voice.

"The deceased appears to be a Hispanic male. About five feet four to five feet six. His weight looks a little light for his height. Cause of death appears to be a slit throat. From what we could see the cut seems to be clean and deep. The Forensic Pathologist will let us know more. The Doc estimates time of death to be forty-eight to seventy-two hours ago. The body does not appear to have been killed here. Maybe just dumped. Soon as the Doctor is done, forensics will start documenting the scene and we will look for evidence. The Doc did say that the body had been badly beaten prior to death."

Quinn checked his notes on the little pad he carried. Buck

figured he wasn't much into technology. He looked over at Romero. Romero looked at his tablet and continued.

"Body was found at 11:30 by two hikers who had been out on a day hike from the resort. They hadn't noticed the body when they started out this morning, but they said they weren't really looking. Something caught their eye as they were coming back. They think it might have been a flash from the sun hitting his belt buckle at just the right angle. As Mark said, no ID that we could find. The first deputy on the scene called it in right away and started taping off a perimeter. The body is not located in an easy place to get to. Wasn't placed carefully as far as we can tell. Maybe just thrown off the side of the road. If you look over there, just above the pathology tech, you can see a lot of broken branches leading to the culvert. Since it didn't rain yesterday or today we can't determine when it was dropped. We told the Doc that the victim appeared to have a streak of something white on his shirt. The tech took a field sample."

Romero stopped, looked at his tablet and appeared a little uncertain as to where to go next.

"Nice report guys," said Buck. "Thanks."

He signaled for the Sheriff and Terry to follow him and left the two detectives talking to Silvio.

"Anything that connects this to our guys?" Buck asked.

The Sheriff replied. "The first deputy on the scene was one of the deputies who was working with Terry on the surveillance. He is the one who took pictures of the guy who threw the toy over the fence before he got grabbed by one of the guards. He didn't get too close to the body, but he swears it looks like the guy from the pictures. The Forensic Pathologist has the pictures down there with him to see if we can get a comparison."

"Ok, good. By the way, were you able to get the Material Witness Warrant?" Buck asked.

The Sheriff said. "Oh, I almost forgot. Yes, we have it in the office, signed by the judge. Where do you want it?"

Buck reached into his pocket and handed her a card with a phone number with a 303 area code on it. He asked her if she could have someone fax the warrant to this number. He told her about the phone call with the Director just before he arrived and that they were waiting for the warrant to go in and grab Claire Ringsby. The Sheriff stepped away and made a phone call. Spoke a few words, read the number off the card, hung up and handed the card back to Buck.

"Done", she said.

Buck pulled out his phone, stepped away and called the Director. The Director answered on the second ring.

Before the Director could speak, Buck said, "Director, the warrant should be coming through on the fax line now, so we should be good on Claire Ringsby,"

"Anything on the body?" the Director interrupted.

Buck explained what they knew so far and that they were waiting for the Forensic Pathologist to give them the all clear on the site. He would call back as soon as he had anything.

Chapter Twenty-Six

Blondy was furious. Even Mustache had never seen him this mad. If it was possible for a human to explode, then this would have been that moment. The Mexican kid was lying on the floor in a ball. When the guard brought him back into the warehouse, Blondy had proceeded to beat the kid mercilessly. He hit and kicked him multiple times in the head and gut with his balled-up fist. Hard enough that the young folks who were working on the production line thought he was dead.

Blondy finally stopped beating on the unconscious kid and turned. Gritting his teeth, he looked at the guard who was supposed to be watching the door. "How the hell did you let this asshole get out the door?"

The guard looked like he wasn't sure if he should answer the question or not. He just looked down at the ground. This made Blondy even madder and before the guard knew what was happening Blondy hit him full force in the face, busting his nose and breaking off a couple teeth. The guard hit the ground hard. Everyone stopped what they were doing. Not knowing what would happen next.

Blondy reached down and grabbed the guard and with one big hand on his throat, lifted him off the ground and pushed him against the wall. The guard was a pretty good size guy. A former Mexican Federal Police Officer who knew how to dish out pain, yet Blondy was able to lift him up with one arm so that his feet were dangling three inches off the ground. Blondy looked him dead in the eye and with that sadistic sneer said, "If you ever let one of these kids escape again, I will cut your balls off and feed them to you. DO YOU UNDERSTAND?"

The guard didn't answer, so with his other hand Blondy pulled a twelve-inch KA-Bar knife out of the sheath hanging from his belt and pushed against the zipper on the guard's pants. The guard's eyes got as big as saucers.

Repeating each word, slowly for emphasis, Blondy repeated the question. "Do…You…understand?"

The guard answered this time that he understood. Blondy smiled, pulled the knife away from the Guard's crotch and slowly let the guard slide down the wall. He then walked over to the kid lying on the floor.

He turned to face the rest of the kids who work working on the production tables, still holding the knife in his hand. The fun he had with the guard hadn't seemed to appease the anger he felt inside. He walked along the production tables and stared, or more like glared, at each kid. When he reached the end of the tables, he turned and started back to the other end. Halfway there he stopped, grabbed the young boy who was standing in front of him and put the knife to his throat. A little trickle of blood started to slide down the kid's throat. Blondy looked at the rest of the kids. In Spanish, he told the kids that if anyone of them ever tried to escape, not only would he kill the one who tied to escape, but he would pick someone else at random, and kill them as well. He promised them it would be very painful.

The kid he was holding, with his arm wrapped around his throat, pissed in his pants. As the urine flowed down his leg he froze not knowing what to expect. Nobody breathed. Blondy looked down as the wet spot expanded down the front of the kid's pants and smiled an unbelievably hideous smile. He pushed the kid down on the ground and told him to clean up the mess.

Blondy moved down the line, eyeing each kid as he walked. He then walked over to the kid who was lying on the floor and in one lightning swift move, lifted the kid's head, push the knife blade into the side of his throat and swept it across his windpipe to the other side of his head. The knife went through the kid's throat like a hot knife through butter. It was over in less than two seconds.

The kids and the guards all stared in disbelief and gasped as a pool of blood formed under the partially severed head of the kid. One of the girls passed out and several of them started crying. Even Mustache looked on in stunned silence. He knew Blondy could be brutal, but this was a whole other side. Mustache decided at that point that he needed to be a little more careful around this crazy Gringo.

Blondy looked at the guard who was wiping the blood from his nose and said, "Get this piece of shit out of here and clean this mess up. Make sure no one can find the body." Then he walked off toward the guard's office and closed the door.

Two guards picked up a plastic tarp from under one of the work tables and dumped the body into it. They grabbed two of the girls and told them to get the mess cleaned up. With the body wrapped in plastic, one of the guards went outside and pulled one of the SUVs over to the side door of the warehouse. Looking around carefully to make sure no one was watching they quickly loaded the body into the back of the SUV and closed the door. Broken Nose then jumped in the SUV and headed for the gate, which opened electronically as he approached.

Broken Nose had never seen anyone get their head almost cut off. He was still shaking as he exited the truck yard. He had to stop for a minute, so at the end of the street he pulled over to the side of the road and tried to settle down. No matter what, he would make sure no one found the body. He never wanted to be on the receiving end of one of Blondy's outbursts.

Finally, somewhat composed, he headed east, turned onto 550 and headed north looking for a good spot to dump the body. After about twenty miles or so, he came to a very sharp hairpin turn and noticed a creek running under the highway. He pulled onto the shoulder of the road and turned off the lights. He sat for a minute. He could see for quite some ways and since there was no traffic visible, he climbed out, opened the rear hatch and pulled out the body.

He pushed the wrapped body closer to the edge of the road and started to unwrap the plastic. His intention was to slide the body down the slope and let it drop into the culvert. His mistake was unwrapping the body so close to the edge of the road that when he pulled the plastic away from the body the body went crashing down into the shrubs below the culvert. "Shit," was his first thought. Now what? He tried to climb down into the creek, but the slope was too steep, and he started to slide himself. Pulling back, he thought, "Damn it. No one will find it down there."

He quickly threw the tarp back in the rear, closed the hatch, jumped in the driver's seat and turned the SUV around and headed back to town.

Chapter Twenty-Seven

Buck, Terry and the Sheriff stood on the edge of the road near the culvert and watched as the La Plata County Search and Rescue team assisted Dr. Robert Kramer up from the bottom of the culvert. Dr. Kramer is a semi-retired medical doctor and licensed Forensic Pathologist under contract to La Plata County as well as the surrounding counties to perform autopsies. Colorado is one of several states that still operates under the Coroner system instead of the Medical Examiner system. Since the Coroner in La Plata county, Jennifer Bishop, is not a medical doctor, any deaths that require an autopsy, by code, must be performed by a licensed Pathologist. The county hired Dr. Kramer to perform autopsies on an as needed basis.

Dr. Kramer was assisted up the slope, disconnected from the climbing harness and stood to the side as the rescue team pulled up the body, which was wrapped in a black body bag and secured to a rescue sled. The body was then placed in a waiting ambulance to be delivered to the Sheriff's office, where a small autopsy suite along with coolers was set up in the basement. This was a lot more convenient than a few years ago when the bodies had to be taken to Grand Junction for autopsy.

Once Dr. Kramer was comfortable that the body was secure,

he signed a transportation order and his pathology assistant entered the ambulance for the ride down the mountain to the Sheriffs' office. The body would be accompanied by his assistant until it was safely locked in one of the four coolers available. This overabundance of caution was needed because the body, especially in a foul play situation, was part of the chain of evidence. The ambulance was followed by a deputy. Just one more precaution against tampering with evidence.

Dr. Kramer walked to his car and removed his Nitrile gloves and his Tyvek one-piece jumpsuit. He rubbed disinfectant on his hands, turned and headed towards the assembled group.

"Sheriff, gentlemen," he said as he approached.

"Dr. Kramer, this is Buck Taylor from CBI and the lead deputy on this case, Terry Rubin." Everyone shook hands and then waited as the Doctor assembled his thoughts.

"Cause of death is pretty obvious," started the Doctor. "His throat was slit pretty much from ear to ear. Deep enough that it was almost severed. Death would have been instantaneous. My experience tells me the assailant had to be a pretty good size guy and was also well trained. The autopsy will reveal more, but my guess is the knife went in just under the right ear and was swiped across the throat to the other side. This is a method that has been refined by the military over the years because the larynx is cut through almost immediately so the victim has no chance to yell out."

Buck interrupted. "So, you're thinking special forces training?"

The Doctor looked at Buck. "First blush. Yes, that would be a good starting point." The Doctor continued. "I will tell you this. That young man suffered one hell of a beating before he was killed.

Anyone of the blows he suffered could have probably killed him at some point. The knife was final."

Terry asked. "Doctor, were you able to compare the face of the victim to the photo we gave you?" Is it the same guy?"

The Doctor pulled the photo from his shirt pocket and handed it back to Terry. "Hard to tell for sure, not a great picture, but I would say ninety-five percent yes."

Everyone stood for a minute, then the Doctor turned to leave.

"Oh. I did take a couple samples from the cuts on his face. We might get some usable DNA from the blood. Gave the samples to Dani. She will bring them up with the rest of the stuff she found. Not much so far. I will start the autopsy as soon as I get back to the office. Sheriff, will one of your guys be attending?"

The Sheriff waved over Quinn and Romero, who were talking with Dani Walker, the forensic tech, who had just climbed up from the culvert. They walked over and stood with the group.

The Sheriff said, "The Doc is going to start the autopsy as soon as he gets down the mountain. Would like at least one of you there, can you work that out?"

It was obvious from the reaction of Romero, that he wasn't thrilled with the idea of attending the autopsy, but he waited for his partner to talk. Quinn, who had probably seen quite a few autopsies in his career told the Sheriff that he would head down for the autopsy and that Romero could finish wrapping up the scene. Romero looked relieved. The homicide team walked off towards the cars and Buck figured Quinn was giving Romero last minute instructions for closing out the scene.

The Sheriff looked at Buck and Terry. "For right now I am going to let the homicide team deal with this. Your plates are full. If this turns out to be related to your case, we will decide then what to do."

Buck and Terry both nodded in agreement.

Buck said, "Let's get those blood samples over to the state lab in Pueblo and see if we get any DNA. I will call the lab and let them know it's coming."

Buck checked his watch and realized he had missed lunch, so he hopped in his car and headed down 550 and back into Durango. At College Ave, he turned left until he got to East 8th Avenue, turned left and headed up the hill to Fort Lewis College. He knew of an awesome taco truck that usually parked at the campus. It was right where he thought it would be. He ordered two beef tacos and a bottle of Coke and sat down at the park bench opposite the truck. Lunch was gone in a couple gulps and he got back in his car and headed back down the hill.

Chapter Twenty-Eight

Buck, the Sheriff and Terry had agreed to meet back in the conference room at the Sheriff's office to go over today's interviews. Buck wanted to stop in and talk to the sneak and peek team and see if they had anything that was usable from the wiretaps. Buck headed for his car and just as he sat down his phone rang. It was Hank Clancy, FBI.

"Buck," said Hank. "Have you spoken to Josh or his guys yet today?"

"I was just on my way back to talk to them."

Buck proceeded to tell Hank about the body found in the culvert. He emphasized the fact that the body may not be related to their investigation, but they believed it might be based on the picture from the surveillance team. He told him that the Forensic Pathologist was getting ready to start the autopsy and that they had some blood samples they needed to get to the state crime lab in Pueblo to see if they could get any DNA.

Hank was not pleased that he hadn't been told about the body earlier, but he seemed to get over it pretty quickly.

He said, "Ok. Keep me posted. Go see Josh and have him fill you in on the electronics. Also, we did pick up an encrypted sat phone from the NSA satellite survey. The boys in Washington are working on the encryption and once they crack it we will see what's there. They did tell me that the encryption software is top notch, maybe even government or military grade."

Buck told him he would call him in a bit and closed his car door and pulled away. As he did his phone rang again. Jess Gonzales, DEA.

"Buck, it's Jess. Can you talk?"

"Sure Jess, whatcha got?"

"We may have nailed down one of the US enforcers for the Sonoma Cartel. I am sending the info to your phone. This guy is bad news. Name we have on him is Harry Crank. Staff Sergeant. Not sure if that is an alias or real. He spent 6 years in special forces, Green Beret. Dishonorable discharge in 2010 and forty-eight months in a military prison after almost killing four guys in a bar fight. Claimed they jumped him and all he did was defend himself."

"According to the Military Police report from Fort Benning, Georgia, Staff Sergeant Crank and two of his trainers were having drinks in a strip joint off base when some guys in the audience started hassling one of the strippers. Somehow, someone got pushed and Sergeant Crank ended up getting a beer spilled on him. According to witnesses, Crank went nuts and started slamming the guys at the other table. By the time he was pulled off by his two buddies, the four college kids at the table looked like they had been through a meat grinder, the bouncers were injured, the dancer had a split lip from getting punched by accident when she tried to run behind the table these guys were sitting at, and they had caused about four grand in damages to the bar."

"Everyone who didn't need hospitalization went to jail. The four college kids went to the hospital. MPs were called and the cops turned over the soldiers to them. Might have been the end of it except Sergeant Crank took exception to being turned over to a black MP and decided to teach him a lesson. Back at the military police jail on base, the MPs removed the cuffs and before anyone could move Sergeant Crank had the black MP in a headlock and almost broke his neck. Took six MPs to separate them."

"The result of the bar fight was that of the four kids Crank had put in the hospital, two were released with bandages and casts, one suffered a concussion and a couple broken ribs and one ended up in rehab and will most likely spend the rest of his life in a wheelchair as a quadriplegic. Crank had the book thrown at him. Seems the bar was owned by a state legislator and he knew all four of the kids. Crank got busted down to a private, spent forty-eight months in a military prison and received a dishonorable discharge. Once out, he fell off the grid and hasn't been seen since."

"Why do we think this is one of our guys?" Buck asked.

"Was talking to a couple of our guys who used to work across the border. They said that when the Sonoma Cartel was just getting started there were a lot of violent endings for members of the other cartels. According to rumors, the guy running the ops for the Sonoma Cartel was a tall blond ex Green Beret, who had a real gift for creating violent endings."

She went on to tell him that the guy they heard rumors about was a real whack job. "These stories, especially the bad ones, have a way of turning into legends. At some point, all the stories, true or not, end up as part of this guy's street cred. The bad part is we don't know what is truth or fiction. We do know that he has traveled between Mexico and the US on several occasions over the years and someone always gets dead. And always in a violent way."

"With this cartel war going on across the border things are

changing rapidly, almost daily, and the bodies keep piling up. If this guy is now working for the Sonoma Cartel, then whatever we are dealing with is a big deal."

"Jess, do we know what this guy did in special forces?" asked Buck

"Hold on, let me look through his military record." Buck heard her clicking keys on her computer. "Holy shit, Buck. Lots of redacted stuff in his file. From what I can see, this guy was one badass. Here it is. Last posting was Benning as a hand-to-hand combat instructor. Specialty was blade weapons."

Buck whistled. He told Jess about the body dump he had just left. Could be a coincidence that the kid was killed with a knife in a very military manner. Buck didn't think so; neither did Jess.

"Buck, if this is one of our guys in the warehouse, he has about a dozen outstanding warrants on him. He might be our way in."

"Jess, is his picture in the stuff you just sent me?"

"It is," replied Jess.

"Thanks," Buck said. "I will call you later."

Chapter Twenty-Nine

Buck hung up and pulled into the parking lot behind the Sheriff's office.

His first stop was the conference room to talk to the sneak and peek guys. Toby was manning the computers this afternoon and he was listening intently through the headphones that covered both ears. He waved a hand at Buck to acknowledge his presence and pointed to the chair. He then held up one finger, signaling to Buck to wait. He clicked a bunch of computer keys and removed the headphones.

"We are getting some good stuff," he said.

Then he swung the second computer monitor around so Buck could see what he was looking at. On the screen was a live feed from the camera they had placed in the air conditioning duct. Buck put on his reading glasses and leaned in to get a better view of the screen. He was looking at what appeared to be a long assembly line table with a couple dozen people sitting around the table opening boxes of toys, removing a piece of the toy, using a knife to cut a small opening and then feeding pills of some kind into the body of the toy. The part that was removed was then reinstalled, the toy was replaced in the box and the box was sealed. It looked like any small factory in America.

"Can you pan this camera?" Buck asked.

"Unfortunately, no. This one is not moveable. I can zoom in quite a bit."

The view from the camera began to grow larger and more defined. Toby took it to maximum zoom. It gave Buck a closer view of the people working but not a great view of the pills. At least not enough to identify the product. He watched for a few more minutes and then leaned back from the screen and scratched his head.

"Any way we can identify the pills?" he asked.

Toby shook his head. "I did have a view last night when someone placed a huge industrial size pill bottle on the table. Couldn't read the words on the bottle so I sent it to Washington to see if they can do anything with it."

"Ok," said Buck. "What else have you got?"

Toby clicked a few more keys and the screen changed to a view of a computer worksheet. He proceeded to explain to Buck that they were able to isolate one computer from the workspace and three computers from the office area. The ones from the office didn't give any indication of what was going on in the warehouse. The analysts worked all night on the computers and from what they could tell, it was almost like two different businesses were being run out of the space. The books for the trucking company were clean. No odd write-offs, no mysterious entries. Just a very simple accounting program. All the billing receipts match up with deliveries and all the manifests looked normal. The analysts even compared past invoicing to the invoicing for the past couple weeks and nothing had changed.

"The other computer is another story. We gave access to the NSA and they are still having trouble getting in. The encryption is first rate and very high end. They think they are making progress. The NSA was able to crack the encryption on the one sat phone they locked on." According to Toby, there was only one call made today and it sounded like a very simple report. All is good, on schedule, that kind of thing. Nothing was said that was definitive about a shipping date.

Buck sat back. He was hoping for more. He was almost disappointed. Then Toby dropped the bomb. "Since the building's electrical system was being used as a gigantic voice tap, it can pick up even the quietest conversation. Basically, no place to hide. It seems that one of the guards must have gotten beat up by the boss and the guard was still pissed off that he had been disrespected. He told the guy he was talking to that he would get even with the boss as soon as they got this first shipment out of the way. He would settle the score." Toby reminded Buck that this conversation had taken place in Spanish. He offered to play it for Buck, but Buck's Spanish was rudimentary at best.

He shook his head and Toby continued the debrief. "The guard, it seems, was really pissed at himself for letting that kid almost escape, but that did not give the boss cause to punch him in front of all those kids. The boss had disrespected him and to make matters worse, he made him dump the body. The guard sounded like he had a strong connection to the big boss and would make the other boss pay. His pal reminded him that the Gringo boss was crazy. That he slit that kid's throat without even thinking about it. At that point, someone else walked into the room and told them their break was over and get back to work."

Buck pushed forward in his chair. He looked at Toby with a surprised look on his face. Almost to stunned to talk.

"Is that what they actually said? That the Gringo boss slit the kid's throat?"

Toby nodded. "That's how we translated it. Does this mean something?"

Buck replied. 'We found a body dumped off the highway north of town today. Young Mexican kid with his throat slit. Can't be a coincidence."

Toby replied. "Holy shit. But does this give us enough to go after him? Right now, all we have is two guys talking."

Buck thought for a minute. "At this point, we don't even know who this guy is. We have some info from the DEA on a possible guy but no proof he is even here. If it is the same guy and we can prove he is here it might help our cause and give us a way in. It might not get us a warrant on its own but with everything else we have, it might be enough. Let's see what the Sheriff thinks."

Toby said, "You think this kid was killed in front of the others as a lesson?"

Buck thought for a minute. "Yeah. That would be my read. Anything else?"

Toby nodded. "Just typical work environment chatter. These kids are being abused by the guards, but they don't say much. I think they are just plain scared. Last night after we activated the voice taps, we picked up some crying coming from somewhere in the space. Possibly from the cages we spotted when we set the camera. The guards make small talk, but nothing about what's going on."

Toby looked unsure about the next part of the debrief. Buck looked at him.

"You got something else?" Buck asked.

"Not sure what it means but I think one of the bosses is having sex with some of the young girls. We picked up some, what I guess you could call, grunts and some screams. The whole lead up to the grunts made it sound like the girl did not want to go and she kept pleading with someone else to stop it. The second voice sounded American, definite Sothern accent. He just laughed. The sex sounded pretty rough."

Buck looked at Toby. "Ok. Keep listening. Can you copy the conversation about the body to a disc, so the Sheriff can get it to the District Attorney?"

Toby said he could and Buck told him that they had done good, but to keep working on the computer.

Buck got up and headed towards the Sheriff's office. If this is the same guy Jess had sent him the info on then they could possibly go after him on one of the outstanding warrants. They needed to prove it is the same guy.

Buck hated this point in an investigation. Things were starting to open up but they were still missing a lot of pieces. He thought back on the picture of the kids working at the table. How had they been able to sneak that many people, as a group, into the US without someone noticing? He wanted to dismiss the first thought he had but it sat there nagging at his brain. These guys had help getting across the border and they were getting help bringing in huge quantities of pills, probably Oxy, but from where? He knew anything manufactured in the US was carefully controlled. But if not from here, then where? After all, the papers were full of stories about the huge rise in opioid addictions. The President had just recently declared it a National Medical Emergency. This was serious stuff, yet from looking at the pictures and the number of trailers sitting in the trucking company yard, they were bringing this stuff in without any trouble.

Chapter Thirty

Buck stopped off in his temporary office, sat down at his desk, pulled out his phone and dialed the number for Max Clinton. Dr. Maxine Clinton was a matronly woman in her early sixties, about five feet five with short gray hair. She probably thought she carried around an extra fifteen pounds she didn't need but she was still a handsome woman. Married for 40 years, Max had 4 children, eleven grandchildren and 6 great-grandchildren. She lived in a 150-year-old farm house in Pueblo, where she liked to tend her garden and sit on her porch and drink iced tea. She was also a bourbon girl and could easily drink most people under the table. She was loud and outspoken, but she knew her job.

Max received her Ph.D. in Biology from the University of Colorado and had worked as a biology professor for 20 years before joining CBI. Currently, she was head of the state crime lab, a job she thoroughly enjoyed. She was a tough taskmaster, but she had a belief system that didn't allow for defeat. Her goal was to give the crime investigator, no matter which department or municipality they worked for, all the information they would need to solve any crime. She held that as a sacred obligation to the victims. She was incredibly dedicated and her team at the lab practically worshipped her.

Buck would have been included in that group. Many times, during a tough investigation, it was Max and her team that lit the spark that led to a breakthrough. Max was one of Buck's favorite people and she felt the same way about him.

Maxine answered her phone on the fourth ring. "Hey, Buck. How's my favorite cop?"

"Doing great," Buck replied.

"I bet not if you're calling old Max. What can I do to make your day?"

"I have some blood samples heading your way from Durango. I need to see if we can get DNA from the samples for anyone other than the victim. It's a pretty crucial ask."

Max asked. "Is this for the possible cartel thing? The Director already called me and told me to put everything on the back burner if you called. He didn't go into details but said this was a top priority. He even authorized us to spend the money for an overnight DNA test. Those are not cheap, and he told me it didn't matter. God, Buck, what have you gotten yourself into now?"

Buck filled Max in on some of the details about the case and what they had to date. When he spoke the words out loud, it really didn't seem like they had much of a case. But then when he thought about the fact that he had only arrived yesterday morning, maybe things weren't so bleak.

Max agreed. She was always good for his ego. She seemed to always know just the right words to say to keep his head on straight. She always said, if she could deal with her huge family, she could deal with pretty much anything. She had proven that time and again and Buck was always grateful for her insights. She may not have been a cop, but she knew more about crime than anyone he knew.

She listened carefully as Buck spoke. Not interrupting until he was finished giving her the high points.

"You know Buck. It sounds to me like you guys are pretty much one break away from closing this thing down. It will either come from the science or it will come from the electronics, you just watch. In the meantime, I will get the blood samples going as soon as we have them in our hot little hands."

Buck thanked her, and she ended the conversation the way she always did. "God will watch over you, Buck Taylor. You are a good man. Stay safe."

Buck wasn't much of a religious man. He hadn't been to church in probably forty years. He had been raised Catholic but left the church right after Confirmation. He always had too many questions about the teachings and too many people telling him that he had to have faith. That wasn't the answer he was looking for. He had a lot of friends, Max among them, who always offered up a prayer and especially when Lucy was dying. He never once rejected any of those offers. Often smiling and thanking them for their kind thoughts.

Buck had realized a long time ago that it wasn't God and faith that he had a problem with, it was organized religion. In his many years in law enforcement, he had seen too many times the after effects of someone's religious beliefs. It amazed him that so many people of faith could cause so much hatred and crime. But then non-believers created just as much havoc.

Buck always believed there was probably a higher power out there but he didn't believe that whatever that power was that it really cared about one individual over another. His football coach always offered up a prayer before each game asking for help in defeating the other team. He always suspected the other team's coach probably was doing the same thing. How did God decide which team should win?

He knew a lot of people who said a lot of prayers for Lucy over the five years she was sick, but in the end, she still died. And she was the last person who should have gotten cancer. But Buck didn't carry any hatred. Who could he possibly get mad at? Who could he blame?

Buck believed that there were spirits or a force all around us and he always thanked them for allowing him to enjoy the hike, or for allowing him to catch fish, or see the sunrise and the sunset. It wasn't a religion. It was something deeper. Something Buck really didn't understand. He just accepted it. But no matter what, he always appreciated it when Max told him that God was watching over him. After all. What could it hurt?

Buck hung up his phone and sat back in his chair. He picked up his phone and dialed Jess Gonzales, DEA.

Jess answered. "Hey Buck, what's up?" He filled her in on the electronics results so far. She listened intently.

"Sounds like this could be the same guy. We just need to prove he is actually in the warehouse."

"Yeah," replied Buck. "Easier said than done. But that wasn't all I called for. If we are dealing with huge quantities of oxy, where is the stuff coming from?"

She thought for a minute and said. "Great question. We have been wondering the same thing since this all came to light. We have tight controls on everything manufactured in the US and Canada, so we are certain it is not coming from inside the US, especially with the possible quantities involved. Some of my guys are wondering if it is coming from someplace way off, like China or Pakistan or somewhere else out there. Probably getting shipped into Mexico. At this point, we don't have a solid answer."

Buck replied, "Ok, let's say it is from overseas. How is it getting across the border?"

Jess was a little hesitant. "We have some thoughts but I am going to keep those in house for a while yet. We may have a better idea once this is over."

"You think the cartel is getting help on our side, don't you?"

"Look Buck. Let's wrap this up first. Anything else is federal and we will deal with it. Sorry I can't be more specific."

"No problem Jess. I gotta run. Let's talk later."

Buck hung up the phone. He sensed Jess knew more than she was saying. He understood that whatever she knew was federal and he was just a local cop, but he also respected the fact that she had a much bigger job to do than he had, and he was grateful for the help.

Buck got up from his desk, walked down the hall to the kitchen and grabbed another Coke out of the refrigerator. He opened it, took a big gulp and looked out the window. How did we get here, he thought as he looked out over the sleepy little town? How could something so ugly show up in a place so beautiful? Buck knew one thing for certain. Evil might have arrived here but he would make sure it didn't stay and that it didn't go anywhere else. This was the world he lived in and he wasn't going to let anything ruin it.

Buck left the kitchen and went in search of the Sheriff and Terry Rubin.

Chapter Thirty-One

Blondy was sitting in the little guard's office in the warehouse talking on the encrypted sat phone. The conversation was in Spanish. Mustache was sitting on the other side of the desk. He had spent the last 15 minutes filling in the Boss about progress and about the kid he had to make an example of. He knew the Boss would approve. The Boss would have done the same thing and it would most likely have been a lot more brutal. In the two years since he started working for the Sonoma Cartel, he had seen and done a lot of horrific things but the things he had witnessed the Boss do were so much worse.

When Carlos Rojas wanted something, he didn't care who got in his way, men, women, old people, kids. It didn't matter. Carlos would have probably cut off his own mother's head if it got him what he wanted. Brutal was an understatement when it came to Rojas and the more brutal the better.

Blondy stopped talking and listened. He said. "No problem, sir. We can make that happen."

Blondy hung up the phone, looked at Mustache and said, "The Boss wants to move up the timetable. Instead of shipping out the first loads on Tuesday, he wants to do it Sunday morning. He has already alerted our other locations to expect the shipments and be ready to re-ship within a couple days. What do you think? Can we be ready?"

Mustache thought for a moment and said, "That only gives us two days. We still have one and a half trailers to load. We should be ok. We will need to push these kids to get done. It would be better if we had that kid you sliced. He was a hard worker."

Blondy smiled. "Yeah, well that's too damn bad. We needed to make an example of the kid. Water under the bridge."

"Ok. You're the boss. I will start pushing the kids. No sleep tonight."

Mustache stood up to leave. Blondy said, "Sit a minute. Couple other things. I told the Boss that I am getting a twitchy feeling in the back of my brain. Not sure what's going on, but when I get the twitch I always pay attention. Make sure the guards keep their eyes open. Second. He's concerned that Dick and Hector might not be fully onboard. We may have to handle them."

Mustache interrupted. "This is a small town man. Somebody gonna notice one of those guys goes missing. Maybe we can increase the money each month, see if they come around."

Blondy thought for a minute. "Ok. Offer them another hundred K each and let's see if that makes them more cooperative. Last thing. When we are done here the Boss wants his nephew to take over running the operation and he wants us back home. He is having some problems and he needs us to deal with them. He wants his nephew to run a minimum of four trucks a week out of here and he is thinking about bringing up the first load of liquid cocaine and meth. He wants this place fully operational by the end of the month'.

Mustache looked at him. "O, but you and I both know that kid is an idiot. He let that kid almost get over the fence. You also better hope he didn't somehow get word to his uncle that you punched him in front of everybody. These wackos have pride and you twisted his up a bunch. You sure we ain't going home to get slaughtered?"

Blondy got a serious look on his face. "Don't know for sure."

"Look man. We got us a boatload of money. Maybe it's time to move on. Maybe Europe or someplace like that."

"Knock that shit off. You know the Boss could find us anywhere. We're in this for the long haul. Besides, if we bailed, Rojas would not stop looking for us until we were dead. I don't want to spend the rest of my life looking over my shoulder."

Mustache nodded, got up from the chair and headed into the warehouse. Blondy sat and thought for a minute. He hadn't considered when he punched the Boss's nephew, that he was stepping over a family line. He was maintaining discipline. He hoped that this time his temper hadn't gotten him in trouble. Blondy opened the screen on the encrypted laptop, pulled up a contact list and sent out a group email to his drivers letting them know to be at the warehouse at four AM Sunday morning. He wondered why the Boss moved up the timetable, but then what did it matter? He needed to be ready no matter what.

Mustache walked along the production line and started yelling in Spanish that they had to get the last truck loaded by the end of the day tomorrow. No one would be sleeping tonight. The kids never flinched. They just kept their heads down and kept working. He then headed over to the guard that Blondy had punched and pulled him towards the loading dock door and out of earshot of the office.

"Your uncle is going to leave you here to run this operation after we are done," he said to the guard. "Your uncle wants us back in Mexico after the loads go out. Did you somehow get word to your uncle about getting punched?"

The guard looked at him with surprise. He was ready to deny anything. He didn't trust Mustache and thought this might be a test or something. He answered in Spanish, "hell no, man. You know me better than that. Rojas would kill him if he found out."

Mustache knew he was lying. Pride was a big factor in the cartel world, as was family until it wasn't. He wasn't sure how the nephew had gotten the word back to Rojas, but it was obvious that he had. Mustache smiled.

"Maybe you should say something," he walked away.

The guard wasn't sure what just happened, but he was starting to get the idea that maybe things weren't all that rosy between Blondy and Mustache and that Mustache was covering his bets. Something to think about.

Chapter Thirty-Two

Claire cringed whenever the door between the old warehouse and the other warehouse, as she referred to it, opened. Blondy made her nervous but when it was Mustache who came into the office she felt almost dirty. It was probably the way he stood in front of her desk and leered at her. No one had ever looked at her like that and it made her feel cheap and used.

The door to the other warehouse opened and in walked Mustache. He stopped at her desk and with that lecherous smile asked her how her day was going. Trying to be polite, the way she had been raised, she told him her day was fine. He told her he could make her nights fine too and then he laughed a disgusting laugh and headed back towards the offices. After each encounter with him she wondered to herself, how was she ever going to be able to stay in this job if he was part of the package. She felt like she needed a shower.

Mustache found Hector sitting at his desk working on the computer. Hector smiled and invited him to have a seat, which Mustache did. Mustache was thinking that Hector was coming around to having them as part of his business. He felt that Hector was beginning to like the money, even though he had only received one payment so far, but he seemed to be adapting better than Dick was.

Hector was starting to enjoy the money. He was very careful how he spent it and he hadn't yet told his wife about the off-shore account, but he was able to take her to dinner a couple times and to buy her a pretty bracelet for no reason at all. His wife felt it was extravagant but she didn't force him to return it and she wore it every day.

Hector stopped clicking computer keys and looked at Mustache.

"Everything Ok?" he asked.

"Where is your partner?" Mustache asked.

"He is meeting with a prospective client. Can I do anything for you or do you need to see him?"

Mustache liked the fact that they were still chasing business. It made him feel more like they were getting the hang of working for the cartel and were trying to keep their piece of the business working.

"The Boss thinks you might not be comfortable with our arrangement. Is that true?" Mustache asked.

"No," replied Hector. "We are fine. Dick had a little trouble coming around but he seems ok now. We have tried to stay out of your way just as we were told to do."

"That is good because we wouldn't want you to be unhappy. Unhappy people cause problems." Mustache smiled.

"Did we do something wrong?" asked Hector looking very nervous.

Mustache told him that the Boss liked to have happy employees and partners and so towards that end he was going to give them each an additional fifty K each month. Just so they would feel appreciated. He wasn't sure why he lied about the amount that he and Blondy had agreed on. Maybe he was starting to think too much. He and Blondy had known each other a long time and they trusted each other. Or did they. Hector smiled, said thank you and was there anything else he could help him with.

"Just make sure your partner appreciates our generosity."

Mustache stood up and walked out the office door. Hector was relieved that there was no problem and pleased with what he had just heard. A couple months of this and we might be able to get out of this little town he thought, and go someplace far away. Now he had to make sure Dick went along. He would hate to see something terrible happen to Dick.

Hector told Dick about the increased monthly payment when he got back to the office. Dick was not pleased. He had been quiet for the last couple weeks about this new arrangement but he hadn't accepted this whole thing yet. It also bothered him that Hector seemed to be going along quite willingly.

Dick walked out of Hector's office, sat down at his own desk, put his hands up to his head and pushed his hair back. He was concerned that once whatever was going on next door was finished that either he or Hector would be expendable. He knew that the work next door wasn't a onetime thing and that he would have to keep up a false face from now on. He was also concerned that he could end up in prison and that scared him to death.

Chapter Thirty-Three

Buck found the Sheriff in her office. She was talking on her desk phone and pointed to the chair opposite her desk. Buck sat down. The chair was an old padded black leather chair and although it had seen better days it was still comfortable. Buck sat back and waited for the Sheriff to finish her conversation. The Sheriff clicked off.

"Hell of a day," she said. "I am glad we don't have many days like the last couple. People are running a little ragged. By the way. That was Dr. Kramer. He was calling with the preliminary autopsy results. Just as we figured. The kid died from massive blood loss caused by the slice through his neck. Nothing unusual there. The Doc did say that the facial contusions and the body bruises were recent, probably within a couple hours of his death. One thing he noticed that was a little strange, was a lot of earlier bruising. Doc figures this kid has been getting beaten for months. Some of the old bruises were almost too faded to see."

Buck thought about that for a minute.

"I'm guessing," he said "This is probably how they keep these kids in line. Beatings, drugs, you name it. Any early tox info?"

"No tox screen yet. Too early. He did take a few more swabs

and he pulled some material out from under his nails. Who knows? Maybe the killer left us some DNA. He packaged up the clothes and the new swabs and along with the earlier blood swabs he sent it all to the state crime lab, by courier service. The lab should get it later tonight or first thing in the morning."

"Detective Quinn is finishing up with the Doc and will be up in a bit to write it all up. At least right now there is nothing that points to any connection between the murder and the warehouse except for the electronics, which right now is uncorroborated."

Buck said, "Maybe after we get the labs back. Let's wait and see. In the meantime, I think we should take a run at the two guys who own the trucking company. Maybe we can get something from one of them."

"You think that's wise?" asked the Sheriff. "We don't know how deep these guys are in. Might tip our hand."

"Yeah. Been thinking about that. I know this guy Dick has been crying in his beer and now with Claire on the run, maybe Dick is our in. Let's wait til our guys pick up Claire and get a chance to talk to her. Might give us some new insight into which way to go. They should be picking her up right about now."

"Ok," said the Sheriff. "The local newspaper hound keeps calling the desk wanting to know about a possible dead body. That's gonna be a big story around here. How do you think we should play it?"

"Can we hold him off for a little while until we know if it is connected or not? Somebody tried to hide the body, and as of right now, they probably don't know we found it. I'd like to keep it that way."

"Got it. Let me see what I can do to keep stalling him."

"Where you headed?" she asked.

"I was gonna grab some food and head back to the hotel. Need to fill out a report for the Director on progress so far. Gonna be a short report. Call if you need me."

Buck got out of the comfortable chair, walked out the door to the Sheriff's office and headed for his car. He was just opening the door that led to the parking lot when Terry Rubin pushed it open.

"Hey, Buck. I was looking for you."

"Well," replied Buck. "Here I am. What's up?"

Terry was concerned with the lack of progress they had been making. Buck liked this young fella. He had a lot of drive. He also wasn't as young as Buck thought. Buck figured when he met Terry, yesterday that he was in his late twenties, early thirties. He couldn't have been more wrong. Terry was actually forty-six. He had received a Bachelor's degree in Criminology from the University of Colorado in Boulder and had graduated from the FBI Forensics Academy, which the FBI ran each year to teach local law enforcement officers how to run an investigation and gather evidence. It was a highly sought after program and the FBI prided themselves on only taking the best the states had to offer. On some occasions, the FBI made job offers to the top-ranked students in the class. Terry had been offered a job but had turned it down due to his family situation.

He spent ten years with the Salt Lake City Police Department before transferring to La Plata County. He had been with the Sheriff's Office for nearly ten years. At first, he wasn't thrilled with the pace of life in Durango, but he had no choice. His wife's mom was ailing, and his wife wanted to be close. Even though his mother in law had passed away five years ago Terry had gotten comfortable in his new surroundings and his family had set down roots. With his young looks, he was a perfect fit for undercover drug work, considering Durango was a college town, and he thrived in his new job.

Terry followed Buck to his car.

"What do you think if we go after either Dick or Hector? Maybe we can shake something loose."

Buck smiled. "Sheriff and I were just talking about that very thing. We are going to wait until the CBI team talks to Claire Ringsby and see if she might be able to give us some insight into which one might be best. Good thought though."

"Great minds," said Terry. "You gonna call it a night?"

"Yeah. Why don't you wrap up for today and we can pick up fresh in the morning?"

Terry said that he had some paperwork to do to and he would close up in a little while. He wished Buck a good night and headed back to the side door of the Sheriff's Department. Buck got in his car and sat for a minute trying to decide what he wanted to eat. What he really wanted was a good steak, so he headed out to 550, turned north and headed for Charlie's Roadhouse, a little steak place just out past the northern edge of Durango.

Buck loved Charlie's and tried to get there at least once anytime he was in the area. It was a unique little place. From the outside, it looked like an old log cabin. Inside it had an old west charm. Dark wood, worn red vinyl cushions but it was the menu that was unique. They offered four different cuts of steak: ribeye, NY, filet and sirloin. They recently started offering a chicken dish. The steak came with a baked potato and vegetable. You could get a salad, but they only had ranch dressing. That was the entire menu. Buck didn't know where they got their meat from but he had never tasted meat so tender in his life. He liked the simplicity of the place and he was never disappointed with the meal.

Buck finished the last little bit of the ribeye he was eating and the waitress came by and refilled his glass of Coke. She took his plate and he sat back to just enjoy the moment. He tried to focus for a minute on the case but with all the background noise in the restaurant, it was hard to concentrate. He finished his Coke, paid the check the waitress had left on the corner of the table for him and stepped out into the night air. The last couple days had been hot but the nights were almost perfect. In the mountains, the air cools off fast as the sun is going down but in the summer it never gets too cold. Just comfortable. The sun was starting to cast long shadows across the parking lot. Buck headed for his hotel.

Chapter Thirty-Four

Terry Rubin was just wrapping up his reports and was getting ready to head home. Tonight, was spaghetti night and his wife Maria, who was of Italian descent, made some of the best meatballs Terry had ever tasted. He always thought it was her cooking that attracted him to her when they were first dating. Her parents had owned an Italian restaurant in Salt Lake City and it was obvious that she had learned to cook from the best.

Deep in thought about meatballs and fried mozzarella sticks, Terry snapped out of it as he walked past the conference room. Randall was sitting at the table with Josh and they were very rapidly typing on their laptops. Josh saw Terry standing in the hallway and waved for him to come in. Terry stepped into the conference room and walked over to the table. He was watching the computer screens on both laptops and was amazed at how fast Randall was typing away on the keyboard. The screens stopped moving and they all read what was on the screen in front of them.

Terry looked at the two men. "Is this for real?" he asked.

Josh nodded. "We just confirmed it with NSA. They picked up the whole conversation on the encrypted sat phone. We only had one side."

Terry looked confused. "Can you explain this to me so I understand what you have?"

Randall took over. "You bet. We picked up a conversation between two people. They were talking quietly, but like we said, the whole space is one big voice tap so we get everything nice and clear. Just prior to these guys talking, one of the guys was talking on the sat phone. Even though it was in Spanish the guy definitely had a southern accent. Anyway, after we heard the conversation between the two guys on site we hooked up with the NSA to confirm what we heard and to see what was being said on the other end of the phone since they get both sides of the conversation. They just sent us the translation transcript and we were confirming it with our translation from the site."

"Ok," replied Terry. "Whatcha got?"

"The local guy must have been talking to the big boss. He told the boss about making an example of one of the kids who tried to escape and that he had to slit his throat. The boss seemed pleased but also concerned. He wants to move up the shipping date to Sunday morning."

Terry almost couldn't breathe. "He actually said he had to slit a kid's throat?"

"Yeah," replied Josh. "And he told the guy on the other end of the phone that he had the guard dispose of the body in the mountains."

"Holy shit. If we can figure out which one did it, we got them. Nice work. Now, what about this shipping date thing?"

Randall took over. "Sounds like they were originally going to ship on Tuesday, but the big boss is edgy and wants to go Sunday morning. They just sent out a blast text to what is probably their drivers to be at the warehouse at four AM Sunday morning."

Terry was almost giddy. "Awesome. Now we have a date and time. We have been waiting for this kind of break." Terry was pulling out his phone when Josh stopped him.

"Hold on cowboy. There's more. The southern accent guy is getting twitchy. Told the other guy he is getting this itch in the back of his neck that somethings up and he always pays attention to the itch. It might be because he punched the guard who let the kid try to escape and it turns out the guard is the big boss's nephew and he is supposed to be running things once this shipment leaves. The two guys talking are being recalled to Mexico. One guy questioned if it might be to get slaughtered for punching the nephew. They talked about running, but southern accent guy shut him down. Now here is the good part. A few minutes later, heavy Mexican accent asked another guy, we are thinking the nephew if he had reported the punch and the disrespect to his uncle. The guard denied doing it, but heavy accent suggested maybe he should. Not sure what that was all about."

Terry sat down in one of the chairs at the conference table and thought about this development. The two guys who seem to be running things have been recalled by the big boss. They don't know if the guard he punched, the nephew, told the uncle anything but there is some concern that being recalled to Mexico might mean payback for the disrespect. Then the one guy talks to the nephew and practically tells him to tell his uncle about the punch. Randall suggested it sounds like heavy accent is trying to protect his ass and maybe even get the other guy killed. Everybody kind of nodded in agreement.

"Have you called Buck?" Terry asked.

"Not yet. You got it first," replied Josh.

"Ok. Can you put this all together and send it out to the

whole team, your boss, DEA and CBI and I will call Buck? He went to dinner, so I am going to go home, grab a bite and then call him. Give him a chance to digest his food. Nice job, guys."

Terry headed for the door, hopped in his car and headed home for a quick dinner. Things were coming together.

Chapter Thirty-Five

Buck pulled into the parking lot of his hotel, turned off the car, opened his door, got out and walked around to the rear hatch to grab his backpack. He opened the backpack to make sure his laptop was inside and zipped it back up. He wanted to spend time tonight going over the file that Jess Gonzales, DEA, had emailed him about Harry Crank. He felt that what she had read to him over the phone earlier was a possible match for the guy who killed the Mexican kid, but he wanted to really sit down and digest the file. Buck always believed the devil was in the details in any investigation. He felt the file on this guy was a good break.

He slung one of the straps of his backpack over his right shoulder and started walking towards the door to the hotel. Just as Buck was passing the last row of cars, the door to the hotel opened and out stepped a tall rangy looking blond guy. He had a physique that told Buck he was in excellent condition. All sinew and muscles. His hair was not too long and was what you might call scraggly. What stopped Buck in his tracks was the tattoo he saw on his right arm, visible just below the sleeve of his green T-shirt. The tattoo showed a skull with a dagger through it. Definitely Green Beret.

Buck had seen those tattoos way too many times while he

was an MP during his time in the army. Buck's mind was trying to grasp what he was looking at when he heard a voice on his left side calling his name. Buck turned his head to the left just in time to see Jess Gonzales coming out from between two cars and waving at him. At the very same moment, he heard a voice from his right yell out "Hey Cop." Buck looked to his right and saw two guys coming from either side of the row of parked cars. Each guy had on a baseball cap and was carrying a semi-automatic pistol.

Now Buck had never really dealt with metaphysical stuff and he didn't believe in coincidence, but when he would look back on this entire incident it was like some weird cosmic convergence. Here was Buck, here was the possible Green Beret bad guy, here was Jess Gonzales and here were two guys with guns. It seemed to Buck that at that moment everything went into slow motion.

Buck threw his backpack off his right shoulder, flipped the thumb break on his holster and grabbed his gun. Somewhere behind him, someone yelled "GUN!!" The Green Beret looked first towards Buck and then towards the two guys with guns, not sure what to do. He started moving to his right away from where this was all taking place as the two guys with the guns raised them up into firing position and started pulling the triggers as they were closing the gap. Three other people, coming out the front door of the hotel, stopped for a moment and then dove back inside the hotel.

Buck, using his peripheral vision while keeping an eye on the two shooters, looked for cover. Not seeing any, he dropped to a crouch just as the first bullet flew over his head, pretty much where his chest had been just a nanosecond before. Now instinct and training kicked in as Buck drew his pistol firing just as the weapon cleared his holster. Then firing twice more as he brought the gun up to his shooting position. Two of his rounds found their mark and he could see a big splash of red blossom across the chest of the shooter on the right. More bullets flew past him as he turned his sights on the other shooter. At that instant, he could hear a volley of explosions from behind him and the other shooter's gun flew up in the air and he smashed into the car behind him, slid down the door and sat there not moving. Buck spun around with his gun up and quickly saw Jess Gonzales standing about fifteen feet away, leaning over the hood of a car with her gun positioned in front of her.

Buck swung back around, keeping his gun aimed at the two shooters lying on the ground.

"You Ok?" he yelled.

"Good." Came the reply from Jess who was now running across the rest of the drive aisle with her gun pointed at the shooters.

Buck had moved in on the guy he had taken down and kicked the gun out of the way. Looking back to make sure Jess was nearby, he bent over and touched two fingers to the neck of shooter number one. It was obvious from the amount of blood on the ground around him that the shooter was dead, but Buck checked for a pulse anyway.

Jess was standing about five feet behind him watching him while also keeping an eye on shooter number two. As Buck stood back up, she moved to the shooter now propped up against the car door and checked his pulse. Buck was now covering her with his gun. She looked up at Buck and shook her head. Shooter two was also gone.

She holstered her weapon and walked towards Buck. Sirens, lots of them, could be heard in the distance coming from all directions. Buck holstered his gun. His hands were shaking. The two dead shooters didn't bother Buck. He had been involved in several shootouts during his long career. A lot of cops go through their entire careers never using their weapon. In his career, Buck had used his weapon three times and each time a bad guy had died. No, it wasn't the dead shooters that bothered him, it was how close that one bullet had come to ending his life.

Jess's face was ashen. This was the first time in her career that she had killed a man. She had been in shootouts before, but never one on one. She steadied herself and looked at Buck.

"What the hell, Buck?" she asked. "Who the hell are these guys?"

"No idea."

Buck knelt back down next to shooter number one and pushed his baseball cap off his head. He stood up, walked over to shooter two and did the same thing. His mind was clearing and then the realization set in.

"The Slattery brothers," he said.

"Who the hell are the Slattery brothers and why did they just try to off you?" she replied. "Are these guys part of what we are working on?"

Buck shook his head. "No. A case I was working in Teller County. Triple homicide. We were waiting on DNA before we arrested these guys. Prime suspects."

Three Durango Police Department cars rolled into the parking lot with lights flashing and sirens wailing. The cops stopped about twenty feet away and exited the cars with guns drawn. Buck held up both hands, as did Jess, to let them know there was no threat and in his right hand was his badge, which he had removed from his belt.

"Cops, on the job," he yelled.

Still cautious, the first officer to his left approached Buck and Jess. The two other cops held their positions and covered their man.

Buck told the officer that he was going to reach slowly into his back right pocket and pull out his ID. Gun still trained on Buck, the officer said, "slowly."

Buck removed his ID and handed it very slowly to the cop, who took it with his left hand and opened it up. Looking at the picture and then looking at Buck, he closed the wallet, handed it back. He then looked at Jess and asked her to take out her ID, also slowly, and hand it to him. Jess complied and he went through the same exercise. Convinced the situation was under control, he handed Jess back her ID and holstered his weapon. His fellow officers did the same and then moved up to see what had transpired. The first officer clicked the microphone he had hooked to the collar of his shirt and called for an ambulance and a supervisor. He reported the shooting and that there were law enforcement personnel involved and gave the all clear.

By this time two more Durango police cars had entered the lot and the officers were starting to put up barricades at the driveway entrances so no one could leave or enter. At almost the same time, two Sheriff's department cars arrived and a black civilian car. One of the marked cars contained Sheriff Sinclair who got out and walked over to Buck and Jess. Terry Rubin badged his way past the cops putting up the barricades. They all stood around looking at the two dead shooters.

Chapter Thirty-Six

The ambulance was cleared into the parking lot followed by another Durango Police Department marked unit. This one contained Chief of Police Gilbert Chandler. Gil was a solidly built man of forty-five, with slightly graying hair. He stood about five-ten and weighed about one sixty-five. He had been the Chief of Police in Durango for the past ten years. He was well respected in the community. He immediately took charge. The Chief and Buck went way back and he knew Jess from a DEA raid that his department had been a part of a couple years back. He shook hands and looked at the two shooters on the ground.

"Well, Buck. You sure know how to keep things interesting. Any idea who these two are?" He pointed at the bodies.

"Yeah. The Slattery brothers. This one is Mike and that one is Todd." Buck pointed towards each body.

"They part of what you guys are working on?" the Chief asked. He had been apprised of the current investigation by Sheriff Sinclair. He had offered her his help as needed.

"No," replied Buck. "These two are, were, prime suspects in a triple homicide in Teller County I was working on before I got the call to come here. We were stalled in the investigation and waiting on DNA results."

"Any idea how they tracked you here?" asked the Sheriff.

"No idea at all. Teller County was supposed to be sitting on these two until we were ready to make an arrest. Might have overheard something while we had them in for questioning. Not sure."

The Chief looked at Jess. "And what's your story young lady?"

Jess replied. "I had just gotten here so I could talk to Buck about the investigation. I saw Buck at just about the same time these two showed themselves and then all hell broke loose."

"Sounds like you were in the right place at the right time, Jess." replied the Chief. Jess just stood there with her arms wrapped across her chest.

The Chief next directed one of the police officers two get two evidence bags and asked Buck and Jess to hand over their weapons. They both pulled the magazines, racked the slides to dump the next round out of the chambers and handed the weapons and the mags to the officer, who placed them in the bags, noted the date and time on the bags, sealed the bags and signed his name on the flaps. He handed the bags to the Chief.

The Chief then pulled out his phone and called Dr. Kramer, the Forensic Pathologist, and asked him to hurry over to the hotel. That done and while he had his phone out, he snapped several pictures of the bodies in situ, as they lie. He directed his officers to cordon off the area around the bodies and asked everyone in the area to step outside the police tape. Since this was not related to the drug investigation, he asked the Sheriff if her homicide detectives could handle the interviews and he directed two of his officers to go into the hotel lobby and see if they could get the names and contact info for anyone who had seen the incident. He told them to get preliminary witness statements. The Chief asked Jess and Buck to head over to the Durango Police Headquarters. He put them in separate patrol cars.

The Sheriff called Quinn, filled him in and asked him to grab Dani Walker, her Forensic Tech, and head over. They would be handling the investigation. She told him to send Romero over to Police Headquarters and start the interviews. She had been filled in by Josh about the new timeline at the trucking company and she wanted this shooting investigation wrapped up ASAP. The Chief had one of his officers call the city public works department and get a couple big lights brought over. It was getting dark fast.

Once at Durango Police Headquarters, Jess and Buck were put in separate interview rooms. The officer escorting them asked if they needed anything and Buck asked for a bottle or can of Coke. Jess still had the water she was carrying when the whole incident started.

Detective Romero arrived at police headquarters on the heels of Christine Brewer, the District Attorney. She wanted to observe the interviews. Romero was extremely thorough. Even though Buck was very familiar with the Miranda Warning and understood his rights, Romero read him his rights and asked him if he wanted a lawyer. Buck declined and signed the letter waiving his right to counsel. Step by step Romero walked Buck through the events of the evening. Buck was impressed with Romero. He asked the right questions at the right time, he made copious notes on his notepad, even though the entire interview was being videotaped and he walked him through the events several times until he had a complete understanding of what happened.

Satisfied that he had everything he needed from Buck,

Romero pushed back from the table stood up and turned for the door. He stopped turned and extended his hand toward Buck. Buck shook his hand. Romero said, "Buck, I'm glad it was them and not you." He opened the door and walked out. He followed the exact same procedure with Jess, including the handshake at the end.

By the time the interviews were over, the Chief, DA Brewer, Sheriff Sinclair and Detective Quinn were all standing outside the interview rooms. The Chief directed everyone into a small conference room and closed the door. He asked Romero to give them all a rundown of the interviews. Romero consulted his notes and then in clear strong voice explained that both interviews were consistent in their content, both agents had covered the events thoroughly and in his opinion, unless there was evidence to dispute the facts as he knew them, that he believed this was a good shooting.

Detective Quinn gave a recap of what had been discovered at the scene. Dani Walker, the Forensic Tech, had cataloged a total of fourteen rounds of various calibers. It was possible, he explained, that they might have missed something since the area was huge. Most of the bullets recovered had been found in vehicles in the parking lot. He also explained that he had gone over witness statements from those people they were able to interview and that their stories were consistent with the information just provided by Romero. He also concurred that this was a good shooting. He then mentioned that according to the witnesses, Buck would probably be dead if it wasn't for the fact that he kneeled at the right time and that Jess was there. Most of the rounds were directed at where Buck was. Almost like the bad guys hadn't even seen Jess.

He did make one note that got everyone's attention. He said three of the witnesses had asked him if they had talked to the tall, blond guy. They all felt that he had the best view from where he was standing at the time. Quinn had thus far been unable to locate a tall, blond guy at the hotel.

The Chief then looked over at Christine Brewer, the District Attorney, and asked her for her opinion. She had witnessed both interviews and was satisfied that they had the full story. She would recommend that no charges be filed and the that the events of the evening be classified a good shooting and closed. Buck and Jess were to be released.

Before they concluded, the Chief told the group that he had been in contact with the Sheriff in Teller County and that the information Buck provided about the case up there was accurate. The Slattery brothers were the primary suspects in the triple homicide. The Teller County Sheriff had asked if it would be ok if he sent two of his detectives down to review the evidence they had. The chief said he had allowed that and that the detectives would arrive sometime in the morning.

His final comments were about the preliminary findings of the Forensic Pathologist. According to Dr. Kramer, both men were hit multiple times. Shooter A was hit in the lower torso and in the neck, which would probably prove to be the fatal wound, and shooter B was hit three times in center mass. As a side note, he had told the Chief to tell both Buck and Jess that they had been extremely accurate under the circumstances and he was proud of them. Smiles all around the table.

"Ok," said the Chief. "Let's get Buck and Jess out of the interview rooms and let's talk this through one time and then get everyone out of here. It's getting late and it's been a long night."

Chapter Thirty-Seven

Buck and Jess joined the group. Handshakes and congratulations all around. Jess still looked a little shaken up and Buck tried valiantly to keep everyone from seeing his hands shake as he talked. Buck told them about walking towards the hotel entrance and seeing the tall, thin, blonde guy come out of the building and how something caused them each to stop and look at each other. Then Jess had called to him and as he turned towards her all hell broke loose. He asked if they had been able to interview the blonde and was told that no one could find him after the shooting.

Jess opened her laptop, pulled up the file she had sent him earlier and push the computer over towards Buck. "Is this the guy you saw?"

Buck, who hadn't had a chance to look at the file Jess had sent him, studied the picture. There were several pictures from his imprisonment in the military prison and it was in one those pictures Buck spotted the special forces tattoo. He was certain it was the same guy. His mind flashed on the tattoo on his right arm. The skull with the dagger through it.

Buck looked up. "Ninety Eight percent. I didn't realize it

when I first saw him since it was just a glance, but I remember seeing the tattoo on his arm. I think that's what I first focused on."

Terry Rubin, who had joined the group a few minutes before asked. "Do you think he set this up?"

Buck thought for a minute. "Don't think so. He has never seen me, or Jess, and I think it was just happenstance that he was there at that time. I remember thinking about how I was going to handle the encounter when the shooters showed up. It would have been obvious to him that I was a cop. We were twenty feet apart and my badge and gun were both clipped to my belt."

The Sheriff looked around the table. "Anything else before we head out?"

Terry stood up. "I had a conversation with the FBI computer guys. We have a timeline now."

All eyes were on Terry as he explained the conversations the computer guys had picked up. He told them about the conversation regarding slicing the kid's throat and the little power play that seemed to be going on. He talked about the timeline being moved up to Sunday morning.

Terry said, "I asked them to get the transcripts to everyone and then I headed home for a quick dinner. I knew Buck had said he was going to dinner but I wasn't sure where he was going so I figured I'd give him time to eat. After I finished dinner I was heading over to his hotel to fill him in when the shots fired call came over the radio."

Everyone kind of looked around the table. Jess finally broke the silence. "We don't have a lot of time to put this together. We need to get moving."

The Sheriff looked at DA Brewer. "Well, Chris, what do you think. We have enough for a murder warrant at least?"

Brewer looked at Terry. "Get me all the transcripts and the packet that Jess sent Buck and send it to my office. I will have my guys write up the warrant and get it over to Judge Houseman. I think we are on a good footing, especially since there are other outstanding warrants on this guy."

Jess spoke up. "I will call my Director and see if we can get a search warrant for the drugs. I think we have enough to take it to a federal judge."

The Sheriff looked around. "Ok, everyone. We got a lot to do. Buck, Jess hang back a minute, ok.? Everybody else, let's get ready to put this to bed. We will hook up in my office tonight at seven and let's get all the SWAT team leaders there as well. Thanks, everyone. Nice work tonight."

After everyone left the room, the Sheriff and the Chief sat down and pointed to the empty chairs. Buck and Jess sat down. The Sheriff started the conversation. "You guys were incredibly lucky tonight. I am very glad you guys weren't hurt. I stood at the scene where Buck was kneeling and for the life of me I can't figure out how you didn't get hit. You've got one hell of a guardian angel." She paused a beat.

"I just want to make sure you guys are going to be ok. From the sound of it, we are going to have a pretty big operation going on and I need everyone in top shape. If either of you feels you might have trouble dealing with this it is ok to step away now. I have already spoken with both your directors and the feeling all around is that you guys get to make the call. I have a preacher and a psychologist available at a moment's call if you need to talk through this and both the Chief and I are available for you, too. So here it is. Are you good to go?"

Buck looked at Jess and then back to the Sheriff. "Good to go," he responded.

The Sheriff looked at Jess. "Jess?"

Jess looked at Buck. "Good to go Ma'am."

The Sheriff looked at the Chief and then back to Jess and Buck. "Ok then. You two get some sleep and let's meet up this afternoon."

She reached into her backpack and pulled out the two evidence bags containing Buck's and Jess's guns. She opened the bags and slid the guns and magazines back to their respective owners. Buck and Jess thanked the Sheriff and the Chief and headed for the door. A deputy was waiting to drive them back to their cars. He already had both their backpacks in the car since they had been dropped at the scene when all the shooting started. They drove back to the hotel in silence.

Chapter Thirty-Eight

Blondy pulled his rental car into the truck yard, hit the bottom on the garage door opener for the smaller delivery door, drove up the ramp and pulled the car into the warehouse. He had been doing this every day since he arrived at the warehouse. He knew there were a lot of people looking for him and the less he was seen the better. The garage door rolled down and when it was closed he stepped out of the car.

Mustache headed over to him. "What the hell is going on out there? With all the sirens I thought for sure we were getting raided. I was getting ready to pull the plug and get the hell out of here!"

Blondy looked at him. "Damn, that was unreal! Felt like I was in a war zone again! Couple cops got into a shootout in the hotel parking lot. Damn bullets flying all over. I was like twenty feet away when the first shots rang out. Got my head down and headed for the car so I wouldn't get caught up in the lot when the cavalry arrived. God damn cops came from every direction. It was freakin nuts!" His whole body was shaking from the adrenalin rush.

Mustache looked at him with concern. "You think the cops were here for us or for the shooters?"

"Can't say for sure. I had this weird sensation, as the older cop

"

was walking towards the hotel, that he actually stopped and looked straight at me, but then bullets started flying and I got the hell out of there."

"Anyone see you there?" Mustache asked. "They might be looking at you as a witness."

"Can't be sure. There were other people around. I am going to stay here until we head back to Mexico. Swing by my room when you go back to the hotel and grab my stuff."

Mustache filled him in on progress so far. They had filled the last half of the one trailer while he was gone and had just started on the last trailer. The last shipment of toys had also arrived and the kids were busy filling them up. He didn't see any problem making the deadline. He also let Blondy know that he had to up the amount of Oxy some of the kids were getting. They were running without sleep and some of them were starting to crash.

Blondy shook his head in agreement and headed for the office. He needed to sit down and get to his calm place. His body was still shaking. He closed the office door, sat in the chair, kicked back and stared at a spot on the ceiling. He focused every part of his being on that one spot. He had learned to do this from an old army Sergeant he had trained under during his first year with the Green Berets. At first, he thought it was bullshit, but after a while, he found it got easier and easier to get to a calm place. That's what he was looking for now.

He thought about what Mustache had asked him. Was it possible the cops were aware of what was going on inside the warehouse? He hadn't seen any signs that they were being watched, but he still had the twitch in his neck. The twitch was never wrong. The twitch had kept him alive in some of the most inhospitable places on earth and he always trusted the twitch. His mind started to focus in on the spot, his breathing became regular and he could feel his heartbeat returning to normal. But for some reason, he could not get the nagging feeling out of his head. They swept the warehouse three times a day with some of the most sophisticated anti-bugging software that was available. He never knew where Rojas got this stuff from but it was way high tech. So far, they had found no anomalies. Was it possible they missed something?

Then a weird thought crept into his psyche. Mustache was the one who ran the scans every day. Was it possible… No, he had to stop thinking like that. They had worked as a team for a long time. But then again… Could he be working for someone else? Another cartel boss perhaps? Rojas had wiped out a lot of the other cartel bosses in his rise to the top, thanks to him and Moustache, but was it possible? Those guys had families and families sometimes have long memories. He decided that his thinking was wrong. He also decided to keep a closer eye on Mustache and the other guards, especially Rojas's nephew. Can't ever be too safe. The twitch hadn't gone away.

Chapter Thirty-Nine

Buck and Jess thanked the deputy for the ride, grabbed their stuff and stepped out of the car into the early morning air. The air felt cool and Buck took a deep breath as the deputy drove off. He stood for a minute looking at the last of the stars as the dawn was starting to break. He looked at Jess.

"You ok?" he asked. "For real?"

Jess looked at him, tried to answer and wrapped her arms around him. Buck was surprised but he just let her hold him for a minute. He rested his hand on her back.

"It's ok," he said.

She let go of the bear hug, stepped back and looked at the ground. She wiped the tears from her eyes. "Look at me. What a mess," she said. "Big tough DEA agent and here I am crying like a little girl. What the hell is wrong with me?"

Buck just stood there for a minute. He wasn't quite sure what to say. Finally, he said, "look Jess. None of us are perfect and we all deal with shit differently. I almost died tonight and if it wasn't for you, I probably would have. You saved my life and I am truly grateful."

He went on to tell her about the first bullet sailing just over his head when he knelt down. He hadn't mentioned how close it had come to anyone else. She looked at him and moved her hand up to her mouth. She hadn't realized how close it had come, either. Had he not dropped to his knees it would have hit him right in the chest and he wasn't wearing his body armor.

"What made you kneel?" she asked. "That was a strange reaction to the situation."

Bucked looked at her. "Not sure. I remember looking around for cover in that split second between seeing the guns and hearing the shot and I knew I needed to get small. If I had dove to the ground, I would not have been able to grab my gun and fire, so kneeling was the only option. I heard all those bullets flying by me and all I kept thinking about was that Lucy would kick my ass if I got myself killed."

His face almost lit up. He was never that spiritual, but there is no way he should have survived tonight. No way in hell. Yet here he was.

"Looks like Lucy and I did a good job keeping you alive," Jess replied.

There seemed to be an awkward moment coming so he pulled out his phone and pulled up his messages. He had eleven messages. Jess did the same and looked at the seven messages she had. Buck suggested they head inside and start returning messages and try to get some sleep. They agreed to meet at the Sheriff's office at one. Buck closed his phone and nodded a silent thank you. Jess nodded back and they headed inside.

Chapter Forty

Buck opened the door to his room, stepped inside and locked the deadbolt. He walked over to the desk and set his gun and badge on the desk. He sat on the edge of the bed and cried like a baby. He missed his wife so much and he would love to see her again, but getting killed today was not in his plans. Had Lucy reached out and helped him tonight? He had no idea, but every time he replayed the events of tonight in his head he got the same result.

The first bullet fired at him was definitely a kill shot. No doubt in his mind. Had he not dropped to his knees, he would be lying on a slab. The first shot he fired just as his gun cleared the holster was way off the mark. A complete miss and the second two shots he fired, once he got both his hands on the gun and out in front of him, were off too. Or so he believed. He could still see it as clear as while it was happening. He was tracking towards the shooter and pulled the trigger even though he was not lined up. Pure muscle reaction. He was certain the shots had missed, yet the shooter went down. He ran it through his mind several more times, each time more and more certain he had not been on target. He didn't know how to explain it. Maybe Lucy was there tonight. He did know one thing for certain. He owed his life to Jess Gonzales.

Buck walked into the bathroom and washed his face with cold water. He dried off, pulled his phone out of his pocket and sat down at the desk. His first call was to his Director. Even though the sun was barely up, he figured his boss would be. He was right. The Director answered right away.

"You ok?" he asked. No one says hello anymore.

"Yes, sir," Buck replied. He went on to tell him what happened, even though he knew that the Director had already had the same conversation with Sheriff Sinclair. The Director listened carefully, asked a couple questions and then told Buck he was grateful that he had survived. He then filled Buck in on the interview with Claire Ringsby.

Claire Ringsby had been intercepted just prior to boarding the flight to La Guardia airport in New York. Tracy and Doonen said she came along willingly. Buck had worked with both Tracy and Doonen on several occasions. Rachel Tracy was a single mom with a ten-year-old son. She worked mostly property crimes, burglary and things like that. Faith Doonen was a former basketball player for the University of Colorado. She was just short of six feet tall and wore her hair short. Doonen typical worked in cybercrimes.

The Director continued. "After the initial shock of being pulled out of line at the airport wore off, she opened right up. Tracy and Doonen just had to sit there and listen. According to her statement, a couple weeks back a lawyer from Denver, supposedly representing potential trucking clients, walked into the office and asked for one of the owners. At the time Hector Vegas was the only owner in the office and he met with the lawyer. After the lawyer left the office, Hector was very shaken up. She didn't know what went on in the office but later, when he told Dick Dillon about the visit, Dick went nuts. She had never seen them go at it like that as long as she had worked there. Within a couple days she was introduced to two guys, one blonde, one Hispanic. They were introduced as new partners. She was afraid of them both. The warehouse was walled off and she was no longer allowed in the larger space. She seemed to have no idea what was happening in the closed off space. She just did her job and hoped that neither one of the new partners came into her office."

"Two days ago, Dick took her aside, told her he had set up an offshore bank account for her and deposited fifty thousand dollars into it and he told her to finish up work that day and then disappear. She was afraid at this point, so she did what he said. Booked a flight out of town and headed to Denver. The impression Tracy and Doonen got was that Dick had not accepted the new arrangements and was planning to take his family and run. Hector, she told them, just looked nervous all the time. They said she seemed more concerned about her two bosses than herself. She also wondered if she would have to give the money back that Dick gave her."

"For the time being, we have her stashed away in a hotel at the airport until we close this up. Bottom line, she doesn't seem to know much."

Buck responded. "Her statement lines up with what we have been speculating. The lawyer is a new angle. I have been wondering how they made contact. Can you get someone to check out the lawyer?"

"Already in the works. Denver Police are keeping an eye on Ringsby, I have the computer guys pulling everything they can find on the lawyer. Ringsby remembered his name and I have Tracy and Doonen sitting on his office."

"We probably don't have enough to get a warrant and we don't want to spook him or his bosses," Buck replied.

"Let's see what we can find out about him. The computer guys will pull his life apart and we will see what shakes out."

They talked for a few minutes about the raid for Sunday morning and the Director offered once again to send help. Buck told him he would let him know by the end of the day. They clicked off.

Buck looked at his messages and decided he needed to call his kids before returning any other calls. He dialed his daughter first. Cassandra was the middle child and she was every bit a middle child. In high school, she played soccer, ran track and played volleyball. She lettered in all three sports. She was also the one who got in trouble for violating curfew, drinking, and whatever other mischief she could find to get into. Buck was surprised when she was accepted to the University of Arizona with a full scholarship for volleyball. He was even more surprised when she was accepted into law school. Cassie was never much for regimented education.

Two years ago, she suddenly dropped out of law school and her career path took a different track. She joined the Forest Service and was now working as a wildland firefighter with the Helena Hotshots. The Helena Hotshots were one of the elite firefighting teams based out of Helena, Montana. Buck was not surprised. He never saw her sitting behind a desk as a lawyer. She loved the outdoors and she was as tough as they come. Lucy wasn't pleased that she quit school without any discussion and she worried constantly whenever Cassie was called out on a fire, but she also knew her daughter and if this was where she was happy, then so was her mom.

Cassie's phone went straight to voicemail, so Buck figured she was probably on a fireline someplace. He left a message asking her to call him when she got the chance and to tell her that he loved her and missed her.

Next, he called David, his oldest son. David looked just like his dad at that age, he was slightly taller at six feet two and was a little heavier, but the resemblance was almost scary. David was a patrol officer with the Gunnison Police Department. He also played guitar in a local bluegrass/country band. David answered on the second ring. "Hey Dad, how are you?"

Buck spent a few minutes on pleasantries, how were the grandkids, how was the job going, the wife ok?. Then he told him about the shootout. David had heard something on the news this morning as he was getting off shift but the reporter didn't have many details. He asked a few questions, was glad his Dad was ok and then they hung up, promising to get together soon.

Jason, his youngest son, answered the phone sounding like he was still half asleep. Jason was an architect and he lived in Boulder with his wife Kate and their three children. He listened in stunned silence as Buck told him about the shootout. Of all of Buck's kids, Jason was the one who had continued to follow Catholicism, just like his mom, and seemed to get more involved in his church after Lucy died. He told Buck that he believed that his mom had been there to watch over him. Buck asked him if he had heard from his sister. Since Jason and Cassie were closer in age, they had stayed the closest and typically spoke every week. He told Buck that the last he heard she was working on a fire in Northern California. They talked pleasantries for a few minutes then Buck signed off.

He felt a lot better after those calls. His family was important and they all stayed close. During the past year, since Lucy died, they had made an extra effort to include him in family things, and he was glad they had. It was the kids who kept him sane when in the beginning all he wanted to do was work and forget the pain of the loss. They were his rock.

Buck decided to wait on the other calls. He needed to put

his head down on the pillow and crash. For the first time in his life, he thought that maybe he was too old for this kind of work. Even though he had survived the encounter, he was concerned that his reaction time was off. His body began to shake and tears formed in his eyes. He opened his wallet took out the picture of Lucy and stared at it for a few minutes. Before he put it back into the sleeve in his wallet he thanked her for looking out for him last night. He laid back on the pillow and went right to sleep.

Down the hall, Jess got off the phone with her Director. He, too, was glad she had survived and based on the information he had received, she had handled herself in an extraordinary manner and had done the DEA proud. He was planning to put her in for a heroism award. She told him that wasn't necessary, but he insisted. They discussed the planned raid and he offered more assistance if needed, to which she told him she would let him know if she saw a need for more people. They also discussed a few other operational things that were in the works and he told her to get some sleep and hung up.

Jess stripped out of her clothes, turned on the shower and stepped in. Out of nowhere she was hit with a huge wave of emotion and found herself sitting on the floor of the shower with her arms wrapped around her legs and the water running down her head. She cried like she hadn't ever cried before. By the time she got out of the shower, she was emotionally drained and she was asleep as soon as her head hit the pillow.

Chapter Forty-One

Buck woke up with a start. He could hear something ringing in the distance, but he was unsure what it was. He looked around the room trying to focus on where he was. The phone continued to ring. Slowly his brain kicked into gear and he realized he was in his hotel room. He could also see sunshine coming through the gap in the curtains. He located the source of the ringing and picked up his phone. He recognized the number.

"Jimmy", he said. "What's up?"

"Jesus Buck. Are you alright? The Chief just stopped in for lunch and told me what happened."

Buck focused his clearing head. "Yeah, Jimmy. I'm ok. It was a hell of a night. Thanks for asking."

"Ok. Hearing your voice makes me feel better. So, you guys took out two bad guys in a shootout in a parking lot. Hell of a story to tell the grandkids. Someday."

"Yeah. Maybe not for a while though."

Jimmy laughed. "Listen, Buck. The other reason I'm calling is that Dick Dillon is in here crying in his beer again. The Chief is keeping an eye on him until you can get here."

"Ok. I will be there in fifteen. Don't let him leave."

"You got it," replied Jimmy.

Buck climbed out of the bed. Put on a clean pair of jeans and a clean t-shirt, clipped his badge and gun to his belt and grabbed his backpack. As he was walking through the front doors of the hotel he found himself slowing his pace and looking around the lot, carefully. Not seeing anything out of the ordinary, he headed for his car. As he neared his car, he called Terry Rubin.

"Hey, Buck. Everything ok?" Terry asked.

"Yeah. You doing anything right now that can't wait?"

Terry replied. "Nothing that can't wait. What you got going on?"

"I am heading over to LaBon Café. Dick Dillon is there getting sauced. I want to take a run at him and see if we can confirm how many bad guys are on site and if Blondy is amongst them. You want in?"

Terry said, "hell yeah! I will meet you there, ten minutes."

Buck hung up and his phone rang. A number he didn't recognize.

"Buck Taylor."

"Agent Taylor. This is Detective Ronny Briscoe from Teller County."

"Hey, Ronny. What's up?" said Buck.

"First off, the Sheriff said you had a shootout. Glad things turned out alright for you. Heard you put down our suspects. Thanks. I just wanted to let you know that we just got to the La Plata Sheriff's office and we are heading down to watch the autopsy on the Slattery Brothers. Wanted to thank you for closing this one up for us. Crime lab called this morning and they were able to pull a partial print off one of the bullets from Pop Grayson. It's a match for Mike Slattery. Case closed."

"That's great Ronny. Glad I could help."

"Listen, Buck. The Sheriff said to tell you that if you ever need anything, all you need to do is call. We owe you big. Thanks."

Buck thanked Ronny for the call and hung up. Another satisfied customer he thought to himself. He pulled out onto the highway and headed for the café.

Buck found a parking space a half block from the café, got out of his car and headed for the café. Terry Rubin and Durango Police Chief Chandler were standing outside the door to the café.

Chief Chandler said, "Hey Buck. You get any sleep? I spotted Dick Dillon when I stopped in for lunch. I knew you were thinking about talking to him, so I figured I would give you a call before he got too shitfaced."

Buck looked through the front door and saw Dick Dillon sitting at the end of the bar nursing a beer, a shot glass sat in front of him, half full of a slightly brown liquid. The bar was fairly crowded with lunchtime patrons, but Buck didn't really want to wait. They were running out of time and Buck needed as much information as he could get.

Buck thanked the Chief, who said he would stand by at the front door, just in case Dick got belligerent. Terry and Buck walked into the bar and headed straight for Dick. Jimmy gave him a slight nod as he walked along the bar. If anything weird happened, he knew Jimmy would also have his back. Just as a precaution, he unsnapped the thumb break on his holster.

Terry grabbed the stool next to Dick and sat down. Buck stood next to Dick at the end of the bar. Jimmy looked at them both with droopy eyes.

"What the hell you guys looking at!" exclaimed Dick.

Buck started. "Hey Dick, my name is Buck and I work for the

Colorado Bureau of Investigation and that's Terry, he works for the Sheriff. We'd like to talk to you for a minute about a couple things."

Dick sat up taller on his stool and with a couple slurred words said. "I don't have to talk to you, so get the hell out of my face." He started to get up from the stool, but Buck put his right hand on Dick's shoulder and gently, but firmly, held him in his place. Then Buck leaned his head down and whispered in Dick's ear.

"If you try to move again I am going to slam your face into the bar top. Then I am going to arrest you and let all these people sitting around us know that you and your partner allowed a Mexican drug cartel to get a foothold in their town."

Dick looked startled. Buck would swear that at that moment Dick went from falling down drunk to stone cold sober. Total waste of all the money he had spent to tie one on. Dick looked up at Buck.

"You can't do that?" he said rather meekly.

"Go ahead and try me," said Buck in return.

Dick looked unsure of what to do next, so he leaned into the bar and took a sip of his beer. Buck wasn't sure if what happened next was just stupidity on Dick's part or if it was a smart move to protect himself and his family, but no matter what, Buck was ready. As Dick, holding the handle of his beer mug, started to swing the mug towardsBucks's head, Buck reached out with his left hand and caught Dick's hand and the mug while at the same time, using his right hand, he drove Dick's face into the bar top. The crashing noise of Dick's face hitting the bar and the mug smashing into the floor made everyone in the bar jump. They all looked towards the end of the bar.

Several of the people sitting at the bar and the tables started to get up and head for the end of the bar. Jimmy smacked his sawed-off Louisville Slugger onto the bar top. Jimmy always kept the bat under the bar. Just in case. The crack it made when it hit the bar stopped everyone in their tracks. He just stared at everyone and slowly everyone sat back down in their seats.

Terry, who really hadn't expected the move, reached across Dick and held him down on the bar top. Jimmy started to move down the bar, but Buck held him off with a nod. By this time, Chief Chandler was at their side and had his handcuffs out. He reached past Terry, grabbed Dick's right arm, swung it behind him and put the cuff on his wrist. Buck slid the other arm around and the Chief did the same thing to that arm. Dick was bleeding all over the bar from what was probably a broken nose. Buck looked over at Jimmy and shrugged his shoulders. Jimmy just smiled and waved him off. Wasn't the first person who had ever face planted on Jimmy's bar and it wouldn't be the last.

Together Buck and Terry half carried and half dragged the semi-conscious Dick down the bar and headed for the door. The Chief had pulled out his radio and called for a patrol car for transport. Everyone in the bar watched silently. Once outside, Dick started to come to and started moaning about his nose. Jimmy had handed Buck a bar towel as they were getting ready to leave and he was holding the towel against Dick's nose. People on the street stopped and stared. It only took a minute for the patrol car to arrive and they loaded Dick in the back seat. Dick asked Terry to go with the police officer and to stop by the hospital on the way to the Sheriff's office and get Dick's nose taken care of. Buck would interview him later.

As the patrol car drove away the Chief looked at Buck. "I gotta tell ya, Buck. You sure have a way of keeping things interesting when you're in town."

Buck laughed. "Yeah and here I thought small-town life was boring."

They both laughed. Buck told the Chief he would let him know what Dick had to say as soon as he could get him in the interview room. He thanked the Chief for his help, they shook hands and the Chief headed back to his car. Buck stood there for a minute. As he turned to walk back to his car, his phone rang. Buck didn't recognize the number, but he answered it anyway.

Chapter Forty-Two

"Buck Taylor."

"Hey Buck, It's Randall with the FBI. Wasn't sure when you were getting back here so I wanted to let you know the latest from the voice tap."

Buck got back to his car, opened the door and sat down on the seat. "Go ahead Randall."

"The guy with the southern accent got back to the warehouse just after your shootout in the parking lot. He told his friend all about it and told him that he was only a couple feet away when it all started. Since you saw him and can ID him and he saw the shootout and headed back to the warehouse, we can now definitively place him in the warehouse. He said he was going to stay in the warehouse until they head back to Mexico and he asked the other guy to get his stuff from the hotel."

"That's great Randall. I am heading to the Sheriff's office now."

"Oh, one more thing. The other guy mentioned that he had to up the dose on the kids since they hadn't had any sleep and some of them were crashing. If that is true, then we can confirm that those kids are being drugged to keep them there. I gave this to the

Sheriff and the DA and they are going to add kidnapping and illegal imprisonment to the charges on the warrant."

Buck thanked Randall, hung up and sat back in his seat. This confirmed what he already believed. Those kids had been tortured and drugged, probably with Oxy, and in all likelihood, have no idea where they even are. They are like zombies. The more he thought about it the more pissed he got. Then a new thought crept into his head. Once ICE took those kids into their possession they would most likely be transported to a holding facility in Alamosa and then transported to either Tucson or Houston where they would await deportation. They would be prisoners again, this time courtesy of Uncle Sam. He was having a real problem with that. These kids had been through enough.

Buck pulled up a number on his phone and then stared at it for a couple minutes. Buck was definitely a law and order person and he was not a fan of illegal immigration, but this was something else. These kids never asked to come here and the idea of keeping them as prisoners until they were deported back to almost certain death was more than he could fathom. Once Rojas found out that his distribution dreams had been dismantled, he would have his revenge on everyone he could get to, and that would probably include these kids. Their lives were in serious danger if they were sent back to Mexico.

Buck dialed the number. If word of what he was about to do got out, his credibility with the Feds would go right out the window. It was a risk he was willing to take. His thought, just before the Director answered his phone, was that Lucy would approve. He was doing the right thing.

"Hey Buck", the Director answered. "What's up?" Someone finally said hello.

Buck gave the Director an update on what they had gotten off the voice tap and about the incident with Dick Dillon, then he got to the real reason for the call.

"Sir, do you have a phone number for that human rights lawyer, the one who gave the talk on human trafficking at the police conference a few months back?"

"Are you talking about Sandi Calhoun?" asked the Director.

"Yes sir, I think that was her name."

"What's going on Buck?"

Buck explained about the kids being drugged and held prisoner and that he was concerned that unless someone stepped in that they were just going it be imprisoned someplace else.

When he finished, the Director was silent. Finally saying, "Buck. What are you planning on doing if I get you her phone number?"

"Well, sir. I'd rather not say. I don't want to get you involved and the less you know the better. If the shit hits the fan with the Feds, I will take the heat. This is my move."

Silence. Anyone who knew Buck would know that he would not knowingly circumvent the law and the Director, more than anyone else, knew that Buck did not take things like this lightly.

"I'll tell you what I am going to do. The Governor knows her quite well. They worked on several anti-trafficking bills when he was in the legislature. I am going to call him and see if he will call her and ask her to call you. If the shit hits the fan, he can cover for both of us. He never passes up an opportunity to thumb his nose at the federal government and this could be a huge humanitarian feather in his cap come the next election."

"Do you think he will do it?" Buck asked.

"Are you kidding? He is still pissed about the whole sanctuary city thing the feds tried to pull on Denver. He would do this in a heartbeat. Answer your phone when it rings." The Director hung up.

Buck headed back to the Sheriff's office.

Chapter Forty-Three

The Sheriff's office was buzzing with activity. In the conference room the three SWAT Commanders, La Plata County, DEA and FBI, had one of the construction plans for the warehouse and the site pulled up on the big screen at the front of the room. Sitting around the room were twenty-five SWAT team members. The FBI SWAT Commander was walking the teams through various breaching strategies. He was pointing out the possible breach points into the building. Buck stepped into the room and stood in the back so as not to get in the way.

There were three breach points circled in red on the screen; the front door to the office, the smaller roll-up delivery door at the front of the building and the rear door, which would hopefully give the teams access to the cage area. The commander was pointing out that all the doors opened out or in the case of the delivery door rolled up. The office door was ninety percent glass so that one would be easy to shatter. At six AM in the morning they were not expecting anyone to be in the office.

It was decided after a lengthy discussion that part of the FBI team would breach the office. At the same time the La Plata team, with the help of the additional FBI SWAT guys, would use one of the heavy personnel carriers to smash through the delivery door. They knew from surveillance that the roll-up door was electric and that they would be unlikely to raise it from outside. Immediately upon crashing thru the door, the breach team would lob in a couple flash-bang grenades to cause a distraction and hopefully disable the guards.

One of the big concerns with using the flash-bangs was the presence of the kids. They would be unprotected and would probably feel the full effects. No one was happy about that but there was no other way to breach and disable the guards safely and they didn't want the guards shooting the kids. Unfortunately, it was an acceptable risk.

At the same time as the two front of the building breaches were taking place, the DEA would use an explosive charge and blow the rear door. Part of the DEA team would also remain outside the facility after the breach to pick up any runners.

The FBI Commander reminded everyone that the first priority was to protect the kids inside. The rules of engagement were simple. Take whatever steps were needed to protect the kids and the SWAT teams from being harmed by the guards. This was going to be a tall order.

After a little more discussion everyone agreed with the plan and the Sheriff got up from her seat and stood behind the podium.

"First, I want to thank you all for your help with this. We have never been involved in anything of this magnitude and we appreciate all the work you have done and will do to make this raid a success. I want to go over a few more operational details so we are all on the same page. Even though this is a joint operation involving multiple agencies, it was decided after discussion with all those agencies that the Sheriff's Office will be in operational control. Terry Rubin, my narcotics investigator and the guy who got this all rolling, will be in tactical command. I will be right there with him at the command center. So you are all aware, the command center will be established in the auto body shop across the street from the warehouse. We have been using this for our surveillance and it will give us good visibility. The other person in the command center will be Buck Taylor. Buck is standing in the back corner and he is with the Colorado Bureau of Investigation. Buck is pretty much the reason you are all here tonight."

Everyone turned and looked at Buck, who gave a slight nod of his head.

The Sheriff continued. "At five AM we will leave this office and stage in our respective areas. Access to the warehouse property will be through the back corner of the fence. The FBI sneak and peek team used that access for their entry into the complex. Once inside, teams will take up positions at their assigned entry points. The FBI team will be responsible to disengage the electronic lock on the front gate and clear the way for the breaching vehicle. The breaching vehicle will stage at the end of the street out of sight of the warehouse. There will be two FBI snipers on the roof of the body shop and two more on the roof of the building behind the warehouse. They will be designated overwatch one and two respectively. The Sheriff used a laser pointer to point to both locations on the big screen, as well as, the back entry point.

"The La Plata SWAT team is designated Team Able, FBI SWAT is Team Baker and DEA SWAT is Team Charlie. My Patrol division will block off all the streets surrounding the warehouse at fifteen minutes before the raid. Durango Police will set up a roadblock at the same time on US 550 south and north of the warehouse. There will be Colorado State Troopers stationed south and north of the city on 550 and west and east of the city on 160.

They will be there to stop any of the trucks that might leave the yard before we are ready. The FBI computer team has all the trailers GPS tagged and will keep us apprised of any early movement. The Southern Ute Tribal Police will cover 550 south of the city if any of the trucks should make it onto reservation territory. They will be backed up by the New Mexico State Police. Any questions so far?"

The Sheriff looked around the room. No questions from the teams.

She continued. "Once we have breached the warehouse all focus must be on the safety of the kids. The guards are to be disabled in any way that makes sense and does not put any of you folks in harm's way. We know there are at least six armed individuals on site. It is possible there are others we are not aware of, but we have tried to identify them all. While all of this is happening on site, the Durango Police along with several members of the FBI will be executing a "No Knock" warrant on one Hector Vegas. He is one of the owners of the trucking company. The other owner, thanks to Buck Taylor, is already in our custody and as soon as he is finished up at the hospital he will be put in a cell." Everyone again looked at Buck and many of those in the room smiled and nodded their approval.

"One other item, just so you all have the full picture. CBI will also be executing a "No Knock" warrant this morning on a cartel lawyer in Denver. As you can see this is a wide-ranging operation. If we can successfully shut this down, we will put a huge kink in the distribution network of the cartels. Please be careful. The people on site at the warehouse are incredibly dangerous. Jessica Gonzales the DEA Agent in Charge of the Grand Junction office would like a minute."

Terry Rubin entered the room, stood next to Buck and softly said. "Dick is in the interview room as soon as you are ready. He has a broken nose and slight concussion, but the emergency room doctor said he should be fine." Buck nodded. Jess Gonzales walked up to the podium.

"Good evening. This operation is huge. If this distribution network is as big as we assume, it will be months before we know the impact we will make after the raid. We will document every move we make. Make sure your body cameras are fully operational. We don't want some lawyer screwing up our good work. Once the space is secure, my team will immediately start documenting the evidence with the help of the FBI Forensic team. Evidence gathering is important, but the safety of the kids and our teams is priority one. Be safe and be careful." Jess sat back down in her chair.

Terry Rubin walked to the front of the room and stood behind the podium. "For those of you I haven't met, I am Terry Rubin with the La Plata County Sheriff's Department. I have been asked to be in tactical command of this operation. I don't want to go back over everything we have covered so far. Check your gear and communications equipment. We will reassemble back here at four AM to go over any final details. We want everyone to go home tomorrow after we are finished. So be safe."

"One more thing. SWAT will take control of all the kids until ICE can get onsite. We have ICE staging just outside of town, so they wouldn't be in the way during the raid. We will have medical help and several ambulances available since some of these kids might be starting to go through withdrawal. As soon as we can clear everyone at the scene, we will transport the kids by bus to here, where we will begin interviews. At this point, we still don't know who is who inside the warehouse so until we clear each person, everyone is a suspect."

The meeting broke up and the SWAT Commanders

separated into teams to discuss the actual onsite procedures in more detail. Several of the SWAT members from the various units had worked with Buck in the past and they stopped at the back of the room to congratulate him on the shootout and to talk about how he managed to survive. Buck recounted the events and many of the team members just scratched their heads as they listened. Jess Gonzales joined the group and corroborated Buck's telling of the events.

As the group broke up, Jess took Buck aside. "Did you get any sleep?" she asked.

Buck replied. "A little. You?"

"I didn't sleep much, but I think I am doing ok."

Buck looked at her. "Why don't you stay with us in the command center until the raid is over? Let your SWAT guys handle it."

"I may take you up on that offer. Hey, I heard you had a little more excitement this afternoon at some bar. Broke a guy's nose. You are one badass, Buck Taylor."

Buck smiled. "Yeah, takes a real badass to take down a drunk," he laughed, as did Jess.

Just then Terry Rubin came through the door. "I've got Dick in interview one."

"Excellent. Let's go see if he wants to cooperate. Can you find the DA and have her meet us there? I'd like her to observe." Terry headed to find the DA, just as Buck's phone rang.

Chapter Forty-Four

Buck pulled out his phone. Unknown number. Buck answer the call.

"Buck Taylor."

"Agent Taylor, this is Sandi Calhoun. Are you able to talk?"

Buck asked her to hold on for a second and he headed out the side door and into the parking lot. Once clear of the building he reestablished the call.

"Yes, Ma'am and thanks for calling me back."

"I must say Agent Taylor that this seems quite unusual. I don't often get a call from the Governor asking me to call a police officer and to keep the conversation totally off the record. I will also say that the Governor told me that you are highly respected and that whatever you tell me, I can count on. Now would you mind telling me what this is all about."

"Yes, Ma'am. I have a problem that I think might be right up your alley."

Buck proceeded to tell her as much about the raid as he felt comfortable talking about with a civilian. He then got to the heart of the conversation.

"These kids have been drugged and tortured for God knows

how long. I am worried that once ICE takes control of them they are going to end up in a detention facility with minimal medical help. I am hoping you might be able to work something out to get them the help they need in someplace other than a prison. These kids, as far as we know, haven't done anything wrong and they probably have no idea that they are someplace other than Mexico. They will be scared, most likely traumatized after the raid and many will be starting withdrawal."

There was silence on the other end of the phone as Sandi Calhoun tried to wrap her head around what Buck had just told her. She finally replied.

"Agent Taylor, how many young men and women are we talking about?"

"We do not know for sure, but we think it could be as many as thirty or thirty-five. We also have no idea of their ages. One other thing you should know. Some of the girls have been sexually assaulted while in captivity."

"Oh my God," Sandi replied. "Agent Taylor, the Governor said that it is totally out of character for you to do this and he will take full responsibility for the information getting to me. But I would like to know for my own peace of mind, why are you doing this?"

Buck thought for a minute. "Well, Ma'am, I'm not quite sure. I have a real problem with kids being abused, no matter where they are from, and these kids have been through hell. I guess I just don't want them to be hurt anymore. To be totally honest with you, if these kids get sent back to Mexico their chances of survival are pretty much non-existent. This is one of the worst cartels we have ever seen."

"Good answer, Agent Taylor. I am going to hang up and make believe this call never happened. I will do everything I can to see that these kids are treated fairly and given the chance for asylum if that is what they want. I will not contact you directly unless it is something important but know that this has my full attention. Thank you, Agent Taylor." Sandi Calhoun hung up.

Buck was a little conflicted. He did what he believed was the right thing to do but he also did something that as a cop he shouldn't have done and that was get a lawyer involved. He put away his phone and just stood there for a moment all alone in the parking lot.

He dialed the Director, who answered on the second ring. "Hello, Buck. What's going on?" he said Hello.

Buck filled him on the raid details and then said, "I just spoke to the lawyer. She sounds like she is onboard."

The Director replied. "That's great news. The Governor will be pleased and from this moment on, I have no idea what you are talking about."

Buck asked. "Are you ready to go after the cartel lawyer?"

The Director replied. "Warrants are in place. I have a team on his residence and a team on his office. We've been sitting on both locations but so far, we haven't seen him at either location. We are hoping he hasn't rabbited. We issued an All-Points Bulletin on him and his car and we alerted Homeland and TSA in case he heads for the airport. They have flagged his license and passport."

"Thanks, sir. I need to get back inside to interview one of the owners of the trucking company."

"Hey, Buck? Be careful tomorrow. I don't want to lose you."

Buck hung up and was just about to enter the building when his phone rang again. This time it was Hank Clancy, FBI.

"Hey, Hank. What's up?"

"Great news Buck. First, we have all the warrants in place. Copies are being sent electronically to the Sheriff as we speak.

Second, we were finally able to ping the encrypted sat phone at the other end of the call. We have a location on Carlos Rojas."

"That's great news Hank. Any chance we can get to him?"

"Not likely," replied Hank. "He is living in a huge hacienda about forty miles south of the border, south of New Mexico. The hacienda used to belong to that Mexican American movie producer, Simon Rivera and is in the middle of nowhere."

Buck thought for a minute. "Isn't that the guy who disappeared a couple years back with his entire family?"

"One in the same, Buck. Everyone always assumed he bolted to avoid a huge tax bill the IRS was planning to drop on him. Maybe we were wrong and he and his family are buried somewhere out in the desert."

"Jesus, that takes balls, to kill someone and then move into their house."

"You are right, Buck. Who knows what goes on in this guy Rojas's head. Hopefully, we will cripple his operation enough that the other cartels, what's left of them, will figure out a way to retaliate against him. Would be good for us."

"You got that right," replied Buck.

"Alright, I need to run so I can meet with the forensics team. We will arrive by military transport right at dawn and will stage at the airport until we get the all clear from you to come in. Good luck tomorrow and keep your head down."

Hank hung up. Buck headed upstairs to interview one.

Chapter Forty-Five

Dick Dillon was sitting handcuffed to the table in interview room one when Buck opened the door. He had a bandage covering his broken nose and the start of what were going to be two amazing black eyes. He was holding his head, either from the pain of the slight concussion or the pain of the hangover he was most likely starting to experience. He looked up as Buck entered the room.

"Hey. I ain't talkin to you. You broke my damn nose." His words were muffled by the bandage and the cotton that had been stuffed up his nostrils to stop the bleeding. Buck just smiled and sat down opposite Dick. Opening a manila folder, Buck took out his Miranda card and read Dick his Miranda warning. When he was finished reading the warning he asked Dick if he understood his rights. After several attempts, Dick finally acknowledged he understood his rights.

"You have no one to blame but yourself. I told you what was going to happen if you got smart with me, so you had to test it." Buck hesitated for effect. "Or was that your plan from the minute I walked up to you. Get yourself locked up so we could protect you."

A muffled voice. "I don't know what you're talkin about.

Why don't you go bother someone else and leave me alone? I'm gonna sue you guys for breakin my nose."

"No problem, Dick," Buck said. "We will let you go as soon as you tell us about the cartel taking over your business and setting up a drug distribution network in your hometown. Your neighbors are going to love hearing about that."

Dick looked angry. "You don't know anything, so why don't you get out of my face and get me a lawyer."

"Good idea, Dick. Maybe we can call that cartel lawyer that you and Hector went into business with. I'll bet his boss will be really happy when he tells him you have been arrested and are cooperating with us."

Dick suddenly went ashen. "You can't do that. I haven't told you anything."

"That's true Dick, you haven't told us anything. But we have been tapping your phones and computers for a couple days now and once we let that information slip to your attorney, the big cartel boss is going to think it came from you."

Buck pushed his chair back and stood up to leave. "I'm going to call your attorney. I hope you have a way to protect your family. Cartel guys don't mess around."

Dick suddenly lost all his fight. "Wait. I don't want my family hurt. On second thought, I don't want a lawyer. Ask me what you want."

"Ok, Dick. Why don't you start from the top and I will fill in the blanks as we go?"

Dick started from the beginning when he first heard about the cartel lawyer. He told Buck how he lost his temper with Hector and how they almost got into a fist fight that afternoon in the office. He told him how he hated the idea, how he hated the money and how he gave part of the money away to Claire Ringsby, his office manager, so she could get out of town. He told Buck he was working on a plan to get him and his family out of town as well. He also told Buck, reluctantly, of being knocked down by Blondy when he asked what they were doing in the sealed off portion of the warehouse. He figured it had to be drugs, but he never got to see inside the space.

He wanted Buck to believe that he wanted no part of what was going on, but that Hector seemed to be starting to come around to working with the cartel guys. He told Buck he was afraid for his family's safety and the only reason he tried to hit Buck in the bar was because he had too much to drink and his inebriated mind thought if he got himself arrested he might be able to protect his family. After about forty minutes, he stopped talking and answering questions, put his head in his hands and cried.

Buck sat back in his chair. During the conversation, Buck had shown Dick the picture of Harry Crank and Dick identified him as the blond guy in the warehouse. He looked almost petrified when he saw the picture.

"Alright, Dick. You did really good. In a few minutes a Deputy is going to bring in a copy of everything we just talked about. I need you to sign the statement after you read it and make sure it is what you told me."

Dick looked up and tried to wipe the tears from his eyes with his hands still in handcuffs. "What's going to happen to my family? Can you protect them?"

"For right now, we are going to put you back in a cell. You are being held for assaulting a police officer. Tomorrow morning, the FBI will execute a search warrant on your house. At that point, it will be up to the feds how they are going to deal with you and your family. If what you have told me is true, it might be possible for your lawyer to get you into witness protection. That's not my call. Continue to cooperate and we will see what happens. I am going to have the DA get you a public defender for now. Just sit tight."

Buck got up from the chair and when the door buzzed he opened it and stepped out. The Sheriff and DA were waiting.

Buck looked at the DA. "Do we have what we need to execute the warrants?"

DA Brewer responded. "I think we are golden. I will call the Public Defender as soon as I leave here and explain the situation. We will make sure they keep this under wraps until after the raid."

The Sheriff looked at Buck. "You think we can get the FBI to recommend witness protection?"

"I will talk to Hank Clancy in the morning and get his take. In the meantime, can you call Durango PD and have them put someone on Dick's house until this is all over? Let's try to keep his family safe."

"You got it Buck. Why don't you go get some dinner and we will see you back here in a couple hours?"

The Sheriff and DA Brewer walked out together, and Buck headed for the back door. He needed some air and a good meal. One of Jimmy Palumbo's burgers would probably fit the bill.

Chapter Forty-Six

It was high summer tourist season in Durango and the sidewalks, shops and restaurants were packed with people. Buck had to go over three blocks before he could find a parking space. He pulled in and sat for a minute and just watched all the people. Buck was a student of human nature and he thought back on the days when the family would take driving vacations and in small towns all over the west, just like this one, Buck would watch the people on the streets and make up stories about them for the kids. He could keep the kids entertained for hours and even weeks later, long after the vacation was over, the kids would still make mention of the characters Buck had described. He found himself in a melancholy moment as he thought about his life with Lucy. His eyes got moist and he wiped them with the back of his hand.

Buck took out his phone and dialed his daughter Cassie. He expected to get her voice mail and was ready to leave a message when she answered the phone.

"Dad are you alright? I just came in out of the field and got Jason's voicemail and was just getting ready to dial your number. A shootout, Oh my God."

"I'm ok Cass," Buck replied. "It could have been worse."

"Dad, Jason said all the shots were directed at you and that mom protected you. Is he joking?"

"Well, some of that is true. Most of the shots did come my way and I am alive and unscathed. I don't know if your mom was looking out for me or what. Must have just been my lucky day."

"What happened to the guy who was shooting at you? Did you arrest him?"

"Well, not quite. There were actually two shooters." Buck paused a minute.

"Dad, what happened to the shooters?"

"Both shooters are dead. I got one and Jess Gonzales, you remember Jess, she works for the DEA, she took out the other one."

Cassie was silent for a second. "I'm so sorry Dad. It must have been horrible. I'm glad Jess had your back."

"Yeah, me too. Listen kiddo, I need to go. I have to work tonight and need to get some food. You stay safe ok and we can talk in a couple days if you have some time."

"Ok, Dad. Try to stay out of harm's way. Love you, Dad."

"Love you too, Kiddo."

Buck hung up and just sat for a minute. Then he shut off the car, climbed out and headed for the La Bon Café.

The café was packed to the doors, but as soon as Jimmy saw Buck he pulled his stool from behind the bar and set Buck up on the end of the bar. Once again, he didn't ask what Buck wanted. He dropped a huge slab of meat on the grill and brought over a bottle of Coke.

"Hey, man. How's Dick Dillon? Man did you slam him."

Buck smiled. "Broken nose and a mild concussion. Hey, sorry about the mess on the bar."

"No worries, man. Not the first time somebody bled on the

bar. Won't be the last." Jimmy laughed a hearty laugh. He walked off, flipped Buck's burger, dropped a handful of fries into the hot oil and headed to the end of the bar to refill some glasses. He walked back to the grill, put a big chunk of cheddar cheese on the burger, delivered another burger to someone halfway down the bar and then put the burger on the bun, piled on the fries and delivered the plate to Buck.

"Enjoy, man." Then Jimmy headed off to take care of the rest of his customers.

Buck dug in like he hadn't eaten in days. The noise level in the narrow space was intense but Buck loved the environment and Jimmy looked like he was truly in his element. Jimmy worked the room like a politician, shaking hands with newcomers, filling glasses, flipping burgers. It was a sight to see. It was also the first time Buck had seen Jimmy handle the bar on a busy night without Loraine. He would have to tell her what a great job Jimmy did while she was gone.

Buck finished his burger and fries, put the cap on the bottle of coke and dropped a twenty dollar bill on the bar. Jimmy was having a spirited conversation with another biker down the bar, so he just waved to Jimmy as he left. He walked out into the night and headed for the car.

This was the time of night when Buck missed Lucy the most. Whenever he was on an assignment out of town, he would always call her at nine o'clock. They would talk about how her day went and he would always assure her that he would be ok, even though there was never a guarantee. As her disease progressed he always tried to minimize the worry for her and tried to keep the conversation light. He missed wishing her a good night. As he slipped into the car, his focus switched over. He let the melancholy go and put his head in what he liked to call mission mode. He focused all his attention on what was coming up in the next couple hours. He pulled out of the parking space and headed for the Sheriff's office.

183

Chapter Forty-Seven

Buck pulled into the parking space right opposite the side door of the Sheriff's office, grabbed his backpack and headed inside to the conference room. His first stop was to talk to Randall from the FBI sneak and peek team. Randall was busy listening to his headphones and typing furiously on his computer. Buck tapped him on his shoulder. Randall held up one finger to indicate he needed a second. He finished typing and pulled off his headphones.

"Sorry, Buck. Wanted to make sure I got that final conversation transcribed for Agent Clancy. What's up?"

"Anything new on the taps?"

Randall slid his computer over so Buck could get a better look at the screen and scrolled back up to the top of the most recent page. Buck read what Randall had transcribed. There were no new earth shattering revelations. What he read sounded like a group of people trying to wrap up a project. Lots of activity, very little conversation. Buck finished reading.

Randall spoke first. "We checked texts earlier and all the drivers responded back that they would be on site by four AM."

Buck responded, "Awesome. This thing is coming to an end. Any word from the NSA on the encrypted laptop?"

"No, sir. Agent Clancy has given our SWAT guys orders to grab all the computer equipment they can find. He wants it shipped immediately after the raid to the NSA at Fort Meade. They are thinking they might have better luck breaking the encryption if they have the machines on site."

"Has Terry Rubin asked you if you are able to block all the bad guys' communications during the raid? Is that possible from here?"

"No, sir." He hasn't discussed it with me. He might have spoken with Josh or Toby. The answer to your question is, yes. We can shut down their entire network from right here."

"Good," replied Buck. "Let's kill everything as soon as the word is given to breach the warehouse. Also, have the Colorado and New Mexico State Troopers and the Southern Ute Tribal Police been given access to the GPS tags on the trailers so they can track them if they leave before we hit the warehouse?"

"Yeah. The Sheriff and Terry had a conference call with all three agencies a little bit ago. We gave them each access to a secure cell phone app that they can use to track the trailers."

Buck thanked Randall and headed off to find the Sheriff and Terry Rubin. They were both sitting comfortably in the Sheriff's office. The Sheriff waved Buck in.

Buck said. "I just spoke with Randall and asked him to shut down all communication from inside the warehouse as soon as we are ready to breach. He said you guys have already spoken to Colorado, New Mexico and the Tribal Police and they have access to the GPS tags on the trailers."

Terry replied. "Great idea on the communications. It never crossed my mind. Yes. Everyone has the tags and access to a cell phone app Randall had. They are all ready and will have their units stationed per our discussion by five AM. They will not move to intercept any of the trucks until you give the word."

"Excellent. I'm going to check in with SWAT. Oh, remember, you are in tactical command of this operation, so you will be the one to let our partners on the road know when they can move on the trucks. Are you up for all this?"

Terry smiled. "Yes, sir. You can count on me."

The Sheriff smiled and nodded her head in agreement. Buck looked at Terry.

"I have no doubt you are ready. The Sheriff and I will be right there with you, but you know what needs to happen and I am confident you can do this."

"Thanks, Buck. I really appreciate that. Means a lot coming from you."

Buck nodded and headed out the door. He found the three SWAT Commanders in his temporary office leaning over the desk, studying the blueprints they had gotten from the building department.

"You guys ready?" Buck asked.

The FBI Commander looked up from the blueprints. "Ready as we can be. We were just going over this again. Sure wish we had an easier way to breach the space. We are worried about the time between blowing the rear door, crashing into the cargo door and setting off the flash-bangs. The bad guys may have enough time to start spraying those kids."

Buck looked at the blueprint. "Are you planning to kill the power to the space just before we hit it?"

The Sheriff's SWAT Commander responded. "We talked about it, but then we are going in blind with possibly forty people running around in a panic. We could miss one of the bad guys and end up getting someone killed"

The DEA SWAT Commander spoke up. "The other concern is that the roll-up door could crash down on the assault vehicle and block our access into the warehouse. That would put all the burden of the breach on my guys coming in the back door. Not great."

Buck pointed to the door that had been drawn between the office and the warehouse space. "We don't know exactly where this door is, but what would happen if we made a stealth entry into the office and breached through this door? Can you do that?"

They all looked at Buck. "Great minds," said the FBI Commander. "That's what we were just talking about as you walked in. We can pick the lock on the office door instead of breaking it. The office should be empty. We can clear it quickly and then set up on the inner door. If it opens into the space, we are golden. If it opens into the office, we still have a timing issue, but not as bad."

Buck stood up. "Let me find out." And he walked out the door and headed down the hall to the holding cells.

Dick Dillon was not happy to see Buck walking towards his cell. His head and nose still hurt like hell. Buck stopped at the cell door.

"The door the cartel guys installed in the wall they built between the office and the warehouse. Which way does it open? Into the warehouse or into the office?"

Dick scratched his head and thought real hard. "It opens into the warehouse."

"Are you absolutely sure?" Buck asked.

"Yeah. No doubt."

"Thanks." Buck headed back down the hall leaving Dick to

wonder what that was all about. The SWAT Commanders were still where he left them.

"According to the owner we have in custody, the door opens into the warehouse."

"That will work", said the FBI Commander. "Now all we have to do is get into the office without them hearing us. This just improved our chances of keeping those kids alive. Nice work Buck. Thanks."

Buck nodded. "Always happy to help." He walked out of the office to find another bottle of Coke. It was gonna be a long night, so he decided to find a quiet corner in the conference room and take a nap.

Chapter Forty-Eight

Buck's internal alarm clock went off at three forty-five AM and he sat up and tried to stretch the kinks out of his back and shoulders. Sleeping in chairs was for younger folks. He thought to himself. "I'm getting too old for this crap." He took a long gulp out of what was left of his bottle of Coke, tossed the empty into the recycle bin in the corner and stood up. Both knees creaked like they really objected to waking up from sleeping in a chair.

Josh was now working at the listening station and transcribing his notes as he listened to the taps. He looked up as Buck approached gave him a thumbs up signal and went back to typing. Buck headed for the ground floor.

The SWAT guys had started to arrive and were busy checking their gear. Everyone was dressed in black from head to toe. Ballistic vests were being put on and communications gear was being checked and rechecked. Each SWAT member had a balaclava wrapped around his neck for easy access to conceal their faces during the raid. Helmets were put on and then weapons were checked. Pistols were holstered, and assault rifles were connected to a lanyard hanging around each person's neck.

Outside in the parking lot, the breachers were checking their fuses and setting up the quantities of Semtex they believed they would need. Buck was surprised at the lack of noise. Each team member knew his or her job as well as the jobs of the rest of the team. If one person was to fall, everyone on the team knew how to pick up the slack.

Each team member also checked their medical pouch. They all carried a modest supply of first aid supplies. In situations like they were about to enter, if someone was hurt, seconds counted. They all understood the risks and they were all well prepared for what lay ahead.

Buck walked over to his Jeep and opened the rear hatch. First, he unlocked the secure lockbox that was welded to the rear floor. He removed a tactical thigh holster, removed the semi-automatic pistol, dropped the magazine and check the bullets. He replaced the magazine and racked the slide. He then flicked the safety on and holstered the weapon. He then checked the three other spare magazines and replaced each one back in its assigned slot. He grabbed his ballistic vest and slipped it over his shoulders, slid the zipper up and checked to make sure he had his extra handcuffs and a supply of flex cuffs, his flashlight and a couple additional magazines all loaded with forty-five caliber shells. He placed his expandable baton in the holder at the side of the vest. Checking to make sure he had everything he needed, he slipped on his thin black nylon jacket, emblazoned with CBI in large letters on both the back and the left side front. He covered his head with a CBI ball cap and shut the rear hatch.

As he headed back to the building he ran into Jess Gonzales. From their clothes and equipment, they could have been twins, except Jess's vest was emblazoned with DEA. She also carried a Taser attached to the left side of her belt. She would normally wear the Taser on her right hip, so it was instinctively the first weapon she would grab. Tonight, was different. Tonight, the rules of engagement were different and the situation more dangerous.

"Hey, Jess. You ready?"

"You bet Buck. The teams are loading up and we are ready to roll out. Hey listen, things are going to get a little crazy later and if I don't have a chance to say it, thanks for calling me in on this one."

"No worries, Jess. Wouldn't want anyone else at my side."

Jess nodded and headed for the SUV that her SWAT team was climbing into.

Terry and Sheriff Sinclair walked up to Buck. Everyone was in plain clothes and everyone was weaponed up.

"Buck", Terry spoke. "You ready to head over to the command center?"

Buck nodded and they all headed toward the Sheriff's black GMC Tahoe. Several Sheriff's Department marked police cars rolled out of the parking lot and headed in different directions. The deputies would be setting up roadblocks a few minutes before the breach.

Chapter Forty-Nine

The Sheriff drove past the warehouse, turned off her lights and pulled into the parking lot for the auto body shop across the street. She pulled around behind the building and shut off the engine. Terry still had one deputy on surveillance inside the auto body shop and he unlocked the door as they approached.

Terry asked the deputy. "All quiet?"

"Yeah. Drivers started arriving a little bit ago and they have been firing up the semis and hooking up to the trailers. There is still one semi backed up to the loading dock. They closed the dock door about ten minutes ago, so I think they are done loading the last trailer."

Terry picked up the binoculars from the desk and looked out the window. The truck yard was lit up like the county fair. Not great for our side, he thought. One thing he saw that was a plus was that the electric gate was open, probably in anticipation of the trucks leaving. This was good for the SWAT guys.

"Snipers here yet?" Buck asked.

The deputy nodded. "Got here about an hour ago. They are on the roof."

The SWAT teams arrived at the building behind the

warehouse, parked the cars and started moving quietly through the empty parking lot and up to the corner of the fence that the sneak and peek team had used for their entry. They had left the fence bolts loose, so it was just a matter of removing the nuts and slipping out the bolts. Quietly one by one, the DEA and the FBI SWAT teams passed through the opening in the fence and moved cautiously towards the back of the building. When they arrived at the back of the building each team headed for opposite ends of the building. The FBI team moved around the corner of the building and headed towards the front corner. They would hold at the corner until it was time to access the office.

The DEA team headed towards the back door. Once there, they assembled on each side of the door. The breacher attached a small wad of Semtex to the doorknob and inserted the wireless fuse. He would set it off from his cell phone. They actually had an app for setting off explosives. Technology was amazing.

While those two teams got set in their respective positions, two FBI snipers found the roof access ladder for the building behind the warehouse and climbed to the roof. Once there, they moved to separate ends of the building, staying below the parapet as they ran. Once in position, they sighted in their rifles and started their overwatch duties. These guys took their role in all this very seriously. They were responsible for all those other guys on the ground. They had a big job.

The Sheriff's SWAT team pulled to a stop at the corner, just down the street from the warehouse and shut off the lights on the assault vehicle. Once more each member of the team checked their gear and then checked the gear of the person next to them.

At this point, all movement stopped. Everyone was in place. Terry Rubin began contacting each unit on his radio. The radios were all set to a special frequency that was reserved for only the highest law enforcement use. The SWAT team commanders on the ground and the snipers on the buildings responded with a single click over the microphone. Everyone was on radio silence.

He was just about to contact the deputies and the Durango police officers to set up the roadblocks, when the first semi started roaring and pulled away from the fence at the far end of the yard, heading for the gate. Three additional semis pulled out right behind the first.

Terry picked up his radio. "All units, hold position, semis leaving the yard."

Terry, Buck and the Sheriff all breathed a sigh of relief when the trucks all turned the same way and headed toward 550. They were all worried that one might turn the opposite way and drive right past where the SWAT vehicle sat.

Terry gave the trucks five minutes to clear the area and then he radioed the Deputies and Durango PD to set the barriers. He then radioed Josh back in the conference room and asked him to contact the Colorado and New Mexico troopers and the tribal police and let them know which way the trucks were heading. He also reminded Josh to tell them not to intercept until they received word that the raid was in progress.

Terry checked his watch. It was now five minutes to six in the morning and the sun was just a slight pink swathe of color coming over the mountains. He looked at Buck and then the Sheriff. Each nodded. Terry picked up his radio.

"Team B. You are clear to access the office. Drivers are all inside."

One audio click.

"Team A. Time to roll."

One click.

Buck looked down the block and saw the SWAT assault vehicle turn the corner. Lights off and several figures hanging on either side of the vehicle.

At the same time, one of the team B members picked the front door lock, opened the door and six bodies entered the space. Two members remained at the corner of the building to keep an eye out.

Inside the office, four of the team members quickly and quietly cleared the space while the breacher placed a small wad of Semtex on the doorknob, inserted the wireless fuse and the entire team moved down the wall and found cover.

A muffled voice came over the radio. "Team B, ready."

Terry picked up the radio. "Team C get ready to breach." Click.

The SWAT vehicle arrived at the entrance drive and turned in and moved towards the electric gate, which thankfully, still sat open. It started to move into position, ready to hit the roll-up door.

Buck looked at Terry. He nodded.

Terry picked up the radio. "All teams, BREACH!"

Two simultaneous explosions could be heard at either end of the warehouse as the SWAT teams breached the two access doors. Immediately followed by the sound of four flash-bangs going off. The SWAT assault vehicle roared up the ramp and hit the cargo door right dead center. The door flew in and landed on top of Blondy's rental car. The Swat vehicle hit the back of the car and drove it ten feet forward until it hit the fence and stopped.

Buck, Terry and the Sheriff threw open the front door of the auto body shop and ran towards the warehouse. Over the radio, the various units were yelling. "Police, we have a warrant!" "Federal Agents, everyone on the ground!" "Police, on the ground!"

"GUN!"

Terry, Buck and the Sheriff stopped short of the building as automatic weapons fire could be heard from several locations in the building.

"Drop the weapon!" From multiple voices. More shots fired.

Screams could be heard coming from inside.

"Man Down, Man Down!!"

"Runner, back door!" Multiple shouts.

Chapter Fifty

Mustache had just walked into the guard's office and Blondy was just walking out of the restroom when the first explosions rocked the building and the door to the main office blew into the warehouse and almost off its hinges. One of the guards had been standing right in front of the door when it blew and the door hit him square in the back and knocked him to the ground. He was down for the count. At the same time, Blondy felt the concussion from the blast that took out the back door. He dove back into the restroom just as two flash bangs were thrown into the space and exploded simultaneously. The same thing happened as two more were thrown in from the main office.

The noise and smoke from the flash-bangs had the desired effect and the kids started screaming and covering their eyes and ears as they fell to the floor. The space was soon flooded with people wearing all black and sporting ballistics vests and heavy weapons. Mustache was in the office and didn't get the full effect of the flash-bang, but he still came out the door of the guard's office staggering and clawing at his ears. The roll-up door suddenly came crashing down and almost hit him as it landed on the rental car. Even though he was having trouble seeing, Mustache raised his weapon and tried to aim at the people rushing around the smashed door.

"Police, we have a warrant!" "Federal agents, everyone on the ground!" "Police, on the ground!" "GUN!"

The first bullet hit Mustache in the chest. The next four followed suit and Moustache died before he hit the floor. Two of the other guards were able to recover enough from the flash bangs and even though they were having trouble standing and seeing, they managed to pull the triggers on their guns and spray bullets where they thought the intruders were located. Both men died in a hail of gun fire.

"Man Down, Man Down!"

Another guard came around the corner of the cages and raised his weapon.

"Drop the weapon!" The guard fired and was immediately put down by multiple rounds.

Blondy had a good idea who these guys were, and it puzzled him for a moment. "How did they know?" He had been careful. Then he hit on it. "That damn kid who tried to escape. He must have thrown something over the fence. Shit, Shit, Shit." He picked himself up off the floor and cracked the restroom door. It looked like the cops were all inside the space, so he opened the door and moved toward the back door.

He was almost to the door when he heard a cop yell. "We have a runner."

Without looking back he ducked into the cage and picked up one of the girls who was lying on the floor crying and holding her ears. He backed out of the cage and immediately raised his gun and placed the barrel against the back of her head. Even though she could barely stand, Blondy was able to crouch down enough to stay behind her and not give the approaching cops a shot. He continued slowly backing up towards the back door. He heard a chorus of voices,

"Drop your weapon!" and "Let the girl go!" His hearing was finally clearing, and he was able to see a little more clearly. He reached the threshold of the door and pinned himself and the girl against the wall. Decision time.

Chapter Fifty-One

Buck, Terry Rubin and Sheriff Sinclair, with guns drawn, entered through the glass door into the office and slowly stepped through the door into the warehouse. The inside of the warehouse looked like a war zone. The production tables they had seen on the camera were tipped over. Bodies were lying all over the floor, many crying and writhing in pain. Many had blood coming from their ears. To his left, Buck watched as one of the SWAT members was putting flex cuffs on the unconscious guard who had been hit by the door.

Buck headed towards the back of the building. As he approached the SWAT officers, he spotted Blondy pinned against the wall next to the back door holding a young girl in front of himself for protection. The officers were yelling for him to drop the weapon he held against her head and let the girl go. Buck stepped forward and was immediately grabbed by a SWAT officer. He shrugged off his hand and looked at Blondy.

"Sergeant Crank," he said. "Is this how you want to go out? Protected by a girl."

Buck held his gun at his side. The room went silent. Weapons were lowered as Buck was now in the line of fire. Everyone froze.

Terry Rubin turned his back and spoke quietly into his radio.

"Overwatch two, hostage situation. If you have a shot, you have the green light."

"Roger," came the response.

Buck looked at Blondy. "You were awarded a bronze star and a silver star for bravery. I bet you didn't get them by hiding behind a kid. Why don't you let the girl go and drop the gun? You don't need to die today."

Blondy looked up and Buck could see instant recognition enter his eyes. The cop from the parking lot shootout. What are the odds? He also started to calculate in his head his odds of staying alive. He would either die in prison from a lethal injection or from the shiv of one of Carlos Rojas's paid killers. He was screwed no matter what he did. He made a decision.

Buck took another step forward and stopped. He looked at Blondy and then he saw it in Blondy's eyes. Blondy had made his decision. Blondy started to slide step towards the door keeping the girl in front of him. Buck started to raise his pistol. Blondy's foot hit the threshold and he looked down at his foot. He glanced over his shoulder and saw two more SWAT cops pointing automatic weapons at him, from outside the building. He looked at Buck and smiled. Buck started to race forward. He was too late. Blondy stepped over the threshold and raised his head two inches over the girl's head. It was just enough. The sniper's bullet entered his skull between his left ear and his left eyebrow. The back of his skull blew out and splattered bone and brain matter over the wall behind him.

Buck caught the girl just as Blondy let her go. It was a completely involuntary movement because Blondy's life ended as soon as the bullet hit his brain. Blondy's body jerked to the right and slid down the wall, smearing more blood and brain as it went. Buck, holding the girl in one arm, holstered his pistol. It was all over.

Two SWAT officers walked up and took the girl out of Buck's arm. He looked down at Blondy. He stood for a moment. Such a waste. He turned and walked back down the hall toward the warehouse. Several of the SWAT officers patted him on the back as he walked past. Buck simply nodded.

The scene in the warehouse was improving. Paramedics had arrived and were applying a pressure bandage to the left leg of one of the FBI SWAT guys. As it turned out, one of the guards, unable to see, had gotten off a lucky shot before he was hit with numerous bullets. Not so lucky for the SWAT member who was in the wrong place at the wrong time.

Paramedics were also working on some of the kids. It didn't look to Buck like their injuries were too severe. Some of them might suffer a little hearing loss, but they were alive and that was what mattered. Two of the kids had already been transported by ambulance. They were the most severely hurt, having gotten caught in the crossfire.

Terry spotted Buck and walked towards him. "What you tried to do back there was amazing."

Buck just nodded. He had mixed feelings about what had happened in the back hall and he would need to sort those out once he was alone.

Terry continued. "The troopers stopped all four trucks. One was headed for Salt Lake City, one was headed east on 160 toward Denver and two were headed south. The Ute Tribal Police stopped one just before it got to the state line and the New Mexico State Police stopped the other one just north of Farmington. FBI agents and the DEA guys out of Santa Fe are already on their way to all four stops. No one resisted."

Buck looked pleased. "What about the other drivers here?"

"Two of them were catching a nap in their rigs and three more were found safe inside the little office. They will all have headaches, but they are alive. Oh, the guy with the mustache, Claire Rinsgby had mentioned. He was the first to die." Terry walked away to take a call.

Sheriff Sinclair walked up. "All in all, not a bad morning." Then she looked around the warehouse. "Could have been a lot worse. Not sure if we could have done it without you. Unfortunately, I am going to have the Feds in my county for a long time trying to sort this all out."

Buck smiled. "You got that right." He stepped away from the Sheriff and headed for the main office.

Inside the office, the SWAT guys were taking pictures of each laptop as they sat on the desks and then placing them in evidence bags. They had already grabbed the encrypted laptop. It had been sitting in the little office in the back. Buck nodded to the officers and walked out the front door into the morning air.

Buck sat on the front steps leading to the office and looked out into the parking lot. A crowd was starting to gather outside the yellow police tape that two deputies were putting up around the property. The first news trucks were arriving. He wondered if the Governor had alerted them. He just shook his head. That's when he noticed Jess Gonzales having a very animated phone call on the other side of the parking lot. She hung up the phone and spotted Buck sitting on the steps. She walked over.

Jess was out of breath and more excited than Buck had ever seen her. "Buck, this is huge. I was just on the phone with my

Director. If the amount of drugs we found in the one trailer is the same in all the others, this raid could be worth upwards of one hundred million dollars and that's conservative."

Buck looked at her, disbelieving. "Seriously. Holy shit! That would make this one of the biggest drug busts in history. Carlos Rojas is not going to be happy about this."

Jess laughed, as did Buck. "I need to run," she said. "We need to start inventorying all this stuff. The Director is flying in twenty more agents from other jurisdictions to help. See you later."

Terry Rubin found Buck a minute later. "I just spoke to Chief Chandler. They executed both warrants on Hector Vegas and on Dick Dillon's houses. Everything went fine. Lots of tears and crying. I guess they scared the crap out of Hector's wife and kids when the used the battering ram on their front door. FBI is gathering evidence and Hector is in lockup at Durango PD."

Buck stood up and held out his hand. "You did an awesome job on this Terry. First class police work." Terry shook Buck's hand.

Terry just stood there speechless. Buck let go of Terry's hand and said. "I will catch up with you later. Time to make some calls. If this thing is as big as Jess thinks it is, the Governor is gonna want to be involved." Buck stepped away from Terry and pulled out his phone.

Chapter Fifty-Two

The Director answered on the first ring. "Is it over?"

"Yes, sir. And it is going to be a whole lot bigger than any of us expected. This could potentially be the biggest drug bust in history." He proceeded to fill in the Director on all the details.

When Buck finished, there was a moment of silence on the other end of the phone. Then the Director said, "Ok Buck. I am going to call the Governor and fill him in. Max Clinton and the mobile crime lab should be there in a couple hours. I will let the Governor know that you would prefer to stay in the background and let the locals get all the credit. Awesome job Buck. Please let everyone on the team know I said so, ok?"

"Yes sir. That will be fine. And thank you sir. I am going to stay here for a couple more days to help wrap up what I can and then I am heading home. If you need me, that's where I will be." Buck disconnected the call.

The next couple hours were a blur as Buck and Terry Rubin continued to coordinate the work going on in the field. Max Clinton arrived a little after noon, with her forensics team and the CBI mobile crime lab. Her arrival was followed within minutes by the FBI forensics team, out of Denver, and their mobile crime lab. Max immediately introduced herself to the FBI's lead forensic analyst and they began coordinating the work of gathering evidence. There would be plenty of work to go around.

A couple hours after the raid on the warehouse, the trucks that had left the yard early began to arrive back at the warehouse. It was decided by all concerned, that it would be easier to have the trucks escorted back to Durango so that all the evidence could be processed in one location and the contents of the trucks could be properly inventoried and documented.

While the first two trucks that returned were opened, Buck noted the arrival of Robert Townsend, Special Agent in Charge of the Denver office of ICE, Immigration and Customs Enforcement, and several carloads of ICE agents. Buck walked over to greet Townsend. They talked for a few minutes about the shootout and exchanged pleasantries. Buck then informed Townsend that there were still a couple of the kids on site. They were being held in the office area and were being interviewed by a couple Spanish speaking deputies. Each young person, except those that had been transported to the hospital, were photographed, fingerprinted and were advised of their Miranda rights. Since there were so many people on site inside the warehouse, it needed to be determined what role each person played, before they were released and transported to the Sheriff's office where they would be held until ICE could take them into custody. They were also being evaluated as to their medical conditions. Many were already starting to show signs of opioid withdrawal.

Townsend informed Buck that he would send his team over to the Sheriff's office to start processing the kids. He told Buck they would be transported, as soon as they were medically released, to a holding facility in Alamosa and that deportation proceeding would start immediately. Buck thanked Townsend for his help and walked back to the two trailers that were being inventoried.

Hank Clancy, FBI, pulled into the truck yard followed by three more black, government issue SUV's containing a dozen more agents on loan from several different field offices. He spotted Buck and waved. The remaining two trucks arrived at the same time, escorted by Colorado State Troopers and two Southern Ute Tribal Police units. The trailers were backed up to the loading dock. Jess met Buck and Hank Clancy at the back of one of the trailers. The FBI videographer started documenting the scene as Jess had one of her agents cut the lock on the trailer with a pair of bolt cutters. As the videographer had done twice before, he carefully documented the lock being cut and being removed from the hasp.

Two DEA agents then cleared the hasps and swung open the doors. Everyone stared at what they saw, some hardly believing their eyes. Inside the trailer were crates marked as containing AR type assault rifles. When the inventory was completed, in the next couple days, it would be determined that there were two hundred such crates with each crate containing six brand new rifles. The inventory would also reveal over four hundred handguns of varying calibers and almost a half million rounds of ammunition. Enough firepower to arm a small army. It looked like Carlos Rojas was preparing for war.

However, the biggest surprise was what sat strapped down in the middle of the trailer. Most of the observers had never seen that much money in one place. The money had been shrink wrapped together to make a solid block four feet long, four feet wide and almost six feet tall. Buck and Jess both let out a whistle. Hank stood speechless. Terry Rubin had just arrived on the dock with the Southern Ute Police Chief and the officer who had made the initial stop of this particular trailer. They were all having trouble understanding what they were looking at.

The Ute Police Chief was the first person to speak. "Holy Cow."

Buck looked at him and responded. "You can say that again."

Jess Gonzales, DEA, smiled. "There are millions of dollars there. Man did we put the hurt on the Sonoma Cartel."

Everyone started to come out of their stupor. Hank Clancy immediately phoned his SWAT Commander, who was somewhere in the warehouse, to have one of his men bring around the FBI SWAT vehicle, which was fully armored and secure and to have several of his SWAT officers assemble at the trailer. He directed his commander to disconnect the semi from the trailer and park the SWAT vehicle in front of the trailer. He then ordered the trailer doors closed and he assigned four SWAT agents to stand guard over the trailer. He needed some time to figure out what to do with all that money.

Buck had stepped away from the group and immediately placed a call to Gerald Choo. Gerald Choo was the Agent in Charge of the Denver office of Alcohol, Tobacco and Firearms. The ATF would take possession of the weapons from the trailer, inventory everything and then open an investigation to determine the origin of the weapons. When Gerald answered his phone Buck said, "Jerry, have I got a deal for you."

Buck went on to tell him about the raid and the trailer full of weapons they had just opened. After a few minutes of conversation, Gerald told Buck that he would have a team on the ground inside of two hours to take possession of the weapons and start investigating how the cartel was able to lay their hands on that many weapons. Choo told Buck that he was not aware of any large arms thefts recently or any missing weapons from any military weapons depots. Choo thanked Buck and hung up.

Buck had gotten several texts and calls from his kids, but he didn't have time to talk so he sent them a group text to let them know he was OK and he would talk to them later.

Chapter Fifty-Three

The area around the truck garage had taken on almost a carnival atmosphere. In spite of the fact that the streets surrounding the warehouse had been cordoned off and no one was allowed near the warehouse. The streets outside the barricades were filled with people from all over the county. Many of the business parking lots surrounding the blocked streets were filled with various types of media vehicles and Buck was amazed to see that in just a short period of time, even the major national networks had arrived on the scene. He wondered to himself, again, if maybe the Governor had something to do with the large turnout

Buck was a familiar face to many of the local and statewide reporters, so he tried to stay back from their view. Even so, several times he had heard someone call out his name and shout out a question or two. Several reporters, who had his cell phone number, tried to call. He ignored them all. He was not interested in being part of the story.

The Sheriff had called Jimmy Palumbo to see if he could arrange to get food and drinks sent over to the warehouse. By this time in the day, everyone was running on empty and she hoped some food might help. Jimmy had jumped on the phone and started calling his network of restaurant contacts and charity groups he worked with and within two hours several Durango police officers were rolling into the lot, their patrol cars filled with food and drinks for all.

Buck grabbed a sub sandwich that had been donated by a local shop and a cold bottle of Coke and found a shady spot on the street side of the parking lot. He sat under a tree and devoured his sandwich. July in the mountains still got hot and everyone appreciated the break. Buck looked around the parking lot of the warehouse. There wasn't a parking spot to be had and he doubted they could fit many more people in the lot.

Buck leaned back against the trunk of the tree and within minutes found himself nodding off. He was almost asleep when he snapped out of it and decided he needed to keep moving. That's when he noticed Jess Gonzales, DEA, and Hank Clancy, FBI, heading his way. They each had a sandwich and a bottle of something cold.

"Mind if we join you?" asked Hank

"Pull up a piece of shade. You two look as beat as I feel."

They both sat down in Buck's shady spot and went to town on their sandwiches. As they ate, Jess filled Buck in on what had taken place in the last hour or two. She told him that the drivers' paperwork had proved to be a treasure trove of information. Jess had collected all the destination and delivery information from each of the semis and had forwarded the information to her boss in Washington. The information proved invaluable. Her office had the locations of eight smaller local distribution centers that had been set up by the cartel in eight major western and southwestern cities.

The DEA office in Washington, in conjunction with the FBI and local law enforcement in each of those cities, had used the information from the raid this morning to get search warrants for all eight locations. As of an hour ago, raids had been mounted and were now taking place at each location. Several of the locations raided so far did contain small amounts of drugs, mostly local stuff the cartel had been able to get their hands on while they waited for the big shipments coming from Durango, but they also netted eight more encrypted laptops, which were being bagged up and would soon be headed to the NSA.

Buck said. "That's awesome Jess. Sounds like we really hit Carlos Rojas where it hurts."

Jess smiled and was just about to answer when Buck's phone rang. He checked the number and answered the call.

"Yes sir", said Buck. The Director was calling to fill Buck in on the cartel attorney they were staking out last night and this morning. Buck listened intently and hung up the phone. He filled Jess and Hank in on what the Director had just told him.

It seems the attorney was not hiding from anyone. He hadn't been seen at his residence or his office because he had taken his wife to dinner at a fancy downtown Denver restaurant to celebrate their anniversary and had gotten a room at a hotel for the night. He was unaware he was under surveillance until he turned on the Sunday morning news and saw a developing story about the raid in Durango. The lawyer and his wife quickly dressed, had the valet bring their car around and raced home to get their two kids and their pre-packed emergency suitcases.

The attorney was a smart guy and he circled the blocks around their house several times to see if it was being watched. Not seeing anyone in the neighborhood who didn't belong, he pulled into the driveway, ran into the house, grabbed the kids and their "Go" bags and headed for the car.

While he was grabbing everything they would need to travel,

his wife was paying the babysitter and scooting her out the door. They all jumped into the car and he pulled out of the driveway and headed for Centennial Airport. First, they had to pass back through the security gate at the entrance to the neighborhood. The attorney lived in a gated community.

On the way home, his wife had called the charter jet company he already had an account with and arranged for an immediate flight to Cabo San Lucas, where they had a beautiful townhouse that looked out over the ocean. The charter service always kept pilots on standby for their more discerning clients and she was told that the pilots would be at the airport within half an hour.

CBI agents Tracy and Doonen had found a nice place to park their car just inside the entrance to the golf course across the street from the attorney's gated community. They had been able to park in the very first parking space, which gave them a great view of the main gate and they had spotted the attorney's car as soon as it entered the driveway and stopped at the security gate. There were only two ways to get in and out of the community. Through the main entrance or through a rear service entrance. Tracy and Doonen had asked the Arapahoe County Sheriff to have a deputy posted across the street from the service entrance. They called him to let him know the attorney had come home.

The Attorney exited through the main entrance and headed south on University Blvd. He eventually turned at Arapahoe Road and headed east. Tracy and Doonen were four cars back at the light. The Arapahoe County deputy was two cars behind them. The little parade proceeded east on Arapahoe Road until the attorney turned right at the sign for Centennial Airport. Two blocks up, he turned right, into the parking lot for Centennial Charters. Tracy lit up her flashers and hit the siren. The attorney hit the gas, drove around the parking lot and was stopped dead in his tracks by four Arapahoe County Sheriff's cars. The deputies were out of their cars with guns drawn. Tracy pulled up behind him. While Tracy held her position at the back of the car, Doonen, with gun drawn, approached the driver's door. She ordered the attorney and his wife out of the car while two deputies positioned themselves to either side of the passenger door.

The arrest of the attorney and his wife continued without incident and they were booked into the Arapahoe County Sheriff's jail. The attorney immediate requested a meeting with the US Attorney for Colorado. The US Attorney, Ernesto Salvatore, and his attorney were now sitting in a conference room negotiating a spot in the Witness Protection Program, in exchange for everything he knew about the Sonoma Cartel. Additional CBI agents and Arapahoe County Deputies along with a couple FBI agents from Denver were now executing a search warrant on the attorney's house. His neighbors stood on their lawns and looked stunned that this was happening in their little private paradise.

Chapter Fifty-Four

Doctor Kramer, the county's Forensic Pathologist, was just walking out of the warehouse as Buck was crossing the parking lot. Buck looked up to see the Doctor standing on the loading dock.

"Hey, Doc. You doing ok?" The Doctor looked as tired as everyone else.

"I'll say one thing, Agent Taylor. Things sure get interesting when you're around." The Doctor smiled. "Haven't been this busy in years."

The Doctor had spent most of the day examining the remains of the deceased guards. He had just finished with the last body, the one by the back door, and had given the all clear for the paramedics and ambulance crews to start removing the bodies from the scene and taking them to the autopsy suite at the Sheriff's office. He was going to run out of refrigerator room and was trying to find some additional storage. He told Buck that he had requested help from Montrose County and Grand Junction and that two more certified Forensic Pathologists would be on site first thing in the morning to assist with the autopsies. This was going to be a busy couple of days.

He looked at Buck and Buck noticed the sadness in his eyes. "What a damn shame. And for what? Those young folks are going to go through hell until they get the opioids out of their systems and then they will have to face the reality of what they had been put through. Some of them may never recover. Such a shame." He nodded to Buck and headed for his car.

Buck made a slow pass through the warehouse stopping now and then to talk to one of the evidence techs. As he passed by the small office, he stopped to watch the paramedics placing Mustache into the body bag. He thought to himself. "I wonder if we will ever find out who this guy was?"

He walked towards the back door where one of the ambulance crews was just wheeling in the gurney. He stopped and looked at Blondy. He was no longer propped up against the wall. Dr. Kramer had laid him down to conduct his field examination. Buck looked at the bloody streak on the wall. He had to agree with the doctor. What a waste. Buck thought back to the moment Blondy raised his head up. Buck had seen the smile and he knew that Blondy had chosen the best way out. He knew when he raised up his head that his life was already forfeit. Carlos Rojas would never allow this betrayal and failure to go unpunished.

Buck found Terry Rubin sitting in the small office. He was just sitting there staring at the wall. Terry was bone weary and he had every right to be. Buck gave Terry a little salute with his right hand and turned and headed for the door. For the most part, his job was finished. This investigation had moved into other states and had now become mostly a federal affair. He would now be on the periphery and that would be fine with him.

The Sheriff left the warehouse several hours earlier and had taken Buck's tactical gear with her. Buck stood outside the warehouse. It was a beautiful night and he decided to walk the half mile back to the Sheriff's office. He unclipped his badge from his belt and put it in his pocket and untucked his shirt to cover his gun. He headed toward the deputy who was manning the entrance to the crime scene, signed himself out and started walking. He wasn't in a big hurry to get anywhere. He was also glad to see that most of the people who had surrounded the warehouse earlier had left and no one noticed him walk away.

As Buck entered the parking lot for the Sheriff's Department, he saw that several of the news trucks were now parked in the lot and the Sheriff and Durango Police Chief Chandler were standing in front of the building and were speaking to the media. Much of the crowd of onlookers from the warehouse were also present. The Sheriff was explaining the events of the day and wanted to assure all the citizens of the city and the county that the situation was under control and there was no further danger. She also explained that there was still a lot of evidence to examine and that there would be a press conference early the next morning and the FBI and DEA would be available to answer questions.

One of the reporters, Buck recognized from one of the Denver TV Stations, asked about the shootout that had happened in the hotel parking lot the night before. Chief Chandler explained that the events of the night before were not related, at all, to the drug raid today. He went on to explain that an agent with the Colorado Bureau of Investigation had been ambushed in the parking lot by two individuals, who later were identified as prime suspects in a triple homicide in Teller County.

The CBI agent was in Durango following up on a lead and had no idea the two suspects had followed him from Teller County. He explained that both individuals had died at the scene from multiple gunshots and that the CBI agent had been uninjured. He further explained that his office and the Sheriff's office had conducted a thorough investigation and determined the Agent's use of deadly force was justified. Due to the nature of the Agent's work, he would not be identified at this time.

Chief Chandler concluded by telling the reporters that they would need to contact the Teller County Sheriff's Department or the Colorado Bureau of Investigations for more information.

The press conference continued, but Buck was done. He entered the side door and headed up the stairs to the conference room. He was hoping to say goodbye to the FBI sneak and peek team but when he stepped into the conference room, the space was empty. They had already packed up their gear and were probably headed back to Denver. They were good people and he was grateful for their help. He would make sure to let Hank Clancy know how much they had helped this investigation.

Chapter Fifty-Five

The young folks who had been cleared by ICE agents were being held in the public meeting hall that was attached to the Sheriff's Office. Many of them were asleep on the floor while others sat shaking in chairs. Opioid withdrawal had taken hold of many of the kids and Buck felt sorry for them. They had been through so much already and now this. Buck spotted Robert Townsend, the ICE Agent in Charge and walked over to him.

"Hey, Bob. How are they doing?"

Townsend, who had just hung up his phone, turned to Buck. "Some of them are doing ok right now. The doctors at the hospital said we need to get them to a holding facility as soon as we can. The withdrawals will only get worse." Townsend hesitated for a moment.

Buck said, "What?"

"We don't really have the facilities to take care of illegals going through opioid withdrawal, especially this many. I have been calling everyone I know for ideas and I have a lot of people working on this, but this is way beyond anything we have ever dealt with.

"Perhaps I can help with that?" The voice came from the main doors leading to the public meeting room and both Buck and Townsend looked towards the voice.

Sandi Calhoun, Attorney at Law, stood in the doorway holding what looked to Buck like a legal document. Buck had never met Sandi and his first and only contact with her had occurred just the other day when they spoke on the phone. Buck had been in the audience at the National Police Chiefs Conference in Denver this past April when Sandi Calhoun had given the opening night keynote speech. The subject of her speech was human trafficking and Buck had been very impressed with what he heard.

Sandi Calhoun had been born and raised Catholic in a primarily Hispanic neighborhood in West Denver. Divorced early in her marriage, she found herself as a single mother left to raise her three young sons on her own. At the same time, she was struggling to raise her sons she was also putting herself through school. First at the University of Colorado in Boulder and then at the University of Denver Law school, where she graduated at the top of her class. Sandi had initially gone to work for a large Denver law firm, but she never found satisfaction in the job. Her passion was to help those less fortunate, so she finally left the huge firm and put up her shingle above the door of a rundown little storefront in Five Points, a mostly downtrodden neighborhood just north of Downtown Denver.

Over the years her practice outgrew the little storefront and she moved her firm to a larger building a few blocks away from the original location, but she kept the original storefront location. She staffed it with new, young attorneys who wanted to change the world. The old storefront would keep them closer to the people she had grown to love.

Sandi's practice originally started out handling immigration cases and cases involving people who were being stepped on by the system, and by life. A lot of her work involved pro bono cases and many of her clients, when they could, paid with food and things they had made. No one was ever turned away because they couldn't pay. To make ends meet and pay her staff, she also had attorneys working for her who handled typical legal cases, DUI's, contracts, mergers and acquisitions, personal injury and some small criminal matters. For Sandi, though, it was the helpless and the hopeless that got her full attention.

Over the years, Sandi had become the go-to lawyer in Denver for those seeking asylum in the United States. She never shied away from a controversial case and she became a familiar face on the nightly news, always fighting for the rights of the oppressed. She never cared about her clients ethnic or religious backgrounds. If you were oppressed or lived in fear of going back to your original country, Sandi was the person you wanted in your corner.

Sandi was a powerful force to be reckoned with and as the years progressed, she found herself being invited to speak at rallies for various causes all around the state. She became a vocal activist for many causes, but she still focused mostly on causes that dealt with human and sex trafficking. She was on the Board of Directors of several charitable foundations. She also became a leading expert on human trafficking and was in high demand as a speaker and as a guest lecturer at law schools all around the country.

Five years before Buck had heard Sandi speak at the Police Chiefs Conference, she was diagnosed with Metastatic Breast Cancer. The breast cancer had been found during a routine mammogram and additional scans had found that the cancer had also spread to her spine. Sandi was devastated. She did not accept the fact that her life could be over. There was too much left to do and too many people who depended on her, especially her three sons. Sandi's life was about to be turned upside down, but she vowed to fight the cancer with everything she had. She had faced many powerful adversaries in court and this would become the biggest fight of her life. Her faith in her doctors was strong, but her faith in God was an even more powerful force in her life. She would fight hard, but she would also pray to God for help. Her support network of family and friends was huge, and she felt their love and support every step of the way. Sandi had set goals for herself as she battled this dreaded disease, but the most important goal would be the one that would stay with her through the entire fight. She would live to dance with each one of her sons at their weddings and that became her focus.

So far, Sandi Calhoun was winning the battle. She fought like a trooper through the double mastectomy, the numerous chemo treatments and the reconstruction. The cancer in her spine had completely disappeared and she thanked God every day for that incredible miracle. Her ongoing scans had shown no new cancer over the past three years. Sandi believed that God had chosen her for a mission and she would not let him down. Her passion for the less fortunate amongst us continued to grow and was now stronger than ever. She would move heaven and earth to help those in need.

All that love, support and her incredible faith in God had paid off. During the past year and a half, Sandi had danced with two of her sons at their weddings. She had one more wedding to go. She had also been at the hospital for the birth of her first grandchild. Something she never thought might happen. She felt truly blessed and fortunate. Now her attention would turn towards helping the young people from the warehouse.

Chapter Fifty-Six

Sandi Calhoun was an attractive Latina with shoulder length brown hair and a smile that lit up the room. But the first thing Buck noticed were her eyes. Buck had never seen eyes that were so expressive. Just looking at them and you could feel the passion she had for her job and the compassion she felt for her clients. Sandi Calhoun's presence filled the room. She was smart, soft-spoken and charming. Buck had dealt with a lot of attorneys over the years and he knew one thing immediately. Sandi Calhoun was good at her job because people who met her instantly liked her.

She reminded Buck a little of his late wife. Lucy was the social butterfly in their family and just like Sandi, here in this moment, Lucy's presence had filled any room she entered. Buck missed her terribly.

Sandi wore an impeccably tailored light grey business suit, grey suede shoes that matched the color of her suit perfectly and a burgundy blouse that was cut a few inches below her neck. Around her neck, she wore a small silver cross on a very fine silver chain. She walked into the room and reached out her hand.

"Agent Townsend, it is nice to see you again." Bob Townsend shook her hand.

"Good evening Counselor", he said. "What brings you here?"

She turned toward Buck and extended her hand. "Sandi Calhoun, Attorney at Law, and you would be?"

Buck shook her hand. "Buck Taylor, Ma'am. Colorado Bureau of Investigation, nice to meet you." Buck noticed that she gave him a very slight wink with her right eye. She turned back to Townsend.

"Agent Townsend. I am going to make your day." She handed him the paper she was carrying. "What you have there is a Cease and Desist Order signed by US District Court Judge Henry Morales ordering you to stop all contact with the individuals involved in this case and to stop any deportation proceedings you have either already started or will start in the immediate future. It further orders you to place all those individuals under my custody effective immediately."

Bob Townsend read the order in full. Buck could have sworn he almost saw the typically stoic agent in charge smile an almost imperceptible smile. Townsend stopped reading the order and lowered the paper.

"Ms. Calhoun. How did you get involved in this and how did you get this order so quickly? The raid only happened this morning and the press didn't even have the story until much later. You have a source in this investigation?"

Sandi smiled. "You know I can't discuss that with you, Agent Townsend. Attorney-client privilege. Now if you have a problem with this order, we can certainly give Judge Morales a call at home. I'm sure he wouldn't have any problem explaining this order to you, this late on a Sunday night. Shall we give him a call? I have his home number right here." She held up her phone.

Townsend really wanted to act like he was in charge, but this was one fight he was definitely going to lose. Judge Morales was a real hard ass when it came to protecting the rights of undocumented individuals and the last thing he needed today was a judge chewing on his ass. Buck had to turn his head and make believe he was checking his phone for messages, so he could silently chuckle to himself. Sandi Calhoun was good. Very good.

Buck turned back and broke the silence. "Ms. Calhoun, do you have a plan in place to take care of all these kids? They will all need special care due to the opioid addiction and they have all been tortured and some of the girls have been sexually abused for most likely a fairly long period of time."

Buck looked around the room at the kids. What they were going through and were about to go through broke his heart. Townsend nodded his head in agreement. He was glad Buck had asked the question.

"We certainly do Agent Taylor," Sandi responded.

Sandi went on to explain that she had made arrangements with several medical transportation companies to head down to Durango to pick up the young people who had been cleared by the police and were medically able to be moved. Most would be taken by ambulance. The kids who were hardest hit with withdrawal symptoms would be transported by air. They would all be under constant medical supervision until they reached one of three drug rehabilitation facilities she had arrangements with in Denver. Those facilities had agreed to donate their services and would supervise the kids as they went through the withdrawal protocols.

She also had several doctors and nurses who were willing to volunteer their services to make sure all the medical needs of the kids were met. She assured Townsend that all three facilities were top tier, secure facilities and that the kids would not be allowed to leave the facility without supervision. While they were receiving treatment, her office would make them available to the authorities for any interviews that might be needed in the preparation of the case against the people who had perpetrated this heinous crime. Each young person would be represented by an attorney from her office or another volunteer attorney and the attorney would be present at all interviews.

Once the kids were medically cleared by the doctors and if the authorities no longer needed the kids to be available for legal proceedings, the kids would be given two choices. They could choose to return to Mexico, knowing full well that their lives might be in considerable jeopardy from the cartel or they could choose to seek asylum in the United States. If they chose the latter, lawyers from Sandi's office or other volunteer lawyers would file all the necessary paperwork needed to request asylum. Those who chose to return to Mexico would be sent home by plane, as soon as they were able to travel, to the closest major airport to their final destination. They would not have to go through deportation proceedings.

Bob Townsend knew he should ask questions or object to something, but this late in the evening he was tired and ready for this day to be over. The plan as outlined was sound and deep down inside he was grateful that someone was taking this out of his hands. He knew he would sleep easier tonight knowing these kids were in good hands.

He looked at Sandi. "Sounds like you have done your homework on this. I don't see any reason to bother Judge Morales this late. I will forward a copy of this order to my office in Washington and let them know about the arrangements you have made. I doubt anyone will have any issues."

Buck couldn't agree more. For ICE and the Border Patrol,

this was going to be a public relations nightmare. A lot of powerful people in Washington were going to be asking a lot of hard questions in the next few weeks to find out how thirty some drugged kids had been snuck across the border. One of the biggest battles the newly elected President had been waging was a huge effort to make our borders more secure. This was going to cut deep.

Sandi smiled. "Thank you, Agent Townsend. Now if you have another minute we should step outside and make sure we have all the documents you will need to release these kids into my custody. The medical transports should start arriving in a couple hours."

Buck decided it was time to head back to his hotel. He shook hands all around and told Sandi Calhoun that it had been a pleasure meeting her. He wished them both a good night and walked out into the cool night air.

Chapter Fifty-Seven

The incessant ringing of a phone woke Buck from a really deep sleep. It took him a second to realize where he was and he almost fell out of bed as he reached for the phone. He had crashed hard last night when he got back to his hotel room and was asleep as soon as his head hit the pillow.

He looked at the screen, but he was having trouble focusing so he just hit the green button.

"Taylor!" Buck said in a voice that sounded a little too loud.

Director Jackson was on the other end of the call. "Wake the hell up Buck. The Governor is holding a press conference at the warehouse in little over an hour and he wants you there."

Buck tried valiantly to get his brain to engage. "Sorry Director. Didn't realize it was you. Please repeat that."

Speaking more slowly this time, almost exaggerating each word, the Director replied. "Ok, Buck. I am in Durango with the Governor. We arrived a little bit ago. The Governor is going to hold a press conference at the warehouse in just about an hour. He wants you there."

Buck finally focused. "Yes, sir. Got it. I am on my way."

The Director hung up.

Buck grabbed a quick shower, found a clean T-shirt in the pile on the floor and put it on. He clipped his badge and gun to his belt and headed for the car. He wasn't surprised that the Governor would be in town. This case was huge and the Governor would get all the political mileage out of this that he could. This bust would go a long way to appeasing the law and order crowd who typically had nothing good to say about the liberal Governor. Not that Governor Richard J Kennedy cared much about what most people thought. He had won the election for Governor, little over a year ago, by one of the largest margins in the history of the Colorado Governor's race. Regular people loved him.

Buck had to park on the street leading to the warehouse. There was no way to get near the place with the crowds of people and the massive amount of news trucks. Buck was amazed. The news media's presence had grown huge since he left the site last night. He even spotted news vans from several international stations and quite a few from Mexico. He wondered how a news conference like this was going to go over in the house of Carlos Rojas, the leader of the Sonoma Cartel. He had a feeling people down there were going to die. Carlos Rojas had a bad temper on a short fuse.

The Governor was setting up for a hell of a show. The money trailer had been pulled into the middle of the yard and the doors were wide open. Inside stood some very unhappy looking FBI SWAT guys, wearing full tactical gear and covering their faces with black balaclavas. Standing off to the side of the trailer, Hank Clancy, FBI, was in a somewhat heated discussion with Kevin Jackson, the Director of the Colorado Bureau of Investigation. Hank looked as unhappy as his SWAT guys. Director Jackson was pointing his hand at the Governor and was obviously trying to make a point. Hank didn't look like he was buying whatever the Director was selling.

DEA agents, Colorado State Troopers and Sheriff's deputies surrounded the trailer. All of them were armed with assault rifles.

All the doors to the warehouse were closed. Inside, the forensic teams were still collecting evidence and processing the scene, the DEA was sorting and cataloging the drugs and the ATF was inventorying all the weapons that had been seized. There was still a ton of work to be done and it would be another very long day for everyone involved.

The huge block of money had been pulled forward, so it sat right in the open doorway of the trailer. A lower platform had been erected in front of the trailer, so the Governor would be standing slightly below the block of money. This would make for some great pictures. The Governor was in his element. Governor Richard J Kennedy was a multi-millionaire businessman and a seasoned politician, having spent 20 years in the Colorado legislature before running for Governor. For most public appearances the Governor was usually seen in a stylish three-piece suit. Today he was dressed for the people. Governor Kennedy was wearing jeans, western boots and a denim shirt, open at the neck with his sleeves were rolled up. The Governor was extremely fit for a gentleman of seventy years old and Buck thought he looked good standing up there with all that money.

The Governor stepped up on the stage, followed by a decent sized contingent of folks representing the various agencies that had been involved in the raid. Standing to both sides of the stage and positioned so as not to block the Governor and the big block of money, the Governor introduced his partners. Everyone was represented. FBI, DEA, Sheriff's Office, Durango Police Department, ATF, ICE, Colorado and New Mexico State police and the Southern Ute Tribal Police. CBI Director Jackson stood right next to the Governor.

The Governor started out by saying how thrilled he was to be back in Durango, a part of the state he really loved. He thanked the news media for coming to cover this press conference. He then proceeded to explain the events of the past twenty-four hours. Hank Clancy, FBI, had given the Governor's Aide a detailed but relatively vague outline to follow. There were still elements of this investigation that Hank wanted to keep out of the media. For the most part, the Governor followed the outline as he spoke. He, of course, mentioned the huge block of money, as the cameras all around him started clicking once again. He told the press that although they were still counting, the Treasury Department estimated that the block of money could contain as much as a hundred million dollars.

He told them that it was estimated by the DEA that the street value of the drugs seized here in Colorado and at the eight other smaller distribution sites was estimated to be over two hundred and fifty million dollars. Buck thought that estimate might be a little high, but the Governor was having fun with the facts and he had the press eating out of his hand.

So far, the investigation had resulted in at least fifty arrests directly related to the crime and the investigation would possibly yield as many as two hundred arrests by the time it was completed. He verified that five suspected cartel members had been killed during the raid, that one FBI SWAT officer had been injured and that two of the thirty-four kids that were being held as slaves, were in the hospital having been caught in the crossfire during the raid. One of the kids was clinging to life and had been airlifted to Denver for surgery to remove a bullet near her spine and the other was still in Durango and was now listed in stable condition.

The Governor told those assembled that this would go down

in history as one of the largest drug raids ever conducted in the United States and that they were expecting the prosecution of those responsible to go on for years. He didn't mention Carlos Rojas by name, but he did say that they felt that this was a huge blow to the suspected growth of the Sonoma Cartel, north of the border. He then spent a long time praising all those involved and thanking them all for their efforts.

Governor Kennedy was never afraid to be shown up by anyone and he was more than willing to share the spotlight. For the next hour, the Governor answered questions and as much as possible, pushed those questions over to the rest of the folks onstage with him. Buck felt the news media was getting a pretty good picture of what had transpired, and he was pleased that the Governor had given credit where credit was due. He was also glad the Governor hadn't dragged him into this circus.

Chapter Fifty-Eight

Buck was standing just off to the side of the trailer, talking with Max Clinton, the head of the state crime lab, when the press conference broke up. The Governor spotted him and made a beeline straight for him. Grabbing Buck's hand, the Governor said,

"Buck, you guys did a great job here. Excellent police work. I've already personally thanked the Sheriff and her team. I am very proud of the way they handled this. I will make sure to thank everyone I haven't thanked so far before I leave. I also wanted to tell you that I am very pleased you were not injured during the shootout. What a crazy thing to happen in the middle of an investigation like this. Wow."

The Governor was ecstatic. Buck thanked him and told him he was glad he survived as well. Director Jackson came up and shook Buck's hand. The Governor's aide also walked up and told the Governor that they needed to leave soon. They had other appointments in Denver that they needed to get to.

The Governor shook Buck's hand again. He leaned in a little closer and said.

"I understand that all those kids are going to be turned over to Sandi Calhoun and she has arranged to get them the help they need.

I am so glad ICE was able to work things out with Ms. Calhoun. I wonder how she was able to get that order from Henry so quickly." Then he smiled at Buck and walked away.

There was no doubt in Buck's mind that the Governor had probably had a lot to do with Sandi Calhoun getting that cease and desist order. He was well aware that the Governor and Judge Henry Morales had attended the same law school and were brothers in the same fraternity.

Director Jackson smiled as the Governor walked away.

"He's a sly old fox, ain't he?"

Buck nodded in agreement and the Director laughed. "When you feel you are wrapped up here head home for a break. I'll call you in a couple days." The Director walked off after the Governor.

Buck spotted Hank Clancy and Jess Gonzales talking to the FBI SWAT Commander. The rest of the SWAT team was in the process of locking up the trailer and breathing a sigh of relief that they could now get that money out of here. Buck had noticed that all the crates of weapons had been removed from the trailer.

Buck asked Hank if they had come up with a way to get all that money someplace safe, so they could count it. Hank told him the plan. It was decided by people a lot higher up the food chain than Hank, that the best way to transport the money was exactly like the cartel had intended. They would leave the money in the trailer. As soon as the press was clear of the truck yard two semis would leave the yard an hour apart. Each semi would be part of a convoy of SWAT teams, State Troopers, FBI and DEA agents. The State Patrol would also provide air support over each group. Having a decoy semi and a huge convoy of cops should stop anybody from trying to ambush the convoys. Their destination would be the

Federal Reserve Building in Denver. They had the equipment to count huge quantities of money and the means to safely store it.

Buck told Hank that he thought the plan was probably the best option, then he took Jess by the arm and walked towards the warehouse.

"You doing ok?" he asked her.

"Nothing a little sleep won't cure," she responded.

"Good," said Buck. "I just wanted you to know that I owe you and if you ever need anything, all you have to do is call."

"That's not necessary, Buck. We are friends and friends always have each other's backs." She gave him a big hug. Buck held her tight for a minute.

"I heard a rumor that there might be a Deputy Directors job in your future," Buck said.

Jess backed away and looked at him. "How do you do that? Is there anything you are not plugged into?"

Buck held up his hands in surrender. "Hey, what can I tell you? I'm a detective. Comes with the job."

Jess just smiled and headed back to her team. Hank was getting all the various agencies set up for the drive back to Denver. At this point, two identical trailers attached to identical semis were facing the road. Everyone was taking their places.

Sheriff Sinclair walked up and stood next to Buck. She had dressed in her class "A" uniform for the press conference. She looked sharp. She also looked as tired as everyone else. Standing side by side, they watched silently as the first semi and the parade of cops left the yard.

"I am so glad that all that money is finally leaving my county. I haven't slept a wink since we discovered it."

Buck just nodded. They watched in silence as the last State police car in the first convoy left the yard.

"Gonna be pretty quiet around here after all of this," said Buck.

"That's ok, Buck. I think we have all had as much excitement as we can stand. It will be nice to get back to just regular old boring police work."

Buck smiled and the Sheriff looked at him. "You are a hell of a cop, Buck Taylor, and if you ever want to settle down in one place I can find a spot for you right here. It would be an honor to have you in my department."

Buck looked back at her. "It would be an honor for me to work here. You guys are top notch. Speaking of top notch where is Terry Rubin?"

"I told Terry to leave after the press conference and get some sleep. He was dead on his feet. You know, Buck, Terry may be too shy to say something but you letting him run this investigation and sticking by him meant a lot to him. Another big fan in the Buck Taylor fan club. Ok. I'm heading home to see my husband and get some sleep. Thanks, Buck. You need anything just call. Stop and say goodbye on your way out of town."

Buck shook the Sheriff's hand and she headed for her car. She looked back and said. "Oh, stop by your temporary office. I left all your gear in there. Later Buck."

Buck gave a small salute and headed towards his car.

The events of the past couple days hadn't completely sunk in yet and Buck found it hard to believe that this all happened in less than a week. What had happened in this small mountain town this week was incredible and Buck felt privileged to have been able to work with such amazing professionals. Not a bad word could be said about anyone involved in this investigation. Buck felt very proud. He also wished that he could call Lucy and let her know everything had turned out OK. He realized that she probably already knew. The thought made him smile.

On the way back to the Sheriff's office, Buck called each of his kids. By now the story was big news on every TV and radio station in the country, possibly the world, and Buck wanted to make sure they knew he was OK. They were all amazed at the news reports and all expressed how proud they were of their dad.

Chapter Fifty-Nine

Buck spent most of the next two days wrapping up loose ends and filing his reports for both this investigation and the triple homicide in Teller County. Buck was a stickler for details and his reports always reflected that. Earlier this afternoon, he had spent a couple hours fly fishing in the Animas River just north of town. He loved living in Colorado and never wanted to be anyplace else.

The La Bon Café was fairly empty when Buck walked in. He was heading back to Gunnison tonight and he wanted one more of Jimmy Palumbo's monster cheeseburgers. He also wanted to fill Jimmy in on the investigation. Loraine had gotten back home the day before and they both stood there listening to Buck tell his tale. They were fascinated. Occasionally one of them would walk away to take care of a customer, but for the most part, they just stood behind the bar and listened.

Buck was just finishing up his burger and fries when the door to the bar opened. Sandi Calhoun stood in the doorway for a moment and removed her sunglasses so her eyes could adjust to the "ambiance." She walked over to Loraine at the cash register and said,

"I was told I might find Buck Taylor here?"

Loraine looked her up and down. Sandi was wearing black

jeans, black running shoes, a white button-down blouse open at the neck and a little silver cross around her neck. She had on a black Colorado Rockies ball cap. Loraine must have approved of what she saw because she pointed towards the end of the bar. Sandi spotted Buck sitting on the last bar stool.

Buck looked up as Sandi approached. He said, "Evening Counselor. Surprised to see you here."

Sandi looked around the room. "What a great place. I can understand why you come here. Chief Chandler told me I might find you here. Hope you don't mind?"

Buck smiled. "Not at all. Can I get you something?"

She looked at the back bar. "Do you think they have Dr. Pepper here?"

Buck laughed. "Boy are you in the right place. If Jimmy stopped drinking Dr. Pepper, the company's stock would drop like a rock. Hey Jimmy. One Jimmy's private reserve for my guest please."

Jimmy walked over and set a glass and a cold can of Dr. Pepper on the bar. Buck introduced him to Sandi and they chitchatted for a minute. Buck suggested they move to a table along the wall and he led her to the last table. Buck sat with his back to the wall facing the door. Force of habit.

Sandi said. "I wanted to thank you again for the call. Those kids would have just gotten lost in the system if it hadn't been for you"

Buck asked how they were doing and Sandi filled him in on the last couple days. All the kids had been transported back to Denver and were currently undergoing detox. The last two kids were still in the hospital. The one that had been airlifted to Denver was now in stable condition and the one here in Durango was being released today. That's why Sandi was still in town. She wanted to make sure the kid was taken care of. She had a charter flight later this evening and would be taking the kid with her. Buck was pleased to hear that things were going well. He felt bad for those kids. None of them had asked for this and they certainly didn't deserve what happened to them. They were going to need long-term care and a lot of support to get past this nightmare.

Buck's phone was sitting on the table and his text notification alarm chimed. He looked down at the phone, saw a message from Hank Clancy, FBI. He clicked on the text and smiled. The message read simply. "WE GOT HIM."

"Something good?" Sandi asked.

"Let's just say that the kids who decide to return home will find the danger considerably less than it was earlier today."

Sandi looked at him. He turned his phone around and slid it over to her. She looked at the message, her mouth opened, and her hand moved up to her mouth.

She looked at Buck. "Does this mean what I think it means?"

Buck nodded. "I believe it does."

She slid the phone back to Buck. "Oh my God. That is great news."

They chatted about the investigation for a few minutes and Buck told her how impressed he was with the way she handled Bob Townsend, the ICE Agent in Charge. They both laughed. Then Sandi got a serious look on her face.

"I understand you lost your wife recently. I was very sorry to hear that. How are you doing?"

Buck thanked her for asking and told her he was doing alright. His kids made sure of that. He told her that Lucy had fought metastatic breast cancer for over five years, but that once it metastasized to her brain, it was just a matter of time. Sandi mentioned her own battle with breast cancer and that she understood what he had gone through. She asked if Lucy had passed away at home. Buck's eyes got a little moist.

"She passed away in her sleep. We were lying in bed and I was reading a report. Lucy had been sleeping twenty hours a day by then. At one point she snuggled up against my chest and nestled in. I must have dozed off and when I woke up about an hour later Lucy was gone."

Sandi had tears in her eyes. "I am so sorry Buck. I shouldn't have brought that up. What a beautiful way to go. She was very lucky to have you."

Buck just nodded. It took him a minute to compose himself. "Yeah. We were lucky to have each other."

They talked for a few more minutes then Sandi looked at her watch. She had a plane to catch and Buck needed to hit the road. They stood up and Sandi came around the table and gave Buck a big hug.

"You are a good man Buck and God has blessed you."

Buck smiled and thanked her. He wasn't so sure that was true but coming from her he almost believed it. Sandi waved goodbye to Jimmy and Loraine and left the bar. Buck sat back down and finished his drink. It would be nice to get home. He hadn't been there much lately. He was ready for a little downtime. He had a lot of chores to take care of and there were still a lot of memories of Lucy in the house that he hadn't dealt with yet. It was time.

His phone rang and Buck looked at the number. He answered his phone.

"Yes, sir."

The Director asked him if he had seen the news yet tonight. Buck said he hadn't. It appears that the investigation had discovered how the trucks got across the border. The FBI was reporting that four Border Crossing Agents assigned to the area around Aqua Prieta in Arizona, had been working for the cartel. The FBI was calling it a huge break in the Durango investigation and the arrests would close a huge hole in our border security.

Buck was pleased. He thanked the Director and hung up. Well, that was one question answered. He wondered if they would ever find the answers to the other questions.

Buck walked over and said goodbye to Jimmy and Loraine and they promised to get together soon. Buck headed home.

Epilogue

In a windowless bunker, somewhere in a secure location in the mountains of central Georgia, two US Air Force drone pilots sat at their control panels and looked at the video feed from the two Predator drones that were now flying high over the desert in Mexico about 40 miles south of the New Mexico border. Below the first drone was a huge hacienda. Over the last several hours, the pilot using his Hi-Def camera had been watching as several dozen cars had arrived. The occupants of the cars had entered the hacienda and were greeted by a dark-haired man wearing a white suit. Each car also contained several men, all armed with assault rifles, who remained outside the hacienda. If the pilot so desired, he could have zoomed in enough with the camera to read the serial numbers on the guns.

The other drone was on station about five miles west of the hacienda and was observing a long one-story block building. It appeared to be a warehouse of some kind. At this moment there was no movement outside the building. The pilot waited patiently.

In another windowless room, deep inside the Pentagon, a dozen high ranking civilian and military officials were watching two huge Hi-Def monitors mounted to the wall. They were seeing the same thing the drone pilots in Georgia were seeing.

A technician, seated at a computer console, looked up from his monitor.

"General. Target is confirmed. The man in the white suit is Carlos Rojas."

The General looked across the table at the United States Attorney General.

The Attorney General looked around the room and each person nodded in agreement.

"Give the order General," he said.

The General pushed the talk button on the console in front of him.

"Stingray One One, this is Ranger. Target is confirmed. You are clear to execute under my authority."

In the secure bunker in Georgia, the first drone pilot responded. "Roger." He lifted a bright red cover on his console and flipped a switch. "Weapon is armed. Target is locked." He pushed the red button next to the cover. "Weapon released."

Back in the basement room in the Pentagon, everyone was silent as they watched the video. Thirty thousand feet above the hacienda, the latching pins released and a massive bomb began to fall. The United States had just declared war on the Sonoma Cartel. Technically, we had also just secretly attacked a foreign country, but all those denials would come later.

The weapon that had been dropped was a fuel-air bomb, typically identified as MOAB, mother of all bombs. This was a smaller version of MOAB, but was still unbelievably powerful. According to military sources, the MOAB was the most powerful, non-nuclear explosive device in our arsenal. Several years ago, the Russians had tested their own device dubbed FOAB, father of all bombs. The explosion that resulted was the most powerful explosion ever recorded. It was rumored that they had developed an even more powerful bomb but that they were afraid to test it for fear it might set the atmosphere on fire.

The device technically explodes twice. Five hundred feet above the target the first explosion released billions of atomized, highly explosive fuel particles into the atmosphere, a nanosecond behind this release a second explosion ignited the particles, unleashing a massive fireball on the target. Everything within two hundred yards of ground zero was immediately incinerated. Anything that might have survived the initial fireball was immediately destroyed by the shock wave that emanated from the center of the explosion. Nothing would survive in an area a half mile surrounding ground zero.

Back in the desert, Carlos Rojas had no idea he had only seconds to live, along with many of his hand-selected inner circle. He thought nothing could ever touch him. He thought he was protected. He was sadly mistaken and because of his arrogance, his family would pay a heavy price.

Even from thirty thousand feet, the explosion was massive and everyone in the Pentagon room had to turn away as the flash filled the screen. When the Mexican authorities finally arrived on the scene later that day, all they would find was a smoldering crater in the ground two hundred yards wide and almost twenty feet deep. They would be unable to explain what had happened.

At that very moment in the National Earthquake Information Center in Golden, Colorado, several seismographs would register a five-point-two magnitude earthquake. The epicenter of the quake was located in the Mexican desert approximately forty miles south of the New Mexico border.

As the bomb was being dropped on the hacienda, the second

drone's camera was focused on eight figures that seemed to suddenly rise up out of the desert like some kind of hairy plant. Only these hairy plants were armed with the latest high-tech assault rifles. The Pentagon group watched as those eight figures raced toward the block building. A small explosion happened at the entry door and six of the eight figures entered the building while two remained outside. Unlike the video feed from the hacienda, this one had both video and audio.

Everyone in the Pentagon room was mesmerized. It felt like they were watching a video game, only this one involved real bullets, which were now systematically taking out other bad actors with assault rifles and pistols. The automatic weapons fire stopped, and a voice confirmed the all clear. The video showed padlocks being cut and someone yelling for everyone to get out.

The drone video confirmed the action as the front door swung open and dozens of people ran from the building and scattered into the desert. The six Special Operations team members ran out and joined up with their two teammates outside. The entire operation had taken less than two minutes to complete.

A voice came over the loudspeaker. "Ranger, this is Striker One. Building is clear. Mission accomplished."

The General keyed his mike. "Roger, Striker One. Confirmation received."

The video showed the men running across the desert and jumping into a waiting Blackhawk helicopter. The video ended and was replaced with the video feed from the drone.

"Stingray One Two, this is Ranger. Target confirmed. Execute on my authority."

Inside the bunker in Georgia, the second drone pilot acknowledged the order and followed the same procedure as the first pilot. As he pushed the red button, two Hellfire missiles headed on an unstoppable course toward the block building. Two massive explosions occurred almost simultaneously. The block building was destroyed.

Without any further communication, the two drone pilots headed their drones back to a secret drone base operating out of the White Sands Testing Center in New Mexico. Once the drones were secure, the pilots shut down their console and left the structure.

In the room deep in the Pentagon, the Attorney General congratulated the General on a successful mission. They had just sent a strong message to the other active cartels that the United States would not sit idly by if they chose to move their business north of the border. The General then nodded to the technician seated at the computer console. The technician pushed the delete button on the keyboard and all evidence of the attacks disappeared. The President nodded and left the room.

Buck Taylor Book II

Crime Delayed

A BUCK TAYLOR NOVEL

BY

CHUCK MORGAN

Chapter One

How could they be so dumb? All they had to do was stash the carcass and come back for it later. Why did that lady ranger and her dog have to show up? Up to that point, everything was perfect. The bull elk was huge with a monster rack. He was the biggest elk they had seen in the last month at least.

Sure, they were a little out of season and they didn't have a permit for a bull elk, but they weren't hurting anyone. The elk was just standing there waiting to be shot. What did it hurt? God must have intended for them to shoot it or he wouldn't have put it there, right?

They were going to stash the elk in their hunting camp. Well, not much of a hunting camp. It was basically a lean-to made of sticks and pine boughs but it was a great place to hide out when they weren't hunting. They had all the comforts of home. They had a gas lantern for light, they had a small cooler for drinks and they had a couple sleeping bags for when they stayed out at night. They really didn't need the sleeping bags because the nights were still warm even at this altitude.

Tonight, they would have come back and butchered the elk. The sled they use to haul out the meat was hidden in the ravine next to the lean-to. All they had to do was load it up and drag it back to the cabin. It was only a couple miles and they had done it a lot lately. They always took a different track back so that the undergrowth wouldn't get worn down and show the way back to the cabin.

They were the hunters, and everyone depended on them for food. They were the best shots in the group and they knew how to skin and gut what they shot. The elk would have lasted them a week or two. But now this. The Teacher is not going to be pleased.

The lady ranger came out of nowhere. One minute they were dragging the elk back to camp and the next minute there she was standing on the little ridge with her stupid dog. All she had to do was walk away. Her and that stupid dog. But she didn't.

They had hidden in the bushes. She should have walked right by them and not seen them, but no. The dog had to sniff them out. He had to start barking. She could have kept walking but she must have sensed them because she pulled the gun out of her holster. They couldn't let her find them or the cabin.

The first rifle shot hit her in the thigh. There was no ballistic armor around her thigh. She went down hard and rolled down the ridge into the ravine. The dog tried to go after her but the second bullet hit the dog right in the chest. The dog went down hard too. There was a lot of blood. They broke cover and rushed over to the edge of the ravine. The lady ranger was trying to reach her pistol with one hand and she was trying to key the mic on her shoulder with the other.

When she saw them, she just froze. Blood was pumping out of her leg. A crimson fountain exploding with each heartbeat. She looked at them and began to plead with them to help her. She had tears in her eyes. They just looked at her. The lady ranger started to shake. Her breathing got shallow. She looked so helpless just lying there in the ravine. The Teacher had taught them not to let anything they hunted suffer. They understood the kill shot. He raised up his rifle and without any hesitation or doubt shot her in the forehead.

Where was the dog? They had seen the crimson stain explode from the dog's chest. He went over the ridge, so he must just be on the other side, but he wasn't. Where could he have gone? They wanted to make sure he didn't suffer like the lady ranger, but he wasn't on the other side of the ridge. They looked around trying to spot the blood trail, but there was none.

Maybe he was some kind of mystical forest creature. Just like in the stories the Teacher use to tell them around the campfire. It would be a grand prize to take back to the Teacher. He might award them with a knife or a hatchet. But, where is he? He couldn't have gone far, but after an hour searching, there was no sign.

They went back to the lean-to and found a camp shovel and headed back to the lady ranger. The Teacher had told them that all life was sacred, so they knew that he would not be happy if they didn't give the lady ranger a proper burial and that's just what they did. The covered her body with dirt and rocks, cut some pine boughs and further covered the grave in the ravine. Then they said the Lord's Prayer just like the Teacher had taught them. Finished, they headed back to the elk carcass.

Instead of waiting til tonight to butcher it they decided to do it now. Someone might have heard the extra shots and they also figured that sooner or later someone would come looking for the lady ranger and her dog. They finished dragging the carcass to the lean-to hunting camp. They spent the next two hours butchering the huge elk, loaded up the sled and hauled it back through the woods to their cabin. They would have a big feast tonight.

They would tell the Teacher about the lady ranger. He would

be happy that they had protected the others. They were not sure if they should tell him about the missing dog. The Teacher might not be pleased that they had missed the shot and not killed the dog. He might give one of the others the rifle and let them go on the next hunt. The more they thought about it, the more they convinced themselves that they would not mention the dog.

Chapter Two

Buck Taylor, Colorado Bureau of Investigation Agent and his son David had volunteered to work the burger and hot dog tent at the annual Gunnison Labor Day community picnic and were doing a brisk business. Buck tried to make the burgers the same way his friend Jimmy Palumbo did at the La Bon Café in Durango. Jimmy's burgers were huge and legendary and the only food item besides french fries that Jimmy sold in his café/bar but Buck just couldn't get them to taste the same. Someday he would find out Jimmy's secret.

Gunnison, Colorado, population of roughly 6,200 people, sits at an elevation of 7,700 feet and is the largest city in Gunnison County. Situated along the Gunnison River, the city was incorporated in 1880. The area is a mecca for hunters, fishermen and anyone who enjoys the outdoors. It is home to Western State Colorado University which was founded as The Colorado State Normal School for Children in 1901.

One interesting historical fact is that during a two-month period at the end of 1918 the residents of Gunnison isolated themselves from the rest of the area to prevent the introduction of Spanish Influenza. All roads were blocked at the county borders and people traveling through the area by train were not allowed to leave the train. Because of the isolation, no one in Gunnison died of the flu.

North of Gunnison lies Crested Butte, a ski resort community which helps contribute to the winter tourist trade since you must pass through Gunnison to get to the Crested Butte ski area. Gunnison is a picturesque little community in the heart of the Rocky Mountains and appears to be a perfect place to raise a family.

Buck Taylor stands six-foot-tall and weighs in at 185 lbs. Very little of it flab for a 58-year-old man. Buck's hair is salt and pepper with what seemed like a lot more salt than pepper and he wore it slightly longer than was typically the fashion of the day. Buck lived in Gunnison all his life. He spent seventeen years with the Gunnison County Sheriff's Department before accepting a position with the Colorado Bureau of Investigation. He met and married his high school sweetheart Lucinda Torres and they raised three children, David, Cassie and Jason. Life was good until Lucy was diagnosed with breast cancer and for five years she and Buck fought the battle of her life. A little over a year ago Lucy lost the battle.

They were just finishing up the latest rush of people when his son's cell phone signaled an incoming call. David looked at the call and answered.

"Taylor," he said. He listened intently to the call then hung up. David was a police officer with the Gunnison Police Department. He looked a lot like his dad when his dad was his age. Slightly taller than his dad and slightly heavier than his dad but the resemblance was striking. Unlike his father, David still moved with the ease of a young man.

David had recently been promoted to sergeant and was now the night shift supervisor. He liked working the night shift and had been a patrolman on that shift for many years. He enjoyed the calmness and quiet of a small mountain town in the early morning hours. He also enjoyed those rare occasions when he was able to spend time with Buck. They had a lot in common and he enjoyed hearing about Buck's latest investigations.

The pair didn't have a lot of time to talk today. The picnic was in full swing and the park was packed with locals and tourists alike. This weekend was the unofficial end of the summer tourist season and most of the tourists should have already gone home but the weather was perfect and the town was still living the good life.

Tourism was essential for the survival of the town. In the fall, the hunters would descend on the town to get themselves outfitted for the annual trek into the mountains in search of elk and deer and an occasional moose. As soon as the hunters were gone the skiers would start showing up.

Fishermen would show up all year round and it was not unusual to see a fly fisherman standing in the middle of the Gunnison River stalking a beautiful Brown or Rainbow trout while the snow came down around him. If there was open water on the river, there would be a fisherman standing in it no matter the weather. Buck Taylor was typically one of those fishermen. Buck's passion for fly fishing was only exceeded by his love of his job as a criminal investigator.

Fly fishing was also his escape from having to deal with the death of his wife of 35 years. Lucy Taylor had spent five years battling metastatic breast cancer. She lost the battle when the cancer metastasized into her brain. She held out as long as she could but eventually, the chemotherapy and the radiation were no longer effective. She died peacefully in her sleep wrapped in Buck's arms. Buck was devastated by the loss and now more than a year later he still missed her. She was his rock and his soul mate.

Buck and the family had gathered one Sunday morning to scattered Lucy's ashes in the Gunnison River, not far from where Buck and his son were now cooking burgers. It was supposed to be a private family affair but somehow word had spread around town and a huge group of people showed up. The private affair turned into a huge picnic and celebration of Lucy's life. Lucy would have loved it.

Buck looked at his son as he hung up the phone.

"Something up?" Buck asked.

"Yeah. I need to go into the office. We got a call from the Pitkin County Sheriff's office. They are searching for a missing Division of Parks and Wildlife ranger and they have asked for us to start on our side of the mountain and work towards them. She's been missing almost twenty-four hours. The Sheriff has activated the Gunnison Search and Rescue team and we have been asked to assist."

"Do you need some help?" Buck asked.

"Who's gonna cook the burgers and dogs for this crowd if you leave. I will let you know later if we are looking for volunteers. Can you make sure Judy gets her tent closed up and gets the kids home?"

David's wife Judy was in charge of the dessert tent. She also ran the little deli/ice cream shop that Lucy owned and ran for a significant part of her life. When Lucy passed away, Buck had been thinking about selling the little place but Judy offered to take it over and eventually buy the shop from him. Buck was pleased that Lucy's legacy would continue and besides the people in town loved her little place.

But today Judy's assistant was working the shop while Judy and her and David's three kids, Amy, age 16, David Jr also nicknamed Buck, age 14 and Rosalie, age 10, named after Lucy's mom, ran the tent in the park. Buck told David he would take care of everything and not to worry. He also told him to be safe.

David shed his apron and headed towards the dessert tent to let Judy know where he was heading and dashed for his car. Buck threw some more burgers on the open grill and prepared for the next group of hungry tourists. The Mayor of Gunnison, Pamela Sanders, saw Buck working alone and jumped in to help. Buck's mother in law Rosalie, who had been sitting in the shade, also walked over and put on an apron.

Rosalie Torres was one of the elders of the community. Pushing seventy-five and five feet two, she was a force to be reckoned with. What she lacked in stature, this still active Latina more than made up for with drive. She was still on the organizing committee for the Labor Day picnic and she served on almost every volunteer committee that functioned within the county. Nothing went on in Gunnison that Rosalie was not a part of.

Fernando Torres, Rosalie's husband and Lucy's father, had run a small horse ranch just outside the city border. He had also been an outfitter and hunting guide. His love of the outdoors was something he was proud to have passed on to his two daughters, Lucinda and Rachel and his son Michael. Life was not always easy for Fernando and Rosalie, but they did the best they could and made sure that their children never wanted for anything.

It was a sad day five years ago when Fernando suffered a heart attack while guiding a couple of hunters up near Monarch Pass. Although the hunters had made a valiant effort to revive him and had succeeded several times, by the time search and rescue had reached them Fernando was gone. The family still missed Fernando every day, but it was ok. His daughter Lucy was with him.

By the end of the day every one of the fifty or so volunteers were dog tired, but they all had a wonderful time. Buck had also volunteered to be on the teardown team so after clearing out the burger tent and making sure Judy and the kids had torn down the dessert tent he spent the next couple hours helping clear the rest of the tents and clean the park. Just before he left the park he walked over to the little handicapped fishing dock where the family had scattered Lucy's ashes and spent a minute in quiet reflection. He said goodnight to Lucy and headed for home.

Buck was due in the office in Grand Junction the following afternoon for the monthly staff meeting and he had a bunch of paperwork that needed to get turned in for the cases he had recently closed.

Chapter Three

Buck is assigned to the Grand Junction office of the Colorado Bureau of Investigation but he typically works from home and handles cases in the central and southwestern parts of the state. He is highly regarded as an investigator by those who know him and he is often called upon by Governor Richard Kennedy to handle special cases of a sensitive nature.

The phone call he received just as he was getting ready to leave the house for Grand Junction was regarding one of those sensitive cases that required special handling.

Buck recognized the number on his phone as one of the main numbers for the CBI office in Grand Junction. He wasn't sure who was calling but he hit the answer button.

"Buck Taylor."

"Hey Buck, this is Paul Webber. Did I catch you at a good time?"

Paul Webber had just recently joined the Colorado Bureau of Investigation as a field agent and had been assigned to the Grand Junction Office. He came to CBI from the Dallas, Texas Police Department and was very highly regarded as an investigator. Paul was a big guy. He stood six feet four and weighed in at two hundred forty-five pounds. A former college football standout at the University of Texas, Paul had spent four years in the Marines before joining the Dallas, Texas Police Department where he spent six years and was most recently assigned as a homicide detective.

Paul Webber had been assigned to work with Buck on a corruption case out of the city of Montrose, Colorado. The governor had been approached by the Montrose Chief of Police and asked to have CBI start an investigation of the five city council members. A complaint had been filed by a local real estate broker indicating that something shady had gone on during the annexation negotiations for a new subdivision. The Chief of Police was concerned that handling the investigation out of his department might ruffle some feathers. Montrose was a small western slope town and everyone knew everyone. He wanted the investigation to be impartial.

Buck had liked Paul Webber from the first time he met him. Paul was smart and he had a tremendous amount of drive. Like Buck, he was also very passionate about investigating crimes.

Buck and Paul had been investigating the entire annexation process for the past couple weeks and had finally gotten a warrant to look at the finances of each person involved. They were expecting a call from the forensic accountant any time now.

"Hey, Paul. I was just getting ready to leave the house and head to the office. What's up?"

"The forensic accountant just called. We were right. Councilman Meyers definitely tried to hide fifty thousand dollars. The accountant was also able to backtrack the money to the developer's daughter's personal bank account. He is emailing us the findings. We should have enough to make an arrest."

"Great news, Paul. Go ahead and type up the arrest warrant for the developer, his daughter and the councilman. Fax that to the city attorney in Montrose and have her call the judge to get the warrants. I am leaving the house now and will meet you at police headquarters in about an hour. See if you can pull Richards and Baxter away from their desks. We could use them to arrest the developer."

"Will do Buck. See you in a bit."

Paul hung up and Buck smiled. He hated when elected officials disregarded their oaths and violated the trust of their constituents. Besides Councilman Meyers was an arrogant prick. He pushed the speed dial button on his phone and heard the Director's phone ringing.

Colorado Bureau of Investigations Director Kevin Jackson answered the call.

"Hey, Buck. What's going on?"

Kevin Jackson was the youngest person ever appointed to run the Colorado Bureau of Investigation. He had spent years working his way up the administrative side of the Colorado Springs Police Department and had made significant changes along the way. But he wasn't just an administrator; he was also a cop and a very good one. Buck had become very familiar with the Director, and sometimes it seemed as though he worked for the Director instead of for the agent in charge of the Grand Junction field office.

Buck filled the Director in on the events getting ready to unfold in Montrose. He explained what the forensic accountant had discovered and that he had Paul Webber preparing the arrest warrant. He also asked him if it was ok to borrow Agents Richards and Baxter to help with the arrests? He would use the Montrose police as back up. The Director told him that he would call the governor and fill him in. He had no issues with anything Buck had told him and told

Buck to let him know when the arrests were finished. He told Buck to stay safe. Buck hung up

Richards was Agent James Richards, a ten-year veteran with the Colorado Bureau of Investigation. Richards had spent several years with the Ann Arbor, Michigan Police Department before deciding to relocate his family to Colorado. He had a slight build and a very bookish look about him. Buck thought he was an accountant the first time he met him.

Baxter was Agent Ashley Baxter. Ashley was five feet four with long blond hair that she usually wore in a ponytail. She joined CBI five years before, right out of the University of Wisconsin. A Denver native, she had no issues moving to Grand Junction and had thrived in her new environment. She typically worked with Richards and their focus lately was mostly on property crimes like burglary. They had just wrapped up a successful investigation into a series of home invasions and were waiting for their next assignment.

Chapter Four

Jimmy Corey was concerned when he woke up Labor Day morning and his mom still wasn't home. She had promised to be home last night. They had planned to spend Labor Day together and then they had an important meeting at his school on Tuesday.

Susan Corey had worked as a ranger for the Division of Parks and Wildlife since graduating from Colorado State University in Fort Collins, Colorado seven years earlier. She had earned a bachelor's degree in animal biology and had jumped at the chance to work for the CPW. At five feet seven and one hundred forty pounds she was in excellent condition to hike the backwoods of the Colorado mountains to enforce hunting and fishing laws and protect the animals in her charge. It was not unusual for her to spend several days in the field searching for poachers or anyone else breaking the law. She didn't mind working alone since she always traveled with Duke, her five-year-old golden retriever.

Jimmy took out his cell phone and pressed the number one key. His mom had always told him that if anything ever happened to her that he should call the first preprogrammed number in his phone.

Miguel Vargas answered on the second ring. "Vargas."

"Hi Mr. Vargas, this is Jimmy Corey, have you heard from my mom?"

Miguel Vargas was the Chief Ranger at the Colorado Parks and Wildlife office in Glenwood Springs. Vargas was fifty years old, five feet ten and weighed one hundred seventy pounds. He was in excellent health from spending almost thirty years as a CPW ranger. A job he loved.

"Hi, Jimmy. Last I heard she was due back home yesterday. Did she not get home?"

"No sir," responded Jimmy. "I have been trying her cell phone since last night and it just goes to voicemail."

Vargas was now concerned. It wasn't like Susan Corey to stay out of touch.

"Jimmy let me see if I can find her. Keep trying her phone and if she comes home have her call me. I will be back in touch as soon as I hear anything."

Vargas hung up and dialed the CPW dispatcher. Because of the holiday and the perfect weather, most of the eleven rangers that worked out of Glenwood Springs were on duty. There were still a lot of campers in the woods and encounters with wild animals were always a concern. He asked the dispatcher to call the troops and have them start looking for Susan Corey's car.

Vargas knew Susan Corey was working a poaching case somewhere south of Aspen but he didn't have an exact location which was going to make this tough. He was going to need some help. Susan Corey could be anywhere.

Vargas's next call was to the Pitkin County Sheriff. Vargas and Sheriff Earl Winters had been friends for years. The Sheriff recognized the number on the screen and answered his cell phone immediately.

"Hey, Miguel. What's up?"

"Mornin Earl. Hate to bother you on the holiday but I have a missing ranger and could use your help."

Vargas went on to explain the situation and that she could be anywhere in the area. Vargas knew Susan Corey was heading into the mountains south of Aspen looking for elk poachers but she could have been heading home and encountered another issue. The last time the dispatcher had talked to her was three-days earlier and she told them she would be hiking into the area around Hunter Peak. The problem is, Hunter Peak is not easy to get to and there are several old Forest Service roads that you can use to get into the area. After that, it is still good couple hours to hike in.

The Sheriff listened intently, asked a couple of questions and told Vargas that he would have his deputies start looking for her truck. He would also activate the Pitkin County Search and Rescue team and call Gunnison County to see if they could start looking from their side of the mountain. There were several old access roads she could have used from Gunnison County as well. The more folks they could get out on the roads looking for her the faster they could find her truck and narrow down the search area. The Sheriff hung up.

The Sheriff was good to his word and his first call was to Gunnison County Sheriff James McCauley who listened to him and then promised to have his deputies start looking along the back roads and to also have his search and rescue team start covering what the deputies couldn't.

His next call was to his dispatcher to call in all his deputies and his search and rescue team and have them meet at the Sheriff's office. His plan was to spread as many cars around the county as possible to try to find Corey's truck.

Meanwhile, Miguel Vargas was doing the same thing with his

rangers and after assigning search areas, he jumped in his truck and headed for Aspen. As more time passed the more his concern grew. He knew Susan Corey could take care of herself but anything could have happened. She could have fallen or somehow gotten injured, she could be lost, although that was unlikely, or, god forbid, she could have encountered the elk poachers and things could have turned ugly fast. He hoped it wasn't the last scenario.

Vargas called Jimmy Corey back on his cell phone. When Jimmy answered, he explained what was going on and that a lot of people were going to be looking for his mom. He also asked him to look around her small office and see if she left any notes about where she planned to go when she left the house. Jimmy promised he would.

Finally, as he was getting ready to head to Aspen Vargas asked his wife to head over to Susan Corey's house and sit with Jimmy. His wife could read the concern in his eyes and told him not to worry. She would take care of Jimmy and she would also call his grandparents in Pueblo and let them know what was going on.

Chapter Five

The Sheriff arrived at his office and waited for his search teams to assemble. While he waited, he pulled up Susan Corey's truck registration through the Division of Motor Vehicles website. The ranger drove a state-issued 2014 Chevy Tahoe, white, with the Division of Parks and Wildlife logo on the front doors. Just to be on the safe side, he asked dispatch to put out a BOLO, Be On The Lookout, for her truck, just in case she was stranded someplace. He also put in a request through her cell phone provider for the last location her cell phone had been used. This might help narrow down the search area.

Once his search teams and deputies arrived at the office, he provided them with Susan Corey's picture, her vehicle registration and assigned each searcher with an area to search. The search teams headed out. The day did not go well and by nine PM that night the Sheriff called the searchers in and asked them to meet again the next morning to start searching again. Susan Corey had fallen off the face of the earth and the Sheriff hated to call off the search but with darkness setting in it would make looking down old access roads even harder. Best to wait for morning.

Tuesday morning dawned clear, bright and warm. Strangely

warm for a September morning in the mountains. The searchers started to arrive at seven AM and were just getting their assignments when the Chief Deputy walked into the room and asked everyone to just sit tight for a little bit. The Sheriff was out on a call which might prove helpful to the search.

The Sheriff and another deputy were on their way to talk with a couple of hikers who found a dog that appeared to have been shot and was lying under a Colorado Parks and Wildlife Chevy Tahoe.

Pitkin County Sheriff Earl Winters was the epitome of a western Sheriff. Tall and broad at the shoulders, Earl wore jeans, a button-down shirt and a broad-rimmed Stetson. He had a bit of a gut hanging over his belt but was still an impressive man. The large handlebar mustache only added to the old western look. Earl had been Sheriff for over twenty years and had no intentions of retiring anytime soon. He loved his job and he loved his county.

The Sheriff was first to arrive at the location of the call. County Route 13 led south from the Aspen Highlands ski resort and the road ran out at the Maroon Snowmass trailhead. This was a very popular trail that led to Maroon peaks and the parking lot was still crowded even though it was late in the season. The Sheriff didn't have to look hard to find the hikers who had called in the report. There was a crowd of hikers standing around the white Tahoe that was parked down a small side road that led to the parking lot restroom.

The group separated as the Sheriff walked up. The reporting party, Henry and Lidia Franklin, were kneeling next to a full-size golden retriever. On the other side of the dog another hiker was cleaning the wound and talking softly to the dog while working out of a first aid kit. The dog was shaking. The Franklins introduced themselves to the Sheriff.

The Franklins had started on a day hike just after dawn and had not noticed the dog at first. As they were walking to the restrooms they heard what sounded like someone whimpering. That someone turned out to be the golden retriever. He was lying under the truck crying and when Lidia crouched down to see if he was ok, she noticed the blood on his chest. She was able to pull him out from under the truck and that's when she had her husband call 911.

The other hiker who was working on the dog identified himself as Steven Blair. Blair was a registered nurse who had started for the trailhead a few minutes after the Franklins and immediately pulled out his first aid kit and started working on the wound. He reported that the blood around the wound had mostly congealed but he couldn't be sure if there was any internal bleeding. He felt the wound might be a day or two old. The dog was too weak to stand and did not look good but he still managed to lick Blair's hand while he spoke to the Sheriff.

The Sheriff knelt next to the dog and stroked his fur. He slid the dog's collar around and found a name tag. "Duke." The name on the back of the tag was Susan Corey with a phone number.

While the Sheriff was checking the name tag, the deputy arrived and knelt next to him. The Sheriff showed him the name tag and the deputy nodded. The Sheriff told the deputy to get an emergency blanket out of the back of his patrol car, a Ford Explorer and he then asked Blair to help him carry the dog to the back of the car. They gently placed the dog in the back of the Explorer and the Sheriff told the deputy to head for the Pitkin County Emergency Vet clinic.

The Sheriff called dispatch and told the dispatcher to call the emergency clinic and let them know that the deputy was on his way and that the dog looked critical. He then thanked the Franklins and Steven Blair and took down their contact info in case he needs to contact them later on.

The Sheriff went back to his truck and pulled a Slim Jim out of his toolbox and made quick work of getting into the ranger's truck. Once inside, he found the registration and confirmed that it was indeed Susan Corey's truck. Other than some papers sitting on the passenger seat he couldn't find anything that might indicate where she had gone. The Sheriff was very concerned and it was now time to call in the cavalry. He locked up the ranger's Tahoe and headed back to his truck.

"Dispatch, come in."

"Go ahead, Sheriff."

"Dispatch, activate search and rescue and have them report to me at the Maroon Snowmass trailhead. Call in all off-duty deputies and reserve deputies and have them assemble here as well. Contact Gunnison County and ask if they could activate their search and rescue and coordinate with me when they are ready. I will try to give them a search perimeter as soon as I can. Then put out a statewide broadcast that we have a missing and possibly injured law enforcement officer and we are requesting assistance to search a massive area. Foul play is assumed at this point. Got it?"

"Yes, sir. Do you want a call for volunteers for the search?"

"Not until we know what we are dealing with."

The Sheriff then called Miguel Vargas and filled him in on what they had just discovered. Since all of Vargas's rangers were also armed law enforcement officers, he would mobilize the entire team and have them head to Aspen to assist with the search. The Sheriff asked all the hikers who were still in the area to remove their cars from the parking lot and evacuate the area. This was about to become a crime scene. He used a couple of old buckets and a chain to close off access to the parking lot. It was going to be tight trying to get a lot of vehicles in here but they would figure it out. Now he just needed to wait for the troops

The Sheriff stood at the trailhead and looked deep into the woods.

"Where are you, Susan Corey?"

It was time to get organized.

Chapter Six

Buck Taylor turned left off Main Street onto S Park Avenue, turned right onto S 1st Street and pulled into the Montrose Police Department parking lot. He parked his state-issued Jeep Cherokee in one of the visitor's spaces and headed for the building. Once inside he identified himself to the duty officer at the desk and was buzzed into the back and headed for the Police Chief's office.

The Police Chief, Paul Sawyer, was seated at a small conference table across the hall from his office. Also in the room was the City Attorney, Beverly Jensen, Paul Webber, James Richards and Ashley Baxter from the Colorado Bureau of Investigation. Two Montrose police officers Nunez and Harding were also in attendance. Buck was pleased. He had worked with Nunez and Harding before and knew they were top notch cops. Buck shook hands all around.

"Ok," he said. "Do we have the warrants?"

Beverly Jensen nodded. Beverly was a twenty-eight-year-old, medium height black woman who had landed in Montrose after completing her law degree at THE Ohio State. She was looking for a place to start over after a failed marriage and had fallen in love with the area during a trip early in her college years. From the few encounters Buck had with her in the past, he knew she was smart and dedicated.

"You bet. We have arrest warrants for City Councilman Benjamin Meyers, Reginald Carstairs and his daughter Regina Carstairs. We are good to go."

"Great," said Buck. "I will take Meyers with Officer Nunez. Paul, you and Harding will take Regina Carstairs and Richards and Baxter will take Reginald Carstairs. You all have the addresses. This should be simple but keep on your toes. You never know how people are going to react. Chief you will be our back up if the shit hits the fan. We all good?"

Everyone nodded and they headed out the door to their cars. The Chief stopped Buck before he left the building.

"Hey Buck, I really do appreciate the work you guys did. This was going to get hairy if we had to deal with one of the city fathers and you are really saving our bacon. Thanks."

"No problem, Paul. As far as we are concerned the information we received came from a source outside the city and the first you guys found out about the investigation was when we showed up just now with arrest warrants. That should give you plenty of cover."

Paul Sawyer smiled and they headed to their cars. Buck, followed by Officer Nunez in his patrol car, pulled out of the lot and headed back down South 1st Street, turned right onto South Park Avenue and turned left onto Main Street. Benjamin Meyers and Associates Real Estate office was just four blocks down on Main street so just before they got to Junction Avenue the two cars pulled over to the side and double parked. Buck put his red and blue flashers on, grabbed the warrant and exited the car.

Walking briskly, he pushed open the front door to the real

estate office and walked right past the receptionist who started to say something but Buck wasn't listening. He turned the handle of the door marked Benjamin Meyers and pushed open the door. Meyers was seated behind his desk talking to two clients one male and one female and he looked startled when the door burst open and in walked Buck followed by Officer Nunez.

"Benjamin Meyers. We have a warrant for your arrest on public corruption charges. Please stand up, step around the desk and keep your hands where I can see them."

Meyers looked at his two clients who started to get up and were immediately told to remain seated by Officer Nunez. Nunez then looked at Buck.

"Agent Taylor, this is Reginald Carstairs and his daughter Regina."

"Well well," said Buck. "You two are under arrest as well. Please do not move. Nunez, call it in."

Regina Carstairs started to give Buck a lot of lip and reached into her purse, which was in her lap. Nunez who had the better angle saw the handle of the gun before Buck did and immediately drew his service weapon and placed it at the back of Regina's head. Buck grabbed Meyers who had just started to stand up and pushed him flat down on his desk and drew his own weapon and pointed it at Reginald Carstairs.

Carstairs looked bewildered until Nunez pulled the gun all the way out of his daughter's purse and then he looked scared. Regina just looked hostile and continued to yell profanities at Buck. She finally ran out of steam and sat back in her chair. Nunez called dispatch and told them to send everyone to the real estate office and proceeded to search each person, one at a time and put flexicuffs on their wrists while Buck held Meyers down and held his gun on the Carstairs.

The Police Chief was the first to arrive, followed immediately by the rest of the crew from his office. They were each read their Miranda rights and were then walked through the real estate office and out past the crowd that had gathered on the street. Each suspect was placed in a different patrol car and driven back to police headquarters to be booked, fingerprinted and formally charged.

Paul Webber watched the booking process and said to Buck.

"What are the odds that they would all be together at just the right time?"

"You got me Paul but boy that Regina sure wanted to go down swinging. I can't believe she went for a gun. What an idiot."

"You got that right," Paul replied. "I will stick around and make sure all the paperwork is covered if you want to head to the office."

Buck nodded told Richards and Baxter that they could clear out as well and stopped and shook hands with the Chief and officers Nunez and Harding and asked Beverly Jensen if she needed anything else from him.

Beverly told him she was good and she would call him if anything came up. Buck wished everyone well and headed for his car. Once in the parking lot he called the Director and filled him in on the arrests.

The Director said, "she actually went for a gun in her purse. What the hell did she think she was going to do? Shoot her way out of the office."

"You got me, Director. I was as surprised as anyone. This could have gone from simple to messy in a heartbeat. I'm heading up to the office. Call if you need me."

Buck disconnected the call, slid into his car, turned onto Highway 550 and headed for Grand Junction. Buck had just gotten to Delta, Colorado when he pulled over to the side of the highway and turned up the police radio. Buck hardly ever used the police radio in the car. It was mostly there just for emergencies. He preferred to do most of his calling on his cell phone. It was a little more private.

Buck listened to the statewide officer assistance call. This must be the same ranger his son David had mentioned. It sounded to Buck like the situation had gone from a missing ranger to something else entirely especially when the bulletin mentioned that her dog had been shot. Buck never ignored an officer assistance call. He always figured that someday it could be him on the other end and he would want everyone to respond. He pulled out his phone and called the duty officer at the Colorado Bureau of Investigation office in Grand Junction. He told the woman who answered that he was responding to the officer assistance call from Pitkin County and would be in touch.

There was no easy way to get to Aspen from where he was in Delta, so he turned onto Route 92. At Hotchkiss, he turned onto Route 133 which would eventually take him to Carbondale where he would turn south on Route 82 and head for Aspen. All told the drive would take him almost three hours and he would arrive late in the afternoon. He had no choice. A law enforcement officer was in trouble. Buck flipped on the emergency flashers in his engine grill and hit the gas. He needed to shave some time off the three-hour drive.

Chapter Seven

The Sheriff was standing next to the Pitkin County Search and Rescue mobile command center when Buck walked up. Buck had to park almost a mile down the road leading to the trailhead. Between tourist cars and all the emergency vehicles, there was barely room for all the people.

"Sheriff," said Buck. "Heard you could use a hand."

The Sheriff turned and shook Buck's hand. "Buck Taylor. How the hell are you? Been a while."

It had been a few years since Buck had worked with Sheriff Winters and he was amazed to see that the Sheriff looked exactly the same as the last time he saw him.

"Doin good. Want to fill me in on what you got goin?"

"You betcha," said the Sheriff. "Hey, by the way, was really sorry to hear about your wife passin. Always liked that lady. And hey, nice job in Durango last month. Knocked the shit out of the cartel boys." Bucked nodded.

The Sheriff filled Buck in on the search so far. Since Susan Corey hadn't left any information in her car, so the Sheriff had no choice but to use it as a starting point for the search and send his teams out in several different directions. Because the dog had been shot, the Sheriff had assigned a deputy or an armed ranger to work with each two-man search team. He wanted someone armed with each group just in case. He was happy to report that the dog was out of surgery and the emergency room vet felt good about his chances.

The Sheriff walked Buck through the search grids on the topographic map he had laid out on a table inside the command center. Right now, he had fifteen search teams working from several directions and all heading generally toward Hunter Peak. The Gunnison County search and rescue teams were working their way toward Hunter Peak from the south. From this point on it was just a matter of waiting. And it would be getting dark soon and he wanted everyone back before dark.

Buck looked at the grids. "Lot of area to cover. Any tracks from the dog?"

"No," responded the Sheriff. "None that anyone could find."

"You got PIS out there? Anyone could find tracks it would be him."

"Can't find him. Truth is I think he is pissed at me."

Buck waited for an explanation. The Sheriff went on to explain that one of his newer deputies had gotten curious about PIS and had pulled his prints off a soda can and ran them through AFIS, the Automated Fingerprint Identification System. As in the past, the prints came back as unknown and as in the past, PIS found out that they had run them and he stormed off to god knows where.

Buck let out a low whistle. "You guys violated his trust. No wonder you can't find him. Geez. We promised we wouldn't do that anymore. Try to find out his identity."

"I Know. Jumped all over the deputy. But nothing I can do now."

"Ok," said Buck. "Since your search teams will be heading

back in a little bit, I am going to check into the hotel and I will try to find PIS and see if I can get him to help."

Buck shook the Sheriff's hand and started the long walk back to his car. Good thing he was in good shape. Buck reached his car, managed to turn around on the narrow road and headed for Aspen.

Aspen, Colorado, playground of the rich and famous, is the county seat of Pitkin County, Colorado. Aspen had a population of around 7,000 people and sat at an elevation just shy of 8,000 feet. It was originally built as a mining town in the 1880's and was almost abandoned after the collapse of the silver mines in the early 1900's. In the 1930's skiing started to take the place of mining and Aspen started looking towards the future but all that got put on hold during World War II. In 1946, skiing took off for real and Aspen hasn't looked back since. Once the county seat of the counterculture movement in the United States, Aspen is now home to movie stars and corporate CEO's and boast the most expensive real estate in the country. A lot had changed over the years and Buck was never sure if it was a good thing or a bad thing. Mostly it just was and Buck accepted that.

One thing Buck loved most about Aspen was that it still had its share of quirky characters and in spite of efforts to "clean up the city," the city still had a fairly good size homeless and counterculture population. Buck was on a mission to find one of those quirky characters as he pulled his car into a parking space along South Monarch Street next to Wagner Park.

Buck had first encountered PIS about ten years back. PIS, as he was affectionately known, had arrived in Aspen about twenty years ago and had immediately stood out. At that time the counterculture movement was in full swing and drugs were everywhere. Everyone in Aspen had either heard of or knew PIS except that no one really knew much about him. PIS was tall, about six feet two and gangly as folks used to say. He probably weighed one hundred fifty pounds soaking wet. He had long gray hair pulled back in a ponytail and a three-day growth of stubble on his face. The odd thing is that no matter what day or time of day you encounter PIS his stubble was always the same. It never seemed to grow out or look untidy.

Unlike most of the homeless characters at the time, PIS never smelled like a homeless person. He wore the same clothes every day but never looked dirty or unkempt. His outfit hadn't changed since Buck first met him. He wore calf height, brown leather lace-up moccasin style boots, light gray tuxedo pants with a dark gray stripe down the legs and a worn white dress shirt now frayed and yellow with age. Around his waist he wore a bright red cummerbund and around his neck he wore a bright red ascot.

No matter what time of year or what the temperature was PIS always wore the same tattered brown linen coat and a black beret. He looked rather elegant for a homeless person. His only other possession was a well-worn leather backpack that looked like it had traveled the world. The initials, P-I-S, were engraved on the flap and since no one knew his name, everyone just called him PIS, which he never seemed to mind. His demeanor was always jovial and friendly and no one ever complained about feeling threatened by his presence. Most striking was his British accent. Not the harsh Cockney accent you associate with street people but a very elegant silky-smooth accent that just exuded sophistication.

No one ever saw him panhandling for money, yet he always seemed to have enough to visit one of the local pubs for his nightly glass of cognac. As it turned out, PIS also had an incredible talent which helped him generate some income on a fairly regular basis. PIS was an amazing tracker. There wasn't anything he couldn't find whether it be an animal or a missing child and his abilities had come to the attention of many of the local hunting guides who paid him a daily fee to help them find game for their out of town clients. PIS's tracking skills had also come to the attention of the local police and Sheriff and over the years he had been involved in finding many lost hikers or missing persons in the rugged mountains surrounding Aspen.

Early on, when he first arrived in Aspen, many people tried to engage him in conversation to try to determine his real name or his background. It was rumored that several times people had tried to follow him as he left the downtown area and headed for the forest at the end of the day. No one was ever successful. Within minutes of entering the forest PIS would completely disappear leaving his followers bewildered. No one had any idea where he went at night or where he slept but every morning he was right back downtown walking the alleys between East Hopkins Avenue and East Hyman Avenue rummaging through trash dumpsters. If you asked people to guess PIS's age you would get answers from forty to eighty. He truly was a mystery.

The Sheriff had run his fingerprints once when an overzealous deputy had tried to arrest PIS for vagrancy and his prints came back as unknown. PIS had become furious at the intrusion into his privacy and ever since there was a truce between local law enforcement and PIS. He would provide his tracking services for free to any agency that had a need for such services, in exchange local law enforcement would no longer try to determine his true identity. That truce had lasted almost twenty years, til now.

Buck had first met PIS during a missing person's case Buck had been working in the Aspen area. The case involved a missing heiress, a thirteen-year-old girl, who had disappeared from her home in the Woody Creek area. It was never clear if she had walked away from her home or if she had been taken. Security had been tight around the family home and there were no signs of a break-in. No ransom had ever been demanded and no body was ever discovered, even though Buck and PIS with the help of the Sheriff's department had worked tirelessly for two weeks and had scoured every inch of the forests around Aspen. It was Buck's only case that remained unsolved and the case file sat in a prominent place on Buck's desk as a reminder of the one he couldn't solve.

Buck had gotten to know PIS pretty well during those two weeks. More so than anyone else had ever been able to and had developed a fondness for this unusual character. During those two weeks of hiking around in the woods, Buck had learned two things about PIS that he had kept a secret to this day. He found out that PIS's real name was Pheasant Iverson-Smythe. PIS had refused to say anything more about why his first name was Pheasant and Buck let it go. The other thing he learned, while they sat around a small campfire one afternoon, was even more of a mystery. PIS had pulled an old tin cookie box out of his backpack. Inside the cookie tin wrapped in fine silk was a beautiful china cup and saucer, a silver spoon, a small tea ball for brewing tea and a tiny silver teapot. PIS had also removed a smaller tin containing loose leaf Earl Gray tea which he proceeded to brew up for himself. The whole image seemed completely out of place. Buck had spotted a worn black and white picture of a very beautiful young woman sitting in the bottom of the cookie tin but when he asked PIS about the picture, PIS almost reverently closed the tin and softly explained that some things were best left unsaid. Buck could have sworn he saw a tear develop in PIS's eye.

Those two weeks had created a strange bond between these

two men. Buck couldn't really explain it and he never tried. He had worked with PIS several more times over the years and it became clearer and clearer to Buck, that as he got older PIS never seemed to age. PIS also seemed to understand how much it troubled Buck that the case of the missing heiress remained unsolved.

Chapter Eight

Buck had spent the next couple hours until well after dark walking the streets and alleys of downtown Aspen searching for PIS. His inquiries with local shopkeepers, hoteliers, bartenders and the homeless he encountered had netted the same response. No one had seen PIS for a couple of days. Most couldn't remember the last time they saw him, but they would be happy to let Buck know if he showed up.

Buck checked into his hotel and crashed for the night. Tomorrow was going to be a very long day. Before he nodded off to sleep, he asked the spirits of the woods to keep an eye on PIS and Ranger Susan Corey and keep them safe. Buck wasn't religious in the typical sense of religion. He had been raised Catholic and he and Lucy had tried to raise their children Catholic but only Jason, their youngest son, had kept organized religion in his life. Buck was more spiritual than religious. He had very little use for organized religion but he always believed that there were spirits out there keeping an eye on things. He always thanked the spirits for allowing him to catch fish or for allowing him to witness a beautiful sunrise or sunset. Lucy never questioned his beliefs and she never minded when he discussed his attitudes with his kids or grandkids.

Buck's internal alarm clock went off at five AM and he showered and dressed, clipped his badge and holster to his belt and headed out to get something for breakfast before heading down to the trailhead. Stopping at a small gas station and convenience store just before the turnoff for Route 13, Buck grabbed a couple bottles of Coke and water and a few snacks to take with him. He was sitting in his car eating a microwaved burrito and drinking his Coke when there was a knock on the passenger side window. Buck glanced over and there, standing beside the car was PIS. Buck hit the button to unlock the door and PIS climbed into the passenger seat.

"Good morning Agent Taylor. How very nice to see you again. What a pleasant day it is going to be."

Buck loved listening to PIS's accent and for a second he just stared. He had no idea how PIS had found him, especially this far from downtown. He swallowed the piece of burrito he was chewing on and smiled.

"Where have you been?" Buck asked. "People haven't seen you in a couple days."

"I've been around. I heard you were looking for me. Will we be embarking on another grand adventure?"

Buck nodded. "We have a missing person we need to find. I am heading to the trailhead now and could use your help."

PIS looked serious for a moment. "I told the Sheriff that I would not be available to work with him for a while. Did he send you to find me?"

"No. The Sheriff was very clear that you were pissed. I told him I would find you. This one is important PIS. A female ranger is missing and her dog was found shot. We need your help."

PIS stared at Buck for a minute without saying anything. His trust had been violated once again and Buck understood how important that was to him but he also had no doubt that PIS would do the right thing.

"I didn't realize it was a ranger who was missing. Had I known, I would have found the Sheriff and offered my assistance."

Buck simply nodded, started the car and pulled out of the convenience store parking lot. The sun was just starting to come over the mountains and Buck knew from past experience that the earlier PIS got on the trail, the better and morning light was the best for finding obscure footprints or trail signs.

Buck was able to pull into the Maroon-Snowmass trailhead parking lot and parked next to the rescue command center. The Sheriff, coffee in hand, was standing over the table looking at the search map with the head of the Pitkin County Search and Rescue team. They both looked up at Buck and PIS approached.

"Buck, PIS. Nice to see you," said the Sheriff.

Buck nodded but PIS reached out his hand, first shaking the hand of the head of the rescue team and then shaking the Sheriff's hand.

"I must apologize Sheriff. My behavior of late has been in very poor taste and if you will allow me, I would like to offer my services in the search for the ranger."

Buck had never seen PIS seem this contrite. He had filled PIS in on the events thus far and PIS seemed to be extremely concerned about the fate of the ranger's dog. Buck wondered if the wounded dog had somehow struck a nerve with PIS. Something from his past that triggered a serious response.

The Sheriff accepted his offer of help and Buck and PIS joined the Sheriff around the map. The Sheriff explained that the rest of the teams would be arriving soon and then he reviewed where they had searched yesterday and what the game plan was for today.

PIS studied the map very carefully as if he was memorizing every trail and landmark, although Buck believed deep inside, that PIS knew these forests like Buck knew his own house.

PIS looked up from the map. "Is it possible to see where the dog was found?"

The Sheriff explained that the ranger's truck was still at the scene and he led Buck and PIS over to where it was parked. PIS got down on his knees and looked under the car. He had spotted a small splash of blood on the rocks under the truck and he reached in and touched it with his hand. He then crawled under the truck as far as he could go and started scanning the area around the truck. He basically had a dog's eye view of the forest around the truck.

The sun was just starting to cast long shadows across the parking lot as PIS slid out from under the car. PIS was focused on something in the distance and both Buck and the Sheriff knew better than to interrupt PIS when he was this focused.

Chapter Nine

The Teacher was not pleased. Not pleased at all. They had never seen the Teacher this mad. They brought home all that nice elk meat and had the others cook up some for dinner. Some of the others had found some canned vegetables at one of the houses they raided and also some soup. It was a good meal.

The Teacher then asked them to tell the others how they had shot the elk and that is when the trouble began. Being the oldest, the hunter told the story the way the Teacher had taught him too. He used words and visualization to bring the others along on the trail as they stalked the huge animal. The others sat and listened, enthralled with the story. Even the youngest sat still during the telling.

They described seeing the animal in the distance, how they crawled and crouch stepped to within a couple hundred yards and how they had drawn a bead on the elk, sighted in on his massive chest, took a deep breath, just like they had been taught, held the next breath and fired. The shot was perfect and the elk had only been able to run a couple yards before it fell down in some grass. They chased after it and when they found it it was still breathing so, they slit its throat to stop the pain. Just like the Teacher had told them to do. The Teacher looked pleased.

They told the group about dragging the elk back to the hunting camp in the woods and how they were going to hide it and come back to butcher it later but that the lady ranger and her dog had spotted the camp. The Teacher froze. He asked them to repeat the part about the lady ranger which they did. A little more nervously this time.

They described how the dog had sniffed out their hiding spot and how they had no choice but to shoot the lady ranger in the thigh since she was wearing a ballistic vest. They described how they had found her lying in the ravine and how the blood was pumping out of her leg and she had pleaded with them to stop the pain and they told everyone that they shot her in the head, so she would no longer suffer, just like the Teacher had taught them.

The Teacher's face grew red with anger. He demanded to know what had happened to the dog. They were now too afraid not to tell the whole truth so they told everyone that they had shot the dog and had seen it fall but that after searching for a long time they were unable to find the dog. They explained that they had gone back to where the lady ranger was lying in the ravine and had covered her body with dirt and sticks so no one would be able to find her.

The Teacher could no longer contain his anger. He yelled at them for taking a human life, something he had always told them never to do. He understood that they were trying to protect the others but taking a human life was forbidden. He told them that they would be punished for taking the human life and he told them he was very unhappy that they could not find the dog. If the dog made it back to where it had come from there would be hell to pay and that they had put the others in peril.

The Teacher was certain that the outsiders would come looking for the lady ranger and her dog and he now feared that after all this time they would have to move their camp. He told them that it was all their fault for being so stupid and to get caught by the lady ranger. He called them dumb and stupid and a bunch of other words they did not understand and they knew the Teacher was mad, very mad. He said that if the outsiders found the cabin that they would take the others away to a bad place where they would no longer be able to see each other and that the hunter and the younger one would have to go to jail because of killing the lady ranger. They had no idea what jail was but the Teacher made it sound like a terrible place and the younger one started crying which just made the Teacher madder. He took the rifle that was in the corner and put it under his bed. He told them not to touch it again until he had come up with a suitable punishment.

The Teacher told the girls to clean up the table from dinner and then to start moving everything out of the cabin and deep into the mine. They needed to be prepared for when the outsiders came. He told the hunter and the younger one to go out into the woods and make sure the traps were all set. He did not want to be surprised by the outsiders.

The others had never lived anywhere else but the cabin. They were scared and nervous about having to leave. All their stuff, the Teachers books, and the awards he had given them for doing good things were here in the cabin. Momma was buried not far away and they were worried that they would never be near her again. Some of the others started to cry.

The Teacher, sensing their worry and concern, started to calm down. He told them all to come back to the table for a minute. He had them all hold hands and then he read his favorite passage from the bible. "Yea, though I walk through the valley of the shadow of death…" The other listened carefully to the words. They always felt better upon hearing the words.

The Teacher finished reading and told them that he loved them all, even the hunter and the younger one, and that he was sorry he had gotten so mad. He told them that human life was precious and that it was wrong to take a life but that they might now have to take more lives to protect their home. This would make him sad. He hoped that they could get deep enough into the mine so no one would find them and that someday they might be able to come back to the cabin.

The Teacher asked them all to gather up their things as quickly and quietly as possible and start moving things into the mine. They all followed his orders and the hunter and the younger one left to check on the traps.

Chapter Ten

While the Sheriff headed back to the rescue command center to help organize the searchers and give them their assignments, Buck stood next to Susan Corey's truck and watched PIS work. PIS was methodical in his approach to tracking and it would take all his skills for this one. The dog had left almost no trail to follow, so PIS gradually started to expand his circle around the truck. Moving out five yards each time he completed a circle around the vehicle. Several times he had gotten down on his knees or his belly to get a better view of the area.

Buck waited patiently. The rest of the search was going to be organized but not too precise since they had no idea in which direction Susan Corey had traveled. They knew from the Chief Ranger that she was supposed to be searching for the illegal elk camp in the area near Hunter Peak and that several of the search teams had been in that area but had found nothing. Once she arrived in the parking lot something could have changed her mind and she could have gone off in any direction. This was needle in the haystack time.

Buck's thoughts were interrupted by a call from PIS.

"Agent Taylor. Over here please."

Buck had tried for years to get PIS to call him Buck but to

no avail. Even if no one was around, he still called him Agent Taylor. Buck walked over to where PIS was kneeling on the ground looking at something in the dirt. Buck knelt down next to him and looked at the spot PIS was pointing at. Buck got closer and finally pulled his reading glasses out of his back pocket. He looked at the ground next to PIS's finger and could barely make out a single, very light pad impression and contained in that impression was a tiny spot of something reddish brown. Blood.

Knowing where the first trail mark was, gave them a direction of travel from the ranger's truck and with that PIS started moving in that direction. Buck could hardly see the trail but there was enough indentation in the undergrowth to give PIS something to follow. Buck ran back to the rescue command center to let the Sheriff know that PIS had a trail and to pick up one of the search team radios. The Sheriff was still going to send out his search teams per the plan they had come up with earlier, just in case the trail PIS was following didn't pan out.

Buck headed back to his Jeep, put on his ballistic vest, grabbed his backpack, a topographic map, handheld GPS unit and his back up semi-automatic pistol and headed back to the ranger's truck. PIS was already fifty yards up the trail looking for the next sign which he found just as Buck was walking up behind him. A spot of blood on a leaf eighteen inches off the ground. Buck could barely see it but he trusted PIS so off they went.

The trail they followed was hardly more than a slight impression in the undergrowth but it made sense to Buck. If you were a guide running an illegal elk camp you wouldn't want to have it anywhere near one of the established trails. This trail looked like an old game trail that hadn't been used in years. It was perfect. The last thing you would want is for a tourist to stumble on your camp and this area was filled with tourists hiking on the many established trails.

PIS was like an old hound dog on a scent. Periodically he would stop and kneel down to look at something, or he would stop, scratch his beard and then move ten or fifteen paces into the woods around the trail and circle back toward the trail. Buck soon realized that this was how PIS maintained the sign. If he lost the trail he would move left or right until he could reestablish the trail. For the most part, the dog seemed to have traveled a fairly straight line. Several times over the next couple hours PIS would stop and point out where the dog had laid down to rest. Buck could hardly imagine how much the dog must have been hurting as it made its way back to the ranger's truck.

Buck was in pretty good shape for a fifty-eight-year-old man but after four hours of hiking over uneven ground, he needed to take a break. PIS, on the other hand, looked like he hadn't walked anywhere at all. He still wore his linen coat and his beret and he wasn't even sweating. Buck was mystified. It was early September but it was still extremely warm for this time of year. Buck was sweating profusely. PIS did agree to hold up so that Buck could take a breather and he didn't refuse the bottle of water and the trail mix bar that Buck had offered him.

Buck unfolded the topographic map and pulled out his handheld GPS unit. He had been marking waypoints on the map as they had been traveling. PIS came over to look at the map with him. They had traveled in pretty much a straight line from the ranger's truck but what they both noticed was that they were not headed to Hunter Peak, at least not directly. If this trail continued, they were actually traveling to the west of the peak. Away from where most of the rescue units were searching.

"What do you think?" Buck asked.

PIS pondered the question and looked once more at the map. "If I had to venture a guess I would say that something distracted the ranger or she had some new information that we were not aware of. There are several trails that lead to Hunter Peak that she could have followed more easily than this trail, yet she chose to bushwhack through the trees. Very odd indeed," replied PIS.

Buck had to agree. He folded up the map, put it back in his pocket and they headed out again. Twice over the next hour PIS lost the trail in some rocky terrain and it took a little bit of time to reestablish the trail. Buck had spent that time listening to the other search teams reporting in. No one had anything good to report.

Buck and PIS had traveled for about another hour when PIS suddenly stopped and put his hand out so Buck couldn't move past him. At almost that same instance the radio crackled.

"Search team four to command. We have a serious problem, over."

"Go ahead search team four, this is command."

"Command we have a man down. One of the rangers stepped on what appears to be some kind of booby trap. He was impaled in the leg with a sharp stick that just popped out of the ground. He is bleeding badly and we need a paramedic."

"Search team four. Please begin first aid and try to stop the bleeding. We are sending in the paramedics. Please provide coordinates."

The search team leader gave them the coordinates and Buck pulled his map out of his pocket. The search team was in the grid next to the one he and PIS were working. Probably a little over a mile from their present location. Buck put the map back in his pocket and started to move in the direction of search team four but PIS stopped him again. Buck looked annoyed until he saw where PIS was pointing. Just above the surface of the trail, Buck spotted the monofilament fishing line. It was tied to a bush off to their left and was pulled tight across the trail.

"Booby trap?" Buck asked.

PIS nodded. "Yes. Be very careful. Let me see where this goes. Please stand back a couple paces."

PIS got down on his knees and slowly followed the line without touching it. Five feet off the trail and in fairly dense underbrush he stopped. The string was attached to a very rudimentary crossbow that had been anchored between two shrubs. The bolt was nothing more than a sharpened stick but with the tension on the line, it could have delivered a nasty surprise to whoever tripped it. PIS pulled a knife from his pocket, snapped it open with one hand and proceeded to cut the tripwire and disengage the bolt. He crawled back out of the underbrush.

"Could have been a bit of a nasty surprise for whoever tripped this," he said while handing the bolt to Buck. "It was low enough to the ground to cause some damage but I don't think it was intended to kill. Just wound."

Buck examined the bolt. "Crude but effective."

"How the hell did you spot the trip wire? I was looking at where you were pointing and I didn't see it until you touched it."

"Experience Agent Taylor. Someone does not want us to find this elk camp."

Buck pulled out his radio. "Command this is Buck Taylor. Please put the Sheriff on."

"Go ahead, Buck. This is Earl," replied the Sheriff.

"Earl, have all the search teams stop immediately. We just

disarmed a booby trap along the trail we are following. There could be more out there."

"All search teams. You heard the man. Stop immediately until we figure this out. Buck, how do you think we should handle this?"

"We are certain we are on the dog's trail. Let us continue forward and clear a path and see where the trail takes us. In the meantime, I would suggest you pull everyone back to the parking lot. Right now, our trail is taking us to the west of Hunter Peak. We will call in as soon as we reach the end of the trail."

"Ok Buck. Stay in touch. All search teams, backtrack the way you went in and return to the parking lot."

Buck looked at PIS. "Let's keep moving. Slowly."

PIS nodded and started back down the trail.

Chapter Eleven

She had to park along the road leading to the Maroon-Snowmass trailhead parking lot. There were a lot of emergency vehicles ahead and it appeared that the entrance to the parking lot was closed. She had no idea what was going on. She had overheard a conversation at the restaurant that there was some kind of police search going on at the trailhead and she decided to come see for herself.

She decided to leave her car on the side of the road and walk down to the crowd to see if she could find out what was going on. She pulled the long brown wig down a little snugger on her head, pulled it back in a ponytail and put on her Denver Broncos ball cap. She climbed out of her car, grabbed her backpack out of the trunk and slung it over her shoulders. She looked just like all the other hikers that were walking down the road to the trailhead.

As she walked towards the barricade that was set up at the entrance to the parking lot, several disgruntled hikers came walking back from the barricade. Several people told her that the trail was closed until further notice. She thanked them as they passed, figuring that was what most friendly hikers would do.

She stepped into a crowd of hikers and day users who had gathered at the barricade and listened as the park ranger told the crowd that the authorities were in the process of looking for a lost hiker and the park would be closed until the search was concluded.

Most of the hikers took the information as gospel and turned to head for their cars. Some chose to stay and either grumble about the inconvenience or ask questions to try to get more information from the ranger. She stood quietly to the side of the group and listened. She had learned long ago that you got a lot more information from people if you stopped and listened and watched their body language.

As the other hikers conversed with the ranger, she heard his words but more importantly, she noticed his eyes. It was obvious to her that he was not being completely truthful. He was trying to be polite with the crowd but there was an underlying tension in his face and voice. Answering the same questions a dozen or more times gets old pretty fast but the ranger answered each query with a polite forced smile.

Satisfied that she was not going to hear anything new, as more hikers and curiosity seekers came and went, she turned and headed back to her car. Being the polite, friendly hiker, she was, she let those just heading for the barricade know that the trail was closed indefinitely. The other hikers politely thanked her before continuing on to the barricade to hear it for themselves.

She reached her car, put her backpack back in the trunk and stood for a minute looking down the road at the barricade. She knew the ranger was only being partially truthful. It was obvious the trail was closed. So that was the truth. The missing hiker was another story. From the trailhead she could see the Pitkin County Search and Rescue mobile command center, so obviously, there was some kind of search going on. Typically, in small communities, when a hiker is lost or missing the Sheriff's office calls for volunteers but that was not the case here. Most of the volunteers she could see were uniformed searchers and she also noted a lot of law enforcement types. A lot more than you would see at a simple search and from the cars she observed the law enforcement folks had come from many different jurisdictions. She would need to think about this some more.

She climbed into her car and just sat for a minute. Was it possible they had found it? Is that why all the cops were on the scene? In all the time it was there no one had ever stumbled onto it. Was it possible that someone spotted the newer lock? She had purposely taken an old looking padlock from her grandfather's garage so it would not be obvious to anyone looking that the lock was recently changed.

She started to feel a little nauseous and took a sip of water from the bottle between the seats. It couldn't be. She was just getting started. She had tried to be careful, just like she had been taught. She made certain she wasn't followed and she covered her tracks well. No, it was not possible. No one had discovered it in forty or fifty years. Why now? She started to shake and she wrapped her arms around her chest and squeezed. The shaking finally stopped.

She decided that she was just being paranoid and that the cops would not be waiting at her house when she got home. After all, how would they even know about her? She started her car, pulled off the side of the road and headed home. Even though she felt more confident that this didn't concern her and it was just a coincidence that something was going on in the same area, she had this little nagging bug in the back of her head. She would need to be very careful until she worked this all out.

Chapter Twelve

The trail was becoming more obvious as they moved forward. They were finding more and more dried bloodstains on the undisturbed undergrowth and PIS told Buck that with the amount of blood he was finding, they must be getting close to the end of the trail. He also had to stop once more and expose another booby trap. This time it was a shallow pit about a foot deep covered with a thin layer of sticks and leaves. Almost impossible to see, but it could have been quite effective. Buried in the small pit were a dozen sharpened sticks pointing up so anyone who happened to step into the pit would have had their foot impaled on any one of the spikes.

PIS spent a few minutes removing the spikes, which were buried a foot or so deep in the soil to keep them upright. At one point he commented about the fact that what they had encountered so far were very similar to the types of booby traps the Viet Cong used to set during the Vietnam war. Crude but highly effective.

Buck started to ask him about the comment but PIS just ignored him and finally stood up and said they should keep moving. Buck let it slide but wondered if he had just been privy to another little tidbit about PIS's life.

PIS moved down the trail with a little more urgency, or so

it seemed to Buck. He seemed to be much more focused and they covered a lot more ground until they arrived at a small rise and PIS stopped and knelt down and touched something on the ground. Buck climbed up the little rise behind him, stopped to catch his breath and looked to where PIS had his hand. This blood spot was so obvious that even Buck could see it.

Without saying anything, PIS stood and moved a couple feet to his left and repeated the process. Buck looked and noticed the second large blood spot. PIS still hadn't said anything. He stood up and moved down the backside of the ravine where he found more dried blood. He stood and looked around the area. Then he looked at Buck. There was a seriousness in his eyes that Buck had never seen before.

"The dog was shot there." He pointed to the spot where Buck was now standing. Buck stayed silent. "It would appear he fell off the ridge in this direction and landed here." He pointed to another big blood stain. "There is a good blood trail leading back to the trail we came in on. I am amazed, that with the amount of blood that is here, that the dog was able to walk back four point four miles and get back to the ranger's car. He must have been in terrible pain."

Buck pulled out his handheld GPS and looked at the data. They had traveled four point five miles. He hadn't told PIS how far they had gone but he hit the number almost exactly. Buck didn't know how PIS had known but he decided to keep that knowledge to himself. PIS was certainly an anomaly.

PIS climbed back up the small ridge and looked around.

"What do you think happened to the ranger? Any chance she might be still alive?" Buck asked.

PIS stood for a moment and Buck thought he saw PIS's eyes get a little misty.

"I don't think so." He pointed to the other large spot of blood on the ground a few feet to the right. "This is arterial spray. Notice the many small droplets. I believe the ranger was shot here." He slowly stood up. He pointed to a pile of leaves and sticks at the bottom of the ravine.

"I believe we will find the ranger under that pile of leaves."

Buck pulled his cell phone out of his pocket, clicked on the camera and took a couple pictures of the various blood stains as PIS pointed to them. He then put his camera away and looked at PIS. He nodded and they carefully made their way down into the ravine making sure to disturb as little as possible.

At the bottom of the ravine Buck took over and PIS stood back to let Buck do his job. Very carefully, Buck began to remove the leaves and sticks from the pile. Below the leaves and sticks, Buck found a layer of loose dry dirt. His heart sank. It was obvious, even to him, that the dirt was recently disturbed and he moved even more carefully.

Using his hand to brush away the dirt, the face of Susan Corey gradually revealed itself. Her eyes were still open and Buck could almost sense the horror she must have felt knowing her life was slipping away. The dark hole in her forehead and the lack of blood on her face told Buck that the kill shot had come almost too late. Buck figured Susan Corey must have been at the end of her life when someone put her out of her misery. He stopped and stared at her face.

Buck had seen a lot of death in his long career in law enforcement but he had never gotten jaded by it. He was still impacted deeply and seeing Susan Corey's lifeless face made him sit back for a moment and reflect on his own life. It also made him angry that this young woman's life had been cut short and he silently vowed to do everything he could to find and punish the person or persons who had done this.

PIS joined him and together they removed the dirt and debris from the rest of her body. PIS pointed to the bullet hole and the massive amount of blood that stained her green pant leg. Buck nodded and pulled out his camera again. He took pictures of the wounds and of her body as it lay and pictures of the debris that had been piled on her. He finally looked at PIS.

PIS said, "whoever shot her knew what they were doing. Shot her below her ballistic vest. She rolled down the slope ended up here and then the shooter shot her in the forehead. Such a terrible waste. I am truly sorry Agent Taylor."

Buck nodded. "Without your help, we might never have found her. Thanks for helping to bring her family closure. Now we need to call in the troops. This is now a crime scene."

Buck climbed back up to the top of the ridge and found that he had 2 bars of cell service. He decided not to broadcast the find over the radio, so he used his phone and dialed the Sheriff.

The Sheriff answered on the second ring. "Buck, does this mean what I think it means?"

"Yeah. Didn't want to broadcast it on an open frequency. We found Susan Corey. We are gonna need the Forensic Pathologist and the crime scene guys."

Buck told the Sheriff about what they had discovered. He pulled out his handheld GPS and gave the Sheriff the coordinates for the body and told him how to follow the trail from her truck. He would send PIS back up the trail to meet them halfway and he would lead them in the rest of the way. He asked him to send in a couple search and rescue guys to carry out the body when forensics was finished and he requested as many deputies as the Sheriff could spare.

This was going to be one tough crime scene to process. He asked him to keep all the other law enforcement folks and rangers away from the scene.

The Sheriff mentioned that there were several Gunnison County deputies not that far from his location and he would request assistance from the Gunnison County Sheriff and have his deputies meet up with Buck to help work the scene. This deep in the mountains, jurisdiction lines sometimes get blurred and Buck told the Sheriff he would be grateful for all the help. The Sheriff would also be calling his homicide team.

Buck hung up and headed back to PIS and the body. He asked PIS if he would head back up the trail and meet the teams coming down. PIS slapped Buck on the back and headed up the ridge. Buck was now alone with the body and he said a silent prayer and asked the spirits of the forest to watch over her family.

Chapter Thirteen

Buck pulled a silver and orange survival blanket out of his backpack and used it to cover Susan Corey's body. He had also checked to make sure she still had her weapon, her radio and her cell phone. It was obvious that robbery was not a motive, so he quickly dismissed that idea and moved on to the next idea. Ambush. Was Susan Corey ambushed? And if so by whom? Buck was all too familiar with ambushes having barely survived an ambush while investigating a drug distribution network in Durango, Colorado a month or so back. If it hadn't been for luck and his friend Jessica Gonzales, the DEA Agent in Charge of the Grand Junction office, he would not be here today.

The Slattery brothers were prime suspects in a triple homicide Buck had been investigating in Teller County, when he was reassigned to the cartel investigation in Durango. Somehow the brothers had followed Buck to Durango and tried to ambush him in his hotel parking lot. Jess Gonzales was walking through the hotel parking lot on her way to meet Buck just as the shooting started. Buck and Jess had killed both brothers but Buck would never forget how close he came to getting killed that evening. He knew his late wife Lucy would not have been pleased.

He stopped and cleared that memory out of his head. Susan Corey needed and deserved Buck's full attention and he would not let her down. Buck stood up and looked around the area. The trees were not as dense in this part of the forest, as a lot of what they had passed through. The shot could have come from almost anywhere, so he needed to narrow that down a bit. He walked back up to the top of the ridge to the first blood stain. He looked down at the blood stain and noticed the spatter that PIS had first pointed out to him. Most of the spatter appeared to be on one side of the larger stain, so he decided to concentrate his initial search in that direction.

Buck walked back down into the ravine and headed in the direction he thought the shots might have come from. He noted one thing almost immediately. Whoever had buried Susan Corey's body had left almost no footprints. Whoever this person or persons were, they had skills. Buck moved carefully away from the body. He was still worried about additional booby traps, so he was very careful where he placed his feet. Remembering how PIS had used a circular pattern each time he lost the trail Buck followed a similar pattern. Every five feet or so he would stop and then move right and then left in a semi-circle around the body location.

Buck was just completing his fourth semi-circle when he heard some leaves and sticks crackling in the distance. Buck unsnapped the thumb break on his holster and removed his semi-automatic pistol. He slowly knelt down.

"Gunnison County Sheriffs!" a voice called out. "Coming in from the south."

Buck replied, "All clear. Come ahead." He rose and holstered his gun but kept his hand on the back strap. Just in case.

Buck spotted the two Gunnison County Sheriff's deputies coming through the trees, followed by two Gunnison County Search and Rescue members. He snapped the thumb break on his holster shut. Buck recognized Walt Jenkins. Walt was a corporal and had been with Gunnison County for about six years. The other deputy he didn't recognize.

Walt stepped up and extended his hand. "Buck Taylor, how the hell are you?"

Buck shook Walt's hand and Walt introduced him to deputy Jimmy Sanchez. Buck shook Jimmy's hand and then shook hands with the two rescue team members, Mike Brill and Connie Hancock, both of whom he knew quite well.

Walt walked over to the body and pulled back the corner. He stood there for a minute said a silent prayer and crossed himself. Walt was a devout Christian. He put the blanket over Susan Corey's face and looked around the area.

"Heck of a crime scene Buck. What do you want us to do?"

Buck explained about his semi-circle search pattern and that they were looking for the shooter's nest. He also reminded them of the possible booby traps. Walt told Buck that they had encountered a booby trap on the way up the hill.

"If Jimmy hadn't tripped over his own feet he would have gotten an arrow right in his backside," said Walt. "Luckily the arrow passed right over him and embedded itself in a tree. Who would have ever thought about booby traps in Colorado?"

Buck agreed and the four Gunnison searchers headed off to continue Buck's search pattern. Buck took the opportunity to take a breather and pulled a bottle of Coke and a trail mix bar out of his backpack. They had been going nonstop since this morning and Buck was beginning to feel his age. Finishing the Coke and the trail mix bar, Buck headed in the direction of his initial search to help the

Gunnison County team. He was just coming up on the first searcher when he heard Jimmy Sanchez call his name.

Jimmy was about forty yards from the body and was looking at something on the ground as Buck walked up. He was soon joined by Walt Jenkins and they looked at what Jimmy was looking at. The spent shell casing was lying on the ground in plain sight. It didn't appear that anyone had tried to hide it, unless someone had missed it.

Buck pulled out his phone and snapped a picture of it. Walt pulled a clear evidence bag out of his backpack and handed it to Buck, who had already gloved up and he picked up the shell casing between his two fingers and placed it in the bag and sealed it. Buck signed his name to the bag and Walt placed it in Buck's backpack.

The group also noticed a large puddle of blood near the shell casing. From the way Buck read the scene, it appeared that whoever shot Ranger Corey was probably hiding behind this downed log and pretty much hidden from view. From this vantage point, Buck could clearly see the top of the ridge where Susan Corey was shot. But what was the blood?

Jimmy had moved off from the group and was following the blood trail that led to the little hideout. He called to Buck.

"I think I know what the blood is from."

Buck and Walt walked over to where Jimmy was standing. Jimmy was standing next to a huge pile of bloody guts.

Jimmy remarked, "I think someone gutted an elk here. It's not a fresh pile so I would say a couple days."

Buck and Walt agreed with his assessment. A picture started to form in Buck's mind. He explained his theory to Jimmy and Walt.

"My guess, at this point, is that someone was hunting out of season, possibly the illegal hunters that the ranger had been following. The hunters heard her coming and pulled the carcass over behind the downed tree and hid. Something the ranger or her dog did must have spooked them and someone shot her in the thigh. Shot the dog too but the dog managed to crawl away. Susan Corey wasn't as lucky. She fell into the ravine bleeding badly. Someone then shot her in the head, either to shut her up, or put her out of her misery or something."

Walt looked at Buck. "Man Buck, if that's the way it went down that is pretty cold. Using a kill shot on an animal is one thing, but to kill a person up close, that's something else entirely."

Buck just nodded. He tried to visualize what Susan Corey had been feeling at the time. Lying in a ravine feeling her life pumping out of her thigh and then watching as her killer stood in front of her and calmly points his gun at her and pulls the trigger. Whoever did this was going to pay. Buck made himself that promise.

Chapter Fourteen

She sits alone in the dark in her room. One small lavender candle burning in a small mason jar on her dresser. The night air is still unseasonably warm so she has the window open and she can hear the hubbub of mountain life as it passes by her home. Her parents had gone out to dinner as soon as she got home. They looked frazzled, even more so than usual. It has been hard on them, especially the last three years since she was away at college. They knew she would be leaving again very soon and she wondered if they hated her for her decision.

She had lived in Aspen all her life and for the most part, it had been a good life. Her parents were not rich and they didn't get involved in the Aspen social scene. They lived in the same little Victorian house on West Hallam Street that her grandfather bought in the nineteen fifties. She was the third generation living under the same roof and sometimes things got a little crazy.

Her father's father, her grandfather, had come to Aspen a few years after the end of World War II. He had been a soldier in the 10th Mountain Division as the war neared its end and had learned how to ski. Some of his fellow warriors were settling in small communities throughout the Colorado mountains and were working to build up the fledgling ski industry. He thought it might be fun to be a part of the movement.

His best friend, Gus Murphy, found a job with the recently formed Aspen Skiing Corporation and had offered her grandfather a job working as a mechanic on the ski lifts. Having been mechanically inclined all his life, her grandfather took to the job like a fish to water. As the years progressed, his life became more and more fulfilling and he felt he was living the American dream. He met and fell in love with her grandmother, bought the small Victorian house on West Hallam Street and raised a son there. It was a perfect life except that the demons were still working hard in the back of his mind.

The demons had always been there as long as he could remember and his time in the army had only deepened the lust they brought out. He had practiced his craft, as he called it, with great abandon as a young man. Many of the townsfolk around Lynchburg, Virginia thought he was odd and some actually feared him. He had grown up on a very rural farm outside Lynchburg. The family's water came from a pump and an outhouse served their more personal needs. To say they were dirt poor would have been an understatement. His father was a sharecropper and didn't even own the dirt under their meager house.

Life had not been easy growing up. He was constantly picked on when he was able to get to school, which was not often, and as things got worse his father would take to drinking and he was a terrible drunk. No one was safe from his rage especially his mother and younger sisters. Numerous times he had watched as his father left his middle sister's room and he heard her crying inside. As his younger sister got older, the same thing would happen to her. His mother would often come out of her room with a black eye or a bruised lip. He wasn't saved from his father's rage because he was a boy. His father would belittle him all the time about not being good at anything or not being a man. He would work him from dawn til dusk and then if the mood was right would beat him senseless for even the most minor infraction.

His escape often took him into unknown territory. He took to following in his father's footsteps and started abusing the animals on the farm. But it didn't stop there. Many of the neighbors complained to the local Sheriff about their pets disappearing. The Sheriff had visited the farm numerous times but never found any evidence that anyone on the farm was involved but the neighbors knew the truth. What they had no way of knowing was how deep the depravity went.

One afternoon one of the neighbors had confronted him about a missing goat. He had seen the goatskin hanging in a tree along the creek behind the farm. The neighbor confronted him and his father with the evidence and a fight broke out. By the time the Sheriff arrived the neighbor was dead. His father, who was covered in blood, tried to put all the blame on him but the Sheriff didn't buy it. They were both arrested. His father was convicted and died in prison a few years later. He was convicted and given a choice, jail or the army. He chose the army.

The army was a great place for him. They taught him how to kill. A skill he honed with great enthusiasm. He was so good at it that he was often the first soldier called upon when a Nazi guard needed to be dispatched silently. His knife became his friend and he used it most effectively when an enemy officer needed to be encouraged to talk. He was a skilled craftsman and his actions often turned the stomachs of even the most hardened soldiers.

He had been able to keep the demons under control for the first couple years after he moved to Aspen but they had become too strong for him to ignore. He needed to feed the demons but Aspen was a small mountain town. Missing people would be noticed. At first, he tried to feed the demons with animal sacrifices. He stayed away from family pets, too close to home, so he focused on wild animals which were in abundance in the forests around Aspen.

Killing forest creatures with his bare hands was certainly a lot of fun but it didn't satisfy the demons for long. He needed the sensation and the arousal that came from killing another human being. The incredible satisfaction it would bring as he felt life slowly slip away from someone who had been a living breathing person. He also missed the thrill of the hunt. Finding the right person and stalking them until just the right moment. He loved the challenge.

Her thoughts were interrupted by the commotion down the hall, so she stood, blew out the lavender candle and walked down the hall to her grandfather's room. Her grandmother was trying to get the very agitated man to calm down. Her grandmother looked up as she entered the room and her eyes pleaded for her granddaughter's help. Her grandfather had been getting more and more agitated lately. The past few decades had not been easy for the family. Since the accident that had left her grandfather a quadriplegic, he had been confined mostly to his bed but for the past five years, the Alzheimer's Disease had taken a terrible toll on his mind. He struggled to keep his sanity but his memories were all but gone and she feared that the demons were winning the final battle for what was left. She knew what to do so she sat down on the edge of the bed and started to hum a lullaby. It didn't matter what lullaby she hummed; it seemed it was the sound that would calm him down. Her grandmother took the opportunity to increase his morphine drip and he finally fell asleep. Her grandmother looked relieved. She sat for a few more minutes and then left his room, grabbed her jacket and headed out into the night.

Chapter Fifteen

Buck and the others stopped their searching as they heard the first sounds of the parade of law enforcement personnel approaching the small ridge. Buck wanted to try to keep the crime scene as untouched as possible, so he headed back to the body just as PIS and the Sheriff came over the ridge. The Sheriff looked as solemn as Buck had ever seen him. Buck took a minute to review with the Sheriff what they had discovered and they planned out the perimeter of the crime scene. They would tape off the area from the top of the ridge, down into the ravine and over to where they had found the probable shooting location. The area was huge.

Since Buck was on scene as a courtesy more than anything else, he let the Sheriff take charge of the crime scene. He would step back and let the locals handle the investigation and would offer his services as needed. The Sheriff called his two homicide investigators over to where he and Buck were standing.

Moe Steiner was a twenty-year veteran of the Sheriff's Department. He was about five-ten and maybe one hundred seventy pounds. He had thinning hair and a large brown mustache. He was dressed in jeans, T-shirt and light jacket. His partner was Jane Fitzpatrick. Fitz, as she was affectionately known around Aspen, was a sixteen-year veteran and had been working homicide for almost ten years. The mother of three and grandmother of two she was five six and maybe a little overweight. She also had on jeans, a light flannel shirt and her dark blue nylon police jacket.

Buck shook hands all around. He had first met both investigators when he was investigating the missing heiress ten years ago. His only unsolved case. He knew them both to be exceptional investigators and extremely detail oriented. He had a feeling that this investigation, because of the location and the size, would be a challenge for both of them.

They had just begun discussing the overall crime scene when the Sheriff's two forensic techs, Claudia Gomez and Holly Flynn, crested the ridge followed closely by Dr. Emily Parker, the Forensic Pathologist for Pitkin County.

Colorado is one of about a dozen states that still use the Coroner system instead of the Medical Examiner system. The coroner for each jurisdiction is an elected official and that person did not have to have any experience at being a coroner or even be a medical professional. Anyone could run for coroner. The system was gradually evolving so that the coroner needed to complete a formal training program in death investigations but it was a slow process. Since unlike in the Medical Examiner system, the coroner did not have to be a doctor, each coroner would contract with a licensed Forensic Pathologist to handle any investigations that required an autopsy. These Forensic Pathologists were usually highly trained doctors, who in a lot of cases, split their time between several jurisdictions to keep costs down.

Dr. Emily Parker had been the licensed Forensic Pathologist for Pitkin County for five years. She had been a medical examiner in Los Angeles before growing tired of the rat race and had decided to relocate her family to the Colorado mountains. A graduate of Harvard University and John Hopkins Medical School, she was very highly regarded and the ultimate professional. Instead of working as a pathologist for several counties, Emily Parker had opened a family medical practice in Aspen, where you could still find her most days. At the time she wasn't sure if she wanted to go back into the medical examiner profession. That changed five years ago with the sudden death of her predecessor, Dr. Ross Malone, who died in a freak skiing accident on Aspen Mountain. Since Dr. Parker was already licensed as a pathologist, she took the job on, temporarily, until they could find a permanent replacement for Dr. Malone. The county was still looking.

She walked up to Buck and the Sheriff and extended her hand. Buck shook her hand.

"Nice to see you again Agent Taylor. I wish the circumstances were better."

Buck nodded. "Good to see you too Doc. Sorry for the long trek."

"No worries," she replied. She looked down at the body in the ravine. "Why don't you give me the tour since you found her. Ok with you Sheriff?"

The Sheriff told her it was fine with him but he wanted one of his homicide folks down there with them. Fitz stepped forward and the small group started down the side of the ravine. Buck had worked with Dr. Parker several times before and knew that she would prefer to view the body first before asking for his report. She never wanted her first impressions tainted by the opinions of others. There would be time for that later. Buck and Fitz stood off to the side as Dr. Parker gloved up and knelt down next to the body.

While Buck, Fitz and Dr. Parker worked around the body,

the Sheriff had a couple deputies tape off the area and he asked his forensic team to start working towards the body from the shooter's nest, for lack of a better term. Gomez and Flynn grabbed their gear and headed over to where the two Gunnison County deputies stood watch over the possible nest. Once there, they shook hands all around, gloved up and started working the scene. Walt Jenkins had grabbed the evidence bag with the shell casing in it from Buck's backpack and handed it to Holly and showed her where they found it. He told her that Buck had the pictures of the bullet insitu, as it lay, on his phone.

Walt and Jimmy Sanchez proceeded to walk the two forensic techs through what they had discovered during their initial search. They showed them the gut pile from the elk and indicated the direction the carcass had been dragged and finally hidden behind the downed tree where they found the shell casing. Gomez and Flynn worked the area as thoroughly as possible considering all the leaves and undergrowth and then started working towards the body. They needed to work fast as the light was starting to fade.

Chapter Sixteen

Dr. Parker carefully examined both bullet holes, took a liver temperature, and with the help of Buck, rolled the body over to look for exit wounds or other wounds that might indicate a struggle. The bullet that had penetrated Ranger Corey's forehead had exited out the back of her head and was buried in the debris under the body. It had made quite a mess coming out. Dr. Parker called over Claudia Gomez and asked her to carefully collect the skull fragments and brain matter and then see if she could locate the spent bullet.

The bullet that penetrated Ranger Corey's thigh had not exited and was likely buried in the bone. Dr. Parker would dig that out during the autopsy. Buck picked up Ranger Corey's pistol from the ground next to the body and dropped it into the evidence bag that Fitz was holding. He did the same thing with her radio and cell phone.

"Sheriff," Dr. Parker called. The Sheriff looked down from the top of the ravine.

"You can go ahead and have the rescue team bring down the body bag. Ranger Corey is ready to leave the scene."

She stepped out of the way as the rescue team came down into the ravine and placed the black PVC body bag next to the body.

One of the rescue team members was an Episcopal minister and he knelt next to the body. As the rest of those in the area bowed their heads, he said a prayer for Susan Corey. He then made the sign of the cross and nodded to the rest of the team. The team gently lifted Ranger Corey and placed her in the body bag. Several deputies climbed down into the ravine and everyone pitched in to get the body to the top of the ravine. The trail was too narrow for vehicles, so the team would need to carry the body back to the parking lot. With permission from the Sheriff, they headed out. The light was fading fast.

Dr. Parker stowed her gear and removed her gloves. "Agent Taylor since you were the first on the scene I would like to hear your impressions." She pulled out her cell phone and clicked on the voice recording app.

Buck waited for Fitz to pull out her phone as well and then he began.

"PIS and I followed a very poor blood trail from the dog until we arrived at the top of the ridge above us." Dr. Parker looked at PIS who had been standing off to the side and out of the way and smiled. PIS nodded back.

"Once we arrived on the ridge, we found two larger blood spots, one from the dog and one from Ranger Corey. The dog's blood trail went off the ridge to the opposite side and we were able to follow it back to the trail we came in on. The other spot, which according to PIS appeared to indicate arterial spray, appeared to point in this direction. We followed the direction of the spray and at the bottom of the ravine, we found a large pile of debris. I took photos of everything we did and found, from this point on, including the blood stains on the ridge. After removing the loose leaves and sticks, we found a layer of disturbed soil which we carefully removed and exposed Ranger Corey's face. The bullet hole in her forehead was obvious. We knew that the forehead wound was not the cause of the blood pool on the ridge, so we carefully exposed the rest of the body and discovered the wound in her thigh. After exposing and photographing the body and with the help of the deputies and rescue team members from Gunnison County, we continued to search the area. About forty yards out we found what appears to be the shooter's nest and we also found a gut pile a couple dozen yards beyond that."

Buck stopped to catch his breath and see if they had any questions.

"And your opinion Agent Taylor?" asked Dr. Parker

"My opinion is that Ranger Corey happened upon someone or more than one person who had illegally killed an elk. It appears they had been dragging the elk back in this direction when they heard Ranger Corey and her dog and hid the carcass and themselves behind the tree at the end of the crime scene tape. Either Ranger Corey or her dog did something that spooked the hunters and they shot her through the thigh. Missing her ballistic vest. Ranger Corey then rolled down into the ravine and was subsequently shot in the forehead and buried."

Dr. Parker and Fitz turned off their voice recorders.

"Thank you, Agent Taylor. Your assessment of the crime scene jives with my initial findings. The rest we will confirm during the autopsy."

Buck helped Dr. Parker and then Fitz back up to the top of the ridge and they headed towards the Sheriff. He was talking with his forensic techs as well as two of his deputies. The available light was fading and with the fear of additional booby traps the Sheriff had asked all his people to clear the crime scene before it got completely dark. He would leave two deputies to guard the crime scene and they would be relieved in four hours. He would continue this pattern until everyone returned to the scene first thing in the morning to continue looking for evidence.

The Gunnison team headed back south, with the deepest thanks from Buck and the Sheriff and Buck and PIS followed the rest of the group out of the woods.

"I would like to come back with you in the morning Agent Taylor if that is acceptable? I feel I can be of use in tracking these evil doers."

"No problem PIS. We can meet where we met this morning. Let's say five AM. I'd like to get here before the crowd shows up."

"Very good sir."

The Sheriff's group, including Buck, the Doctor, PIS and the homicide detectives caught up with the rescue team carrying the body bag. The rescue team had stopped just shy of the entrance to the trail and one member of the team was in the process of unfolding an American flag which he then placed over the body bag. He looked at the Sheriff who nodded and the somber procession headed into the parking lot.

The path from the trailhead to the waiting ambulance was lined with several dozen rangers, law enforcement officers and rescue team members who all now stood at attention and saluted as the body bag was carried past them. It seemed to Buck that even the forest creatures had stopped to show their respect. You could have heard a pin drop it was so quiet. The body bag was very gently placed in the waiting ambulance and those assembled began to head back to their various vehicles.

Miguel Vargas walked up to Buck and PIS who had moved off to the side of the trail. "I wanted to thank you personally for finding Susan Corey's body." He shook hands with both Buck and

PIS. "I don't know how I'm gonna tell her son. They were extremely close and he is gonna be devastated. We're all devastated. It's been years since we've had a ranger killed in the line of duty. Susan Corey was one of the best."

Tears formed in his eyes and he turned and walked towards the ambulance. He would ride to the Aspen Valley Hospital in the ambulance with the body. He didn't want Susan Corey to have to travel alone. The ambulance pulled out of the parking lot followed by the contingent of officers, rangers and rescuers all with the emergency lights flashing. It was another incredible show of respect.

Dr. Parker stepped up and thanked Buck and PIS for their help. She told them she would perform the autopsy first thing in the morning and the Sheriff asked Detective Moe Steiner if he could attend the autopsy. Fitz would be back at the crime scene coordinating the search for evidence. Moe simply nodded.

The Sheriff said, "Ok folks. It's been a long, sad day. Let's all meet up tomorrow morning and see if we can find the bastards who did this." They all headed for their cars and pulled out of the parking lot, checking out with the deputy who was manning the barricade.

Buck asked PIS if he could buy him dinner but as Buck expected PIS graciously declined so Buck dropped him off in Wagner Park. Buck then headed to a local deli, grabbed a sandwich and a couple bottles of Coke and headed for his hotel.

Chapter Seventeen

The younger one sat high up in the tree and watched the people below him. He had been watching when the older man and the crazy man with the funny hat had found the lady ranger. The Teacher was not going to be happy. Once they found the lady ranger the older man with the ponytail left and the other man stayed and started looking around. He was soon joined by four other searchers and together they found the hiding spot behind the downed tree.

Now he sat watching as more people arrived led by the older man with the ponytail. Some of them gathered around the lady ranger and others searched the area inside the yellow string. He would have to wait until dark before he would be able to climb down from the tree and run back to the cabin to let the Teacher know what he saw.

He was fascinated by the little boxes some of the people had. They would hold them out in front of themselves and then a light would flash. The first time he thought they were shooting the lady ranger again and this confused him but they also did the same thing behind the downed tree. He didn't understand. Maybe the Teacher would know what this odd behavior was all about.

As darkness started to settle into the ravine, he watched some of the people put the lady ranger's body into a black sack and then they took her away. The others soon followed. Maybe they didn't like being out in the woods at night. He always liked night in the woods. It was peaceful. The others made a lot of noise and sometimes he just needed to get away and he would find refuge in the woods.

He waited until almost full dark before he climbed down from the tree. He knew he shouldn't but he couldn't resist walking back to see where the lady ranger had been buried. Just before he got to the ravine, he was startled by the two men in dark clothes who were hiding up on the ridge. He froze. He knew how to walk in the woods like the Indians the Teacher used to tell them about when they would have story time. He knew they would never hear him, so he silently moved a little closer.

These people were dressed in black clothes and they carried funny looking rifles. They didn't look anything like the rifle he and the hunter had used on the lady ranger. He wondered why they were there. Could it be a trap? The Teacher had told them about the war and how the bad people would hide in the forests and then attack without warning. Were there others around? He hadn't spotted anyone else.

He sat for a minute and listened but they were very quiet. Maybe he should take out the big knife the Teacher had given him for being smart in his lessons and sneak up on them and put them down. He was so close to the one man leaning against the tree that he could stick him before he even knew he was there. Maybe the Teacher would reward him for protecting the others. He might get to use the rifle and become the new hunter. Then he remembered that the Teacher had been very upset that they had killed the lady ranger. He had told them that life was sacred and that killing people was wrong.

He was undecided as he watched the two men. He reached out and touched the handle of the small metal object that was wrapped in leather and hooked around the man's leg. The man jumped and looked around. The other man laughed and asked him if he was afraid of ghosts. The man continued to look around but he never saw the younger one who had scampered back a couple feet into the undergrowth.

It could be fun scaring the men in the black clothes but he knew he needed to get back to the mine and tell the Teacher. Slowly he backed away from the ridge and circled around the far side of the yellow string. He decided to take the long way back to the mine. He did not want to leave any kind of trail for the people to follow. He needed to protect the others.

An hour later he arrived back at the mine. Even though there was no light coming from the tiny hole in the mountainside he was able to find it without difficulty. The others were all asleep but the Teacher was sitting at the old wooden table drinking that foul-tasting liquid from the old bottle. He called it hooch and he wouldn't let any of them touch it. The younger one had taken a taste of the last little bit that was in the Teacher's old mug after he went to sleep one night and it burned his throat and belly as it went down. He never touched the foul liquid again.

The Teacher looked up from his cup. He had sad droopy eyes. He told the Teacher all about the people and about them finding the lady ranger. He also told him about the two men in the black clothes with the funny looking rifles. He waited for the Teacher to tell him he had done a good job of protecting the others but the Teacher just looked sadder and turned back to his cup.

The younger one knew better than to push the Teacher when he was drinking the foul-tasting liquid, so he silently walked away and climbed into his bed. He was soon asleep. The Teacher finished his drink and slowly lowered his head to the table. His last thought was that he hoped he could protect the others.

328

Chapter Eighteen

Buck and PIS arrived at the parking lot before dawn and checked in with the bored looking deputy who was sitting in his patrol car next to the barricade. He reported to Buck that all was quiet and that the third twosome of deputies had checked in about two hours before and he was expecting the second twosome to be walking into the parking lot any time now.

The morning was much cooler than the day before had been and Buck snugged his insulated Carhart jacket up against the breeze that came rushing down from the higher peaks. Fall was definitely in the air this morning but it didn't seem to bother PIS. He was dressed in the same clothes he had on yesterday and his linen coat was unbuttoned. Buck had never seen PIS sweat no matter how hot the weather got and he had never seen him look uncomfortable in the cold. His three-day stubble looked neatly trimmed. Just like always.

They headed down the trail leading back to the ravine. Buck had wanted to get there before the crowds showed up. He wanted to see if they couldn't pick up the killer's trail. Buck was always amazed to watch PIS in the woods. He looked so completely comfortable. The sun had barely started to lighten the sky and Buck needed a flashlight to see his way down the trail but PIS just forged ahead like he had walked this trail a thousand times. The conversation was kept to a minimum as they walked.

About a half hour into the trail they heard the second shift deputies approaching and Buck called out a greeting so they would not be surprised. Buck never liked the idea of surprising people with guns in the dark. The deputies stopped for a minute and exchanged pleasantries. Talked about how cold it had gotten overnight and told Buck about the earlier deputy who thought he felt someone touch his thigh holster. Scared the crap out of him and everyone had a good laugh.

Buck and PIS told them to have a good day and moved on. Buck stopped for a minute just after they left the deputies. He looked at PIS.

"Any chance what the deputy felt wasn't just his imagination?"

PIS thought about it for a minute. "What is it you Yanks often talk about, the killer coming back to the scene of the crime? That would be pretty ballsy I must say."

PIS and Buck continued down the trail until they arrived the ridge. The sun was just starting to come up over the mountains but the chill remained in the air. Buck called out to the two deputies on duty and announced themselves. Buck introduced himself to the two deputies. They were familiar with PIS. While Buck talked with the two deputies, PIS took a walk around the perimeter of the ridge. Curiosity about the deputy being touched got the better of PIS and he started examining the area for tracks or a disturbance of some kind. He found what he was looking for behind the big tree.

"Agent Taylor, a minute if you please."

Buck and the two deputies walked over to where PIS was

standing. PIS knelt down next to the tree and pointed to a small depression in the leaves.

"Someone was definitely out here last night. I don't think the deputy imagined anything."

Buck and the deputies got closer and could barely make out a small boot print in the ground where PIS had scraped aside the leaves. Buck pulled out his cell phone and snapped a picture of the print.

"How can we be sure it wasn't from one of us yesterday?" Buck asked.

"From my recollection, none of us were near this tree. Besides, this print is way too small. Looks almost the size of a child's print or possibly a very small female." PIS responded.

Buck noticed the two deputies move their fingers a little closer to the trigger guard on their rifles and start to look around. Concern was definitely imprinted on their faces. Buck found his own hand sitting on the backstrap of his pistol. He slowly looked around the area.

PIS had stepped back away from the tree and was now down the opposite side of the ridge clearly looking for a trail. He gradually disappeared from view. The others stood their ground. In the distance, they could hear the rest of the investigators and searchers coming down the path.

As the Sheriff approached, he noted the concern and the tension of the small group on the ridge.

"Buck, what's going on?" he asked.

Buck recounted the conversation they had been having just before the Sheriff arrived. At this point, Fitz joined the group as did the two forensic techs. Fitz was the first one to speak up.

"You seriously think that the killer came back here last night and tried to sneak up on our deputies? For what purpose?"

Buck started to respond when PIS returned to the top of the ridge.

"The deputies definitely had a visitor last night and whoever it was, knew this forest very well and was very skilled. The trail disappeared back behind the tree and circled around the crime scene. This individual was out far enough that in most cases we would probably not have even looked for a sign that far out. If I hadn't been following the trail from the tree, I would never have seen it. Very clever."

The group looked at each other not sure what to say, so PIS continued. "I also think this person might have been sitting up in a tree yesterday afternoon watching what we were doing. Found a heavy impression under that big aspen just past the downed tree. It looks like someone dropped down off the lower branch."

"How can you be certain?" asked the Sheriff.

"I had checked that area under the tree right after we found the shooter's nest. Those impressions were not there yesterday afternoon. I lost the trail about a quarter mile from here, heading northeast."

Chapter Nineteen

The Sheriff was not happy. His first thought was that he had left two of his deputies out in the woods by themselves and that they could have been killed. His second thought was "Who the hell are we dealing with?" The perpetrator was in the woods within the past twelve hours. That was a big head start and they had a lot of ground to cover. He was going to need some reinforcements and everyone was going to have to be armed. This was not a job for the search and rescue team.

He called the group together. He explained his plan. The forensic team and Fitz would continue to work the scene under the watchful eye of two deputies. He would contact the Sheriff's in Eagle, Garfield and Gunnison counties and ask them to call out their SWAT teams and any deputies they could spare for a manhunt. He asked Buck to call his Director and see if he could remain on the investigation and then he and PIS would start scouting the area and see if they could narrow down the search area a little. He was still concerned about the booby traps they had found so far and that would hinder the search.

Buck took a minute to step away from the group and pulled

out his phone. He was amazed that he actually had cell service this far back in the woods. He dialed the Director.

Kevin Jackson answered on the second ring. "Hey, Buck. You still in Aspen?"

"Yes, Sir. Things just got a little more complicated."

He went on to explain the most recent events to the Director and told him that the Sheriff would like him to remain on scene and help with the manhunt. He explained about the tracks they found this morning and about the booby traps.

"So you think that someone, possibly the killer, actually snuck up on the two deputies last night? To what end?"

"Can't say for sure sir. But it sure changes the dynamics of the investigation."

"Ok Buck. You stay. What do you need from me?"

"We could use a little help from the Grand Junction office. Whoever you can spare. Might also be wise to get some troopers down here. This manhunt is going to leave the county stretched pretty thin."

"Ok Buck. I will do what I can. In the meantime, you watch your ass. I came close to losing you once. I don't want to go there again." The Director hung up.

Buck put his phone away and went back to talk to the Sheriff. He told the Sheriff it was ok with Director Jackson that he stay and help. He also told him he had requested some help from Grand Junction and had also asked the Director to get in touch with the Colorado State Patrol and have some troopers fill in for his deputies around the county. The Sheriff thanked him for the idea about the troopers. He hadn't gotten that far in his thought process.

Buck pulled out his topographic map from his backpack and laid it on the ground. The Sheriff and PIS knelt next to Buck and

Buck asked PIS to point out where he lost the trail. PIS took a minute to orient himself and pointed to a location about a quarter mile from where they sat.

"I think we should start at the shooter's nest and work out. We know where PIS lost the trail from last night but what bugs me is that we haven't found the trail to their elk camp. We know they killed the elk and dragged it as far as the nest. What we haven't found is where they went after that. I doubt they butchered it here. We would have found evidence of that. They had to continue dragging it out of here but to where?" Buck said.

PIS agreed. Buck looked to the Sheriff who nodded in agreement. He also agreed that Buck and PIS should try to find that trail to the elk camp. The Sheriff then pointed to three locations on the map. He was going to have his SWAT team follow Buck and PIS from the crime scene. He would have a couple of his deputies or reserve deputies meet up with the SWAT teams from the other counties and come in from three other areas. He would request that Gunnison SWAT approach from the Crested Butte Ski area and head north. One of the other SWAT teams would meet up at the Conundrum Creek trailhead off Route 15 and head southwest and the other team would start from Ashcroft off Route 15 and head northwest. They would all converge on where ever Buck and PIS ended up.

Buck agreed with the plan and the Sheriff asked his two SWAT deputies who had been the last team on the site this morning to accompany Buck and PIS. The Sheriff would have another deputy meet up with them later and bring them some sleeping bags and some supplies. He would start the SWAT teams out first thing in the morning. This should give Buck a chance to narrow down the trail. The Sheriff stood, shook hands with Buck and his team and told them to stay safe. He then headed back to the parking lot. He had a lot of calls to make and a lot of people to get organized.

Buck looked at PIS. "You good with this. I can't make you stay."

"No problem Agent Taylor. Happy to serve." PIS replied.

Buck grabbed his backpack and headed down the ridge to the shooter's nest. They needed to follow the elk. But first, they had to find it. That might be easier said than done. Either way, they had a lot of people who were going to be depending on them to get the job done.

PIS started working in a semi-circle around the shooter's nest. He surmised that since they had dragged the elk from the gut pile to the downed tree that they must have been heading in that direction when they encountered the ranger and her dog. He was both amazed and perplexed that whoever they were following was good enough to outsmart him. That didn't happen often.

PIS was out about a quarter mile from the shooter's nest and he was getting more and more aggravated with himself for not being able to spot the trail. Elk carcasses are not light and this one was being dragged across the ground. There had to be a sign. No one is that good. He stopped and looked back through the trees to the shooter's nest. He was on a straight line directly from the gut pile and though the nest. It had to be here. He slowly scanned the area and then he spotted it.

At first, he wasn't sure he was looking at it. It blended in almost perfectly with the surrounding area. He slowly walked forward scanning the area for booby traps as he went. The closer he got the more obvious it became. The undergrowth was denser than in the rest of the area. The sign wasn't much but to a trained eye; it was just enough. He stepped around the growth now noticing for the first time the cut ends of the branches. He stepped to the front of the mass and spotted the blood on the ground. He marveled at the cleverness of the camouflage. No wonder the ranger hadn't found this camp. It was practically perfect in its disguise.

PIS gave a short shrill whistle and waved to Buck and the two deputies who had been following farther back. He waved them over.

"Agent Taylor," he said as Buck and the deputies approached. "I believe we have found the hunting camp." Buck looked at the makeshift lean-to and the blood stain on the dirt floor. He was impressed with its simplicity. He looked around the area and even to his older tired eyes he could see the double track that went off to the Northeast. It was obviously a trail made by some kind of sled. A very heavy sled.

Chapter Twenty

She had discovered her grandfather's trophy box a couple months back and wondered about the significance of the baubles. She knew it was her grandfather's because no one in the family remembered the old cigar box that was hidden in a hole in the wall behind her grandfather's big Craftsman toolbox. She had mentioned it one night at dinner and no one reacted. Well, that's not exactly true. She thought she saw some kind of recognition in her grandmother's eyes but that disappeared as quickly as it arrived.

She waited until the family was asleep and entered her grandfather's room. He was sleeping soundly and she hoped that he might wake up in one of his, getting rarer, lucid moments. She hated to disturb him, so she started to leave his room when a low frail voice stopped her in her tracks.

She approached the bed and stood there with the trophy box held out in front of her. Her grandfather stared at the box in her hands and smiled. She hadn't seen him smile much since she had gotten home from college and it surprised her. He asked her to open the box so he could look inside.

She opened the box and held it so he could see inside. His heart monitor reacted almost immediately and she was afraid the change of tone from the monitor might wake someone else in the small house. She closed the box and pulled it away from him but his expression indicated that he wasn't done. She glanced towards his bedroom door to see if anyone might have heard them and then she reopened the box and he looked deep inside. She asked him what all these pieces meant. He smiled and asked her to remove the gold edged cameo necklace. She held it up for him to see and he told her that this was the first one.

She was a pretty runaway from somewhere up near Chicago. Her family life had been brutal, so she headed west to find her own way in the world. The Korean War was over and a lot of people were leaving their familiar homes to look for financial opportunities out west. The fledgling ski industry and lax laws were drawing people from far and wide and Aspen was no exception. The young woman had found work in a small diner just off the highway and she had found a room with several other young women. Her grandfather had befriended the young woman and they started seeing each other at night. Her grandmother never knew.

After a few weeks, she told him that she was tired of the cold and had decided to head to California. Her grandfather sensed an opportunity about to disappear so he told her he would drive her to the train in Glenwood Springs. He knew she hadn't told any of her friends about him, so he wasn't worried about getting caught. That night, as she slipped out of her rooming house, he met her up the highway and loaded her one suitcase in the trunk of his car. She was dressed in a long skirt, pretty white blouse and around her neck was the cameo neckless. A gift from her mother.

Instead of heading north up highway 82, he turned south and headed out of town. He turned down route 15 which at the time was just a narrow dirt road and found the old fire road that led to Conundrum Creek. She asked him where they were heading and he told her that he wanted to show her a beautiful sight before she left. He finally reached the end of the road, parked the car and reached his arm around her shoulders. The syringe bit deep into her shoulder and she started to yell but he put his hand over her mouth and held it there until the sedative had time to work.

The snow was not that deep on the old trail through the wood as he carried her over his shoulder. The old mining cabin was falling down but it wasn't the cabin he was interested in. Years before when he first arrived in Aspen he spent a lot of time exploring his new home and discovered the old cabin a mile or so down Conundrum Creek. It sat back about a quarter mile from the trail along the creek and was completely hidden from view. What interested him most about the cabin was the shaft the old miners had dug under the wooden floor of the cabin. The shaft went down about thirty feet and then opened into a large long tunnel. He found old broken down and decayed wooden shelves and a lot of old mining equipment.

When he first found the cabin he thought it would be perfect for his needs. He spent several weeks tracking down the owner of the property and discovered that the mining claim that the cabin sat on was owned by a man in Pittsburg who had almost completely forgotten about the old claim. Through a series of letters and telegrams, her grandfather was finally able to get permission to work the old claim and use the cabin.

He spent the next couple months cleaning out the space and installing the things he knew he would need. Along the walls, he bolted in chains and shackles for hands and feet. He purchased several kerosene hurricane lamps and built a bed with a straw mattress. The biggest improvement he was able to make in the machine shop at the ski resort maintenance shed. He fashioned a large metal hatch door that he installed over the old rotten wooden shaft door and put heavy duty hinges and a hasp on it.

The old miners had left an old kerosene stove in the tunnel that they had vented up through the ground a few feet behind the cabin. It would help to keep the chill out of the air and make it a more comfortable space to work in. He also placed his pride and joys in the tunnel. Over the years working at the ski resort he had managed to use the metal shop and had fashioned several beautiful knives and scalpels. Since he made them all himself, there was no record of him buying them. His space was finally complete and his body had tingled at the thought of what would soon be taking place in his secluded little world.

Her grandfather's voice seemed to grow stronger as he told her the rest of the story. He had carried the young woman to the cabin and had unlocked the trap door. He lowered her down the old wooden ladder and placed her on the bed while he fired up the kerosene lanterns and the old kerosene stove. Once the space got warmer, he stripped off all the young woman's clothes and tied her to the bed frame. She had a beautiful body, young and subtle. Her breasts were small but perky and she moaned through the gag as he repeatedly penetrated her. Twice he had to inject her with more sedative to keep her quiet. This was the first time he had ever had sex with someone other than his wife and he was surprised at how much he enjoyed it but the night was fading fast and he needed to get home before his wife woke up.

Now that he was totally spent he untied her from the bed and carried her over to the first set of shackles that he had bolted to the wall. Still naked, he hooked the shackles to her hands and feet. She had started to wake up and the fear in her eyes made him get excited all over again but he didn't have the time to penetrate her again. He was running out of time. He opened an old cabinet that was hanging on the wall and removed a leather bundle. He carefully placed it on the wooden table under the cabinet and unrolled it revealing his assortment of custom made knives.

He chose a thin four-inch-long scalpel from the bundle and admired it in the light from the kerosene lantern. He loved how the scalpel glowed under the yellow light of the lantern. He walked over to the young woman and held the scalpel so she could see it. She squirmed hard against the shackles and started to bleed where the metal shackles cut into her hands and feet.

Slowly and almost delicately he slid the sharp edge of the scalpel along her exposed abdomen. He had used this same technique on several high ranking German Officers during the war. They were a stubborn lot but eventually, they all talked. He didn't care if the young woman talked or not. This was not an interrogation. This was pleasure.

He could hear her screaming through the gag. He spent the next hour slowly slicing the young woman's torso, legs and arms until she finally passed out. She just didn't seem to have the stamina of the German Officers. It was almost disappointing. He walked over to the leather bundle on the bed and using an old rag, cleaned the blood off the scalpel and his hands. He got dressed and then walked back and turned off the kerosene stove and put his bundle back in the cabinet. If she was still alive when he returned he would finish the job but for now the demons were satisfied. He turned off the kerosene lanterns and climbed out of his workspace. He closed the hatch, made sure the padlock was shut and covered the hatch with the decaying floorboards.

The night had gotten colder and it had started to snow. He stood for a minute and just gazed at the beauty of the scene. He felt at peace for the first time in a long time. He walked back to his old car and headed home.

Chapter Twenty-One

She could feel the heat rising as her grandfather told her the story of his first civilian kill. She hadn't realized how sexually aroused she felt as he described the details of the kill. She felt embarrassed that she was feeling this way and didn't understand what was happening. Her grandfather knew exactly what was happening. He could sense that she had the same feelings he did when it came to taking another's life. He finished his story and looked at the vibrant pink color in her cheeks and the little beads of sweat that had formed on her forehead and cheeks.

He told her that he knew she was the one who would follow him. He could feel it deep in his soul. He told her that he would help her find her way along the path that had been taken from him so long ago. She stared in disbelief at what he was saying. She could never take a human life. She had never killed anything nor had the desire to do so. Or did she? His description of the kill had certainly stirred something deep inside her. Something scary but also something wonderful.

Her grandfather started to speak in dribble and incomplete sentences and then he slowly closed his eyes and went to sleep. The lucid moment had passed but she had certainly learned a lot. She looked at the rest of the pieces of jewelry in the little box. Her grandfather just admitted to being a serial killer. One of the first in modern history, yet there had never been any hint that this was the case. She wondered how many more pieces of jewelry would have found their way into his little treasure box if he had not been injured so many years ago. She also wondered how he had kept the demons from destroying him since he was no longer able to feed their needs.

She also wondered if her grandmother knew about his proclivities. She had definitely noticed the change in her grandmother's eyes when she mentioned the old cigar box she had found in the garage. Yet her grandmother never said anything about it.

She looked again at the trophies her grandfather had collected. She wondered about the people they had belonged too. Most of the jewelry appeared to be pieces that would have been worn by young women of the time. She wondered if she would ever be able to get their story from her grandfather. She would need to hurry. She was due back at school in early September. If she was going to act on the feelings that had been stirred up by her grandfather's story, she would need to do it quickly.

She closed the lid of the old box, leaned in and kissed her grandfather on the forehead and left his room. The house was quiet as a church cemetery and she was grateful. She headed back to her room and once inside closed the door and hid the trophy box in the back of her closet. She needed to understand the feelings that her grandfather's story had generated. Was it possible she was a serial killer too?

She had taken psychology classes at school and she understood that serial killers were psychopaths. She always believed they were evil incarnate and that they would stand out in society like freaks at a carnival. Even though she had never had the opportunity to see her grandfather in his early years, she never considered him to be odd. He had never spoken before of his craft. But now. His story had aroused something deep inside of her. Something she now both feared and found interesting and exciting.

Could it be true that he could sense in her the things that made him do the evil deeds he had told her about? It made her sick to her stomach and she ran into her tiny bathroom and vomited in the toilet. No, there was no way she could ever be the evil thing her grandfather had suddenly become in her eyes. But she was also envious of him. If the way she felt while he was telling his story was real, the sensation was amazing. She felt more satisfied, sexually, at this moment than she had with any of the college boys she had slept with over the years.

She knew she needed to pursue the feelings to see if they were real. She was afraid of what she might find and of what she might become but she needed to find out. She laid down on her bed, her head full of strange thoughts and feelings. She decided the first thing she needed to do was to try to find her grandfather's old cabin and see if the shaft was still locked up tight. She would check that out first and then decide on the next step. She fell asleep quickly.

Chapter Twenty Two

Buck took pictures of the makeshift hunting camp with this cell phone camera and noting that he still had one bar sent the pictures along with the GPS coordinates he took from his handheld GPS unit to the Sheriff and to Fitz. Fitz would have to bring the forensic techs down to the camp as soon as they were finished processing the crime scene at the ravine. Buck pulled a roll of crime scene tape from his backpack and with the help of one of the deputies ran the tape around the makeshift hunting camp.

Satisfied with the day's progress so far and with the light beginning to fade the small team decided to wait at the elk camp for the deputy bringing them in supplies and hole up there for the night. With the possibility of booby traps still out in the woods, Buck didn't want anyone getting hurt. At first light they would follow the sled tracks and see where they led. Buck also asked the Sheriff to have the deputy bring one more assault rifle with him. The idea that someone snuck up on the two SWAT deputies at the ravine had everyone a little jumpy.

While one of the deputies cleared the fire ring that someone had worked very hard to try and hide, Buck looked around the elk camp. There wasn't much to see. The blood stains on the ground that had been covered up with leaves gave Buck the impression that the camp had been used for a long time. There were obvious signs that someone had been butchering animals but no evidence of tools. Whoever had cleared out of this camp had done so with a great deal of skill. There was not going to be much physical evidence for the forensic techs to find.

In the distance, Buck could hear the sound of a small high-pitched motor. He assumed the deputy bringing in their supplies was on a dirt bike or a small ATV, all-terrain vehicle. Just then, the driver came through the trees and stopped at the yellow crime scene tape. He had, in fact, been able to maneuver his small ATV along the trail they had left. That was actually quite an accomplishment considering there was not much of a trail to follow.

The deputy shook hands all around and then offloaded two backpacks and a couple sleeping bags from the small cargo cage on the back of the ATV. He had a Remington AR15 slung over his shoulder which he handed to Buck.

"Sheriff said you asked for this," the deputy said. "He also sent along some deli sandwiches for dinner, some water bottles and danishes for breakfast."

Buck was also glad to see that the Sheriff sent along a couple bottles of Coke. He would make sure he thanked the Sheriff.

"Sheriff wanted me to tell you that he has several deputies watching all the known trailheads on both Routes 13 and 15 and that the SWAT teams will head out at first light according to the plan you guys came up with earlier."

Buck thanked the deputy for the supplies and the information and the deputy climbed aboard the ATV and headed back up the trail. He wanted to get out of the woods before total dark. PIS had taken the food bag and was in the process of handing out sandwiches and water bottles. They each found a little piece of the forest and set their tired bodies down for a breather and nourishment.

The two deputies smiled at each other as they watched PIS open his backpack, remove his little tin and start to brew himself a small pot of tea. Everyone had heard the stories of PIS and his china tea set but few had ever seen it for real. Buck watched them but said nothing. Buck understood that for PIS this was a very private moment and he didn't want to interfere.

PIS looked up at the deputies as he took his first sip of tea from the china cup. "Even in the wilderness, gentlemen, we must remain civilized and there is nothing more civilized than a good cup of tea."

Everyone chuckled and dug into their meals. The sandwiches were excellent and as the sun set and the forest became darker everyone settled in for the night. It would be chilly tonight but the sleeping bags the Sheriff had sent them would be most welcome.

Buck rolled his sleeping bag out on a bunch of leaves and pine boughs he had cut and made himself a nice insulated platform to sleep on. He crawled into the sleeping bag and rested his head on his backpack. He had found a spot near the fire pit that gave him a small opening through which to look at the milky way above. This far into the forest the view of the Milky Way was incredible.

Buck looked up at the sky and thought back to the camping trips his family had taken when the kids were younger. After the kids had gone to sleep, he and Lucy would lie next to each other and stare at the stars. With no city lights to lessen the view, they were able to see billions of stars and even the swirling celestial cloud that flowed through the milky way. It was always magical, only this time it brought a tear to his eyes knowing that he would never be able to share another moment like that with Lucy. Buck closed his eyes and drifted off to sleep.

Buck had asked one of the two deputies to take the first watch. Everyone was concerned about having a repeat of the night before and did not want to face the possibility of someone sneaking up on the group.

The night had gotten cold as Buck slowly opened his eyes. He wasn't sure what had woken him but he sensed something was not quite right. He snapped open the thumb break on his holster and put his hand on the gun. He slowly looked to his left and noticed PIS lying flat on his back with his eyes wide open. PIS slowly turned his head toward Buck.

"We are not alone," PIS said in a whisper. Buck tensed and looked towards the two deputies. They both appeared to be sound asleep.

"Where?" asked Buck.

"Not sure. Could be maybe twenty yards out behind the lean-to. There might be two of them. Can't tell for sure."

"How do you want to handle this?" asked Buck

The fire had settled down into just a pile of hot embers and the forest was almost as dark as being inside a cave. PIS slowly slid out of his sleeping bag and still lying flat on the ground, crawled deeper into the woods behind them. Buck pulled his pistol out of his holster and slowly unzipped the sleeping bag. He would be ready to move if PIS needed help.

The deputy on the other side of Buck must have sensed something going on but Buck signaled for him to stay put. The deputy lowered himself back down on his backpack but Buck saw him pull out his service weapon and place it on top of his sleeping bag. Buck wasn't sure how long PIS was gone but his internal alarm clock told him it was about twenty minutes. Twenty very tense minutes.

Chapter Twenty-Three

PIS called out from somewhere behind the lean-to. "PIS coming in." Slowly he emerged from the right side of the lean-to. Buck and the first deputy crawled out of the sleeping bags, guns in hand. The other deputy suddenly woke up and wondered out loud what was going on. Buck grabbed a log off the pile they had collected earlier and dropped in on the fire. The embers caught the dry wood and the flames exploded adding much-appreciated light to the dark forest.

PIS stood next to the fire. "I could account for two of them. I think that was it. The first one was about thirty yards out behind a group of shrubs to the north. Had a very good view of our little camp. The second one was up a tree to the south. No more than fifteen yards. They must have heard me moving through the undergrowth because they moved off quickly. I will check for tracks in the morning."

The one deputy swore under his breath. Buck looked around. "Sounds like the same MO, modus operandi, from the other night at the ravine. You certain they are gone?"

PIS nodded and Buck and the two deputies holstered their pistols. No one was going back to sleep anytime soon. Buck was amazed at how easily PIS had been able to move around in the dark forest. The guy had some mad skills and even though Buck never asked specifically, he wondered where PIS had received his training. It certainly didn't come from being a homeless guy in Aspen.

The one deputy asked the question that everyone had on their minds. "What the fuck are we dealing with? What kind of criminal stays in the area of the crime and follows the police around?"

"Good question," responded Buck. "Not any kind of criminal I've ever encountered. Good thing is, we know they are still in the area and we know there are at least two of them."

Everyone agreed with Buck's statement but Buck felt uneasy. He wondered why the killers hadn't tried to run. What was keeping them in the area? Buck didn't have enough evidence to be able to answer that question, so he pushed it to the back of his mind. He would definitely figure out the answer before this was over.

Buck sat back on his sleeping bag and watched the fire. PIS walked over and sat down next to him. Buck noticed the perplexed look on PIS's face.

"What's got you bugged?" he asked.

PIS thought for a minute. "Either my skills are getting rusty, or we are up against people who have skills that far exceed mine."

PIS was quiet for a minute and Buck could see he was replaying the whole thing in his head. He finally spoke. "I was as quiet as a church mouse when I moved through the woods, yet they had me before I even got close to them and they were able to scamper off without me having any idea they were moving."

Buck sensed his frustration. PIS had skills in the woods that Buck could only marvel at. If PIS was concerned, then the people they were after were incredibly dangerous. They had already shown themselves to be cold-blooded enough to shoot a human being in the head at close range and they had proven they were not afraid to sneak up and observe armed law enforcement personnel.

Buck assured PIS that it wasn't his skills that were lacking. It was obvious that the people they were chasing knew the woods better than they did and they would just need to be a little more diligent. Buck sensed that they were getting close. They all needed to stay focused.

As dawn started to break over the mountains and the sky turned a pale shade of pink everyone in the camp felt a little relieved. They were now able to see around them and some of the concerns from the night before lifted. Each man packed up his sleeping bag and they each ate a danish for breakfast. PIS had disappeared into the woods as soon as it was light enough to see and he finally came walking back into camp.

"Agent Taylor, there were definitely two culprits last night as I had suspected. They both headed off in different directions but they met up again about a quarter mile from here. I also found the rest of the trail we spotted yesterday. They had done a bang-up job trying to hide it but the grooves from the sled were too deep to eradicate completely."

"Excellent, then we have a trail to follow." He looked at each man individually. "We need to stay alert. We know they are good at building booby traps and they are also not afraid to get close to us. Let's douse the fire and get moving. The SWAT teams will be starting soon. We need a target."

With that, the one deputy emptied a water bottle on the fire embers and stirred them around with a stick. The last thing they needed out here was a forest fire. PIS slung his backpack over his shoulders and started for the sled trail. The others followed a couple yards behind.

Chapter Twenty-Four

They had been following the men for almost an hour when the men finally settled in for the night. They had lit a small fire and then all slipped into their sleeping bags. The hunter had a good observation spot just beyond the lean-to and he had watched them all settle in. The younger one was on the other side of the camp up in a big aspen tree.

Once he was confident that the men were asleep, the younger one had silently climbed down from the tree and carefully snuck up to just outside their camp. He could hear the men softly breathing he was so close. At one point he was going to see if he could reach one of the rifles but the old man with the ponytail started to move around, so he thought it best to back off. He wasn't sure what he would do if he did get one of the rifles.

The men had rifles that didn't look anything like the old rifle the hunter used. Theirs were all black and had lots of things that seemed to be attached. The rifle the Teacher had given the hunter was just a wooden stock and a barrel. Nothing fancy but it did a good job on the animals they hunted.

The Teacher had told them all stories about a big war in the jungle and that he had used a rifle that was black and had things attached to it. It sounded just like the rifle the men were carrying. The younger one thought it would make a great prize to bring one of these back for the Teacher and the Teacher might reward him and let him use the black rifle to hunt with. Since the Teacher's hands shook really bad sometimes he didn't think the Teacher would be able to use the rifle anyway.

The men had remained quiet for quite some time, so the younger one moved back towards the tree he had been hiding in. The almost unperceivable clicking sound alerted him that something was wrong. The hunter had seen something, so he froze where he was. He glanced back through the trees just in time to see the old man with the ponytail slide quietly out of his sleeping bag and crawl into the woods. The old man with the ponytail made almost no noise as he scooted along the ground.

The younger one watched him for a minute. The old man with the ponytail had skills just like he and the hunter had. He had found their trails and traps. He wondered if the old man had been taught by the Teacher. The Teacher had told them that he had taught a lot of men during the jungle war how to survive in the woods. Maybe the old man with the ponytail was one of the Teacher's students. They would need to be careful if that was the case. He might know how to set traps like he and the hunter knew how to do and that could be dangerous.

The younger one knew he should head back to the safe place but he wanted to test the old man with the ponytail, so he started to move away from the men's camp. He would work his way back to the trail by making a big circle around the camp. He wanted to see if the old man with the ponytail would be able to track him so he decided to lead him towards one of the old animal trails that would take the men away from the safe place.

He made small noises as he went, crackling a leaf or snapping a small stick. He was having fun but then the old man with the ponytail stopped and looked at something really carefully on the ground and while still kneeling looked around. He then quietly set off in a different direction. The younger one wasn't sure what the old man with the ponytail had found but he was now heading back towards the hunter.

The younger one gave a soft, low-pitched whistle that he knew most people would never be able to hear but he knew the hunter would hear it. The low-pitched whistle was something momma had taught them all and it meant danger and for everyone to head back to the safe place. He continued down the old animal trail for a ways and then circled back around through the trees and headed home.

The younger one caught up with the hunter just down the trail from the safe place and then hid in the undergrowth and watched the trail for a while to make sure they had gotten away. Feeling confident that they had not been followed by the old man with the ponytail, they reset the booby trap on the trail and headed for the mine.

When they got back inside the mine, the Teacher was just starting breakfast for the others. They told him about the old man with the ponytail and that maybe he was one of the men the Teacher had taught how to survive in the woods. The younger one told him about playing with the old man with the ponytail and that he was as good as they were in the woods.

The Teacher listened to their story and looked concerned. His hands were shaking badly today and he was having trouble using the knife to put the jelly on the bread. The older girl finally took the knife and started making the sandwiches. They were running out of bread and some other things and they would need to plan a raid on one of the big houses.

The Teacher reassured them that everything would be ok and that once the men left the woods, they would sneak into the big empty house up by the ski lift and raid their food stores again.

The teacher sat down on the old chair and rested his face in his hands. The others went about their business of cleaning up the living area in the mine but the hunter sat down next to the Teacher and rested his hand on the Teacher's arm. The Teacher looked at him and the younger one and they saw the concern on his face. The Teacher told them to go back down by the cabin and make sure the traps were set just like he had shown them.

The hunter grabbed his rifle and the younger one went to the old box and took out some metal spikes and a hammer and a spool of old fishing line. The teacher led the younger one to the old green box and using the key from his pocket he unlocked the box and opened the lid. The younger one had never seen what was inside the old green box. The Teacher had told them never to touch the box and they never did.

The Teacher pulled out several old cardboard tubes with strings hanging out of one end. The tubes looked very old and they were covered in some kind of white powder. He also took out some metal tubes with wires attached to them along with a metal box with a T handle stuck in it. He put it all in an old backpack. He told the others to stay in the cave and that he, the hunter and the younger one would be back in a while. The Teacher slung the backpack over his shoulder and the three of them headed for the mine entrance.

Chapter Twenty-Five

Once outside and away from the mine the hunter and the younger one watched the Teacher as he very carefully slid one of the metal tubes into each of the cardboard tubes. He then took a big spool of wire that he had taken from the cabinet in the kitchen area and handed it to the hunter and the younger one. He told them to run the wire from the mine entrance back to the cabin. He needed six wire runs to different spots around the cabin and he pointed out where to run them. They took the spool and headed back towards the mine entrance.

The Teacher was worried. Many times, over the years, people had gotten close to the cabin or the mine entrance but this felt different and each time they had been able to either run them off with animal noises or simply hide in the woods or in the mine until they passed. These men were on a mission. He had seen determination like that during the war. These men were dangerous and he was convinced that they were only a scouting party. He was sure that sooner or later the woods would be crawling with people looking for his little family. The hunter had killed one of theirs and they were out for blood.

The Teacher had promised momma that he would do

everything he could to protect the family and he had been successful for a long time. Now, however, he was worried that he might not have enough left to do the job. He was getting on in years and each day his hands seem to shake a lot more. He was also having trouble talking and doing even the slightest of chores. He was worried about what would happen to the family if he didn't wake up one morning. His thoughts went back to that day so many years ago.

He joined the army right out of high school and had found the family he never had before. His mom worked nights as a waitress at a local greasy spoon and his dad worked at the car plant in town. His dad was also a drinker and he had no problem beating on his wife and son when he tied one on, which seemed to be almost every night. The day after graduation he had headed for the army recruiting station and enlisted. The war in Vietnam was in full swing and he was able to leave for boot camp within two days of enlisting. He left that little west Texas town and never looked back.

Years of getting beat up by his father had given him an inner strength and he was able to handle everything the army threw at him. His test scores and his skills during boot camp got him noticed and he was offered a chance to become an Army Ranger. He thrived in this new environment and was soon proficient with every weapon the army had to offer and his escape and evasion skills put him at the top of his class.

He was in the middle of his third tour of duty in Vietnam when something inside snapped. Maybe it was too many close calls while on patrol, or maybe it was that he just could no longer stand seeing the kind of destruction and death that war caused or maybe he just got a conscience, but anyway, he had finally had it with war and killing.

His unit had come upon a small village in the Vietnam

highlands that they believed was being used by the Viet Cong. They interrogated the local elder who denied it but his unit wasn't satisfied. To force the elder to talk they started shooting the civilians one by one. There was screaming and tears and then all of a sudden he lost control of the situation and his unit. He tried to stop the frenzy but by the time his men were finished, there was nothing they could do except set the village on fire and move down the road. He was grief-stricken and after brooding about it for a couple days, he swore to his men that he would see to it that they all paid for the terrible massacre.

A week later his unit was involved in a horrible battle for a valley that he cared nothing about and after three-days of intense fighting, he finally had enough. Sometime during the third night of the battle, he slipped away from his tiny foxhole and silently disappeared into the forest surrounding the valley. For several weeks he used his escape and evasion skills to hide from enemy patrols until he finally crossed into Laos and eventually made his way to Bangkok in Thailand.

No longer in uniform and with long hair and a heavy beard he looked like some kind of homeless beggar. During his days in Bangkok he looked for ways to get out of the country and at night he would rummage through trash to find anything edible. Eventually, he found work on a tramp steamer with an Indonesian captain who didn't care about papers. He only cared about hard work.

For six months he sailed around the Indian Ocean before finally leaving the ship in Abu Dhabi in the United Arab Emirates. With money in his pocket he was able to fly to Spain and then on to Central America, eventually making is way across the US/ Mexico Border in New Mexico. Airport security at the time was pretty much nonexistent and no one ever questioned his driver's license. He assumed the army figured he had died in the battle for the valley and had never even looked for him.

He hitchhiked his way north through New Mexico and eventually found himself in Aspen, Colorado. He fit right in. The counterculture scene was in full swing and there were drugs and women everywhere. With his long hair and dirty clothes, he looked like everyone else but he found that he just couldn't deal with all the people. One day he headed back into the forest and after a few weeks of just being alone in his own thoughts, he stumbled on an old miner's cabin.

The cabin hadn't been lived in for years but it had good bones and he was able to use the scraps from the original cabin to fix it up, so it was livable. The miner, whoever he was, had tapped into a small spring so the cabin had running water and he also found the old mine a few hundred feet back behind the cabin. He spent the next several years fixing everything up so he had a rugged but comfortable home and more importantly he found the privacy he so badly wanted.

Before leaving Aspen, he bought an old M1 carbine from a pawn shop along with a box of 30 caliber ammo. He was a crack shot and had no problem making sure he had plenty of food to eat. All in all, he had a good life.

Chapter Twenty-Six

His thoughts turned to the morning he had found them. The snowstorm had been furious and had lasted three-days and when it was over, there was probably three feet of fresh snow on the ground. The temperature had dropped way below freezing but the little miner's cabin was warm and cozy. He hated the idea of having to go out in the cold but his fresh meat supply was running low and he had decided before the storm set in that he needed to do some hunting to replenish his stock. The fact that the storm lasted three-days only made his situation worse, so he put on his long underwear, every sweater he owned, which was only two, and his coat, hat and gloves and head out into the snow.

The day had dawned beautiful. The sky through the trees was a bright robin's egg blue and there wasn't a cloud to be seen. The fresh mat of snow on the ground was untracked and sparkled in the morning sunlight. He just stood in the doorway of his little cabin and admired the beauty that surrounded him. He closed the cabin door and headed out.

He found the old Ford station wagon on an old Forest Service fire road that hardly anyone ever used. The car was almost buried to its roof. The front wheels were sitting in a ravine off the side of the road. He thought it might be abandoned until he heard a faint cry coming from inside the car. Fearing the worst, he dropped the bundle of snowshoe hares he had shot and with his hands he started digging for the driver's door.

It was hard work and he was soaked to the bone and cold as hell when he finally cleared enough snow to open the driver's door. He would never forget the sight he found inside the car. The woman sitting in the driver's seat was barely conscious. She was wrapped in a coat and had wrapped herself up in a blanket, but it hadn't helped. Her skin was cold to the touch and he feared she was dead until she slowly opened her eyes. She stared at him and was able to mutter a short sentence. "Help my babies."

He looked behind her and couldn't believe his eyes. There, filling the back seat and the rear back facing seat where eight kids all wrapped in blankets with just their little faces visible. He was shocked. Most of them were barely moving and he knew he needed to do something before they froze to death. He had no idea how long they had been in the car but their situation was desperate. He told the woman he would go and get help but with a soft almost dying voice the woman pleaded with him not to bring the authorities.

He spent the next hour clearing the doors so he could get the kids out of the car one at a time. The whole gang of them were stiff and barely able to move but night was falling and he needed to get this little troop to his cabin before the temperature dropped even more. They would not survive another night in the woods.

Still wrapped in their blankets the kids helped each other as they struggled through the deep snow trying to follow the man's tracks. The woman, barely able to walk, managed to carry one of the youngest children and he had two of them in his arms besides the bunch of snowshoe hares. It took several torturous hours of trudging through the deep snow but his little troop finally reached the little cabin. He opened the door and ushered them all inside. It was going to be a tight fit but the closeness of their bodies would help them thaw out. Once inside they all crashed on whatever piece of real estate they could find and within a matter of minutes, the warmth of the cabin had everyone asleep.

He awoke to the smell of rabbits cooking in the big cast iron pot. Shaking the cobwebs out of his head, he remembered finding the woman and kids in the car in the woods and hiking back to the cabin. He raised his head from the table he had fallen asleep on and there, standing in front of his little wood stove, was an angel with a wooden spoon. The woman was taller than he thought she was the night before and she had the most beautiful long blond hair hanging down her back almost to her waist. For a minute he just sat there and looked at her.

She turned and was startled to see him looking at her. Her face glowed in the early morning light coming through the old lead glass window. She turned back to the stove and continued to stir the rabbit stew she had prepared. Gradually the children awoke and soon the little cabin was filled with more noise than he was used to. It was almost scary. He had lived alone for such a long time that having people around, especially this many, made him uneasy.

The whole gang gobbled down the rabbit stew like they hadn't eaten in weeks, which might have been the case and then everyone settled down and sleep overtook them once again. While everyone was asleep, he hiked back to the car and made several trips carrying what meager bits of luggage they had. He had hoped to find something in the car that would explain who she was and how she came to be stuck in the middle of the mountains in a snowstorm with eight kids.

Back at the cabin with their meager belongings he finally got some of the answers he was seeking. She told him that she had been driving through the mountains heading for a new start in California. She had family out there who were going to help her with her kids. She had taken a wrong turn after leaving Aspen and then the storm hit and she was completely lost. When the front tires went into the ravine, she knew they were in trouble so she wrapped everyone up in what she could and prayed for a miracle. God had sent him as an answer to her prayers.

She told him she was from Florida and that two of the children were hers from a failed marriage and the rest were either adopted or in foster care. She said she had permission from Florida to take the kids to California to a new life. He doubted the story right from the first minute she opened her mouth. He had interrogated enough prisoners while he was in Vietnam and he knew when people were lying to him. This woman was nothing but one big lie.

She never ever did give him a story he could believe but over the years he had finally stopped asking and they settled into a quiet life. The kids were growing and he found a new purpose in teaching them things, important things, like reading and writing but also necessary things like how to pick locks, set up traps and survive. The kids became very good at breaking into the huge mansions that had begun to spring up around Aspen over the years. Many of these were second homes for rich celebrities and business people and they were empty a good portion of the year.

They expanded the cabin to accommodate the entire gang and had also set up a second home back in the old mine. This was their safe place in case someone got too close to the cabin. They had used it several times especially recently as it seemed there were a lot more people hiking in the woods

Things went along fine until one morning two years ago when the woman woke up feverish and exhausted. She had tried to stand at the stove to cook breakfast but had passed out. Luckily, he was standing behind her and he was able to get her into the bed they shared. Over the next several days she woke up delirious and had very little idea of who anyone was. The Teacher, as the kids had been calling him, was beside himself with worry but he knew she would never let him go for help. On the third day, she didn't recognize him or the children. On the fourth morning she didn't wake up at all and her breathing was shallow and labored. She stopped breathing later that day.

In all the years they had lived in the same cabin the Teacher had never really gotten the whole story from her. He was able to glean that she had actually started out in West Virginia and that somewhere along the road she had decided to start kidnapping small children who were too young to know any better. She never told him how she chose the kids to kidnap or what she really intended to do with them and she never explained why their parents didn't come looking for them but over the years they had all become one big family and he finally stopped asking.

The children had chosen a beautiful spot above the mine for her grave. From there she would have a view of the entire area and they were very pleased with their choice. They had dressed her in a dress she had made that she always intended to wear for a special occasion but never had. She looked beautiful. The Teacher wrapped her in a blanket, carried her up the mountain to the grave site and slowly laid her in the shallow grave the oldest boys had dug. Each child had been told to find something special in the woods that they thought momma might like and they each placed their special treasure in the grave with her. The Teacher then shoveled the dirt back into the grave and then they all said the Lord's Prayer.

The Teacher knew that any chance of ever finding out her true story was now gone forever and he decided that the most important thing at this point was to keep his little family together. He had grown very fond of the children over the years and took great pride in teaching them the things they would need to know as their lives progressed. He also wondered what would happen if they eventually decided to leave the cabin. They were approaching that age where they would probably want more out of life than what was available in their little family group.

And now here they were setting up defenses and traps to protect their little family from the outside world. He had no doubt his children would be able to survive in the real world. He often would sneak into Aspen at night to steal food and other things they needed and he always tried to bring back a current newspaper or a new book to help them with their education. He was amazed at how smart the children were and how quickly they learned new skills. He was also amazed at how quickly and easily they learned to break into houses or stores without leaving any signs of having been there. Their survival skills, thanks to him, were top notch.

He had known for a while now that his days were numbered. He had read up on Parkinson's Disease in a medical book the children had stolen from a doctor's house and he believed that this was the ailment that was causing the hand tremors. He didn't think he had long to live but as long as he had a breath to take, he would do all he could to protect his family.

Chapter Twenty-Seven

PIS was very quiet as he scanned the ground around him. Once they found the first booby trap, in a spot that PIS had checked during his nighttime chase of their two followers, it was decided that Buck and the two deputies would stay several yards behind PIS. He had been able to disarm the trap but they didn't want to take any chances. Whoever they were chasing had been able to set up the trap in the dark, while being pursued by PIS.

Buck had spoken with the Sheriff by radio right after they had gotten on the trail. He finally had a decent signal and he was able to give the Sheriff their coordinates from his handheld GPS unit. The Sheriff reported back that the SWAT teams were just starting to enter the woods and based on Buck's coordinates they should meet up in a couple hours.

"Sheriff please be sure to remind everyone about the booby traps. We have uncovered several more since we left yesterday." Buck said.

"You got it, Buck. Everyone has been told to be really careful. By the way, the guys from Gunnison are coming up on horseback so they may get there before the rest of the teams. You guys stay safe."

Buck wrapped up his radio call and they started back down

the trail. PIS had moved ahead and Buck and the two deputies had lost sight of him. Buck wasn't sure where the feeling came from but his head told him to stop and he held up his fist. The two deputies knelt down and raised their assault rifles in a defensive position.

Buck had his assault rifle slung over his shoulder and he immediately pulled it around and took the same position as the deputies. They stopped, barely breathing and listened. All Buck could hear was the breeze rustling through the trees. Then the deputy, Manning, pointed to his ear and then pointed off to the left. Buck strained to listen. Then he heard it. There was definitely movement off to the left. Buck couldn't tell how far off but it was just within his hearing range.

Buck looked ahead for PIS but he still couldn't see him. Deputy Manning moved slightly to his left while staying in a crouch while Deputy Sanchez shifted to the right and covered the trail they had just come down with his rifle. They waited.

Buck had learned a little bit about the two deputies while they were eating their sandwiches the night before. Deputy Rick Manning had been with the Pitkin County Sheriff's department for about three years. He had been born and raised in the county and his Dad owned a gas station and convenience store in Carbondale. He was single and had served two tours in Afghanistan as a Marine before joining the department.

Deputy Michael Sanchez had been with the department about six years. He had been a standout bull rider in high school in Waco, Texas and had hoped to move into the PBR, Pro Bull Riders Association, after graduation but a bad trip on the back of a fiery bull ended with a career stopping knee injury. Unable to fulfill his lifelong dream to be a pro bull rider, Michael had spent a couple years just bumming around the western US before he settled in Dillon,

Colorado. When he heard about an opening in the Pitkin County Sheriff's office, he applied and was surprised to be one of three people chosen for the three jobs available. Two years ago he married a local girl and they had a beautiful baby girl. His promotion to the county SWAT team had been a highlight of his life to this point.

Buck wasn't sure what to do at this point. He didn't want to move deeper into the woods because, with booby traps still a real possibility, this could be a trap to draw them in. He was just about to decide on a plan when he spotted a bright red spot coming through the trees. Everyone tensed until they spotted PIS.

Buck and the deputies stood as he approached and he stepped onto the trail and stopped to catch his breath. Buck looked at him with a questioning expression.

"Sorry Agent Taylor. Didn't mean to cause a stir." He caught his breath. "We were being followed again. Only one this time but close enough that I spotted him through the trees. I didn't want to lose him, so I broke off the trail and tried to circle around him."

"It looks like you didn't catch him. What happened?" asked Buck.

"Didn't need to. I think we are getting close," replied PIS

"Well, what are we waiting for? Let's go get him!" said Deputy Sanchez.

"Hang on there young fella. This one is very crafty and it could be a trap."

PIS looked at Buck. "There is an old miner's cabin up ahead about half a mile. I didn't get too close but it looks abandoned. The person I was following disappeared into the woods behind the cabin." PIS went on to tell them that he had encountered two more traps while following the person of interest.

With booby traps still lurking in the woods, they would need to approach the cabin with caution. Since PIS was unarmed Buck suggested he remain back on the trail once they got close to the cabin. PIS just laughed and headed down the trail. Buck looked at the two deputies who both just shrugged their shoulders. Buck nodded in agreement and they headed off after PIS. This time they kept a little more distance between each other and Sanchez covered their rear.

The trail they had been following had almost completely disappeared when Buck and the deputies caught up with PIS who was now kneeling behind a downed tree. He pointed over the tree and Buck and Manning knelt next to him. Sanchez had taken a position behind another tree and was acting as lookout.

Buck spotted the little cabin about fifty yards off through the trees. It sat in a little clearing in the trees. Buck slowly scanned the area. As far as he could tell the little cabin appeared to be abandoned. But where had the person gone that PIS had followed? There were no visible trails leading away from the cabin.

Deputy Manning handed Buck a small pair of binoculars and Buck carefully studied the area around the cabin. It looked abandoned, just like PIS had told them but he had an uneasy feeling. They needed to clear the little cabin so they could continue trying to follow their person of interest. Buck had the two deputies move off the trail to the right and left. PIS reminded them to watch where they placed their feet and they both acknowledged that they understood. The two deputies would approach the little cabin from the sides while he and PIS approached the cabin head on. Once again Buck suggested that PIS stay back while he approached the cabin but PIS just smiled.

Buck started moving down what was left of the almost invisible trail and PIS followed a couple yards behind him. That was the agreement they had reached since PIS was unarmed. Both deputies had moved off the trail about twenty yards and were slowly working their way toward the cabin always keeping Buck and PIS in sight. Buck with his rifle up to his shoulder moved slowly at a slight crouch. Whenever he could, he would step slightly off the trail and hide behind an available tree. He continually scanned the area with his rifle as they approached the cabin.

The explosions caught them completely off guard. The first explosion went off just to the right of Deputy Manning and knocked him to the ground. The second explosion went off a few seconds later between the cabin and Deputy Sanchez who dove for cover behind a large aspen tree. Buck and PIS had just reached the cabin when the first two explosions occurred. Immediately after the second explosion PIS reacted and threw himself against Buck driving him away from the cabin. They both hit the ground just as the front of the cabin exploded. The air was filled with flying pieces of wood and glass. Buck and PIS covered their heads with their arms and tried to bury themselves deeper into the leaves and the undergrowth. The sound was deafening.

Chapter Twenty-Eight

She had spent a good part of her summer vacation trying to locate her grandfather's torture chamber. She knew it was somewhere along Conundrum Creek but she was having a great deal of difficulty locating it. She didn't have much time to spend with her grandfather since she was working in a local restaurant, so she missed out on a lot of lucid moments. Those few times she was able to sit and talk with him he didn't make a lot of sense.

The last time she found her grandfather in a mood to talk he spent most of the time talking about his second kill. He had asked to see his treasure box again and she went and pulled it from the hiding space behind the big toolbox in the garage. He spent a lot of time looking at the small treasures but he kept coming back to a thin silver bracelet. He would stare at it for a few seconds, look at something else and then repeat the process as if drawn to it.

She knew better than to interrupt his train of thought, so she waited patiently until he was ready to tell his story. She took the bracelet from the treasure box for him, he stared at it and sat back against his pillow.

The young woman who owned the bracelet was from Maine. He couldn't remember the city but he sure remembered her. She was petite and pretty. He couldn't remember how old she was but she was old enough to drink and that was where he found her. She was on her way to Oregon to meet up with some friends from high school.

Her family didn't know she was in Aspen. She had told them she was going to Florida for spring break but she changed her mind at the bus station and decided to go to Oregon where her high school boyfriend was going to school. He found out that the boyfriend had no idea that she was on her way. She would be perfect. He discovered that the girl from Maine had no place to stay in Aspen and almost no money for food, so he found her a place to sleep in an old shed behind the maintenance shop.

Even though he was older than she was he liked the way she flirted with him. Her attention got him very excited. When he would visit her after work, she always seemed pleased to see him and she seemed to enjoy teasing him. He figured that the bright red lipstick was just for him. He told her about a hot spring located south of Aspen and that they could go there. Clothing was optional which didn't seem to bother her.

Telling his wife he had to work a night shift he met the girl at the shed and they headed for the old forest service road that led to the hot spring. Before they had even gotten to the spring, she had started to take off her clothes in the car. She reached over at one point and ran her hand along the zipper in his pants. He almost smashed into a tree along the narrow dirt road.

He pulled the car off the road and into the forest in a spot he had picked for its privacy. Once he stopped the car, she started to unbuckle his pants. He was more than ready as she straddled him in the front seat. He was so preoccupied that he almost forgot the syringe he had placed in the door pocket. She was so preoccupied that she never even flinched when he pushed the needle into her shoulder. They both exploded together and then she passed out in his arms. He pushed her off and got out of the car. Pulling up his pants he finished dressing and went to the passenger side door and pulled her out onto the ground.

The area was as dark as a cave but he had memorized the trail back to his little house of horrors and a half hour later he was unlocking the hatch under the floor of his little miner's cabin and lowering her down into the shaft. Once he got her down to the bottom of the shaft, he tied her to the bed just as he had done the first time and raped her for several hours until he was completely exhausted.

He then dragged her over to the shackles attached to the wall and bolted her in. He admired her naked body for quite a while before he got started. She was almost perfect. Once again, he opened the cabinet and removed his knife collection and after careful examination, he chose a ten-inch-long filet knife.

He stripped of his clothes and approached the still unconscious young girl. He had read an article about an old Chinese torture technique called lingchi or death by a thousand cuts. The Chinese had used this technique to torture people prior to its abolishment around 1905. Basically, it involved using non-lethal cuts and slices to ensure that the victim survived for a long period of time. He was excited to see how many cuts he could make on this young girl before she died. He wanted to wait for her to regain consciousness but he was getting excited, so he decided to begin.

At some point early on the young girl woke up and the fear in her eyes only made his excitement greater. He realized that although he was enjoying the experience that he needed more practice in controlling his cuts. He felt that some were way to deep and after only an hour the young girl was bleeding profusely. He knew he should slow down and take his time but he kept getting more and more excited.

He was disappointed when the young girl finally passed out for good. He had been keeping count and had only gotten to two hundred slices.

He would need more practice. He sat for a minute on the end of the bed and admired his handy work. He really liked what he saw.

He cleaned up his tools, got dressed and turned off the kerosene lantern. He was completely exhausted but excited by the prospect of practicing this technique some more.

She tried to ask her grandfather for better directions to the shaft but he just leaned his head back into his pillow and fell asleep. She found herself getting more and more excited as he described the technique. She wondered if she would have the strength to perfect what her grandfather had started. She put the bracelet back in the box and headed back to the garage to hide the box.

She felt very pleased with herself that she was giving her grandfather the chance to relive his life from so long ago. She hoped when he finally rested for the last time that he would feel good about his life. She was glad she could help him relive those memories.

She would need to continue her quest to find the hidden shaft and the old cabin on her own. She felt like she was getting close. She felt she was ready to follow in her grandfather's footsteps and maybe even develop a technique of her own. She wanted nothing more than to make her grandfather proud of her.

Chapter Twenty-Nine

The Teacher's hands were shaking so badly that he had to show the younger one how to insert the blasting cap into the dynamite instead of doing it himself. He stressed the need for total concentration. The dynamite had been in the mine for years and was very unstable. He told the younger one that one wrong move and he would blow them all up but the younger one was a fast learner and he was able to finish the prep work without incident.

The Teacher now led them out the front door of the cabin and showed them the locations he wanted them to place the dynamite sticks. Each one was buried slightly in the ground and covered with leaves, sticks and rocks. The hunter completed running the wires from the cave entrance to each location.

The Teacher showed them how to connect the wires to the blasting caps and then they headed back to the mine entrance. Once there, the Teacher went back inside the mine and returned carrying a metal box with a metal T-shaped handle sticking out of it. He explained that when the time came to protect the family, they needed to connect one wire from each set to the two little posts in the top of the box. Before connecting the wires, they would need to pull up on the T-shaped handle so it was ready to work.

The hunter laid out each wire run, in order of placement, on the ground just outside the mine entrance so they were ready. The Teacher then took the first set of wires and connected one wire to each post, tightening the two wing nuts down on the wire. He told them that when the time came they would need to push down on the T-shaped handle. That would set off the dynamite.

The Teacher wanted them to follow a specific order if they had to set off the explosives. Right outside first, followed by left outside, and then the one that was set inside the cabin door. If that wasn't enough they had a second set of explosives between the cabin and the mine and they were to follow the same procedure. He explained that this was a similar procedure to one that the US Marine mortar crews used in Vietnam during the jungle war. They would drop a mortar round into each of the four corners of a grid and then drop the fifth round into the middle. The idea was to cause the enemy to move from outside the grid into the middle and then drop a round right on their heads. He told them it was a very effective strategy. They both told him that they understood.

The Teacher also had them add a few more booby traps between the cabin and the mine entrance. He then cut down a few small aspen trees and had the hunter and the younger one stack them at the mine entrance to hide the door. He looked around the area between the cabin and the mine entrance. He had done everything he could to protect the family.

He told the younger one to head off into the woods and keep an eye on the men and he had the hunter hide in the large aspen tree that was about twenty yards away from the door and keep his rifle handy. He was hoping the men would get to the cabin, find it abandoned and keep going but he needed to be ready.

While the Teacher headed back into the mine to check on

the others, the younger one headed off into the woods being careful not to trip over the wires that they had run along the ground. He was very proud that the Teacher had chosen him for this task. He was the best tracker in the family and someday he would be able to take the rifle and become another hunter.

The younger one caught up with the men about a half mile from the cabin. He stayed off the trail about fifty yards and hid amongst the trees and the undergrowth. He watched them for a while and then he suddenly realized that the old man with the ponytail was no longer with the group of men on the trail. Panic set in as he quickly looked around the area but couldn't find him. He decided to move to a different location.

As he quietly slipped through the woods, he almost ran into the old man with the ponytail. If he hadn't pulled back at the last moment and crawled under a downed tree the old man with the ponytail would have seen him for sure. He waited for the old man to pass and then snuck around the tree on the opposite side and headed back toward the cabin. The old man with the ponytail was very good and the younger one spotted him through the trees at the same time the old man spotted him.

The old man was moving straight towards him, so he ducked down into a small ravine and headed back in the opposite direction from which he was traveling. His path would take him away from the cabin but he needed to shake the old man. He stayed in the ravine for about half a mile then climbed out and circled around the trail the men had come in on and headed back towards the cabin on the opposite side of the trail.

He looked around but could not see the men. He felt good that he had been able to get away from the old man. He had gone a long way out of his way to escape the old man and he was worried that he might not get back to the cabin before the men got there. He made it to the mine entrance just as the men split up and started to approach the cabin. Two of the men moved off to the right and left side and the other man and the old man with the ponytail headed towards the cabin. They were all pointing their rifles in the direction of the cabin except for the old man with the ponytail. He didn't seem to have a gun. Maybe their group was set up just like the family. The men with the guns were the hunters and the old man with the ponytail was like him, the tracker.

The younger one took up his position behind the aspen trees they had cut and stacked at the mine entrance and pulled the metal box with the T-shaped handle closer to the door. The Teacher had closed and bolted the mine entrance door to protect the others. It would be up to the hunter and the younger one to hold off the men. The younger one could barely see the hunter in the aspen tree but he knew he was there. Now they just had to sit and wait. Unfortunately, they didn't have to wait long.

Chapter Thirty

The first explosion almost bounced the Teacher out of bed. He had laid down on the bed to try to get rid of the headaches that seemed to plague his days lately. The others were doing their studies and were for the most part quiet. The explosion caused dust and bits of rock to fall from the ceiling of the mine and as he tried to stand up, the others screamed, scattered and hid under anything they could find.

The Teacher was disoriented for a moment and when he tried to stand up his legs gave out from under him and he crashed to the floor. He covered his head with his arms as bits of rock and dust rained down on his head. He looked around the mine to make sure no one had been injured and then was able to get his legs back under him and he headed for the mine entrance.

The second explosion caused him to stagger and bang into the mine wall. More dust and debris came down from the ceiling and he told the others to cover up. Some of them had crawled under the table and a few had crawled under the bed. They all looked confused and frightened.

He reached the mine entrance and was about to unlatch the door when the third explosion knocked him completely off his feet and his head slammed into the dirt floor of the mine tunnel. He reached up to his head and his hand came away covered in blood. His disorientation was back with a vengeance and he was having trouble figuring out where he was. His first thought was that he was still in Vietnam and that the base was under attack. He looked around for his weapons but he had none. He knew that wasn't right, so he must not be in Nam. His mind started to clear as two of the others ran up to him and tried to help him move so he could prop against the wall.

He was having trouble focusing and having troubling trying to figure out why there were kids sitting in the dark with him. Slowly his mind cleared and he started to remember. He could hear the others choking on the dust that had now filled the dark mine. He didn't understand what had happened. Could it have been a cave in farther back in the mine? He just couldn't get it worked out in his head.

All of a sudden his brain cleared enough and he remembered that he had been working with the hunter and the younger one and that they had set explosive charges around the cabin in case anyone got too close to the mine. It still wasn't making sense in his already fragile and now probably concussed mind. He knew he needed to help the others but he was having trouble getting his legs to work. He needed to get them out of the mine before they all choked to death.

It's amazing how sometimes one thing or event can bring about clarity. For the Teacher, that event was a series of gunshots coming from the other side of the mine entry door. He heard the first shots and realized that the hunter and the younger one were outside the mine and they were in trouble. He had left them to protect the others and he had gone to sleep. He needed to get to them to help them. It was his job to protect the others, not theirs. He had made a promise to momma. He had to do something.

He managed to get up on his feet with the help of two of the others and then he told them to run back and hide with the others. He found the latching bolt on the door and was just in the process of swinging the door open when he heard semi-automatic gunfire and lots of it. The men who were searching for them must have found them. Someone had blown the first three charges, probably the younger one and then the hunter had opened fire from his concealment spot in the big aspen tree. Now the men had opened fire on them both. He felt helpless and knew he needed to do something to help them.

Staying low he looked out of the mine entrance and spotted the younger one right next to the door. The plunger sat on the ground next to him and he was leaning back against the wall of the mine with his knees up against his chest and his hands covering his head. The Teacher had never seen him looked so frightened.

The Teacher crawled out the door on his belly and slid under the stacked aspen trees and wrapped his arms around the younger one. He held him as the bullets flew. While he held the younger one, he could still hear the unmistakable sound of the M1 carbine going off to his right. The hunter was making a valiant effort to defend their home but the semi-automatic fire he heard was withering. The hunter didn't stand a chance.

Staying low to the ground the Teacher half crawled and half ran towards the big aspen tree. He no longer heard the M1 carbine. All he heard was the semi-automatic weapons fire. As he neared the tree, he realized his worst fear. The hunter's body hung limply from the branch about eight feet off the ground with a lot of blood flowing from the bullet holes in his chest. The M1 carbine lay on the ground under his body.

With a lull in the rifle fire, the Teacher was able to reach up and pull the hunter's body down from the tree. He reached into the hunter's pocket and pulled out two more clips for the rifle. He ejected the spent clip and slapped in a new clip.

His mind was suddenly back in Vietnam and he needed to protect the men he had abandoned during the firefight. Feeling suddenly twenty-four again the Teacher jumped up, raised the rifle to his shoulder and charged towards the cabin. He had been able to get off two rounds before the first bullet hit him in the shoulder, but he didn't stop. He pulled the trigger twice more as he ran forward. The next couple rounds hit him square in the chest and he flopped back onto the ground.

He looked to his left and saw the younger one hooking up the next set of wires to the plunger. He had to stop him before he got killed too. The Teacher tried to turn on his side but the pain was intense. He held up his hand and tried to get the younger ones attention. He was too late. The explosion went off two feet from where he had hit the ground and he felt his body being flung into the air. The last thing he saw as he hit the ground were the bullets slamming into the younger one as he tried valiantly to get the next set of wires connected to the plunger. Then the lights went out and the Teacher was finally at peace.

Chapter Thirty-One

Buck was lying on the ground trying to catch his breath. PIS was lying partially on top of him. His first thought was, "this must be how all those quarterbacks felt when I pummeled them into the ground as a defensive back for the Gunnison High School Cowboys all those years ago."

Buck had been a standout high school football player and could have gone to almost any college he chose with a full scholarship, but he chose to join the army instead. With his teammate Hardy Braxton covering the left side of the line, they had broken just about every state high school record for defensive play. During senior year they had been called the "Wrecking Crew," and many of those records still stood today.

Buck had his arms over his head as debris rained down on top of them. He tried to shake the cobwebs out of his head but was having trouble focusing. He could feel blood dripping down his neck and his ears were ringing. He tried to move but he was pinned to the ground. Finally, the debris falling from the sky slowed and PIS slid off Buck. Buck looked over at PIS and noticed the pain in his eyes.

"You ok?" he asked.

"I think I caught a piece of shrapnel in my shoulder," replied PIS

Buck picked his head up off the ground and reached over PIS. Buck was amazed at what he saw. Sticking out of PIS's shoulder was a five-inch-long piece of wood. Buck slid closer. He didn't see a lot of blood but he knew this wasn't good. He told PIS not to move.

He was trying to get his radio off his belt when the first shots hit the wood that had fallen around him and PIS. He dragged PIS closer to the wood pile and then picked up his rifle off the ground. He needed to locate the sniper. He raised his head just slightly over the fallen logs but couldn't pinpoint where the shots were coming from. The remains of the cabin partially blocked his view down range. He rested his rifle on the top of a log and started to sight in through the scope when he heard rapid gunfire coming from both sides of him.

Deputies Manning and Sanchez were both behind trees and had engaged the sniper with withering fire. Buck looked through his scope in the direction they were firing and saw the bullets as they tore big chunks of wood out of an aspen tree about forty yards to their left.

Both deputies stopped firing and for the moment silence returned to the forest. Buck scanned the area with his scope. The movement from the right side was low to the ground. He had to look twice not certain he had seen any movement at all. As he watched the big tree, he spotted another person stand up and pull something out of the tree. Deputy Manning must have seen the same thing as he once again opened fire at the tree.

With his clip empty, Manning dropped the clip and was ramming a new clip home when a figure jumped up from the ground under the aspen tree and charged towards them. Several bullets hit the tree that Manning was hiding behind as the figure ran forward firing as he came. Buck and Sanchez returned fire and Buck saw the man falter and a red stain appeared on his right shoulder. Remarkably the man kept coming and was firing again. This time towards Manning who had regained his position behind the tree

Buck sighted in on the man the best he could and both he and Sanchez opened fire at the same time. Buck could see the bullets as they struck the man square in the chest and he flew backwards and hit the ground. Everyone froze for a minute.

Manning had come out from behind his tree and with his rifle raised had started to move towards Buck. Buck slowly climbed to his feet and kept scanning the area for any other danger. The explosion caught them both off guard and the dove for cover. Buck looked up just in time to see the body in the woods fly thought he air and land hard on the ground. He wasn't sure what had just happened but there was someone else out there with them and that someone still had explosives.

Sanchez looked up and something led his eye to a tight stand of aspen trees. The stand didn't look natural as the trees were too close together and from his location the trees looked more like they were leaning against something. He spotted movement behind the trees and fearing the worst he opened fire on the trees.

Buck, Manning and Sanchez held their positions and looked around carefully. PIS was now lying quietly against a fallen log from the cabin. Buck was amazed at how calm he appeared. Like getting stabbed in the back with a huge chunk of wood was an everyday occurrence. Buck put his hand on PIS's good shoulder and signaled for him to stay where he was.

Manning and Sanchez converged on Bucks position.

"Fuck Buck. What the hell just happened?" asked Sanchez.

Buck shook his head. "Got me. I feel like we've been in a war zone." He shook his head to try to clear the ringing in his ears.

The forest had been quiet for a few minutes and Buck suggested they head toward the big tree and see what they could find. The three men spread out and with rifles raised they moved slowly towards the tree. Buck was the first to reach the guy who had charged them. Kneeling next to body, he touched his two fingers to the side of the guy's neck and checked for a pulse. There was none which he pretty much figured after watching the guy get shot repeatedly and then blown up.

He picked up the rifle that was lying next to the body. An old M1 carbine. Buck hadn't seen one of those in years. It was a good rifle in its day and was still used by the military. He slung the rifle strap over his shoulder after checking the body to make sure there were no other weapons. He looked up as Sanchez waved him over to the big aspen tree.

He was almost to the tree when he heard a voice coming from his radio. He pulled the radio from his belt and keyed the mic. "Go ahead Sheriff," he replied.

"Are you guys ok? We heard explosions and gunfire. What's your status?"

Buck was just about to answer when he heard rustling in the trees coming from the trees to the left of where they had entered the little clearing. Buck, Sanchez and Manning immediately found cover and scanned the area.

"Buck Taylor. Gunnison County Sheriff's Office." Came a shout from the woods.

Buck stepped out from behind his cover and still with rifle raised called out.

"Come ahead. Slowly!"

The four Gunnison County deputies, all wearing camouflage, stepped out of the woods into the clearing and looked around. Buck lowered his rifle.

Walt Jenkins, with the Gunnison County Sheriff's Office, had been with Buck when they found Ranger Susan Corey's body. He walked up to Buck and they shook hands.

"Jesus Buck. What the hell happened? You guys ok?"

"Yeah, mostly," replied Buck. "Got one man injured."

Jenkins looked towards PIS. "Masters take a look. Masters has paramedic training." Deputy Masters headed towards PIS pulling out his first aid kit as he went.

Buck held up his hand to Jenkins and lifted the radio to his mouth.

"Sheriff, we are good. PIS has been injured and we are going to need transport. We are also going to need the Forensic Pathologist and Forensics. Gunnison County just arrived. Over." Buck gave the Sheriff the coordinates from his handheld GPS and clipped the radio back on his belt

Deputy Sanchez yelled for Buck and ducked back behind the tree. Buck and Walt Jenkins headed for Sanchez while the other two Gunnison County deputies headed for the stand of aspen trees with Manning. As Buck approached, he saw Sanchez kneeling next to a body on the ground.

Sanchez looked up as Buck approached. "He's just a kid for Christ sake. We killed a kid." Sanchez had tears in his eyes.

Buck and Jenkins knelt next to him and looked at the body on the ground. Sanchez was right. Buck figured the kid couldn't be more than fifteen of sixteen. He had blond hair and blue eyes that were now clouded over in death. He had been shot multiple times.

Buck put his hand on Sanchez's shoulder. Nothing he could say right now was going to change the way Sanchez was feeling.

Buck looked at Jenkins who just nodded. They headed over to where Manning and the other two deputies were standing and the scene was even worse. Lying behind the stand of aspen trees was the body of another young boy. This one was probably no more than twelve or thirteen. Next to him on the ground was an old plunger for setting off explosives. The plunger looked to be a hundred years old and Buck was amazed that it still worked. Manning did not have tears in his eyes but Buck could sense that he was going through the same emotions that Sanchez was feeling.

Walt Jenkins tapped Buck on the arm and pointed to two sets of wires lying on the ground next to the body. "Looks like the kid wasn't finished."

"Yeah," replied Buck. "We better see where those go. Very carefully."

Buck headed off, following one set of wires, while Jenkins followed the other. They each found what they expected about forty yards from the body. The dynamite was very old and coated with white residue. Although he knew the dynamite was not connected to a timer, Buck also knew that this dynamite was probably very unstable. He found a stick and stuck it in the ground. He then pulled a piece of yellow crime scene tape from his backpack and tied it around the top of the stick. He walked over to where Jenkins was standing and repeated the process.

Chapter Thirty-Two

The Sheriff was following closely behind his SWAT team as they traveled along an old fire break that they had picked up on the west side of Conundrum Creek. Based on the radio report he received from Buck earlier in the morning they should be within a mile of Bucks current location. The two other SWAT teams were coming in from Gunnison County to the south and from the Maroon Snowmass trailhead to the west.

The first explosion stopped everyone in their tracks as it reverberated through the valley. The high peaks helped to amplify the sound but it also made it difficult to determine the direction from which the sound came. The second and third explosions did nothing to change that but that didn't lessen the concern the Sheriff felt. His SWAT team had already disarmed two booby traps, so there was concern with moving through the woods any faster.

The rifle fire immediately following did nothing to alleviate the Sheriff's concerns especially when the semi-automatic weapons opened up. "What the hell is going on?" he thought to himself. It sounded like a full-scale invasion was happening in his county. He grabbed the radio off his belt and called Buck Taylor. The lack of a response was not unexpected. Buck and his team were deep in the woods and he might be having getting out a signal.

He called the other two teams to see if they might have a better feel for which direction the sound was coming from. The Gunnison County SWAT team reported that they were about ten minutes from the location Buck had last reported and they were certain the shooting was coming from there. They told the Sheriff they would forego a little bit of safety and pick up their pace. The team coming from the trailhead was still too far away from Buck's last position but they would pick up the pace since they were following Buck's trail and assumed that all the booby traps along the trail had been exposed.

The shooting had stopped and the Sheriff was finally able to reach Buck. "Go ahead Sheriff," Buck replied.

"Are you guys ok? We heard explosions and gunfire. What's your status?"

There was a lengthy delay and the Sheriff started to get impatient. He was about to key the mic again when Buck responded. "Sheriff, we are good. PIS has been injured and we are going to need transport. We are also going to need the Forensic Pathologist and Forensics. Gunnison County just arrived. Over."

The Sheriff was not happy to hear the request for the Pathologist. That meant that somebody was dead. He keyed the mic and called his dispatcher. He asked the dispatcher to call the county Forensic Pathologist and his two forensic techs. He also asked the dispatcher to call the paramedics and activate the Pitkin County Search and Rescue team. Finally, he asked the dispatcher to call Olaf Gunderson and have him bring a couple of his ATVs and a couple of his guides to the Conundrum Creek trailhead. Olaf had been a fixture in Aspen for longer than anyone could remember and he owned an adventure company. The trail the Sheriff and his team were on was somewhat decent for the most part and Olaf's experienced mountain guides should be able to maneuver their ATVs along most of it.

Finished talking to the dispatcher, the Sheriff put away his radio and directed his SWAT team to start moving towards Buck's last GPS fix. The Sheriff had no way of knowing how many people were dead but he was glad the shooting had completely stopped and that Buck sounded like everyone except PIS was ok. In spite of their most recent disagreement, he liked that old curmudgeon and he hoped he wasn't hurt too bad.

It took the Sheriff and his SWAT team another forty-five minutes to reach Buck's location. He stood at the edge of the clearing and looked around. In the middle of the field stood a smoldering pile of what he imaged was once a miner's cabin. The field was covered with debris. He spotted the two sticks in the ground with the yellow caution tape hanging from them and he directed his deputy who was trained as a bomb tech to carefully go have a look and see what needed to be done.

He spotted PIS propped against a log. One of the Gunnison County deputies was carefully taping around the huge chunk of wood so it wouldn't move. They would not attempt to remove the piece of wood until PIS was safely at the hospital. The Sheriff walked over and knelt next to PIS.

"You doing ok?" asked the Sheriff.

"Don't worry after me, Sheriff. Been hurt a lot worse than this," replied PIS.

The Sheriff looked at the Gunnison deputy and noticed him frown. He separated the back of PIS's shirt, that he had cut open to access the wound and the Sheriff could see scars all over PIS's back. It looked like someone had whipped him unmercifully at some point in his life. The Sheriff was stunned. There was so much they didn't know about this Brit. Maybe someday they would get the whole story.

He patted PIS on the shoulder and stood up. The deputy told him that PIS should be fine. He didn't think the piece of wood was embedded too deeply and PIS didn't seem to be in too much pain. He had even refused the painkillers the deputy had offered him. The tape job should hold the wood in place as long as they didn't jostle him too much. The Sheriff thanked the deputy and asked where Buck and the others had gone.

The deputy pointed toward a huge aspen tree and the Sheriff and his SWAT guys headed in that direction. Some noise to his right attracted his attention and he stopped. The rest of the SWAT team came through the trees along the trail that Buck had cleared. The Sheriff asked them to secure the area and start hanging crime scene tape around the entire clearing. The rest of the team was directed to grab some evidence flags and cones and start walking the clearing and marking anything they found that didn't look natural.

He headed off in the direction of the voices he could hear through the trees and stopped short as he reached a point where he was able to see the mine entrance. He could not believe his eyes.

Chapter Thirty-Three

Buck had asked the remaining Gunnison County deputies to search the area between the cabin and the mine entrance to make sure there were no other threats. He had checked the younger one for a pulse but found none which didn't surprise him. Sanchez was holding up ok. He kind of set in his head that maybe the bullets that had killed the two boys hadn't come from his gun. It gave him some solace even though he knew that he was one of the top shooters in the department, but with all three of them shooting, anything was possible.

Buck and Manning were standing to the side of the mine entrance discussing the safest course of action to enter the mine when they heard what sounded like coughing coming from deep inside the mine. They both raised their rifles and looked into the deep recesses of the pitch-black mine.

Buck gave a short shrill whistle to get the attention of the Gunnison deputies and waved them over to the mine. Deputy Sanchez had composed himself and joined the group by the entrance. The Gunnison deputies each had night vision goggles in their backpack, so Buck asked them to lead the way. Unfortunately, the dust was so thick in the air that the night vision goggles proved useless, so the deputies raised them off their eyes. With rifles raised and minimal light from Buck's flashlight and the flashlights on the rifles, they entered the mine entrance.

Buck noticed that the door they entered was a substantial piece of construction, definitely designed to keep people out of the mine. He wondered if the guy lying dead in the clearing built the reinforced door and also wondered what he was trying to hide behind it. Once inside even the flashlights had trouble cutting through the inky black darkness and dust that surrounded them.

Buck kept his flashlight pointed forward and followed behind the three Gunnison SWAT deputies who had separated and now walked down both sides of the tunnel hugging the walls as best they could. Manning followed Buck and Sanchez remained by the mine entrance door to cover their backs.

After what seemed like an eternity to Buck but was actually only a few minutes, the little troop entered what appeared to be a large room and they immediately crouched lower and moved to opposite sides of the space. Buck and Manning held their position in the tunnel and waited.

"POLICE. NO ONE MOVE!!" came a shout from Walt Jenkins. "We are armed and we will shoot!"

Buck could hear quiet movement along with sniffles and tiny coughs. The room was heavy with dust and even Buck coughed as they stood listening. Walt Jenkins moved back down the tunnel and moved next to Buck.

"We can see a couple people and they look like more kids. They are hiding under a table. Can't tell how many. What do you want to do?" asked Jenkins.

"Let's get as much light in the space as we can and see what we are dealing with. Be ready for anything," replied Buck.

"You got it," Walt responded. He keyed his mic. "Ok guys. Let's get all the flashlights turned on. Stay cool."

All at once three more flashlights lit up the space. The seven flashlights combined made a dent in the darkness and it was enough for Buck and the others to see four faces looking up at them from under a table. The faces appeared to be covered with soot. They looked scared.

While the deputies held their guns at the ready Buck moved into the room and knelt down next to the table. He told the kids to crawl out from under the table one at a time. At first, there was hesitancy, then finally one of the girls crawled out. She was soon followed by two more girls and a boy. Buck heard movement on the other side of the room and all guns turned that way. Two more girls crawled out from under a small bed that was pushed against the wall. To say the deputies and Buck were stunned would be an understatement.

Buck looked at the first girl who had crawled out from under the table. "Are there any more children in here?" he asked.

The girl, who looked about ten or eleven years old, looked around the space and then looked at Buck and shook her head no. Some of the kids were still coughing and Buck and the deputies were finding it hard to breathe themselves, so they pointed the kids towards the door and started walking.

Buck was the first one to exit the mine and was glad to see that Sanchez had pulled an emergency blanket out of his backpack and covered the young boy lying next to the mine entrance. He was followed by six children all of whom appeared to be around ten or eleven. Once outside, Buck and the deputies pulled some water bottles out of their packs and gave the kids a chance to get the dust out of their throats.

Buck noticed that each kid looked at the rescue blanket as they came out of the mine but no one said a word, they just looked sad and confused. Manning looked at Buck and Jenkins and signaled for them to follow him away from the kids. When they were far enough away for the kids not to hear, he said,

"What the hell did we just uncover?"

Buck looked back at the kids who were now sitting on the ground in a small group.

"Be damned if I know. One old guy and eight kids. I can't even imagine. I better radio the Sheriff and let him know what we found."

Jenkins nodded in agreement as did Manning and Buck pulled out his radio. He was just getting ready to push the mic when they heard movement at the front of the cabin and spotted the Sheriff and the SWAT team entering the clearing.

Chapter Thirty-Four

The Sheriff approached the group of kids sitting on the ground and just stared. He finally turned and headed over to where Buck and the others were standing.

"What the hell Buck?" he asked.

Buck shrugged his shoulders. "You got us. We were just wondering the same thing."

The Sheriff looked back at the kids and then back at Buck. Buck went on to explain about the explosions and the shootout. He excused himself from Manning and Jenkins and he and the Sheriff walked over to look at the dead kid by the mine entry. The Sheriff pulled the cover back just enough so the other kids couldn't see and then replaced the blanket. They next walked over to the aspen tree and Buck showed the Sheriff the body of the older boy. The Sheriff didn't say a word.

Their last stop was the body of the old man. The explosion had done a little damage to the body but it was the bullet holes in his chest that were what had killed him. The Sheriff stood for a long minute and then looked at Buck.

"I checked on PIS as we came in. He doesn't seem to be the least bit concerned that he has a chunk of wood embedded in his shoulder. I've got transport coming so we can get him out of here." He stood for a second as if deep in thought. "Honest opinion Buck. What do you think we have here? Is this some kind of cult or some weird sex thing or what?"

"I have no idea Sheriff. This is a new one on me. I've seen a lot of abused kids in my day but these kids don't look abused to my eyes. The way they held hands coming out of the mine, I almost get the feeling they are some kind of family."

The Sheriff looked at Buck. "Seriously? And who's this old guy, the father of these kids?"

"Possibly," said Buck. "But I don't think so. These kids all appear to be about the same age. The kid under the tree looks to be the oldest we have seen so far and the one by the mine entrance looks to be a little bit older than the rest. I doubt they are siblings in the typical sense."

"Fuck Buck. This is going to be a mess. I better let social services know. This is going to make their day." The Sheriff walked off pulling his radio off his belt as he went.

Buck took the opportunity and walked over to check on PIS. The Gunnison deputy who had been working on him explained that all things considered, PIS seemed to be doing remarkably well. Buck sat on the ground next to PIS and looked at him.

"I hate to be a bother Agent Taylor. Much ado about nothing," said PIS.

Buck looked at PIS. "You have a five-inch-long chunk of wood stuck in your shoulder. I don't think that's much ado about nothing."

PIS didn't say anything further, so Buck continued. "You pretty much saved my life back there. Thank you for that. How did you know the cabin was gonna go up?"

PIS smiled. "You are quite welcome even if all I did was push you out of the way. About the cabin. The pattern suggested an old tactic your US Marines used to use in Vietnam. The Marine mortar crews would drop their mortar rounds in a square pattern starting with the four corners. The enemy would move away from the corners into the center of the square and then the Marines would hammer the center with successive rounds essentially obliterating the enemy. It was highly effective."

Buck thought about it for a minute. "You think the guy we killed could be former military and might have spent time in Nam?"

PIS said he thought it was a good possibility. He hadn't seen the man before he was killed but based on the techniques it was possible. Buck wanted to talk to the Sheriff about PIS's thought, so he stood up patted PIS on his good shoulder and headed off to find the Sheriff. It was just about the same time as the final SWAT team group showed up.

Buck found the Sheriff and they both stood watching the Sheriff's bomb tech, slowly remove the blasting caps from the two sticks of dynamite that Buck had marked earlier. The bomb tech walked over and told the Sheriff that the dynamite was very old and even removing the blasting caps wasn't going to make the dynamite safe. He suggested leaving them where they lay and just keeping everyone away from them. The Sheriff agreed.

Buck told the Sheriff about his conversation with PIS. He also suggested they might run his prints through the military and see if there was anything to PIS's idea. The Sheriff agreed. He told Buck that the transport would be onsite in a few minutes along with the Pathologist and Forensics. He was planning to send the kids back first along with a couple deputies. PIS would go out with the kids so they could get him to the hospital. The Sheriff told Buck about the scars on PIS's back. Buck had no idea.

They heard the ATVs before they saw them. Olaf Gunderson had delivered in spades as ten ATVs drove into the clearing. Olaf waved to the Sheriff who waved back. Dr. Emily Parker walked up to Buck and the Sheriff followed by the two forensic techs, Gomez and Flynn. The Sheriff walked off with the two techs and left Buck standing with the doctor.

"Looks like we meet again, Agent Taylor," she said. "Do you always make a habit of being where the bodies are?" She smiled and Buck laughed.

"Seems so Doc. It's my curse I guess," he replied.

Buck asked her to follow him and he would show her the bodies. It would be getting dark in a couple hours and the Sheriff wanted to get everyone out of the forest by nightfall. They stopped at the older male's body first and the doctor knelt down and looked at the wounds. She noted the pieces of wood and debris that were buried in his back and side and Buck explained that besides being shot he had also been blown up. She looked at Buck with a confused look.

Buck suggested he show her the other two bodies and then he would be willing to answer any of her questions. He led the way to the boy under the aspen tree. She knelt down and gave the body a quick perusal. She stood up and her face said it all. Nothing needed to be said, so they headed for the younger boy over by the mine entrance. As they approached, she looked at the kids sitting on the ground.

Buck took her by the elbow and led her to the blanket that covered the third body. She pulled back the blanket and just stared for a minute. The age of the young boy was easy to see. The bullets that had killed him had done a huge amount of damage and she quickly counted about a half-dozen wounds. She looked up at Buck and then replaced the emergency blanket over the body.

"This is all so senseless. Was there no other way?" she asked.

"Sorry, Doc. We were under attack from several directions and we had to defend ourselves. We didn't know two of them were kids until it was all over. Everybody feels bad."

Just then a small figure appeared behind Buck and a soft voice asked. "Excuse me, sir. When will the Teacher be coming back?"

Buck and the doctor looked at each other. Buck knelt next to the young girl.

"What's your name sweetie?" Buck asked

"I'm Sarah. It's my turn to cook but I don't know what to make."

She was so calm, it was almost unnerving. Buck thought for a minute. "Is the Teacher what you call the older man?"

"Yes, sir. Will he be back soon?"

Buck thought carefully about his answer. "The Teacher is not going to be coming back. He was hurt badly and…"

"Is he dead?" she interrupted without batting an eye.

Buck looked at the Doctor and then back at Sarah. He decided to be straight with the young girl and see what would happen. The Doctor nodded.

"Yes, Sarah. I am afraid he is dead."

"Can we put him in the ground next to momma?"

Buck asked Sarah where momma was buried and she pointed to a trail that ran up the hill beyond the mine. He asked her if she would show them and she started to walk away. With Sanchez keeping an eye on the rest of the kids, Buck waved for the Sheriff to follow them and he and Dr. Parker followed the little girl up the trail.

About a quarter mile up the trail the little group with Sarah in the lead stopped at a small clearing that overlooked the valley below. The view was incredible. Sarah stopped next to a pile of stones and pointed. There was a wooden cross stuck in the rock pile. "This is where we put momma so she could visit god. Teacher said she would be happy here."

Buck, Dr. Parker and the Sheriff just stood for a minute and watched the activity in the clearing below. Finally, the Sheriff suggested they head back. The ATVs were ready to make their first trip back and they were burning daylight. Dr. Parker took Sarah's hand and they all headed down the trail to the ATVs.

Chapter Thirty-Five

Her grandfather's lucid moments were fewer and fewer as the summer progressed and even helping him look through the treasure box didn't bring out any more stories or more importantly the location of the mine shaft. She grew more and more frustrated thinking she was not going to be able to fulfill what she felt was her destiny. Time was running out.

She spent most of her free time when she wasn't working at the restaurant searching the area along Conundrum Creek. She even enlisted the help of some of her friends but to no avail.

Her luck changed just two weeks before she was scheduled to head back to Florida for school. Two miles from the Conundrum Creek trailhead she found what looked like an old seldom used game trail that she had promised to come back to but over the summer she had completely forgotten about it. It was a bright Saturday morning and the main trail was busy with tourists. She finally remembered the tiny trail and decided that this was the day she would follow it. Her frustration level and this strange sudden need had been building the last couple weeks and she felt like she was going to explode. If she didn't find the mine shaft soon, she might have to improvise which was never a good idea.

Over the summer, the little game trail had become even more overgrown and she actually walked past it twice that morning before she finally saw the faint trail as it snaked off deeper into the woods. Bushwhacking through the trees and the undergrowth, she walked for about a quarter mile before she found what looked like the remains of an old cabin. There wasn't much left, just some old logs in a pile. She could make out bits and pieces of what looked like old wooden shingles and also what might possibly be the remains of an old door.

Pulling on a pair of work gloves she brought along she started to move the logs and debris until she exposed what looked like part of an old wooden floor. Her excitement grew as she struggled to clear more of the floor. She tried to be as quiet as a church mouse so as not to attract the attention of any of the hikers using the main trail. Several back–breaking hours later she finally had almost the entire floor exposed and her heart sunk. There was no obvious trap door or loose boards and she sat for a minute and just held her head. All that work. Could she be in the wrong place? She knew this would probably be her last chance to explore before leaving for college and she felt terrible.

She was about to leave when she noticed one board that kind of stuck out above the others. The sun must have just cast the right shadow because she hadn't noticed the board earlier. Grabbing a thinner stick, she wedged the stick against the edge of the floorboard and applied pressure. It took several tries to get the stick to finally catch and she almost fell over when the board popped loose from the floor. She dropped her stick and pulled up the board with her hands.

She stood there for a moment and just stared. There, below the floorboard, was a rusted metal hatch. She almost screamed out with joy but then remembered all the hikers. She began carefully removing the rest of the floorboards until she exposed the entire hatch. It was just like her grandfather told her except for a lot of years of rust. She removed a small *pair of bolt cutters she had taken from her grandfather's garage and set the jaws around the old lock, which it surprisingly cut through with almost no effort.*

She stood for a moment and thought about what she was about to do. She had hunted for this place all summer and now it was hers. She also realized that once she opened the hatch and climbed down inside her life would change forever. Any smart person would call the authorities and have her grandfather arrested. He was a serial killer, possibly one of the first. He was also someone she had always looked up to. Could she possibly turn him in?

She thought about the two choices she could make. She could put all the floorboards back and walk away never to return, or she could continue on the path that felt more and more right and follow in her grandfather's footsteps. Did she really have it in her to take a human life? Unlike most of the serial killers she had read about this summer, she had a good life. She had never killed an animal. Hell, she never even thought about killing anything until she had discovered her grandfather's treasure box. Now it was all she could think about. The idea was enough to get her aroused.

She finally cleared all the thoughts out of her head and slowly opened the hatch. Her heart skipped a beat when the old rusty hinges made a loud squeak. She froze and listened for a minute hoping the noise hadn't attracted some unwanted attention. She made a mental note to bring some oil from her grandfather's garage and oil the hinges.

Looking down into the dark void, she spotted the old metal ladder hanging against the side wall of the shaft. It looked like it had hardly any rust on it. The smell emanating from the shaft was not at all unpleasant and just smelled dry and old. Pulling her flashlight out of her backpack, she turned it on and scanned the bottom of the shaft, which looked a long way down. She was hoping she wouldn't find the shaft filled with spiders or rats or even snakes but the floor of the shaft just looked dusty.

Gathering up her courage, she set her foot on the first rung of the ladder and, using the door for support, she started to climb down into the tunnel below. She reached the floor of the shaft without incident and scanned the tunnel before her with the flashlight. The tunnel was roughhewn with an occasional brace supporting the roof but to her amazement, the tunnel was only about ten feet long before it opened into a chamber that was exactly as her grandfather had described it.

There against one wall was an old wooden bed. The mattress was old and was covered with an old horsehair blanket. She had to stop for a minute as she visualized her grandfather having sex with the women he brought here. She couldn't picture her grandfather as a rapist, so her mind made the image more pleasant than it probably had been. She spotted the shackles on the opposite wall and could still see faint brownish stains on the dirt floor. She assumed that must be blood and she suddenly felt unsure of her path. Her stomach twisted into a knot and she felt like she wanted to vomit but she forced it back down and continued her search.

The old cabinet was hanging on the wall above a very old wooden table and she opened the cabinet. The leather roll was still neatly tied as she picked it up and placed it on the table. She unrolled the bundle and stepped back. The various knives her grandfather made shined bright in the light of her flashlight. They looked brand new. She picked up one of the thin scalpels and was amazed at how sharp it still was. It was as if time had stood still since the last time her grandfather was here. She put the scalpel back and carefully examined some of the other knives.

A sudden thought occurred to her and she put down the knife and pulled a pair of blue nitrile gloves out of her backpack along with a clean white rag. She wiped down the handles of the knives she had touched and carefully rolled them back up in the leather bundle and returned it to the cabinet. She closed the door and wiped the small knob on the cabinet. She would need to be careful from here on out.

She looked around the chamber and spotted another tunnel running deeper into the mountain. Following the tunnel, she came to another chamber a little ways back. This chamber contained several stacked beds with very rickety frames. She assumed this must have been where the miners would have slept but as she got closer, she noticed the lumps that were lying on each bed. She pulled back an old oilcloth cover which pretty much fell apart in her hand and jumped back startled

Stacked on the bed were two mummified bodies. They were brown with age and appeared to be women. She quickly recovered and checked the other beds. The bodies were stacked on top of each other several to a bed. They all appeared to be naked. She counted fifteen bodies which seemed odd. Her grandfather's treasure box contained sixteen trinkets. She wondered where the sixteenth body was. She spent a few minutes examining the bodies without touching them and she could barely make out lots of tiny cut marks in the now withered skin.

She had never asked her grandfather how he had disposed of the bodies after he was finished with them. The sight before her put an end to any speculation. The answer was he didn't, which is most likely the reason he had never been suspected of a crime. No bodies were ever discovered, so no crime was committed. It made sense.

She threw what was left of the oilcloth tarps back over the bodies and left the chamber. She found the old kerosene stove and the lanterns as she was walking back through the first chamber but she had no idea how to work them so she decided she would bring down a couple lanterns. She could make improvements to the space when she came home from school for her next break. She climbed up the ladder remembering to wipe the rungs clean of her fingerprints. Once back above ground she closed the hatch and wiped the old hasp.

She had been carrying with her the entire summer an old padlock that she found in her grandfather's garage and she hooked it through the hasp. She figured an old lock would draw less attention than a new one if someone found the hatch. She carefully replaced the floorboards and then covered the floor with the debris she had removed earlier. Satisfied and very excited she headed for the trailhead and her car.

Chapter Thirty-Six

Once the Sheriff felt confident that there were no other threats in the area, he released the SWAT teams. Each group headed back in the direction they came. The mood was somber and there was very little conversation as they departed the scene. The kids had been taken out, along with PIS, on the first ATV run. The ATVs had returned a little bit ago and were waiting for Dr. Parker to release the bodies so they could transport them back to the trailhead and the awaiting ambulances.

The Sheriff spent a few minutes in conversation with Buck and then with a hearty handshake thanked him profusely for his help the past couple days. The forensic techs had taken Buck's rifle along with the rifles of Manning and Sanchez. They would now be evidence. Manning and Sanchez would be placed on paid leave until the investigation into the shooting was over.

The Sheriff asked Buck to stop by the Sheriff's office as soon as he could and write out a statement. Since Buck was not going to be part of the investigation, the Sheriff released him and he and the two deputies started the long walk back to their cars which were up at the original trailhead.

As they approached the original crime scene, they ran into

Moe Steiner and Jane Fitzpatrick. They had hiked back to the scene of Susan Corey's death one last time and were getting ready to head back to the trailhead when they heard all the explosions and shooting. The SWAT team passed them a while before and they started to follow in the same direction. The Sheriff had called Fitz a little bit ago and asked them to head his way.

Fitz waved to Buck as they approached. "Crazy day, huh?" she said.

Buck and the deputies filled her in on what had transpired. Moe had opened his notebook when the conversation began and he was carefully taking notes as the conversation progressed. Buck told them about PIS's conjecture that the older victim might have had military training possibly from Vietnam and Moe made a note to contact the military. He also told them about the gravesite that the young girl Sarah had told them belonged to momma. Fitz pulled out her phone and dialed a number.

Gary Cummings, the elected Coroner for Pitkin County, answered his phone on the second ring. He exchanged pleasantries with Fitz and then Fitz asked him if they were able to exhume a body that was buried in the woods without an exhumation order. Gary explained that since it was part of the investigation, they should have no issue but that he would issue an exhumation order anyway just in case. She would be covered. Fitz thanked him and hung up.

Buck wished her and Moe good luck and told them to call if they needed anything and he and the two deputies continued up the trail. There was very little conversation as they walked. Sanchez still seemed to be having issues with the death of the two boys. It was true that they were killed while trying to kill Buck and the deputies but he was still having a hard time dealing with it.

When they finally reached their cars, Buck thanked the two

deputies for all their help and told them to call if they needed anything. He held Sanchez back a minute and reached into the glove box of his car. He handed Sanchez a business card for Susan Lewis, Psychologist.

"If you need someone to talk to, give her a call," Buck said. "She is really good and she helped me a lot after the shootout in Durango. Tell her I sent you."

Sanchez looked at the card and was about to say something when he hesitated and put the card in his pocket. "Thanks, Buck. I might give her a call."

They shook hands and Sanchez headed for his car and a couple days off. Buck slid into his car after putting his gear in the back of the Jeep and just sat for a minute and enjoyed the quiet. He had mixed feelings about not being involved in the investigation but he also knew that Steiner and Fitzpatrick were very good at their jobs and he had no doubt they would get to the bottom of it.

He thought about the kids for a minute and what a strange situation he had walked into. He would check on them in a couple days and make sure they were good. He pulled out his phone and called his boss.

Kevin Jackson, the Director of the Colorado Bureau of Investigation, answered almost immediately.

"Hey, Buck. I was ready to file a missing person's report on you. You ok?"

"Yes, sir. It's been a hard couple days," Buck replied.

The Director, no surprise to Buck, had been kept apprised of the entire chain of events by the Sheriff and told Buck he was proud of him. He was also sad that it was Buck that was the one to find the body of Ranger Susan Corey

Buck filled the Director in on the latest events and the

Director listened carefully. He told him about the explosives and about the shootout and the two dead kids and about the other kids they found in the mine. When he was finished there was a long silence on the other end of the phone.

Finally, the Director said. "Two dead kids, that's rough. You going to be ok, or you need to talk to someone? And another shootout. Is there something you're not telling me?"

"No sir," replied Buck. "My head is on straight. Besides, I still have the number for the Psychologist you had me see after Durango. Things are really good."

Buck changed the subject. "I am going to stick around here for a couple days. I need to fill out a statement for the Sheriff and be available for the shooting investigators. May get in a little fishing while I am here."

"Ok. Call if you need anything." The Director hung up.

Buck was an avid fly fisherman and he tried to get in a little fishing whenever he could. Besides the statement he needed to give the Sheriff he also wanted to head over to the hospital to check on PIS. He started the car and pulled out of the lot.

Chapter Thirty-Seven

PIS had just come out of surgery when Buck arrived at the hospital. He was in recovery and still a bit groggy when Buck badged his way past the charge nurse and walked into the room. PIS looked up and smiled when he saw Buck.

"Agent Taylor, how good of you to come by."

Buck stood by the side of the bed. "You look pretty good for a guy just had surgery. They taking good care of you?"

"Surgeon says I should be able to get out of here in a day or two. The piece of wood only penetrated about three inches and it didn't hit anything vital. Going to be sore for a while."

"Good to hear," said Buck. He shook PIS's hand. "You need anything you call me. I owe you." PIS just nodded his head and then sunk back into the pillow and closed his eyes. Buck left his business card on the table next to the bed and walked out the door. His next stop was the Sheriff's office.

He left the hospital, turned left onto Route 15 and turned right onto Main Street. He reached the Sheriff's office in about five minutes and pulled into the parking lot. He walked into the office presented his ID to the desk officer and was buzzed through. He headed down the hall to see if the Sheriff had gotten back from the crime scene yet.

The Sheriff was sitting behind his desk. He was talking to a deputy who was seated in one of his visitor's chairs but he waved Buck in. The deputy stood up, nodded to Buck and walked out the door. Buck took a seat.

"Statement could have waited til tomorrow Buck."

"That's ok. Want to get it down on paper while it's still fresh in my mind," replied Buck.

They spent a few minutes discussing the events that had transpired and Buck told the Sheriff he had visited PIS at the hospital and not surprisingly he looked like he was hardly bothered by the whole thing. They chatted about PIS for a few minutes and speculated on the source of the scars they had seen on his back. He certainly was an interesting fellow.

The Sheriff stepped around his desk and shook Buck's hand. He thanked him for his help and led the way to the conference room down the hall. He found a pad of paper and a pen and told Buck to take his time. The Sheriff walked out and closed the door. Buck started writing and by the time he was finished, two hours later, he had written a small novel. Buck prided himself on details and he double and triple checked his statement before he stood up to find the Sheriff.

The Sheriff was on the phone, so Buck set the pad down on his desk and turned to walk out. The Sheriff held the phone against his chest and called after him.

"Funeral procession for Susan Corey is tomorrow afternoon. We are starting from the hospital parking lot at 1 PM. The family is not planning a church service, so the procession will head from here to the cemetery in Glenwood Springs for a graveside service. Thought you might like to be there."

Buck thanked the Sheriff and headed for his hotel. He needed a shower and a bunch of sleep. Buck was surprised that it was so dark when he walked out the front door of the Sheriff's office. He hadn't realized he had spent so much time writing his statement. He swung by a local deli that was still open, grabbed a sandwich and a bottle of Coke and headed for his hotel.

Buck had just opened the door to his hotel room when his phone rang. He recognized the number and answered the call.

"Hey, dad. Are you ok?" asked his oldest son David.

"Hey, David. Yeah, I'm good. A little tired. It's been a long couple days."

"I just ran into a couple of the Gunnison County SWAT guys in the bar and they said you were involved in another shootout. For real?"

Buck took a few minutes and gave David the Reader's Digest version of the events of the last couple days. About the hunt for Susan Corey and then the hunt for her killers and finding a family of children living in the woods south of Aspen with an old guy. He also acknowledged that there was, in fact, another shootout.

"Must have been rough finding out you guys shot two kids. Not sure how I would have reacted."

"Yeah," replied Buck. "The one deputy, Sanchez, took it pretty hard. Gonna take a while to put this one behind us."

"Listen, Dad. You need anything you let me know. And you better call Cassie and fill her in. Her team was heading to a fire along the Arizona/New Mexico border but she might have seen something about the shooting on the news. I haven't seen the news story yet but according to the SWAT guys they mentioned that you found the ranger's body.

They said their goodbyes and Buck hung up the phone. He really didn't want to listen to Cassie, his middle daughter, tonight but he knew she would be pissed if he didn't call. Cassie had quit law school a couple years back and took a wildland firefighters job with the Helena Hotshots out of Helena, Montana. Much to her mother's dismay, she had thrived in her new job. Right up until her death, Lucy still didn't like the idea of her daughter willingly putting herself in danger. It was bad enough that her husband faced certain danger all the time in his job.

Buck dialed Cassie's number. Cassie answered on the fourth ring.

"Hey, dad. Everything good? We are just getting ready to head into the woods. What's up?"

"Hi, kiddo. I just wanted you to hear it from me first and not the news. There was another shootout today. I am ok."

Buck gave her the same quick version of the story he had just given his son. When he was finished, there was silence on the other end of the line and he wondered for a second if he had dropped the call.

"Did you shoot one of the kids?" she asked.

"Won't know for a couple days. There were three of us shooting and we were pretty much shooting blind. The people shooting at us were well hidden."

"Ok. I've got to run but I will call when we come out of the field. Please be careful. I don't know if I could handle losing you too." Cassie hung up and Buck just sat there for a minute and looked at the phone. Cassie had been very close to her mother and she had taken her death hard even though they had all been expecting it for over five years. When it finally happened though, it still hurt and Cassie was still grieving, as were they all. Buck's whole world revolved around Lucy. She really was his soul mate.

Buck stripped off his clothes and jumped into the shower. The water felt good and he could feel a little life drifting back into his sore, tired body. He dried off and was getting ready to crawl under the sheets when his phone rang. He looked at his watch. Any time his phone rang this late, it wasn't good.

Buck answered his phone. "Buck Taylor."

"Buck. It's Earl Winters. Hope I didn't wake you but I may need your help with something."

Chapter Thirty-Eight

Buck listened carefully as the Sheriff explained the reason for his call this late. A young couple were heading back to their car after hiking along Conundrum Creek and had stopped near an old collapsed mining cabin to have dinner and they noticed a terrible smell like rotting flesh or spoiled meat drifting around the cabin. The took a cursory look around the clearing but couldn't find anything.

The smell was enough to run them off and they headed back to the main trail. They ran into a couple of the Sheriff's SWAT guys in the parking lot and told them what they had encountered. The two SWAT deputies followed them back down the trail to the turnoff for the side trail and smelled it almost immediately.

They followed the trail up to the old cabin and after looking around they noticed a couple loose boards and when they pulled up the boards, they found what appeared to be a locked metal hatch. The deputies reported that the smell was really bad near the hatch. Since it was getting pretty dark, they GPS marked the location of the cabin and escorted the young couple back to their car.

The Sheriff told Buck that he was able to catch Judge Franklin before he went to bed and the Judge was in the process of signing a search warrant for the hatch.

"Buck, my guys are going to be focused on the Susan Corey investigation for a while. I could use your help with this. If it doesn't turn out to be anything you can bug out but I would like some experienced eyes on this till we know what we are dealing with."

"No problem Sheriff. I know where the trailhead is. I can meet your guys there in say fifteen minutes." Buck was about to hang up when he had a thought. "Sheriff, can you get someone from public works to bring a small generator and a couple work lights to the site? Might help if we are going underground."

The Sheriff thanked Buck and hung up. It looked like Buck wasn't going to get any sleep tonight. He knew he should call Director Jackson and let him know what was going on but he decided to wait until they knew what they were dealing with before he made the call.

Buck put on clean jeans and a clean T-shirt, clipped his gun and badge to his belt and headed out the door. The Conundrum Creek trailhead was about a ten-minute drive through town, so he jumped on Main Street and headed southeast until he reached Route 15. He turned south on Route 15 and a few minutes later turned right at the turnoff for the Conundrum Creek trailhead. He pulled into the space behind two Pitkin County Sheriff's cars.

Buck climbed out of his car and walked around to the rear and opened the hatch. Just to be on the safe side, he slipped his ballistic vest over his shoulders and zipped it up. He put fresh batteries in his flashlight and added three more clips for his 45-caliber pistol in their respective pouches. He added his nylon CBI windbreaker and his CBI ball cap. He locked the rear hatch and headed to the small group of deputies assembled just at the entrance to the trailhead.

Buck shook hands with the four SWAT deputies. Sergeant Jamie Winters, the Sheriff's daughter, would be the lead officer on this little excursion into the unknown. She apologized for dragging Buck out after what he had been through but she appreciated his help. Buck nodded and suggested they get moving.

It took about an hour in the dark to get to the almost hidden turnoff for the cabin. Without the GPS Buck doubted they would have ever found it in the dark. Buck stopped for a minute and checked the air. There was definitely a foul smell in the air. The SWAT officers led the way and they all commented on the smell as they got closer to the cabin. Buck had a lot more experience than the young SWAT officers and he was willing to bet good money that they were going to find a dead body. The smell was unmistakable.

The old cabin was just as the Sheriff had described. The old timbers were laying every which way and most of what lay on the ground was rotten from years of being in the weather. Even the remaining floorboards had seen better days and Buck saw where the first deputy on the scene had pulled up one of the floorboards. The metal hatch lay below the floorboards, so Buck and the deputies removed the debris and pulled up the remaining floorboards.

Once they exposed the metal hatch, Buck took a few pictures of it from different angles with is cell phone camera. The hatch was covered in rust and still appeared to be sound, so Buck didn't think the metal had rusted through. The smell was intense. Buck took a picture of the padlock while it was still locked. It was definitely not a new padlock. It reminded him of the padlocks his father used to lock up his tool boxes.

Satisfied with the pictures he switched over to video and asked the deputy with the bolt cutters to cut the lock and remove it. Buck videoed the entire process. Buck stepped back away from the hatch and snapped open the thumb break on his holster. He rested his hand on his gun. The SWAT deputies raised their weapons to the ready position and Jamie Winters removed the padlock and lifted the hatch making sure she stayed out of the line of fire from her team.

The smell was overwhelming and one of the younger SWAT officers disappeared into the woods and threw up his dinner. Everyone stood back to try to let the air clear. Buck took a small jar of Vick's Vapor Rub out of one of the pockets in his ballistic vest and rubbed some under his nose. He passed the jar around and the SWAT officers followed suit. It helped but not as much as he had hoped. He was glad that he hadn't put on a good pair of jeans or T-shirt. These were definitely headed for the trash once they were finished. Buck had learned over the years that you can never get dead guy smell out of your clothes. He also knew it would take five or six showers to get the smell out his hair and nose.

Jamie looked at Buck and asked. "Should we wait for the lights from public works or should we go in with flashlights?"

"Let's not wait," replied Buck.

Jamie removed a portable electronic gas monitor from her backpack, attached it to a length of rope she carried and lowered it into the shaft. It would be a bad thing to walk into a mine full of methane gas. She watched the monitor as it reached the floor and then pulled it back up. Nothing so far. Just to be safe, she had her guys pull out their full-face gas masks and once snug she stepped onto the top rung of the ladder and climbed down into the dark. She was followed closely by her team. Buck would remain topside until they had cleared the mine.

Chapter Thirty-Nine

The bar was packed and she had been nursing the same beer for most of the evening. Two of her girlfriends were heading back to college on Monday and tonight was girl's night out. The noise from the crowd and the laughter at their table made it hard to concentrate but she was running out of time and she needed to find the perfect subject.

She had never been able to discuss with her grandfather how he chose his victims. What little she did know didn't help. She knew he chose women who were traveling alone or women who wouldn't be missed, but how did he know. There were well over two hundred people in the bar tonight and she was having trouble focusing on one or two who might make the cut.

Getting asked to dance every couple songs didn't help either and her girlfriends kept getting on her case about not drinking. She still had doubts that she would be able to do this. She was still struggling with the fact that she didn't have any of the signs that came with being a serial killer. She had spent time over the summer in the library reading everything she could find on serial killers and she didn't seem to fit the profile.

Of course, the more she thought about it, her grandfather didn't fit the pattern either, at least the part she knew about him. She wondered how far he would have gotten and how many women he would have killed if he hadn't gotten into the accident that night. The story the family always told was that he was coming home from visiting a friend in Glenwood Springs.

According to family lore, there was a terrible rain storm that night and the roads were slick as glass. In those days, the late fifties early sixties, very few vehicles were available with four-wheel drive, especially in family cars. Her grandfather had been coming around a sharp corner, lost control on the slick road and the car flew off the road and crashed down into a creek bed before flipping over several times and wrapping around a tree. Her grandfather hadn't been found for several days until a county road crew noticed the damaged guardrail on the side of the road.

By the time they were able to get him out of the car and into the hospital, he was, for all practical purposes, dead but the doctors believed that the cooler temperatures had actually slowed his body down enough to keep him from bleeding to death. Her grandmother, her dad and his brother Stewart had raced to the hospital as soon as the Sheriff called.

The county had mounted a search for him but the weather was so poor that for several days the searchers couldn't stay out more than a couple hours. He was lucky the road crew had noticed the guardrail, or he wouldn't have made it. What her grandmother found at the hospital that night was a broken man. The doctors weren't sure he would survive more than a few days but he surprised everyone and lived another fifty or so years.

His body was broken almost to the point of not being recognized. He had broken his back in several places and the doctors were certain he would never walk again. Of course, they weren't sure he would ever wake up, so they weren't concerned about his being able to walk. That time would come if he survived. The story was he was in a coma for several weeks and when he finally woke up, he was a quadriplegic. He had completely lost the use of his arms and legs. Her grandmother had been devastated.

She never doubted that her grandmother loved her grandfather but she imagined there must have been times when she would have preferred that he had died in that accident. Her grandmother had spent the rest of her life being his twenty-four hour a day caregiver. She never saw her grandmother complain.

So here she sat in a crowded bar trying to wrap her head around her grandfather's life and what his legacy might have been had he survived to continue his craft.

She was just about to give up her quest and order another beer when she spotted a tall, good-looking young man who had just entered the bar with some friends. She could feel the excitement build in her very private areas. She wasn't sure if the urges she felt were to make him her first victim or just to have sex with him.

She wondered how she would be able to do it. If she drugged him how would she get him to the old cabin? There was no way she could carry him that was for sure. She hadn't really considered that part of her plan. This changed everything.

If she invited him into the woods to see something, go skinny dipping in a hot spring or just to have sex she might not be able to overpower him when the time came. If he fought back, she would lose. She had never been very athletic. Suddenly she needed a new plan. She thought about how hard this serial killer stuff was going to be. So many decisions had to be carefully made and evaluated to make sure one didn't get caught.

She turned back to the conversation going on at the table and she danced a few more dances. Then suddenly in a moment of clarity, she had a thought. Maybe she was looking in the wrong direction. Female serial killers were not all that common but if she chose a female victim instead of a male that would throw the whole thing out of whack. If the authorities did discover her little torture chamber, they would start looking for a man.

This could work. She would most likely be able to overpower a woman at least until she got good enough and developed her real technique. With all she needed to learn she needed to make the first kill as easy as possible. She still didn't even know if she could do it.

The initial problem solved she still had to think about how to get her victim to the cabin. She decided that this first time she would try to lead the victim to the cabin before she completely passed out. The hot spring thing might work. She could find a woman to befriend. Someone who had a little too much to drink and might need a ride home. No one would notice one woman helping another woman who was a little tipsy. It's what women do to avoid predators.

She had been able to score some ruffies from a guy she had dated for a while. She had no idea why he had them but it didn't matter. He needed money and he sold her a small bag without any questions. Ruffies were typically called the date rape drug but the reality was that only a very small percentage of rapes were actually attributed to being drugged. Most rape victims were either drunk or under the influence of some more common drug. If she could slip her victim a ruffie away from the bar or even down by the cabin, she wouldn't have to worry about getting the body there by herself.

Chapter Forty

The SWAT team assembled at the bottom of the ladder and immediately assumed a defensive posture. Sergeant Winters signaled the team to move forward and with rifles at the ready position and flashlights on they moved down the tunnel side by side. As they entered the first larger chamber, they broke off to either side of the tunnel and covered the room with their lights.

Two of the SWAT members moved down the right side of the room and two moved down the left. Sergeant Winters and her teammate had just reached the old broken-down bed when she heard a yell from the other side of the room followed by.

"HOLY SHIT!!!"

And "what the Fuck!!"

She turned towards the sound and saw, in the lights, what had caused such a reaction from her teammates. The body appeared to be hanging from some old shackles that had been mounted to the wall. It was blackish-purple and bloated so as to be almost unrecognizable. Sergeant Winters stepped over to her teammates while the fourth SWAT member cleared the rest of the room. She looked the body up and down. Even with their masks on, the smell was almost overpowering. The skin was already starting to slough off the bones and in another couple days the body would have ended up in a lump on the floor.

She lowered her rifle and pointed to the cut marks that covered the body. They were coated in dry blood and were starting to spread open as decomposition caused the body to expand. There was a dry pool of blood under the body that had mostly disappeared into the dirt floor.

Suddenly the room was bathed in light and the three SWAT members almost jumped out of their skins. The other team member who had cleared the room had discovered a couple battery operated lanterns on an old wooden table and turned them on. That was when they noticed the victim's eyes. They could almost feel the fear that this person had experienced. It was utterly ghastly.

Sergeant Winters directed two of her members to continue searching the tunnel that they could now see at the opposite end of the chamber from where they had entered. She and her other teammate began searching the body chamber. She spotted the old cabinet hanging on the wall over the table with the lanterns on it and opened the door revealing a rolled-up leather bundle. She left it where it was. She would let Buck or the forensics team do the honors. Her job was to secure the space.

A voice came over her radio. "Sarge, you need to come back here and see this."

"What is it Eddie?' she responded

"Not sure I can describe it. You better come take a look."

She closed the cabinet and her and her partner headed down the tunnel following the lights from their flashlights. They had gone a few yards down the tunnel when they saw another room and the faint light of her team's lights. She entered the room and stopped in the doorway unable to believe what she was looking at. Her teammates had removed some old deteriorating covers from some old rickety beds and there on the beds were a whole shit load of mummified bodies. All appeared to be naked and all appeared to be female.

"What the hell did we just walk into?" she asked no one in particular.

One of her teammates responded. "Looks like one of those old Egyptian tombs they show on the Discovery Channel."

She couldn't agree more.

"Ok. Don't touch anything else. Let's go back the way we came. This is a crime scene and we need to clear out."

She left the room and headed for the ladder followed by the rest of her team. Once up the ladder they all quickly removed their masks and tried to breath clean air but the air around them still smell like dead guy. They moved away from the hatch and Buck followed. He gave them a minute to catch their breaths.

"Ok, Sergeant. What did you find down there?"

"Not sure Buck. There is a fresh body hanging up that looks like it was tortured unmercifully and we found a room full of mummified bodies. Looks like all women and looks like they were all tortured as well."

"Alright. Let's tape off the area and prepare for a long night. I called the Sheriff a little bit ago and asked him to have the public works guys bring out an exhaust fan and one hundred feet of flexible air duct besides the lights and generator. See if we can get rid of some of the smell. I need to call the Sheriff back. He is not going to be happy."

The Sheriff was still at his desk. It had been a long couple days and he had a bunch of paperwork to still get through. His cell phone rang and he looked at the number.

"Fuck, Buck. I guess I ain't gonna get much paperwork done tonight, am I?"

"Sorry, Earl. This might be as bad as it gets."

Buck went on to describe the scene that Sergeant Winters had described to him. The Sheriff listened quietly. Buck asked the Sheriff to call Dr. Parker, the Forensic Pathologist, and also have the fire department bring out some Scott Pack breathing tanks. The Sheriff asked Buck about forensics. His forensic techs were still at the other old mine gathering evidence and so were Fitz and Steiner. He was spread pretty thin.

"You want me to call Denver and see if they can spare me to work this with you guys?"

"Sure would appreciate the help. Thanks, Buck," the Sheriff replied.

Buck hung up from the Sheriff and dialed the Director.

A very sleepy voice answered the phone. "Buck, don't you ever sleep?"

"Sorry to wake you sir but it's important."

"It always is when you call. Ok, I'm awake. Let's hear it."

Buck described the scene, just as he did with The Sheriff along with the Sheriff's request for help. Although Buck had statewide jurisdiction, it was always the policy of the Colorado Bureau of Investigation to work with local law enforcement only when they requested help. Buck had for the most part always abided by that time-honored tradition. When he finished, the Director gave a low whistle. "I assume you are thinking serial killer? Should we call in the FBI?"

Buck replied. "I'd like to hold off until we know more. The Sheriff's team is spread pretty thin. I'd like to roll the forensics team from Grand Junction and also bring in Paul Webber to give me a hand. He did really good on the Montrose thing."

"Ok, Buck. I will call Stan and have him roll everyone. Anything else?"

Stan Greenheck was the Agent in Charge of the Grand Junction office of the CBI and technically Buck's direct boss. However, over the past couple years, Buck had been working more for the Director and the governor than he had for Stan and it always bothered him, but Stan was always good natured about it because Buck got results and he was Buck's boss. That was good for him.

"Yes, Sir" Buck replied. "Do we have any Forensic Pathologists on standby that we can call? Dr. Parker out here is already up to her hips in dead bodies and I am sure she would appreciate the help."

"I will start making calls Looks like we are going to be waking up a lot of people. How do you always get involved in shit like this?"

"Just right place, right time I guess. Thank you, sir." Buck hung up his phone.

Chapter Forty-One

The public works crew and the fire department arrived while Buck had been on the phone with the Director. Sergeant Winters and her team were helping them set up the generator and two of her guys went back down into the mine to string up some temporary lights. The smell in the area around the shaft had dissipated a little and it was easier to breathe.

Buck's phone rang and he answered. "Hey, Paul. Sorry to get you out of bed."

"No worries Buck. Don't usually get a call from the Director at three o'clock in the morning. He filled me in but I wanted to check with you before I left Grand Junction to see if there was anything else you needed from here?"

"Thanks, Paul. No, I think we have everything covered. Get here when you can but don't kill yourself. We aren't going anywhere anytime soon. Oh, and Paul. Wear your oldest clothes. Something you won't have a problem throwing away when we are done."

"That bad, huh?" Paul replied.

"Yeah. That bad. See you soon." Buck hung up. It was time to head down into the mine. Buck was glad he wasn't claustrophobic. This would be a bad week to have that problem. Buck walked over to the two firemen who had brought in the Scott Pack breathing apparatus and they helped him put on one of the tanks. Buck was familiar with the system and had used one on several occasions.

Buck checked his cell phone battery to make sure he had enough juice for pictures and climbed down into the shaft. His first mental note was to have forensics check the hatch cover side walls and ladder rungs for prints. He stepped foot on the dirt floor and was pleased to see that the lights were working just fine.

Sergeant Winters stepped foot on the floor next to him and told him to follow her. She proceeded down the short tunnel and into the first chamber. With the lights on, it wasn't nearly as foreboding. Buck asked her to hold up as he took out his cell phone and took a couple overall pictures of the chamber. They then proceeded over to the body.

Buck took multiple pictures of the body, insitu. What Sergeant Winters had described was even more gruesome under the lights. The body was completely naked and obviously female. Both hands were shackled to the wall and her feet were shackled as well. The body was covered with hundreds of slices, some deeper than others. The number of very shallow cuts was amazing and varied in length from a small knick to one across her stomach that must have been a foot long.

"You ever see anything like this before?" asked Sergeant Winters.

"No, but I have read about it. It's an ancient Chinese method of torture. Can't recall the Chinese name for it but it translates to something like death by a thousand cuts."

"You must read some really weird books," she responded

Buck laughed. It actually helped to break the mood a little.

"Ok, Sergeant. Let's see the rest."

Sergeant Winters showed him the bed, which he photographed from several angles and then she opened the cabinet to reveal the leather roll. Buck took pictures of the roll and then carefully removed it from the cabinet and laid it on the old wooden table. While he did that, he also took pictures of the LED lanterns that were on the table. They appeared to be fairly new.

Buck switched his phone camera to video and asked the Sergeant to open up the roll. She carefully untied the two leather strings and unrolled the bundle. She stepped back as Buck panned his camera along the length of the bundle and then he put his phone away.

"Oh my god!" exclaimed the Sergeant.

"Yeah," replied Buck. With his gloved hand he picked up one of the scalpels and brought it closer to his face mask. "Beautiful workmanship," he said.

He placed it back in the bundle and stepped aside as the other two SWAT members pulled the flexible duct past him. He heard the exhaust fan fire up and almost immediately the air seemed to get better. Buck lifted off his facemask and took a breath. He could work in here now without the Scott Pack. He lifted it over his shoulders and set it on the ground turning off the airflow. Sergeant Winters did the same thing.

Buck left the bundle laid out on the table and followed the Sergeant down the next tunnel. They stepped into another small chamber and sure enough, there were four rickety wooden bunk beds and on each bed were several mummified bodies. Buck pulled out his phone and photographed each bed and then a couple overall shots of the room itself. He slowly walked around the room stopping at each bed and looking carefully at each body.

Even through the mummification he could see that these

women had all been tortured with the same method as the newest victim in the other room.

Sergeant Winters voiced the question he had been forming in his mind.

"It looks like these women all died the same way as the woman out front but these bodies look positively ancient. Can't be the same killer, can it?"

Buck looked at her. "Excellent question, Sergeant. I would think not but the methods look very similar." He turned around and headed back to the front chamber. Dr. Parker had just entered the room and was looking at the body hanging off the shackles. She looked at Buck.

"Remind me the next time you come to town to take a vacation, ok?" She smiled and Buck and the Sergeant laughed. He knew she was partly serious.

They followed the same path as he and the Sergeant had followed earlier and returned to the front chamber. Dr. Parker looked depressed. She had never performed an autopsy on a mummy before and now she had fifteen of them. She told Buck that CBI Director Jackson had called her on the way over and told her he was flying in several experts on mummies from the Museum of Nature & Science in Denver. He also had two more Forensic Pathologists in route and they should be here in a couple hours.

"Alright," said Dr. Parker. "Let's start with the newest body."

She and Buck gloved up and she approached the body. Dr. Parker was very thorough as she probed the body, carefully examining every cut mark. After about forty minutes she stepped back and removed her gloves.

Chapter Forty-Two

She had spotted the girl about an hour before, while she was dancing with that hunky Rusty Grover. The girl was moving past the empty tables and sneakily drinking what was left in the empty glasses. She could see the girl was getting pretty loaded.

The girl was cute, with shoulder–length blond hair pulled back in a ponytail. She had a faded blue streak in her hair on the right side. She was wearing a pair of ripped jeans, an old sweater and sneakers that had seen better days. The girl made it through several empty tables before the bouncer came and spoke a few words to her and escorted her out the front door and into the street.

She excused herself from the group and headed for the restroom but veered off and after checking to make sure her friends didn't see her leave, she walked out the front door. The night had gotten a lot cooler than it had been a few hours ago and she shivered as she pulled her jacket tighter around her.

She wasn't sure if she was really that cold or if her nerves were kicking in. Was she really about to do this? She still had doubts about her role as a killer. On some level, it felt right but on other levels, she wondered if she was just doing this because she was fascinated by her grandfather. She always looked up to him and finding out he had killed several women in his younger years didn't change her opinion of him.

She got into her car and pulled out of the parking lot. She had no idea where the girl had gone, so she started driving up and down the streets and alleys. She had only gone through two alleys when she found her behind one of the hotels looking in the dumpsters and then staggering down the alley.

The girl looked a little startled when she pulled up next to her and rolled down the window. She asked the girl if she would like to get some real food and as it penetrated through her booze fogged mind, the girl told her that she would like that. The girl climbed into the passenger seat, put her head back into the headrest and fell asleep.

She stopped at the all–night convenience store and bought the girl a burrito and a bottle of water. She slipped the ruffie into the bottle of water and shook it up to make sure it dissolved. The girl was still sound asleep, so she headed for the trailhead. This might be easier than she imagined.

She pulled into the trailhead and pulled the car as far off the road as she could. Next, she walked around to the passenger side of the car and opened the door. She shook the girl a couple times until she started to wake up. She told the girl that she had food for her and a place to stay but she needed to get out of the car and walk with her.

The girl took the burrito, unwrapped it and started to eat like she hadn't had food in a couple days. She washed the burrito down with a big swig of water. The girl half stumbled out of the car and she held her by the arm and started down the trail. She wasn't sure if it was the ruffie or the booze but the girl just stumbled along with her like a little–lost puppy. There was no conversation.

By the time they reached the old cabin, the girl was almost incoherent and proceeded to pass out. She had to drag her limp body the last twenty feet to the shaft. She unlocked the padlock and opened the hatch. She stopped for a minute and listened to the sounds around her. She didn't hear any people, which was just as she expected. She grabbed the coil of climbing rope that she had left at the top of the ladder and ran the rope around the girl's chest. She put on her gloves and lifted the girl over the edge of the hatch. Even though the girl couldn't have weighed more than a hundred pounds it surprised her how difficult it was to lower her and the roped slipped through her hands and the girl fell the last fifteen feet down the shaft. She hit the ground hard.

She stepped onto the top rung of the ladder and started down pulling the hatch closed as she went. She reached the bottom and stepped onto the ground. The girl was still unconscious, so she untied the rope and dragged her to the chamber. Once there she stripped off the girl's clothes and threw them in a corner.

She had trouble holding the limp girl in place and hooking up the shackles, and by the time she was finished, she was sweating. She stood back and looked at the girl hanging against the wall. Her body was fairly thin and she had small pert breasts. She looked like she hadn't eaten well in quite some time.

She walked over to the old bed and slowly undressed while watching the girl. She laid down on the bed and tried to get herself excited but it just wasn't happening. Maybe it was the nerves or maybe, unlike her grandfather, there just wasn't a sexual component to her needs. She decided to just get on with the cutting.

She opened the cabinet and pulled out the old leather bundle. Once untied, she rolled it out on the table and pulled out a thin scalpel. She walked over to the body and stood for a minute. She was trying to figure out how to begin.

Her first slice was very tentative and the scalpel barely drew any blood. She was almost disappointed. The second slice was across the girl's stomach and that one drew a lot of blood. The girl twitched. After a few more slices she finally figured out just how much pressure to exert and she began to make progress.

By the time the girl started to wake up, she had lost so much blood that she wasn't able to offer much resistance. She tried to scream through the gag but nothing came out. The girl's eyes showed the fear she was experiencing and it made her cut even faster as she watched the life slowly leave the girl's eyes. The ground at her feet was covered in blood and she stepped back and admired her handy work.

She had been keeping track and she had gotten to almost five hundred slices before the girl died. She was proud of her accomplishment. Not bad for a first-timer. She used a container of water she had brought down earlier to scrub her scalpel and wipe the blood off herself. Surprisingly there wasn't much.

She put the scalpel back in its place in the bundle, rolled-up the bundle and placed it back in the cabinet. She walked back to the old bed and put her clothes back on. She once again looked at the girl. She was pleased and she felt no remorse. As a matter of fact, she didn't really feel anything. Maybe she did have the killer gene in her like her grandfather. She checked to make sure she hadn't left anything, turned off the lanterns and climbed back out of the shaft.

Morning was still a few hours away, so she locked up the hatch replaced the floorboards and the debris and headed for her car. She felt very tired. Killing someone slowly, was hard work. She might have to pick up the pace on the next one.

Chapter Forty-Three

Dr. Parker stepped back from the body and leaned against the table under the cabinet. "Death was probably from massive blood loss. I counted roughly five hundred slices of varying depth and length. The autopsy will tell more but I think the cut along her throat might have knicked the artery. But even if it didn't, she wouldn't have lasted much longer than she did. Based on the decomp I'm gonna guess she has been down here about a week, maybe a week and a half."

"Can you tell anything about the killer from the cuts?" Buck asked.

"Not really. There are a few cuts that look like they might have been tentative. Possibly the first couple slices. What surprises me is that there are no signs of resistance in the cuts. It looks like she didn't fight back or try to twist out of the way. I will bet we find some kind of drug in her system when we get her on the table."

Dr. Parker told Buck it was ok to remove the body. She was going to go see if she could do some preliminary work on the mummified bodies in the other room. Buck asked Sergeant Winters to have the paramedics come down and take out the fresh body. She told him that his forensic team had arrived from Grand Junction and they were carrying in their equipment. And also that Paul Webber was upstairs. Buck thanked her and asked her to send everyone down. He would wait for them here so that Dr. Parker wasn't alone.

The paramedics and the firefighters were the first to climb down the ladder and some of them openly gasped when they walked into the chamber and saw the body hanging there. The paramedics pulled out a poly body bag and laid it on the ground in front of the body. The firefighter using a cordless side grinder proceeded to cut through the shackles and they gently lowered the body onto the body bag and zipped it up.

Paul Webber and the CBI forensics team entered the chamber. They were all wearing one-piece white Tyvek overalls with their hoods up, Tyvek booties, surgical masks and nitrile gloves. Buck watched as they each stopped and looked at the body as the firefighters and paramedics lowered her onto the body bag.

"You ok Paul?" Buck asked. Paul looked a little green.

Paul answered hesitantly. "Yeah. I'm good. Been a while since I saw a body like that. Wow."

Buck walked Paul and the forensic team through the mine just as he had Dr. Parker. He pointed out areas he definitely wanted printed and swabbed for DNA. They ran into Dr. Parker in the second chamber. She had had one of the SWAT officers help her move the bodies very gingerly off the first bed and was kneeling next to the three mummified bodies taking pictures. She looked up as Buck and his team entered the already crowded chamber.

Buck introduced her to Paul Webber and the forensics team. She would be spending a lot more time in this chamber, so they needed to strategize so as not to be tripping over each other. Until the bodies were removed completely from the mine, Dr. Parker was in charge and she would direct the forensic team to gather evidence she felt was important while they also followed their own procedures. It was going to be a very long day for everyone.

Buck could see that Paul Webber needed some fresh air, so he suggested they head topside. Once outside the shaft, Paul took off his mask and unzipped his jumpsuit.

"Oh my god Buck. What the hell have you gotten us into?"

Buck was just about to answer when his phone rang. Buck looked at the number and answered the call. "Yes, sir Director?"

"Hey, Buck. I think I have everyone you need headed your way. Can you fill me in?"

Chapter Forty-Four

Buck described the scene inside the mine to the Director while Paul stood next to him and listened. Buck told him about the condition of the fresh body and about the mummified remains in the back chamber. He told him about the knife set they had discovered. He thanked him for getting the team assembled so quickly and especially for the help he had summoned to help Dr. Parker with the autopsies.

The Director asked Buck to speculate on the scene. Buck never liked speculation. He preferred to have the facts in front of him, but he knew that anything he told the Director would stay within a very small circle.

"Well, sir. It looks like we have two different crimes here. We have what appears to be some very old multiple murder serial killings and then a much more recent kill, carried out in what appears to be a very similar manner. We have no idea how long the mummified bodies have been here but we know that the most recent murder occurred within the last week to week and a half. No way at this point to know how the two crimes are related but from my very cursory observation I would say they definitely have a relationship."

The Director listened as Buck spoke. He interrupted only

once with a question which Buck answered as best he could and then he told Buck to stay in touch and call if he needed any help. Buck hung up his phone. He was just going to talk to Paul as the Sheriff entered the clearing followed by several people who looked like grad students and an older gentleman wearing a safari hat.

"Buck, ran into Professor Frederick Standish in the parking lot. These young folks work with him." Buck introduced himself to the Professor and his team. The Professor shook his hand.

"Pleasure to meet you, Agent Taylor. I am a Professor of Archeology at the University of Colorado Boulder and these young men and women are some of my top grad students."

The Professor was probably in his fifties but appeared to be very fit. He wore green cargo pants and a safari shirt with his sleeves rolled-up. He and each member of his team carried a backpack. They all looked like they came ready to work.

The Professor continued. "When Director Jackson called me this morning and described what you had found I was intrigued, to say the least. He expressed the urgency of the situation, so I gathered up my team and headed right out. We'd like to get to work right away."

Buck asked Sergeant Winters to escort the Professor and his students back to the rear chamber to help Dr. Parker and they all disappeared down the shaft. The Sheriff followed them down the ladder.

Buck hadn't noticed that the sun had come up and he looked at his watch. He needed some sleep but there was a lot to do. "Paul, I need you to head over to the county clerk's office and the tax assessor's office and see if you can figure out who owns this cabin. If it was part of a mining claim, the path might get a little convoluted but see what you can find out. Second, take some pictures of the lanterns on the wooden table. They look brand new. See if you can find out who in town sells that brand and then see if maybe someone has security footage of the purchase."

Paul zipped up his suit and replaced his hood and mask and headed back down into the mine. Buck found his backpack and pulled a warm bottle of Coke out of the mesh sleeve on the side. He took a long drink and sat down for a minute on the pile of logs that used to be a cabin.

The Sheriff climbed out of the hatch and walked over and sat down next to Buck. The sun had cleared the mountains and it was shaping up to be a beautiful fall day. The aspen leaves around the cabin were starting to turn yellow and the contrast to the green of the pine and spruce trees was a magical sight. The summer had been unusually wet and that meant that along with the yellows there would also be a large amount of red and orange colors this year.

Buck was thinking about the times that he and his late wife Lucy used to sit on the handicap dock at the park in Gunnison and look out over the Gunnison River at the aspens on the other side. Lucy always loved the fall colors. Buck wiped a tear from his eye. He missed her very much.

"You ok, Buck?" The Sheriff asked.

"Yeah," Buck replied. "Well, what did you think down there?"

"Not sure what to think. I'm worried that we have someone trying to imitate a bunch of killings from a long time ago. Scares me to think we might have a serial killer in our little town. Was also wondering if I should call the FBI and get them involved.?"

Buck looked at the Sheriff. "Let's hold off on the FBI until we know more. I will take care of them. You have enough on your plate right now. How is Fitz coming with identifying the old guy at the other mine?"

The Sheriff filled Buck in on the investigation so far. The Doctor had pulled the two bullets from Susan Corey and the state crime lab had determined that they came from the old guy's M1 carbine. The woman's remains had been unearthed from the mountaintop grave but they were waiting on Dr. Parker to perform the autopsy. So, nothing on that front yet. Moe Steiner had taken pictures of all the kids along with DNA swabs and fingerprints and he was running them through every system available both state and federal looking for any matches to missing kids. He mentioned that Fitz had been having trouble getting any kind of response from the military on any possible ties the old guy had to one of the services.

Buck stopped the Sheriff and pulled out his phone, looked up a number and dialed.

"Hey Buck, how are you brother?" answered Jess Gonzales, the Agent in Charge of the DEA's office in Grand Junction.

"Doing great, Jess. Good to hear your voice," Buck replied.

Jess gave Buck a little rundown on where things stood with the Durango investigation and Buck gave her a quick debrief on the shooting of the ranger.

"We all heard about the ranger getting killed. Heard you were involved. You got a drug angle on this one?" Jess asked.

"Sorry, Jess. No drug angle but I need a favor for Sheriff Winters over in Pitkin County. His homicide folks are looking into a possible military angle on the old guy that was killed and his investigator is not getting much help from the military. You did such a great job getting us the info on the Green Beret in Durango I was wondering if you might be able to push someone to help the Sheriff?"

"For you Buck, anything. Let me make a few calls. Can you text me the contact info for the lead investigator?"

Buck said he would and they chatted for a few more minutes. Buck hung up the phone and immediately pulled up Fitz's contact info and texted it to Jess.

"Thanks, Buck. I appreciate that," said the Sheriff. He looked at his watch.

"I need to run. The procession for Susan Corey starts in less than two hours. See if you can make it." The Sheriff stood up, shook Buck's hand and headed down the trail. Buck had almost forgotten about the procession for Corey. He would need to make some time to be there.

Paul Webber came out of the hatch and took off his mask. He had pictures of the lanterns and he also had digital fingerprints from the girl in the front chamber. He had gotten them from the forensic tech and told Buck he was going to swing by the Sheriff's office and run them through AFIS.

Buck stood up, grabbed his backpack and told the deputy who was now manning the crime scene entrance that he would be back in a while. They both signed out with the deputy and then he and Paul headed down the trail towards their cars. Buck needed to shower before he went to the service for Susan Corey. He stunk of dead guy and he didn't want to offend anyone. He told Paul where he would be and they parted company in the parking lot. Buck headed for his hotel.

Chapter Forty-Five

The funeral procession for Ranger Susan Corey pulled out of the hospital parking lot and turned onto Main Street. The procession was led by a Pitkin County Sheriff's patrol car with lights flashing. It was followed by a Colorado Parks and Wildlife Department pickup truck full of flowers that had been delivered to the coroner's office over the past couple days. The pickup was followed by the black hearse bearing the flag-draped coffin carrying the body of Susan Corey. Behind the hearse was the Sheriff and then a contingent of over one hundred cars and emergency vehicles from Pitkin County as well as several of the towns and counties surrounding Aspen.

Buck pulled out of the parking lot as the last emergency vehicle passed in front of him. He had gotten back to the hotel and taken three showers to try to get rid of the smell. He wore his cleanest pair of jeans and a clean T-Shirt. He hadn't expected to be here this long, so he hadn't packed anything more than the three-days supply of clothes in his GO bag.

The procession traveled along Main Street and then continued on as Main Street turned into Highway 82. Buck was amazed at the outpouring of love and support as they traveled through town. All along the sides of the road people were standing and waving American flags. Even after the highway had begun, there were crowds of people on the road. Susan Corey was getting a heroes send-off. Something she very much deserved.

As the procession crossed the line between Pitkin and Garfield Counties, several Garfield County Sheriff's patrol cars and emergency vehicles joined the procession. The procession turned off Highway 82 and proceeded up Grand Avenue to the Rosebud Cemetery. The procession stopped behind a black limousine and everyone exited their vehicles and lined up along both sides of the pathway leading to Susan Corey's grave.

Buck felt a little underdressed with all the spit and polished class "A" uniforms that were lined up on the walkway, so he walked behind the honor guard and stood off to one side. Miguel Vargas, the Chief Ranger for the Glenwood Springs office of the Colorado Parks and Wildlife Department stepped up onto the path. He was dressed in his class "A" uniform, forest green pants and short jacket, tan shirt with green tie and his green "Smokey the Bear" hat. He was escorting an older woman and man whom Buck figured must be her parents. Behind him, a female ranger, also in Class "As" escorted a young man in a dark suit. This must be her son.

The flag-draped casket was carried by six CPW Rangers and followed the family. Everyone along the path stood at attention and saluted as the casket went by. Buck placed his hand over his heart. Buck was surprised as a shadow crossed his side and he turned to find PIS standing next to him. His right arm was in a sling and he was dressed as always, except today instead of a bright red cummerbund and ascot, PIS was wearing a forest green cummerbund and ascot. He stood alongside Buck and placed his hand over his heart.

To say Buck was surprised to see the Brit was an understatement. He just had surgery yesterday and here he was looking like his old self, except for the sling. Buck also noticed that the hole made by the piece of wood that had pierced his linen coat was sporting a brand new black patch.

The casket reached the grave site and everyone along the path filled in around the family who were sitting in the front row. Miguel Vargas gave a moving eulogy and several rangers from her office also spoke about Susan Corey. A local chaplain continued with the service. Buck gathered from the service that Susan Corey was not really a religious person. It was a beautiful service under a clear blue Colorado sky but it didn't have much of a religious tone to it.

The chaplain finished the service and the six Rangers who had been part of the honor guard folded the American flag and presented it to Susan Corey's mother. In the distance a bugler played taps. The family stood and headed back to the limo and Vargas announced that there would be food and drinks available at the CPW office. Buck and PIS silently followed the crowd and Buck offered PIS a ride to the CPW office, which he accepted.

Once in the car, Buck looked at PIS. "Surprised to see you here today. Did you escape from the hospital?" he asked PIS.

"Doctor said I was a miraculous patient and that I could leave whenever I was ready. Couldn't stand being locked up inside that long. The sheriff was nice enough to give me a ride up here. It was quite a moving procession."

Buck agreed and they headed over to the CPW office for refreshment. In the parking lot of the CPW building was a huge white tent, so Buck and PIS headed that way. Once inside they each grabbed a sandwich and a bottle of water and began milling about. Buck was amazed at how many people showed up and PIS was amazed at how many of those people Buck actually knew.

Buck and PIS walked over to the table where the family

was sitting and Miguel Vargas stood and introduced Buck and PIS to Susan Corey's parents and her son. He mentioned that they had been instrumental in finding Susan and her parents thanked them profusely. Buck was a little embarrassed but PIS was his jovial self and had launched into a lengthy conversation with the family. Buck stepped away and signaled for Miguel to follow him.

Away from the table, Buck asked Miguel how the son was holding up. Miguel explained that even though his grandparents lived in Pueblo, they had agreed to move up here and stay in Susan's house until Jimmy graduated next year. Buck knew that a fund had been set up for the boy asked Miguel how they were doing with raising money. Buck had donated money this morning before he left his hotel room.

Miguel said. "Craziest thing. A lawyer showed up at the bank in town that was handling the donations and gave the bank a certified check for one hundred thousand dollars. He also had a letter telling the bank that a college fund had been set up in James Corey's name at a bank in the Bahamas and that the bank would cover all of Jimmy's college expenses for a four-year degree to any college Jimmy chose to attend. The bank manager had been totally floored but he checked it out and both the check and the account in the Bahamas were real."

"That's amazing. No idea where the funds came from?" asked Buck.

"Not a clue. Jimmy has a guardian angel someplace." Miguel shook Buck's hand. "Thanks for everything you did for Susan. You ever need anything you give us a call. We owe you." He walked back to the family and sat down at the table.

Buck watched as PIS shook hands with Jimmy and his grandfather and gave his grandmother a big hug. He shook hands with Miguel and headed back to where Buck was standing. Buck had an idea running around in his head but it didn't want to land. Buck had watched PIS interact with Jimmy Corey and he wondered silently, if it was possible, that the money and the college fund somehow came from PIS. "Nah. How was that even possible? After all, this is PIS we are talking about. But then again, who was PIS, really?"

Buck and PIS headed back to Buck's car. Once inside, Buck told PIS about his conversation with Miguel and about the money. PIS never reacted. He just said how nice it was that someone was looking out for the young man, then he closed his eyes and went to sleep. Buck woke PIS as they pulled into the parking lot of the hospital and PIS thanked him for the ride and stepped out of the car. Buck watched him walk through the front door to the hospital. He pulled out his phone and called Paul Webber.

Chapter Forty-Six

The thrill of the kill had started to fade. She had gone home that night and slept like a baby. The next morning, she still felt wired. The response hadn't been sexual but the kill had still excited her. She felt better and better about her technique as the night wore on. She really got an adrenalin jolt when the girl woke up and realized what was happening to her. If only it had lasted. The cut she had made across her neck must have hit the artery. She thought she was shallow enough but there was a little spurt of blood that wouldn't stop. She would have to remember that for the next time.

She had been hoping there would be a next time before she had to leave for college but it was not meant to be. She had been back to the bar every night after work, since the first kill and this would be her last night in town and she had not been able to find the next victim. She finished her drink and told her friends at the table that the next round was on her. Instead of waiting for the waitress, she walked up to the bar.

The woman behind the bar was the owner. She hadn't really met her but this was where she and her friends hung out all summer, so they got to know who was who. The bartender/owner walked up and asked her what she needed. She gave her the order for three beers and laid a twenty-dollar bill on the bar.

The bartender/owner came back with three beers and stared at her for a minute. She was beginning to feel a little self-conscious when the bartender/owner finally spoke.

She had admired the necklace she was wearing and wondered where she had found such a pretty piece? She told the bartender/owner that she had found it in a pawn shop in Florida. The bartender/owner looked at it a little closer and then said something that chilled her to the bone.

The bartender/owner told her that she had once had a neckless very similar to that one but that she had lost it when she was involved in a car crash many years before. The neckless had belonged to her grandmother and she had borrowed, well actually stole it, when she ran away from home. She had been in a crash just outside of Aspen and the necklace had disappeared. No one at the hospital remembered seeing it.

She asked the bartender/owner if she remembered anything else about the crash but she said that she must have fallen asleep after she was picked up hitchhiking on the highway and when she woke up in the hospital several days later, she couldn't remember anything about the crash. The police told her that the man who picked her up was probably going to die and that she was very lucky to be alive.

She left the twenty on the bar, picked up the three beer bottles and walked back to her table. She was too stunned to even talk. Luckily her friends were doing enough talking, so they never noticed.

She had taken the jade necklace out of her grandfather's treasure box. She had admired it since she found the box and she decided that it would be one thing to remember her grandfather with. He had been slipping in and out of consciousness for the past couple weeks and the family was not holding out much hope. Since it was her last night in town and she was certain no one would have any idea where the necklace came from, she decided to wear it out. How in the hell could she have ever guessed that someone would recognize the necklace? What a huge cluster fuck.

She needed some air, so she excused herself and walked out the front door and stood on the sidewalk. The air was fall crisp and it felt good. Her thoughts turned to the woman at the bar. She didn't remember anyone ever mentioning that there was a passenger in the car with her grandfather the night he crashed. Is it possible this woman was in the car with her grandfather? How could that have gotten missed in the family stories? More importantly was it her necklace that was in her grandfather's treasure box?

She put her hand up to her open mouth. "Oh my god." This woman was supposed to be her grandfather's sixteenth victim. That's why there were sixteen mementos in the box but only fifteen bodies in the mine. He was on his way to the mine to kill her when the crash occurred. But why had no one ever mentioned a second person in the car?

The bartender/owner did not appear to know who was driving the car that night. She had no recollection of the accident. Her grandfather must have already drugged her when he crashed the car. She didn't know what he used as a sedative but whatever it was, it had to be fast acting and very powerful. Powerful enough to induce amnesia?

She felt a strong chill run up her spine and then in a moment of clarity, she struck on an idea. One that would hopefully keep her focused while she was away at school. She would finish what her grandfather had started that fateful night so long ago. She would take care of his sixteenth victim. She would need to devise a very good plan for this kill. It would take time and it would need to be perfect. The bartender/owner was no slouch. She ran a bar. She would probably be tough to deal with and she had a pretty good build, even after so many years. She pictured the woman in her younger days and understood why her grandfather had chosen her. She was probably a real looker in her day, because she was gorgeous now.

This was awesome. What better way to honor her grandfather than to finish his journey? She felt her excitement build just like it had the night of her first kill. It was a shame. If she only had more time. But that's ok. She would be back at Christmas. She would start working out the plan in her head and by Christmas, it would be perfect. She just knew it. Her grandfather would be so proud of her.

She stepped back into the bar and shook off the chill from the night air. Her body was warm and tingling. She sat back down at the table where her friends were still talking away and took a sip of her beer. She looked over the top of the bottle and stared at her next victim.

The next morning her father and mother packed up the car and drove her to Denver for her flight back to Jacksonville. She hugged them and stepped into the security line. She wrapped her hand around the jade necklace and said a silent prayer that her grandfather would live long enough to see her complete his final act. She smiled as she went through security and waved goodbye to her parents.

Chapter Forty-Seven

Buck left the hospital parking lot, turned right onto Main Street and pulled into the parking lot for the Sheriff's office. He entered through the front door showed his ID to the officer at the front desk and was buzzed into the back. He found an empty desk in the bullpen, sat down and pulled his laptop out of his backpack.

The first step in any murder investigation is the creation of the murder book. This was pretty much the entire investigation in one place and would include interviews, forensic reports, autopsy reports, and crime scene photos. It was also a chronological listing of how the investigation has progressed.

Over the years, Buck finally caught up with the rest of the world and started to use the murder book template in his laptop. In the old days, everything was done with paper and pencil. The problem was, that there was only one book and anyone who needed access had to go to wherever the physical book was located. This was tough since Buck was very rarely in the same place for long. The laptop made it simple since it was always with him and it also gave instant access to anyone who needed to either review something or add a report.

Buck started with the title page and entered the name of the community and the date. The File automatically opened a new case number and that number would be everyone's source of reference for anything related to the case. His next task was to build the chronology of the crime.

Buck was very meticulous about his investigation notes and between the chronology and the case summary he spent over two hours sitting. He got up to stretch his legs and walked over to the soda machine in the corner and bought another Coke. His third of the day, so far. He found a couple boxes of cold pizza in the refrigerator and grabbed two slices and popped them into the microwave. "Hell of a lunch," he thought, as he walked back to the desk he had been using.

Buck pulled out his cell phone and connected the micro USB cable to his laptop and downloaded all his crime scene photos. He spent the next two hours reviewing each picture and attaching a label to them before placing them in chronological order. His final task, for the moment, was to enter the emails for everyone involved in the case and send them an alert that the file had been uploaded and was now available for use. He closed his laptop and went to see if Fitz or Moe Steiner were in the office.

He spotted Moe Steiner walking back from the central printer and followed him back to the office he shared with Fitz. He was just about to ask Moe if they were making any progress on identifying the old man from the cabin when Fitz walked in followed by a tall sharply dressed black man with close-cropped hair. He wore civilian clothes but his military bearing was obvious. He had on a nylon jacket with a patch on the front right and ARMY CID emblazoned in white letters on the left.

Fitz introduced Buck and Moe to Major Richard Cranston. They shook hands all around. Moe suggested they get out of the cramped office and move to the conference room down the hall. Once seated around the conference room table, the Major opened the computer bag he had slung over his shoulder and pulled out a file. He slid the file over to Fitz and sat down.

"First I would like to apologize for taking so long to get back to you. Didn't realize the urgency until I received a call from headquarters in Washington. I was told this was a top priority," said the Major. Buck silently thanked Jess Gonzales.

The Major continued. "The fingerprints you uploaded caught us all off guard." He pointed to the file. "They belong to First Lieutenant James Michael Forester. Lt. Forester has been listed as missing and presumed dead since 1968. He was awarded a bronze star posthumously for bravery during the battle from which he disappeared. Although an extensive search had been made after the battle, his body was never found. He has been in our POW/MIA registry since that time, until today."

Fitz read through the file and slid it over to Buck. Buck had seen his fair share of military files just like this one as an Army MP. He quickly scanned the file. Lt. Forester had entered the Army in 1965 as a ninety-day wonder. Basically, he went from civilian to army officer with only ninety days of training before he was shipped off to Vietnam. It was said during the Vietnam war that the lifespan of a fresh Lieutenant was about sixteen minutes. Forester had beaten the odds and had been involved in several large-scale operations while in country.

Buck closed the file slid it to Moe and looked at the Major. "Why are you here Major? I am sure the Army has better things for a Major to do than to drive all the way from Denver to Aspen to deliver a simple file. Could have sent the file by email. What's not in the file?"

Fitz and Moe looked at Buck and then at the Major. They weren't sure what was happening. The Major looked at Buck and pulled another file from his computer bag and slid it over to Buck. Buck opened the file and started to read. He finished and slid the file to Fitz and Moe.

The Major sat back in the chair and said. "Lt. Forester and his unit were being investigated for an attack on a village just south of the DMZ. This was right after the My Lai massacre and the army was very sensitive to having its units running amuck and killing civilians. Lt. Forester and several of his soldiers were slated to be arrested within a day or two of the battle they were in. No one outside CID had been told of the arrest, so we doubt he ran because of it. The information that was gathered during the investigation was that Forester tried to stop the carnage and he threatened to have the men responsible brought up on charges. Our sources indicated that he took the massacre to heart and was extremely depressed that he had not been able to stop it. Our first assumption when we couldn't locate him was that he might have been fragged by his own men. We could never prove it, so we were back to, he was either killed during the battle, taken prisoner or he finally had enough and just disappeared into the forest. Until your fingerprint inquiry came through, we just weren't sure. Now we are."

The Major sat quietly. Buck looked at Fitz and then Moe. He said to the Major, "what is the Army's interest in this moving forward.?"

The Major thought for a minute. "We have a conflict. He was cleared of all charges and awarded the bronze star. He is also now a deserter, possibly a kidnapper and if I read your report correctly, was involved in a shootout with police. He is an MIA who has been located and should be treated as a hero but the circumstances make that almost impossible."

Buck closed his eyes and scratched his forehead. "Unless Fitz or Moe disagree, all indications are that he was protecting the children he was with. How he got those children is still under investigation but you are correct, he is still a deserter and as a former soldier myself, I cannot see the army giving this man a military burial. My feeling is that the body will remain with us until the Army can notify any existing relatives and if they choose to take the body, that will be up to them. I would suggest the army remove his name from the POW/MIA registry and close his file."

Moe and Fitz had nothing to add. Buck had spoken from his heart and he felt the Major agreed with him. The Major handed his business card to Fitz. "We are already in the process of making the notification. If no one claims his body, please give me a call. No matter what happens I will see that he gets a decent burial even if not necessarily a military funeral."

The Major stood, shook hands all around and Fitz led him down the hall to the main entrance. Moe and Buck discussed the Major's visit and came to the same conclusion. They weren't sure what the Army was looking for but they didn't find it here. Fitz had returned to the conference room and they spent a few minutes discussing both cases thus far.

Moe had been bringing back a report from the printer when he had first encountered Buck and he showed the report to Buck and Fitz. The report came from the State Crime Lab in Pueblo. The bullets that had killed Ranger Susan Corey had come from the M1 Carbine they had found at the old cabin. Now they just needed to figure out who pulled the trigger.

Buck was beat and he said goodnight and headed for his car. He couldn't remember the last time he slept.

Chapter Forty-Eight

Paul Webber spent most of the day behind the counter at the Pitkin County Clerk's Office going through book upon dusty book of property ownership records trying to pinpoint the owner of the old mine and cabin. Not all of the mining claims were digitized, so it was pretty much all hand work. He was able to find the general location of the cabin on the county plat map but after that, his trail hit a lot of roadblocks trying to identify individual mining claims in an area that had several dozen claims.

With the help of several of the nice ladies in the Clerk's Office, he was finally able to narrow down the claim to just a couple and then finally he hit pay dirt, as the old miner's use to say. He found the original claim for the land under the cabin and spent the rest of the day following sale after sale until he finally got to what he believed was the last purchase.

He felt good about what he found since the last time the mining claim changed hands was in the early 1940's. The claim had not changed hands since. Now he was working his computer trying to locate the person who had last purchased the claim. He was just about to give up for the day when he found a motor vehicle registration for one Marvin Bishop Jr. He had been searching for Marvin Bishop and this was the closest he had gotten.

The only problem was that Marvin Bishop was fifty years old. He couldn't possibly have purchased a mining claim in the 1940's but perhaps his father or grandfather had. He was able to run a reverse directory search and found a number for Mr. Bishop. Marvin Bishop lived in Castle Rock Colorado. Actually, based on his address he lived in Castle Pines, a very exclusive gated community just south of Denver and full of huge mansions.

Paul dialed the phone number he had found and was pleased when the call went through. The call was answered by a woman with a heavy Spanish accent. "Hello, Ma'am," he said. "I am looking for Mr. Marvin Bishop. My name is Paul Webber and I am an Investigator with the Colorado Bureau of Investigations."

"Dr. Bishop is not home right now. Could I take your number and have him call you back?" she responded. Paul gave her his cell phone number and told her it was urgent that he speak with Dr. Bishop as soon as possible. She promised to pass on is number and hung up.

Paul hoped his next task would be a bit easier but as he dove back into the internet, he soon realized that it was probably not going to be. It seems that half the outdoor stores in Aspen carried the lantern they had found in the mine. Plus, it was also available online through Amazon.

Paul decided to let that search wait and he pulled the picture he had taken of the victim's face and decided to hit some of the bars and restaurants in town and see if anyone had seen her. He needed to get something to eat anyway, so this would be a great opportunity

Since he had been cooped up all day in the musty archives, he decided to do his search on foot. He left the Clerk and Recorder's

Office, crossed Main Street and headed south on Galena Street. His destination was Wagner Park but he stopped along the way to grab a deli sandwich and a bottle of water. Once sated, he continued on his journey.

Paul worked his way through the homeless people in the park and was getting frustrated. The picture he had was not the best sample of what someone looked like and the more squeamish in the park turned their heads away when he showed it to them. He finally found a small group of young men and women sitting together at a picnic table and approached them with the picture.

As each person looked at the picture, one young girl mouthed "Oh my god," and covered her mouth with her hand. It was too late. Paul heard her and he asked her to look at the picture again.

"Do you know this girl?" Paul asked.

The girl looked at the picture again. "It looks like Blue, but she left town a couple weeks ago." Paul asked her to look at it again. Then one of the young men in the group asked to see it again and he agreed with the young girl.

"What do you know about this girl, Blue?" Paul asked.

The group didn't really know much. She had shown up in Aspen a couple weeks back and was only around for a little while before she left. One young man said he thought she came from some a small town in North Carolina or someplace back east. The group kind of agreed. She wasn't all that talkative and she stayed mostly to herself. The girl who first identified her said she use to spend a lot of time in the alley behind the Jackpot Bar.

Paul spent a few more minutes talking to the group and then thanked them and headed for the Jackpot Bar and Grill. Halfway there his phone rang and he answered. "Paul Webber."

"Uh, hello Detective Webber. This is Dr. Marvin Bishop. My housekeeper said you left an urgent message. How can I help you?"

"Thanks for calling back Dr. Bishop." Paul went on to explain the reason for his call and that he was trying to reach a Marvin Bishop who owned a small group of mining claims in the Aspen area. Dr. Bishop thought for a minute and then told Paul that it was possible that his father had once owned some worthless mining claims but he would need to talk to his father and look through his father's papers.

Paul asked him to please do that and then asked for his address and asked if it would be possible for him to come by tomorrow and meet with Dr. Bishop's father. Bishop explained that his father had suffered a stroke about five years back and he couldn't guarantee if his father would be able to have a conversation but that the detective was welcome to come by at around noon. His father was best in the mornings.

Paul thanked the Doctor and hung up. He felt good about his progress, so he continued walking to the Jackpot.

Chapter Forty-Nine

The Jackpot Bar and Grill had been an Aspen institution for years. It was dark and smelled like old beer and vomit and it was one of the most popular places in town for the younger set. They had live music five nights a week during the summer and the food was marginal at best. Paul walked through the front door and almost gagged but he squared up his shoulders, stepped up to the bar and asked to speak with the manager.

The bartender looked him up and down. "Maggie Stevens. This is my place. You a cop?"

Paul pulled out his CBI ID card and held out his hand. "Paul Webber, Colorado Bureau of Investigation." Maggie shook his hand. She had a firm handshake. Paul also noticed that she was a very attractive woman. He figured she must be in her fifties but he would find out he was wrong.

Maggie Stevens was actually in her seventies. She told Paul she had owned the bar since the early 1970's. She bought it with her ex-husband. Paul asked her how long she had been in Aspen and she told him that she had been involved in an auto accident in 1964 and spent several months in the hospital in a coma. She went through several months of rehab and when she was finished, she decided to stay in Aspen. Over the years she worked in several bars until her and her ex-husband were able to buy the Jackpot.

"What can I do for CBI?" she asked.

Paul explained the reason for his visit and asked her if he could show her a picture of the person he was looking for. He told her the picture was a little disturbing. He opened up the gallery app on his phone and held the picture up for Maggie to see.

"Girl doesn't look too good," commented Maggie. She looked closer, and then she yelled across the floor for the big guy who was setting up a podium at the front door. Boomer was her lead bouncer and she showed him the picture.

"This look like the girl you threw out of here about a week or so ago?" she asked him. He looked closer at the picture. "She looked much better that night than she does in this picture, but yeah, sure looks like her. Found her wandering around from table to table finishing off anything that was left in the glasses after people left the bar."

"Anyone pay any particular attention to her while she was here?" Paul asked.

Boomer thought for a minute. "Not really. She was pretty much by herself until I sent her packing."

Paul thanked Boomer and Maggie and walked back out into the clean mountain air. He stopped a few more young people as he walked down the sidewalk but he wasn't able to get any more information on the woman they called Blue. He was a little discouraged but he had made progress. He headed back to his car, but first, he wanted to stop off at the Sheriff's office to see if anything came back on her prints.

He walked through the front door of the Sheriff's office, presented his ID to the desk officer and was buzzed through the locked door. He found the young woman who had helped him send the prints through the AFIS system and asked her if anything had come back on his prints. Nothing yet.

He sat down at the empty conference room table and dialed Buck. Buck had just gotten out of the shower and was getting ready to put his head down when his phone rang. He checked the number and answered his phone.

"Hey, Paul. What's up?"

Paul filled him in on the conversations with the young people in the park and the conversation with the owner and the bouncer at the Jackpot. He told him about what he found on the mining claim and his conversation with Dr. Bishop. He told Buck he was going to drive over to Denver in the morning to interview the doctor and hopefully his father. Buck told him he had done a good job and to let him know how things went in Denver. Buck was going to meet up with Dr. Parker and the archeology team and see if they were making any progress. He was also going to check with forensics and the crime lab. He reminded Paul that the murder file had been uploaded and to make sure he recorded the information from his multiple interviews.

Buck disconnected the call. He pressed speed dial one and heard the Director's phone ringing. The Director answered and Buck filled him in on the progress so far. He told the Director what an excellent job Paul Webber had done with tracking down the mining claims and getting somewhere on the girl's identity.

He also told the Director about the visit from the Army CID agent. He relayed the conversation as best he could remember it and then voiced the same question to the Director.

"I just can't figure out what the Army was after today. I got the feeling that maybe they wanted us to clear this guy so they could honor him. Seemed a little weird."

The Director agreed and then asked Buck a question he hadn't thought of yet. "What's the possibility that this guy Forester has friends or relations in high places?"

Buck thought for a minute. "Hadn't thought of that possibility. I'm going to suggest to Fitz that they take a little bit deeper look into their suspect. Thanks, Director."

The Director hung up and Buck dialed Fitz's cellphone. When she answered, he told her about his feelings about the army's visit and suggested she look into Forester's background a little deeper now that they had his military file. They talked for a few more minutes and then she hung up. Buck finally crawled into bed and shut off the light.

Chapter Fifty

Paul Webber turned off Highway 287 onto Happy Canyon Road and pulled up to the main gate for Castle Pines. He presented his ID to the guard at the gate and gave him the address he was seeking. The guard walked into the guard shack, made a phone call and returned to the car. He handed Paul back his ID, gave him directions to the address and opened the security gate.

Paul missed his turn once and managed to circle back and find the home of Dr. Marvin Bishop Jr. Dr. Bishop lived on a quiet cul-de-sac. The house, although not as large as Paul expected, was set back amongst the trees. He could see a nice view of the mountains from behind the house as he pulled into the driveway.

Grabbing his computer bag, Paul walked up the sidewalk and rang the doorbell. The door was answered by an older Latina wearing a lavender maids uniform.

"Mr. Webber?" she asked. "Please come in. The doctor is waiting for you."

Paul stepped into a beautifully appointed entry foyer with marble tiles and light wooden millwork. He followed the housekeeper to an open door where she stepped aside and directed him in. Dr. Marvin Bishop Jr. rose from his desk and met Paul with a strong handshake.

"Is it Agent or Detective Webber?" he asked.

"Paul will be just fine Doctor and thank you for seeing me so quickly." Paul sat down in one of the leather guest chairs across the desk from Dr. Bishop.

"I only hope you haven't driven all this way for nothing. My father seems to be having a fairly good morning but I am not sure how much he will be able to answer. He suffered a stroke five years ago and we brought him back to Colorado from his home in Pittsburg. His memory skills are a little off and he has very little use of his left side."

Paul told the Doctor that anything that might help would be appreciated. The Doctor handed Paul a stack of legal documents and explained that these were all the documents he could find related to his father's dalliance with buying up mining claims in the Colorado Mountains. It seemed that his father had seen the writing on the wall when it came to World War II and he thought the country would need plenty of gold and silver if it entered the war. He thought he would get rich.

Marvin Bishop Sr. had, over the years just prior to World War II, purchased eleven small mining claims in the Colorado high country. All sight unseen and all pretty much worthless. Dr. Bishop explained that his father had never been to Colorado prior to five years ago after he suffered his stroke. He was just always fascinated with the old west and wanted to be able to say he was a part of it. A law firm in Denver, that specialized in mining claims, handled all the purchases.

He went on to explain that his father had joined the army, as every able-bodied man had done after Pearl Harbor and had seen action as an Army Engineer. Once the war was over, he had returned to Pittsburgh and began a career as a Mechanical Engineer until he retired in 2000 after the death of his wife.

Paul had listened intently as Dr. Bishop spoke and made a lot of notes in his little notebook that he always carried. He now looked at the papers that Dr. Bishop handed him. The Doctor was correct. There was not much new information in the stack. He pulled out the documents for the claim he was interested in and looked through the pages. He had gotten pretty much the same information from the Clerk and Recorders Office in Aspen.

"Would you like to meet my father now, Paul?" asked the Doctor.

Dr. Bishop stood up, as did Paul, and they walked down a hallway to a room off the kitchen. Dr. Bishop knocked and opened the door.

"Dad, you have a visitor," he said as they entered the room. Paul looked around the room and the first thing he noticed was a larger version of the mountain view he had seen from the driveway. He also noticed that other than a hospital-style bed there was very little medical equipment in the room. The Doctor was standing next to a leather recliner.

The gentleman sitting in the recliner was quite old. He was wearing a white button-down shirt with a red, white and blue striped bow tie. He looked very dapper.

"Dad," said the Doctor. "This is Paul and he would like to ask you a few questions about some of your old mining claims. Would that be alright?"

Paul stepped up to the recliner and shook a very frail, almost translucent, hand. There was a noticeable droop on the left side of

Marvin Bishop's face but his eyes were bright and shiny. Paul sensed there was still a lot of Marvin Bishop behind those eyes.

Paul sat down in the chair the doctor had brought over.

"Mr. Bishop. Thank you for seeing me today. I only have a few questions if that's ok?"

Marvin Bishop responded with a garbled answer and Paul looked at the Doctor who translated that it was ok and to please proceed. Paul showed Marvin Bishop a picture of the old cabin from his phone and asked him if he recognized the building. Marvin Bishop shook his head no. The rest of the conversation didn't go much better. Marvin Bishop confirmed what his son had said, that he had never even been to Colorado prior to 2000. Paul was able to make out some of his words but a lot of what Marvin Bishop said was garbled and Paul could see the frustration building in Marvin Bishop.

Paul was looking through his notes. He asked Mr. Bishop if he had ever leased his claims to anyone or allowed anyone to work the claims? Bishop said something that he couldn't make out. Dr. Bishop moved next to his dad and asked, "Dad can you repeat what you just said?"

Marvin Bishop looked frustrated but he repeated what he had said. Paul looked at the doctor who shrugged his shoulders. It had sounded like Marvin Bishop had said, "wicked smilley."

"Dad, we don't understand what you are trying to say."

The Doctor looked at Paul. "I think he is getting tired. We should let him rest. I am sorry you came all this way for nothing."

Paul stood up and gathered up his papers. He followed the Doctor back to the door when they both turned, startled by the noise. Marvin Bishop was using his good right hand and was banging furiously on the metal tray table next to his chair. He kept repeating the same thing. "Wicked smilly." Dr. Bishop rushed to his side and tried to calm him down but he kept banging and trying to communicate.

Paul knelt down on the other side of the recliner and in a very soft voice said. "Mr. Bishop, did you let someone work this claim after you bought it?"

Marvin Bishop stopped banging and smiled at Paul, who dug into his computer bag and pulled out a blank piece of paper and a wide tip black marker. He put it on the tray and slid the tray closer to Mr. Bishop. He took the cap off the marker and placed the marker in Mr. Bishop's good right hand.

Very slowly and with an engineer's precision, Mr. Bishop started to write on the paper. The Doctor looked at Paul and Paul just smiled. It took a few minutes and then Mr. Bishop reached out and handed the marker back to Paul. Paul put the cap back on the marker and picked up the paper. "Richard Smiley."

Paul shook Mr. Bishop's frail hand and thanked him for his time. He put the paper in his computer bag and followed Dr. Bishop out the door, gently closing it behind him.

Dr. Bishop looked at Paul. "How did you know what he was trying to say?"

"I didn't," said Paul. I just had a feeling he was trying to tell us something important. My dad, after his stroke, always tried to write down things he wanted to say. Thought it was worth a try."

"Well thank you for your patience and I sure hope this helps your investigation."

Paul thanked him for his hospitality and walked out the front door. He put his computer bag in the trunk of his car and pulled out his phone. He called the CBI office in Grand Junction and asked for Agent Ashley Baxter.

"Hey Bax, it's Paul," he said when she answered the phone.

"Paul. What's up? Thought you were with Buck?"

"Right now I'm in Denver. Have you got a few minutes to do a computer search for me?" He gave her the information he had gotten from Marvin Bishop and told her he would be back in Aspen in couple hours and if she found anything to call Buck.

He disconnected the call and dialed Buck's number but the call went straight to voicemail. He left a message telling Buck what he had found in Denver and that he had Ashley Baxter running it down on the computer. He hung up, started the car and pulled out of the driveway. Today was a good day.

Chapter Fifty-One

Buck stopped by the hospital to check on PIS only to find out that PIS had checked himself out of the hospital late the night before. He thanked the nurse and walked out of the hospital, got in his car and headed for the Conundrum Creek trailhead.

He was just pulling into the parking lot when his phone rang. He looked at the number and answered the call.

"Hi, Max. What's up?"

"Hi, Buck. How's my favorite cop?" she said.

Maxine Clinton was the head of the State Crime Lab in Pueblo. A former Biology Professor, Max had been running the lab for the past twenty years. She was about sixty-four years old, slightly overweight and had been married to her husband for just about all her adult life. Buck had seen Max converse fluently and eloquently with college professors and business leaders and he had seen her drink just about every cop she ever met under the table. She was a bourbon girl and proud of it. She considered Buck Taylor one of her closest friends and Buck felt the same way about her.

"Doing good Max."

"Are you working with Jane Fitzpatrick on the Aspen shooting?"

Buck explained that although it was not directly his case, he was still helping out when and if he could. Max told him that she used an open order for an overnight DNA test to run the DNA from the female that had been buried. The Director had originally approved it for the investigation into the drug cartel in Durango but she hadn't used it because that investigation had moved so quickly. She knew this case in Aspen was a top priority, so she went ahead and authorized the test.

That's what Buck liked about Max. She wasn't afraid to step up and make decisions. "Did you get any results?" Buck asked.

"You bet. I just emailed them to Fitz but since it was your DNA test I wanted to let you know I had used it." She gave Buck a quick rundown. "DNA belonged to Corrine Everheart. She's a real piece of work. She has a juvenile record that will need to be unsealed. She has an impressive arrest record for someone who was only thirty-five when she fell off the planet and disappeared. Drugs, gambling, prostitution, assault and oh yeah, kidnapping. She was only out of lockup for five months when she left West Virginia and was never seen again."

"Nice work Max. I will follow up with Fitz later today. Thanks."

Max ended the call the same way she had been doing for years. "God will watch over you, Buck Taylor. You are a good man. Stay safe." She hung up.

Although Buck hadn't been to church since he received his confirmation, he always appreciated Max's little blessing. It wasn't that he didn't believe in god. He wasn't sure what he really believed in. He didn't like organized religion but he never held that against anyone. A lot of people prayed for his wife during the five years she fought metastatic breast cancer but in the end, Lucy still died.

Although he was mad at first, he soon realized that in order to be mad at god he first had to believe in god and he just never got there. He always felt there were forces in the world that he couldn't explain and he always thanked the river spirits whenever he had a chance to do some fly fishing. He just didn't have a place for one god in his life. He never held Max's beliefs against her. He always figured that it couldn't hurt if she believed he was worthy.

Buck stepped out of his car, grabbed his backpack and started down the trail. The day had dawned a little overcast and there was definitely a chill in the air. The leaves were changing colors and almost every day it seemed there was more gold in them thar hills. He enjoyed this time of year. Fall was Lucy's favorite time of year and they had enjoyed many fall walks together on the trails around Gunnison before she was no longer able to walk without a cane. The walks had stopped completely when she needed a wheelchair to get around. Then it was just little jaunts on the concrete sidewalks in the park along the river. Even after all this time he still missed her every day.

Buck reached the old mine cabin just as Professor Standish and his archeology students were taking down their tent and packing up their tools. He had passed a couple firefighters on the trail who were carrying out the last body bag. Professor Standish stood with his hands on his hips looking around the site. He spotted Buck as he entered the clearing.

"Morning Professor. Looks like you guys are wrapping up. How did it go?" Buck asked.

"Oh, good morning Agent Taylor. We had a fascinating time. It isn't very often we get to use our archeological procedures on a modern site. We learned quite a bit."

Professor Standish went on to explain to Buck the procedures they had followed and some of their preliminary finding. He mentioned that much of what they had uncovered would need to be verified in the lab but he spoke with a very nice woman at the State Crime Lab and she was making sure his tests had top priority.

Buck saw how excited the Professor had gotten and he listened intently but he needed a few answers, so he interrupted the Professor's debrief.

"Professor, is there any way from your exam to determine if this was the work of one person or several?" The Professor asked one of his students to bring over his laptop and he fired it up and opened to a series of photos. Buck moved in for a closer look.

The Professor pointed his pen to some of the pictures that contained very detailed images of some of the cut marks and slices. He pointed out some similarities and also some incongruities as he called them. Then he stepped back.

"Based on what we were able to see it is our opinion that all these bodies were killed in the same manner by the same person."

"Any idea how long ago? I'm guessing this cabin has been around since the late 1880's but obviously, the hatch appears to be newer."

"Quite right, Agent Taylor. We did a little research and determined that the screws in the hatch were most likely purchased sometime during the 1950's. We are having one of the welds tested but we feel confident that it will show about the same age. The wooden furniture in the mine is from the early 1900's, as is the old kerosene stove."

"How about the bodies, Professor?" Buck asked.

"The lab tests on the skin and the carbon dating will probably corroborate our findings but we would estimate that based on several factors the bodies were killed and left in the mine sometime during the mid-fifties to early sixties."

Buck thanked the Professor and asked him if he could email him a preliminary report of their findings as soon as possible. The Professor said that would not be a problem and he should have something ready first thing in the morning. He took Buck's business card with his email address on it and headed off to join his students in their packing.

Chapter Fifty-Two

Buck put on a pair of nitrile gloves, slung his backpack over his shoulder and climbed down the ladder into the mine. He noticed the blue fingerprint dust on the ladder and he reminded himself to check the murder book and see what evidence the forensic team had sent to the lab.

He stood at the entrance to the first chamber and scanned the area. He had been over the space several times himself and he knew the forensic team had gone over every square inch with a fine-tooth comb but Buck had found over the years, that no matter how thorough the teams were, sometimes things got missed. It was even more important now that there was no one in the space and all the evidence had been removed.

The space looked different. The bed frame was still there but the old straw mattress had been removed as had the little wooden cabinet and the leather roll of knives. He noted that the team had also removed a significant amount of dirt from under the old shackles. He assumed they would be looking for a DNA match but he figured if they found one it would have to be a modern connection since DNA hadn't even been discovered in the mid-fifties. He continued to scan the chamber.

Finding nothing else, he moved down the tunnel to the back chamber, where the mummified bodies had been found. Here too, the old straw mattresses had been removed. He pulled his flashlight out of his backpack and shined the light under all the bed frames and along the ceiling. Nothing much to see here.

Buck was turning to head back to the ladder when he had a thought. He had no idea how far back into the mine the forensic team had gone. He knew the SWAT deputies had done a cursory check just to make sure there were no other bodies around but he wasn't sure if the tunnel had been thoroughly searched. He turned on his flashlight again and headed down the tunnel.

The beam of light from his flashlight was barely holding its own as the darkness of the mine tunnel surrounded him. Buck had never been claustrophobic but the darkness in the mine was blacker than anything he could remember and it filled him with dread. Shaking off the closeness of the dark he continued down the tunnel until he came to the end. He panned his flashlight around the tunnel.

There was nothing to see at the end of the tunnel. Whatever work had happened here happened a long time ago. He had no idea what he was even looking for. Maybe just a clue to who had been the last person to do any kind of work in the tunnel.

He could barely see the light from the back chamber as he turned and started back down the tunnel the way he had come. He was swinging the flashlight beam back and forth and almost missed it on the first pass. He took a step back and moved the flashlight slowly over a small pile of debris that was pushed up against the wall.

A glint from something shiny caught his eye as the flashlight passed over the pile on the third pass. Buck knelt down and started to slowly move the debris around. He spotted a flat metal object about the size of a quarter and picked it up. Although it was slightly rusted and dirty Buck recognized it immediately. It was a partially rounded square with two red swords crossed over a blue background and the banner across the top said "Mountain". This pin belonged to a member of the 10th Mountain division. He also knew right away that this pin was a lot younger than the mine.

Buck pulled a small plastic evidence bag out of his backpack and noted the date and time. He also set it back on the ground where he found it and took several pictures with his cellphone. He placed the pin in the evidence bag, sealed it and signed his name across the flap.

Buck continued his search of the tunnel but found nothing else of interest and finally headed for the ladder. Once outside, he closed the hatch and removed the Sheriff's padlock from the hasp.

Buck called the Sheriff and he answered on the second ring. Buck told him what he found in the tunnel and they discussed what the pin represented. One issue the Sheriff brought up was the fact that there were several men who lived in the county who had once been part of the 10th Mountain Division. Many of the men who trained with the 10th, essentially America's first skiing soldiers during World War II, were involved in the startup of America's recreational skiing industry. A lot of former soldiers had settled in Aspen, Vail and Steamboat and had been the driving force in opening skiing up to the masses. The Sheriff personally knew of at least 10 former members who lived in the county. He would have one of his deputies put together a list for Buck.

The Sheriff also asked Buck if he could stop by the office when he had a minute. There were two investigators from the Arapahoe County District Attorney's office who wanted to interview Buck about the shooting involving the two kids. The County

Attorney had requested an outside agency handle the shooting investigation especially since two kids had been killed.

Buck told the Sheriff he was on his way and that he could also have the Public Works guys come get the generator, the lights and the fan. He asked the Sheriff to see if they could weld the hatch shut so no one could enter it.

Buck hung up and checked his messages. Paul Webber had called with the name of a person of interest. There was also a call from his youngest son Jason, just checking in to make sure he was alright. He had heard about the death of the ranger and about Buck's involvement. He didn't mention the shooting, which Buck was glad of. Jason was much more sensitive than his brother and sister and he took everything to heart. He had been very close to Buck's wife Lucy and he still seemed to be struggling with her death.

Buck called Jason, got his voice mail and left a message telling him that he was fine and he would call soon. He grabbed his backpack, slung it over his shoulder and headed for the car. He felt good. The pin in his pocket was their first solid lead.

Chapter Fifty-Three

Buck pulled his car into the Sheriff's office parking lot and turned off the engine. He sat for a minute and then pulled out his cellphone and dialed Hank Clancy, Special Agent in Charge of the FBI's Denver office. Hank answered on the second ring.

"Buck Taylor. How the hell are you?"

Hank had been an integral part of the investigation of a Mexican drug cartel trying to set up a distribution network in Durango that Buck had headed. With the help of several local, state and federal agencies, they eventually broke up the cartel's operation and, in the process, made the largest drug bust in history. Hank, in spite of being a FED, was good people and he and Buck had a good working relationship.

Buck and Hank chatted a few minutes about the results of the drug bust in Durango and where things stood with the investigations that continued as a result of their raid. He then took a few minutes to fill Hank in on this new serial killer investigation in Aspen. Hank listened carefully and asked a few questions.

"So, the real reason for my call is to see if the FBI has any record of a serial killer operating in Colorado in the late fifties early sixties?"

"Geez Buck," said Hank. "You don't want much do you? I will admit that I am intrigued. Fifteen mummified bodies in a mine shaft. How crazy is that?"

"Yeah," replied Buck. "I've never run across anything like this before. New one on me."

"I'll bet the Sheriff is just thrilled?" said Hank.

Hank went on to explain that multiple murderers were not called serial killers back in the fifties and sixties. That wouldn't happen until the early seventies. He told Buck that it was unlikely their records had been digitized that far back but he would have one of his clerks start researching and see if they had anything that might help. He asked Buck to keep him informed and if he needed the FBI to get involved, to just give him a call. Buck hung up.

Paul Webber was just starting up the stairs to the front entrance to the Sheriff's office when he spotted Buck walking across the parking lot. He waited at the top of the stairs.

"Hey, Buck. Did you get my message?"

"Yeah," replied Buck. "Sounds like making the drive to Denver was worthwhile."

Paul filled him in on the visit with the Doctor and his father as they walked through the doors, showed their ID's and were buzzed through. Buck set his backpack down on the conference room table and grabbed a seat. He removed the 10th Mountain Division pin in the evidence bag from his pocket and laid it on the table.

While Buck opened his laptop to the murder book page, Paul examined the pin.

Buck looked up from his laptop. "Any chance that this Doctor Bishop or someone in his family might have known about the mine?"

"I doubt it," Paul replied. "His kids are teenagers and he told me that they were all fascinated when they found the mining claim deeds. His father, Marvin Sr., had never mentioned ever owning the claims and the deeds were locked away in an old safe that had been in Marvin Sr.'s garage in Pittsburg up until 5 years ago. I don't see any involvement on their part."

Paul went on to tell Buck about the outburst from Marvin Sr. and that it appeared that Marvin Sr. had allowed someone to work the mine. Since Marvin didn't really believe there was anything of value in the mine he gave this person permission with no written contract or anything.

Buck pulled out his cellphone, hooked it up to his laptop and downloaded the pictures of the pin he took in the mine. He then looked over the forensic reports that had been uploaded so far. The forensic team had found some fingerprints. Many were degraded, but they were working through them. They had found a bunch of residue on the old mattress and were separating out the stains to run DNA. They were not hopeful.

He had an email from Dr. Parker saying that she would be doing the autopsy on the young woman this afternoon and asked Buck if he could join her. He checked his watch.

His email notification chimed and he looked to see what had come in. There was a new email from Professor Standish. He opened the email and read the preliminary report. The report covered everything they had discussed earlier in the morning. Buck saved it to the murder book.

"Paul, I am going to drop in on the autopsy of our newest victim. Why don't you follow up on the information you got about her so far?"

Buck stood up and started to close down his laptop when

one of the deputies walked in and handed him a piece of paper with eleven names and addresses on it.

"Sheriff asked me to put this together for you. It's everyone we know of who were once in the 10th Mountain Division."

"Thank you, deputy," said Buck. He looked over the list and handed it to Paul.

"Go ahead and start working through this list. I will call you when I am done at the autopsy and we can split up what's left of the list."

Paul grabbed his computer bag and headed out the door. Buck walked down the hall to find Fitz when a voice called his name. Buck turned around to find two people walking towards him.

"Agent Taylor. Detectives Young and Lee, Arapahoe County District Attorney's office. Do you have a few minutes for us?"

Buck checked his watch. He had about an hour before the autopsy, so he followed the detectives into an interview room. They asked him to hand his service weapon and any backup weapons he had to a deputy standing outside the door, which he did and then they closed the door and asked him to take a seat.

Detective Young was about forty years old, Buck figured. He was tall and appeared to be very fit. He had blond hair which was starting to turn gray and bright blue eyes. His partner Detective Lee was a short Asian woman. She looked to be somewhere in her thirties and she had dark hair and dark eyes. She smiled at Buck as he sat down.

Chapter Fifty-Four

Detective Lee read Buck his Miranda rights, which was a standard part of an interview like this and Buck declined counsel and signed the paper indicating such. Buck had nothing to hide. They asked Buck if he minded if they recorded the interview and he told them that was fine. Detective Young asked him to tell them about the events leading to the shooting. Buck knew that they probably already had a copy of his statement and that they would use his words now to corroborate what he had put in his written statement.

Buck spent the next twenty minutes describing the events of the search for the ranger's body and the subsequent search of the area that eventually led to the old cabin and the mine. He explained about the explosions and about returning fire and about finding the kids dead along with the old soldier, who had since been identified.

The detectives listened and took a lot of notes on the pads they had in front of them. Buck finished and sat back in his chair. Detective Young opened up a manila folder that sat on the table in front of him and started looking through the pages.

"Any ill effects from the shootout in Durango? I understand you sought professional help?" asked Young without looking up from the papers. He then looked up and stared at Buck.

Buck was caught a little off guard but he remained calm. He had used the same technique himself many times. He was curious how they got his personal medical records. The psychologist he had seen, once, had been at the request of the Director.

Buck calmed his breathing. "No ill effects," Buck said. "I went to the psychologist once, as is routine in CBI for any agent involved in a shooting."

Lee made a note on her pad. Young continued. "From your report, you and the two deputies came under fire and returned fire. Were you able to identify who was shooting at you?"

"Have you ever been involved in a shootout Detective?" Buck asked.

Detective Young looked a little offended. "My record has nothing to do with your actions Agent. Please confine your answers to the case at hand."

"As I stated in my report and also to you just a minute ago. We came under attack as soon as we entered the field. The explosions occurred followed by the shooting. When the cabin exploded, I was thrown to the ground by our tracker who received a serious injury. The deputies identified where the shooting was coming from and they returned fire. The older man charged out of the woods firing as he ran and we all shot back. When the next explosion occurred, we spotted movement in the trees and fired. We had no idea that kids were involved until we cleared the scene. My view of the scene at the large tree was partially blocked by the remains of the cabin."

The questions continued along that same vein for a few more minutes and Buck was getting annoyed. He answered every question truthfully but he started to sense a bit of hostility on the part of Young. Lee hadn't said much during the interview so far. Buck decided it was time to put an end to the interview. He looked at his watch.

Young kept at it. "Do you have any remorse, Agent, for the two kids that were killed or is it just another day for you?"

"Look," said Buck. "No one likes to see kids get hurt or killed. We were in a shootout with an unknown number of individuals. We didn't have time to ask them their ages. We are all saddened by their deaths but it was them or us. They chose the course of action that resulted in their deaths. Now if you have no further questions, I have an autopsy to get to."

Buck pushed his chair back and stood up. He turned for the door when Young said. "So you're a big deal hero cop and you're too good to answer our questions. You have a trail of dead bodies following you Agent and I mean to find out if you're a hero or a killer!"

Buck stopped at the door and turned to face Young who was now on his feet. He started to step towards the table when Detective Lee grabbed Young's arm.

"Tom you're out of line. I need you to back off."

Young looked at Lee and then at Buck. Buck had misread the dynamic. He now realized that Detective Lee was the lead investigator and Young was the pit-bull. It was his job to get under Buck's skin and try to provoke a response and Buck had almost fallen for it.

Detective Young walked away from the table in the opposite direction from Buck. Detective Lee came over to Buck and held out her hand.

"I apologize, Agent Taylor. You have been truthful with us today and I allowed the line of questioning to drift away from the reason we are here. You are free to go."

Buck shook her hand and she signaled the deputy outside the interview room to unlock the door. Buck walked out, retrieved his weapons and ran into the Sheriff, who indicated for Buck to follow him. Once inside the Sheriff's office he closed the door and sat down behind his desk.

"Shit Buck. I am really sorry about that interview. I watched most of it and if you hadn't stopped it, I was going to. Young was way out of line. The interviews with Manning and Sanchez went just fine. Any idea where the hostility came from towards you?"

"No idea. I've never met either one of them."

Buck and the Sheriff talked for a few minutes about both cases. The Sheriff told him that Professor Standish called and reported that his students were having some luck rehydrating the fingers of some of the mummies and were working with his fingerprint tech to try to get some clear prints. They had also shipped the samples off for quick DNA analysis.

Buck thanked the Sheriff and went in search of Fitz and Steiner.

Chapter Fifty-Five

Buck found Fitz and Steiner in their cubicles. Both were on the phone but Fitz held up a finger and pointed to her visitor chair. Buck lifted a pile of file folders off the chair, set them on the floor and sat down. Fitz spoke for a few more minutes and then hung up.

"Hey, Buck. How's the serial killer case coming?" she asked.

"Good. Heading for the autopsy in a few minutes. Did you talk to Max Clinton at the State Crime Lab?"

Fitz told Buck she had spoken with Max and had gotten the information on Corrine Everheart. She told him she had just gotten off the phone with a very nice detective in Charleston, West Virginia and that he was familiar with her disappearance in that city and would send her everything they have on her. She was no stranger to the police in West Virginia. He was also going to start running down missing children around ten years old and see what turns up. She told him that Moe was in the process of uploading the kid's pictures to the missing and exploited children's database and was going to send out a national alert to see if they could figure out where she grabbed the kids.

"I heard you had a little run-in with the Detective Young. Also heard you kept your cool. Thought you might be interested in knowing that I have the ballistics report. Came in about an hour ago. They only matched one bullet from the rifle you were using and that was a non-fatal wound in the old man's shoulder."

Buck let that sink in a minute. "I wonder what his deal was then? I felt like he was mad at me and I have no idea why."

"Shit, Buck. You've been through more on the job in the last two months than most cops deal with in a whole career. My guess is he was just jealous and wanted to see how far he could push you. Good for you that you didn't respond."

"Thanks, Fitz. Hey, do me a favor and ask the Sheriff if you can send a copy of the report to my Director. I'd really appreciate that. By the way, does it say who had the kill shot on the two kids?"

She clicked open a page on her laptop and turned the screen so he could see. Buck read the report and then stepped back. His expression said it all.

"Thanks, Fitz."

Buck headed down the hall to the Sheriff's office. He stuck his head in the door. "Earl, you got a minute?"

The Sheriff waved him in and he shut the door.

"Looks serious Buck. What's up?"

"Fitz just showed me the ballistic report on the two kids. I just wanted you to know that Sanchez took the death of those two dead kids really hard and was struggling with the possibility that he was the one who killed one or both. I thought you should know his mental state before you show him the report. I also asked her to send a copy of the report over to CBI if it is ok with you."

"Sure thing Buck and thanks for the heads up on Sanchez. This is gonna hurt him bad if that's the case. He's a good deputy. Would hate to lose him over this."

Buck stood up and walked out of the Sheriff's office. He

walked out the front door and headed for the hospital and the autopsy on the girl from the mine.

Dr. Parker was already underway when he entered the autopsy suite and apologized for being late. Buck stood in the corner as Dr. Parker and her assistant went through the autopsy step by step recording everything she did on both video and audio. Buck had stood through many an autopsy in his career but he never got used to seeing young people on the table. He noted that the girl seemed very thin for her height. She also had other scarring on her body that looked older than the cut marks. Now that the body was washed, the number of cuts and slices was impressive.

Dr. Parker concluded the autopsy while her assistant closed up the Y incision. She removed her gloves and apron and walked over to Buck.

"Afraid there is nothing unusual here Buck. She died of massive blood loss caused by the cuts. She does have evidence of some superficial bruising but those appear to be several weeks old. I do not think they are related. She is also very malnourished. Probably twenty maybe twenty-five pounds under average weight for her height. We'll have the results of the tox screen in a week to ten days. I hope they find something because the idea that she suffered through this torture while she was awake is going to keep me up nights."

"Thanks, Doc. By the way. How you doing with the mummies?"

"Last time I spoke to the pathologists next door, they had gone through ten of the bodies and were going to stop for the day and pick it up tomorrow. I will email you a preliminary report tonight but it will be almost identical to the report on this young lady."

She turned to leave but Buck stopped her. "Almost identical Doc. What's different?"

She signaled for Buck to follow her and they headed to the room next door that was being used as an additional autopsy suite. One of the mummies was still on the table and she pulled back the sheet to expose the body.

"I will tell you Buck, in all my years of doing this work in LA I never worked on a mummy before. Professor Standish and his team were incredibly helpful. It was quite the learning experience, if you like to learn stuff like this." She pointed to the cuts on the chest of the mummy.

"Professor Standish and Dr. Richland both agreed that the cuts on the mummies appear to be deeper than those on our young lady next door. Their opinion is that the mummies they have looked at so far were mutilated by a man. There was also vaginal tearing evident. In other words, these ladies were raped just prior to their deaths."

She continued. "Our young lady has no sign of being raped or sexually abused in any way. In comparing the cut marks from our victim to the others, they cannot say with one hundred percent certainty that our victim was the work of a man. They feel the cuts were done with a lot less pressure and some even appeared to be tentative. They were not as smooth and clean as on the mummies even though the same knives were used. The end result was the same. She still bled out and died just like the mummies, but my guess is it took longer."

Chapter Fifty-Six

Buck leaned back against the counter and let what Dr. Parker just said sink in. Because all the mummies were women and the latest victim was also a woman he hadn't really thought about the fact that the serial killer could be a woman. He felt a little sexist. Women were just as capable as men at creating evil but his mind automatically went to a man because of the conditions. The brutality of the torture, the work being done in a mine, the bodies just left to mummify and the fact that the crimes were committed during the late fifties or early sixties. It all added up to a man being the perpetrator.

Since the latest crime imitated the original crimes in such great detail, his mind just went to the same place for some of the same reasons. The doer was a man. Could he be that wrong? He was going to have to change the way he looked at the crime.

"You ok Buck? You look perplexed," said Dr. Parker.

"No, not perplexed. Pissed off," replied Buck. "I feel like such an idiot. It never crossed my mind that the killer of our latest victim might be a woman. I made a judgment without having all the facts."

"It's ok Buck, we all do it. Now you have the facts so go look at this case from a different angle."

Buck thanked the Doctor for her time and walked out of the

hospital to his car. He opened his phone and called Paul Webber. Paul answered and Buck asked him if he had eaten dinner yet? It was getting late and Buck had realized, too late, that he had already missed lunch. He asked Paul to meet him at "The Ranch." "The Ranch" was a really good steakhouse in town. It was mostly a local joint and didn't have the same kind of prices some of the other restaurants in town had.

Paul Webber found Buck seated at a booth at the back of the restaurant. Buck had his back to the wall. Force of habit. Paul slid into the booth and the waitress came by. He ordered a beer and pulled out his notebook.

Buck filled him in on his conversation with Dr. Parker including the possibility that the latest victim was killed by a woman. Paul looked at Buck with a surprised look in his eyes.

"Wow, Buck. Never even considered that as a possibility. A woman serial killer? There aren't many of them."

He looked pensive for a minute and Buck said. "Paul. What are you thinking?"

"I was just wondering if our current serial killer could be a female relative or someone like that who has or had a close relationship to the old serial killer?"

Buck thought about that but held is thoughts as the waitress came by to take their orders. Once the waitress left Buck took a sip of his soda and looked at Paul.

"Great thought Paul. Let's put that on the back burner for a minute. Fill me in on your conversations with the 10th Mountain veterans."

Paul opened his notebook. "Of the eleven names on the list I was able to meet with nine of them today. I'll tell you Buck; it is really sad. These guys gave everything for their country and half of them can't even remember their names. Six of the ones I met today have serious Alzheimers. Their families let me look through some of the memorabilia they kept but I couldn't find anything related to a Richard Smiley. Two of the vets still had all their faculties. One guy thought he remembered a Richard Smiley but he wasn't sure. The other one didn't recall the name but he had some great stories to tell me. The last poor fella has been bedridden for decades and is in some kind of comatose state. I have two more to see tomorrow."

He read through his notes. "Oh, here it is. One guy suggested I call Sam Brinkman; he operates a small 10th Mountain Division museum in Minturn. He said they used to keep records of the guys who went through training. Might find something on Richard Smiley there."

The waitress delivered their steaks and the conversation lagged while they ate. Paul mentioned that he had talked to Ashley Baxter at the office but she hadn't had any luck looking for Richard Smiley either. She was expanding her search to other states and she was waiting for the army to get back with her. Paul asked if Buck knew how the other case was going and Buck filled him in on the identity of the man and the woman. He told him that they were publishing the kid's pictures to see if they could attract some leads.

Once finished with dinner Buck laid out the plan for the next day. He asked Paul to follow up with the last two vets. He took the phone number for Sam Brinkman and said he would follow up with him and he told Paul to meet him at the Sheriff's office at lunchtime and they would strategize further. The got up, paid their bill and headed for the parking lot.

Paul hopped in his car and headed for his hotel. Buck decided to take a walk. The night was cool and fall crisp and he needed to clear his head. He was mad at himself for almost getting lured in by

Detective Young. He was also mad that he had been so focused on the location of the crime and the fact that, old mines and rough men go together, that he ignored the possibility that the new killer could be a woman. He wondered if he was losing his touch.

Buck walked a couple blocks and stood looking out over the Roaring Fork River. This time of year the river was fairly low and it sparkled in the moonlight. He wished he had grabbed his flyrod out of his car. There was nothing like fly fishing to clear one's mind. Once that little fly hit the water, all your focus had to be on the interaction between the fly and the fish. You couldn't think of anything else.

He thought about the times when Lucy use to sit on the bank of a river somewhere and watch him fish. Even though she never took up the sport, he just loved having her there and she seemed to feel the same way. She would sit on the bank and later, after she got sick, in a lawn chair and read or crochet. He missed her alot and he was also glad she wasn't here right now because she would kick his ass for having doubts about his abilities. She was one tough Latina. Buck stepped away from the river and pulled out the phone number Paul had given him. It was late but this was important.

"Sam Brinkman."

Buck introduced himself and apologized for the lateness of the call. Sam told him not to worry, that since his wife died a few years back, he usually was at the museum late. Buck explained the reason for his call and the information he was looking for. Sam promised to get back to him as soon as he had anything to share.

Chapter Fifty-Seven

Buck had just finished entering the latest information in the murder book on his laptop and was getting ready to look through the latest forensic updates when his phone rang. He looked at his watch and noted the lateness of the hour but he answered the phone.

"Buck Taylor."

"Agent Taylor. Sam Brinkman here. I hope it's not too late?"

"No, Mr. Brinkman. I was just doing some computer work."

Sam interrupted. "I found some information for you and I knew you said this was important, so I wanted to get back to you right away."

Buck smiled. "Mr. Brinkman, I didn't expect you to work on this tonight."

"Not to worry, Agent Taylor. I don't have anything to go home to and I do love a challenge, so I got right on it. Took a bit to find the right timeframe but I do believe I found the information you were looking for."

Sam Brinkman went on to explain that there was indeed a Richard Smiley in the 10th Mountain Division during World War II. He had been in the training class during the winter of 1943 at Camp Hale in Minturn. Sam went on to explain that when he left the training camp, he was a corporal. He also told Buck that Corporal Richard T Smiley was killed in action in Italy in April 1944.

Buck had started to feel upbeat when Sam called. Now his bubble just burst. "Mr. Brinkman. Any doubt about the information?"

"Unfortunately, not. I have a copy of the telegram from the army to his mom and dad. Sad. He was only 22 years old. War is such a waste of young lives. Sorry I don't have better information for you."

"That's ok, Mr. Brinkman. You have been a huge help." Buck stopped short as an idea bounced around his brain. "Sir, if I could ask you one more thing? Does your information list where the soldiers are from or where they enlisted?"

"Yes, sir. It actually lists both, if that information was available at the time. You need to remember that this was during war, so the record keeping might be a little messy. A huge number of young men joined the various services during the war. Many were underaged and used fake ID's and many joined to escape the law or a bad marriage or some other reason. Patriotism was not always the reason for joining the military."

"Can you possibly email me a list of the soldiers who were in the same training class as Corporal Smiley along with their home cities or where they enlisted?"

"No problem. I will get on it right away."

Buck knew there would be no arguing with Sam Brinkman. Sam was on a quest and Buck figured he'd have the list on his computer in the next couple hours. He gave Sam his email address and thanked him for his help. He sat back in the desk chair and thought about the information Sam Brinkman had given him. Someone had given false information to Marvin Davis when that person asked for permission to work one of Marvin Bishop's mining claims. Unless Bishop was mistaken and had the name totally wrong, the person who had used that name didn't just pull it out of thin air. That person had some kind of relationship with Richard Smiley.

Buck started viewing the forensic results when his computer notified him of an incoming email. Buck was wrong. It didn't take a couple hours for Brinkman to pull together the information Buck had asked for. It took less than an hour. He made a mental note to stop in and visit Sam Brinkman the next time he was in the Vail area.

Buck opened the email and clicked on the attachment. He looked at the list that Brinkman had put together. There were one hundred and fifty names on the list and he slowly perused the list. He found Richard Smiley about two-thirds of the way down the list. Richard Smiley had listed his hometown as Monroe, Virginia and he had enlisted in Roanoke, Virginia. He ran his finger down the list. He was able to find six other enlistees with some town in Virginia listed as their home address. He found that seven men enlisted in Roanoke. There were also six more who had nothing listed for the state of their enlistment. He copied down the names on the pad on his desk.

He started to look for the list of the local 10th Mountain vets when he remembered that the list was printed and he had given it to Paul Webber. He hated to stop when he felt he was just starting to get momentum but he didn't want to wake Paul. Besides he needed some sleep himself. He closed his laptop, turned off the lights and laid down on the bed.

The ringing phone snapped Buck awake out of a deep sleep. He grabbed his phone off the table next to the bed and looked at the number.

"Hey, Hank. What's up?"

"Mornin Buck. Did I wake you?" Hank Clancy asked.

"No. I had to wake up to answer the phone," Buck said and he heard Hank laugh on the other end.

"Listen, Buck. Check your email when you are fully awake. One of our clerks worked overtime but she thinks she might have found something for you. She could not find any kind of active multiple victim murder investigation from back in the fifties and sixties in Colorado but she did find old records of six women who went missing around the same time period."

"What makes her think these six women might be connected to our case?"

"According to the reports from local investigators, these six women were traveling across the country for various reasons and the last place anyone ever saw or heard from them was in Colorado."

"Excellent Hank. I will pull up the email and take a look at the files. Any chance there might be fingerprint cards on these women?"

"These six have print cards but remember this was a very transient time in America. After World War II and Korea, a lot of people were on the move. I looked at the files and most of these women were escaping something. Abusive husbands, bad relationships and some just had a whim to travel. Not a lot of people were fingerprinted in those days unless they got caught. A couple of them were picked up as vagrants or prostitutes. Not unusual for a single woman on the road. Take a look. My clerk is continuing to follow up and I will call you if we find anything else."

Buck thanked Hank and climbed out of bed. He opened his laptop, put on his reading glasses and opened the email and the attachment. Hank was right. Most of these women had lived horrible lives but the thing that struck him most is that most of these women probably had tried to disappear. It was just pure luck that someone had actually missed them.

Buck was just about to call Paul Webber when his phone rang. It was Ashley Baxter from the office. "Hey, Buck. I found Richard Smiley. The Army is sending me his file. Should have it in a few minutes."

"Nice work, Ashley," said Buck. "Send it to me as soon as you get it and thanks."

Buck hung up and called Paul Webber. Paul had just arrived at the home of the tenth name on his list. Buck asked him to take a picture of the list and email it to him. Buck hung up and headed for the morgue. On the way, he called the Sheriff.

"Hi, Earl. Can you have your fingerprint tech meet me at the morgue?"

"Hey, Buck. She is already there. The Professor and the pathologists think they have had good luck rehydrating a couple fingers on each mummy and they want to get them into the system."

Buck told the Sheriff about the files that Hank Clancy had sent him and said he would meet the tech there; he was on his way. He hung up his phone jumped in the shower and then found his cleanest shirt and pair of jeans. Buck could feel the momentum building.

Chapter Fifty-Eight

The fingerprint tech was uploading a print scan into her computer when Buck walked into the morgue. He opened his laptop and pulled up the files from the FBI and clicked on the fingerprint cards. He slid his laptop over to the fingerprint tech and stepped back to give her room to work. The two pathologists were at the other end of a long row of morgue tables and were working with Professor Standish and two of his students as they ran the digital fingerprint scanner over the hand of the next body.

"Professor. Looks like you've had some success?"

The Professor turned to look at Buck. "Much more than we dared hope for. We used some different techniques that have been used on mummies by other archeologists over the years and we found two methods that worked really well. We are now in the process of checking with the scanner to see if the prints are legible."

Buck was just about to ask about the process when he heard a shout from the fingerprint tech. "GOT ONE!!"

Buck and the Professor turned and headed over to the tech. She was almost shaking with excitement. Buck looked at the scan and the old print card side by side, just as she had and he could see it as clear as day. They had their first hit. He slid his laptop back around and clicked on the file for Martha Collins.

Martha Collins was 22 years old in 1963 when she ran away from an abusive marriage. She was originally from Appleton, Wisconsin. Her mother reported her missing two weeks after she left her home. No missing person's report was filed by her husband. Buck just shook his head. She had been arrested in Denver in June of that year for vagrancy. She never made her court appearance and an arrest warrant was issued for her. She was never heard from again. That is until now.

Buck stepped away from the tech and called Hank Clancy. Hank answered and Buck filled him in. Hank sounded almost as excited as the fingerprint tech was. He told Buck that the clerk had found two more possibles and she was emailing them over to him. Buck hung up and congratulated the tech and the Professor and his team. Nothing they had so far would help them find out who the killer was but it would go a long way to giving some of these families closure.

Buck transferred the rest of the fingerprint cards to the techs laptop and closed his computer. He would let them get on with their work. He headed for the door when he ran into Dr. Parker coming down the hall. She too, looked very excited.

She held up a paper as she approached. "We identified your victim." She handed Buck the paper. It was a copy of an AFIS report. "Her name was Margret Mary Trumaine. According to the report she was listed as a runaway. She had just turned twenty-one years old and her prints were on file in New Orleans because she was involved in a bar fight and had been arrested with her boyfriend. A bench warrant was issued a month ago for failure to appear."

Buck looked over the report and pulled out his phone. He dialed the number on the report.

"Stevenson."

"Hi Detective Stevenson, my name is Buck Taylor and I am an agent with the Colorado Bureau of Investigation. I think we found a young woman you have been looking for."

Buck took a few minutes and explained the circumstances surrounding his call. He told the Detective about what they had found in the mine and the hit they just got back from AFIS.

"That's really a shame, Agent Taylor. That young girl never had a chance. She had an abusive father and an extremely abusive boyfriend. By the time I had contact with her she was so far under his thumb I couldn't get her back. She was very meek and mild. Unfortunately, the fact that she is dead doesn't surprise me. I expected her boyfriend would do it but a connection to a decades-old serial killer case. That's fascinating. You get done with this case you should write a book. Can you send me a copy of the autopsy report for my files?"

"Sure can, Detective. Would you be able to email me a copy of whatever you have on her? I'd like to get to know her a little better."

"You bet and thanks for the call." Buck and Detective Stevenson exchanged email addresses and Buck hung up.

Dr. Parker looked at him. "You don't let any grass grow under your feet do you Buck?"

"Can't afford to. The dead can't speak for themselves. That's my job. This young girl didn't ask to die this way and I won't let her death be meaningless."

Dr. Parker could see the intensity in Buck's eyes. She realized that everything she had heard about his dedication and his pit-bull attitude was true. Buck thanked the Doctor and headed for his car. He headed for the Sheriff's Department. There was a bug in the back of his brain and he couldn't quite get it to development.

Buck pulled into the parking lot, grabbed his backpack out of the hatch and headed inside. The desk officer buzzed him in without checking his ID. He walked into the empty conference room and pulled out his laptop and his notepad. He grabbed a bottle of Coke from the small refrigerator in the corner and sat down.

The first thing he pulled up was the forensic reports. He searched through until he found the evidence summary. The techs had found several fingerprints and it always amazed him that they could pull prints that were decades-old but under the right conditions there was no telling how long prints could last.

It was obvious from the report that the killer hadn't used gloves or he had and just got careless. They found partial prints on some of the knives in the leather bundle. They pulled a decent print off a ceramic coffee mug that was also in the cabinet with the leather bundle and they pulled a couple usable prints off the kerosene can and off the fuel cap on the kerosene stove.

The forensic techs had run the prints through AFIS and also through the military but so far hadn't gotten any hits. This didn't surprise him. Fingerprinting was only used in dealing with criminals so if the perp had never had any contact with the law the chances of his prints being in the system were slim to none. He didn't know if the military printed enlistees but he doubted it. During the war, he imagined they just ran as many men as possible through the enlistment process with very few questions asked.

Chapter Fifty-Nine

Buck was going through the report looking for the evidence that could relate to the newer killing when Paul Webber entered the conference room. Paul looked exhausted.

"What's going on Paul?" asked Buck. "You look beat."

Paul explained that he had just spent four hours with two 10th Mountain Division vets in a retirement home just north of town. "These guys love to talk about their time in the 10th. Their stories are incredible. I wish I had the time to write their stories down. Someone should. What incredible men."

"So, besides the stories, were they any help with Richard Smiley?"

Paul opened his notebook. "Both men remember a Richard Smiley but they couldn't agree if he was killed in Italy. One thought he was and one thought he wasn't. They had a lot of arguments like that as they were telling me their stories. They did both remember that Smiley was one of the hillbilly boys. They said that several hillbillies from back east somewhere, had all come into the unit together. Said they were thick as thieves and pretty much stuck together. Said the other guys in the unit used to call them squirrel eaters and most of the unit stayed away from them."

Buck asked Paul to pull out the list of the vet's names he gave him and he opened his laptop and clicked on the attachment from Sam Brinkman the 10^(th) Mountain Division museum curator. Paul slid him the list. Buck opened his notepad to the list he had created from Sam Brinkman's list of the men who enlisted in Roanoke Virginia. It was a long shot but then, so far, everything was. He checked the names on Paul's list and then on his list. No matches. Paul could see the frustration on Buck's face.

Buck pulled his laptop closer and started working his way down the list from Sam Brinkman. Buck had listed only the men who indicated they were from Virginia and had enlisted in Roanoke. He remembered that Sam had told him that some names on the list didn't have that information. Buck had planned to go back to them after he checked out the ones on his list. Now was the time.

Buck found six names on the list that did not contain either their hometown or their place of enlistment. Buck pulled out his phone and dialed Sam Brinkman. Sam answered his phone and listened as Buck told him what he was looking for. Sam Brinkman told him he would get back to him as soon as he had what he needed. Buck hung up.

Buck now took the time to update Paul on the morning's activities in the morgue. Paul was fascinated with the whole idea of fingerprinting the mummies. He was also thrilled that they had identified their victim. The conversation reminded Buck of something he meant to do and he opened his email and sure enough, there was the email from Detective Stevenson. The file from New Orleans was attached. The note in the email from the Detective said, "Thanks for the autopsy report and the photo. Definitely our girl. Heading over to her mom to make the notification. Let me know if you need anything else and good luck."

Buck opened the file. The first thing he noticed was how much the young girl had changed. The girl on the morgue table was much thinner than the girl in the booking photo. Her hair was also shorter now and had a tint of blue color in a streak down one side. Her booking photo showed a girl with bright eyes and blond hair. She looked ten years younger in the booking photo. She had gone downhill fast.

Buck read the booking information and read through the arrest report. Detective Stevenson was very thorough and Buck appreciated how well organized the reports were. He stopped reading and turned his computer around so Paul could see it. Paul read the report and commented about a tragic life. Buck couldn't agree more.

Buck had just stood up from his chair when Fitz walked into the room. She looked as tired as Paul did. She filled Buck in on her case. The pictures they had posted on the Missing and Exploited Children's website had been paying off, at least in the quantity of information they were getting, if not the quality. They had a few decent leads on several of the children and had already arranged with the police in Kansas City and Omaha to take DNA swabs of possible extended family members for two of the kids. DNA had already linked the momma, Corrine, with one of the kids. The oldest boy that had been killed, was her biological child.

Fitz excused herself so she could get back to answering calls. They had brought in several of the volunteer reserve deputies to help out with the calls, many from the news media around the country. Their case had gone viral. Fitz wasn't sure that was necessarily a good thing. She picked her coffee mug up off the table and headed out the door. Buck started to pace when his phone rang.

"Agent Taylor, I have the information you were looking for," said Sam Brinkman.

Buck had no doubt that Sam Brinkman would come through. "Thanks, Mr. Brinkman. Go ahead." Buck grabbed his pen and his notepad.

"Only one of the six names you gave me came from Virginia. Thomas Hawkins listed his hometown as Lynchburg, Virginia and he enlisted in Roanoke. Can't tell you why it wasn't in the report. Like I said last night. This was war and a lot of things slipped through the cracks. I also called one of my contributors in Vail. He wasn't in this unit but was in the unit that completed training just before this group but he remembers the hillbilly boys. Said they were an odd group and they stuck to each other like glue. Didn't have any contact with them after he shipped out. I hope that helps?"

"Thanks much Mr. Brinkman. Helps a lot." Buck hung up his phone and filled Paul in on the conversation. Paul read through his notes. "I spoke with Mr. Hawkins's son yesterday. This is the guy I mentioned who was bedridden and comatose. His son said his father was injured in an accident and had been bedridden ever since. He has been comatose the last two weeks. The doctor doesn't hold out much hope."

Buck sat back in his chair. Something was really nagging at him but he just couldn't put his finger on it. He was just about to say something when his phone rang.

"Buck Taylor."

"Agent Taylor, Frederick Standish here. Do you have a minute?"

Buck said he did and the Professor filled him in on their progress. They had identified five of the women so far and had just opened up the fingerprint cards for the two most recent reports that Buck had sent the fingerprint tech. The Professor was ecstatic about their success and Buck was impressed with what they had been able to do so far. The Professor hung up and promised to report back. Buck filled in Paul.

Buck's phone rang again and this time he recognized the number and answered the call.

"Yes, Sir?" he said

"Buck, I just heard from Max that Professor Standish and his team are having some pretty good luck with getting prints from the old victims. Anything on the newest victim?"

Buck told the Director that, so far, they didn't have anything on the killer. He filled him in on the information they received from Sam Brinkman and also from the detective in New Orleans on the latest victim. The Director seemed very interested in the 10th Mountain connection to the original crime. They talked strategy for a few minutes then Buck hung up.

Buck pulled up the forensic report on his computer and looked through the evidence collected section. He found what he was looking for on the second page. The techs had pulled a relatively fresh DNA sample from the old straw mattress. There was a small stain on the old horsehair blanket that covered the mattress. The note indicated that they had not found a DNA match in the database.

Chapter Sixty

Buck asked Paul if he could run down the street and pick up a couple deli sandwiches. Paul headed out the door and Buck spent the time going back through the murder book on his laptop. That little nagging bug was still in the back of his mind and he couldn't shake it. He knew that solving crimes as complex as this were in the details, so Buck went back to the details.

Buck was still reviewing the photos and the evidence notes when Paul returned with a couple Italian subs. They took a break and ate their sandwiches. Buck got up to throw away the sandwich wrapper when his phone rang. It was Max Clinton, the head of the State Crime Lab. Max was excited. She told Buck that they had gotten a DNA hit off one of the mummies. It wasn't a solid match but it was definitely familial. She said it was possibly a cousin or an aunt or uncle. She forwarded the information to the Galveston, Texas police department since the DNA report had been filed by them. She was waiting to hear back.

Buck and Max talked a while about the progress and how much success they had been having with this case and how nothing related back to the killer but the fact that they could identify these victims was pretty amazing. Buck was just about to say something else when the nagging little bug hit him right in the forehead. He told Max he would call her later and hung up.

Buck sat down and looked at the list from Sam Brinkman and looked at the notation he had made next to Thomas Hawkins's name. He looked at Paul.

"You said Thomas Hawkins was bedridden and comatose right?" he asked.

Paul checked his notes. "Yeah. Bedridden for several decades, comatose in the last two weeks. What are you thinking?"

"Was Hawkins injured in the war?" asked Buck.

Paul looked at his notes. "His son just said he was injured in a car crash. Didn't say when or if he did I didn't write it down. What are you thinking?"

"What would cause an active serial killer, who had already killed fifteen women, to suddenly stop killing?"

Paul thought about it for a minute. "Typically, it would be death or imprisonment." Then Paul's face lit up. "Or an accident that left him a quadriplegic. Shit!"

"Exactly," Buck replied. "Head downstairs to the archives and see if the clerk can find a report on an accident from some time in the sixties that left the victim a quadriplegic."

The Sheriff stuck his head in the door. "You guys are getting pretty loud. You got something?"

While Paul grabbed his notepad and headed out the door, Buck filled the Sheriff in on what they had discovered today. The Sheriff sat back and listened. He was aware of all the activity at the morgue. The thought about the accident he felt was on the right track. He told Buck to let him know if he needed more help and he headed for his office.

Buck picked up his phone and dialed Virginia Gonzales, the

Pitkin County Attorney. Virginia picked up her phone. "Hi, Buck. Figured you'd be calling sooner or later. What do you need?"

Buck spent the next twenty minutes walking her through the evidence they had developed so far. She too, was impressed with the work the Professor and his team had been able to do. Science was amazing. Buck asked her about the possibility of getting a warrant for fingerprints and a DNA sample from Thomas Hawkins. Virginia thought for a minute.

"Buck, I agree with your theory. We are a little light on physical evidence linking Thomas Hawkins to the mummies but I think I can get Judge Donnelly to issue a warrant for the samples. Give me a little bit and I will call you back."

Buck hung up. The momentum was definitely building. He pulled his laptop closer and started inputting what they had learned in the past couple hours. He also shot a quick email to the Director to let him know what the latest theory was.

Buck hated waiting but he had no choice. They had a lot of irons in the fire and Buck just needed to wait to bring it all together. The samples from Thomas Hawkins could seal the deal. He pulled up the evidence report from the murder book and went back to the second page. As he had read before, the techs had found what they felt was a fresh stain on the old mattress blanket but they had not been able to find a match in the national DNA database.

Was it possible that someone related to Thomas Hawkins had decided to start down the same road? The mine shaft was not easy to find. He doubted that someone who just happened upon it, would suddenly decide to become a serial killer or that someone who had the makings of being a serial killer, would go looking for a great place to kill people and would think the shaft was perfect. Those were just too far in the extreme to be plausible. But someone who knew the original killer and had been able to discuss it. That was more of a reality. Especially the methodology of the crimes.

It was not easy to discern from the mummies, how they were killed. As the bodies shrunk, a lot of the slices and cuts had closed up. The only way someone would find out how they died was to discuss it with the killer. Buck thought for a minute. Paul had mentioned that he had spoken with Thomas Hawkins's son. Buck figured that this son would be Buck's age or older. Buck couldn't recall ever reading about a serial killer who started his career that late in life. Of course, it was possible that the son was a killer for a long time and had just not been caught but Buck recalled the conversation with Dr. Parker and about the uncertainty about the killer being a man.

Buck picked up his phone and called Max Clinton at the crime lab. "Hey, Buck. How's my favorite cop?" Typical Max. Always answered his calls the same way.

"Hey, Max. Got a question. The stain the techs found on the old mattress blanket that they have listed as sample 17. Do we know if it came from a man or a woman?"

Buck could hear Max clicking the keys on her computer. "According to the report the sample came from a woman. What are you looking for Buck?"

"Just a wild hair. Did the lab do a DNA comparison between the victim and the sample?" More keys clicking

"The lab did do a comparison," said Max. "The sample did not come from the victim. That should be in the notes in your murder book."

Buck looked at the note section of the forensic report. "I don't see that in the report. When was the report you are looking at uploaded?"

Max put Buck on hold for two minutes. She came back on

the line apologetic. "Sorry Buck, the tech just uploaded the latest report twenty minutes ago. If you have had the report open it probably didn't refresh, so you don't have the latest version."

Buck said, "no worries Max." He hit the refresh button on the report and sure enough, there was the note. He thanked Max and hung up.

Buck called over to the Clerk and Recorders Office and asked the Clerk if she could check a few birth records for him. He had no idea how long Thomas Hawkins had lived in the valley but it was worth a shot. He gave her the information and she promised to call back as soon as she had something. Buck sat back and closed his eyes.

Chapter Sixty-One

The Clerk from the Clerk and Recorder's Office called back and gave Buck the information he had been waiting for. There were four birth records related to Thomas and Judith Hawkins. Thomas and Judith had two sons, Thomas Jr. born in 1950 and Mathew born in 1952. She also found a death certificate for Mathew in 1953. Cause of death was listed as undetermined. Buck assumed it was probably SIDS related. Back in those days, many children's deaths, if spontaneous, were listed as SIDS. Sudden Infant Death Syndrome. It was a catch-all phrase for "we don't know what caused the death."

She also found two birth certificates under Thomas Hawkins Jr. and Sarah Jane Westover. They had two children. Thomas the third, born in 1985 and Alicia born in 1995. Buck thought, "a change of life baby." He thanked the Clerk and hung up.

Paul came rushing back into the conference room carrying in a very old dusty file folder. "It took some time to go through the boxes but we think we found it."

He laid the file on the desk and caught his breath. Buck waited.

"Thomas Hawkins was involved in a single-vehicle rollover accident in July of 1964. It happened between Carbondale and

Aspen. According to the report the car slid on the rain-soaked highway and crashed through a barricade and rolled down the embankment. It wasn't discovered for three-days, until a highway road crew stopped to check out the damaged guardrail and spotted the car in the ravine. Thomas Hawkins was the lone occupant in the car and had been crushed when the car slammed into a tree at the bottom of the ravine. Hawkins suffered serious internal injuries and a broken neck. The investigating deputy made a note in the accident report that the doctors did not think that Hawkins would survive." Paul stopped to catch his breath and Buck pulled the report across the table and started going through it himself.

Paul came around the table and Buck slid the report over to him. There was obviously something else he wanted Buck to see. He flipped a couple pages and slid the report back to Buck. He pointed to a faded note written by the deputy along the edge of the page. Buck pulled out his reading glasses and looked at the note.

Paul saw that Buck was having trouble reading the note, so he filled him in. "The deputy made a note to check on the condition of the female victim. Identity unknown."

Buck looked at Paul. "You just said that Hawkins was the lone victim. What does this mean?"

Paul smiled. "I think someone doctored the final report. The official accident report makes no mention of a female victim. I think someone missed this note from the deputy when they typed up the final report. Someone hid the fact that Thomas Hawkins was not alone in his car at the time of the accident."

Buck removed his glasses. "Shit Paul. Do you think this could have been victim number sixteen and the accident happened before he had a chance to finish the job?"

Paul responded, "it's possible but why would someone cover

it up? Do you think someone in the Sheriff's office, at the time, knew about the killings and was trying to protect Hawkins?"

Buck looked at the signature on the report. Deputy Ernest Rivers. Buck grabbed the report and headed out the door to find the Sheriff. He found him sitting in his office reading a report. The Sheriff looked up.

"Do you remember a Deputy Ernest Rivers?" Buck asked.

The Sheriff thought for a minute. "Ernie was a deputy back in the sixties. Why? What up?"

Buck set the accident reports on his desk and explained the anomaly. The Sheriff looked at the reports, reread the accident report from the deputy and the final accident report and set the reports back down on his desk.

"Got me, Buck. Old Tom Glover was Sheriff back in those days. He was a tough old bastard and he ran a tight ship. Nothing happened in this county that Tom Glover didn't know about. I can't believe one of his deputies would fake a report. To what end?"

Buck replied. "Maybe to hide a serial killer?"

The Sheriff sat back and scratched his head. "Fuck, Buck. How confident are you that Hawkins is the guy? Maybe it was just a simple clerical error."

"Is this Ernie still around? Can we talk to him?" asked Buck.

"No, Ernie died about ten years back," responded the Sheriff.

Buck gave the Sheriff the rundown on what they had. When Buck finished, the Sheriff just sat there. "Ok. What's the next step, the DNA and fingerprint samples?"

"Yeah. Soon as I hear back from Virginia. Do you know the family?"

"No," replied the Sheriff. "Let me know when you are ready to head over and I will come along."

Buck left the Sheriff's office and headed back to the conference room where he filled Paul in on the conversation he just had with the Sheriff.

"Do you really think a cop would cover up multiple murders?" asked Paul.

"I don't think so. I mean it's possible Earl is right and it's just a clerical error. What bothers me is that there is no follow up from the deputy. That I can't explain."

Buck had just sat down at the conference table when Paul grabbed his notebook and started furiously flipping pages. He stopped and read his notes.

"Fuck," Paul said. "Excuse me. I thought so. Maggie Stevens."

"Maggie Stevens what?" replied Buck.

"Maggie Stevens is the owner of the Jackpot Bar and Grill. I spoke with her early on when we were trying to get a line on our victim. She mentioned that she had lived in Aspen since her accident. She said she was involved in an accident in the sixties and had no memories of the event before waking up in the hospital."

Buck looked at him. "Go talk to her and see if you can jog some of her memories. We might have a living breathing victim of our serial killer?"

Paul grabbed his notebook and his backpack and headed out the door.

Chapter Sixty-Two

Buck was starting to get a little antsy, so he decided to take a walk down to the river. He hated waiting for things to happen and it seemed that that was all he was doing today. They had made a great deal of progress in a short amount of time and he felt they were right there. As he stood at the river's edge and watched the water flow by, he felt that they were close to wrapping this one up.

He was about to head back to the Sheriff's office when his phone rang. He checked the number and answered the call.

"Hey, Virginia. Are we good?"

Virginia Gonzales responded, "got your warrant. What are you waiting for?" She laughed.

"Awesome. Can you fax it over to the Sheriff's office? Oh, I hate to do this but do you think you can get warrants for the rest of the family as well?"

Buck explained why he needed the rest of the family's DNA. He waited for a response.

"You think someone else in the family is our new killer. Seriously. A family of killers living here in Aspen and no one knew. You have got to be kidding. Ok, I will try but see if you can get them to give the samples voluntarily."

Virginia hung up and Buck walked back the three blocks to the Sheriff's department. As he entered the building, the desk officer handed him the fax copy of the warrant. He buzzed Buck through the door and Buck headed for the Sheriff's office.

The Sheriff was talking on the phone, so Buck waved the fax and pointed to the conference room. He nodded and Buck headed for the conference room. Buck was closing up his laptop when the Sheriff entered the room. He slid the warrant over to him and put his laptop in his backpack.

"Can you have your fingerprint tech meet us there?"

The Sheriff pulled out his phone, called the tech and gave her the address. He told her to stay in her van until he called her to come in.

Buck called Paul who, said that he was just wrapping up with Maggie Stevens and he would meet them at Thomas Hawkins's house. Buck and the Sheriff walked out of the building and climbed into the Sheriff's car. He pulled out of the parking lot and headed for the address on West Hallam Street. He pulled to the curb behind the county's forensic van and signaled the tech to wait. He and Buck crossed the street and walked up to the cute little Victorian house.

The Sheriff knocked on the door. The door was opened by a middle-aged, heavy set women with gray hair and glasses. He introduced himself and Buck and asked if they could come in. Once inside Buck closed the door.

"How can I help you gentlemen?" asked Sarah Jane Hawkins.

They had agreed on the way over to let the Sheriff do most of the talking since these were his people. Buck was never offended at being considered the outsider. Many times it proved valuable to have the locals handle the locals.

"Ma'am, we have a warrant to get a fingerprint scan and

DNA swab from your father-in-law." The Sheriff handed her the warrant.

She looked at the warrant, confused and unsure what to do. She stepped to the door to the living room and called out. "Tom, can you come here a minute? The police are here."

Tom Hawkins came walking in wiping his hands on a rag. He was medium height, slightly overweight and he had a short haircut and a neatly trimmed beard.

"What do you mean the police are here. What do they…" He stopped short and looked at the Sheriff and Buck. His wife handed him the warrant. He pulled a pair of reading glasses out of his pocket and read the warrant. He looked up at Buck and the Sheriff.

"What the hell is this all about? You want fingerprints and DNA from a man who is on death's door and has been bedridden since 1964. Are you kidding?"

The Sheriff looked at Buck. Buck responded. "We have reason to believe that your father was involved in several murders during the late fifties early sixties."

Sarah Jane Hawkins put her hand in front of her mouth. Tom Hawkins looked at Buck as his anger seethed. "What the fuck are you talking about? You think my dad is a serial killer? How dare you come into my house and make that kind of accusation! Get the fuck out!"

Buck stepped forward. "Mr. Hawkins, I know this may be a shock but we wouldn't be here if we didn't have proof. The warrant gives us permission to be here and to take the samples. You are welcome to call your attorney but he will tell you the same thing."

Buck watched as Tom Hawkins slowly balled his fists and he stared daggers at Buck. Buck looked him in the eye. "Mr. Hawkins," Buck said softly. "Please think very carefully about what you are about to do. We understand your anger but the samples are important and you do not want to make the situation any worse."

"Thomas step back." The voice came from a short elderly woman with a walker who entered the room. Her words to Tom seem to diffuse the situation instantly. He turned and was about to say something when she held up her hand and silenced him. "He may be your father," she said. "But he is still my husband and I will deal with this."

Tom Hawkins started to protest but once again his mother raised her hand for silence. Tom backed off and sat down at the kitchen table.

"Gentlemen, I am Judith Hawkins. If you would follow me, please."

The Sheriff pulled out his phone and called the fingerprint tech to come in. He was just putting it away when Paul Webber arrived at the door. Paul looked around at those assembled and wondered what he had missed. The Sheriff, Buck, the fingerprint tech and Paul followed Mrs. Hawkins through the house to what was obviously an addition that had been built onto the original house.

Chapter Sixty-Three

She pushed open the door and they all entered a very cozy if not very large room. The oxygen tank in the corner hissed as Thomas Hawkins breathed. He was lying in a hospital bed with the blanket pulled up to his chest. He had on striped pajamas and was clean shaven. It was obvious to everyone that Thomas Hawkins was well taken care of.

Mrs. Hawkins sat down on the chair that was next to the bed and held her husband's hand. She nodded to the fingerprint tech who pulled the portable digital fingerprint scanner out of her backpack and ever so gently slid it across his fingers. She then pulled a DNA swab out of her pack, broke the packaging and gently lifted the old man's lip and swabbed the inside of his mouth. Mrs. Hawkins sat silently and watched, holding her husband's hand the entire time.

The fingerprint tech opened her laptop and pulled up the prints that had been recovered at the mine. She spent a few minutes comparing the prints from the mine to the scans and then she looked up at Buck. She nodded her head. Mrs. Hawkins lowered her eyes and a tear fell on her hand.

Buck turned his head and noticed Tom Jr. and Sarah Jane

standing in the doorway. They both looked stunned. Tom finally broke the silence. "Mom, did you know about this?"

She looked at her son. "I would like to talk to these gentlemen alone for a minute. Will you please excuse us?"

Tom Jr. looked hurt and like he wanted to fight but instead he just turned around and walked out. Sarah Jane followed closely at his heels. Buck asked the fingerprint tech to go back to the kitchen, finish her analysis and log the report. She nodded and left the room.

Buck, the Sheriff and Paul Webber stood and watched Mrs. Hawkins. She was looking at her husband and no one wanted to disturb her. She finally reached over and took a tissue from the box on the table and wiped her eyes. She looked up at Buck and the others. She asked Buck to close the door.

Mrs. Hawkins kissed her husband on the forehead and then began. "My husband was a good man. Up until his accident he took very good care of the boys and me." She wiped her eyes and Buck could see the sadness in that statement. "He was a loving husband and father but I always sensed that there was something beneath the surface. He worked a lot of late hours in those days but his paychecks never revealed any extra money. Up until you walked in I always believed that he was having an affair or many for that matter. He would always shower before coming to bed, after a long night but I could always smell the sex on him. It never occurred to me that he might be a killer. He never seemed the type but I know he was troubled. I was young and naïve and despite what I have just told you I always loved him. I still do. When our little Mathew passed away, he was the rock I depended on."

She sat for a minute and looked down at her husband. She wiped more tears away from her eyes. No one spoke.

"I can only assume that from the young lady's reaction, that his fingerprints match fingerprints that were found at a crime scene. What will happen now? He doesn't have many days left and I assume you can't arrest him. What's next?"

Buck looked down at Mrs. Hawkins. "I am not sure Ma'am. That will be up to the county attorney. May we ask you a couple questions?" She nodded yes and asked Buck to please open the door. Buck turned and opened the door and saw a new person in the room. He was the spitting image of Tom Jr. This would be Thomas the third. They all rose from the couch.

Paul pulled out his laptop and turned on the voice recorder app. He nodded to Buck. As the others all listened, Buck walked Mrs. Hawkins through the evidence they had gathered over the last couple days. She had no idea that her husband had been in contact with the owner of the mining claim. She told them he had worked as a mechanic for the Aspen Skiing Company almost from its inception. They talked about his skills as a metal worker and welder. Periodically there would be a gasp from one of the family members especially when Buck described the scene in the mine.

Mrs. Hawkins held her husband's hand through all of Buck's questions. For a frail little old lady, she was amazingly strong. He hoped the crash wouldn't come later but he knew it would. It always did.

Buck asked Mrs. Hawkins if she would allow them to search the house and property. She said she would and then he asked if the rest of the members of the family would allow them to take DNA and fingerprint samples. They still needed to eliminate them as suspects in the recent murder. They all agreed. Buck asked Tom Jr. if his daughter was around. Tom told Buck that she had left the week before to go back to college in Florida.

Mrs. Hawkins looked up at Buck. "I assume you will want to

see his jewelry collection? He thought I didn't know about it but I did. I just assumed it was to help him relive his conquests. I had no idea they were what you would call trophies."

Buck looked stunned, "yes Ma'am."

"Tommy, would you please show these gentlemen your grandfather's toolbox? The trophy box is in a space in the wall behind the toolbox."

Paul stepped through the door and followed Thomas the third. The Sheriff stepped out of the room and called dispatch to send out his forensics team and he asked that they dispatch a couple deputies and to notify the Aspen Police and let them know what was going on.

Buck sat with Mrs. Hawkins. He needed to clear up the anomaly with the accident report. He waited until the Sheriff returned. "Mrs. Hawkins, have you ever read the report about the night your husband was injured in the accident. We found a discrepancy and unfortunately there is no one left alive, except you, who might be able to explain it."

Mrs. Hawkins sat there for a minute and looked at her husband. She finally smiled through the tears and looked at Buck. "I had asked Tom not to change the report but he wanted to do it for me."

"I'm sorry Ma'am. Who is this Tom that you are talking about?" At this point, Tom Jr. and Sarah Jane stepped into the doorway. Mrs. Hawkins looked at them and then back at Buck.

Chapter Sixty-Four

The affair with Pitkin County Sheriff Tom Glover had started innocently enough. Tom was a deacon in her church and they had met at several of the church's social events. Her own Thomas never wanted to attend church with her. She never understood why until today.

It had started out as just coffee but she was feeling that her husband was growing more distant from her every day. A few months before the accident it had turned into something more than just coffee. She had been feeling seriously underappreciated and she needed someone to talk to. She called the Sheriff to see if he would like to stop by for coffee. Her Thomas was at work and her son was in school.

The coffee visit had turned into two hours of intense lovemaking. It was funny. Judith didn't feel any regret after it happened. She still loved her husband but the time she spent with Tom Glover was something else entirely.

Tom was the one who came by the house that day to tell her they had found Thomas's car in the ravine and that he was on his way to the hospital. It was touch and go whether he would live or die. Tom Glover now became her rock.

"Tom told me about the woman they had found in the ravine. She had been thrown from the car and was seriously injured. He wanted to protect me from public ridicule, so he told me he would take care of it." Mrs. Hawkins said.

She had begged him not to do anything that would jeopardize his career and he had laughed at her. He was the Sheriff of the county and he could do anything he wanted to. "He asked Ernie to remove any mention of the girl from his notes. Tom wrote the accident report up himself and Ernie signed it without question."

A tear formed in her eye. "Tom helped me get through all the hard days that would follow, as I had to deal with Thomas's injuries, get a job and keep my son fed and clothed. Tom was always there for me."

Buck asked her how long the affair lasted. She looked down at her hand holding Thomas's hand. Softly she said, "it lasted until the day Tom died, almost ten years ago. That was the saddest day of my life."

Her family just stood in the doorway in shocked silence. Their whole world had been torn apart today. It was horrible to watch. Tom Jr. and Sarah Jean excused themselves and walked out the front door. The forensic team arrived just as they were leaving. The Sheriff stepped away to give the team instructions and asked the fingerprint tech to get the swabs from the rest of the family.

Paul returned with Thomas the third and walked into the room. In his hands was an old cardboard cigar box. He handed it to Buck. Buck opened the box and just as Mrs. Hawkins had said, the box was filled with jewelry. Buck was no jewelry expert but nothing in the box looked expensive. Some of it looked like it might have sentimental value.

Mrs. Hawkins held out her hand and asked to see the box.

Although it was evidence, Buck wanted to gauge her reaction now that she knew the truth about where the pieces came from. He handed her the box and she slowly opened it. She sat for a minute and just looked inside the box. Finally, she reached in and started moving pieces around. She got a funny look in her eyes. Buck watched her as she seemed to count the pieces one by one. She did this several times. She looked up and Buck thought he could see fear in her eyes.

"Ma'am, is something wrong?" Buck asked.

Mrs. Hawkins sat quietly for a few minutes just looking in the box. She closed the box. "There is a piece missing," she said.

"Are you certain?" Buck asked. He took the box from her hand and opened the lid.

"There were sixteen pieces in the box. I checked it every now and then to be reminded of how many women he had cheated with. The piece that's missing was a little jade horse on a silver necklace."

The house was now full of forensics people and Mrs. Hawkins asked Buck if he would close the door. Paul reached behind him and pushed the door shut. Buck was trying to understand what was happening. There were fifteen pieces of jewelry in the box and they had fifteen bodies in the morgue. The numbers worked unless one of the pieces belonged to the sixteenth victim. The woman who almost died in the accident that night. Paul was thinking the same thing as he looked through his notes.

"Agent Taylor. What I am about to say is very hard for me and it will destroy my son and his wife." She paused for a minute and let go of her husband's hand.

"My granddaughter Alicia found the jewelry box. I saw her with it one day when she thought I was asleep on the couch. She was coming out of this room and headed back to the garage. She had spent several days in here talking with her grandfather, over the summer, when he had a lucid moment." She started to cry.

She looked at Buck with pleading eyes. "Please don't say anything to my son."

Buck looked at Paul. "Would you have one of the techs look through Alicia's room and quietly see if they can find anything that might contain DNA? Toothbrush, hairbrush, anything."

Paul left the room and Buck reached over and rested his hand on Mrs. Hawkins's hand. "I hope I have done the right thing?" she said.

Buck stood up. He left Mrs. Hawkins sitting there with her husband. The poor woman's entire life had just unraveled. He felt bad for her. He walked through the house and stepped out onto the front porch. The Sheriff walked up beside him. Together they just stood there in silence.

The Sheriff finally broke the silence. "Hard day my friend. Wouldn't want to be these folks."

Buck looked at him and shook his head. He told the Sheriff about the conversation they had had about her granddaughter. "What are we going to do?" he asked.

Buck knew exactly what they were going to do. "As soon as the DNA results are back and we confirm what Mrs. Hawkins told me, we are going to issue an arrest warrant for Alicia Hawkins and have the Jacksonville, Florida police arrest her. I will let Hank Clancy at the FBI know. He might want his guys to track her down since she could be considered to have fled the state to avoid prosecution."

The Sheriff pulled out his phone. "I'd better call Virginia Gonzales and see how she wants to handle this. We certainly can't arrest the old guy but I'm not sure what to do." He stepped away and walked across the lawn.

Paul stepped out on the front porch. "I just spoke with Maggie Stevens at the Jackpot Bar and Grill. She confirmed that she had a little jade horse pendant on a silver chain but that it had disappeared from the hospital after the accident. She never saw it again until a young girl showed up at the bar a week or two back and was wearing a little jade horse pendant. Something in her mind triggered a memory and she asked the girl where she got the necklace. The girl told her she found it in a pawn shop in Florida. Maggie didn't think anything of it once the bar got busy but she swore that the girl was watching her the rest of the night."

Chapter Sixty-Five

Buck asked Paul to head back to the Sheriff's department and upload his notes to the murder book. Paul headed for his car. Buck took another pass through the house. Mrs. Hawkins was still sitting quietly next to her husband. As Buck looked in the door, she smiled at him and lowered her head. Buck checked in with the forensic team. He found the Sheriff and told him to call if they needed him. He would be back in the Sheriff's office in the morning to file his reports and put the finishing touches on the murder book.

As he walked towards his car, he pulled out his phone and dialed Max Clinton. He told her what had happened in the last couple hours and asked her to rush through the DNA samples she would be receiving for Alicia Hawkins. She promised to get her team on them as soon as they arrived. She ended the call the way she always did.

"God will watch over you, Buck Taylor. You are a good man. Stay safe."

Buck hung up his phone and walked to his car. He sat in his car and pulled out his phone again. He called the Director, who answered on the first ring.

"Hey, Buck. What's up?"

Buck filled him in on the day's events. The Director listened carefully. He asked a few questions and then said, "you guys did a great job, Buck. You solved fifteen decades-old serial killings and are about to close out a serial killer who is just getting started. Congratulations."

Buck thanked him, hung up and sat for a few minutes. He started his car and pulled out. He had intended to go back to his hotel and work on the murder book but the car seemed to have a mind of its own and he found himself parked along the river. He stepped out of the car and walked to the edge. The moon was full and the water sparkled. He stood there just watching the current when he sensed a presence behind him. His hand went instinctively for his gun.

"Sorry to have spooked you, Agent Taylor." Buck relaxed and turned around. PIS stood behind him and smiled.

"I heard it was rather a rough day."

Buck smiled and filled PIS in on the events of the past couple days. PIS listened quietly. Buck asked PIS how his shoulder was doing and PIS told him that he had been hurt worse and not to worry. When Buck was finished, he sat down in the cool grass and looked out over the river. PIS sat down next to him and that is where they stayed until the sun came over the mountains. Buck finally stood, shook PIS's hand and walked to his car. When he turned and looked back at the river, PIS was gone. Buck laughed and started the car.

The next few days were a blur as Buck and Paul continued to pull together forensic reports and log incoming information into the murder book. Virginia Gonzales had decided to indict Thomas Hawkins for the murders in the mine. She did not issue an arrest warrant because she knew he wasn't going to be alive that much longer. Professor Standish and his team had continued making progress and had identified nine of the fifteen women. He wanted to keep going but he had serious doubts that they would ever identify all of them. Hank Clancy agreed and by the end of the week he had pulled his clerk off the case and assigned her other work. Buck found out later that the clerk received a commendation for her excellent work in piecing together the victims.

Fitz and Moe Steiner continued to follow leads on the kids from the other mine. They had solid DNA matches on two of the kids and were waiting for the families to arrange flights to Colorado. The Missing and Exploited Children's Network had led to the possible identification of two of the other children and those leads were being followed up by police departments in St. Louis and Fort Collins, Colorado. The phones were still ringing but not as often. Corinne Everheart's uncle in West Virginia had arranged to have her remains and the remains of her identified son shipped to him for burial.

Major Richard Cranston, the Army CID investigator, arranged to have James Michael Forester's remains shipped to an Army base outside of Washington, DC. Buck had no idea how the Army was going to handle his burial and he decided he really didn't care. As far as Buck and the Sheriff were concerned, it was now an Army matter.

Buck had stopped by the Hawkins home a few days after that fateful day. To say the family was morose would be an understatement. The family moved around like zombies. All but Mrs. Hawkins. Buck found her sitting, in the cool afternoon air, on a love seat on the front porch. She was wrapped in a blanket and was just staring into space when Buck walked up the sidewalk.

Buck sat next to her and she put her hand on top of his. Softly she said. "Thomas will be at rest soon. He will face the lord and have to answer for his deeds. My solace is in the fact that you might give closure to those who have lost loved ones. Thank you for all you have done."

Buck started to stand up when she said, "please find my granddaughter."

She pulled her blanket around her a little tighter and looked across the yard.

The DNA from a toothbrush, that the forensic team found in Alicia's room, was a solid match for the stain on the old mattress blanket from the mine. Virginia Gonzales issued an arrest warrant for the murder of Margret Mary Trumaine. The FBI had also issued a federal arrest warrant for murder and interstate flight to avoid prosecution. The FBI, along with the Jacksonville Police, raided her dormitory but there was no sign of Alicia. All her belongings were still in her dorm room but Alicia was nowhere to be found. The FBI reported back that there was no sign of a little jade horse pendant on a silver chain.

Buck and Paul finished compiling the murder book and Buck emailed a copy to the Sheriff and to Virginia Gonzales. They boxed up all the physical evidence that had been returned from the state lab along with samples from the morgue. The Sheriff had his evidence clerk label and seal the boxes and take them to storage.

Paul headed back to Grand Junction the next morning. Buck found himself standing knee deep in the cool waters of the Roaring Fork River. After several hours, he had only landed one fish but it didn't matter. He could feel his mind clearing more and more as he focused on the fish.

Epilogue

Alicia Hawkins was hardly recognizable. She had a dark tan and she had cut her hair short and died it purple. The phone call from her older brother had come just in time. He didn't want to believe the things they were saying about her and he wanted her to come home to clear her name. She promised she would. She had made a promise to her grandfather. She would finish his legacy. One day soon, she would return to Aspen and finish his job.

Alicia hated the fact that she couldn't go home for her grandfather's funeral. She now, more than ever, understood him. She understood the force that drove him to do what he had done. She could feel that force growing stronger in her every day.

She had managed to get out of her dorm room and across the street to the park just before all the cops showed up. She was surprised to see the men and women with their FBI emblazoned jackets. It made her feel important. She sat in the park and watched for several hours as they carried out her stuff and talked to the other students in the dorm.

She waited until dark and then hitched south until she got to Tampa. She bought some purple dye at a local drug store and rented a cheap hotel room. When she was finished, she looked in the mirror and was pleased with the transformation. Over the following couple weeks she made her way farther south until she couldn't go any further.

Alicia walked out of the bar and stepped into the warm Key West sun. She put on her sunglasses and looked from side to side. She spotted the young girl a block down the street. The girl had arrived on the bus two days ago and looked lost. Alicia had been watching her since she arrived. She looked like a runaway and she was perfect.

The sun was setting and all the tourists were heading to the beach to wait for the green flash. People swore that the flash was visible, for just a second, just before the sun went down but Alicia had never seen it. She really didn't care. She watched the girl walk along the beach looking in the trash cans as she passed. Occasionally she would pull something out of the trash look at it, sniff it and eat it.

Alicia watched the young girl walk along the rocks towards the small tropical forest. She reached her hand into the back pocket of her shorts and felt the thin knife. She reached up to her neck and wrapped her hand around the little jade horse pendant on the silver chain. She smiled a wicked smile and headed off after the girl.

Buck Taylor Book III

Crime Unsolved

A BUCK TAYLOR NOVEL

BY

CHUCK MORGAN

Chapter One

The hike through the valley had been long and arduous, especially since they were carrying four five-gallon jerry cans full of gas. They had stopped earlier in the day at the local twenty-four-hour convenience store and filled the four cans. The trailer they were towing held two four-wheel ATVs, so no one at the store gave them a second look when they filled the cans up with gas. They filled them with the cheapest gas. No sense using high test gas and paying more just to burn it up.

They started down the trail just after full dark. They chose this night because there was no moon. They almost missed the old game trail they had spotted a couple of weeks before, but after doubling back a couple times, they finally located the trail. Access to where they were heading was very limited.

When the wealthy developer traded this piece of isolated land with the Forest Service for the parcel he owned on the back side of the new Elk Mountain Ski Resort, the property did not have any access easements. There was so much controversy when the land swap was made public, that due to the enormous amount of local pressure, the Forest Service agreed as part of the deal not to allow an access easement through the remaining public land.

The opposition figured that would be the end of the lodge project, but the developer was not going to be deterred so easily. He fought through the courts and was faced with countersuits all along the way by local outdoor associations, fishing groups, and conservation groups. In the end, none of this mattered. The fishing lodge that the wealthy developer intended to build would be entirely exclusive. A play place for his rich and famous friends, so the less access, the better. All of these wealthy snobs would be flown in by helicopter, so they would never have to deal with the local riff-raff.

There was an old fire road that led just inside the property line so as part of the compromise the court allowed the developer to use this for construction access only. Once construction was completed, the developer would be required to close down the road at the edge of his property. The only people who would be allowed access to the road were local law enforcement and the local fire department.

This part of the compromise didn't make anyone happy. In the end, the locals blockaded the road, and no one had access. The developer chose to just fly in all his labor and materials. He wasn't going to let a bunch of local yokels stand in his way.

As the two guys carried their gas cans down the old game trail, they believed that tonight this would all end. They would take care of the problem when the courts and the locals could not. The environment would once again rule the day.

The game trail skirted the security shack that had been built just inside the property line along the old Forest Service road. They had spotted six, armed security guards on their last excursion, and they had no interest in messing with them. Stealth was the name of their game, and they were very good at what they did.

On their last trip they had scouted out a great hiding spot just on the edge of the forest, and they were now just sitting quietly and observing the guards as they made their rounds. Almost all the construction workers had been airlifted off the site over the past couple days. The lodge was finished, and soon the staff would arrive to make sure it was clean for the first group of guests. If all went according to the plan, there should be no collateral damage.

They worked their way slowly to the service door at the back side of the kitchen and were preparing to pick the lock. Phase one of their plan would happen once they were inside the lodge and was essentially pouring out the contents of their gas cans. They had little doubt that all this wood would burn like a bonfire. Once they were satisfied that they had covered everything with the gas, they would pull a couple cellular igniters out of their backpacks and position them in the middle of piles of rags they would have taken from the supply closet and doused with gas.

Phase two of their plan involved opening all the valves for the propane equipment in the kitchen. They also had to access the mechanical room and shut the valve that controlled the water for the fire sprinkler system. The mechanical room was in a large closet behind the kitchen. The door was kept unlocked, but they knew there was a chain and padlock around the sprinkler system valve, which was there to prevent someone from closing the valve and preventing the water from reaching the sprinklers in the event of a fire. They would make quick work of the lock with the bolt cutters they brought with them.

They had gone over the plan several times over the last couple days, and each man knew his part. They had used this same plan several times in multiple locations, and it had always worked as planned. They had been working together long enough that they could almost read each other's thoughts. Tonight would be no different. The only issue that concerned them at this point was the weather. The winds were always unpredictable, and the last thing they wanted was to find themselves in the midst of a sudden wind shift and set more than the lodge on fire. So far, the weather report, when they last checked as they started their hike through the woods, was on their side. The front wasn't expected for several hours yet.

They knew from experience that something wasn't right as soon as they pushed open the kitchen door. There was a sudden rush of air that pushed into the building, and they heard the unmistakable sound of the backdraft as the inrush of fresh air fed the unseen fire smoldering somewhere in the building.

They both looked at each other and simultaneously yelled, "FUCK RUN!"

They only made it a couple steps before the explosion from inside the lodge blew out all the windows, and the concussive blast sent them flying head over heels. They picked themselves up off the ground and made a mad dash to the forest, leaving the gas cans where they had landed near the back door. When they looked back, the entire lodge was engulfed in flames, and the heat was intense.

They both knew it was time to leave. They had no idea what just happened, but they wanted to get as far away as possible from the fire before the authorities arrived. Whatever just happened was not part of their plan, and they needed to get the hell out of there. Someone had gotten there ahead of them and set a smoldering fire, but who could that be? And why?

Chapter Two

Buck Taylor stood behind the fire command center that had been set up in the parking lot of the Vaughan Lake campground just off Rio Blanco Route 8.

Buck was six-foot-tall and weighed in at 185 lbs. Very little of it flab for a 58-year-old man. Buck's hair was salt and pepper, with what seemed like a lot more salt than pepper and he wore it slightly longer than was typically the fashion of the day. Buck was always pleased when he looked in the mirror, since other than getting older, he was in as good a shape as he had been when he played defensive linebacker for the Gunnison High School Cowboys, back a long time ago. He still tried to jog five miles every day when he could, and he tried to ride his mountain bike every weekend, weather permitting. The bike was always hanging off the back of his state-provided Jeep Grand Cherokee. Except for a couple of sore knees, coming mostly from age, Buck was in good shape, which was necessary in his line of work.

Buck was an Investigative Agent with the Colorado Bureau of Investigation. He was currently assigned to the CBI field office in Grand Junction, Colorado, but he hadn't been in the office much during the past year. Somehow, he had become the favorite "go to" guy for the Governor of Colorado, Richard J Kennedy, who was, in fact, one of "those" Kennedys. The governor had been in office about eight months, and Buck had been instrumental in closing several high-profile investigations during that period, that made the governor look good. As a result, when a situation came up that might get a little hairy, the governor always asked to have Buck assigned.

The sun was still a few hours away from rising over the mountains to the east, but the glow from the fire a few miles away lit up the sky. Buck stood there almost mesmerized by the flames he could see in the distance.

The William's Fork fire, as it was being called, started a week before and had consumed nearly a thousand acres of some of the most pristine forest in Colorado. The Forest Service brought in a Level One incident commander and several hotshot teams from around the region. The air and ground battle had been relentless and once the winds had finally died down the air tankers and hotshot crews had been able to achieve twenty-five percent containment.

The fire may have been twenty-five percent contained, but there was still a lot of fire out there, and Buck wasn't sure if he would be able to get to the crime scene anytime soon. He took a sip from the bottle of Coke he had brought with him.

The call had come while Buck was in the middle of cleaning out the closet in his home in Gunnison. Buck's wife, Lucy, had been diagnosed with metastatic breast cancer five years earlier and lost her battle a couple of months back. It had been a valiant fight, and Buck missed his wife of thirty-five years every day. The pain of the loss had finally lessened, and he knew it was time to face the task of clearing out the memories. That started with donating all of Lucy's clothes to her church. Some volunteers would be by the next day to pick up all the donated clothes, so Buck had set his mind to finally getting it done.

He soon realized that this was going to be one of the hardest jobs he had ever taken on. Each piece of clothing brought a memory, and Buck felt like he spent most of the day fighting back the tears. He was not winning the fight. His daughter-in-law Judy, who is married to his oldest son David, had already cleaned out a lot of the house, with the help of Buck's grandchildren but Buck wanted to tackle their room and closet by himself.

He finally decided that going through each piece of clothing was going to make the process even more difficult, so he just started pulling everything off the hangers and putting it all in big black contractor trash bags. He then carried the bags out to the living room and piled them up in the front corner.

He was just cleaning out all her personal items, toothbrush, combs and her medicines when his phone rang. He looked at the number on the screen and considered not answering it. He was back at work following Lucy's death, but his bosses had kept his schedule reasonably light. It looked like it was time to get back in the game.

Chapter Three

"Yes sir," Buck answered.

"Hi, Buck. Hope I didn't catch you at a bad time. You doing ok?" asked Kevin Jackson.

Kevin Jackson is the Director of the Colorado Bureau of Investigation. He had a stellar career with the Colorado Springs Police Department before being tapped for the top post at CBI. He was more bureaucrat than cop, having spent most of his career on the administrative side of things, but he was well respected in law enforcement, and so far, Buck was impressed with him. He was also the youngest person ever to be picked for the Director's position.

"Doing good sir. Ready to get back into the trenches. What have you got?"

"Got a call from the governor this morning. There is a wildland fire underway in Rio Blanco county that started with the destruction of a huge, controversial fishing lodge. The lodge belongs to a couple of big opposition donors, and they are making a big stink about the governor not being able to handle the issue. It seems there have been several fires over the last couple years and a group calling itself the National Environmental Task Force is claiming responsibility for this fire as well as several others."

"Excuse me for interrupting sir, but did you just say that a group, that is at the forefront of fighting for the environment, set fire to a forest while burning down a fishing lodge. I've heard about these guys over the years, and this seems like kind of a rookie mistake. Are we sure the group claiming credit is legit? Seems a little odd, sir."

"You picked up on that, huh?" asked the Director.

"Yes, sir," replied Buck.

The Director continued. "We don't know for sure. That's where you come in. It seems that they set this brand-new lodge on fire and didn't pay attention to the latest weather report because a front blew through and the winds jumped up to thirty-five miles an hour with gust up to seventy. Anyway, the governor wants us to get all over this, and he asked for you, personally. But before you start to feel flattered, one of the guys making the most noise is Hardy Braxton. He is even threatening to run against the governor when he comes up for re-election in a couple years. You got any kind of conflict you can't work through with that?"

Buck didn't hesitate. "No conflict sir. I can deal with Hardy and his friends."

The Director went on to fill Buck in on the rest of the crimes that the NETF had taken responsibility for. Over the years there have been several mysterious fires involving controversial projects around the state, including the destruction of a new lodge and restaurant at the top of Vail Mountain. The NETF was considered, by many in law enforcement, to be the special forces unit in the war to protect the environment. They were fearless and deadly, and, no one had been able to get close to this group.

He told Buck to use whatever resources he needed and to check in with the Rio Blanco County Sheriff. The Sheriff had already been briefed, and he knew Buck was coming. The Director told Buck to be careful and stay in touch.

Even though the Colorado Bureau of Investigation had the authority to work anywhere in the state, it had always been customary to wait to be invited into an investigation by the local authorities, be it police or sheriff's office. This time would be a little different since this investigation would cover several locations throughout the state and it was at the request of the governor. Buck would have full authority to handle the investigation as he saw fit.

Buck hung up the phone and walked into his home office and sat down at his laptop. True to his word the Director had sent Buck several files on the various crimes connected to the NETF. There wasn't much information in the files as well as a severe lack of any cohesive investigation into their activities. Buck vowed that he would fix that.

Buck pulled out his phone and dialed a number. The phone rang three times, and Bax answered.

"Hey, Buck. What's up?" asked Baxter

"Hey, Bax. You working on anything that can't wait?"

Bax was CBI Agent Ashley Baxter. Baxter was five feet four with long blond hair that she usually wore in a ponytail. She joined CBI four years before, right out of the University of Wisconsin. A Denver native, she had no issues moving to Grand Junction and had thrived in her new environment. She was also one of the best internet and social media researchers Buck had ever worked with.

She typically worked with Agent James Richards, and their focus lately was mostly on property crimes like burglary. Richards was a ten-year veteran with the Colorado Bureau of Investigation. He had spent several years with the Ann Arbor, Michigan Police Department before deciding to relocate his family to Colorado. He had a slight build and a very bookish look about him. Buck thought Richards was an accountant the first time he met him. He was also a top-notch investigator.

Buck went on to explain the conversation he just had with the Director. He asked Bax if she could pull together everything she could find on the National Environmental Task Force and any environmental groups that might be associated with it. He told her he was looking for a really deep dive. As he expected, Bax told him not to worry, and she was all over it.

Buck hung up, jumped in the shower, toweled off, got dressed and packed a bag with a couple days of clean clothes. He clipped his gun and badge to his belt, grabbed his CBI windbreaker out of the front closet and headed for his car. Once in the car, he dialed his daughter-in-law, Judy, and let her know where he was headed. She promised to keep an eye on the house and make sure the church volunteers picked up all the donated clothes from the living room.

Buck started the car and pulled out of the driveway. He felt good about getting back in the game. He headed for Meeker, Colorado and the Rio Blanco County Sheriff.

Chapter Four

There is no easy way to get from Gunnison to Meeker. No matter which of the two options you take, it still takes almost four hours to make the drive. Buck left Gunnison on Highway 50 and headed west. Knowing he had a while to kill he decided to call his daughter.

Cassie was the middle child, and she was every bit a middle child. In high school, she played soccer, ran track and played volleyball. She lettered in all three sports. She was also the one who got in trouble for violating curfew, drinking, and whatever other mischief she could find to get into. Buck was surprised when she was accepted to the University of Arizona with a full scholarship for volleyball. He was even more surprised when she was accepted into law school. Cassie was never much for regimented education.

A year and a half ago, she suddenly dropped out of law school, and her career path took a different track. She joined the Forest Service and was now working as a wildland firefighter with the Helena Hotshots. The Helena Hotshots were one of the elite firefighting teams based out of Helena, Montana. Buck was not surprised. He never saw her sitting behind a desk as a lawyer. She loved the outdoors, and she was as tough as they came. Lucy wasn't pleased that she quit school without any discussion, and she worried whenever Cassie was called out to a fire, but she also knew her daughter and if this was where she was happy, then so was her mom.

The Director had mentioned that several hotshot teams had been called in to fight the Williams Fork fire and he wanted to see if her team was one of those called in. Her phone went straight to voicemail, which Buck knew meant that she was in the field. He left a message that he was heading for Meeker and to call when she got in from the field.

The rest of the drive was quiet, and Buck spent a lot of the time thinking about all the family drives that he and Lucy used to take when the kids were younger. Those memories brought tears to his eyes, knowing that there would no longer be road trips with Lucy at his side. Several times he had to pass through songs on his iPod that brought back memories of their time together until he finally just turned it off and drove along in silence. He missed Lucy so much. She had always been there for him, and he worried about going through life without his constant companion.

Buck arrived in Meeker just before dark, and as he turned off Highway 13 onto 4th Street, he let the memories clear from his mind as he focused on the job at hand. He crossed Main Street and pulled into the parking lot behind the Rio Blanco County Sheriff's office.

Buck walked through the front door of the Sheriff's office, presented his ID to the deputy on duty at the front desk and was buzzed into the back. Sheriff Caleb McCabe was sitting at his desk reading a report when Buck walked in.

"Buck Taylor, as I live and breathe. It's great to see you." The Sheriff stood up, walked around his desk and gave Buck's hand a hearty shake.

Rio Blanco County was named for the White River, which

flows through the county. The county borders the state of Utah on its western edge and is predominantly an agricultural area. Covering over 3200 square miles, the county has a population of around 6600 people, of which ninety-five percent are white and is predominantly a Republican stronghold. In 1936, Rio Blanco County along with just two other counties west of the Mississippi River voted for Alf Landon over Franklin Delano Roosevelt for President.

Meeker, Colorado is the county seat and was founded in 1880. With a population of just over 2500 people, the city sits in the east-central portion of the county and although mostly agricultural, is also a mecca for outdoorsmen and women. The county was named for Nathan Meeker, an Indian Agent, and was rich with the history of the old west. Nathan Meeker was killed with 11 other people during the Meeker Massacre of 1879. The massacre eventually led to the expulsion of the White River Utes from the area.

"Sheriff, good to see you. It's been a long time," replied Buck. "Sounds like we have a problem we need to deal with."

"Yeah. I spoke with Director Jackson this morning, and he said he was sending you up here at the request of the governor. You know that the governor is not well thought of around these parts so you may want to downplay that part a little."

"Thanks for the advice. You want to fill me in on what's going on?"

The Sheriff pointed to the empty visitor's chair in the corner and walked back around his desk and sat down. Buck sat down and took the file the Sheriff handed him.

Caleb McCabe had just started his second term as the Sheriff. Born and raised on a hardscrabble ranch near Rangely he had served in the military for four years and had seen action in both Afghanistan and Iraq. With a silver star and purple heart, Caleb was a shoo-in for the Sheriff's job when the former Sheriff, Clint Powell, was arrested in Craig, Colorado on sexual assault charges stemming from a drunken party.

Caleb stood only five foot eight, but he was one hundred and fifty-five pounds of pure muscle and being a local who was well respected, gave him an advantage which came in handy in such a large county where most of the residents would rather solve any problem themselves rather then calling in the authorities. Life was hard in this wind-swept county, and the people were even harder.

Chapter Five

The Sheriff gave Buck the Reader's Digest version of the events leading up to the fire at the lodge.

"By the way. Sorry to hear about your loss. My condolences. Your wife was one tough lady."

Buck nodded and choked back a tear.

"No one was happy when Mark Richards, the hedge fund guy, and his buddies decided to build their lodge. Anywhere else in the county would have been fine. You know we have a bunch of private lodges here, but this one was on a piece of pristine forest, and no one liked the idea of the Forest Service doing a land swap with this guy for a chunk of land at a ski resort."

Buck looked at the pictures of the property in the file the Sheriff handed him. The Sheriff continued. "Worst part was they closed almost a mile of both rivers for their own use. That was some of the best fishing on the river. I will say they did a really nice job improving the trout habitat along that stretch, and I've heard tales of some huge fish coming out of there now, but the locals were not happy."

The Sheriff and Buck discussed the terms of the land swap and the access issues that had been the catalyst for a bunch of local rallies against the project. Buck sat back and looked through the thin file.

"How do we know the National Environmental Task Force was responsible for the fire?" Buck asked.

The Sheriff handed Buck a separate piece of paper. "Bastards sent a press release to the local paper. Can you believe that?"

Buck read the press release. It was full of environmental buzzwords, vague accusations, and innuendos, which Buck would need to follow up on. There was a lot of legalese that hinted at corruption and payoffs on a broad scale. It did not paint a very nice picture of Mark Richards or his partners, but it stopped short of making any specific accusations towards them.

"Mark Richards and his friends are not happy, and they are making serious threats towards the county, the federal government, and the governor. I bet I get three or four calls a day looking for a progress report and I keep telling them we can't even get to the crime scene until the fire is out. They don't want to hear it. They even sent a private investigator by yesterday. Not a very pleasant fellow so watch your ass."

The press release was signed by NETF, but that alone was not an admission of responsibility. The Sheriff noted the look of uncertainty in Buck's eyes.

"I know, Buck. This could have been written by anyone. Truth is we really won't know who set the fire until we can get in there and take a look. The incident commander says we might be able to get into what's left of the building sometime tomorrow."

"Ok," replied Buck. "I spoke with Jack Spencer, the State Fire Investigator, on my way up here and he will be here sometime tomorrow morning along with a couple forensic techs from the state crime lab. In the meantime, I am going to check into a hotel and crash. I will see you on site tomorrow morning."

Buck and the Sheriff both stood and shook hands and Buck walked out of the Sheriff's office and headed for his car. Once in his car, he realized he hadn't eaten in a while, and he needed nourishment. He left his car in the parking lot and walked across the street to the "Cozy Up Bar and Grill."

Buck hadn't been in the Cozy Up in years, but he knew nothing had changed since the last time he was there as soon as he opened the door. The bar had operated under several names over the previous hundred years and was listed on the Register of National Historic Places as one of the oldest, continually operating bars in the country.

The original building had been a log cabin, and parts of it were still visible although the low light made it hard to see anything. As Buck's eyes adjusted to the lack of light, he saw that the old vinyl chairs and laminate tables were still in place. A few old ranchers were sitting at the massive wood bar having a heated discussion about something that had them all riled up. They stopped their debate as Buck stepped up to the bar and they all looked at him and nodded before going back to their discussion.

Buck grabbed a seat at the end of the bar and looked around. Nope, nothing had changed since the last time he was there, including the bartender who made her way down the bar towards Buck, with a big smile on her face.

"Oh my God. Buck Taylor. It's been a long time," said Sam. She grabbed a can of Coke out of the cooler as she passed.

Samantha Reynolds set the coke on the bar, walked through the opening at the end of the bar and gave Buck a huge hug. Buck thought she might have held on a little too long but he didn't mind, and he felt his pulse quicken just a little. Sam did that to people.

Sam had grown up on a working horse ranch just outside Meeker and had taken over the bar when her mom decided to retire about ten years back. Now somewhere in her mid-fifties, Sam had gone through three husbands and had raised four kids. Sam was also drop dead gorgeous. At five feet eight, one hundred thirty pounds with long red hair pulled back in a ponytail and incredible hazel eyes, Sam stopped the conversation in any room she walked into. It might also be that there was no way she would ever be able to close the top three buttons of any shirt she wore. Sam was what most men would have commonly called, stacked, and she was proud of it.

Sam finally let go, walked back around the bar and grabbed a clean glass off the huge Montana back bar and pour the Coke into the glass before sliding it over to Buck.

"I heard your wife passed away a couple months back. I was sorry to hear that. You doin ok?" she asked.

Buck thanked her for the Coke and filled her in on the last couple months. Sam listed intently, only stepping away to fill a couple beers down the bar. He told her about how the chemo and radiation were no longer working on the brain tumors and that they made the decision, as hard as it was, to stop treatment.

He also mentioned how the family had all gathered at a small handicap fishing dock in a park along the Gunnison River, in Gunnison, one Sunday morning to scatter Lucy's ashes. It was supposed to be a quiet, family affair but somehow word had gotten out, and three hundred people had quietly gathered behind them on the grass. The private affair had turned into a huge picnic in Lucy's honor. Even though Lucy didn't want any kind of service Buck thought she would have loved the idea of a spontaneous party.

When Buck was finished, Sam handed him a stack of napkins and wiped the tears from her own eyes. She handed Buck a menu, and he ordered the cowboy ribeye steak and a baked potato.

After calling Buck's order to the cook, she leaned across the bar which required Buck to force himself to look into her eyes and she whispered, "Don't take this the wrong way but if you need anything while you're in town and I do mean anything, give me a call."

She smiled and walked back down the bar. Buck knew Sam was sincere since she flirted with him every time he walked into the bar. He hadn't really thought about dating yet, but if he did, she would be his first call.

Chapter Six

Buck finished his steak, gave Sam a kiss on the cheek and a hug and stepped through the front door into the cool night air. He was going to head to his hotel when he looked to the east and could see the fire lighting up the night sky. He climbed into his car and headed back out to the highway, turned left and headed for Route 8. After turning onto County Route 8, it took a little over an hour to get to the Vaughan Lake campground parking lot, where the Forest Service had set up their incident command center.

Buck pulled into the parking lot and parked his car next to the huge white tent that was serving as the command center. He climbed out and zipped up his CBI windbreaker against the chill in the air. Stepping into the tent, he was amazed that there was hardly anyone on duty. Except for a couple young folks looking at weather patterns on their computer screens the only other person stood in front of a large topographic map of the area.

Buck stepped up to the map. "Lookin for the incident commander."

Without turning, the tall guy in the yellow firefighter shirt responded. "That'd be me. Can I help you?"

"Buck Taylor with the Colorado Bureau of Investigation."

The tall firefighter turned and extended his hand. "Pat Sutton. I was told to expect you. Nice to meet you." They shook hands.

"Can I ask you how it's going?" Buck asked.

"Well, the good news is that the winds have died down and tonight the humidity has started climbing, which is helping lay down the fire. Right now, I've got four hotshot teams working the front edge and with any luck, by tomorrow morning we should have this beast about sixty percent contained."

Buck looked at the map on the wall. "How about the area around the lodge? Can we get in there tomorrow to start looking around?"

"Probably, as long as the weather holds. We knocked down all the leftover hotspots this morning, and I have a mop-up crew working that area tonight to make sure nothing flares back up."

He looked at Buck and Buck could see the seriousness in his eyes. "I know you have an investigation to get started but I need you to understand that this is a very erratic fire and once you get in that area I cannot guarantee your safety. If the winds whip up again like they did three days ago that fire could run over you in a heartbeat. Understand?"

Buck nodded. "Got it. We won't move unless you tell us we are good. I would like to have one of your radios if you can spare one and if you tell us to get out of there, we are gone. Fair enough?"

Pat nodded. "I'll do better than that. If I can break away, I will escort you up there myself. When they told me I was gonna be babysitting a state cop, I expected you to come in here and start ordering everyone around. Thanks for not doing that. This job's hard enough as it is."

"No problem. You will find I'm pretty easy to work with. By the way, have you got the Helena Hotshots working this fire?"

Pat pointed to a spot at the center of the fire line on the map. "They are working this point. Pretty tough terrain. You know them?"

"My daughter, Cassie Taylor, is on that team. Wasn't sure they were out here."

"Your daughter is Cassie? She is one tough girl. Damn good at reading the fire and she works harder than most of the guys on her team. I'm always glad to have someone like her around."

Buck thanked Pat and told him that the team would assemble sometime late morning. They shook hands, and Buck walked out through the tent flap. He stepped around behind the tent, found a spot at the edge of the parking lot and watched the flames.

Hardy Braxton walked through the lot and stood next to Buck, who didn't seem to react at all to his presence, but Hardy knew better. He knew that Buck had heard him coming and even though Buck didn't acknowledge him, he was well aware that Buck had his hand on the backstrap of his pistol and had unsnapped the thumb break.

Hardy stood there for a few minutes in silence and watched the flames. From behind they could have been twins, except Hardy had gained a few pounds since high school and now wore a wide-brimmed Stetson to cover his receding hairline. Buck and Hardy had played football for Gunnison High School. They were the team's defensive backfield and were called the "Wrecking Crew" during senior year. Between them, they broke every defensive high school football record in the state, many of which stood to this day. They had also been friends, on and off, since first grade.

Buck had passed up several full-ride scholarships and instead joined the army and later the Gunnison County Sheriff's Department. Hardy, on the other hand, accepted a full-ride scholarship to Stanford and spent the next four years as an All-American football player and later went on to play in the National Football League until a knee injury sidelined him for good.

Hardy left the NFL and took over the reins of his father's small livestock company. Over the years he turned that small company, based out of Gunnison County, into the premier bucking stock and livestock company in the world. A rodeo didn't happen anywhere that didn't have numerous animals from Braxton Bucking Stock in its corrals. He also invested heavily in energy exploration companies and owned the largest private fracking company in the country. By all measures, Hardy Braxton was hugely successful. He was also Buck's brother-in-law.

Hardy married Lucy's younger sister, Rachel, the year after Lucy and Buck got married. Their marriage was blessed with four children, all of whom were now involved in the numerous family businesses. Businesses that now numbered at least a dozen and stretch from Gunnison to California and even dipped down into South America. Hardy was the big dog in Gunnison County, and he was not afraid to use that power to his family's advantage.

Buck knew that Hardy was somehow involved with the controversial fishing lodge project, but he didn't know to what extent. He knew one thing about Hardy Braxton. He never walked away from a fight, and he wasn't afraid of a little controversy.

Chapter Seven

Buck took a sideways glance and went back to looking at the fire. After a few minutes of silence, he finally spoke.

"Hardy," said Buck.

"Buck," replied Hardy.

They both stood quietly looking at the flames for a few more minutes until Hardy broke the silence.

"Rachel and I wanted to be at Lucy's service. We were on a livestock buying trip through South America and couldn't get back. Rachel was devastated."

"Not a problem," replied Buck. "We knew you were tied up."

"I want you to know," Hardy continued, "we are working with the county to buy a one-mile strip of land on the west side of the river where you scattered Lucy's ashes. We want to turn it into a river walk in honor of Lucy. She meant a lot to us. I asked Jason if he had a landscape architect at his firm that can do the design work."

Jason was Buck's youngest son, and he worked as an architect in Boulder. Buck was surprised to hear that Jason was involved in the riverwalk project. He saw Jason and the family a couple weeks back, and he never mentioned it. He figured they must have been trying to keep it a secret, which wouldn't have lasted long. Very little happened in the county that Buck wasn't aware of.

Buck turned and looked at Hardy. "Thanks. You don't have to do that."

Hardy started to explain, but Buck cut him off. "What's your interest in this lodge? Heard you were making a lot of noise. Got a bunch of people fired up."

"Mark Richards and I are partners in this venture and several others, and you are damn right I raised a stink. This is the third fire in the past year that has impacted a project like this and we are getting tired of it. I have also had four fracking sites vandalized. Two last month alone and that weasel of a governor doesn't have a damn bit of interest in figuring out who is doing this. So yeah, if I have to make a little noise and threaten to run against him, then so be it. It got you here, didn't it?"

Buck was silent for a minute while he continued to watch the fire. He finally turned and looked at Hardy.

"Ok, Hardy. I will figure out who's doing this, and I will shut them down, but I need you to back off and let me do my job."

"You just make sure you do," replied Hardy. "Because if you don't, we will take care of those fucking environmentalists ourselves."

Buck knew that it wasn't worth fighting with Hardy when he got all riled up. He would talk to Hardy when he calmed down. He turned back to the fire.

"By the way," said Hardy. "Your son designed this lodge. He was very proud of it."

Buck had no idea that his son Jason was the architect for the lodge. He also wondered why he found out two things tonight that he wasn't aware of. Jason and Hardy had always been close, but it seemed strange that Jason failed to mention either project.

Hardy stood quietly for a few minutes and then turned to leave. "Stop by the house when you get time, and I will give you what we have on the NETF."

Hardy started to walk off and stopped. "Is Cassie and her team working this fire?"

Buck answered over his shoulder, "Yeah, her team is on the front edge. Tough terrain."

"We will pray for her safety," Hardy replied.

He turned and walked off leaving Buck standing in the dark. Buck was concerned. He knew Hardy didn't make idle threats, and he also knew that if he had already gathered some information on the NETF, then he would have to move fast before Hardy and his friends decided to take things into their own hands.

He had told the Director that he could handle Hardy and he knew he could. Handling Mark Richards was going to be another story indeed. Mark Richards was a billionaire hedge fund owner and a heavyweight real estate developer, and he had a reputation for running over anyone that got in his way.

Richards had a lot of money, and an incredible amount of power and he had little regard for the government or people in general. All he cared about was getting whatever he wanted, no matter what. Buck smiled. "This is gonna be interesting," he said to himself. He turned from the fire and headed for his car. Before he pulled out of the parking lot, he asked the spirits of the forest to keep an eye on Cassie.

He pulled out onto Route 8 and headed back towards Meeker. It was time to start investigating, and Buck was more than ready.

Chapter Eight

They had been sitting in the forest at the southern end of the campground parking lot and had watched as Buck and Hardy talked. They had no idea who Buck was, but they were well aware of who Hardy Braxton was. They wished they had brought the parabolic microphone with them. The boss would be interested in knowing what those two had been talking about.

They thought about following Hardy Braxton, but they had been told to stay put and keep an eye on the fire efforts. The boss had not been pleased that someone else had set the lodge ablaze and that the fire had set the forest ablaze. Even if it wasn't their fire, it was a significant mistake, and the boss was worried that they would catch all the blame, and that would make for some terrible publicity. They were actually glad that someone else started the fire. They had checked the weather forecast earlier in the day, and the front was still hours away. They had no idea that the front they had been watching had suddenly picked up speed and dropped farther south than was initially predicted. The end result would have been the same, and the forest would still be on fire, but they were glad it was not their fault. They would still need to follow orders, at least for a little while, until the boss got over being pissed.

The big guy pulled out his cell phone, held it inside his jacket so the light wouldn't shine like a beacon in the dark forest and dialed the boss.

"I hope you have a damn good reason for bothering me this late at night," said the boss.

The big guy went on to explain about the meeting between Hardy Braxton and the new guy. He also filled the boss in on the efforts of the hotshots and reported that the fire was partly contained.

There was silence on the other end of the phone, and the big guy knew better than to interrupt. He waited while the boss thought about the report. The boss finally spoke up.

"Can you get close enough without getting caught and get me the license number from the newcomer's car? I have a way to track him down."

The big guy responded that they could and would call back in a few minutes. He hung up the phone, and his partner headed off around the edge of the parking lot, hoping to circle in behind the car and get the plate number. He stopped where the forest met the lot and pulled out a pair of night vision binoculars. Through the green haze in the eyepieces, he was able to read Buck's license plate, almost as good as he if was standing behind the car. He wrote the number on a small piece of paper and headed back to his partner.

Once back together the big guy called the boss again and recited the license plate number. The boss hung up with any further comment. Cinching up their jackets against the late-night chill they settled down and watched the area around the command center.

They couldn't figure out the newcomer. After he had a discussion with Hardy Braxton and Hardy turned and left, the newcomer just stood there staring into the forest at the fire beyond. They decided that the two men must have known each other, but whatever their relationship was it didn't appear to be very friendly. There was no familiar handshake or a slap on the back. They had a conversation in which neither man hardly looked at the other and then Braxton turned and left. He stopped after a few steps and said something to the newcomer who responded but never turned around to face him.

The behavior of these two men confused them. They were students of human nature, and over the years they had developed a sixth sense about people. They had to. It was what kept them alive, and it made them very good at their jobs. But they just couldn't put their fingers on the relationship they had just watched. Now more than ever, they really wished they had the parabolic mic with them.

They watched the newcomer for another twenty minutes before he finally turned and headed towards his car. Through the night vision binoculars, they could see he was an older guy and looked in pretty good shape even though the green haze. As he turned, his jacket flipped open, and the big guy could clearly see the badge and gun clipped to his belt.

"Shit, he's a cop!" exclaimed the big guy.

"Are you sure?" asked his partner.

"Yeah. I saw his badge and gun. We need to let the boss know."

The big guy took out his cell phone and redialed the boss's number. When the boss answered, he explained what they had just discovered about the newcomer. The boss thought about it for a minute and then told them to follow him and see where he goes. The boss told them not to engage him in any way until it could determine who he worked for.

Disconnecting the call, they both stood up and headed back through the forest to the small turnout where they had hidden their truck. They were sitting just off the road with their lights off when the Jeep Grand Cherokee passed by them on Route 8.

They followed the car for several miles until it pulled into the parking lot of a small mom and pop motel in Meeker and the newcomer got out, walked into the office and walked out a few minutes later with the key he used to unlock unit number seven. They parked in the lot of the gas station across the street, shut off the lights and the engine and settled in for a long night of surveillance.

Chapter Nine

The restaurant that was attached to the small motel Buck was staying at was packed to the doors. Every seat was filled, and 5 waitresses, all wearing jeans, and black tee shirts moved seamlessly from table to table taking orders and filling coffee cups. Buck noticed a few tourists, who were probably also staying at the motel, but the crowd was mostly ranchers and farmers. Buck always looked for places like this when he was traveling, and this one was no exception. Good food, and plenty of it, and fast service with lots of coffee. Just what working men and women wanted to start their day.

Buck was just finishing off his fried eggs, sausages and hash browns when he looked up from his plate and spotted Ashely Baxter coming through the door. She stopped for a few seconds, looked around and spotted him sitting in the booth by the window. She waved and headed in his direction. She carried her ever-present backpack, and she looked like a girl on a mission.

Bax was attractive with hazel eyes, and had long blond hair pulled back in a ponytail. She wore jeans and black Nike's and a light plaid shirt under her Carhart vest. Buck watched as several of the ranchers and cowboys looked up to check out the new girl, and he also noticed a lot of them divert their eyes back to their plates when they spotted the gun and badge on her belt. Bax looked more like a college student than a cop, but Buck knew better. Bax was one hell of a cop in Buck's and a bunch of other people's eyes. She was smart, and she was fearless, but she also knew which one of those attributes to use and when. Buck had a tremendous amount of respect for Bax, and although it didn't happen often, Buck liked working with her.

Bax slid her backpack across the booth seat and slid in opposite Buck. Buck finished the bite of sausage that was still on his fork and nodded.

"Hey, Buck. Sheriff McCabe said I might find you here."

"It's nice to see you, Bax. Have you eaten?"

"Not yet. What's good?" she asked.

Buck waved over the waitress and Bax ordered the same thing he was eating only instead of a glass of Coke, she asked for coffee, which almost magically appeared in her cup. She looked at the glass of Coke and smiled. Buck's consumption of Coke was legendary around the CBI office.

Skipping the small talk, Bax pulled out a couple files from her backpack and laid them on the table next to Buck's now empty plate. Looking around and then keeping her voice low she opened the first file revealing several internet articles about the National Environmental Task Force. Buck was about to pick up the first article when he closed the cover of the manila folder. The waitress set a huge plate of food in front of Bax and then stepped away.

Buck opened the first folder and briefly read the first couple printouts while Bax devoured her breakfast. She had used a yellow highlighter to note pieces of information she felt might be important and she had also attached lime green sticky notes to a few of the pages with comments or suggestions. Buck looked up from the papers and smiled. "She must have stayed up half the night going through this information," he thought to himself.

Bax finished her breakfast and pushed her plate to the edge of the table. She looked around the room and then leaned in towards Buck.

"The stuff in the first folder is basically just internet background. A lot of press releases and newspaper articles about the NETF. There is some interesting information, which I highlighted for you. The sticky notes are some thoughts about how we might want to proceed."

She pulled the second file out from under the pile. This folder was much thicker. Buck opened the cover. Bax took over. "I took the police reports the Director sent you and did a really deep dive. Most of the police reports and the investigations that followed are pretty weak, but I went back to the sources and was able to pull a lot more information up that the Director did not have access to."

Buck started to read the first police report for a fracking site fire south of Craig. Bax continued, "I spoke to the fire chief up that way, and he told me he felt certain it was arson, but he couldn't get enough evidence to make a case, so this investigation pretty much died on the vine."

Buck went to interrupt, but Bax was on a roll. He held his questions and waited for a break in the briefing, which he knew from experience wasn't going to happen any time soon.

"All told, there are 14 unsolved fires over the last 5 years, including the big mountaintop restaurant fire in Vail that could be attributed to NETF, but there is almost no evidence pointing directly towards them. Whoever these folks are they are damn good at what they do."

Bax stopped to take a breath and a sip of her coffee. Buck

spent a few more minutes looking through the police reports, then he took off his reading glasses and looked at Bax.

"Nice job Bax. This investigation just got really big. Can you pull away from whatever you were working on and spend a couple days working this with me?"

"The Director called me after I spoke with you yesterday and asked me to work with you on this full time. I think he's a little concerned about you Buck, no offense."

Buck smiled. "No offense taken. He has every right to be concerned, and I appreciate that he sent you to help me out. Lucy's death hit me harder than I expected, but my head is on straight and I'm ready to hit the ground running."

Buck thought for a minute. "Here's what I would like to do. I am heading back out to the lodge fire to meet the State Fire Investigator. Since you already laid the groundwork with the fire chief in Craig why don't you head up that way and see what else you can find out? Have him take you to the site and see if you see anything he missed. Then work your way through the police reports and talk to whoever ran the investigation and get a feel for what happened. Once I finish up with the lodge scene, I am going to have the Sheriff take me to the two other most recent fire sites here in Rio Blanco County. Give me a call tonight and let's see if any of this takes us anyplace."

Bax pulled her backpack across the seat and stood up. She reached into her pocket and set a twenty-dollar bill on the table next to her plate. Buck knew better than to stop her, so he left it there and placed his own twenty under his Coke glass.

"Thanks, Buck. I am really looking forward to working with you again. It's good to have you back."

Bax took a last sip of coffee, flung her backpack over her shoulder and headed for the door.

Chapter Ten

Commander Jack "Fighting Red" Muldoon sat at the center of the tribunal that had been hastily called in the early morning hours. The issue they were about to deal with could conceivably cost the town everything they had built up over the past couple years, but this was also a discipline issue, and Muldoon wanted to get this over with as fast as possible.

Muldoon was an imposing figure of a man, and very few people ever crossed him. At over 6 feet tall and built like a boxer, the red-headed former Marine Corps Captain and self-proclaimed leader of this group of survivalists, demanded full allegiance from his followers. This was going to be the first real test of his "power" since they had established their little town a few years back. Whatever decision was made here today in the back of the old metal Quonset hut would have wide-ranging implications for their future success or failure as a group and as a business.

In the middle of the floor facing the tribunal and duct taped to a metal folding chair sat Elliot Beech. Beech had been recruited from the NSA, the National Security Agency, by Muldoon, where he was a computer programmer and hacker extraordinaire, who had made clear, on social media, his dissatisfaction with the policies of the

United States of America when it came to cyber warfare. It was those same computer skills that had him sitting before the tribunal on this chilly morning, but Beech wasn't chilled, he was sweating profusely and was having trouble focusing after having been "interrogated" for the past eight hours by Muldoon's security team.

The other members of the town sat quietly in the audience and waited to see how far this would go. Everyone who decided to take up residence in the town understood the rules and regulations, but this was the first time anyone had committed a major breach of the rules and how the tribunal would react was anyone's guess.

Muldoon looked at the other two members of the tribunal, and they each nodded in turn. Garret Tillman functioned as the Chief Financial Officer for the town. At five-feet-ten and balding, the fifty-eight-year-old former accounting clerk quit his job at a major accounting firm and moved his family to Colorado to join Muldoon's venture with the promise of becoming wealthy.

Margaret Windsong had dark black hair and a matronly way about her, but she didn't suffer fools lightly. She had told everyone in town that she was of Native American decent, but she couldn't seem to remember which tribe she was from since she told different stories to different people. Truth be told, she was born and raised in a white evangelical family in Odessa, Texas and had joined Muldoon after running away from home. She met Muldoon in a bar in Denver when he was first putting together his scheme. They were instantly attracted to each other.

Muldoon asked one of the security team to remove the tape from Beech's mouth, which he did with some vengeance. Beech immediately started pleading.

"Red, you have to believe me," Beech cried out. "You have to believe me. I had no idea he was a Fed. I swear on my mother's life."

Muldoon picked up the paper off the table in front of him and stared daggers at Beech, who just as quickly stopped talking. He read from the paper.

"Elliot Beech, you have been brought before this tribunal because you violated our most important rule. You involved an outsider in our business in an attempt to enrich your life and your bank account with little or no regard for the other members of the town. In doing so, you brought a DEA agent, an agent for the very government we have all sworn to oppose, into our midst, jeopardizing our entire operation and forcing us to deal with that agent in a manner we had hoped to avoid. We have no way of knowing how badly your actions will impact our business."

He stopped so that the others assembled in the hut could get the full effect of Beech's actions. He was going to use this as a teaching moment for the other members of the town so that none of them would think about crossing him.

Beech looked up through his two swollen black eyes and started to sob as urine ran down his leg. He had never been this scared in his entire life. He was a geek. He should be sitting in his mother's basement trying to hack into the Social Security Administration's website or some other innocuous government site and setting up ransomware, not sitting in a cold metal building in the middle of Colorado awaiting a sentence.

All he was guilty of was trying to set up a side deal between one of the town's Asian suppliers and a friend from his time at the NSA. How was he supposed to know, that his friend was working with a DEA agent who was working outside the box and who offered him a great deal. Of course, the promise of a one-time payoff of a couple hundred grand and a plane ticket to Fiji or some other exotic place had helped to sweeten the deal.

Muldoon continued. "You have been found guilty by this tribunal of crimes against the town, and you will be banished from the town… But first, you will be locked up in our jail for 90 days of hard labor, and you will not be allowed any visitors. We want to make sure that your actions didn't cause irreparable damage."

A gasp came from those assembled as Red handed down the sentence. Many were surprised at the harshness of the punishment, after all, Beech was one of them, there must be a better way. The town all assumed that the DEA agent had probably been killed, even though they didn't know for sure, and no one questioned the action because it was needed to protect the town and their business. They all wanted to believe that Beech would be spared and allowed to leave but there would always be doubts.

Muldoon glared at the audience as the security team cut the tape holding Beech to the chair and dragged him towards the back door of the hut.

He addressed the rest of the town's residents, "Make no mistake, Beech's crime could have brought down our entire operation. I promised to make you all rich, but you also promised to follow the rules."

The tribunal stood up from the table and walked out the door, following the security team and Elliot Beech. The remaining members of the town slowly walked back towards their homes. Everyone was aware that once the tribunal had resolved a matter before it, there would be no further discussion.

Chapter Eleven

Buck pulled his Jeep into the Vaughan Lake campground parking lot and parked next to the fire command tent. He climbed out of his car, stretched, casually looked around the parking lot and walked into the tent. The Sheriff and Pat Sutton, the Incident Commander, were looking over a topographic map of the area around the fishing lodge while one of Pat's assistants was reading from the latest weather forecast.

Buck stepped up to the table. "Good mornin. How we lookin for today?"

Pat and the Sheriff looked up from the map, and Buck shook hands all around.

The Sheriff spoke first. "Pat thinks the weather is going to cooperate, so we should be able to get to the lodge without a problem."

"We are expecting a little rain later today," said Pat, "but the forecast is for the winds to stay low through tomorrow. That should give you enough time to see what you need to see. Our containment is holding, so for right now I can lead you in."

"Great," said Buck. "We can leave as soon as the State Fire Investigator gets here."

Buck and the Sheriff headed out through the tent flap and walked to their respective cars. They each put on a yellow firefighter shirt, grabbed a white hard hat and a backpack full of the things they would need to do as thorough an investigation as possible. Buck threw a rolled-up raincoat into his backpack along with a couple bottles of water and a few energy bars. He looked up as he heard a car pull into the parking lot.

Jack Spencer's white Chevy Tahoe parked next to Buck's Jeep. He slid out of the car, stood up and stretched and opened the back driver's side door. The big black Lab jumped off the back seat and headed straight for Buck and almost jumped into his arms. Buck grabbed hold of the dog in a big bear hug and shook him side to side.

"Hiya, Gus. How are you, buddy?" The Lab, with his tail wagging nonstop, spun around several times as Buck let him go and then licked Buck on the side of his face. Buck laughed hard and stood up. He reached into a side pocket in the back of his car and pulled out a large, dark brown chew stick and handed it to Gus, who laid down at his feet and started chewing away, tail still wagging.

Buck shook Jack's hand. "Jack, it's good to see you. Glad you had the time to join us."

"I'm glad to see you too, Buck. Hey, I was sorry to hear about your wife. Mary and I were heartbroken when we heard the news. Mary sends her best."

Jack Spencer had been the State Fire Investigator for the past fifteen years. He was five feet ten with a firefighter's build, and his almost white, flat top haircut gave him the look of authority. Although his primary duties were with the State of Colorado, Jack and Gus had worked fires all over the country, and his testimony led to the incarceration of a lot of "firebugs."

Buck was just about to respond when the Sheriff stepped

around the car and looked at the dog at Buck's feet. Buck introduced the Sheriff to Jack, and they shook hands. He then knelt down next to Gus, who was still chewing away on his new chew stick.

"This is Gus. He's one of the best ADC's in the country thanks to Jack and a great nose." Buck stood up.

The Sheriff looked at Gus and said, "What's an ADC if I might ask?" Buck was just about to answer when Rick Carmichael stepped around Jack's car and beat him to it.

"Gus is a certified Accelerant Detection Canine, and like Mr. Taylor said, one of the best in the country. Hi, by the way. I'm Rick. I work with Jack." Rick shook hands all around.

Rick Carmichael was a twenty-something with a bald head and piercing blue eyes. Thin and just a shade under six foot, he was Jack's forensic technician, and his job was to analyze any evidence they might find to see if this was a man-made fire or an act of God.

Jack opened the back hatch on his SUV and pulled out a yellow military-style vest, and as soon as Gus saw it, he dropped his chew stick and stood almost at attention while Jack placed it on his back and tightened the straps. The transformation from loveable pet to working dog was something to watch. Once in the vest, Gus knew it was time to go to work.

Jack grabbed his own backpack and slipped it over his shoulder, closed the hatch and everyone headed for the tent.

Chapter Twelve

Pat Sutton shook Jack's hand and rubbed Gus's head. He had everyone gather around the map table and gave a quick update on the course of the fire and the terrain they were about to walk into. Finally, he gave everyone a stern warning.

"This fire is erratic as hell. Right now, conditions are good, but that can change in a heartbeat. I will be with you the entire time you are at the lodge and hopefully you can get what you need, and we can get back, however, if I tell you we have to go, there will be no discussion and no hesitation, understood?"

He picked up a red Sharpie from the table and drew a circle around an area part way between the lodge and the parking lot. "This area in here has already burned. We call it the black. If we have to evacuate in a hurry, we will head for this area first, so if you hear me yell for you to head for the black, this is where we are going as fast as we can."

Everyone nodded in agreement, so Pat grabbed his radio off the map table, his handheld GPS and his hard hat and led the way out of the tent and down the trail.

Within a mile of the parking lot, the first signs of the devastation showed its ugly head. The trees were burned almost to the ground, and there was nothing left of anything that might have grown on the ground. Buck noticed several charred animal carcasses along the trail, evidence of a hot fire that moved faster than the poor creatures could react to. He could still feel the heat rising from the ash, and the air was thick with smoke, making breathing somewhat difficult.

By the time they reached the site of the lodge they were tired, dirty and sweating profusely. It was no one's idea of fun, and the surrounding destruction made them all sad. This once pristine forest looked like an atom bomb had gone off. It was all so pointless.

What was left of the once majestic lodge was now a pile of smoldering logs, the smoke, and heat still visible, swirling up from the huge pile. Buck told everyone to take a breather, drink some water to clear the ash out of their throats, while he walked off to survey the scene first. He took off his hard hat, wiped his forehead and took a drink from the water bottle he had carried in. "This is going to be one tough crime scene to work," he thought to himself.

Jack and Gus stepped up next to him, and he rubbed Gus's head. "We are going to start working the site from here. If we find anything, I will give a holler and mark it with a flag. Once we cover the entire site, we will have a better idea of where to look for evidence."

Jack and Gus started carefully walking over the debris pile with Gus walking very gingerly on the logs. Now and then he would stop and sit down, and Jack would walk over and stick a little red flag into the pile.

The Sheriff walked up and stood next to Buck, the look of pure exhaustion on his ash-covered face. Off in the distance, a new sound entered the forest. Overhead a huge Boeing 747 thundered over the ridge and couldn't have been more than a couple hundred feet over the trees. Buck and the Sheriff watched with amazement as the huge plane flew just over the treetops and then a massive red trail started to flow from the belly of the beast.

"Since the wind died down this morning, we were able to bring in heavy air support," said Pat Sutton. He had walked up while they were watching the plane, and as they stood there, he raised his radio to his mouth.

"Jimmy, that looked like a good drop. When he comes back for his next pass, have him shift about a quarter mile south. Go ahead and have the choppers start their water drops off that big cliff to the east and work along the ridgeline. Let's see if we can stop this mother from running over the ridgeline."

"Ten-four boss."

Buck was about to say something when he heard Jack call his name and he looked up to see him waving his hand for them to come over to where he and Gus were standing. Rather than walk through the crime scene Buck, Pat and the Sheriff walked around the perimeter of the lodge foundation and, stepping carefully, they approached Jack.

"We have a problem," said Jack as he pointed towards the pile of burnt logs in front of him.

Buck looked where Jack was pointing, and at first, he couldn't see anything, so he focused harder, and he could just make out the charred hand sticking out from under the logs.

"Shit," said the Sheriff. "This is now a death investigation as well. Fuck, Buck."

"Yeah," replied Buck. "Ok, let's see if we can move some of this debris out of the way so we can see what we have."

While Jack and Gus continued their search, Buck, the Sheriff, Rick, and Pat, who had wandered over to see what they were looking at, started very carefully removing the logs that were covering the body.

It took almost an hour to clear away enough debris so they could see just about all of the body.

592

Chapter Thirteen

Buck pulled a pair of nitrile gloves out of his backpack and knelt next to the body. The charring made it impossible to determine if this was a male or female and it was so fragile that he didn't want to try to move it. He was more concerned with the body basically falling apart than he was with trying to preserve evidence. The fire and the firefighting operations had all but destroyed any forensic evidence. He was about to stand up when the Sheriff asked him to look at a spot next to what he assumed was an ear.

Buck looked carefully at the spot where the Sheriff was pointing and at first, wasn't sure what he was looking at. He reached into his backpack and pulled a long-handled cotton swab out of a tube. Leaning closer to the body, he cleaned a little of the char away and then probed with the swab. The swab disappeared into what seemed to be a hole. He left the swab in place, grabbed his cell phone and opened up the camera app. He took several pictures from different angles and put his phone back on his belt.

"Is that a bullet hole?" asked the Sheriff.

"I believe it is," said Buck. "We could really use a pathologist and a forensics team up here, but I don't think we are going to have the time. Have you looked to the east recently?"

The Sheriff nodded his head. He had seen the same thing Buck saw. Clouds were building, and the smoke from the fire seemed to be heading more towards them than it had been earlier. He could definitely sense a change in the wind direction. They were running out of time. They were going to have to work the crime scene themselves.

Buck reached into his backpack again and pulled out a neatly folded black body bag. It was not something that your average investigator would typically carry with them, but once before he had a murder scene get destroyed because of a sudden cloudburst and he vowed after that to keep a body bag in his backpack, just in case. This bag had been in there for almost ten years, and he had not needed it since that day. Today he was grateful that he had it.

With the help of Pat Sutton, they placed the body bag behind the body, opened it up and very carefully rolled the body onto the black plastic. Luckily for everyone involved the body held together when they rolled it. There is nothing worse than to have a body fall apart as you're moving it around. Buck zipped it up, and he and the Sheriff carried it away from the crime scene to the side of the foundation.

Passing out new nitrile gloves, he and the Sheriff returned to the scene and began a methodical search of the area. Buck couldn't be sure what part of the lodge he was standing in, so he took a bunch of pictures with his camera trying to get as many landmarks as possible. He figured his son Jason, might be able to help with figuring that part out once the cleared the scene.

By late afternoon, they had surveyed and photographed everything and anything that looked like it might help with the investigation. Jack had located what appeared to be the melted remains of several metal cans, outside the lodge footprint. He guessed they were probably gas cans, the most likely source of the fire. The arsonist left them at the scene because he knew the fire would pretty much destroy any evidence, but Jack had Rick bag a few pieces for analysis.

The smoke from the fire was starting to block out the sun, and it was getting harder and harder to breathe. Buck was just putting the evidence bags in his backpack when he heard Pat Sutton yell that it was time to wrap up and head out.

While Buck and the Sheriff were working the body, Jack and Gus made good time covering what was left of the lodge. By late afternoon they had covered everything that was safe to walk on or around and looking back over the path of little red flags that Jack had placed at all the locations Gus had alerted, Jack felt he had a good understanding of what transpired. He had directed Rick to take samples from several charred spots on the ground and also from the burnt logs. Once the chemical analysis was completed on the samples by the state crime lab in Pueblo, Jack would know for certain what the accelerant was, but years of experience told him that he already knew the answer.

Rick was cataloging the evidence bags before placing them in his backpack when Jack called him over to what appeared to be the remains of a rock fireplace. Most of the rock chimney had collapsed under the weight of the roof falling in, but you could still make out the bricks that were part of the firebox. Since these were heat treated bricks, the fire hadn't destroyed them like it had the logs.

A few feet in front of what remained of the firebox Rick could make out what appeared to be the remains of some springs and a partially melted metal frame, most likely from a couch or love seat. Next to the frame, Jack was kneeling and was using a small foxtail brush to sweep away the debris. When he finished clearing the area, he pulled out his cell phone and took several pictures of the large dark charred spot the debris removal had revealed.

Rick knelt next to him, pulled out a small plastic evidence bag and using a small scraper, scraped up some bits and pieces from the charred mark on the floor. As Jack was about to stand up, he noticed what appeared to be a small pile of unburnt fabric just on the outside of the area he swept. Scooting across the floor and followed by Rick, Jack reached the small pile and used a pair of forceps and lifted the fabric. The pile was most likely the remains of a couch or chair, which both surprised and pleased Jack, but what fell out of the fabric as he lifted it up made his heart skip a beat.

Lying on the floor where the pile was, he saw a small, shriveled up piece of plastic with a circuit board clearly visible. Jack had just hit the mother lode, and he looked at Rick and saw the smile cross his sweat and ash-covered face. Jack had found a piece of the igniter that hadn't burned up in the fire.

They were just placing the circuit board in the evidence bag when they heard Pat Sutton yell it was time to leave, so they quickly gathered up their gear and with Gus at their heals, headed for the trail they came in on.

Chapter Fourteen

The four-mile trek back through the devastation was made even harder by the fact that after a full day of working in a hot, smoky environment they also had to carry back the body bag. Buck and the Sheriff made it look easy, but it was anything but, and not being able to breathe was making it worse.

Pat Sutton told them that the winds had shifted, and they were now experiencing gusts of up to twenty-five miles per hour, which under normal circumstances is not that bad, but when you are trying to beat down a forest fire, even a little wind is not your friend. The bad thing was that the wind was blowing embers into new stands of trees that were already dry due to the drought conditions that Colorado had been experiencing for the past couple of years. He now had new fires starting up in three locations around them, and he had called for reinforcements and increased water and retardant drops.

The planes and helicopters had spent all afternoon making valiant efforts to beat down the new fires, but the fire had already jumped one fire line, and part of Pat's containment area had now disappeared. Two additional hotshot teams were on their way and would join the effort by nightfall. By the next morning Pat would have almost four hundred firefighters working this fire, which was growing rapidly.

Earlier today he was going to pull two of the original hotshot teams so they could get a well-deserved rest. Now, instead, those teams were working their way up the side of a ridge that even a mountain goat would find difficult, so they could try to clear a new fire line. The days had been long, and the work was hard, but none of the teams balked when Pat issued the new orders.

As Buck and his team got closer to the Incident Command Center, the air got a little clearer, and it was easier to breathe. A few hundred yards from the parking lot, they had to cross over a small stream. Gus was the first one to make a move, and as he stepped into the stream, he just plopped down and let the water rush over him. Buck could have sworn the tired dog actually smiled. Finally, after a few minutes, he stood up, shook off and rejoined the team on the other side.

Each member of the team had followed Gus's lead and had, if nothing else, leaned down and washed the day's soot out of their hair and off their faces. The water was cold and refreshing, and it made them feel a little more human.

They walked up the embankment that led to the parking lot, and Pat headed directly for the Command Center. The parking lot was filling up with fire engines and emergency vehicles from all over the area, and Pat needed to get all these units positioned in the best places to fight this new threat.

Buck led everyone over to his Jeep, opened the hatch and placed his backpack down. He passed around a couple bottles of water to each person and then pulled a collapsible water bowl out of the back of his car, filled it with water and set it down for Gus. Jack had already removed Gus's vest, and the dog knew he was now off duty. After drinking his fill, he found a shady spot under Jack's SUV and crashed. His job was done.

The Sheriff had called the County Coroner as they were nearing the parking lot and he was waiting for an ambulance to show up to transport the body to the Forensic Pathologist in Grand Junction. Colorado is one of a handful of states that uses the Coroner system instead of the Medical Examiner system. In Colorado, the County Coroner is an elected official and doesn't need to have any formal training for the job. The Coroner doesn't even need to be a doctor or medical professional. In the event of a suspicious death or crime where an autopsy is required, the County Coroner contracts with a Licensed Forensic Pathologist, a specially trained doctor, to perform the autopsy.

Rio Blanco County, as well as several other west slope counties, contract with the Forensic Pathologist in Grand Junction. This shared jurisdiction is common in counties that can't afford or don't need a full-time pathologist.

Buck pulled the evidence bags out of his backpack and laid them on the floor in the back of his car. Jack did the same thing with his evidence bags. While the others watched, Buck and Jack shared their thoughts. Jack went first.

"From what I can tell, the accelerant used, and there definitely was an accelerant used, was probably plain gas, nothing fancy or complicated. The burned-up gas cans were a dead giveaway, but we will run everything just to be certain. Most arsonists know that it is much more difficult to analyze ordinary gasoline from a fire since it pretty much burns up almost completely. We will run the samples through the mass spectrometer, but it will most likely come back as ordinary gasoline. However, we hit the jackpot."

He pulled out the bag holding the igniter piece and handed

it to the Sheriff who looked it over and passed it on to Buck. Buck smiled. This was a great piece of evidence. More than he had hoped for.

Jack continued. "We laid out a series of flags at every location Gus got a nose full of accelerant, and when we found this piece of the igniter and looked back over our trail, it was obvious what the arsonist had done. The evidence suggests the arsonist had doused a couch or chair with gasoline and set it in the middle of the floor near the fireplace. The fireplace chimney would help draw air from across the room as the fire grew. He then poured gasoline on all the furniture and ran a line of it from the couch to the rest of the furniture."

"We will probably find that this igniter piece is from a remote cell activated igniter. That way the arsonist could be long gone before he hit the button on the app and yes, believe it or not, there are igniters that have cell phone apps. Once he pressed the button, the first thing to ignite would be the fabric inside the couch cushions, and then from there, the fire would just follow the gasoline trail. If we hadn't found the igniter, this type of fire would be almost impossible to solve without a witness. This guy was very good, but we now have a piece of evidence that we can trace. Rick will send these off to the state crime lab tonight if we can get to the FedEx office before it closes."

Chapter Fifteen

Buck handed the igniter piece back to Rick who put it back into Jack's backpack. The Sheriff was looking at the pictures that Jack had downloaded from his phone to his laptop and asked a question.

"Why didn't the fabric burn up if that was where the igniter was placed?"

"Well," Jack responded. "Could be any number of reasons but to keep it simple for right now, let's just say that fire does some funny things. Take a wildfire like this one. I have seen a wildfire rage through a neighborhood and completely destroy everything in its path, and then when the smoke clears, one house sits completely untouched by the fire. We have no real idea why. Lots of theories and opinions, but sometimes, shit happens. I know you were hoping for a better explanation, but right now I don't have one."

The Sheriff nodded and continued looking at the pictures on the laptop. Buck picked up his evidence bags, which numbered far fewer than Jack had, and said.

"We don't have much to go on with the body. If I had to guess, it appears to be a male of indeterminate age or ethnicity. The only thing we found was a hole in the back of the head next to the ear. I can't be sure, but my guess is that it's a bullet hole. So, for now, we are going to treat this as a murder. How he got killed and how he ended up in our fire still needs to be determined as does the theory that the fire was set to cover up a homicide. We just don't know yet."

Buck was about to say something else when they saw the ambulance pull into the parking lot and head their way, around all the emergency vehicles. The Sheriff walked over and spoke with the two attendants, signed the transportation order and led them over to the body bag which they very delicately picked up and placed on the gurney.

As the ambulance pulled out of the lot, Buck looked at his ragtag group of investigators and decided that anything else could wait till morning. It had been a long day, and everyone was beat. Buck suggested they head back to Meeker to clean up. He told them that he would be at the Cozy Up at eight PM and that he was buying dinner for anyone interested.

They all got in their cars and after taking a moment, started up and pulled out of the lot. Buck stood next to his car and thought for the longest time about what they had discovered today. He had a feeling that the body was going to be pretty much worthless, but the igniter piece, now that was a good find, and he knew Jack wouldn't give up until he had identified the igniter. Once that happened, they could start to close in on the killer and the arsonist, possibly one and the same, although Buck had enough experience to know that nothing was ever that simple.

Buck closed up his car and headed back towards the command tent. Inside it looked like organized chaos as Pat briefed the fresh firefighters on the fire and gave out their assignments. His troops now briefed and heading for their vehicles, Pat waved Buck over to the map table. Buck told Pat about the evidence they found.

"We got lucky today with that igniter. If anyone can track

that thing down, it's Jack Spencer. Who would have ever thought we'd uncover a murder?"

Buck nodded. "Yeah. Took me by surprise. However, it could move the investigation in a whole other direction. We'll know more once the autopsy is finished."

Buck stopped for a minute and looked at the map on the table. "How bad is it?" he asked.

Pat ran his eyes across the map and then at Buck. "It's never good when a fire flares back up. Luckily, we have a lot of resources on hand and more on the way. By the end of the day tomorrow we will have five hundred firefighters on the line. And the weather report is calling for rain tomorrow. Every little bit helps. But we will tame this beast."

Buck could see the determination in Pat's eyes, and he knew that the people in the area were fortunate to have this man running the show. Buck thanked him for his help today and headed to his car. He needed a shower and some clean clothes.

Chapter Sixteen

Bax felt like she had been driving on this rutted dirt road, if you could even call it that, for what seemed like hours. It was hot and dusty, and she couldn't wait to get to her destination. As she rolled over the next ridge, she stopped to let the dust clear ahead of her. Finally, there below her was her destination. She also noticed that she was only a mile or so west of the city of Craig, Colorado. It's a shame the road she had to take couldn't have been straight. She would have been there by now.

She pulled forward and passed through the fence that surrounded the site. The sign on the gate read Braxton Global Energy Site 12. She was well aware of who Hardy Braxton was and also his relationship to Buck. She knew she needed to do her best work, just like always.

Bax parked her state-issued Jeep Grand Cherokee next to the fire engine red pickup truck with the Craig, Colorado Fire Department emblem emblazoned on the door. The Fire Chief stood next to it and smiled.

"Hi, Chief Pierce. Ashley Baxter CBI." They shook hands.

"Please call me Clay," he said. "Everyone round here does."

"Nice to meet you, Clay. Please call me Bax and thanks so much for meeting me here."

In front of them was the burned-out remains of what had once been a huge drilling rig, along with what was left of what Bax assumed was the site office trailer, although it was hardly recognizable as anything.

"Clay, can you fill me in on what happened here?"

"Sure thing. Three weeks ago, we received a call from the county dispatcher asking us to assist with a well fire. Even though this is outside the city limits, we tend to help each other out around here. The closest county unit was several miles away working on a grass fire, so we headed on over."

The Chief went on the explain that by the time they arrived, which was just before daybreak, the entire complex was ablaze. It took his entire force of four trucks, as well as, two city tanker trucks to get the blaze under control. He went on to explain that firefighting foam takes a lot of water, yet even with the foam, the fire was a bear to put out, and it almost seemed like the fire only went out when it ran out of anything to feed on.

Once out, they had to wait almost two days before the twisted metal cooled down enough for them to get close to it, to try to figure out what happened.

The Craig Fire Department doesn't have an arson investigator, so they called the State Patrol for assistance. After two days of searching the rig, the findings were inconclusive. The night before, there were thunderstorms in the area and the lightning was pretty fierce, so without any evidence to the contrary, they concluded that it was probably a lightning strike that set the place ablaze and once the oil on the rig caught fire, it was just a matter of time before everything in the yard went up.

Bax noticed that the Chief looked like he wanted to say something else, but he wasn't sure what to say.

"Clay, I sense that you don't necessarily believe the report."

Clay Pierce was not a big man, but he looked like a little kid who had been caught with his fingers in the cookie jar as he shuffled his left foot back and forth in the dirt and scratched his thinning gray hair.

He finally looked at Bax. "Look, I don't want to give you the wrong impression. The State Patrol was very diligent in investigating this, but I don't think nature at its worst caused this. It's true that we had storms in the area but the lightning that night stayed farther to the north. I can see this site from my back porch, and we didn't get woken up by any storm that night. We heard a small boom, which I believe is when the trailer went up."

"No worries, Clay," said Bax. "Anything you tell me will stay between us for now. Why don't we go take a look and see what some fresh eyes might uncover?"

Bax grabbed her backpack from the back of the Jeep and they headed over to what was left of the trailer. Anyone looking at it would never know this had once been an office trailer. The only thing that marked this as a trailer at all were two twisted and partially melted axles. This must have been one incredibly hot fire to cause this much damage.

Bax put on a Tyvek jumpsuit and a pair of nitrile gloves and handed the Chief a pair as well. After slipping on the gloves, they started a very methodical search of the wreckage, beginning at the twisted axles.

She had learned a lot over the years working with and around Buck, and she was very methodical when looking at a crime scene. Several times she pulled out a little yellow evidence flag and stuck it in the ground near something she wanted to come back and look at later on. She never rushed this part of the investigation. She was well aware that many cases are solved because of the science and Bax, like Buck, was a stickler for details.

The pair worked around the entire trailer site, and she took scrapings from several pieces of metal that she bagged and cataloged for the crime lab. She also took several samples of the soil below the trailer. It was while she was digging around in the dirt under the remains of the trailer that she found a small piece of plastic that seemed to have been part of a circuit board. She passed it to the Chief while she slid out from under the metal.

Clay was looking it over when she stood up and dusted herself off. She was grateful she had remembered to pack a pair of Tyvek coveralls in her backpack before she left home this morning.

Clay had lifted his glasses up to his forehead and held the piece about as close to his eye as he could, trying to make out what was imprinted on it. Bax pulled out a bottle of water, and the Chief washed the piece off and then lowering his glasses he looked at it again.

He handed it back to Bax. "Do you think this might be important? Could just be from a phone or radio from inside the trailer."

She took the piece back and looked at it closely. "True, but right now it's evidence until it's not."

She slipped the piece into a plastic evidence bag, sealed the flap and signed it and put it in a manila envelope with the rest of her samples. They headed for the drilling rig.

Chapter Seventeen

He had been watching them through the high-powered scope on his rifle since they had first arrived at the site. He had no idea who the blond chick with the ponytail was, but he was very familiar with the local Fire Chief. Their paths had crossed several times over the years, and he had always come out ahead. Someday his luck might run out, but he never considered it luck. He always believed it was skill that kept him both alive and free.

He had been watching when the Chief pulled into the site this morning, and he wondered what was going on until he saw the black Jeep Cherokee crest the hill and stop for a second. He figured whoever was driving wanted to let some of the dust clear before heading down towards the site. That road was one bumpy son of a bitch.

He finally came to the conclusion that the blond chick was some kind of investigator or something. The way she crawled around the wreckage, without fear, and handled the samples she had taken, made it obvious that she had done this before. He was intrigued by her. She looked to be about the same age as his own sister would have been if she was still alive. This woman carried herself with authority.

He adjusted his position on the ridge and continued to watch through the scope. He was even more intrigued when she handed something to the Chief from under the trailer. He tried to focus in on what they were looking at, but he couldn't make it out.

He knew the other investigators hadn't found any real evidence, but the way the Chief and the blond chick were examining the piece of whatever they found, made him wonder if he had made a mistake. The fire was hot enough that it shouldn't have left any evidence, but they seemed to have found something important.

He watched the blond chick put the evidence into a plastic bag, sign it, and put the bag in a manila envelope. Now he got very concerned. She had evidently found something he missed, and he was not happy about it. He continued to follow them as they walked toward the drilling rig. Without ever taking his eye off the scope, he smoothly pulled back the bolt on the rifle and with three fingers deftly inserted a high-powered ballistic round into the chamber and slid the bolt back into place. He hoped he didn't have to use the round, but he wanted it in place just in case.

Chapter Eighteen

Bax and the Chief started the process all over again once they reached the drilling rig. The damage was incredible. She had been part of several arson investigations since joining CBI, including one industrial warehouse full of chemicals, but she had never seen the kind of destruction she was looking at now. Every piece of metal that wasn't melted into a puddle was twisted and deformed. She thought back to pictures she had seen from World War II after the atomic bomb was dropped on Hiroshima. That was what this site looked like.

She followed the same procedure, placing yellow flags near some items, photographing everything as she went and taking scrapings of anything that looked out of place or unnatural. The work was dirty, and by the time she was finished she was covered in ash from head to foot and sweating profusely in her Tyvek jumpsuit.

As she was climbing around on what used to be the drilling rig base, some of the destroyed piping that wasn't melted together, shifted and she suddenly found herself under a very precarious pile. The Chief rushed over to give her a hand getting out, but she waved him off. A glint of metal caught her attention, just out of reach in the pile.

Bax pushed against a couple pieces of pipe, which seemed to have stabilized, and with the Chief carefully watching, she squeezed between the pipes and pushed herself into the cramped space. The Chief was amazed at her agility.

She had to turn over on her back and let her head dip down under what she believed might have been the control panel, with its now silent and melted gauges and buttons. She momentarily lost focus in the jumble of pipe and sheets of melted metal, but she stopped, took a couple of deep breaths, and finally located the glint of metal she was hunting. Reaching out her gloved hand she pulled out a small metal piece that had somehow become wedged between the base of the control panel and the pieces of the derrick that had collapsed onto it.

With the help of the Chief, she was able to pull herself back out of this man-made hell she had crawled into and emerged back into the sunlight. She was never so glad to be back on real ground, even if it was just dust.

The Chief was looking at what turned out to be a piece of a metal canister about 4 inches long and was most likely cylindrical although there wasn't enough left to be sure of the actual shape. He handed it to Bax after she finished drinking a full bottle of water in order to get the ash out of her throat.

"I think I know what this is," said the Chief. He continued as she slowly looked at all the sides of the piece.

"A few years back we had to clear an ice damn in the Yampa River in order to keep the whole valley from flooding and dynamite just wasn't doing the trick. The Army Corps of Engineers sent a guy down to help us, and he used a Thermite charge, which burns so hot it pretty much vaporized the ice dam. This looks like the same kind of cylinder he placed on the ice."

Bax now looked even closer at the piece of metal. There were what appeared to be a couple numbers imprinted into the outside of the piece, but it was so charred that she couldn't read them. She held it up to the sun and turned it this way and that to try to get a better look.

The bullet slammed into the pile of melted pipe just inches from her head, and it blew a huge piece of metal out of the pile. Bax instinctively dove sideways and slammed into the Chief, knocking him to the ground. She never heard the sound of the rifle shot, so it either came from a long way off, or it came from a silenced rifle. She didn't much care. She had heard the bullet fly past the side of her head, and that was all she needed.

The second bullet hit the pile of metal right behind where she and the Chief had found cover, and it showered them with rust and metal pieces. Bax unzipped her coveralls and pulled her Sig out of her holster. She didn't know who was shooting at them or where the shots came from, but she needed to be ready.

The Chief pulled his radio from his belt, but his hands were shaking so badly that he was having trouble working the radio. Bax placed her hand on top of his and softly said, "It's ok, Clay. I got this."

She took his radio and keyed the mic. "Dispatch, this is CBI Agent Ashley Baxter at Braxton drill site 12. Shots fired. Officer needs assistance."

"Agent Baxter, this is dispatch, is anyone injured?"

"No ma'am," replied Bax. "Shots seemed to have come from south of our position."

"Roger, Agent Baxter. Are you in pursuit?"

"Negative. I am with a civilian and can't leave him alone and unprotected."

"Roger. Deputies are en route. Stay protected. I will notify the Sheriff."

"Thanks. Baxter out."

She handed the radio back to the Chief who was starting to calm down. He was amazed at how calm Bax appeared in spite of almost having her head blown off. She needed to get to her car and get her binoculars so she could try to pinpoint the shooter's position. She told the Chief to stay down, and she slowly raised up. It had been a while since the last shot, so she made a mad dash to the car and pretty much dove in through the open rear hatch, trying to keep as much protection between her and the shooter.

She found her binoculars and slid out of the rear compartment. Keeping as much of the vehicle in front of her as possible she slowly looked around the car toward the hills in the distance. After a few sweeps of the hills, she spotted a dust trail fading off to the southwest.

Chapter Nineteen

He watched the blond chick through the scope as she crawled into the guts of the destroyed derrick. He was actually amazed watching her and almost forgot why he was there. She looked like some kind of fearless monkey. He didn't know if he would have the guts to crawl into the spaces she was in, so he kept watching.

When she finally crawled back out, she was covered in ash, but she held a shiny piece of metal in her hand which she and the Chief were looking at. Even from almost a mile away, he knew exactly what it was. The damn canister should have burned up in the fire. What the hell happened?

He wasn't sure if the decision to shoot at them was a survival instinct or if he was just plain pissed off. But he took careful aim. He didn't want to kill them, because he knew that would just make things worse, but he needed to do something, so he decided to put the fear of God into them.

He aimed for a spot of metal just above her head, slowed his breathing, momentarily held his breath and pulled the trigger. The silencer he had had custom made for his rifle did an excellent job covering the sound of the shot, to the point that he almost didn't hear it himself. He would have to bring the welder some more business as a way of thanking him for the excellent quality.

He watched the blond chick dive into the Chief, and they took cover behind the pile of pipes. Without removing his eye from the scope, he slowly pulled back the bolt, caught the bullet case in his palm and, once again very deftly, slid a new round into the chamber and slid the bolt forward. The second shot slammed into the jumble of melted pipe just above where he figured their heads would be. It, like the first bullet, disintegrated on impact.

He was about to load the third round when the radio next to him crackled.

"Dispatch, this is CBI Agent Ashley Baxter at Braxton drill site 12. Shots fired. Officer needs assistance."

"Agent Baxter, this is dispatch, is anyone injured?"

"No ma'am," replied Bax. "Shots seemed to have come from north of our position."

"Roger, Agent Baxter. Are you in pursuit?"

"Negative. I am with a civilian and cannot leave him alone and unprotected."

"Roger. Deputies are en route. Stay protected. I have notified the Sheriff."

"Thanks. Baxter out."

"Shit," he thought. "She's a state cop."

He took his eye off the scope, placed the third bullet into his pants pocket, picked up his brass, and with his rifle in hand slowly slid down the hill until he was no longer visible from the drill site and raced for his car. He needed to put some distance between himself and the site. This was not exactly the best countryside to find places to hide, but he knew a place where he could go, and it wasn't far.

Chapter Twenty

It was twenty long minutes before the first Moffat County deputy arrived. The whole time she was waiting, one side of her brain kept telling her to get in the car and take off after the dust cloud that was slowly fading to the south while the other side of her brain kept telling her that she needed to stay where she was and keep the Chief safe. After all, she was armed, and he wasn't.

The protection side finally won out, and she was sitting on the ground next to the Chief when the first deputy pulled into the site with lights flashing. He spun his car sideways to the drill rig, so he was facing away from the shooter, jumped out of the car and took up a position behind the patrol car.

"You guys ok?" he yelled from behind his car.

"Yeah," Bax yelled back. "I think the shooter is gone. Saw a dust cloud heading away from us past those hills." She stood up and pointed over her shoulder.

The deputy slowly rose up and holstered his pistol. He stepped out from behind the car and walked over to Bax. The Chief was in the process of standing up.

"Hi, Chief. You ok?" asked the deputy.

"I'm fine Jerry. Thanks for asking."

The Chief dusted himself off and stepped up to where the deputy and Bax were standing.

The deputy looked at the ash covered mess that was Bax and reached out his hand. "Deputy Jerry Garcia, ma'am."

She shook hands with the deputy, introduced herself and looked at his name tag with a questioning grin. The deputy smiled. "Yeah, I know. My parents were sort of hippies in their day." He laughed, and it broke the tension.

Bax was just starting to explain what happened when two more Sheriff's vehicles pulled into the lot followed by a Craig police car. Sheriff Gil Trujillo stepped out of his car, walked up to Bax and the Chief and made introductions all around.

Bax explained what had transpired and showed them the spot where she first spotted the dust cloud.

"Jerry why don't you and Kate head up that way and see if you can find the shooter's nest."

Deputies Garcia and Thorn hopped into Jerry's patrol car, pulled out of the site and headed up the road toward the nearest set of hills leaving a trail of dust behind them.

"Agent Baxter, can you fill me in on what happened? By the way, I appreciate that you checked in with my office when you got into the county. Most state folks don't bother."

Bax smiled and nodded her head. She gave the Sheriff and Craig Police Sergeant Bob Calvin a quick trip through her investigation so far. She showed them the piece of plastic with the remains of what looked like a circuit board on it, and also the metal piece that the Chief was convinced came from a Thermite explosive device.

When she finished her debrief the Sheriff looked at the Chief.

"Clay, looks like you might be right. You said all along you thought this was arson and it looks like this stuff is taking us in that direction."

"Agent Baxter, looks like all the dust and ash paid off. Nice work. We will follow up on the shooter. Why don't you check into a hotel and swing by the office in the morning and write this all up? I am going to join my deputies and see if we can find a trail. By the way, thanks for not leaving Clay by himself. I will make sure your Director knows how you handled yourself. Well done. Clay, you ok to drive or do you need Bob to take you home?"

The Chief just nodded. He was ok.

While the Sheriff was talking to Bax, several more city and county patrol cars showed up, and the Sheriff and Bob assigned them to check out the roads that ran south from the site and head towards the river.

Bax thanked the Chief for all his help and escorted him to his pickup truck. They shook hands, and she promised to keep him apprised of the investigation. She watched him pull out, and she picked her backpack up off the ground and put it in the back of the Jeep along with her binoculars. She sat on the bumper and tried to get her hands to stop shaking. It felt like someone had just let all the air out of her and she felt deflated. She wiped a couple tears out of her eyes and just sat for a minute and breathed deeply. She realized that she had never been more scared in her life than she had been today.

Finally calmed down, she got in her car and headed back to Craig. She needed to get the evidence bags overnighted to the state crime lab, and a good night's sleep. She would start fresh tomorrow. She also made a silent vow to find the son of a bitch who shot at her.

Chapter Twenty-One

Buck had just pulled into the parking lot at the Cozy Up when his phone rang. He pulled out his cell phone recognized the number and answered.

"Hey Gil, long time. Is Bax behaving herself up there?"

"Hiya Buck. Listen, first off Bax is ok, but she's the reason for my call."

Buck listened intently as the Moffat County Sheriff described the events of the day. The concern on Buck's face becoming more and more evident as the call progressed. Even though he wanted to interrupt several times, he had learned a long time ago that the best interrogators listen more than they talk, so he waited for Sheriff Trujillo to take a breath.

"Gil, did you find any tracks or evidence of the shooter?"

"We found an area of disturbed brush up on one of the ridges with a good view of the drill site, but nothing to indicate it was human-caused. Could have been a pronghorn bed for all we know. The spot was over a mile away. That would take one hell of a shooter from that distance. There were lots of tire marks not that far away, but it has been so dry up here for the past couple weeks, they could be weeks old. And you know as well as I do that almost everyone up here drives a truck of one kind or another. We are going to head out tomorrow, first thing, and see if there was anyone in the area who might have seen a truck or car fly by.

Buck asked him how the Fire Chief was doing, and Sheriff Trujillo told him that he had checked on him a little bit ago and he seemed to be doing ok.

"Gil, you need me to come up there?"

"Nah. We're good for now. Bax is back in her hotel room, and I asked her to stop by and write up a statement tomorrow. What she needs now, most of all is some sleep. We'll start again fresh in the morning. I'll let you know if I need any help."

Sheriff Trujillo also told him about the items that Baxter had found at the rig. The idea of the igniter peaked Buck's interest since they had found something that sounded pretty similar at the lodge. The possible use of Thermite was something totally out of the blue. Most eco-terrorists did not have access to things like Thermite. Thermite was extremely dangerous, if mishandled, and the eco-terrorists Buck had encountered almost always tried to use easily obtainable materials that were not easy to trace, like gasoline.

"You think this might be related to your case?" Sheriff Trujillo asked.

"I'm having doubts about that. We don't know much about this group that potentially set this fire, but one thing we do know is that in all the fires they are accused of they never used a weapon. I'm wondering if this is something else. Besides, why would an arsonist hang around a burned-out drill site for more than three weeks? Seems like odd behavior to me."

"You got that right Buck, but you and I both know that criminals do some weird shit. What do you want to do? We are at your disposal."

"I want to send up a full forensics team to take a look around. I've got this bug, all of a sudden, running around in my brain that keeps trying to tell me that something is going on up there. Let me make a few calls and get back to you. Thanks, Gil. Talk soon."

Buck disconnected the call and hit speed dial one. Kevin Jackson, the Director of CBI, answered on the second ring.

"Hey, Buck. How's it feel to be back in the field? I heard that fire took a turn and jumped containment. You all right?"

"Yes sir, feels good to be back, and yeah the fire made things interesting today."

Buck filled the Director in on the fire investigation so far and discussed the body they found in the rubble of the lodge. After answering a few of the Director's questions, he told him about the call from Sheriff Trujillo and about Bax's close call. There was silence on the other end of the phone, and he could hear the Director breathing. He knew not to interrupt. Finally, the Director spoke.

"Fuck Buck. What the hell is going on in Moffat County? Arsonists are known to come back to the scene of their fires, but not three weeks later and armed with a sniper rifle. Doesn't make sense, even for eco-terrorists. What are you thinking?"

Buck told the Director that he was having trouble wrapping his head around the eco-terrorism angle when it came to the drill rig fire. He told him about the possible Thermite link and the possible igniter piece that Bax found.

"Thermite, huh?" said the Director. "When was the last time you heard about a tree hugger using something as sophisticated as Thermite?"

"My point exactly, sir," replied Buck. "That's what's not making sense. I think a few of the well fires that Hardy Braxton is blaming on the NETF are actually something else entirely."

"Ok, Buck. What do you need from me?"

"I'd like to send a full forensics team up to Craig to go over that site with a fine-tooth comb. I would also like to take Hardy Braxton to the site to see if he sees something we may not see."

"Ok, Buck. I'll call Max and let her know you will be calling her and to get the team from Grand Junction rolling. Keep Bax up there working that scene unless you need her with you. Let me know what else you need as you go. I'm going to call the Governor and fill him in."

The Director hung up, and Buck headed into the bar. He hadn't eaten all day, and he was starving.

Chapter Twenty-Two

Jack and Caleb were already seated at a table for four when Buck joined them. They had decided to take Buck up on his offer of a free steak dinner. Both men had a frosty mug of ice cold beer in front of them. The bar was packed, which Buck was glad to see, and the noise level had gone up a few decibels since his last visit. The two waitresses working the floor made sure no one's beer glass ever went dry.

A young waitress, with dark brown hair and an arm full of tattoos, hurried towards Buck, but Sam Reynolds cut her off with a wave and walked up to the table. She set a cold can of Coke on the table alongside an ice-filled glass and gave Buck a hug.

"Steaks will be up in a few minutes, boys. What else can I get you?" she asked.

"Sam," replied the Sheriff. "Looks like we have everything we need for now. Thanks."

Sam headed back to the bar but stopped to pat Gus on the head, which elicited a small tail wag from a very sleepy looking dog. Sam had lost her own dog, Moose, a year or so back but for some reason, she never got rid of his pillow at the end of the bar. Now it was used mostly by special guests.

The guys took a few minutes to discuss the lodge fire and the sudden wind shift that caused the fire to explode all over again. The news had reported earlier that the fire had once again almost doubled in size and was now headed in a westerly direction and might require the evacuation of the lodges on the west side of County Route 8 and the evacuation of the town of Buford.

"We've already evacuated all the campers and fishermen from Trapper's Lake and Pat is pulling some of his teams from the east side of the fire and heading them towards Route 8. I am heading back out there as soon as I finish my free steak," said the Sheriff.

"Hey, speaking of Buford. What's the deal up there?" asked Buck. "Looks like the town is being revitalized. Noticed a bunch of houses and trailers behind the old lodge."

"Well, not sure if revitalized is the right word," replied the Sheriff. "Bunch of survivalists bought up a huge parcel of land and just kind of moved in and took over the town. Started building houses. Not that there was much of a town, to begin with. They pretty much rule their own roost, and I try to stay out of it. I don't have the manpower to mess with them, and the County Commissioners have said to just leave them be. I think everybody up there is armed, and they are not very friendly to outsiders."

"They all wealthy?" asked Jack. "I imagine land isn't cheap up there. Any idea how they support themselves?"

Buck leaned forward, interested to hear the answer. He had been thinking the same thing.

"Don't rightly know what they do. I do know that the local package delivery service in town had to add on two more drivers for all the packages coming and going. I'm guessing some kind of internet business, but until they break the law, I'm staying out of it."

Buck sat back in his chair as Sam delivered three huge

Porterhouse steaks and all the sides to the table. The waitress with the tattoos brought over two more mugs of beer and another can of Coke for Buck. The conversation lagged as the three men dug into their meals.

Between bites, Buck watched the people entering and leaving. He had a good eye when it came to people, and he played a little game with himself to see if he could figure out who was who and what they did for a living. It was a lot more fun when he used to do it while on a family vacation, but it still amused him.

Several times, when he looked up from his plate, he noticed the short guy down the end of the bar. He couldn't be sure, because there was nothing overt, but he couldn't shake the feeling that the little guy was watching them. If he was, he was very good at being subtle about it. Buck just passed it off as curiosity and continued to enjoy his steak.

Finished with the meal and sitting back in his chair, Buck filled Jack and the Sheriff in on what had transpired in Moffat County earlier today. He told them about the close encounter Bax had with a bullet and about the possible Thermite connection.

The mention of Thermite perked up Jack's ears, and he laid his fork down and leaned into the table.

"Thermite is more than just a product. It is also a chemical reaction, and it can be some nasty shit. We used it in Iraq to seal up the guns on the tanks we captured. Burns hotter than almost anything out there. About 2500 degrees C. Turns everything it touches into a molten pile of crap. No wonder it made such a mess of the drilling rig. Rust is actually one of the components needed to cause the reaction. I bet with all those rusty pipes, it made a hell of a puddle."

The Sheriff was the first to ask. "I guess you can't just buy this stuff, right? Sounds like something the military or the government would keep tabs on."

"No Sheriff, you would actually be wrong. There are websites online that will show you exactly how to make the product and how to use it. Anyone can do it. The good thing, if there is such a thing, is that it is tough to ignite, but boy once it ignites, stand back. And just for shits and giggles, there is no way to put it out. It has to burn itself out. Like I said. Pretty nasty stuff."

He looked at Buck who was listening intently.

"I will go out on a limb here, Buck, and tell you that if Thermite was in fact used on the drilling rig, then you are dealing with something a lot bigger than a couple eco-terrorists burning down a fishing lodge. No eco group I am aware of would ever use Thermite. Way too hard to control."

The conversation proceeded along that same line for quite a while longer with both Buck and the Sheriff getting a long lesson from Jack on fire starting and thermite reactions. Buck found it all very informative and also very scary. "What the hell had Bax uncovered?" he wondered to himself.

The Sheriff was the first to stand up and stretch. He shook hands all around and waved goodnight to Sam. Buck and Jack talked for a few more minutes, and then Jack looked at his watch, called Gus and headed for the door. He had a long drive ahead of him, and he said his goodbyes, telling Buck that he would have preliminary results of their samples in a day or so.

Buck said goodnight to Sam, who was running like crazy from one end of the bar to the other and headed out into the cool night air. He could smell the moisture in the air once he stepped outside. Hopefully, it would be enough to help the firefighters.

Chapter Twenty-Three

Buck walked out of his hotel and headed for his car. Once there, he put his backpack in the back and pulled out his phone. He dialed Hardy Braxton's number. Even though it was just past six AM, he knew Hardy would be up. Hardy may have gotten a little soft over the years, but he was still a rancher at heart and ranchers started their days pretty early.

Buck heard Hardy's phone ringing, and after a couple rings, a sleepy Hardy answered.

"You better have a damn good reason for calling me this fucking early," he said.

Buck almost laughed out loud. Well maybe Hardy had gotten softer than he thought. Oops!

"Good morning to you too. You got some time today? I need you to run up to your number 12 site in Moffat County and meet me there. I am leaving for there now, so maybe a couple hours. Ok?"

"Why do I want to drive all the way up there and why the rush?"

"Look," said Buck. "You started all this shit, so either you meet me there or find one of your drilling engineers and have him meet me there. You may have a bigger problem than some eco-terrorists."

Buck could hear Hardy talking to someone in the background, probably Rachel, and then he said.

"Ok. If it's that damn important, I'll be there, but this better be good." Hardy hung up without even a goodbye. Buck just laughed.

His next call was to Max Clinton. He dialed her number and waited for the phone to connect.

Dr. Maxine Clinton was a matronly woman in her early sixties, about five feet five with short gray hair. She probably thought she carried around an extra fifteen pounds she didn't need, but she was still a handsome woman. Married for 40 years, Max had 4 children, eleven grandchildren, and six great-grandchildren. She lived in a 150-year-old farmhouse in Pueblo, where she liked to tend her garden and sit on her porch and drink iced tea. She was also a bourbon girl and could easily drink most people under the table. She was loud and outspoken, but she knew her job.

Max received her Ph.D. in Biology from the University of Colorado and had worked as a biology professor for 20 years before joining CBI. Currently, she was head of the state crime lab, a job she thoroughly enjoyed. She was a harsh taskmaster, but she had a belief system that didn't allow for defeat. Her goal was to give the crime investigator, no matter which department or municipality they worked for, all the information they would need to solve any crime. She held that as a sacred obligation to the victims. She was incredibly dedicated, and her team at the lab practically worshipped her.

Buck would have been included in that group. Many times, during a tough investigation, it was Max and her team that lit the spark that led to a breakthrough. Max was one of Buck's favorite people, and she felt the same way about him.

Max answered her phone on the fourth ring. "Hey, Buck. How's my favorite cop? You doing ok?"

"Hi, Max. Yeah, I'm doing ok. Some days are better than others, but it's good to be back in the field."

"Well, you hang in there. God and your friends will help you get through the loss."

Buck never minded when Max invoked God into the conversation. She was very religious and she really seemed to believe the teachings of her church. Buck had realized a long time ago that it wasn't God and faith that he had a problem with, it was organized religion. In his many years in law enforcement, he had seen too many times the after effects of someone's religious beliefs. It amazed him that so many people of faith could cause so much hatred and crime. But then non-believers created just as much havoc.

Buck always believed there was probably a higher power out there, but he didn't believe that whatever that power was, it really cared about one individual over another. His football coach always offered up a prayer before each game asking for help in defeating the other team. He always suspected the other team's coach probably was doing the same thing. How did God decide which side should win?

He knew many people who said a lot of prayers for Lucy over the five years she was sick, but in the end, she still died. But Buck didn't carry any hatred for them. He was mad mostly at God, but that left him conflicted. In order to get angry at God, he had to actually believe in God and he wasn't sure if he did or not.

Buck believed that there were spirits or a force all around us and he always thanked the spirits for allowing him to enjoy the hike, or for allowing him to catch fish, or see the sunrise and the sunset.

It wasn't a religion. It was something deeper. Something Buck really didn't understand. He just accepted it. But no matter what, he always appreciated it when Max told him that God was watching over him. After all. What could it hurt?

Max explained to Buck that she had already heard from the Director and she had the forensics team from Grand Junction on the way to Moffat County. She was curious what Buck hoped to find, especially since the State Patrol already completed an investigation at the site.

"I'm not sure Max. Someone took a couple shots at Bax while she was on site and there's something about that that doesn't make sense."

"Is Bax alright?" asked Max. The grandmotherly concern taking over her voice.

Buck went on to tell her that Bax was fine and that she had some evidence heading to the crime lab, which should be there today. Max said she would keep an eye out for the package and get her people on it right away. She told Buck to let her know if there was anything else he needed and then she ended the call the way she always did.

"You're a good man, Buck Taylor. God will watch over you. Stay safe."

Buck hung up his phone, hopped in his car and headed to Moffat County to meet Hardy Braxton.

Chapter Twenty-Four

There was a full contingent of government vehicles at the Braxton Global number 12 site as Buck pulled his car through the security gate and parked next to Sheriff Trujillo's cruiser. The Sheriff had several of his deputies standing around the front hood of his car looking over a topographic map of the area. He excused himself from the group when he saw Buck pull in and he stepped away and waited as Buck slid out of his Jeep. Bax spotted him as well and headed for the open door.

Buck shook hands with the Sheriff and then looked at Bax. "Bax, you ok?"

Bax was already fired up and ready to charge ahead. Buck had no doubt that if she hadn't had to wait for him, she would have already been off towards the hills looking for signs of the guy who took a shot at her

"Yes sir, Buck. I told the Director this morning that I was good to go."

Buck smiled. "Ok, Bax. For now, the Director and I want you to work this scene with the Sheriff and his team along with the forensics team. If I need you back in Meeker, I will let you know.

Bax interrupted. "Buck, why the forensics team? The State Patrol already did their investigation?"

Buck explained about the conversation he had with the Sheriff the night before and about the bug in his brain that was tugging at a string and wouldn't let go. He told her that something wasn't right about this site and he wanted a full-blown forensic search. The Sheriff nodded in agreement.

"Buck and I talked, and we can't figure out why an arsonist would still be hanging around a site three weeks later and why he would take a couple shots at you. Arsonists are not known to use weapons. They set fires and then sit back and watch them burn. This is weird."

"Sheriff's right, Bax. Something doesn't add up, so I called up the forensics troops to see what they can find. Who knows, we might not find a thing, but you already found two significant pieces of evidence that were missed. So, let's see what happens."

Bax shook her head in agreement. "The Director said you were going to bring Hardy Braxton to the site. You think he can help?"

"Won't know until he gets here," replied Buck.

Just then they heard a car pull through the gate, and Buck looked around to see Hardy Braxton's huge SUV pull to a stop behind his Jeep. Hardy stepped out of the driver's side, hitched up his jeans and put a tan Stetson on his head. Two other men, similarly dressed, climbed out of the passenger side front and rear seats. Buck had never met these other two individuals, but he could sense that the guy getting out of the back seat was probably Hardy's attorney. He was shorter than Hardy and a lot thinner with a thin mustache and he had a computer bag slung over one shoulder.

The other fellow was tall and rangy with a gray ponytail

and long sideburns. His craggy face was well lined and tan. Not a beach kind of tan but the kind of well-worn tan that turns your skin to leather and comes from having spent most of your life working outside.

Hardy walked up to Buck. "Now you want to tell me what the hell you mean I may have more trouble than a bunch of eco-terrorists?"

"Same ole Hardy," Buck thought to himself. "Never one to mince words when direct and in your face worked just as well."

"We are not sure yet exactly what we are looking at. That's why we want your opinion of the site."

Hardy waved over his traveling companions. "Then let's get started. It's already hotter'n shit out here. This is my lawyer, Irv Tuttlemen, and this tall fella is my chief drilling engineer, Carl Burkholder. Now, what do you want from us?"

Buck introduced them to Bax and the Sheriff and asked them, for starters, to just walk around the site and see what they could see. He didn't expect much with this first pass, but every investigation starts at the beginning.

The Sheriff excused himself and along with Bax headed back to the waiting deputies. Once again pointing at the map, he gave each deputy a section of the topo map to check out. They were looking for any strangers in the area or speeding cars yesterday afternoon or anything that might be odd. He folded up the map and everyone headed for the cars. He glanced over at Buck as he slid into his vehicle and thanked the lord that he didn't have to stay and deal with Hardy Braxton. They pulled through the security gate and headed in various directions.

Meanwhile, Buck stood back and watched Hardy, and his associates wander around the burned out well site. It was obvious that

Hardy was not taking this all that seriously, nor was the attorney, but the drilling engineer, Carl, seemed to be in the spirit of things and several times he got down on his knees to look under something and once he even called over one of the forensic techs to crawl under a pile of molten metal and retrieve something from underneath.

Hardy walked back over to where Buck was standing, pulled out a white handkerchief and wiped his brow under the Stetson.

"You really think there is something here or is this some kind of revenge thing by that no count governor?" asked Hardy.

"Look, Hardy, you know me better than to believe I would ever be involved in something political. Something is not right here, and I told you I will get to the bottom of it. This is how the process works. Did you bring the daily drilling reports from this site?

Buck had sent Hardy a text on the drive over and asked him to bring any daily reports, inventories and any other paperwork that they might have on this site. Hardy waved over the lawyer who pulled a notebook out of the bag he had slung over his shoulder and handed it to Hardy.

Hardy handed the notebook to Buck but held on for just a second. "This information is proprietary, that's why the lawyer is here. You can read it here with us, or you will have to subpoena it later on. This doesn't leave my sight."

Buck nodded and started thumbing through the pages. Most of the information didn't mean anything to him, but he finally found what he thought he was looking for. He opened the tab that read "Invoices."

Chapter Twenty-Five

Sheriff Trujillo and Bax decided to make one more stop before calling it a day. It had been a long hot couple of hours, and they had almost nothing to show for their time driving the back roads along the river, except a long list of contact information. The Sheriff had been getting reports all morning from his other deputies, and none of them were having much luck either. The search teams had been calling into dispatch all morning with ID's and license plates that needed to be run, but so far nothing serious had shown up on the people they had interviewed. It seemed that whoever the shooter was, he had vanished into thin air.

The day was getting hotter if that was even possible, and the air was thick with dust as they pulled into the next small camp area along the river. It was a quiet spot and looked like an oasis. Here in the middle of all this dry, hardscrabble terrain was a just a little bit of heaven. A small copse of trees in an otherwise barren landscape.

There were three tents scattered about in the little oasis, and they could see several people lounging about in folding chairs that they had set in the river. Two people were fly-fishing. It was an idyllic scene.

The Sheriff and Bax parked the patrol car next to a beat-up

looking old Jeep Cherokee and slid out of the car. A young man was sitting in a folding camp chair under one of the trees sipping on a beer, which he set down under his seat as the Sheriff approached. A young woman crawled out of the small dome tent and walked up to meet them.

"Mornin, folks. Looks like you found a nice spot to camp." The Sheriff looked out over the campsites.

"Afternoon Sheriff," said the young man in the chair. "We doin something wrong? The sign said public camp area."

"No, you folks are fine, just checking the area. You folks been here long?"

Bax walked off to talk to the two people who had stopped fishing while the Sheriff spoke to the young couple. They were both pulling out their fishing licenses as she walked up.

"Catch anything?" she asked. Her badge and gun plainly visible hooked to her belt.

"Couple small ones, ranger." They held out their licenses.

"Thanks, fellas, but I'm not the ranger." She did look at their licenses and wrote their names down on the pad on her clipboard. "I am working with the Sheriff's department, and we are looking for a car thief who might have come this way yesterday afternoon. You guys didn't happen to see anything out of the ordinary yesterday, like a car or truck speeding by here?"

"No, ma'am. We just set up camp this morning. We were working in Grand Junction yesterday. Didn't get here til about 2 hours ago and were lucky to find an open campsite."

Bax thanked them for their time and handed back their licenses. As they put their licenses away, she told them to enjoy the fishing. They turned and headed back into the river. Bax wrote down the license plate number on her pad.

Bax rejoined the Sheriff who was just wrapping up with the young couple. They had been camping there for a couple days, but yesterday afternoon they had been shopping in Craig for supplies and had stopped for dinner. The young man was able to find two receipts in his car from the restaurant and the grocery store. Both were time stamped. Bax took down their contact info and their license plate number and thanked them for their time.

They walked over to the other tent on the site, but no one appeared to be around. The young woman told the Sheriff that the owner of the tent was an older man who had been at the campsite when they arrived three days before, and he kept mostly to himself. She said he seemed a bit unfriendly.

The Sheriff thanked them for their time, and as he and Bax walked back to his vehicle, an old yellow Ford station wagon turned into the campsite and parked next to their vehicle. The door made a loud screech as the older fella driving, pushed open the door and stepped out. He nodded to the Sheriff and then walked around to the back door, opened it and pulled a nice size rainbow trout out of an old beat up cooler.

"Afternoon, sir," said the Sheriff. "That's a mighty fine-looking fish you got there."

"Yes sir, it is. Took damn near twenty minutes to land it. Best luck I've had this week."

He had longish gray hair and a gray beard, and he smelled of tobacco smoke. Bax worked her way upwind to avoid the smell. The Sheriff didn't seem at all bothered by it.

"We were wondering if you might have seen a car or truck driving by yesterday? Might have been in a big hurry."

The man thought for a minute and then told them that he had seen a newer model pickup truck fly down the road sometime late in the afternoon. He couldn't be sure of the time since he doesn't wear a watch, but he knew it was later in the day. He told him he didn't think much of it at the time.

The Sheriff asked for the man's driver's license, for his report and made a note of his information on a civilian contact form his deputies carried. It's always nice to know who is in the county. While the Sheriff made his notes, the man told him that he would be around for a couple more days before moving on. His final destination was California.

Just then Bax asked the Sheriff to step over to the man's car. She was standing at the back door, and she had a concerned look on her face. The Sheriff handed him back his driver's license and followed the man back to his car, and they both looked at where Bax was pointing.

Just barely visible under a pile of clothes was a large plastic rifle case. The kind used to protect valuable hunting rifles. The Sheriff asked the man if he would mind pulling out the case, which he did willingly. He turned the case, so they could all see inside, unlocked the padlock from the one latch and opened the case revealing a very old but well cared for rifle and scope.

The Sheriff asked if he could pick up the rifle and the man told him it was fine. He told them it hadn't been fired in some time because he hadn't been able to afford ammunition for it. While the Sheriff examined the rifle and sniffed the chamber, the man told them it had been the only inheritance he received when his father died a long time ago. He also told them that his father, a retired Marine, had been a stickler for keeping his guns clean and in perfect working order. Even though the rifle was probably fifty years old, he felt obligated to do the same. So even though he hardly ever shot it, he made sure to take it out of its case and clean it every week. He hoped his father would be proud.

The Sheriff handed him back the rifle which he very delicately placed back in the case, closed and locked it. He slid the case back under all the clothes. The Sheriff thanked him for his time and told him to enjoy the fish for dinner. He and Bax headed for his car, hopped in and headed back towards the drill site.

Chapter Twenty-Six

Buck wasn't sure of the names for a lot of the materials listed in the invoice section of the report, but he was getting the idea that opening up a new drilling site was a pretty costly operation. He started feeling bad for Hardy. He had a considerable investment in materials and manpower, and now it was all just a melted pile of slag.

The forensics team had spent the better part of four hours crawling all over the pile of metal, and their white Tyvek suits were no longer white. Buck had noted that they stopped several times and took samples of metal or ash or some other unknown substance. At one point one of the techs had even taken a sample of a stain in the parking area. He liked working with these guys. They were incredibly thorough. Of course, Max Clinton wouldn't have it any other way.

He was just starting to read through the daily reports in the notebook when he heard Carl Burkholder call over to Hardy. Hardy, on his phone, as he had been since he arrived, held up one finger and continued to talk.

Carl, who had a similar blue-covered notebook to the one Buck was reading, was standing next to what Buck had been told was the drilling rig control panel and was flipping pages in the notebook.

He watched Hardy disconnect the call and walk over to Carl. He noticed Hardy very seldom smiled and today he looked downright pissed off. Buck thought to himself, "how times had changed." Hardy was always the guy in school who got busted for pulling some lame, dumb stunt. As long as it got a laugh from the other students, Hardy was in on it. Now he was a hard-bitten international businessman, but somehow Buck didn't think he looked happy.

Buck watched from a distance as Carl pointed to the remains of materials in the field and then pointed to some note in the notebook. Hardy would look at the notebook to where Carl was pointing and then say something. A few times Buck thought Hardy was going to have a heart attack. He would gesture and point and then get red in the face, and Carl or the lawyer would say something to try to calm him down. This episode went on for about twenty minutes until Buck decided it was time to get in the middle of whatever this was.

"You guys ok?" Buck asked as he approached the group. Carl immediately closed the notebook and looked at Hardy and the lawyer. "You obviously found something that's not right, so you want to fill me in?"

Hardy threw up his hands and stared at Carl. "Go ahead and give him your theory."

The lawyer looked like he wasn't sure what to do. "Mr. Braxton, we should probably discuss this fully before making any kind of statement."

He started to say something else, but Hardy cut him off with a wave of his hand.

"We came here with the intent to help Buck figure this out, which is what I asked him to do." He looked at Buck. "You don't know this man like I do. He is like a bulldog. He is going to find this out anyway, and I would rather he heard it from us, then from the newspapers."

Buck just stood by silently and waited. He had spent a lifetime developing patience into its highest art form, and his silence had never failed him. Hardy finally looked at Carl. "Tell him."

Carl looked at Buck. "Well sir, something doesn't add up. According to the drilling plan and the daily reports, they were supposed to drill a four-inch shaft down to a depth of forty-nine hundred feet, turn due west and horizontal bore for another thirty-nine hundred feet. This should have put them into the best part of the fracture zone, so when they started pumping in the fracking fluid, the shale would fracture easily and give off the desired amount of oil. What's odd, is that what I see here doesn't match what is in the reports."

"How so?" asked Buck.

Carl hesitated, and Hardy lowered his voice a couple octaves and said, "Finish it."

Carl started again. "These reports follow this plan exactly. Almost too exactly. They didn't miss a date or a depth, and they didn't have one issue arise with either equipment or conditions. This is the most perfect drill site I have ever seen. Problem is, it's all a lie. No site is ever this perfect. I don't care who is running it. The second problem is the inventory and the invoices. Nothing matches what's lying here in the yard."

Carl opened the notebook to the inventory page, and Buck looked at the page he turned to, as Hardy walked away.

"The inventory matches the daily reports. Again, almost perfectly. Except, here where they list four-inch pipe casing. There is none. All the pieces that are left are eight-inch casing. They also list enough pipe to hit their marks. The problem is that the invoice is for twice as much pipe and there are only a couple hundred feet of pipe left in the yard. Now there isn't a drilling company anywhere in the world that will buy more materials than they need or pay more for larger pipe than the engineer calls for."

"Ok. Bottom line it for me," said Buck.

At this point, Hardy walked back up to the group looking only slightly calmer than when he walked away.

"The bottom line is either someone can't read a fucking engineering report, or someone is drilling a larger, deeper shaft for a very specific purpose. I think it's the latter," said Hardy.

Buck thought about what Hardy just said. "What other purpose?"

"Mr. Braxton, you need to be very careful what you are about to…" But Hardy waved the lawyer quiet.

"My name is on this fucking site! Not yours, mine! And it's my responsibility to make this right." He looked at Buck. "I think someone may be using the well to dispose of toxic waste. I could be dead wrong, but I don't think so. Carl?"

"I agree with Hardy. I've seen this before in several third world countries but not here. Waste is a lot more profitable right now than oil, and it takes decades for anything to happen to draw attention to the problem."

"Hardy, how could this happen under your nose and you not know about it?" asked Buck.

"We used a new drilling company on this one." Hardy stopped and got this oh shit look on his face. He looked at Buck and Carl.

"The same company drilled four other wells in this field. We used these guys because Mark Richards insisted we give them a try. Fuck."

Buck was just about to say something when the Sheriff and Bax pulled into the site. He excused himself from the group and walked toward the Sheriff's vehicle. They were all about to step into a hot mess, and Buck was not happy about it.

Chapter Twenty-Seven

The Rio Blanco County deputy slid to a stop on the gravel road that led to the makeshift town. The road was blocked by two Hummers and four men all armed with AR15 style assault rifles. The deputy placed his mic back in the holder and stepped out of the car.

"This here is private property, and you are not welcome," shouted one of the men manning the gate. They all held their rifles at the ready position pointing towards the ground.

The deputy stopped next to his front tire. "The Sheriff has issued a mandatory evacuation order for this town. The fire is out of control and heading this way. You need to gather your things and move out. You will have twenty minutes."

"We are a sovereign nation," shouted the man at the gate. "You have no authority to issue any kind of orders to us. Now turn your car around and get out of here before we are forced to defend ourselves."

The deputy was unsure of what to do next, so he took a step forward and the two men on the outside edge of their group raised their rifles chest high, pointing towards the deputy. The deputy stopped in his tracks and rested his hand on the back strap of his pistol.

"Don't you understand that there is a forest fire headed your way and…"

"No. What you don't understand is that you just made a threatening gesture towards us after we warned you that your laws are not recognized here. Take one more step toward us, and we will open fire."

Now with four guns pointed directly at him, the deputy chose the better part of valor and slowly stepped back towards his car door, never once taking his eyes off the four men. He pulled open his door and slid into the seat and quickly backed down the gravel road until he was far enough away and then made a K turn and headed for the main road.

Once on the main road, he pulled over to the side and sat for a minute. His hands were shaking. He was also getting madder by the minute. Mostly because he represented the county and who the fuck did they think they were talking to him that way. He was almost tempted to go back up to the gate and have it out with them. His smarter brain decided that was probably a bad idea. He headed towards the Vaughn Lake campground to find the Sheriff.

County Route 8 was starting to look like a parade with all the cars and trucks making a run for Meeker. The campers had already been evacuated from Trapper's Lake, and now it was the ranches and resorts to the west of Route 8 that were on the move. The deputy passed a huge number of trucks pulling horse trailers even though he knew that a lot of the ranch and resort owners had chosen to ride out the firestorm. They could get all the people out, but there was just way too much livestock to move in the short amount of time they had to move. Many of them had their own employees, using their own light and heavy equipment, creating fire breaks and clear zones around buildings. They were running whatever sprinklers they had, and they had people hosing down the roofs of the buildings.

The deputy didn't completely understand the fact that many of them chose to stay, but he figured he might think differently if it was his ranch or resort he was trying to save. He didn't have time to second-guess any of them. He pulled into the Vaughan Lake campground to report to the Sheriff.

In the meantime, back down the road in the new town of Buford, Muldoon stood on his front porch and looked east. The wall of smoke was definitely getting closer, and he could see lots of cars and emergency vehicles out on Route 8. He called the front gate on his radio.

"Front gate, this is Muldoon. What did the deputy want?"

"This is the front gate. He wanted us to pack up and leave. Seems the Sheriff ordered an evacuation. We told him to turn around and leave."

"Good. We can deal with our own problems. We don't need them. Keep two men at the gate and send two more back to me. Out."

When the two gate guys arrived in one of the Hummers, Muldoon ordered them to get all the women and children that weren't working and move them into the underground shelter inside the big barn. He then told them to gather up all the men and all the available hoses and start watering down the areas around the houses and the houses themselves.

Even with the smoke only a couple of miles away, he still believed that this was all a setup and that once they evacuated, the government would come in and raid his property. There was no way he was going to let that happen. They had worked too hard to build their little town, and no one was going to take it away from them.

He was positive that the DEA agent had told someone, even though he didn't admit anything during the entire time they tortured him, they still needed to be ready.

Muldoon called back into the house and told Margaret Windsong to gather up the computers and put them in the safe. The safe was rated to thirty-five hundred degrees, and he was told by the salesman that it could pretty much survive an atomic bomb blast. He headed off toward their makeshift jail. He needed to have a few words with Elliot Beech. He had to find out what the government knew, and so far, Elliot hadn't talked. He would make sure that changed and changed right away.

He hopped on his ATV and headed towards the back end of the property where they had located their jail in an old pump house that had been abandoned years ago. It was far enough away from the central part of the town that no one was able to hear what went on inside.

Muldoon pulled up outside and hopped off his ATV just as the door swung open and one of his security guards, wearing a long black apron, like a butcher wears, stepped out and lit up a cigarette.

"Has he talked?" asked Muldoon.

The guard blew a smoke ring and then blew a stream of smoke through the middle of it. "Nah. He still swears that he didn't know the guy was a Fed and that he never told him anything about our operation."

"You believe him?"

The guard looked at Muldoon. "I was pretty hard on him. If he was going to crack, he would have by now. What do you want to do with him?"

Muldoon told him to wait outside, and he stepped in through the old metal door and pulled it shut. Beech sat on a metal chair, naked and strapped down with wire ties and duct tape. His face was a bloody mess, and he had burns and cuts all over his body. Muldoon spotted the battery cables running from the battery. One was hooked to the chair, and one was lying next to it. He also noticed the charred hair around his man parts. He smiled his approval.

He stood there and looked at Beech. "How pathetic," he thought.

"Elliot, looks like you're having a bad day. I can make this all stop if you just tell me the truth about how much you told the government agent. It will all be over in a minute if you tell me." His voice was so soft that Beech had to cock his ear to one side to hear him.

"Nothing," was his only raspy response.

Muldoon had seen too many men tortured during his long military career. He knew that they weren't going to get the truth out of Beech. At least not the truth he wanted to hear. They had been at this for two days. No one could resist that long. There was no sense wasting any more time. Jack pulled his pistol from the holster on his belt, screwed on the silencer and shot Beech through his right ear. He put the pistol away, opened the door and stepped out into the fresh air.

"Go ahead and clean that up," he said, and he hopped on his ATV and headed back towards the center of town.

Chapter Twenty-Eight

Buck filled in Bax and the Sheriff about the conversation he was having with Hardy Braxton and his team as they pulled up. Bax looked confused, but the Sheriff looked like he wanted to walk over and strangle Hardy.

The more Buck explained, the madder the Sheriff got until Buck finally said, "Look Gil. From what I can gather, Hardy was unaware of any of this. He was pretty much hands off on this site as well as the other sites in the county, and he appears to be as pissed off as you are. So, get hold of yourself and let's go finish this conversation so we can figure out a course of action."

Buck and his team walked back to where Hardy, the lawyer, and the engineer were standing, still deep in conversation. Buck looked at the engineer. "Tell me about pumping toxic waste into these wells. We need to know what we are dealing with."

"Without chemical analysis, we could be talking about anything. I once saw an entire village in Africa decimated because some warlord decided to make a ton of money pumping crap into the ground. He ended up contaminating the entire water source for the village, and people started dying terrible deaths. I don't know if that is what we have here, and I hope to God it's not, but we should plan for the worst."

"Do you think the other wells in the county were drilled for the same purpose?" asked Bax.

Hardy hung up his phone and stepped up to the group. "I may be able to answer that, young lady. I just got off the phone with our office, and I am very unhappy to say that we have no oil or gas production information for any of the sites in Moffat County."

The Sheriff looked at Hardy with a fiery stare that could have probably caused the same amount of damage as the fire caused. "Are you telling us that you might have poisoned my county?"

Buck stepped between them before Hardy could answer. He held his hand, palm out, towards the Sheriff and looked him in the eye. "Calm down, Gil. We will get to the bottom of this, so let's just bottle up the anger for a minute. We are going to need everyone at the top of their game. We could have a serious problem here so let's work this out." The Sheriff stomped away from the group.

The lawyer started to say something, but Hardy cut him off with a stare and he just kind of backed away silently. Buck looked at Carl. "Could we also be talking about radioactive waste here?"

"I've never heard it done anywhere else in the world, but I guess anything is possible. I have not heard of anyone trying to get rid of radioactive waste, but I am sure if you check with Homeland Security, they will be able to tell you. From what I understand the government takes a real interest in stuff like that."

Buck was thankful that the Sheriff had walked away before he asked the question. His anger level was about as high as Buck had ever seen it and the last thing he needed right now was for the Sheriff to blow up.

Buck took Bax aside and they had a serious discussion about

where this was going to go. Mark Richards was possibly involved in a serious environmental situation, but right now it was Hardy who was pretty much hung out to dry. Bax nodded a couple times, and then Buck called over the Sheriff, and he and Bax walked back over to Hardy.

"Ok folks, here is what we are going to do. Hardy, I want you and your team to head over to the Sheriff's office and write up a statement about everything we have discussed here today."

The lawyer started to object, but this time Buck cut him off with a wave.

"This is not a statement about guilt or innocence. I want to get the facts as we know them down on paper. This could potentially be used later on at a trial, but right now we need everyone involved to understand that besides the facts about the materials and the drilling records, we have a working theory that will need to be further explored. If I were you, Hardy, I would give Bax copies of the reports we all looked at today, but I can only suggest it. Your lawyer will tell you that we will probably be requesting a subpoena for the records anyway, but for right now, that is your call."

He went on to explain that he would like to have Carl remain available to work with Bax since he was the subject matter expert on the whole drilling and extraction process. Bax nodded in agreement.

"Bax, please call Bill Unger at the EPA. We are going to need an emergency response team out here immediately to investigate this and the other four wells and try to determine if, in fact, they have been used for illegal dumping. Bill will make that happen."

Buck caught the eye of Tim Jacoby, the lead forensic tech on the site, and waved him over. Tim pulled off his mask and Tyvek hood and unzipped his suit. He was sweating like a pig.

Buck explained the situation to him and could see the concern that suddenly appeared in Tim's eyes.

"Tim, please have your team wrap up what they are doing, double bag all your samples and then let's get everyone off the site. We do not know if there is any contamination on this site, my guess being that the fire would have destroyed most of it, but let's err on the side of caution and go ahead and set up a decontamination station and implement basic decontamination protocols."

Tim nodded, zipped up his coveralls, replaced his mask and hood and headed back for his team. The Sheriff pulled out his cell phone and called the Fire Chief and told him to send out his hazardous materials unit to help with the decontamination and to do it quietly. The last thing he wanted right now was to stir up the people of his county. There would be plenty of time for that later if, in fact, they did discover that poison had been dumped in the wells.

Buck took Bax aside. "I need to head back to Meeker unless you need me here. You know what you need to do. Go ahead and open an investigation file and let's take this one step at a time. Keep me posted and be careful. We don't know where our shooter is. Questions?"

Bax shook her head. "I'm good to go Buck. I will have the file set up by the end of the day, and I will call Bill Unger right now. I will let you know if I need anything else. Thanks for your help with Hardy Braxton."

Buck smiled, told her to call if she needed him and headed for his car. He pulled out his phone as he stepped up to the car and dialed the Director. This case had just taken another strange turn, and they were just getting started.

Chapter Twenty-Nine

Buck sat through part of the interview with Hardy and his team at the request of the Director, and he was actually impressed with Hardy's attorney. He requested that before any conversation takes place that they meet with the county attorney and he negotiated a fair arrangement to protect Hardy as much as possible.

In exchange for "informational testimony" regarding the drilling and fracking process, no one was to be Mirandized, and Hardy would not be held criminally responsible for anything that was said during the interview unless new facts came to light that might change that outcome. Buck was well aware that the criminal prosecution was the least of Hardy's worries. If word got out that his company, even without his knowledge, had deliberately caused potential harm to the residents of Moffat County, the civil lawsuits alone would cost him millions of dollars. Buck felt bad for Hardy, who looked utterly spent, but there was really nothing he could do to help him at this time.

After watching an hour of the interview, Buck was confident that Bax and the Sheriff had things well in hand and he decided to head back to Meeker. He needed to shift focus from this investigation to the probable murder and arson investigation he was preparing to roll into. He pulled out of the parking lot and swung through one of the fast-food restaurants that had sprung up all over Craig since his last visit.

He grabbed a burger, fries and a coke and headed for Route 13. He watched in his rearview mirror as the white pickup truck that had been following him since the first time he left the fire command center, pulled onto the highway a few cars behind him. He wondered why they followed as close as they did since there was really no place else to go between Craig and Meeker. It made him laugh at the ineptitude of the two guys in the truck, unless him knowing they were there was part of some plan he was unaware of. He decided not to worry about the two guys and the pickup for now. He would deal with them later.

Buck arrived at his hotel room a little after dark, parked his car, grabbed his backpack and headed for the lobby. Just for kicks, he looked across the street, and sure enough, there in the restaurant parking lot was the white pickup truck. He was almost tempted to walk over and see what they wanted, but he decided that was probably a bad idea. He unlocked his room and stepped inside.

Buck set his laptop up on the small desk table, pulled up the internet and logged into the CBI website. CBI had gone digital a few years back, and Buck was finally getting used to setting up his investigation folder in cyberspace. He used to set up his investigation book in a blue notebook which meant a lot of paper and if someone took the notebook from him to add information, he would have to track that person down and find the book. With Buck very seldom working in the office in Grand Junction, this sometimes made the transfer of information difficult. This new system was so much easier.

Once he filled in a couple blanks on the title page, the file was created and given a case number, he could then email access to that file under the case number to anyone involved in the investigation and they, in turn, could upload documents right into the file. No searching for the blue notebook. And no need to look for documents or reports. Everything in one neat, tidy package.

Buck clicked on the file he had created the night before and clicked on the investigation timeline page. This was a snapshot of each step of the investigation. Each time he opened the file, the first order of business was to note the date and time the file was accessed. Buck was meticulous about his notes, and this was how he ran each investigation. He had never lost a case in court because something was missing from his file.

He noticed that an entry had been made a few hours before from the Forensic Pathologist in Grand Junction, so he closed the timeline and opened the report folder.

Dr. Sima Kalishe had posted the preliminary autopsy report and left a note for him to call her if he had any questions. Buck clicked on the report and spent the next hour reading and then rereading it and making notes on his yellow pad. Even with all kinds of technology available, Buck still, sometimes reverted back to paper and pencils. When he was finished reading the report for the third time, he picked up his pad and looked at his notes. There wasn't much there.

The report was pretty straightforward. The victim was a male of unspecified ethnic background, height, as best as could be determined due to the condition of the body, was estimated at between five feet eight inches and five feet eleven inches tall. Weight was estimated to be between one hundred forty and one hundred sixty pounds. Hair and eye color could not be determined. There were no distinguishing marks on the body as far as could be found. He did have one pierced ear, but no earring was found.

Cause of death was one bullet to the side of the head just above and posterior to the left ear. It was a small caliber weapon, and the bullet had been sent to the state crime lab. The Pathologist noted what appeared to be subcutaneous bruising around the face and chest, but nothing was visible on the surface due to the excessive charring of the skin.

The pathologist had taken X-rays of the victim's teeth, and those were included in the file along with some very gruesome pictures of the body. There was nothing unusual regarding the victim's organs, however, in severe fire victims the organs tend to cook and boil as the body is burned. That was definitely the case here.

She did note that there was no charring inside the victim's lungs or nasal passages indicating that he was not alive when the fire started. The preliminary cause of death was the gunshot to the brain pending the outcome of toxicology tests. Samples of skin, organs, and teeth were sent to the crime lab for DNA analysis.

Buck sat back and rubbed his eyes. He looked at his notes. There wasn't a lot to go on, but it was a start. Hopefully, the DNA results would shed some light on the victim's identity. Buck closed the report and uploaded it to the national missing person's database. It wasn't much, but maybe someone else in law enforcement might be looking for someone who matches some of the information.

With no other reports to review at the moment, Buck decided to shut down his laptop and get some sleep.

Chapter Thirty

Buck was awakened by the ringing of his phone and had trouble locating it on the table next to the bed. He finally found it, noted the time and answered.

"Taylor."

"Buck, Jack Spencer, did I wake you?"

"Hey, Jack. No, I'm good. What's got you up so early?"

"I just got a call from the lab," said Jack, "and I was wrong. The accelerant wasn't gasoline at all. It was something else entirely."

Buck listened as Jack explained the lab results. The remains of the cans that they had discovered outside the structure area definitely contained gasoline. That was confirmed by the mass spectrometer results. The problem was the residue samples they had taken from inside the lodge. The mass spec results showed a cocktail of strange ingredients, which Jack had never seen used in this combination before. He started giving Buck the names of the chemical compounds they had found when Buck cut him off.

"Jack, can we discuss this in English? I flunked high school chemistry."

"Sorry, Buck. What all this gibberish says is that someone made up a custom cocktail to start this fire. This is pretty sophisticated stuff, and you can't just go out and buy this stuff at the local hardware store."

Jack explained that the combination of chemicals made a napalm-like substance that would have an almost putty-like consistency. The final product, besides being very sticky, would smolder for a while before bursting into flames when exposed to a lot of oxygen and burn extremely hot.

"Now the other product we found…"

Buck wasn't fully awake, but he was becoming more focused as the conversation went on and he stopped Jack again. "What other product?"

"That's what I was just getting to Buck. We found the chemical signature for a second accelerant. This product was a liquid, and it had the same chemical properties as white lightning, you know, moonshine."

Buck was now wide awake and looking for his notepad, which he found on the desk next to his laptop.

"Did you just say white lightning and moonshine?"

Jack went on to explain further. It appeared that whoever lit the fire had first covered all the furnishings and the flooring with a product similar to white lighting. This product was almost pure alcohol and would have burned fast and hot. Fast enough and hot enough to catch the rest of the building materials on fire. Once the logs had caught, the whole building would have gone up in a matter of seconds.

The other product was this putty product. Jack's assessment was that this product was stuffed inside the couch or chair and when the igniter was activated it started a slow fire that would have essentially sucked all the oxygen out of the room and then just sat there and smoldered.

What happened next was still just speculation but either someone opened a door or a window or a piece of glass failed in the vacuum and blew into the space, either way, the sudden inrush of oxygen would have caused an almost instantaneous backdraft and boom, the whole place would have exploded.

"The open valves we found in the kitchen from the propane tanks and the chemicals on the floor and the furnishings would have created a massive explosion. The closed valve on the sprinkler system didn't help, but my guess is that the fire would have blown right past the fire sprinklers and they would have been completely ineffective."

Buck, now sitting at his desk was making notes as Jack spoke. He could tell from Jack's voice that this was really exciting for Jack.

"Ok, so let me see if I have this straight. Someone spread a whole lot of moonshine around the inside of the lodge. Then they set up this smoldering fire which worked almost like a timer, to give whoever set the fire a chance to get away, and then, when oxygen entered the space, everything blew at the same time. Is that about right?"

Jack told him it was close enough, but even so, it was all still just speculation as to the sequence of events. Jack went on to tell him that he had never before seen the chemical signature for the putty-like product and had sent it on to the Denver office of the ATF. Alcohol, Tobacco and Firearms has an extensive database of every chemical ever used in a bombing or any other attack, and he was hoping that they might have run across this chemical composition before. If they had, it could be a signature product of the arsonist which might help them find this person.

Buck let Jack take a minute to catch his breath before he started asking the questions he had written down on his notepad. Buck wasn't sure how this information might help them at this point, but if Jack was excited about the information, he would respond accordingly.

Jack finally took a long breath, and Buck filled in the empty air.

"Jack, what about the gas in the can remains we found? Sounds like almost overkill to me."

Jack responded, "Yeah, me too. I can't figure that one out. Anyone who would put together a product this sophisticated would not also bring along several cans of gasoline. It would serve no purpose. It would take a lot less white lighting to get a fire going than it would gasoline, and it would burn hotter and faster."

Buck thought for a minute. That nagging bug was back in his brain. He never knew when it would show up, but he had also learned a long time ago to never discount the bug. He sat and rubbed his temples and then it came to him.

"Jack, suppose, just for an instance, that the arsonist didn't bring the gas with him. We already talked about the fact that these eco-terrorists almost always use gas because it is easy to obtain and hard to trace. We know that the eco-terrorists sent a letter to the local paper claiming responsibility, but the sophisticated chemical used, kind of shoots that idea to hell. What happens if…?"

"Buck, you're thinking that we have two arsonists working the same location at the same time without either one aware of the other. That's almost too bizarre."

"Yeah, but it would also explain," Buck interrupted, "the forest fire. The NETF has never made a mistake like that before. They either got seriously careless, or someone else set the fire to cover up the murder and didn't care about the weather or about what happened later."

"The eco-terrorists could have arrived with the gas and found the fire already happening. They might have dropped the gas cans and just bolted. It would explain a lot, except for why two separate groups wanted to destroy that lodge."

"Fuck, Buck. If you're right, we have a real mess on our hands."

Chapter Thirty-One

Jack uploaded the mass spectrometer report to the investigation file, and Buck took a few minutes to read it and reread it. The chemical names were out of Buck's knowledge base, but the rest of the information was just as Jack had explained. Buck needed to get back out to the lodge. "What was it about that lodge that would cause two different groups of people to want to destroy it?" he thought to himself.

Buck jumped in the shower, got dressed, grabbed his backpack and opened the door. The smoke in the air hit him like he was sitting at a campfire when the wind shifted. There was a distinct haze, and he could see the soot that had accumulated on the cars in the lot overnight. He knew this was not a good sign.

He walked next door to the little restaurant, sat down at the only open booth and picked up the menu. He could overhear the conversations around him, and it seemed that almost everyone was talking about the fire. He also got the distinct impression that a lot of people were blaming the fire on the lodge built by Mark Richards, which was mostly true since the fire was a direct result of the lodge being there.

He put down the menu as the waitress approached and

ordered the ranch special, two eggs over hard, sirloin steak and hash browns with a Coke to wash it all down. He was about to pull out his phone to check messages when a shadow crossed the table, and a woman sat down on the booth seat opposite him.

"Agent Taylor, my name is Stephanie Street." She slid her business card across the table, but Buck didn't reach for it. "I represent the Western Colorado Conservation Alliance and my clients want to be certain that you understand that they had nothing to do with the lodge fire and if you continue your investigation by looking into conservation groups in the region, that I will be forced to file for a restraining order to prevent you from harassing my clients. Have I made myself clear?"

Buck sat for a second and just looked at Ms. Street. She was a lot younger than he was, but then again, he usually felt like most people he encountered were and she was fairly attractive with a round face, deep blue eyes, and jet-black shoulder-length hair. The combination was almost mesmerizing. He finally reached over and picked up her business card and looked at it.

"I'm sorry, Ms. Street, is it? Have we met before?"

The waitress stepped up to the table and set down a huge plate of food in front of Buck. She asked him if he needed anything else and then she looked at Ms. Street, who shook her head no. The waitress walked away, and Buck unrolled the silverware from the white paper napkin and then look at Ms. Street.

"Ms. Street. I have no idea who your clients are. This investigation is in its earliest stage, and at this time I don't have a clue who I will need to interview. Now I appreciate the fact that you have brought your clients to my attention and I will make sure to make a note in my file that I might need to talk to them at some point, but right now I have no interest in harassing your clients, just eating my breakfast."

Ms. Street looked almost perplexed. She had dealt with law enforcement types before, and she knew the direct approach usually worked best, but she wasn't sure what had just happened. She had received information that her clients were being investigated about the lodge fire, and subsequent forest fire, but here was the lead investigator, as far as she was able to determine, and he acted like he had no idea who her clients were. She didn't know what to do next, which was a position she rarely ever found herself in.

"Are you trying to tell me that you haven't spoken to my clients and have no interest in doing so at this time?" she asked.

Buck cut a piece of his eggs, slid it onto the fork and held it poised just below his mouth. "That would be correct, Ms. Street. But I will definitely run a background check on their organization, and if I find the need to interview your clients, I will give you a call." He waved her business card in the air. "If there is nothing else, I would like to finish my breakfast as I have a very busy day."

Ms. Street started to slide out of the booth, and Buck said. "I would be interested in finding out why your clients think they are under investigation for the fire since so far I haven't interviewed anyone."

Stephanie Street didn't lose the perplexed look from her face as she stood up. "Just know this Agent Taylor, I will protect my clients at all costs. Good day, sir."

Buck watched her walk away and smiled. "Did his first lead just walk up and present itself to him?" he wondered. He dug into his breakfast, paid the check, left the waitress a nice tip and headed out the door into the smoky haze.

Chapter Thirty-Two

Sheriff Trujillo arrived at his office early the next morning and found Bax sitting at the table in the conference room that was attached to his office, hard at work. They had wrapped up the interviews with Hardy Braxton and Carl Burkholder late the night before and hadn't had a chance to discuss their impressions of the interviews. She was clicking away furiously on her computer and didn't look like she had slept at all. She didn't notice the Sheriff's arrival until he put a fresh cup of strong black coffee down in front of her.

"Did you get any sleep, or have you been here all night?" he asked, noticing the growing pile of papers that were strewn all over the table.

"That son of a bitch lied to us!" she said excitedly.

"Who, Hardy Braxton?"

"No," she replied, "James Robert Galvin."

The Sheriff stopped and thought for a minute, but he apparently had a confused look on his face because Bax stopped clicking her laptop keys, took a sip of her coffee and filled him in.

"The guy from the river with the fish and the rifle."

"Ok, I remember him but what is this about him lying to us?"

Bax dug through the piles of paper on the table until she found one of the items she was looking for. She handed the first pile of documents to the Sheriff. While he looked through the papers, she explained what she had discovered during the night.

The clerk in the office had run all the names and license plates that the Sheriff and his deputies had collected while checking along the river for anything unusual. Most of the names came back clean, but a couple had some past minor infractions. Nothing very serious. However, James Robert Galvin was a different story.

Galvin's name didn't show up in the motor vehicle database in Colorado or any of the surrounding states, which was odd since he gave Bax a Colorado License. What she did find was an arrest warrant, now closed, for a James Robert Galvin of Lake County, Colorado. The charge was two counts of murder.

Bax had left a message on the voice mail at the Lake County Sheriff's office and was waiting to find out the particulars of the case. It was odd that the arrest warrant was never acted on and even odder that is was closed out without explanation.

She rummaged around on the desk and found a couple more printouts that she handed to the Sheriff. She hadn't been able to find a criminal record in Colorado, but at some point, during the night she started running a deep dive internet search on Galvin and came up with some interesting information. She found a news article about a wrongful death lawsuit filed by James Robert Galvin's attorney on his behalf. "It seems Mr. Galvin's wife and young daughter both died from a rare form of cancer and he tried to sue the chemical company that had sold him some kind of fertilizer he'd used on his land."

Using her superior computer skills, she was able to find a little more information on the lawsuit, mostly from some local press releases. The Galvins owned a small ranch in Lake County, Colorado and Galvin had purchased a new fertilizer combination to use on his vegetables from an unnamed chemical company. There was something wrong with the fertilizer, some cows died and Galvin blamed the fertilizer for his family's cancer.

She hadn't been able to find out any more about the lawsuit except that it had been dismissed because the attorney didn't have any standing according to the judge. This would have been odd all by itself since the lawyer represented the party that has been wronged, but she couldn't find anything else because the records were also sealed.

She had just started working through channels to get the records unsealed. There had to be a reason he wasn't in the motor vehicle database and there had to be a damn good reason to seal the records for a lawsuit that was dismissed. Her interest was piqued, and she wanted answers. She was also pissed that she had been lied to.

The Sheriff looked at the papers in his hands and then looked at Bax. "Ok, Bax. The question now is, how does this connect with the oil well fires?"

"That's what I was working on when you came in," she replied.

"Good, then grab your stuff and let's go see if we can find Galvin. I think we need to have another chat with him and see what he has to say. In the meantime, I am going to have one of the clerks start running a deeper background check on him. "

Chapter Thirty-Three

Buck spent the better part of the drive from Meeker to the fire incident command center talking to Dr. Kalishe. The charred body was in such bad shape that any distinguishing features would have been completely destroyed. Buck asked her about the subcutaneous bruising she described in her report, and she told him that when she opened up the body, she was able to see the bruising on the underside of what was left of the skin.

She told him it was pretty much just luck that led to that find. It was not something she would typically look for in a body with this much damage.

"So, at this point Doc, there is pretty much no way to identify the victim?" Buck asked.

"Unless the DNA is still viable, and we get a hit through the national DNA registry, I'd say the chances are pretty slim. We could hope for a dental match, but if you read farther down the report, several of his teeth are missing. I can't determine if they were knocked out or if they blew out due to the fire."

Buck thanked the doctor and pulled into the Vaughan Lake campground. The fire was running south, so they hadn't had to relocate the fire command center, but the smoke was another matter.

Buck had noticed that it got a lot denser the further he drove up Route 8. At one point, as he passed Buford, he looked over toward the town and noticed they still had their security guys manning the gate to the town, only this time they were all wearing surgical masks and had their heads almost completely covered. Glancing the other way, he could see that the fire looked a lot closer to the town than it had been the day before.

He was contemplating what would possess a bunch of survivalists to stay in an unprotected area when they were looking down the throat of a fire-breathing monster. He decided he had better things to do than to start getting philosophical about what made people do dumb things. His entire career had been based on people doing dumb things, and that wasn't going to change anytime soon.

He stepped out of his car, grabbed his backpack and headed for the fire command tent. Pat Sutton was where he had been for the past couple visits, hunched over his topographic maps while several other people clicked away on their computers with lightning speed. As he walked through the tent, he noticed several of the computers were open to what looked like different satellite views of the fire. None of them looked good.

Pat looked up from his map and keyed the mic on the desktop radio. "Mike three come in."

"Go ahead, Skip," came the reply.

"Mike, can you move your team about a quarter mile to the south? The latest pictures show the fire creeping up on a steep draw, and if it gets in that draw it could make a run for about a mile. We need to stop it there."

"You got it, Skip. Mike three out."

Pat laid down the mic and looked at Buck. The weariness in his eyes was telling.

Buck asked him how things were going, which he realized after he asked it was a really dumb thing to ask, but Pat, good-naturedly, took the time to show him where things stood, and it didn't look good. A small finger of fire had jumped Route 8 just south of the command center, but luckily, they had spotted it pretty quickly, and with the help of the rancher who owned the property, his crew of cowboys, and a helicopter, they were able to beat it back.

The biggest issue right now was that the fire was blowing toward a good size stand of spruce trees that had been killed off by the Spruce Budworm. Once the fire got in there it could burn up a lot of acreage in a very short period of time. Pat was concentrating a vast amount of resources to that edge of the fire. He did mention that the wind had calmed down enough overnight that he could begin airdrops again and he had two huge 747 tankers en route. If the wind held off, he was hoping to get back to about thirty percent containment.

"Pat, what do you think the chances are that I can get back out to the lodge site?"

Pat thought for a minute, checked with one of his weather forecasters and said, "Actually, pretty good today. The fire has done just about all the damage it can do at that end of the burn scar, and the winds are predicted to keep blowing from the northeast so the fire and a lot of the smoke will blow away from the site. You want someone to go with you?"

"No. I don't want to cause you any trouble, you got your hands full. I would appreciate one of your radios though, just in case."

Pat pulled one of the spare radios out of the charger, set it to the correct channel and handed it to Buck who clipped it to his belt.

"Just like the other day, Buck, if I call and tell you to move, you get your ass out of there, ok?"

Buck nodded and thanked him for the radio. He headed back to his car and took his hard hat and his bright orange traffic safety vest out of the back and put them on. He made sure he had his flashlight, a camera, a couple bottles of water and some energy bars. He grabbed his backpack and headed across the parking lot to the trail.

He wasn't sure what he was looking for or what he hoped to find once he got to the lodge site, but things weren't adding up. He understood why the conservation people were upset and why they would want to burn down the building but why would another group decide to do the same thing at precisely the same time. There had to be a damn good reason.

Chapter Thirty-Four

Sheriff Trujillo and Bax left the Sheriff's office by the rear door. Their first stop was at Bax's Jeep so she could get her ballistic vest out of the back, which she put on and snapped shut. She also grabbed her backup weapon and strapped the thigh holster on her leg. She was now ready to go. While she was getting herself ready, the Sheriff was doing the same thing at his car.

He and Bax climbed into his marked unit and headed for the highway. He also unclipped his radio and called dispatch to have Deputies Garcia and Thorn meet him a quarter mile east of the campsite. They had no idea of Galvin's state of mind or his abilities, but they wanted to take every precaution, especially if he was the one who shot at her.

Twenty minutes later, they were parked on the side of the road on the downslope side of a ridge. Garcia had already climbed to the top of the rise with his binoculars and was scanning the area. He came sliding back down the hill and caught his breath.

"Nothing visible Sheriff. There is only one tent under the trees, and all I see are two fishermen in the river," he reported.

The Sheriff decided to err on the side of caution and directed both deputies to follow him down to the camp. Garcia would follow him into the camp while Thorn took up a position at the entrance. He gave the word, and they all jumped back in their vehicles and headed to the camp.

The two fishermen, who were sitting in chairs along the edge of the river, looked startled when the three Sheriff's department vehicles pulled in to the campsite and stopped in a cloud of dust. They looked more concerned when they noticed that everyone had on a ballistic vest and their weapons were drawn. They thought it prudent to stay right where they were, so they set down their beers and sandwiches and waited for the cops to come to them.

Checking all three campsites to make sure they hadn't missed anything and feeling confident that Galvin wasn't hiding in the trees, the Sheriff released Garcia and Thorn back to their patrol routes as he and Bax approached the fishermen.

"Afternoon gents," said Bax as she holstered her weapon. "Did you guys see what happened to the older fellow we spoke to yesterday?"

"Yeah," said the one fisherman. "He cooked up that big trout he had last night, gave us and the young couple next door a bunch of it and then just after dark, packed up and pulled out."

Fisherman number two continued. "He didn't say much, just all of a sudden he was dropping his tent and packing up that old station wagon of his. Didn't seem in a big hurry when he left, so we didn't really think much about it."

Fisherman number one. "He do something wrong?"

"We just had a few more questions for him," replied the Sheriff as he holstered his pistol. They looked at the Sheriff like they didn't quite believe him.

"When did the young couple leave?" asked Bax.

"They left about an hour or so ago. Said they had to be back at work in the morning. We were just getting ready to call it quits ourselves and head back to Grand Junction. Tom here needs to be at work tonight. I get one more day off.”

Bax thanked them and handed them each one of her business cards. She asked them to keep an eye out as they were leaving and if they spotted the old station wagon to please give her a call.

As they walked back to the Sheriff's car, he keyed the mic on his shoulder and told dispatch to issue a state-wide all-points bulletin for the car and the driver. He asked the dispatcher to also include Utah and Wyoming. They climbed in the Sheriff's car, and Bax punched the dashboard with her fist.

“Shit. He could be anywhere by now if he left last night!” She was not happy.

“Well look,” said the Sheriff. “We can't do anything out here so why don't we head back to the office. I'd like to look at the tapes from the interviews with Hardy Braxton and his team. Maybe we can find something we missed while we wait for the EPA to arrive.”

After arriving back at the office, they walked back to the conference room, grabbed a couple bottles of water and some snacks and made themselves comfortable in the conference room. Bax fired up her laptop and pulled up the interview tapes from last night.

After two hours, the tapes finally ended and they both stood up to stretch. The Sheriff walked over to the coffee maker in the corner and poured himself and Bax each a cup of black coffee. Bax slowly sipped hers as she looked over her notes.

“Well,” she said. “It looks like we have plenty of information on the process and we can put together a drilling timeline and comparisons of the inventory, invoices and what's actually on the site. The question is, what do we do with it and can we use any of it to convict someone of a crime?”

The Sheriff replied. "I doubt we have anything right now that is actionable and believe me I wish there was because if this is all true, I really want to make someone suffer. The problem right now is that all we have is the opinion of the people who are responsible for the wells. Mark Richards's name doesn't appear on any of the documents we have seen so far. Everything right now points to Hardy Braxton as the bad guy."

"I know, so here is what I'd like to do. I think we should do a deep dive into Hardy Braxton and his many companies and see if we can make anything fit with the illegal dumping scheme. At the very least we have to try to find anything that can be connected to Richards, but as Buck would tell me repeatedly, the investigation will go where the evidence takes us."

They started to work out a plan of attack and were in the process of deciding on which task was to be completed by whom when one of the deputies knocked on the conference room door. He told the Sheriff that the EPA crisis team had just arrived at the well site.

Bax downloaded the interview tapes and all the papers from the internet searches into her case file, shut down her laptop and headed for the door. She wanted to talk with the EPA investigators before they got too far along.

Chapter Thirty-Five

The fire had devastated the forest around the lodge. What was once a beautiful pristine wilderness was now a charred mess of burned sticks, but even with all the charred landscape Buck could see the first sprouts of Indian Paintbrush pushing their way through the dusty soil, and he stopped for a minute and marveled at the resilience of nature. This was one of those moments he wished he could share with Lucy and he got a little misty-eyed.

His hike to the lodge was uneventful, and the smoke wasn't that bad. He could still hear the sounds of the helicopters as they flew to Trapper's Lake to fill their huge buckets with water for the fight that was still going on south and west of the lodge. He knew this fight wasn't even close to being over. He passed several firefighters hiking back towards the command center, and they looked exhausted. He wondered how Cassie and her team were doing.

Buck reached the lodge and sat down on a burnt log, took off his hard hat and wiped his brow with the back of his hand. He was no expert, but it seemed to him that the humidity was up. Maybe that would mean rain since the storms that had been predicted for the last two days never materialized. He shrugged off his backpack and just sat for a moment looking over what was left of the lodge. He knew from experience that sometimes the best thing to do during an investigation was to just sit and look around. Get a real good feel for the area.

After a few minutes of looking around, Buck pulled a pair of heavy-duty leather work gloves out of his backpack along with a handful of blue nitrile exam gloves. He stood up and started slowly walking around the lodge. He wasn't looking for anything specific, just possible areas to look at further. He had no idea what he was looking for, so this was the best approach.

It took close to two hours to completely walk around the lodge. Every once in a while, he would stop and look harder at something that caught his eye. Several times he stepped into the lodge itself to look at something only to find it was a reflection or something else insignificant.

With his first pass complete, Buck stepped onto the floor of the lodge and began moving about the burned-out logs. He had to push a couple logs out of the way in order to see under them. As he moved, he had a final destination in mind; the couch or chair where they had found the victim. He was trying to get into the killer's head as he moved through the building carrying a dead body and what he did along the way.

Several times he stopped and examined something he found on the floor. He would take a picture of it with his cell phone and then put it in a plastic evidence bag, sealing it and noting the date, time and rough location. He also made a mental note to call his son, Jason, and see if he could email him a floor plan for the lodge.

As he got closer to the area where the body was discovered, he slowed his pace and moved with determination. He was looking for anything that might give him a clue as to what was so important about this building that everyone, it seemed, wanted to burn it down.

The body had been lying under a bunch of massive logs, that Buck assumed, must have come from the roof. It was also very near where the small plastic igniter part was found under a scrap of unburnt material. Buck wondered if the body had been hidden someplace and came crashing down with the roof or if it had been sitting or lying on a couch or chair and the roof had collapsed on top of it. He decided to work from the assumption that someone had placed the body on the furniture and that the fire had caused the roof to collapse on top of it.

He started pushing and pulling the big logs that he could move out of the way so he could get a better view of where the body had been. He found a few more pieces of fabric that had not completely burned up along with some partially melted foam rubber. Most likely the cushion filling of the furniture. He took a couple pictures and then placed the pieces in an evidence bag. There was enough of the material left that they might be able to determine which piece of furniture it came from. That could help with the placement of the body in the space.

Buck spent the next couple hours crawling around on his hands and knees. The fire had done an extraordinary job of destroying just about all the evidence that might be found. During his long career, Buck had never believed that a crime scene was worthless for evidence gathering. He now thought he had encountered his first one. Other than the few pieces of fabric and foam he had found; the fire had destroyed everything else. Buck finally stepped back over to the log where he had left his backpack, put his meager samples inside and sat down on the log.

He had never felt so frustrated at a crime scene. That little bug that had been running around in his brain was not satisfied and continue to stomp around, but he was no closer to getting any answers. He had been confident all along that something would have led him to understand why this building had to burn, but after several hours of back-breaking work, there was still no clear answer. The little bug was just going to have to wait.

He started to wonder if he was losing his touch. He had been at this job a long time. Or maybe he had come back to early after Lucy's death. Perhaps he wasn't ready. Buck hated these thoughts. He had never been the kind of person, even during those tough years of dealing with Lucy's illness, who would fall into self-pity or despair. No matter what happened he always managed to persevere, but he was sitting literally like a bump on a log and filling his head with self-doubt.

Buck took a long drink from his water bottle and poured the rest of the water over his head to clear away the dust. When he shook the water out of his hair, he realized how stupid this was. He'd had tougher cases before, and this one was no different. Besides, if Lucy saw him sitting here thinking like this, she would have kicked him right in the ass. That thought made him smile, and he decided that the little bug was right. Something didn't make sense, but he wasn't going to find the answer here. He picked up his backpack, put on his hard hat and headed back to the command center. This site, as far as being a crime scene, was dead. He would need to look elsewhere for the answers.

Chapter Thirty-Six

Hardy Braxton's face was bright red as he listened to the person on the other end of the call. Rachel, who was standing nearby thought he was going to have a heart attack. She had seen Hardy get mad before, but this was something new and scary. She didn't have all the details yet, but she had never heard him talk to Mark Richards like that before.

"Look, Mark," shouted Hardy. "Who the fuck do you think you're playing with here? I asked you a straightforward question. Are you using our wells to pump toxic waste into the ground?"

"Now Hardy, I have a lot of businesses under my name, I can't remember all of them, for Christ's sake."

"That's bullshit, Richards. Right now, my neck is stretched out about five miles, and I need an answer. Yes or no?"

"Hardy, it's not that simple."

"The fuck it isn't. We are in some deep shit if you pulled this stunt."

"Now hold on Hardy. As I recall, you haven't complained once about all the nice fat checks you get from our ventures, and besides, as you said earlier, your neck is out five miles, not mine. As I recall our business ventures, my name doesn't really appear anywhere, but oh my God, yours does."

Hardy sat back and blew out a breath. He couldn't believe what he was hearing. That smug son of a bitch was going to throw him under the bus and let him take all the blame and the lawsuits. He needed to be careful where this conversation went from here. He knew he had a temper and Richards had just about pushed him over the line. There were two things that Hardy didn't like. Not being in charge and being pushed around by pompous assholes. He had now reached the limit.

Hardy looked at Rachel, who was signaling for him to calm down. He had built this company up from a small cattle company into one of the biggest livestock and energy companies in the world, and he wasn't going to let the likes of Mark Richards tear it down.

Mark was still rambling on with that smooth southern accent, the one Hardy knew was as fake as the guy using it was when he shouted into the phone and cut him off.

"You listen to me motherfucker. I know I haven't done anything illegal, but I am damn sure you can't say the same thing. So maybe I should just call the Attorney General in Washington and have a nice conversation with him."

Mark's voice suddenly changed, and the smooth southern twang was gone, replaced by all New York. "Hardy, are you taping this conversation? Because know this. I am Mark Richards, and there is nothing you can do to hurt me. I will bury you in lawyers and paperwork. As far as I am concerned, you used our business relationship and the oil wells we drilled together to run a side scam involving toxic waste, and I am appalled. I might just call the FBI and swear out an arrest warrant for you and your whole family. And know this also, Hardy, your cop brother-in-law doesn't scare me one fucking bit. So, you chew on that, my friend, because by the end of the week I might just end up owning your ranch and all your livestock, which might be a lot of fun."

Hardy heard the phone disconnect on the other end and just sat there for a minute holding his cell phone. "Maybe I should have taped the conversation," he said to no one in particular. Rachel who was now seated in one of the big leather chairs in front of his desk just looked at him. She could see the fire in his eyes, and she got very concerned. Mark Richards may be worth a lot more than Hardy Braxton, but he had never dealt with Hardy when Hardy was mad. And right now, Hardy was furious.

Hardy opened his cellphone contact page and speed-dialed Irv Tuttleman, his lawyer. Irv and Hardy went back a long way, and Irv had been a big part of all the successes they had enjoyed on the way to this moment. Irv didn't look the part of a tough as nails attorney, but looks were deceiving, and Hardy had found over the years that Irv had one of the best legal minds around.

Irv answered the phone on the second ring, and Hardy explained the phone conversation he just had with Mark Richards. Irv didn't interrupt once as Hardy repeated the conversation as best he recollected. Finally, exhausted, Hardy stopped talking. He sat back in the desk chair and put his feet up on the beautiful burled wood desk.

For a moment there was silence on the other end of the line, and Hardy was afraid he might have lost Irv, but then Irv spoke. He explained that the way they had Hardy's multiple businesses structured, each business was isolated from the others so Mark Richards could try as hard as he liked but there was no way he could own Hardy's companies. He did tell Hardy that any lawsuits coming from the oil well issue could tie them up in court for a long time and might cost Hardy a lot of money.

He told Hardy that threatening to go to the Attorney General was probably a bad move because Mark Richards would now be on the defensive and he was probably already directing his lawyers to destroy any evidence of his involvement in the oil wells. Irv promised that he would do everything to protect Hardy, but they were going to have to go on the offensive and get ahead of this. Once this became a criminal matter, it would be a lot harder to fight.

Hardy listened to everything Irv said and finally started to calm down, much to Rachel's relief. He knew Irv had his back. As he listened, he began to think about how to go after Mark Richards. He was pissed that Mark would hang him out to dry and at this moment he wanted to do nothing but destroy him even though he knew that would be impossible. But he could still dream, couldn't he?

Irv was talking about having his staff gather all the documents related to the oil wells that they had partnered with Mark Richards on, and then they could sit down and see where they stood. Then he said something that Hardy never expected to hear from Irv.

"Hardy, you need to sit down with Buck and fill him in on everything you just told me. You always told me Buck was the most honest guy you ever knew, so it's time to tell him everything we know."

Rachel, who had been listening to the conversation nodded at Hardy. In a whisper, she said, "Call him. I trust Buck a hell of a lot more than the Attorney General. Buck can't be bought."

Hardy knew she was right, and he told Irv to start working on the documents, emails and phone calls. He knew what he needed to do.

Chapter Thirty-Seven

It had been a long time since anyone had talked to Mark Richards the way that Hardy Braxton had just done, and Mark was not happy. No, as a matter of fact, he was pretty pissed, and everyone sitting in his office knew it as he threw his cell phone across the room, shattering when it hit the Frederick Remington statue sitting on the credenza.

He jumped up out of the chair behind his Montana size teak desk and stormed around the office. No one breathed.

"Who the fuck does he think he is? No one talks to me like I'm some kind of piece of shit on the bottom of his shoe! I will crush that son of a bitch! I will crush his entire family! He is nothing but a pompous little asshole! I'm Mark Richards, and I'm like the fourth richest man in the fucking world. No one treats me like I'm filth!"

He looked at his attorney sitting in the chair opposite the desk. "As of right now, our relationship with that fucker is done, finished. I want you to cancel every contract we have with him, and then I want to crush him!"

"When I get done with him he is going to be worthless! And then I'm going to make him suffer! I will own his ranch and his livestock, and then when I have it all I will kill everything he values and burn his new house to the ground, while he sits and watches! He has no idea who he just fucked with!"

This tirade lasted for another twenty minutes, and everyone in the room knew not to interrupt until he was completely finished. They had all seen this behavior before. Behind his back, his staff called it his petulant little boy behavior. He finally calmed down, walked over to the bar and poured himself a big glass full of bourbon and chugged the contents of the glass. He sat down in his chair. Then he looked around the room.

"Everyone get the fuck out of here except for Steve!" he screamed.

It was like someone fired a starter's pistol and everyone made a mad dash for the door like they couldn't get out of there fast enough. Mark watched them all leave and then looked at his attorney, Steve Fletcher.

Steve looked at him. "You feel better now?" he asked with a smile.

Mark let out a huge, straight from the belly laugh and got up and poured himself another glass of bourbon. He poured a glass for Steve, as well, handed it to him and then sat down on the edge of the desk. Of everyone in his company, he knew Steve was the only one who would talk to him straight, and Steve knew it too, which is why he never worried about his job.

Mark asked the attorney how bad this was going to get, and Steve didn't hold back. "I told you when we decided to go down this road that we were going to make an ungodly amount of money. And I also told you that if the shit hit the fan, we could lose just as huge. We may be facing that time right now."

"Civil or criminal?" Mark asked.

"Both," replied the attorney. "if this goes public we are going to get sued by anyone who lives near one of your wells and has ever had a runny nose and the criminal case is going to depend on how good they do their jobs. What do you know about Hardy's brother-in-law? Anything we can use?"

Mark explained that Buck Taylor was pretty much a Boy Scout, but the way Hardy described him, he was going to be a force to be reckoned with. The female agent he had no information on, but if she was working for Buck, she would also have to be a straight shooter.

Mark walked around the desk and sat down in his chair. He kicked his legs up onto the desk and rubbed his temples. The bourbon was starting to dull his senses, but it was also making the headache go away. He looked pleadingly at Steve.

"Look, Mark. I think you need to take the wife and head for your island for a couple weeks." Mark owned a private island in the Caribbean where he had another huge estate, and it was far away from the prying eyes of the government and court system of the US.

"I will get the private investigators to look into the cops, but I am not hopeful. We also need to find that guy you hired to look into Muldoon. With that big fire raging out there, we need to close that investigation up and let it die. You won't be having any of your powerful friends visiting that resort anytime soon, if ever, so we don't need to worry about that one. In the meantime, I will have our people scrub all the files and get rid of anything relating to the waste disposal business. I am also going to talk to our folks at that big east coast newspaper you own and have them start a smear campaign on Hardy Braxton. Now, go tell your wife you are going on a vacation and get packing. I will alert the airport to have the jet fueled and ready whenever you are."

He looked across the desk at Mark, who was now sleeping

with his head back and his legs up on the desk. He had no idea how long Mark would be asleep, but he figured he would just let Mark's wife know to get ready to leave and she would take care of everything. That was the way it always was with Mark Richards. Mark would make these rash, boneheaded decisions and then everyone else would have to pick up the pieces. To be entirely fair, they were all paid a great deal of money to take on that responsibility, but it was also a fact that Mark owed a lot of his success to the people around him.

Chapter Thirty-Eight

Bax wasn't sure what to expect as she crested the ridge leading to the well site. Maybe she expected to see a bunch of people wandering around in space suits carrying fancy instruments in their hands. Boy was she wrong. What she saw as she looked down on the well site was a group of what looked like college students out for a Sunday picnic. She was almost disappointed. There wasn't a space suit amongst them.

She pulled into the parking lot and parked next to a white panel van with government plates. There were no signs anywhere indicating that the van came from the EPA. The Sheriff would be pleased.

As she slid out of her car, a tall, thin man with a straw cowboy hat walked up and introduced himself. Bill Unger was older than she expected but he had an awesome tan and looked to be very fit in his jeans and t-shirt.

"Hi, Agent Baxter, Bill Unger, EPA," he said with an easy-going smile.

"Nice to meet you, Bill. Please call me Bax."

With pleasantries exchanged, Bax asked about the lack of protective gear. Bill explained that since she had asked him to keep this low key until they were sure what they were dealing with, he decided jeans and t-shirts were more appropriate than space suits.

"So, what's the plan, Bill?" she asked.

Bill explained that they were just getting their gear unloaded and once that was done the first order of business would be to cut away some of the melted pipes in order to expose the wellhead. He mentioned that after a preliminary look over the site that there was probably nothing toxic in this well since they hadn't finished drilling it. Once they were confident this well was clean, they would visit the other four wells in the field.

Just then, Bax heard a loud noise as one of the techs, wearing protective gloves and a face mask, fired up a large reciprocating saw with a very sturdy diamond edged blade and started cutting away the pipes around the well. Bill explained that they had first checked the opening on the pipe for natural gas. Not finding any, they had decided to move forward with getting rid of the pipe.

Bax watched as the tech made quick work of the pipe and after about two hours, he and his colleagues had managed to clear away most of the excess debris, continually monitoring the well for any kind of gas. They cleared away enough of the pipe to give them access to a top of the well. It was a dirty job, and it was probably a good thing they weren't wearing white space suits because they would be filthy by now.

With the top of the well casing exposed, another tech slid a tiny detector tip down alongside the pipe that was still in the well. The detector tip bottomed out at somewhere around twelve thousand feet. Hooked up to several very high-tech monitors including a gas chromatograph and a portable mass spectrometer, the techs kept a constant watch on the monitors looking for any change in the readings.

Just as Bill had expected, there was nothing in this well yet, which was evidenced by the drill pipe still in the well. Bill had his team pull all the equipment and load up the van.

Bax was disappointed. It seemed like every step they took led to another dead end.

He invited Bax to join them for dinner in town and she accepted. She wanted to know more about the work they did. So leading the way, she drove them to a decent steak restaurant in Craig.

The conversation was light at first, and Bill and his team laughed about the places they had been and the crises they had seen during their careers. Surprising to Bax was that these young technicians had all worked for the EPA for well over ten years each. She had assumed that Bill was the boss, and the techs were something like college kids working on their degrees. Boy was she ever wrong.

Only one team member had a master's degree. The rest of the team all had Ph.Ds., most in chemical engineering. She came to realize as the night wore on, and the stories got more detailed, that this was a top-notch team. The kind of people you wanted on your side in a crisis. Of course, she should have realized that from the start. If Buck suggested someone to help with a problem, you can bet your last dollar that that person or persons would be the best around. She had never known Buck to work with anyone but the best.

Eventually, the group petered out, and they all headed to their hotel rooms. Tomorrow would be a much harder day and, from the way they were talking a much more dangerous day.

Sitting alone in her hotel room, Bax uploaded her notes into the investigation file. She looked through everything she had loaded and saw a lot of information. Unfortunately, there was very little of any real evidentiary value. She finally closed her file and picked up her cell phone. Buck answered on the second ring. He sounded as frustrated as she felt.

"Hey, Buck. Hope your day went better than mine?"

She filled him in on the hunt for James Robert Galvin and the disappointing results at the first well site. He suggested a couple avenues for her to pursue and then they talked about the lodge fire. The eight-hundred-pound gorilla in the room was Hardy Braxton. It seemed like they were dancing around Hardy's involvement in everything that had happened so far. Right now, Hardy and Mark Richards were the only real common denominator in both events. They discussed the videotape interviews she had recorded the day before and they discussed the fact that there was nothing startling in the tapes.

Buck suggested she focus her attention on Hardy, which didn't really surprise her. Brother-in-law or not, Buck was about the law and the evidence. He told her to keep the faith and to call if she needed anything. Buck hung up, and Bax turned out the lights and just lay on the bed. Hopefully, tomorrow would bring a break in the case.

Chapter Thirty-Nine

After talking to Bax and having already filled out everything he could in his investigation file, Buck decided to walk over to the Cozy Up. He didn't drink, but he felt like he needed a diversion, so he put away his laptop and left his room. He had always been a student of people, and he liked sitting in bars and restaurants just watching the people. It used to drive Lucy nuts because he would try to analyze each person who walked through the door of whatever place they were sitting.

It would have been a beautiful night except for the smoke in the air. You could also feel the humidity in the air, and he was hoping that maybe it was knocking some of the crap out of the air. He stepped out of the front door of the hotel and before doing anything else, he checked to make sure his two shadows were still in the parking lot across the street. He had no idea who they were or what they wanted, but it was almost comforting, in a weird way, to see them sitting there keeping an eye on him.

The Cozy Up was unusually quiet, and he figured most of the locals had already gone home for the evening. After all, this was an agricultural community, and, in his experience, folks involved in that kind of livelihood usually went to bed early.

Buck grabbed the same seat at the end of the bar he had sat in the first time he walked in, what seemed like weeks ago but was only three days. Sam lit up when she saw him come in, and by the time he sat down, there was a cold Coke sitting in front of him. Sam served a couple more customers down the bar and then asked him if he wanted anything to eat. Even though the kitchen was closed, she would make an exception. Buck politely declined.

Since it was slow, Sam stood on the other side of the bar and listened while Buck filled her in on the sorry state of his investigation. She was about to offer him words of encouragement when the front door opened and a dozen tired, smoky Hot Shots stepped into the bar.

The few people who were still at the bar, Buck included, stood and applauded and you could see the firefighters perk up. Sam walked down the bar and started taking drink orders. They asked her if the kitchen was still open and before she could answer Buck stepped up to the group and told them it was, and that dinner was on him.

Sam smiled at him and walked back into the kitchen to stop her two cooks from leaving, and Buck introduced himself and started pouring beers. Sam walked up behind him as he was pouring a beer from the tap and placed her hand on his back. He looked at her, almost waiting for the explosion since he had just volunteered her place but what he found was a big smile.

He was about to say something when the swinging door to the kitchen opened and the two waitresses, who were just about to leave walked back into the bar, tying on their aprons as they walked. Without hesitation, they started taking orders from the firefighters. Sam playfully pushed him out of the way of the beer taps, with her hip and told him to talk to the chef. One of the cooks had already gone home, and the chef was going to need help.

Buck headed into the kitchen, grabbed an apron and the Chef handed him a dozen porterhouse steaks to put on the grill. While the Chef cooked up the side dishes of baked potatoes and corn on the cob, Buck played grill master. It was amazing. For the first time since Lucy died, Buck seemed to really be enjoying himself. Between steaks, he stepped through the swinging door into the bar and was amazed to see that several more people had arrived and suddenly the mostly empty bar looked like a party was going on.

The locals treated the firefighters like royalty and someone had passed around a cowboy hat that was now brimming with money to pay for their meals and drinks. The atmosphere was exciting. One of the firefighters walked up to the small stage in the corner, picked up one of the guitars off the rack and started to play some old favorite country western songs. It turned out that the guy had an excellent voice and soon the whole place was singing and clapping along with the music.

Buck physically worked harder than he had in a long time, cooking steaks and cleaning dishes and by the time last call came around the party was in full swing. Sam was almost reluctant to call an end to the party, when the mayor of Craig walked in with his wife and told her to stay open as long as the firefighters wanted to stay. The mayor and his wife introduced themselves to each of the firefighters, thanked them for their service and the party continued.

Buck, finally finished in the kitchen, took off his apron and hung it over the back of his chair. The party looked like it was winding down, and he picked up the cold Coke Sam had placed in front of him and turned his chair to watch the crowd. One of the firefighters walked up and reached out his hand. "The bartender told me that your daughter is out on the fire line," said the firefighter.

"That's right," Buck replied. "Cassie Taylor. She's with the Helena Hot Shots."

"Wow, that is one tough crew. Those guys have been on the front line of this fire since the beginning. You must be really proud of her."

Then he called over the other firefighters and introductions were made all around. More stories were told, and more songs were sung, and then the party, once again started to slow down. Sam's crew cleaned up the kitchen with Buck's help, and after the firefighters thanked everyone in the place and promised to be back with their friends, everyone left the bar, and it was just Buck and Sam.

Buck started to apologize for volunteering Sam's place, but Sam walked around the bar, touched her finger to his lips to silence him and then kissed him like he hadn't been kissed in a long time. Buck returned the kiss and then Sam took him by the hand.

Buck left Sam's apartment over the bar just as the sun was starting to break through the smoky haze. It had been quite a night, and Buck felt good. He also felt bad if that was possible. It had been five months since Lucy died and tonight, even though Sam proved to be a fantastic lover, he felt like he had cheated on Lucy. She would have told him to stop being such a baby. That it was time for him to get out in the world and live his life.

He smiled at the idea that Lucy would have approved, and he walked down the street to his hotel. He felt invigorated, and he realized that last night, all of it, was what he needed to get his mind back into the investigation. He felt like the next big break was on its way. He didn't know how true that was.

Chapter Forty

Buck had just stepped out of the shower and was getting dressed when his phone rang. He picked it up, looked at the caller ID and smiled.

"Hey, Jess. It's been awhile. How ya doing?" he said as he answered the call.

Jessica Gonzales was the DEA Agent in Charge of the Grand Junction field office. She had worked with Buck on several investigations over the years, and they had become fast friends. She had been one of the first people to show up at Buck's house in Gunnison, the day after Lucy died. She had been to their house several times, and she had developed a real fondness for Lucy.

Jess was one tough girl. Raised in Brooklyn, New York, she was the youngest DEA agent, male or female, ever, to be offered a position as an Agent in Charge. Buck had no idea how old she was and was afraid to ask. She had a thirteen-year-old son from a previous relationship, and they lived with her mother. Jess was about five feet four, weighed about a buck twenty-five and was all muscle. She prided herself on her less than one percent body fat and worked out most days for two or three hours. She was also proficient in several martial arts styles.

She typically wore her gray hair short and spiked, and her favorite outfit was black jeans, laced up boots and a black T-shirt that accentuated some impressive curves. It was rumored that she had several tattoos, but no one Buck knew had ever seen them. Her record at the DEA was impeccable.

"I'm good, Buck. Heard you were back in the field. You doing ok?" she asked.

Buck and Jess spent a few minutes catching up, talking about some past cases that they had worked together and then she asked Buck how his current case was going. Buck filled her in on his lack of progress. She was stunned to hear that Buck's brother-in-law might be the center of attention in both cases.

"You think you might have to arrest him. I'd like to be there to see that," she laughed.

"Too early to tell, but who knows. So, what's up Jess?" he asked during a lull in the conversation.

"I got an odd call last night from the AIC in our Memphis office. He has a missing agent, and he was calling because he saw a post about a burned-up body you have at the Grand Junction Coroner's Office. He called to see if I knew you and if I would check it out."

Buck listened as Jess filled him in on the details of the disappearance. It seems one of the DEA agents told his girlfriend that he was going on an undercover assignment and he would be gone for a couple weeks. Even when he was undercover, he tried to contact her every other day just to let her know he was safe. A couple days ago he fell off the grid and stopped calling her. Being a good agent, he had given her an emergency number to call if anything ever happened to him and she lost contact.

She was worried enough after a couple days that she finally

called the emergency number and got his supervisor on the phone. Well, the supervisor had no idea what she was talking about. He told her that her boyfriend was not working any kind of assignment that he was aware of and that he had requested a couple weeks leave of absence to take care of a sick parent in Oklahoma. The only problem was that both his parents were deceased. The supervisor automatically assumed that he was probably shacked up with some bimbo in a hotel someplace, but because the girlfriend was so upset, he assigned one of his agents to start tracking him.

The agent pulled his phone and credit card records and soon discovered that the last place he used his phone was at the airport in Denver to call his girlfriend and the last time he used his credit card was to rent an RV. Since then, he completely dropped off the radar. Now his supervisor began to worry as well. He knew that this wasn't like him to just drop out of sight like that, so the supervisor opened a full-blown missing person investigation.

According to Jess, the agent investigating spotted the post from the Grand Junction's Coroner's Office on the national missing persons database and here they were.

"Jess. Do you have the missing agent's vitals?" Buck asked.

"Yeah. Five feet seven and about one hundred fifty pounds. Brown over brown. He's Asian. Name's Jimmy Kwon. Could this be our guy?"

Buck thought for a minute. The pathologist had estimated five feet six and about one hundred forty pounds, but with the condition of the body, it was almost impossible to tell exactly.

"It's possible. The body was badly burned, well actually more like charred would be a better description, but based on the pathologist, the stats are close. Do you have any idea what this guy might have been doing here?"

"None," she replied. "Like I said, his boss thought he was on leave."

"Ok. Can you get me his dental records and send me the name of the company he rented the RV from and I will check it out? Don't hold your breath, but I will see what I can do."

"Thanks, Buck. I will send the dentals as soon as I can get them. Shit, I hope your burned body isn't our guy. Shits gonna hit the fan. Washington doesn't like it when our guys go off the reservation."

They talked for a few more minutes, promised to get together for dinner and then Buck hung up.

Chapter Forty-One

Bax was sitting in the conference room running a computer search on everything Hardy Braxton. It had been a long morning already, and she felt like she was getting cross-eyed from looking at the computer screen, but she knew she was making some headway. Many of Hardy's businesses were privately held, so that information had to come from other sources than just the internet, his business ventures with Mark Richards were mostly partnerships, so she was able to get a lot of information from the Secretary of State's website. There was also a lot of internet information because pretty much anything Mark Richards got involved with made headlines.

She began to develop a picture of how Mark Richards did business. He would team up with some local company, especially energy companies, which he seemed to have an affinity for, let them do all the work and sit back and collect huge profits. None of the documents used by those companies, for permits or land purchases, contained any mention of Mark Richards's involvement. He was pretty much isolated in case anything went wrong.

Hardy Braxton, on the other hand, had his name on everything. She had been able to get her hands on some profit-and-loss statements from a couple of his partnerships and had forwarded those over to the forensic accountant. Math was never her strong suit, so she figured a little expert help couldn't hurt.

She was reading through the documents she had printed off when her phone rang. She looked at the unknown number and decided to answer it anyway.

"Ashley Baxter."

"Hi Bax, Bill Unger. Do you have a minute to talk?"

Bax had been waiting for Bill to call but she suddenly felt worried now that it actually happened. She put down the papers she had been reading and told him to go ahead.

"Ok. The bad news is that we have found toxic waste contamination in two of the four wells we checked today. We are certain we will find that the chemicals are probably Persistent Bioaccumulative Toxins or PBTs. The worse news is that the levels so far seem to be much higher than anything we have seen in any of the Superfund sites."

Bax immediately started a Google search for PBTs and what she found did not make her very happy. Bill went on to explain that they were taking samples back to their lab but that he had no doubt that that the lab would confirm his findings. PBTs included chemicals and toxic minerals such as arsenic, lead, beryllium or zinc but, as a class of toxins, it also included Persistent Organic Pollutants or POP's which included dioxins, hexachlorobenzene and a mess of other extremely hazardous chemicals. All in all, the stuff was bad news.

Bax was feverishly working the keys on her computer as Bill spoke, and she almost missed the most important part of the conversation. She suddenly stopped what she was doing and asked him to repeat himself.

"What I said was that while we were on one of the sites, a

small tanker truck pulled into the lot. Since none of us were wearing anything that said EPA on it, he asked us if he could go ahead and dump his load. He needed to get back to the transfer site, and it was a long drive."

"Holy shit. Can you hold him there until I get there?" she replied, excitedly.

Bill told her to take a breath. He already called the Sheriff, and a deputy was being dispatched to the scene to bring the driver in. He told her that their preliminary test of the tanker found the same chemicals as they found in the well.

Bax could not believe their luck. She had a feeling that something was about to give and then this just falls into their laps. This was the break she was waiting for. Bill told her that they were wrapping up and that they would be back at the Sheriff's office in probably two hours. He clicked off, and Bax started printing off another ream of paper on toxins.

She pulled out her phone and called Buck. She could not contain her emotions as she told Buck what she had found out about Hardy's various business and about Mark Richards and his relationship to Hardy and then she told him about the toxins and about the driver.

Buck was overjoyed to hear about the driver. The fact that they had been dumping PBT's into the ground in Moffat County did not make him very happy. He had run into chemicals like that early in his career when a dam holding back a mine tailings pond collapsed, and they found the remains of two bodies in the sludge at the bottom of the pond. Buck had solved the murders and sent several of Colorado's leading mine operators to jail. It was a big case for him and ended up in a huge Superfund designation for the area around the pond.

Buck told her to upload all the information she had so far into the investigation file, and he would read it later that night, then they would sit down and strategize about the next step. A lot would depend on what the driver had to say.

Buck told her about the call he had from Jess Gonzales regarding the missing DEA agent. He told her he had called the RV rental company Jess had sent him the contact information for and that the RV was GPS tagged and he was waiting for the clerk in the CBI office to fax the RV company a copy of the court order requesting the current location of the RV. He also told her Jess was sending him a copy of the agent's dental records. They talked for a few more minutes then Buck clicked off, and Bax sat back in her chair and gave herself a minute to feel good.

Sheriff Trujillo stuck his head in the door as he headed for his office.

"Hey, did you hear that the EPA guys nabbed a driver coming to one of the sites to drop a load?"

Bax told him that she had, and he told her the deputy had just radioed in and that he should be at the office in about twenty minutes. He said she could use Interrogation Room One and he would join her once they had processed the driver.

Chapter Forty-Two

Buck hated waiting, especially on things that pertained to the cases he was working on, so he decided to fill his time doing a little research. He pulled his car into the parking lot at the Sheriff's office, presented his ID to the desk officer and was buzzed into the back. He found an empty desk in the bullpen and fired up his laptop.

He was curious about the young woman who had confronted him in the restaurant at breakfast the day before, so he decided to do a little research on her and her clients, the Western Colorado Conservation Alliance.

Stephanie Street appeared in several of the results of his Google searches. She specialized in environmental law, a field Buck was not all that familiar with. The more he read about her, the more he realized that she basically sued companies for violating environmental law. These cases rarely went to court and usually resulted in some low dollar settlement. If her clients were accident victims, she might have been described as an ambulance chaser, which surprised Buck because her credentials were pretty impressive.

She graduated at the top of her class at Yale Law School and had clerked on the US Court of Appeals in Washington for several years before moving west and taking a job as a litigator for a large downtown Denver law firm. Her record of wins was impressive as well, until three years before when she suddenly quit the law firm.

The next time she showed up was in a lawsuit brought by the Western Colorado Conservation Alliance against a mining company in Leadville, Colorado. The suit alleged that the mine was letting Acid Mine Drainage (AMD), a toxic mix of subsurface water and mining residue, flow into a nearby creek and was destroying the habitat of the endangered Humpback Chubs. The case had gone to trial and attracted national attention. Stephanie and her clients eventually prevailed, and the mine was forced to spend several hundreds of thousands of dollars to clean up the stream.

Buck figured she could have written her own ticket to anywhere after receiving that verdict, but she stayed put. It looked like, for the last couple years, she had filed a bunch of lawsuits on behalf of her clients but none that attained the level of the mine case. Some even seemed a little frivolous.

Buck was now a lot more curious about this woman, so he worked his way through several social networking sites and some attorney associations until he finally found what he was looking for. On a very popular social networking site, he found a page dedicated to the Conservation Alliance and there, in one of the pictures, was a proud Robert and Marilyn Street celebrating the mine victory with their daughter, Attorney Stephanie Street.

That explained a lot. He was still curious as to why she decided to stay and work only for the Alliance, but that would have to wait. His phone rang with an unknown number and Buck answered.

"Taylor."

"Agent Taylor, this is Rosemary at Mountain RV in Denver.

We spoke earlier. I have the location information on the RV you sent over the court order about."

"Thanks for calling me back Rosemary. I really do appreciate it. So where is that RV right now?"

"The RV is located just south of the town of Meeker on Highway 13. I can't be more specific than that, but I did do a Google map search, and there are two RV parks just outside of town. The White River Campground and the Riverside RV Resort."

"Thanks, Rosemary. This is a huge help."

Buck hung up and called Sheriff McCabe and filled him in. The Sheriff, who was out on patrol, suggested they meet at the Riverside RV Resort first since that one was the closest to town. Buck said he could be there in about fifteen minutes, he hung up, and headed out the door.

Fifteen minutes later, Buck pulled into the parking lot of the resort and parked next to the Sheriff's SUV. Buck slid out of his car and looked around. The RV park sat right alongside the White River and was heavily treed and beautifully kept. It was apparent that the owners of the resort were very proud of what they had. Buck noticed about twenty-five RVs of every different make and size.

The Sheriff walked out of the small office followed by a small elderly woman and walked up to Buck. He introduced him to Mrs. Talbot, the owner, and Buck told her that he was very impressed with the resort from what he could see. Mrs. Talbot mentioned that she and her late husband had built the resort back almost forty years ago and after her husband died she had wanted to give it to her kids but neither one was interested, so she decided to just keep doing what she had been doing for all those many years.

The Sheriff interrupted. "Mrs. Talbot remembers the young

Asian man. She said she put him in site twenty-seven because it was closest to the river and furthest from the office."

"He said he was looking for privacy," said Mrs. Talbot. "I hope he isn't a wanted felon. I wouldn't allow that kind of person in here."

Buck smiled at Mrs. Talbot. "No, ma'am. As a matter of fact, he's a police officer on vacation, and his family has been trying to reach him. We are here just as a courtesy."

Mrs. Talbot looked cross-eyed at Buck and then looked at the Sheriff who nodded. Buck knew right away he wasn't putting anything over on this woman. She may have been elderly, but she was as sharp as a tack, and she just read him like a book. The Sheriff asked if she would wait inside the office and they walked off toward the far end of the park, nodding at curious campers as they went.

They reached the end of the park and found spot number twenty-seven. Buck checked the license information on the RV with the information he had received from the RV company and nodded to the Sheriff. The Sheriff stood off to one side of the side door and as inconspicuously as he could, pulled his pistol and held it down against the side of his right leg. Buck stepped up to the door and having already drawn his pistol, knocked loudly on the door and called out Jimmy Kwon's name.

Receiving no response from inside the RV, Buck checked to see if the door was locked while the Sheriff worked his way around looking in all the windows. They now had a problem. This was primarily a welfare check, and since no one was home, they should have walked away and notified his supervisor that they had found the RV. They could have also called a judge and gotten a search warrant and hoped that Jimmy Kwon wasn't inside lying on the floor bleeding. The Sheriff made the decision for them and pulled out his phone and called a friendly county judge.

Judge Elena Morales answered on the second ring. The Sheriff filled her in on their dilemma and asked her for her legal advice. Judge Morales thought for a minute and then told the Sheriff that since the life of a federal agent might be at stake that he should go ahead and enter the RV and do a thorough search. She would have her clerk write up the search warrant and fax it over to the Sheriff's office.

The Sheriff thanked her, and Buck pulled a small zippered leather pouch out of his pocket, opened it and pulled a pair of lock picks out of the pouch.

"Damn, Buck. Do I want to know why you have that?" he asked with a grin.

Buck laughed. "In case I forget my house keys."

With the Sheriff laughing behind him, Buck knelt next to the door and proceeded to unlock it. They both raised their pistols, he nodded to the Sheriff and then he swung open the door. Once inside Buck went left, and the Sheriff went right. From everything they could see, the trailer was empty, and a quick walk through the RV confirmed that.

Buck was looking through the back bedroom when he heard the Sheriff call him. He turned and walked back to the front and looked at the table the Sheriff was looking at. The dining table was covered with photos of people, lots of people. Buck took a pen out of his pocket and slid the pictures aside revealing several manila file folders.

Using the tip of the pen, Buck opened the first file. It contained a series of reports, written in a very professional manner and detailing what appeared to be an investigation into an illegal prescription drug ring. Buck was looking through the files when the Sheriff pulled out a large folded map. He put on a pair of blue nitrile gloves and unfolded the map.

"Buck, this is a map of the area around Buford. There are symbols handwritten on here indicating houses and warehouses with what appears to be the names of the people who live in them."

Buck slid a picture out from under one of the files and pushed it towards the Sheriff. "This is a picture of an EpiPen, but it's not from this country. Lucy kept an EpiPen handy while she was on chemo, in case she had a bad reaction. It didn't look like this one. The packaging is different."

They spent the next hour going through the files and looking at the pictures. The conclusion they came to was chilling.

"This guy was investigating the entire town of Buford. There is information in these files on dozens of people in the town who are involved in selling counterfeit EpiPens and other foreign medications."

"Yeah," agreed Buck. "But who was he investigating for? His boss thought he was on leave and since this is Jess's turf, he wouldn't have been working undercover without her knowing about it."

"Fuck Buck. What the hell was this guy into?"

Buck had no idea at this point, but he knew one thing. He would find out.

Chapter Forty-Three

Antonio Gonzales looked up as Bax, and Sheriff Trujillo walked into the interrogation room, sat down and laid a file folder on the table. Bax had been watching him through the glass for the past fifteen minutes, and this was a guy who was definitely nervous. The whole time he looked like he wanted to be anywhere but where he was.

She removed her pocket copy of the Miranda warning and read him his rights. She asked him if he understood what she had told him. He said he did, and she put the card back in her shirt pocket.

Bax opened the folder and sat for a minute, not saying a word and just looked at him. She had watched Buck do this dozens of times, and she understood what was at play. People hate silence. They feel the need to fill it, especially when they are in an uncomfortable position. She had watched Buck get a full confession out of a murder suspect without asking one question. He just sat there for a couple hours and didn't say a thing. By the time he was finished, the suspect looked like he was ready to climb the walls.

She slid the papers around in front of her and looked like she was intently reading what was in the file. The truth was that there was very little in the file. Mostly it was old printed papers she found next to the printer and borrowed. A deputy was still running his prints through the system, but she had enough to get things started. Antonio watched nervously without saying a word.

"Antonio, we've got a problem," she said. "Not only have you been arrested for illegally dumping toxic chemicals, but…" She picked up one of the papers in the folder. "This report from ICE says you are here illegally."

She sat back and waited for a reaction as sweat appeared on Antonio's brow. He picked up the water bottle they had given him when they first brought him in, and he drank half of it in one big gulp.

"I have a green card." He said softly. "I have been here twenty years. I have a family." Tears rolled down his face.

Bax almost felt bad for him. After all, he wasn't the ringleader of this crime, he was just basically an errand boy. Someone who had the misfortune of being in the wrong place at the wrong time. Truth be told, she had no information about his legal status but she decided to give it a try and see where it went. She obviously hit a nerve.

Bax looked at the Sheriff. "Look, Antonio," she said. "We have not alerted ICE that we have you in custody. So, for right now no one knows but the three people in this room. We don't care about your immigration status. We need to know who you are working for and where you are getting the chemicals. If you help us, maybe we can help you."

Antonio sat for a minute and thought about what Bax had said. If he told them everything they needed, would they really keep him from getting deported? He had spent his whole life, up to this point, flying under the radar. He loved this country, and he loved his family. It would kill him to have to leave them, but back home you never trusted the police.

Bax sat back and let her offer sink in. She was getting pretty good at this patience thing. In her early years, she would have gone after him with both barrels. She knew she could be tough if she needed to be. She had played bad cop several times, but she enjoyed this kind of challenge more. The whole spirit of cooperation thing was pretty cool.

Antonio finally looked into her eyes. "You can keep me from getting deported, but will I have to go to jail?"

Bax pulled her list of chemicals out of the folder and read the names and the description of the kinds of illnesses they could cause. She could see the fear in Antonio's eyes as he listened to her words.

"The chemicals I have been dumping can do those things you described?" he asked.

It was apparent from his reaction that he had no idea what he was hauling. He explained that no one had ever talked to him about using protective gear when picking up and dumping the chemicals. He asked Bax if the chemicals he was dumping could be hurting children. When she told him about the kind of illness and deformities children could get from drinking water tainted with those chemicals, he broke down, put his face in his hands and wept.

Bax and the Sheriff stood up, she picked up the folder, and they walked out of the room. They would give him a minute to let it all sink in.

Outside in the hall, keeping an eye on Antonio through the glass, she looked at the Sheriff.

"He doesn't seem to have a clue what he was dealing with, and right now he is in there thinking about his own kids," she said. "Why don't you call the District Attorney and let's see if we can get him a deal that doesn't involve jail time?"

"What about his immigration status?" asked the Sheriff. "He

has never even had a parking ticket, and he owns a house and pays taxes."

Bax thought for a minute. "Sheriff, this is your jurisdiction. I'm just a guest here. But I know that if Buck was here right now, he would tell me to do the right thing. When I told him I didn't care about his status, I meant it. I will go along with whatever decision you make."

Bax walked back to the door to the room, and the Sheriff headed for his office to call the District Attorney. She sat down opposite Antonio, who looked like he was finished crying, and asked him if he was ready to talk to her. His nod was almost imperceptible. She asked him to say the words for the videotape, and he did. She slid a document across the table to him along with a pen and asked him to read it and sign it. She explained that he was giving up his right to have an attorney present and was willing to talk with them on the record. He picked up the pen and signed the paper.

The Sheriff walked back in, and she slid the paper over to him. He looked at it and nodded.

For the next two hours, Antonio filled them in on the who, what and where of his job. Antonio and several other drivers worked as contract drivers for a larger company. Three times a week they would drive to a large warehouse outside of Rangely, fill up their liquid waste trucks and take the load to a specific location. They never knew which location they would be going to until they arrived at the warehouse. In the last couple of months, he had offloaded the liquid at 3 different locations.

He said that he had spoken with a few of the other drivers and they had been to places in Utah, Wyoming, and Nevada, as well as Colorado. He said there could be as many as fifty other drivers. He wasn't sure. He wrote down directions to the warehouse and then sat back in his chair totally spent. He told Bax that he never liked delivering the liquid because it smelled terrible, but the money was very good. He said he used to pump out pit toilets from campgrounds and porta potties at construction sites, but this was a much better job.

Bax told Antonio that she would be right back, and she stepped out of the room. The Sheriff had stepped out earlier to meet with the attorney from the District Attorney's office, and they were both standing outside the door.

The Sheriff introduce Bax to Amber Hunter, the Attorney and Bax asked, "Do we have enough to go after the warehouse?"

Amber did not look like the answer she was about to give was going to satisfy Bax. "Right now, no. We have a connection between the well sites and the warehouse. But what we need is corroboration. That we don't have. Can you get another driver to confirm his story?"

Bax looked disappointed, but she knew what the answer was going to be before she asked the question.

"Let's find out," she said.

Chapter Forty-Four

Buck and Sheriff McCabe spent most of the day going thru all the information they found in Jimmy Kwon's RV, and as it turned out, he had amassed a lot of evidence against the people of Buford. They found documents relating to the purchase of the property, to the establishing of various companies online and a massive amount of information on the drugs that were purchased. The most critical piece of information they found in the files was the names of the companies overseas that the town had been buying the illegal drugs from.

What Buck and the Sheriff found amazing was that they were running this business right out in the open and no one ever caught on, at least not until Jimmy Kwon came knocking. The big unanswered question was, who was Jimmy Kwon working for? They ran the numbers in his cell phone, and several came back to burner phones which Buck had sent over to his office in Grand Junction and two other agents were now trying to track down those numbers.

The Sheriff asked a local accountant to look at the financial records they found, and he had just finished his initial review and stepped into the Sheriff's office.

"Sheriff, we are definitely in the wrong business," he said. "If these records are correct, these guys were making two hundred grand a month selling these drugs."

Both Buck and the Sheriff stopped what they were reading and looked up.

"Seriously?" asked Buck.

"Quite seriously," replied the accountant. "Last month alone they took in close to four hundred thousand. They have a hell of a scheme going. Take the EpiPens alone. They were buying these low-quality drugs from companies in India, Pakistan, and China for about twenty cents each and reselling them for three hundred dollars each here in the US. That's a huge markup, and that is just the pens. They have entries for at least 6 other drugs that they are buying and selling."

Buck looked at the printout. "What is this stuff listed as clients? These numbers are huge?"

"From what I can tell, they are not only selling to the public through the internet, they are also acting as a wholesale distributor and selling to other companies here in the US and abroad. That is where the bulk of their income comes from."

Buck sat back and looked stunned. "How the hell can this go on and no one is aware of it? This has to be dangerous, selling cut-rate drugs to people who rely on this stuff to stay alive."

Buck was about to dive into another pile of papers when his phone rang. He recognized the number and answered. "Hey, Doc. Did the dental records help?"

Buck listened to Dr. Kalishe. When he hung up the phone, he did not look happy. "The forensic dentist is ninety percent certain that the body belongs to Jimmy Kwon."

"Shit," said the Sheriff. "That means we are going to be crawling with Feds."

Buck walked over to the conference room refrigerator and took out another can of Coke, his fourth so far today, and looked out the window. He noticed the smoke in the air was thicker than it was a couple hours ago. "The wind must have shifted again," he thought to himself.

He walked back to the table. Buck hated situations like this. He hated losing the investigation to the Feds. There were people out there who needed to know about Jimmy Kwon, but the Sheriff was right. As soon as he called Jess, the Feds would be all over this. He also knew that if they sat on this information and Jess found out that they knew, his credibility would be shot. "I need to call Jess and fill her in. While I'm doing that, why don't you call the District Attorney and see if he can come over here and take a look at what we have?"

The Sheriff stood up and then turned to Buck. "I am going to send a deputy over to sit on the RV. Can we get the forensics team out of Grand Junction to go over the RV? It might be a crime scene."

"I will make that call as soon as I'm done. I need to call the Director first." The Sheriff headed to the dispatcher and Buck pulled out his phone.

Director Jackson answered on the second ring. "Hey, Buck. What's up?"

Buck filled him in on the missing DEA agent and all the evidence he had collected about the town of Buford. He gave him a quick rundown on the arson case and the fact that more and more he didn't think that the NETF was responsible for burning down the lodge, but he still hadn't been able to nail down what was bothering him about the whole thing. The Director listened intently, remaining quiet for the longest time. Buck waited patiently.

"Fuck Buck," the Director finally said. "How do you always manage to get into these kinds of messes?"

Buck knew he was joking, but he also knew that he was more than likely half serious too. Buck had made a career out of turning simple cases into complex cases, and this one was proving to be no different.

"Ok Buck, so what's our next move?"

"Well, sir. First, I need to call Jess Gonzales at the DEA. She needs to know. Second, we are calling the DA to come by and look at what Jimmy Kwon had collected. If we have enough for a search warrant, we might be able to move before the Feds get here."

Buck's phone beeped indicating another call coming in, but he ignored it. The Director agreed with the plan. He didn't really see another alternative other than to try to get ahead of the Feds. He was well aware of how quickly his people would react if it was one of theirs that had been killed. They would move heaven and earth to find the killer. He knew the DEA would be no different.

"Ok Buck. Do you need me to send up some help?"

"No, sir. Not yet. But we do need the forensic team from Grand Junction to go over the RV. We have no idea where Kwon was killed, so right now it is a crime scene."

"I'll call and get the CSI's rolling. Keep me posted on how you want to play this. I've got your back, whatever you decide." The Director hung up, and Buck sat back in the chair and rubbed his temples. He picked up his phone, looked at the most recent call list and dialed his voice mail. He listened to the message, hung up and dialed the number from his recent call list.

"Agent Taylor, thanks for calling me back."

"No problem, Mr. Earp is it? What can I do for you?"

"Well, I've got some information about Mark Richards that you are gonna want to see."

Chapter Forty-Five

Bax walked back into the interrogation room and sat down opposite Antonio. She had a feeling this next ask was going to be very difficult for Antonio. She was going to ask him to give up one of the other drivers. This was the part of the job she hated. She held all the power over this man, and his entire life in the palm of her hand. She had already made up her mind that she wasn't going to force him. That just wasn't her style. She wanted his cooperation, not his fear.

She looked into Antonio's frightened eyes and told him she needed his help. She needed someone else to corroborate the information he had just given them. She didn't coerce him, and she never raised her voice. He was just a guy trying to do right by his family and he deserved a little respect. She told him she needed to talk to another driver. Then she sat back and just watched him.

Antonio just sat and stared at the table. He never looked at her, and for ten minutes she just sat. She was actually surprised at herself that she had the patience to sit and wait. That never happened before she met Buck.

Finally, Antonio looked up and asked her if he could use a phone. She knew it probably wasn't the smartest thing to do since he could just as easily call his boss and rat her out, but she had a feeling about Antonio and she decided to play along. She handed him her phone, and he picked it up and dialed a number from memory. Her first thought was, "Who does that anymore?" She couldn't even remember her parents' phone numbers without looking at the contact list on her phone.

Antonio started speaking in rapid-fire Spanish. The conversation often sounded heated, but he kept making his case to the person on the other end of the phone. What he had no way of knowing was that Bax spoke fluent Spanish and she was listening very carefully to his side of the call. Finally, he hung up and slid her phone back to her.

Antonio had convinced his cousin, one of the other drivers, to come in and talk to Bax. He had told him that unlike the police at home in Mexico, this senorita could be trusted. Bax thanked him, stood up and left the room.

Antonio's cousin Armando arrived at the Sheriff's office twenty minutes later and was led back to the other interrogation room by a deputy. Bax and the Sheriff followed them into the room and sat down. They introduced themselves and took down his name and contact information. The Sheriff gave it to the deputy, as he was walking out the door, and asked him to run Armando's name through the various crime databases.

Since Bax had listened to Antonio's side of the conversation, she knew where to start with Armando, so she spent a few minutes talking about his family and his kids. She never brought up his immigration status because she didn't want to spook him. Finally, she showed him the list of chemicals they had been dumping and told him about the way those chemicals could impact the health of the people in the county, especially his own kids.

Armando read down the list of side effects and health issues caused by the chemicals and then looked at Bax.

"All this can happen because of the chemicals we have been carrying?" he asked.

Bax explained this to him in more detail. What she told him caused tears to form in his eyes.

"Is this what made my little Jennifer sick?" he asked. He went on to explain that his six-year-old daughter had been diagnosed with a rare form of brain cancer and that she was getting radiation treatments. The tears flowed freely as he asked. "Did I do this to her?"

Neither Bax nor the Sheriff was sure how to respond, so Bax just reached across the table and put her hand on top of his. She held it there until he was able to calm himself down. She now understood why Antonio called Armando.

For the next hour, Armando told Bax the same story as Antonio had. She asked some clarifying questions, but for the most part, she let Armando just talk. When Armando was finished, Bax thanked him, and she and the Sheriff stepped out of the room.

Amber Hunter met them as they exited the interrogation room. "Nice job, Agent Baxter," she said.

She turned to the Sheriff. "I think we have enough to hit the warehouse. I'll have one of my people write up the warrant if you will call the Sheriff in Rio Blanco County and the Rangely Police and coordinate the raid with them."

She turned and walked down the hall towards the front door. Bax was looking in the window at Antonio. "What do we do with them?" she asked. "I really don't want to turn them over to ICE."

The Sheriff smiled. "ICE doesn't know we have them."

Bax kind of cocked her head sideways and looked at him. "We must have forgotten to include ICE when we were running their background checks. I already chewed out the deputy who did the background checks." He smiled. "I will have one of the deputies work up their release papers." The Sheriff turned and walked towards his office. He had a raid to coordinate.

Bax called Bill Unger to make sure his team hadn't left Craig yet, and when she reached him, she told him about the warehouse. Bill sounded like a kid on Christmas morning, he was so excited. He asked her if she wanted him to call in more federal people, but she told him they could handle it. He said his team would head to Rangely and stay out of sight until they were needed.

Her next call was to Buck.

Chapter Forty-Six

Buck, the Sheriff and a team from the District Attorney's office were sitting around the conference table organizing the files that Jimmy Kwon had collected. The whiteboard at the front of the room was covered with squiggly lines leading from one picture to the others. With the help of several deputies, they had been able to identify most of the people in the pictures and now they were creating a hierarchy chart of the organization. Jimmy's notes were very clear, he just hadn't marked any of the pictures with names or positions.

At the top of the chart was John F Muldoon, AKA Jack Muldoon. From everything Kwon had written, it appeared that Muldoon was the guy in charge. Under his picture was the picture of a heavy-set woman with long black hair. Kwon had identified her as Margaret Windsong, but Buck doubted that was her name. Her skin was way too pale to be of Native American decent, but then again, you never know.

Elliot Beech, the third picture to the left of Muldoon, was much younger than the other two. Kwon had listed Beech in his notes as simply "Hacker." They had no idea what his job was, but his name appeared quite a lot in the notes. From what they could determine they believed that Beech was probably Kwon's contact. Below them were about two dozen other people along with about a dozen children. The deputies had just about finished putting names and faces together, and when they stood back, they were only missing a handful of connections.

Buck was just about to say something when his phone rang. He looked at the number and answered.

"Hey Bax," Buck said. "What's going on?"

She told him about the information they had gotten from the two drivers and about the raid the Sheriff was now coordinating. Buck listened as she filled him in on the rest of her investigation. He was impressed with everything she had accomplished. He told her to make sure to document everything in the investigation file and include all the information she had gotten on Hardy Braxton and Mark Richards.

He asked her about the suspected shooter.

"Nothing yet. We've got an APB out to all of Colorado, Utah, and Wyoming but so far no sign of him."

Buck asked her about his background, if he had ever worked with explosives or chemicals and if she had pulled the death certificates for his wife and daughter. He listened to the silence on the other end of the line.

"Shit Buck. We got so busy with the drivers I totally forgot to dig into his background. God what an idiot. I feel so stupid."

"Hey, Bax. Don't worry about it. You've had a lot on your plate. His info is in the file, I will have someone in the office run it down."

Buck heard the intercom on the Sheriff's desk go off. "Sheriff, Sheriff Trujillo on line one." The Sheriff stepped away from the table and walked into his office, kicked the door shut with his foot and picked up his desk phone.

Bax continued. "Buck, this thing has gotten big. Bill Unger and his team are already heading to Rangely and Trujillo is calling McCabe to coordinate the raid. With any luck at all, we can get something at the warehouse to link Richards and the chemical dumping. I hope it's enough."

Bax finally took a break, and Buck said. "Even if we can't get Richards this time, you guys should feel good that you are about to stop a chemical dumping operation that could have ramifications for years to come and could affect the health of thousands of people. That's not a bad couple days work." Buck hung up his phone.

The Sheriff waved Buck into his office. "I just got off the phone with Gil Trujillo. They are going to move on a warehouse outside Rangely to look for toxic chemicals. I am going to round up a couple deputies, and we will meet them at Rangely PD in two hours. I assumed you would want in."

"Hell yeah. That was Bax on my phone. She filled me in. I need to call the office and get someone to do a deep dive on the possible shooter. Give me a couple of minutes. Can you have one of your clerks start running background on everyone we have on the whiteboard?"

The Sheriff said he would take care of it and that they would head out in about twenty minutes. Buck took a minute to call the Director and fill him in. The Director listened as Buck relayed his conversation with Bax and then gave him the details of the upcoming raid.

"Good news all around Buck. Now give me your take on where Bax is headed."

"She's doing fine, sir. So far, she has followed all the

procedures you would expect someone to follow on an investigation like this. She ran everything by the attorneys, and everyone is good to go. McCabe just spoke with Trujillo, and they are working out the details of the raid, and I think she has done a pretty good job. Good as I would have done, besides we usually talk before she makes a move."

"Ok Buck. What do you need from me, anything?"

"We haven't been able to run background on the possible shooter, Galvin, yet, and I would like to have someone check on the deaths of his wife and daughter. Can you get someone to do that?"

"You got a hunch about something Buck?"

"Not sure, sir. I'm just trying to figure out his motivation."

"Ok, Buck. We will get you what we can. Keep an eye on Bax and stay safe. Now that you're back, I would hate to lose either you or her."

Buck took one more look at the whiteboard as he packed up his backpack. He wished he had more time to spend running background on all these people, but he would just have to rely on the Sheriff's people to take care of that.

He slung his backpack over his right shoulder, grabbed a can of Coke out of the refrigerator and headed for the door. He was almost out of the building when a deputy called to him.

"Agent Taylor, Sheriff said to tell you that the CSIs just arrived at the RV park."

Buck waved his hand over his shoulder, yelled his thanks and headed to his car. He stashed his backpack in the back, jumped in and pulled out of the parking lot right behind the Sheriff. Once on the highway, he flipped on his flashers and hit the gas.

Chapter Forty-Seven

The little caravan of law enforcement vehicles ran south on Highway 13, turned onto Route 64 and headed west. They pulled into the parking lot of the Rangely Police Department and parked behind the building. Bill Unger and his team were already on site with their nondescript white panel van and were briefing the Rangely Chief of Police and two of his officers on the dangers of PBTs. The Chief was extremely concerned that these chemicals were being stored and transported through his community.

The people of Rangely are no strangers when it comes to chemicals. The area is largely agricultural, but there are a great many fracked gas wells surrounding the town. They have been part of the boom and bust cycle of well drilling for years, and they have always had a healthy respect for the fracking industry, but this was something entirely new. People deliberately poisoning the ground and potentially the groundwater. The Chief of Police was not pleased.

Sheriff McCabe climbed out of his SUV, walked over and shook hands with the Chief. The Sheriff and Chief Applegate had worked together many times, and they maintained a very close, friendly relationship. The Sheriff introduced Buck, who had just walked up and joined the little group. Buck thanked the Chief for his cooperation and then stepped over to talk to Bill Unger.

"Bill, good to see you." Buck reached out and they shook hands. "How bad might this be?" he asked.

"Based on what Bax learned from the two drivers, it looks like this has only been going on for a year or so. If that's the case, then it might not be too bad. We'll know more when we can take a look at the disposal company's records." He pulled a sheet of paper out of his pocket.

"I took the liberty of pulling a federal warrant to search for the records and chemicals. I wasn't sure if you guys had thought to include that in your warrant. Besides, since mine is federal, it will supersede yours anyway."

"Good thinking Bill." They were just walking back to join the group talking with the Sheriff when the team from Moffat County pulled into the lot. Bax pulled in and parked next to Buck's Jeep. She walked over to the group, and more introductions were made.

Speaking to the group Bax said, "I want to thank you all for being here today. We are going to do this operation by the book all the way. Once the scene is secured, we will turn the building over to Bill and his team. We do not believe that any of these individuals are armed, but we need to be careful anyway. Stay on your toes. Keep an eye out for anyone trying to destroy records or computer files. This could be the tip of the iceberg and could help us close out several cases. I will now turn it over to Sheriffs McCabe and Trujillo."

Chief Applegate pulled out a set of plans he had gotten from the building department and laid them on the hood of his patrol car. Everyone gathered around. He showed them the two entrances into the building and where the office was. Since they didn't have any idea if there were any PBT's being stored on site right now, he couldn't say for sure where they might be, but he reminded everyone to be careful. The State Patrol had provided an hazardous materials unit with full decontamination capabilities just in case of an accident of any kind.

Sheriff Trujillo continued with the briefing and then broke everyone up into teams. They all headed for their vehicles to gear up. Buck walked back to his Jeep with Bax.

"You guys have done a good job," he told Bax. "Now let's hope this raid will give us what we need to finish this part." He told her about the call he received just as he left Meeker and the offer of documents about Mark Richards.

"Do you think this is legit?" she asked.

"No way of knowing. I told him I would meet with him tonight at the Cozy Up and he was ok with that."

"Do you need me to back you up?"

"Thanks, Bax. Let's see where we end up after the raid."

They both opened their back hatches, pulled on their ballistic vests, checked their pistols and stood by, waiting for the signal. The signal from Sheriff McCabe came five minutes later, and they all hopped into their cars and pulled out of the parking lot, heading west on 64.

Two miles after crossing the White River, they pulled into the dirt parking lot of a nondescript metal building. There were four cars and pickup trucks in the lot. One team pulled behind the building, and everyone piled out of their vehicles. Sheriff McCabe gave the word, and the teams pulled open the doors and moved into the building.

"Police, search warrant!" shouted Sheriff McCabe as the teams spread out and within seconds had three workers lying face down on the ground, with their hands handcuffed behind their backs. Buck and Bax headed for the office in the back corner of the building. As they opened the office door, they saw one man sitting behind the desk his fingers poised over the keyboard.

Buck raised his pistol and pointed it at the man's head. "Touch that keyboard, and it will be the last thing you ever do." The look in Buck's eyes said it all and the man wisely pushed his chair back from his desk and raised his hands over his head.

Bax walked behind the desk, handcuffed one hand and then with a nod from Buck, told the man to stand while keeping her hand on the cuffed arm. Once standing she told him to put his other arm behind his back, and she finished cuffing him. She led him out the door and into the arms of Chief Applegate. She turned around and headed back into the office.

Buck was seated behind the desk. Luckily the guy who was sitting there hadn't closed out the program, so Buck had full access to the computer. Which didn't really do him much good since he was pretty much a dinosaur when it came to operating a computer. Sure, he could enter data into a pre-designed program, and he knew how to do an internet search, but after that, it was all foreign to him.

Buck stepped from behind the desk and let Bax take over. He watched in amazement as her hands flew over the keyboard. While she worked her magic, he checked out the rest of the office including the file cabinets in the corner. He could hear what turned out to be the owner of the company, loudly discussing his rights with Chief Applegate.

Buck had just walked out of the office when Bill Unger called from the back door. "Buck, we think we found it."

Buck noticed that the owner suddenly became very quiet. He walked out the back door followed by Sheriff McCabe. Two members of Bill's team were in the process of donning white hazmat suits while the other members checked the breathing tanks and attached the hoses to the suits. The two men opened the door of a small outbuilding and closed it behind them.

"One of the workers told us to look in the outbuilding, so we did. There is an underground storage tank under it with a very elaborate pumping system," said Bill.

While Bill's team investigated the underground tank and took samples to run through the mass spectrometer, Buck went back inside to see if Bax had found anything on the computer. He stepped into the office just as she was starting to explain what she found to both Sheriffs.

She was able to find files that were essentially hidden within other files, and when she opened them, she hit on a treasure trove of information. It would take a lot of time to decipher all of it, but she had a good idea where the chemicals were coming from and how much had been distributed so far. The answer could have been a lot worse. The one thing she hadn't found so far was a link to Mark Richards.

Buck had stopped listening about halfway through her presentation and was looking at all the pictures the owner of the company had framed and hung on his wall. Suddenly he stopped, pulled down one picture and reread the caption. It was a newspaper clipping from the local paper, and it talked about the new growth plans for the company now that they would have increased operating capital thanks to a new partner. What got Buck smiling was what he saw in the picture that accompanied the article. The picture showed the owner shaking hands with his new partner, Mark Richards.

Chapter Forty-Eight

Buck set the picture down on the desk, and everyone stopped what they were doing and looked at it. Bax was the first to respond.

"Oh my God. We have been searching high and low to find some connection between Mark Richards and the company doing the dumping, and after all that work, it is going to be a newspaper clipping that nails him."

"I think we need to have a little talk with the owner of this company," said Sheriff Trujillo.

Buck and Sheriff Trujillo walked out while Bax and Sheriff McCabe continued working on the files in the drawers and on the computer. Two deputies were standing next to the owner of the company, Randy Stewart, and they stepped to the side as Buck and the Sheriff walked up.

"Mr. Stewart, my name is Buck Taylor with the Colorado Bureau of Investigation, this is Sheriff Trujillo from Moffat County. We'd like to ask you a couple questions if that's ok?"

Stewart looked them both over and said. "I want my lawyer."

"No problem, Mr. Stewart. I am going to read you your Miranda Rights and then the Sheriff and I are going to tell you where things stand. You will be able to call your attorney when we are finished."

Buck pulled his Miranda card out of his pocket and read the warning word for word. He asked Stewart for a verbal acknowledgment that he understood his rights. Stewart was eager to say that he did and reiterated he wanted his attorney.

Buck pulled up a chair and sat with his knees touching Stewart's. "See Mr. Stewart, the nice thing about your rights is that it is perfectly fine for us to talk to you as long as we don't ask you any questions."

Buck started to explain about the toxic nature of the material they had been handling, making sure that he was very clear about the health risks. He talked about federal charges from the EPA as well as county charges for the dumping and the possibility of lawsuits. The entire time he was speaking, Stewart got paler and paler, with little beads of sweat forming above his lip.

"I have no idea what you are talking about, we deal with household and light commercial waste. We would never be caught dead handling PBTs."

Bax walked in and tapped Buck on the shoulder. She handed him a couple pieces of paper she had printed off from Stewart's computer. Stewart could see from where he was sitting that she had circled several items with a red sharpie. Buck looked over the papers.

"The household waste business must pay pretty well, Mr. Stewart. Your bank records, which we found on your computer in a file marked Safety Information, show a very successful business. You should be very proud. Odd though that they would have gotten misfiled in the wrong file. I guess things like that happen sometimes."

Buck smiled and watched Stewart's reaction. He seemed to be turning a lovely pale shade of green. What pushed him over the edge was when Bill Unger walked up with the letters EPA emblazoned on his jacket. Stewart hadn't seen the EPA team since he was in the office. At the sight of Bill walking up, he almost passed out, and one of the deputies had to reach over and hold him up in the chair.

Bill handed Buck a printout from the mass spectrometer. Buck was having a little too much fun watching Stewart squirm in the chair, so he asked Bill to explain what he found even though Buck could read the printout without any issues.

Bill took back the printout and proceeded to explain that they found a roughly five-thousand-gallon tank under the floor of the outbuilding and that the tank contained the same chemicals they found at the two dumpsites in Moffat County. He told Buck that the match was as good as a fingerprint match in people.

Bill also added that just the federal violations alone, would probably net about a 30-year jail sentence plus millions in fines and that didn't include the lawsuits from anyone who gets sick. Buck sat back and watched Stewart. He could see it in his eyes the moment survival mode kicked in.

"I had no idea we were dumping toxic waste," he said.

"Well, that's kind of strange since…" Buck picked up another sheet of paper from the pile Bax had given him. "You were the one who gave the drivers their assignments and destinations. Since there are no legal dumpsites up there for these types of chemicals, I would have to wonder what you thought they were doing with the chemicals once they got there?"

For almost a full minute no one said a word, and all eyes were on Stewart. It looked like Stewart was about to say something when Chief Applegate walked up to the group.

"The municipal court judge just approved the search warrant for Mr. Stewart's house. Sheriff McCabe, two of his deputies and one of my guys are on their way over there right now to execute the warrant."

Buck smiled at Stewart and over his shoulder said, "Bill you might want to have a couple of your people go to his house as well. He might have exposed his family to the chemicals. Maybe they should put on their hazmat suits just in case. Maybe check his neighbors too, for contamination. We will also need to check his employees' houses for contamination."

At this point, poor Mr. Stewart just lost it. The image of people in hazmat suits talking to his neighbors and searching his house was too much to bear. After all, Rangely was a small community. Tears flowed down his face, and he broke out into a major sweat.

"I changed my mind! I don't want an attorney. I will tell you whatever you want, just don't embarrass my family."

"Ok, Mr. Stewart, how much involvement in your company does Mark Richards have?"

Stewart looked stunned. "How do you know Mark Richards is involved in this company? There are no documents with his name on them. This my company and I alone am responsible for this mess. No one else."

Buck had set the picture he had taken from the wall in Stewart's office next to the chair he was sitting in. He reached down and held the picture so Stewart could see it.

Stewart stared at the picture. "Fuck" was all he said.

"Tell us how Mark Richards is involved," said Bax, over Buck's shoulder.

"Ok, ok. Mark Richards gave us the money to expand. He owns eighty percent of the company only it was set up, so his name didn't appear anywhere. The tank under the outbuilding was at his direction. He even provided the specs for the transfer system. We could have gotten a system for much cheaper, but this is what he demanded we install. Eventually, we would have had a dozen five thousand-gallon tanks, but he was having trouble getting them shipped in special from India or China or someplace like that. He told me he had made arrangements to have a special kind of fracking fluid manufactured and we would be the first to have it. It was going to revolutionize the fracking industry. Until you guys showed up today, I really had no idea what the chemicals were. Now I feel awful. My employees have no idea they have been exposed to shit that bad."

Once Stewart got started, he talked non-stop until he finally sat back in his chair exhausted. Buck now had a much better picture of how Mark Richards does business. He buys either entire companies or sets up some kind of convoluted partnerships without his name ever being attached to the businesses and then if things go bad because of some shady deal he worked out, it's the owner of the company that gets burned, and he walks away scott free with a huge profit. Buck was starting to dislike Mark Richards more and more.

Buck stood up and thanked Stewart for his openness. Buck could see in Stewart's eyes, that he suddenly realized he had been hung out to dry by Mark Richards. He told Bax where to look on his computer for other files that were "misplaced."

Buck stepped away, and the two deputies from Moffat County escorted Stewart to a waiting car for the trip up to Craig.

Chapter Forty-Nine

Things had gotten so crazy that Buck had completely forgotten to call Jess Gonzales. He felt bad. Jess was a good friend who had asked him for a favor, and he felt like he blew her off. He wondered if his mind was still filled with too much of Lucy's death. He knew Lucy would never let him think that way when she was alive. The thought of her at that moment brought tears to his eyes, and he was glad he was driving by himself so no one could see him. He wiped the tears from his eyes and shook his head to clear his mind.

He pushed the green phone icon on his steering wheel and said. "Call Jessica Gonzales."

Buck heard the phone ringing on the other end, and Jess picked up. "Hey, Buck. Is this a good or a bad call?"

"Hey, Jess. I'm afraid it's gonna be a bad call."

"Fuck, Buck. It's our guy, isn't it?"

"Pathologist says ninety percent. I'm really sorry, Jess."

"Thanks, Buck. This is not going to go over very well in Washington. Any idea how it happened? Could it have been an accident?"

Buck explained about the bullet hole behind his right ear and the missing teeth, some of which could have been caused by the fire

738

and some may have been pulled out. She listened in silence until Buck was finished.

"Did you find his RV?" she asked.

Buck filled her in on what they found in the RV and about the investigation he seemed to be running. He told her about the pictures and the files and the spreadsheets that they were presently looking at.

"Who the hell was he working for?" she asked, not really expecting an answer.

"Not sure at this point. What can you tell me about the illegal prescription drug market in this area?"

"That's just it. We haven't had any chatter about this kind of drug ring operating in this area. We busted a huge Fentanyl lab in California a couple months back, which surprised everyone because most of that shit comes in from Mexico, but we haven't done any investigating in this area. How could something this big operate right under our noses?"

"Look Jess. Don't beat yourself up over this. The Sheriff was in the dark as well. These guys think they are a sovereign nation and they won't let anyone on their property. They have also been operating right out in the open, and no one was suspicious. I can tell you this, right now the DA's team is going through the stuff we collected from Jimmy Kwon, and if they have enough for a warrant, I am going to find out what's going on. You can take that to the bank."

"Ok Buck. Don't make a move without me. I need to call Washington and fill them in. Keep me posted and thanks."

Jess hung up, and Buck called the Director to fill him in on the call with Jess. One of their own was killed, even if he was working on his own, and they weren't going to sit still very long.

Buck figured they had twenty-four maybe thirty-six hours at the most before Meeker would be crawling with Feds and the Director agreed. He needed to move quickly to figure this out, and the Director told him to call if he needed help.

Buck pulled his car into the driveway for the Riverside RV park and drove down to Jimmy Kwon's RV. The forensic techs were in the process of loading up their van as Buck slid out of his car.

Kelli Vaughan stepped away from the van, met Buck halfway and gave him a big hug. Kelli was about Buck's age and wore a silver-blonde wig. Kelli had been diagnosed with breast cancer about a year ago, had successfully finished her first round of chemo and was now back at work on a limited basis. She had reached out to Lucy and Buck several times during her surgery and treatment and was heartbroken when Lucy passed away.

"How you doing, Buck?"

"Mostly good Kelli. It hits me sometimes that she's gone, but I've been able to work through it. What have you found?"

Kelli explained that they found very little. She told him unequivocally that Jimmy Kwon had not been abducted or killed in the trailer, they found no indications of a struggle of any kind and everything they did find led to only one person. As far as she and her team were concerned, the trailer was clean.

Buck thought about it for a moment. "If Jimmy Kwon wasn't taken from here than it is most likely that the people he was investigating had no idea what kind of information he had collected since it was all here when they arrived this morning. So he was killed someplace else, most likely in Buford. Great job Kelli. Thank your team for me."

Buck gave her a hug and told her to keep in touch that he was always available for her and her family. She handed him the keys to the RV and headed for her van. Buck slid back into his car, turned around and drove down the road to the office. Mrs. Talbot was sweeping off the front porch when she saw him pull up. She set down the broom and walked towards his car. He rolled down the window.

"Mornin Agent Taylor. Did you folks find what you were looking for?"

"Unfortunately, we did," he replied. "I wanted to let you know that I will call the rental company and have them make arrangements to pick up the RV. It may take a couple days."

"So, I assume the young Asian man will not be returning for his package?" she asked.

Buck looked at her for a moment. "What package?"

"He left a package a couple days ago before he disappeared and asked me to hold it until he came back for it. He said if he didn't come back to give it to the authorities. I kind of forgot about it until I was cleaning the office this morning and it was sitting under my desk. Do you want it?"

Buck shut off the car and slid out. "Yes, ma'am. I do."

Buck followed her into the office and waited on the customer side of the counter until she was able to bring him the package. Buck pulled a pair of nitrile gloves out of his pocket and put them on. He pulled out his knife, flipped it open and slit the tape on the end of the package. Putting away his knife he opened the end flap and slid out a pile of papers about an inch thick. Buck leafed through the papers and noted that they were mostly copies of what had been found inside the RV. He looked at the letter on top that was addressed to the Agent in Charge, Grand Junction Field Office.

The first part of the letter was mostly introductory. It explained who he was and that he was running an off the books investigation into an illegal prescription drug ring involving the entire town of Buford, Colorado.

The letter went on to explain that he was being paid by Mark Richards to develop a case against Jack Muldoon and others in the town, which his lawyer, Steve Fletcher, would then present to the proper authorities so that a legitimate investigation could be launched, and the town closed up.

"What I discovered during my investigation is that Mark Richards was an early investor in getting the operation in Buford off the ground. Mr. Fletcher revealed to me during one of our meetings that Mark Richards did not want his involvement in this criminal enterprise getting out to his guests. I was not going to reveal that last little bit of information in my investigation notes."

"I know I have violated a lot of laws and DEA procedures by going off on my own, but the money was too good to pass up, and I used some of it to put a deposit down on a small ranch in Brazil. If you are reading this, then I guess I will not be making the trip since I am either in jail or dead. If it is the latter, please let my boss know that I am sorry about violating my oath and let my mom and sister know that I loved them. The title to the ranch is in my bedroom closet in a fireproof box. The key is in my desk. When you find the box, you will also find digital audio tapes of my initial meeting with Mark Richards and subsequent meetings with Mr. Fletcher."

Buck put the letter down and gave a soft whistle. He sat down in the chair next to the counter and just stared at the letter. Jimmy Kwon, besides being an excellent investigator, had left an insurance policy. He had Mark Richards on tape setting up an investigation that would have sent Jack Muldoon to jail for a long time. Buck needed to hear those tapes. There was nothing really illegal about all this unless it led to the death of Jimmy Kwon.

He put down the letter, pulled out his phone and speed dialed Jess Gonzales.

Jess answered on the second ring, and before she could even say hello, Buck said. "Jess I need you to call Jimmy Kwon's boss in Memphis."

Chapter Fifty

Bax and Sheriff Trujillo had been sitting opposite Randy Stewart in the interrogation room since he had been arrested in Rangely. They reread him his Miranda Rights and had him sign a statement indicating that he waived his rights to have an attorney present. They sat quietly while he wrote out his statement on a yellow pad.

Finally finished he looked up from the pad and slid it over to Bax. She read through all nine pages and then slid it over to the Sheriff who picked it up and read it. The Sheriff nodded and stood up and left the room. Bax looked at Stewart.

"Randy, the DA will read your statement and then come in and talk to you. We have called your attorney, and he is on his way in. Just sit back and try to relax." He raised his cuffed hands and looked pleadingly at Bax.

Bax smiled. "Sorry, Randy. Those have to stay on until we book you. Once we are finished with the booking process, Bill Unger from the EPA will come in and sit down with you and your lawyer. I want you to understand that their investigation is completely separate from ours. We are concerned with the illegal dumping of hazardous chemicals within the county. They will discuss possible civil and criminal proceedings on a federal level. I would urge you to cooperate with them as you have with us."

Randy just buried his head in and hands. Tears flowed as he thought about how this was going to affect his family. They had allowed him to contact his wife, and the Sheriff had suggested that he might want to have them leave town for a while. So far only limited information had spread around town, but as his neighbors learned more about the crimes he was accused of, things might turn ugly.

Bax sat back in her chair. "Randy, how come you didn't ever question dumping these chemicals? You knew the fracking fluid story was false, didn't you think to question what you were handling?"

Randy picked up his head. "The money was too good to pass up. We had struggled for a couple years as oil prices crashed again and everyone basically stopped drilling. When someone like Mark Richards calls you with an offer, you assume it is a good thing. After all the guy is a billionaire. He told me one of his companies had developed a method to render the chemicals safe so he could use them for fracking. I guess I should have questioned the deal a little more."

"Randy, do you know anything about the fires at four of Braxton Global Energy's sites?"

"No ma'am. The news reported that they were caused by some environmental group. That's as much as I know, swear to God."

Bax thanked him for his candor and stepped out of the room. The Sheriff and Amber Hunter were sitting in the Sheriff's office, and Bax stepped through the door.

"Well?" said Bax.

Amber looked at her. "We are going to charge him with the illegal dumping, which will allow us to process him and hold him in a cell. It will also give us time to put together a criminal conspiracy case against him and Mark Richards. We are still a little light on the evidence against Mark Richards, but I think we can at least get an indictment on the conspiracy charge. I also want to look at some health code violations. I want to throw the book at the son of a bitch."

"Do we have enough evidence to at least bring in Mark Richards and question him?" the Sheriff asked.

Amber thought for a long minute. "If nothing else he has been implicated in a crime by Mr. Stewart. We should ask him to come in voluntarily so we can try to clear up the allegations. I will convene the Grand Jury in the morning and see what we come up with. I am also going to issue an arrest warrant for Hardy Braxton. It is still his wells that are being used, and we haven't cleared him of any wrongdoing. Do you have any issues arresting him, Agent Baxter?"

"No, ma'am. I do want to discuss this with Buck to make sure we don't interfere with something he might be working on. After all, the lodge fire involves arson and murder, so I don't want to jeopardize anything."

Bax left the room to call Buck and Amber stood up, thanked the Sheriff and headed for her office at the other end of the building.

Bax pulled out her phone and called Buck, who answered as soon as it started ringing. "Hey, Bax. Good news?" She lost focus as she watched Randy Stewart being escorted away, in handcuffs, to the county jail to be booked.

"Sorry, Buck. They just took Stewart over to the jail to book him. Listen, the DA is going to convene a Grand Jury tomorrow. She is hoping to indict Mark Richards on conspiracy charges, and she thinks we should ask him to come in voluntarily to answer some questions. I didn't want to fuck up anything you might be working on, so I told them I was checking with you first."

"Thanks, Bax. Can you hold off until I meet with the guy

who says he has information on Mark Richards? I am meeting him in a couple hours.”

“I think I can make that happen. Oh, the DA is going to issue an arrest warrant for Hardy. Do you want me to bring him in or do you want to handle it?”

“That’s your case and so far, other than being a part owner of the lodge, we have nothing on him on our end. Go ahead and bring him in. Word of caution though. His lawyer may look like a little nerd, but he is incredibly sharp. Do everything by the book.”

Buck took a few minutes to fill her in on the latest in the Jimmy Kwon murder investigation and about the letter and the tapes. Jess had called him back to tell him that several DEA agents were on their way to Kwon’s house to try to find the lockbox with the tapes in it. She would call as soon as she had something. Her bosses in Washington were interested in hearing what was on the tapes as well.

“Smart guy leaving an insurance policy. You think he knew he had been made?” she asked.

“I think he was just covering his ass in case something happened. We may never know his motivation.”

“You know Buck, it seems like everything we have looked at in these two cases revolves around money. The illegal dumping, probably the fires, the lodge maybe and definitely the drugs. I can understand the little guys getting caught up in all that money but what was in it for Mark Richards? He has more money than God.”

“I don’t know Bax. Boredom maybe or the fact that he can get away with anything he wants because he has all that money. Guys like that usually have huge egos. It could all just be about power.”

“Too weird. If I ever get that rich, please make sure you knock me down a peg or two every now and then will ya, Buck?”

"You got it Bax. I need to run. I have one more stop to make before I meet Mr. Earp. We'll talk later."

Chapter Fifty-One

Buck noticed that the smoke in the air had gotten a lot thicker, that the wind had also been steadily picking up all afternoon and it was blowing toward Meeker. The air was heavy with moisture that had yet to turn into rain. His thoughts flashed on Cassie, and he hoped she was ok. Lucy would never forgive him if something happened to Cassie. He was the one who encouraged her when she told them she was quitting law school to become a firefighter.

He was still focused on Cassie, and he almost missed to driveway on the right side of the highway. He turned in and followed the gravel drive past a small separate garage and parked in front of the house. He sat for a minute and admired the view. The house was an old farm house with a big wraparound deck. The house was not quite dilapidated, but it definitely needed some work, as did the surrounding yard, but what Buck admired most was the stretch of the White River that flowed for a couple hundred yards behind the house.

Buck could almost picture himself standing knee deep in the middle of the river watching that tiny dry fly drift along in the lazy late summer current and hooking a nice size rainbow trout. He spent a lot of time on the river in the months after Lucy died. Fly-fishing was the outlet that got him through the worst moments, and it helped to clear his mind. He knew Lucy would be happy that he used fishing as his release. She always loved sitting on the bank and watching him fish while she read a book or did needlepoint. He missed those days.

Buck shook off the melancholy moment and slid out of the car. Out of force of habit, he touched his pistol that was hooked to his belt. It was a habit developed over a lifetime of being a cop, and he didn't even think about it. He walked up the walkway, up onto the porch and rang the doorbell. He heard footsteps heading towards the door, and the door was pulled open.

Stephanie Street stood in the doorway wearing a pair of jeans, University of Colorado sweatshirt and bare feet. She did not look happy to see him.

"Agent Taylor, I thought I made myself clear the other day that you were not to harass my clients. What do you want?"

Buck looked at her and smiled. "I have come to talk with your parents since they are the clients you tried to warn me off about. May I come in?"

Stephanie seemed a little taken aback that Buck was aware who her clients were, but she really shouldn't have been. She had been told by everyone she had contacted that Buck Taylor was incredibly thorough and that he was a dogged investigator. She hesitated for a minute like she was thinking seriously about slamming the door in his face, but something about the way he asked seemed so unthreatening that she decided to let him in.

Before she could open her mouth, Buck said. "Look, Ms. Street, I am not here to harass your parents. I doubt your parents had anything to do with the fire at the lodge."

Sounding almost annoyed, she asked. "Why would you think

that? They are well known in the international conservation movement and…"

"How long have they been sick?" he asked.

Stephanie stopped dead in her tracks and turned around. She was so close that for the first time Buck could see the heavy lines under her eyes that she tried to hide with makeup. She fumbled for words.

"What are you talking about? My parents are perfectly fine. How dare you?"

Buck raised his hands in surrender. "Look Ms. Street, it's obvious. This was once a beautiful house with what I am going to guess was a perfectly manicured lawn and flower beds, which have now fallen into disrepair. You are here cooking dinner. The roast smells awesome by the way, and you have huge bags under your eyes from lack of sleep which you try to cover up, but they are still there. There are also several unopened bags of pills sitting on the front table we just passed, which probably came in today's mail."

Suddenly tears started to roll down her cheeks, and she turned and walked toward the kitchen. Buck followed her in and spotted a not so elderly woman sitting at the kitchen table. She was wearing a beautiful dress with a sweater, and her hair was combed and pulled back in a ponytail.

She had a crossword puzzle book sitting in front of her that was upside down, and she was filling in the little squares with a black pen. She looked up as Buck entered and smiled. She then turned back towards her puzzle.

Stephanie checked the roast in the oven and then stirred the potatoes that were boiling on top of the stove. She used a kitchen towel to dry her eyes and then she leaned against the counter.

"My dad developed Alzheimer's first about five years ago. He hardly ever gets out of bed anymore, and I have to feed him by hand. Mom developed it last year. She can still do some things when she has a lucid moment, but for the most part, her mind is shot. It's horrible. These two people were both college professors when they go into the conservation moment. They were brilliant and were world acclaimed, especially after we won the lawsuit."

"A year ago, I gave up my practice and moved in with them. Thank God they had the money from the lawsuit or I'm not sure what we would have done. I don't want them in an institution. I promised I would care for them here in the house they have lived in for their entire lives. In the past, whenever there was an issue that put conservation in the limelight, they were the first ones to be questioned by the FBI or some other acronym. That's why I tried to warn you off. As you can see, they are no threat."

Buck listened to her story without comment. He finally said. "I know what it takes to care for someone, and I don't blame you for trying to protect them. When I said I didn't think they were involved, I meant it even before seeing them. From everything I read, it is not their style to set fires. They are more the academic type of fighters." Buck paused. "Do you know where your brother is?"

Stephanie looked surprised by the question. She thought about telling the same old family lie she always told, but she had a sense that this cop was not going to buy it.

"We haven't seen my brother in several years. There was a very public split in the conservation and environmental movements while I was in college and my brother and some of his friends headed in another direction. Mom and dad did not agree with his choices. How did you know I had a brother?"

"There was a picture online of you and your parents celebrating the lawsuit victory in which you and your parents were named, but in the background was a young man who looked exactly like you. I assumed he must have been your brother."

"Yeah," she said. "That damn picture. We didn't even know he was at the courthouse that day until the picture came out in the newspaper."

"Stephanie is your brother part of the NETF?"

"Honestly Agent Taylor. I don't know for certain. He and his friends pulled some crazy shit, but I hope for my parents' sake that he is not an arsonist, but if he is at least they won't know about it. Now if you'll excuse me, I need to get dinner on the table."

She walked him to the door, and as he stepped out on the porch, he turned and said. "There are organizations that can help you take care of your parents."

"I know, but it's my job, and I wouldn't have it any other way. Thanks, Agent Taylor for understanding." She closed the door, and Buck turned and headed for his car. He felt bad for Stephanie Street, but he also understood. He would never call anyone to help with Lucy either. It was his job. He slid into his car and took one more look at the river. He started the car and turned around in the driveway. He had one more person to meet today.

Chapter Fifty-Two

Buck pulled into the parking lot of the Cozy Up and slid out of his car. He was about to open the back hatch to grab his backpack when a huge shadow loomed over him. He instinctively let his right-hand drop down to the backstrap on his pistol, and he unsnapped the thumb break on his holster. He looked up as this mountain of a man stepped between the cars.

The man held up both his hands and said, "whoa there. Didn't mean to startle you. Names Morgan Earp." He lowered his hands. Buck looked up at this man standing in front of him and kept his hand on his pistol. Morgan Earp was a giant of a man. Easily six foot six and three hundred pounds if he weighed an ounce. He had short gray hair, a neatly trimmed gray beard and wore a t-shirt that did nothing to hide his massive biceps or his incredibly flat stomach.

Earp slowly reached his left hand into his front pocket and pulled out his ID. He handed it to Buck, who still keeping a wary eye on Earp, reached out and took the ID. He looked at the picture on the California Private Investigator's license and looked at Earp. The picture did not do him justice. Buck relaxed, handed back the ID and reached out his hand which was immediately lost in this giant's grip.

"Morgan Earp, huh? Any relationship?" Buck asked.

"No. No relationship as far as we know. Dad was a history buff, and he thought it was cute. He didn't realize what a pain in the ass it would be for me growing up."

"I was expecting to meet you inside. Would you like something to eat?"

"No thanks. I'd rather do this out here. Too many pairs of ears in a bar like this. Can we talk out here?"

Buck nodded. Morgan Earp had spent twenty-five years with the Los Angeles County Sheriff's department before retiring and going into private practice. His last ten years was as a homicide investigator. His practice, he told Buck, was very exclusive and a lot of his clients had names Buck would recognize.

He explained to Buck that he had been hired by Veronica Richards, Mark Richard's wife, because she believed her husband was having an affair. Well as it turned out, he was having many affairs, with many women, some famous and some not, which he couldn't understand because Mark Richards was about five foot eight, chubby and was starting to go bald. He was not a very pleasant man.

Veronica Richards, on the other hand, was five foot nine, drop dead gorgeous with an incredible body and was a former swimsuit model. He guessed money made people do odd things. He pulled a folder out of a computer bag he had hanging over his left shoulder and handed it to Buck.

"I want you to understand that I am violating a shit load of confidentiality rules that I don't take lightly, but when I think the law is being broken, I can't just sit by and do nothing."

"Why don't you tell me what you think is going on?"

"Mrs. Richards has known about the affairs for about a year and a half. She didn't really react when I gave her the investigation package like she already knew what was in it. She paid me the remainder of my fee without question, and I left. I guess curiosity got the better of me and I parked my car down the street where I could see the front door and waited. A little while later, a brand-new Jag pulled into the driveway, and a good-looking guy stepped out and approached the door. He was met by Mrs. Richards before he reached the top step and then they entered the house."

"When I got back to the office, I did a little digging, and I think the guy she was meeting with was her husband's attorney Steven Fletcher. I let it go and went about my business, but a few months later I started seeing the reports about the fires at the fracking sites. They began in California and then moved into Arizona, Utah and finally Colorado and that was when Hardy Braxton called me. He asked me to investigate the fires."

"Mr. Braxton was sure that the wells were being destroyed by an environmental group because of the fracking. The problem was that nothing I discovered led me to that conclusion. When the lodge burned down the other night and ignited a massive wildfire, I felt certain that it was not some eco-terrorist nut jobs. I couldn't put my finger on it, but the more I thought about it, the more it seemed like something else."

"I told Mr. Braxton that I didn't believe it was the terrorists, but he didn't want to hear it. When I found out that an official investigation had started, I decided to back off, but I thought you should know what I found out. I have a personal policy that once law enforcement gets involved, I am finished. Call it professional courtesy. I reached out to a friend in the government, and he told me that you were handling the investigation and that you could be trusted, so I reached out and here we are."

Buck was now intrigued, and he opened the file and looked

through the pictures and then read the report that Earp had given Mrs. Richards.

"You said you thought a crime was being committed. Care to elaborate?" Buck asked.

"I think Mrs. Richards is working with the attorney to slowly destroy her husband. I don't have any proof but thinking back on how she reacted when I gave her the report and what has happened since then, and the timing of when the fires started, I just have a gut feeling she is behind a lot of this. After all those years as a cop, I always go with my gut."

Buck knew the feeling. He always followed his gut as well, so he knew how Earp was feeling. Buck thought about what Earp had just told him and sat down on the back bumper of his car. The little bug in his head was back, and he suddenly had some clarity.

He hadn't been able to figure out what the well fires and the burning lodge had in common other than Hardy Braxton and Mark Richards, and more importantly, he couldn't come up with a reason the lodge was so important that everyone wanted to burn it down. And how did Jimmy Kwon's body end up in the lodge? The bug was looking for an answer and suddenly, thanks to Earp, here it was. Revenge.

This wasn't about politics or money or even the environment, it was purely about revenge. Could it be that simple? Mrs. Richards had been wronged by a cheating husband, she was going to get even, and she had the resources to do it. The problem was that the revenge had moved into criminal activity.

Another thought popped into Buck's head. Suppose Mrs. Richards found out that her husband was going to ruin Jack Muldoon and have him put away for years just to protect his luxury fishing lodge? But why would that matter to her? Would she go as far as hiring someone to burn down the lodge? That still didn't tell him how Jimmy Kwon's death fit into the picture?

Buck looked at Earp. "Can I keep this?" He held up the file.

"Yeah. I don't like feeling like this woman used me to get more dirt on her husband, just to hurt him. You do whatever you need to with them."

Earp closed his computer bag, shook Buck's hand and disappeared between the cars. This case just took a significant turn and Buck needed to get someplace quiet and think. He was about to close up his car, but instead pulled out his phone. He speed dialed Bax.

"Hey, Buck. I was just going to call you."

Buck cut her off. "We may have been looking at all of this the wrong way. Can you get down to Meeker right away?"

"Sure Buck. I'm on my way."

The quiet place would have to wait.

Chapter Fifty-Three

Buck had just pulled into the parking lot when his phone rang. It was the main number for the CBI office in Grand Junction. Buck answered the call.

"Taylor."

"Hi Buck, it's Paul Webber."

Paul had just recently joined CBI after spending time with the Dallas Police Department. He was assigned to the Grand Junction office, but Buck had not had the opportunity to work with him yet.

"Hey, Paul. What can I do for you?"

"The Director asked me to do a background check on one James Robert Galvin, formerly of Lake County Colorado. I just finished, and I am not sure if this is the same guy you are looking for."

Paul explained that there is no current record of a James Robert Galvin. No driver's license, no credit cards or bank accounts. Nothing. He did find a death certificate for Amanda Galvin, twenty-seven and Sandra Galvin, seven years old, both at the same address and both died in nineteen ninety-seven. Cause of death is listed as homicide on both.

"I also found a death certificate on file in Lake County for a

James Robert Galvin, forty-three, for later that same year. Cause of death is listed as suicide."

Buck stopped walking and asked Paul to repeat what he had just said, which he did.

"Paul, the wife and daughter supposedly died of a rare form of brain cancer. Are you sure you have the right family?"

"That was my concern, so I double checked and pulled their autopsies. Both the mother and the little girl did have similar forms of brain cancer, but that wasn't what killed them. I sent a request to Lake County but haven't heard back yet. This is really confusing."

"Paul keep looking into their backgrounds. I need to make a call. I will get back to you."

Buck hung up and looked in his contact list. He found the number he wanted and dialed. The phone was answered on the second ring.

"Sheriff Whitmore, how may I help you?"

"Tom, it's Buck Taylor. How are you?"

"Well fuck, Buck, this is a surprise. I'm doing great, how about you? You hanging in there alright?"

Tom Whitmore had been a deputy in Lake County back in the late nineties. Today he is the Sheriff of Lake County and has been since two thousand two. Buck figured if anyone could shed some light on this, it would be Tom. Buck explained what he was looking for and Tom responded in almost a reverent tone.

"Everyone here remembers that day. Amanda Galvin taught second and third grade at the county elementary school. She was really popular. A couple of months before she died, the family announced that she would be leaving the school. It seems both she and her six-year-old daughter developed a rare form of brain cancer.
"

"I still remember the day we found them. It was one cold ass January morning, and Amanda missed her doctor's appointment. The doctor asked us to do a welfare check because they weren't answering the phone and Freddie Jameson and I drove out to their ranch to see what was up. We pulled into the yard, and it looked like the place was abandoned. There was no smoke coming from the chimney, and the windows were frosted over. We drew our weapons and pushed open the front door. It was unlocked just like always."

"We found Amanda in her bed under a couple quilts and blankets like she was trying to stay warm. At first, we thought maybe the heat went out, but then we noticed the blood stain on the pillow. She had been shot behind her right ear with a small caliber bullet."

"We searched the rest of the house and found Sandy in her room. She was also in bed and had almost the same wound. We didn't see any sign of Jim, so we called for forensics and put out an APB for James Robert Galvin. It was a sad day."

"Tom, we found a death certificate for James Galvin. What happened?"

"We got a call from one of their neighbors about four months later because she thought she saw a light moving around in the house. Thought it might be a ghost, so we responded. We found Jim hanging from the loft in the barn. He left a note on the kitchen table. I guess he couldn't stand to see them suffer anymore, so he shot them in their sleep and then covered them up to keep them warm. Can you believe that? He killed them but didn't want them to get cold. Weird, huh? Anyway, it seems he hid out in the mountains for a couple months and then couldn't live with what he'd done so he went back to the ranch, wrote the note and hanged himself. We found him with one of Sandy's stuffed animals in his hand."

"Tom, any chance this was foul play made to look like a suicide?"

"Nah. The State Troopers did a good job investigating, and your people even helped with the forensics. It was just what it looked like. Why are you interested?"

Buck explained what he and Bax had been involved with over the past couple days and Tom listened quietly. He told Tom about the guy that Bax had met who introduced himself as James Robert Galvin. Other information they had gathered indicated that his wife and daughter had gotten cancer from bad water on their farm.

"Well Buck, either that's the damnedest coincidence with the names or someone's pulling your leg. I can assure you. He's been dead since ninety-seven."

Buck asked Tom if there were any incidents in the area involving chemical-tainted water. Tom told him that back around the same time, some of the county residents were complaining about a fracking company that supposedly polluted their wells, but it was never proven, and he hadn't heard a word since.

Buck thanked Tom and hung up. He would fill Bax in when she got to Meeker.

Chapter Fifty-Four

Jack Muldoon stood on the front porch of his house in Buford and looked toward the east. All day long the flames had gotten closer and closer, and they could now actually see the tips of the flames above the treetops on the other side of Route 8. The long procession of cars evacuating the area and heading toward Meeker had slowed to almost nothing, and all they saw now were fire engines and emergency vehicles passing on the road.

The people of the town had been watering the lawns and watering down their houses for most of the day. When the wind kicked up again, a couple small spot fires started in the grass around town. The residents were able to put them out before they spread too far. He set up a fire watch, as night approached.

Just before dark, another deputy came by and told them they needed to get out, but his security team ran him off just like the last one. Some of the residents were starting to make noise about leaving, but Muldoon assured them that they were perfectly safe. They had the underground bunker, and if they all worked together, they would prevail. He was not giving in to a government plot to take over his town. Besides, they still had shipments to receive and send out. About an hour before, he had wondered why the delivery company hadn't come out to pick up the next load of boxes. He was hoping that the government wasn't getting wise to his program.

Margaret Windsong stepped out on the porch wearing a surgical mask against the smoke.

"Jack you need to come in, the smoke is going to kill you."

Jack told her he was fine and that he needed to make the rounds of the town to make sure all was in order. He stepped off the porch, hopped onto his ATV and roared off toward the back of the town.

He swung by the warehouse to make sure the night shift was processing and packaging orders. He found out that several of the team were not at their stations. His intention was to drive over to their houses and, if need be, drag them to work. As he sat back on his ATV, he noticed several shadows heading towards the back gate. He couldn't believe that his people would abandon him. He fired up the ATV and roared towards the back gate, screaming orders into his headset for his security team as he went. By the time he got to the back gate the damage was done and whoever had been trying to get away had managed to do just that.

He was tempted to drag everyone out of the bunker and their houses and find out who was gone. "Ungrateful SOBs," he thought to himself. He was going to make them rich, and they gave it all up because they couldn't stand a little smoke.

He turned his ATV around and headed back to town. The wind had died down a little, and the air was heavy with mist. Not a full-fledged rain, more like a fog, but hell, any moisture was a good thing if it knocked the smoke down. He had orders to get out, and the smoke was making that extremely difficult.

His security chief pulled up next to him, and Muldoon jumped his ass for not having a man stationed at the back gate. The chief promised to take care of it right away and roared off toward the front entrance. He would send one of those guys to the back entrance to secure it.

Since there were no other spot fires in the town, Muldoon headed for home. He needed a good stiff drink to clear the smoke out of his throat. As he sat there his thoughts turned to the Asian Fed who had infiltrated their midst. He wondered, again, how much information Elliot Beech had passed on to the agent. He wished he hadn't been so quick to put an end to Beech's life. He really wanted to know what the Feds knew. He hated looking over his shoulders.

Chapter Fifty-Five

Buck pulled into the parking lot at the Sheriff's office, grabbed his backpack and raced up the stairs. He presented his ID to the deputy on duty at the front desk and was buzzed in. The Sheriff was just walking out of his office with a coffee cup in his hand when he spotted Buck coming down the hallway.

Buck stopped and caught his breath. "Caleb, we may be looking at this all wrong. Bax is on her way down so if you have time, I'd like to run through this again?"

"I have a little time, but I need to head out to the fire command center. Damn thing blew up again. Let me get a refill, and I will meet you in the conference room."

Buck walked into the conference room, dropped his backpack on the table and grabbed a Coke out of the refrigerator. He walked back to the table and pulled the file that Earp had just given him out of the front pocket. He also pulled out the letter and package Jimmy Kwon had put together. He was spreading the papers out on the table when his phone rang.

Buck answered. "Jess. Did they find the tapes?"

"Jeez Buck. I was at least hoping for a hello. Yes, they found the tapes just where Jimmy Kwon said they would be."

Jess went on to explain that Jimmy's office just emailed the audio files to her and she was calling to let him know that they were also on his computer.

"Did you listen to them?" he asked.

"Yes. Right after I sent them to you. Jimmy was definitely working for Mark Richards. The first tape is mostly Richards ranting and raving about the drug operation, and how if his clients found out they would never come to his lodge."

She told him that Richards offered Jimmy one million dollars to put together an investigation package on Jack Muldoon. Richards was going to use it if Muldoon refused to cooperate and move his operation. He mentioned at one point on the tape that even though it was his money that set the whole thing up, he didn't have any of the business records they would need to prosecute Muldoon, and he wanted Jimmy to provide that stuff.

Buck was pulling out his laptop when the Sheriff walked into the conference room with a full cup of coffee. Buck fired up his laptop and opened the email from Jess. He clicked on the attached audio files.

The first tape was exactly what she said it was, so Buck clicked off it and played the next tape. This time it was Jimmy talking to Steven Fletcher. At one point, Jimmy asked why Richards wanted to crush this man so badly. The lawyer responded that Richards was concerned about the possibility of his lodge clients finding out that he was involved with illegal prescription drugs. He figured if he could get rid of Muldoon, then he could give the business to his wife to run and she could take the whole thing to California. She hated living in Colorado anyway and this way he killed two birds with one stone. Get rid of Muldoon and get rid of his wife as well.

The second tape was just more planning and the lawyer

figuring out a timeline to send the information on Muldoon to the authorities. They wanted to move quickly once Jimmy's investigation was complete. The lodge was set to open soon.

Buck turned off the laptop and sat back in his chair. He still had Jess on speaker, and the Sheriff was seated next to him, scratching his head.

"I will never understand rich people I guess," said the Sheriff. "A million bucks to run an investigation that we could have run for free and all to keep a lodge that was miles away from getting tainted by the town nearby that none of his guests would have even cared about. How weird is that?"

"Yeah and to get rid of his wife," said Jess over the phone. "And it led to the death of a DEA agent, and even if he went rogue, he did it with the right intentions. I want these fuckers!"

Buck had to agree. This was a little bizarre, especially since he now knew that Mrs. Richards was planning to destroy her husband and had been for quite some time.

"Maybe she wanted more than just the drug business. Maybe she wanted it all."

Buck and the Sheriff turned to see Bax standing in the doorway. She stepped into the room, dropped her backpack on the table and pulled up a seat.

Jess's voice came over the phone. "Hey, Bax. You might be right. What do we know about the wife?"

Buck slid the file from Earp over to Bax. He filled them in on the conversation he had with Earp and that Earp was confident that the wife was behind a lot of the problems the company had encountered lately and that she might be working with her husband's lawyer to bring down her husband.

"A woman scorned," said Jess. "And one with access to a lot of money. That's a bad combination."

Buck posed a question that just occurred to him. "Could she bring her husband down without destroying the hedge fund? That was where the big money was."

Bax was the first to respond. "We only know of two shady businesses that Mark Richards is running under the hedge fund umbrella. Suppose he has a dozen businesses like this that are all self-sustaining. His wife would have more money than she could ever use, several times over, even without the hedge fund."

Everyone thought this made a good bit of sense, but it was still all speculation. All they had on the wife was a gut feeling from a private detective. Right now, they needed to deal in what they did know. Buck slid the package from Jimmy Kwon over to the Sheriff and Bax slid closer, so they could both look at it together. Buck explained what was in the package so that Jess could hear.

When he was finished, Jess suggested that the next step was to arrest this Muldoon character. They all agreed. Buck told them he would walk the package over to the District Attorney's office and see what they thought.

"Buck," said Jess. "I haven't gotten approval to run an investigation on this town, but if you are ready to move, you let me know. I have six agents and a helicopter ready to go."

Buck thanked her and clicked off his phone. Bax pulled together the files and stood up. Buck picked up his backpack, and they headed out the door.

Chapter Fifty-Six

On the walk over to the District Attorney's office, Buck told Bax about the information he had gotten from Paul Webber and Tom Whitmore. Bax stopped and looked at him.

"What the fuck, Buck. I didn't get shot at by a ghost. That guy was flesh and bones. What the hell is going on?"

"I'm not sure Bax. All I can tell you is that Tom Whitmore was the first officer on the scene and he personally knew the victims. If he says that James Galvin is dead, then you can bet your last dollar that the guy is dead."

"Sounds like we have an imposter on our hands. It also drives me mad that we haven't had any sightings of his car, anywhere."

"Bax this whole case is driving me nuts. Just when something starts to make sense, a new fact pops up that changes everything. I am having trouble keeping up. Just for shits and giggles, I would like to arrest someone. Let's see if the attorney can't help us with that."

Buck and Bax spent the next hour sitting with the Rio Blanco District Attorney, Silvia Garcia, reviewing all the information that they had collected from Jimmy Kwon's RV and also from the package he left at the RV park. Silvia looked through every picture and every document. Buck had worked with other attorneys who were careful, but Silvia was cautious to the extreme. She made sure every T was crossed, and every I was dotted, and she had Bax rewrite the request for the warrant three times before she was comfortable. When they were finally finished, Silvia sat back in her chair and looked at Buck and Bax.

"Ok guys. I feel good about what we have here. This guy Kwon was a hell of an investigator. Let's call the judge and see if he is in."

Silvia picked up her desk phone and dialed the number for County Court Judge Earl Flagg. The judge was just sitting down to dinner, but Silvia was very persuasive, and the judge finally relented and told her to send the two officers over with the evidence, and he would look at it. She thanked the judge and hung up.

She picked up her pen and wrote the judge's address on a slip of paper and handed it to Buck.

"Good luck guys, and be careful, ok?"

Buck thanked her, and they grabbed their pile of evidence, their backpacks, and the warrant application and headed out the door. They loaded everything into Buck's car and Buck pulled up the address on his phone. The judge lived a couple blocks away, so they pulled out of the parking lot and headed north.

Three blocks later they pulled up in front of a beautiful old Victorian style home. Buck admired the craftsmanship as they parked and walked up the walk. Mrs. Flagg met them at the door and escorted them to her husband's office.

Judge Flagg was a lot younger than they envisioned when they saw the house. With dark brown hair and a brown mustache, the judge was very distinguished looking. He looked up from the papers on his desk.

"Good evening agents, why don't you show me what you have."

Bax handed the judge the application and Buck pulled out the files and laid them on his desk. Just like with Silvia, the judge reviewed every piece of evidence. He asked a lot of questions. When they were finished, he picked up the pen from his desk and signed the warrant.

He handed the warrant back to Bax and said, "Agents get these people out of my county and be careful."

They thanked the judge and left his house. They needed to coordinate an arrest, one that was not going to be easy since the person being arrested did not believe that anyone had jurisdiction over him.

Buck pulled out his phone and called the Director.

"Hey Buck. What have you got?"

Buck told the Director about the warrant and filled him in on his meeting with Earp and with the box that Jimmy Kwon had left. He ran through the approach he wanted to take with arresting Jack Muldoon, and the Director offered a couple suggestions. He also told him about the odd situation with James Galvin.

"So, this guy has been dead since ninety-seven. Does he have any family that we know of who could be using his name? He'd be what, about sixty-three now. I will call Paul Webber and have him start looking."

The Director told Buck to call if he needed any help and hung up and Buck felt a little foolish. They had been so busy he hadn't gotten back to Paul, so he never had a chance to ask the same question. Bax had heard the conversation and nodded.

"Makes sense, Buck. Maybe he had another kid who would

be somewhere in his forties. The guy I spoke with appeared to be closer to sixty, but he might have been less."

Buck pulled into the parking lot, and they grabbed their evidence and the warrant. Time to do some real police work.

Chapter Fifty-Seven

Buck was sitting in the conference room working his phone. He wanted to handle the arrest quietly, but the more he thought about it, the more he wished he had a platoon of Army Rangers available. He wanted to start by just knocking on the front door, but he also wanted that platoon of Rangers waiting in the wings in case the shit hit the fan. He knew he couldn't get Rangers, but he could get the next best thing.

Buck called Sheriff Trujillo. Gil, besides being the Sheriff of Moffat County also ran the Northwest Colorado Interagency SWAT team. Because most of the police agencies in the northwestern part of the state were relatively small, they had banded together several years ago to create a mutual aid emergency response unit. Buck knew a lot of the officers and deputies who made up the SWAT team and had the utmost respect for them.

"Hey Buck, what's going on?"

"Hey, Gil. I need you to call out the SWAT team first thing in the morning."

He went on the explain his plan for the arrest of Jack Muldoon and that he wanted to have the SWAT team available as back up if needed. Gil questioned Buck's approach.

"Sounds like you might be better off if we hit them hard and fast."

"I agree, but I don't want to get into a shootout, and we don't know Muldoon's state of mind. He might be a crazy survivalist, or he might still be the battle-hardened soldier the file says he is. We will go in easy at first."

"Whatever you need Buck. Let me know at dawn where you want us, and we will be there."

Buck thanked Gil and dialed Jess Gonzales who answered right away.

"Damn Jess are you ever away from your phone?"

"You know me better than that. What's up?"

Buck explained what he needed, and Jess was eager to help out. She knew her team would be happy to get this Muldoon guy. She only hoped Buck would give her a few minutes alone with him so she could get to the bottom of Jimmy Kwon's death. Of course, she knew Buck would never go along with that idea, but a girl could dream.

Buck thanked her and hung up.

Bax sat at the other end of the table and was coordinating the forensics team. She wanted them ready to go as soon as she called them after the arrest.

Buck looked at his watch and realized they had missed dinner, so he told Bax to wrap up and they headed out the door for the short drive to the Cozy Up.

They walked in the front door and, as always, Buck noticed several male heads turn when Bax walked in and just like always, most of them turned back around when she took off her jacket and they could see the gun and badge on her belt. Bax had that effect on men, and Buck often wondered why some lucky guy hadn't taken her for his own or vise-a-versa. He wasn't the kind of man who thought a woman could only be whole if she was married, but as far as he could tell, Bax was a hell of a catch.

Sam walked around the bar and gave Buck a big hug and Buck introduced her to Bax. The two hit it off right away, and after a few minutes they were talking and laughing like they had known each other for years. Buck just sat back and listened since he was the butt of most of the conversation.

Sam left to put in their order, and a few minutes later a waitress returned with a Coke for Buck and a draft beer for Bax. They sat and looked around the bar which was crowded with locals and tourists alike. The volume on the jukebox was up, and it made it difficult to talk, so they just sat there and watched the people.

Most of the conversations seemed to revolve around the smoke in the air and the fire in the forest. Buck heard someone mention that the fire was now up to four thousand acres and that there was almost a thousand firefighters on the line. Buck thought about Cassie, which made him think about his son Jason. He called Jason when he had first gone out to the lodge to see if he could get a set of blueprints, but Jason never called him back. It wasn't unusual for Jason not to call. Where Buck was very close to Cassie and David, Jason seemed to gravitate towards Lucy, and he took it really hard when she died. He made a mental note to call him later.

Dinner arrived, and Bax dug into her steak and salad like she hadn't eaten in a month. She looked over at Buck.

"Sam seems really nice. Have you known her long?"

Buck nodded, "About twenty years, I guess."

"She's really gorgeous. Are you sleeping with her?"

If Buck wore dentures, he would have swallowed his teeth.

Instead, he felt his face get red, and he started to sweat. Bax smiled at him and laughed.

"Shit Bax. What kind of question is that?"

"You can see by the way she looks at you that you mean something to her. I think you make a nice-looking couple."

Buck was getting redder in the face when his phone rang. He looked at the number and excused himself for a minute so he could go outside to hear.

"Hey, Caleb. What's up?

"Hey, Buck. If you want to hit Buford tomorrow morning and pick up Muldoon, you might want to do it early. Pat says they are expecting strong winds to hit around nine and he is afraid it might jump Route 8. If it does, Buford is going to burn, and those idiots will not evacuate."

Pat took the phone from the Sheriff. "Seriously Buck. If the winds hit like we expect, and the rain doesn't come tonight, I'm afraid we might get overrun. I've got five hundred firefighters converging on the highway in front of Buford right now, and we are going to go like the hammers of hell to push back while we have the chance."

"Pat is there anything I can do to help?"

"You don't happen to have a couple bulldozers in your back pocket? State's resources are spread pretty thin with all the fires, and heavy equipment is just not available so we will do it the old-fashioned way."

Pat hung up, and Buck started to walk back into the bar when he had a thought. He speed dialed a number on his phone and waited.

"Hi, Buck. How are you holding up?"

"Hey, Rachel. I'm doing good. Is Hardy around?"

Buck waited while Rachel went to find Hardy. He knew

what he was going to ask was a little out of line, but this was important.

"Hiya, Buck. What's up? Calling to warn me that there is a warrant for my arrest in Moffat County? I already know that."

"I'm sorry Hardy. I have been so busy today I didn't know. Are you ok?"

"Yeah," said Hardy. "So, if that's not it, what can I do for you?"

"This may be a hard ask, but do you still have that road crew working outside White River City?"

Hardy said he did and asked why. Buck told him what he wanted, and he heard silence on the other end of the line.

"You got some balls, brother. I will give you that."

Buck waited quietly. He knew the old Hardy would never refuse him, but with all that was going on, he wouldn't blame him if he did.

"When do you need them?" Hardy finally asked.

"Now," Buck replied.

"Fuck, Buck. Let me make some calls."

Hardy hung up, and Buck walked back into the bar to finish his dinner. He hoped Hardy would come through.

Chapter Fifty-Eight

Sunrise broke smoky, cold and damp but the fire was still raging as Buck pulled over on the side of the road behind two SWAT vehicles. He wished they had time to scout out the area, but he was hoping that with all the noise and confusion from the fire, they might catch Muldoon's people asleep at the switch. That's why he wanted to try the soft approach first.

He slid out of his car and opened the back hatch, pulled his ballistic vest out of the back and slipped it over his shoulders. He then checked the pistol on his hip, took his ankle holster out of the locked gun safe that was welded to the frame of the car and strapped it around his right ankle. He put his CBI nylon windbreaker on over the vest and put on his CBI cap.

Sheriff Trujillo had assembled his team, and they were looking at Google Earth on his laptop. They found a couple ways to surround the town without being seen, and he was giving his team their assignments. Buck walked up and looked over the map.

"What do you think, Gil? Can we do this without getting anybody killed?"

"I think we can. My biggest worry is that fire. It's getting really close to the road. If the firefighters can hold it back, we might have a chance."

Just then Bax pulled in behind Buck and walked up to the group. She looked like she and Buck shopped at the same store. She was ready for action.

"Are we ready?" Buck asked.

"Yeah. What about the DEA? Are they ready?"

Buck had worked out the details with Jess while it was still dark out. They had re-conned the town and determined that one of the two big buildings was most likely the warehouse. The other building she wasn't sure about, so she positioned her guys between the two. The original plan was for them to chopper in and act as a diversion. The smoke from the fire put an end to that idea, so they had come up with plan B.

Buck picked up his radio. "Jess. You guys ready?"

"Roger," came the response.

Buck looked at Bax. "You ready?"

"Let's go get him," she responded.

Buck shook hands with Sheriff Trujillo, and they headed for his car. Buck slid into his seat, pulled his pistol out of his holster and laid it on the seat between his legs. Bax pulled hers and held it down alongside the passenger seat. She held the arrest warrant in her hand.

Buck pulled off the shoulder and headed for the road into Buford. As he turned up the gravel road, he spotted the two sentries standing by the gate with their assault rifles at the ready. Buck pulled up to the gate and rolled down his window. He put his hand on the pistol on the seat.

"What do you want, cop? We told you guys before we ain't leaving, so back the fuck up and leave."

Buck studied the man holding the assault rifle. He waved him over to the car. The guy was hesitant at first, then he grew a pair and walked over.

Buck whispered. "We have a warrant to arrest Jack Muldoon."

The guy looked at him. His partner asked him what he said. He shrugged his shoulders and stepped closer to the window and leaned in, just a shade too close. Buck pushed his arm out the window and grabbed the strap on the assault rifle and pulled the guy towards the window, at the same time he slid his pistol under the man's chin and told him not to move. His partner started to react, but two black-clad SWAT officers flew around the guard shack and dropped him to the ground.

Buck held his prisoner until the SWAT officers had flexi-cuffed his partner and then grabbed the guy Buck held and forced him to the ground. He was just as quickly incapacitated.

The sun, trying to shine through the smoke and the clouds, was just clearing the trees as the SWAT officers opened the gate and Buck pulled through. He looked in his rear-view mirror and saw the SWAT vehicles turn up the road. He keyed his mic and announced that the guards were down, and they were moving on the house. Buck drove slowly down the main street and pulled to a stop in front of what they had determined was the largest house. According to the map Jimmy Kwon had made notes on, this house belonged to Jack "Fighting Red" Muldoon. Several members of the SWAT team raced down the street and moved behind the house.

Buck and Bax opened their doors and slid out of their seats. Buck could feel the wind starting to pick up. They walked up the walk, onto the front porch and took up positions on either side of the door. Buck knocked, softly, like a neighbor might if she was coming to borrow some sugar. They waited and then heard footsteps approaching the door.

The person on the other side opened the door without ever looking out the window. It was nice to see that survivalists were able to trust each other enough to think no one would bother them. As the door unlatched, Buck slammed his full weight into it, and the woman fell to the floor and screamed.

"Jack!"

Buck stepped over her and saw the blood streaming down her face from where the door hit her in the nose. Bax made fast work of rolling the woman over and cuffing her arms behind her back. She then put a piece of duct tape over her mouth.

"Jack Muldoon!" Buck yelled. "We have a warrant for your arrest."

They both moved cautiously with their guns pointed ahead of them. Just as Buck was thinking how quiet the house was they heard the SWAT team smash in the back door.

"POLICE! WE HAVE A WARRANT!" Came multiple yells as the SWAT team fanned out across the ground floor.

Buck pointed towards the woman on the ground, and the SWAT officers nodded. He pointed up the stairs and following right on each other backs, the three team members head up the stairs. Buck moved toward the living room which was off to the side of the entryway.

The SWAT team yelled that the upstairs was clear and started back down the stairs as a loud boom sounded behind a closed door, and a huge ragged hole appeared in the door. The first SWAT officer on the stairs took a couple pieces of buckshot to his left arm, but he was able to return fire with his assault rifle.

Buck moved around from the living room to the side of the

door that was now destroyed and slammed his foot into it. The door pretty much fell off its hinges. The second blast from a shotgun took out a chunk of the door frame to Buck's left, but he dove back just in time to avoid getting peppered with buckshot.

The SWAT team was now standing on the other side, and one of them lobbed a flashbang down the stairs, which exploded in a loud, blinding flash of light. When the sounds from the flashbang cleared, they heard a door slam in the basement. Buck, with his gun pointing forward and his flashlight now in his other hand, peeked around the door jamb.

Not seeing anyone at the bottom of the stairs he slowly advanced down the stairs followed by the SWAT team. Buck panned his light around the basement and was amazed at the number of weapons that were stored in racks along the walls. This guy could have outfitted a small army. That was when he spotted the steel door that was built into the wall.

"He's got a bunker!" shouted Buck.

The SWAT team leader stepped up to the door and ran his hand over it and banged on it with the end of his Mag-Lite. He turned to Buck.

"I doubt we can blow it. We can try."

Just then Buck heard Bax call out. He told one of the SWAT officers to keep an eye on the bunker door, and he raced up the stairs.

Chapter Fifty-Nine

Bax came running up the front steps and onto the porch just as Buck came out the front door.

"The wind just blew up, and the fire is crossing the road." She pointed over her shoulder.

Buck stood there almost stunned. What just a little bit ago had been a wall of trees on the other side of Route 8 was now a wall of flames. Spot fires were popping up on their side of the road. The wind was howling, and they could feel the heat as the wind, and the fire acted like a blast furnace.

Buck looked around and saw several of the black-clad security guys lying on the ground with their hands bound. A couple of people stood on the street and seemed unsure of what was happening. Buck told Bax to evacuate everyone as fast as possible. A gust of wind blew up and as Buck watched the roof of one of the houses at the outer edge of the town exploded in fire.

He keyed his Mic. "Gil, we need firefighters and evac, now!" He ran down the stairs before Bax could say a word and yelled for her to uncuff all the security people and get them all shovels

Bax spotted Sheriff Trujillo racing up the street.

"Buck wants me to cut the security guys loose and get them

shovels." She looked at the Sheriff with doubt in her eyes. She very rarely questioned anything Buck asked her, but these guys were under arrest, and she was worried about releasing them.

The Sheriff looked over his shoulder. Flames had blown across Route 8 and were now racing across the field towards the town. Bax could see firefighters running from the flames and heading towards them. She knew this did not look good.

"Cut them loose Bax. We are going to need everyone we can get to fight this monster."

Bax yelled over to the SWAT officer watching the guards and to cut them loose and get them on the fire line.

Sheriff Trujillo keyed his mic. "Caleb. The fire has crossed the highway. We need everything you've got!"

"Hang in there Gil," came the reply. "We are sending everyone we can."

The Sheriff looked around. All eyes were on him. The noise from the firestorm sounded like a jet engine, and he could feel the heat on his face.

He started barking orders at the top of his voice. "Grab all the hoses you can find and start hosing down the grass between here and the road. If you don't have a hose, grab a shovel or a rake."

He grabbed one of the firefighters.

"You see that fence line?"

The firefighter nodded. "We need a fire break along that fence line, and we don't have a lot of time to get it done. Get everyone you can and start digging and clearing the brush. Also, get some of your guys and have them start putting out spot fires as fast as they can. Now move!"

"What about the people in the bunker?" someone shouted from the street.

Bax looked at the Sheriff and at the civilians gathering around, who looked terrified. She grabbed a woman standing there with a shovel.

"What bunker?"

"The bunker under the warehouse. Muldoon locked the people who weren't working in the bunker after a couple people fled the compound last night. They won't be able to breathe, and they will cook to death in there. You have to help them!" She ran off to join the others on the fire line.

The Sheriff called over three of his guys. "Get into that building, find that bunker and get those people out!"

"What about Buck?" shouted Bax.

"Can't worry about him now. We have work to do." He handed her a shovel one of his guys found in a tool shed behind the house. Bax took the shovel and headed for the fire line.

She glanced across the field and saw Buck leading about a dozen firefighters toward the house that was burning. Buck was waving his hands and pointing as they ran and then he did something she will never understand. She watched him kick open the door to the burning house and rush inside followed by two firefighters. Her heart skipped a beat at that moment, and she wondered if she would ever see him again.

Suddenly, the two firefighters rushed out of the burning building dragging a woman behind them. "Where was Buck?" She was about to race towards the building when Buck ran out of the building carrying a dog in his arms. He fell to the ground coughing and laid the dog down. The last thing she saw before she raced off to join the fight was Buck getting licked by the dog.

The Sheriff looked towards the fence line. There were hundreds of people scraping at the ground to get rid of the vegetation. Both firefighters and civilians standing shoulder to shoulder. They were making a valiant effort, but as he looked across the field, he knew they would need a miracle to pull this off. He didn't have a plan B.

The first helicopters appeared over the tree line and started dumping their buckets of water on the fire that had crossed the road and was racing towards the town. As the helicopters left to pick up more water, several tanker planes flew over and dumped both water and fire retardant on the field between the town and the road.

The sound of an approaching airplane caused everyone to stop and look as the huge Boeing 747 flew past the town to the south, made a steep left turn to run parallel to the road and dropped a massive amount of water along the edge of the field. Bax was amazed by the accuracy and the daring of the pilots. She couldn't be sure, but she figured the plane was no more than two hundred feet off the ground.

The sound of the water hitting the ground reminded her of a flash flood she and her father had gotten caught in while hiking in the Canyonlands in Utah. She remembered the sound being deafening, and they had been barely able to climb to a ledge almost forty feet above the slot they were hiking in. They spent two days sitting on that ledge until the water receded enough that they could walk out.

What scared Bax the most at this moment was the silence after the planes and helicopter left the area. The only sound was the fire, and she realized that she liked the sound of the aircraft a whole lot more.

The Sheriff was standing next to Bax clearing vegetation when he stopped and looked up. Bax stopped too. The fire line was getting wider, but the flames were getting closer. They had no idea how long they had been at it, but they knew it had been several hours and everyone around them look exhausted, but they kept fighting. The air drops were helping but what everyone there that day wanted more than anything was rain.

Bax had seen Buck several times leading his intrepid band of firefighters from hot spot to hot spot working along the edges of the fire. They were making a valiant effort to stay ahead of the flames, but she wasn't sure they were winning.

"Did you hear that?" the Sheriff asked her. "Sounds like a tank."

Bax heard it too, but she didn't know what it was or where it was coming from. All she knew was that it was getting louder. Several people along the fire line stopped to listen to the clanking metal sound.

Suddenly, a cheer rose up and traveled along the fire line. Out of the smoke came three huge bright yellow bulldozers, followed by a couple front-end loaders and three water trucks. The bulldozers rolled up towards the fence line pushing huge piles of dirt as they went. The water trucks followed behind, spraying the ground that was just cleared and then started working their way towards the town. And leading the fight, sitting atop the first bulldozer, was Hardy Braxton.

The Sheriff tapped her on the shoulder and smiled. "Did you bring the arrest warrant? Looks like Mr. Braxton is coming to us." He let out a huge belly laugh and went back to shoveling.

Just then Bax pointed toward the north, and the Sheriff stopped and followed her gaze. Coming out of the smoke across the field, with what looked like a hundred firefighters was Buck. He looked like a Civil War general leading the charge. The firefighters veered off and headed for the fire line, and Buck ran up to Bax and the Sheriff. He was filthy from his head to his toes, and he was sweating up a storm. "I found a few guys to help," he said. "Pat is throwing everything he has at this spot right now."

A tanker plane flew over and dumped a load of retardant along the front edge of the fire line followed immediately by three helicopters. The fight was definitely on, and Pat was pushing his crews for a knockout.

It was amazing because it looked like everyone got a second wind when the dozers and the new firefighters showed up and now they were all working twice as hard to clear debris and vegetation. Many people raced off to help the firefighters put out spot fires, and a bunch more were hosing down the buildings.

Chapter Sixty

Bax had no idea how much time had passed, but for the first time, as she looked around, she felt like maybe they were winning. The winds had started to die down about an hour ago, and the efforts of everyone on the line seemed to be paying off. She had stopped to take a drink of water from a water bottle someone had thrown to her, and she looked around for Buck, who was nowhere to be found.

The Sheriff looked towards the warehouse, and his SWAT team appeared at the door followed by about a dozen men, women and children, many of whom were coughing and trying to breathe. The Sheriff waved to his men. Just then Jess Gonzales appeared at his side. He had no idea where she even came from. Her face was covered in soot.

"We've secured the warehouse as best we can. They have a massive amount of counterfeit prescription drugs here. We also put all the computers and file cabinets we could find into a room in the back of the warehouse. Hopefully, it will protect them from the fire.

"What happened to you guys? We haven't seen you all day," Bax asked as she walked up.

"Buck asked us to secure the warehouse and protect the evidence. The back wall caught on fire, but we were able to get it out before it spread. We needed to protect the evidence, but we ended up helping your guys get a bunch of people out of a bunker. The day just got worse from there."

She looked at Bax. "Buck blew past us on an ATV a few minutes ago. Last we saw him he was headed for the tree line and it looked like he was following someone on another ATV. What's going on?"

Bax keyed her mic. "Buck, can you hear me?"

A very garbled message came back over the radio. All she was able to make out was "Muldoon" and "ATV." She asked him to repeat what he said, but she got nothing else. She looked at the Sheriff and then at Jess.

"Do you think Muldoon had a back way out of his Bunker?" the Sheriff asked. "My guy reported in a little while back that the door was still closed in the basement. Shit."

Just then, the sky opened up, and the rain came pouring down. Everyone on the fire line stopped and raised their faces towards the sky. The rain felt good, and the Sheriff just stood there and let the rain wash over him. He had said they needed a miracle to survive this, and he got two. The bulldozers that came out of nowhere and now the rain. He turned around to talk to Jess and Bax, but they were nowhere to be seen. He looked across the field and spotted two ATVs racing off toward the west. "I wish I had those two women on my team," he said to no one in particular.

He was worried about Buck, so he keyed his mic and put out a call for his guys to meet on him. He was heading toward one of the SWAT vehicles when he spotted an SUV coming across the field. He raised his hand to keep the rain out of eyes so he could see who it was.

Sheriff McCabe came bouncing across the field in his

department SUV. He had skirted around the fire and come in from the northwest. He pulled to a stop and spotted Sheriff Trujillo. He looked around at what looked like a war zone. He could not believe the number of people on the line still trying to push the fire back. The rain was making their jobs a lot easier.

"I can't believe you guys survived that firestorm! Absolutely incredible!" He saw the SWAT guys running towards them from all different directions.

"What's going on?" he asked.

"Looks like Muldoon got away and Buck is in pursuit on an ATV. Bax and Jess Gonzales lit out after him," replied Sheriff Trujillo. "I was about to send my guys after them."

"Ok, Gil. You and a couple of your guys head out, and I will keep an eye on things here."

Sheriff Trujillo and three of his SWAT team members jumped into the closest SWAT vehicle and headed out across the field on what earlier was a dirt road but now was a small river. The truck fishtailed in the mud, but the driver got some traction and the forged ahead.

Sheriff McCabe now took over the firefighting efforts and continued where Sheriff Trujillo had let off, and he started moving civilians and firefighters around the town like pieces on a chess board. There were still hotspots flaring up around the town, but the rain-soaked grass and dirt were killing most of the embers as they flew.

He knew the fight was not over, but the fight had left a lot of the people on the line. All around the center of the town firefighters and civilians were taking a breather from the fight. No one was looking for shelter from the rain since it felt too good to pass up.

More firefighters were joining the fight as time wore on and he realized that almost the entire firefighting force was now in the town. The water and retardant drops were continuing unabated, and it seemed like everything and everybody were covered in an orange tint. The rain was helping people look human again.

Most of the fire was now contained to the other side of Route 8, and the Sheriff decided to risk bringing in some much-needed food and water. He called Pat on the radio and told him to open the north portion of the road from the command center to the town entrance, and he asked him to send in the supplies.

The small caravan of National Guard trucks pulled into the town about fifteen minutes later, and people started to line up. It reminded him of pictures he had seen of refugee camps. Everyone looked wiped out. He had been a part of many firefighting efforts in his role as Sheriff, but the work that these people did today was unlike anything he had ever seen before. They had saved this small town and a lot of ranches beyond it.

Chapter Sixty-One

Buck was working with the firefighters on one of the houses that caught fire when he spotted some movement in his peripheral vision. He turned and looked around. As he looked past Muldoon's house, he spotted someone running from the house to one of the two outbuildings that sat behind the house.

He squinted through the smoke to see who was running and he realized that it was the woman he had knocked down with the door when they entered the house to arrest Muldoon. He watched as she ducked behind the outbuilding.

"What the hell?" he thought.

He started walking up the street toward the house when a black ATV came roaring out from behind the outbuilding and headed west. The woman was sitting on the back of the ATV, but it was the driver he noticed. Well, actually it was the driver's red hair that he noticed.

Jack Muldoon and the woman were trying to get away in all the confusion. Buck dropped his shovel on the ground and raced towards the house. One of the security ATVs was parked by the walkway to the front door.

Buck looked around, trying to spot either Bax or the Sheriff, but with everyone crowded together working the fire line he couldn't locate them, so he ran up the street and jumped on the ATV.

Buck was an old hand at driving ATVs. He used to take the kids riding in the mountains behind Crested Butte ski area. There were several small streams, and lakes he used to love to fish and an ATV was the only way to get there. He turned the key, and the engine roared to life, so he kicked it into gear and headed after Muldoon.

By the time Buck cleared the town Muldoon was about a mile ahead, and the visibility was terrible. Buck was not wearing a helmet or goggles, and the ash in the smoke stung his eyes as he picked up speed. He could barely see the tree line, but he knew Muldoon had entered the forest, so he bore down on the throttle. The bouncing jarred his teeth, and he felt like his head was going to explode as he raced up the dirt trail.

The sky suddenly opened up, and the rain filled his vision. He was glad the rain was washing the dust out of his eyes, but now he had raindrops stinging his eyes and clouding his vision. He also noticed the trail was getting very slick, and he felt out of control as he raced towards the woods.

He heard his radio crackle and a muffled voice asked, "Buck, can you hear me?"

He keyed the mic that was clipped to his jacket, but the bouncing made it hard to speak. "Bax, Muldoon is trying to get away on an ATV. Need back up."

The ATV started to slip sideways on the slick mud, and he let go of the mic so he could grab the other handlebar. It took everything he had not to flip the ATV, but he pushed the throttle as far as it would go.

Suddenly, out of the smoke he saw the trees and just by sheer luck he stayed on the trail and flew into the forest. He could see Muldoon's tracks in the mud, and he knew he should back off the speed, but he needed to stop Muldoon.

About a half mile into the forest, Buck came around a corner and had to crank down hard on the brakes as the ATV spun sideways and slid in the mud, stopping at the edge of the gulley. He jumped off the ATV, wiped the dirt and mud out of his eyes, unsnapped the thumb break on his holster and pulled his pistol.

He pocketed the ATV key and stepped toward the gulley. The ATV Muldoon had been driving was smashed against the far bank of the gulley and had buried itself in the mud. The dry creek bed at the bottom of the gulley was beginning to fill with water. Buck scanned the area with his pistol and then slid down the slope into the water.

He knew as soon as he saw the position of her head that the woman who had been riding with Muldoon was dead. Her neck had obviously broken when the ATV hit the gulley and even though she appeared to be dead, Buck had learned a long time ago not to take anything for granted. He reached down and checked her neck for a pulse. The woman was definitely dead. Looking around, he noticed a small spot of blood on a rock. The rain was causing the blood to spread out and run off the rock into the now rushing water below.

Muldoon had obviously been hurt when he drove into the gulley. Buck had no way of knowing how bad, so keeping his pistol pointed ahead and using his left hand for leverage, he pulled himself up the bank and scanned the area. He could just make out footprints in the wet undergrowth, so cautiously, he moved forward.

He hadn't walked very far when Muldoon charged from behind a tree and slammed into him. The gun flew out of his hand, and they both tumbled into another gulley that was full of mud.

Buck had been hit hard while playing football in his youth, but this was a whole new experience. Muldoon, a seasoned combat veteran, had grabbed Buck's jacket as the tumbled and flipped Buck over his head as he fell. Buck landed hard on his back and gasped for air. The mud in the bottom of the gulley absorbed some of the pressure, but it still hurt like hell, and he knew he was in trouble.

Muldoon was on his feet and dove at Buck who was able to move just enough that Muldoon was only able to catch him with one of his arms. It helped that Muldoon couldn't get any traction in the mud and slid as he dove.

Still gasping for air, Buck grabbed Muldoon's arm and rolled over him, twisting his arm behind his back in a very unnatural position. Muldoon let out a yell and slammed his fist into the side of Buck's head. Buck saw stars, but he knew he was in the fight of his life, so he scrambled backwards up the side of the gulley and then launched, feet first, and hit Muldoon in the chest as he was starting to stand up.

Buck picked himself up off the ground and charged Muldoon again as he stood up. Muldoon hit the ground hard with Buck on top of him. He was able to get in a couple lucky shots that staggered Buck, but Buck was able to hang on and counter punch. They rolled around in the gulley and Muldoon pushed Buck off and tried to stand but slid in the mud.

By this time Buck had had enough. He was feeling dizzy, and he was afraid he might pass out. He needed to end this and fast. Muldoon, who had both height and the weight on Buck, was trying to stand up, and Buck knew if he did, this fight might be over. Buck dug deep and suddenly five months of holding back the anger of losing Lucy exploded out of Buck like a volcano. He jumped off the bank and in one swift move kicked Muldoon in the side of the head.

Muldoon flopped down in the mud and Buck attacked with everything he had. The fight had gone out of Muldoon who was now moving slowly, but Buck wasn't finished. He grabbed Muldoon by his collar, jerked his head up and pounded his face with his fist until his knuckles started to bleed. Blood poured out of Muldoon's nose and mouth, spraying all over Buck as the blows continued to find their mark. Somewhere during the beating Muldoon lot consciousness, but Buck wasn't finished yet. He had a lot more anger to get out of his system.

He reared his right hand back and just as he started to drive forward, something grabbed his arm.

"Buck, that's enough!"

He spun his head around and standing behind him soaking wet and covered in mud was Jess Gonzales. She let go of his arm and wrapped her arms around him.

"It's ok," she said in a soft, calming voice. "You got him."

Buck, looking half dazed, looked at Jess and then at Muldoon. He climbed off Muldoon's chest, fell back against the bank and looked up at Jess who had slid over to the opposite bank. He looked down at Muldoon and just stared for a minute. Dazed and bleeding he tried to stand up but had trouble keeping his balance, so Jess stood up, grabbed his arm and helped him up. He shook off the dizziness and wiped the mud and blood out of his eyes.

"Fuck, Buck. Looks like we missed a hell of a fight."

The voice came from Sheriff Trujillo who was standing on solid ground above Buck along with Bax and two of his SWAT officers. Buck just smiled.

Chapter Sixty-Two

Buck was able to walk under his own power back to the ATV, of course, Jess and Bax walked on either side of him, just in case. They were ok with him walking, but they drew the line at him driving the ATV back to the town. The Sheriff called for two of the ambulances that had been stationed at the fire command center, and then he and Bax walked back to where Muldoon was still lying, handcuffed and unconscious, guarded by one of the SWAT officers. With the rain coming down it was difficult to get good pictures, but Bax documented the scenes as best she could.

The light was beginning to fade as the EMTs carried the bodies of Margaret Windsong and Jack Muldoon out of the woods to the waiting ambulances. Windsong's body would be heading toward the forensic pathologist in Grand Junction, while Muldoon was heading to the small hospital in Meeker, accompanied by two SWAT officers.

Buck had been checked over by the EMT, who bandaged his right hand, cleaned up the cuts on his face and arms and told him he needed to rest. He told Buck to stop by the hospital and get his head checked since he more than likely had a concussion. Buck said he would, and then he downed a handful of ibuprofens and climbed into the front seat of the SWAT vehicle.

The SWAT vehicle headed back towards the town and Buck put his head back and closed his eyes. The bouncing, as they hit water-filled potholes on the trail, made the pain in his head unbearable. He had to grit his teeth after one pothole because he wanted to scream to make the pain stop. The driver, noting the look of anguish on Buck's face, slowed down and made an effort to miss as many potholes as he could. The rain made seeing difficult.

They had just passed the outer edge of the town when Buck's radio crackled. He opened his eyes and turned up the volume.

"Buck, come in."

He keyed his mic, "Go ahead, Caleb."

"Did you guys pass a concrete block building at the far end of the town?"

Buck said that they hadn't, and the Sheriff explained that one of the security guards was willing to make a deal in exchange for immunity. In good faith, he told him to get someone to look in the old pump house by the tree line.

Buck hated the idea of turning around and driving around looking for a pump house since his head was throbbing, but he told the Sheriff they would take a look, so he asked the driver to turn around and head back the way they came.

Now that the smoke had started to clear out of the air from the rain and the fact that the fire seemed to be on its last legs, the visibility had improved significantly. They made it back to the edge of the woods and then started driving northwards along the tree line. Bax, sitting in the back seat, was the first one to spot an old building in the distance, and she shouted over the engine noise for the driver to head towards it.

The driver stopped a couple yards away from the building, and everyone stepped out of the vehicle and looked around cautiously. They had no idea if this was some kind of ambush, so everyone had guns drawn as they approached the building.

Buck pointed towards the side of the building, and Sheriff Trujillo and one SWAT officer headed around to the back of the building. Buck and Bax took up positions on either side of the old rusted metal door. The building was not very large, maybe one hundred square feet with concrete block walls and a metal roof.

The Sheriff and the SWAT officer came back around the building and joined Buck and Bax at the door. They reported that there was no back door and no windows. Everyone tensed as Buck grabbed the doorknob and turned.

They knew it was going to be bad as Buck pushed the door open and they rushed in and fanned their guns around. The space was pitch black, but the smell was overwhelming. The smell of urine and the coppery smell of blood invaded their nostrils and mouths, but it was the smell of decomposition that was the worst. Buck, already queasy from the head blows and not having eaten anything all day, had to step back outside. Bax came out behind him and helped him lean over. He rested his hands on his knees and tried to breathe. She stood by him until the Sheriff and the SWAT officer stepped back outside and the SWAT officer vomited. The Sheriff looked a little green himself, but he was able to keep it inside.

"We have a body," he said. "Looks like it's been here a couple of days." He keyed his mic and called Sheriff McCabe and explained what they had found in the pump house.

Buck stood up, took a deep breath and pulled out his phone. "Buck Taylor, how's my favorite cop?" said Max Clinton as she answered her phone.

Buck told her he was doing good and then he explained what they found. He asked her to send the forensics team from Grand Junction back up. Bax would be waiting for them.

Max told him not to worry and then she ended the call just as always. "You're a good man Buck Taylor, and God will watch over you."

Bax, Sheriff Trujillo, and Buck got back in the SWAT vehicle, while the SWAT officer remained behind to secure the scene. They drove in silence back to the town.

The Sheriff came to a stop in front of Muldoon's house. It was still raining, but not as hard and it looked like the last rays of the sun were trying to break through the clouds as they exited the vehicle.

Buck looked up to see Hardy standing next to Sheriff McCabe. He walked up, shook hands and said, "You really came through Hardy. Thanks for the equipment but I was surprised to see you here."

Hardy, soaking wet like everyone else and dog-tired, smiled. "I couldn't ask my people to charge into hell unless I was willing to go with them."

He looked at Bax. "Young lady, I understand you have a warrant for my arrest. If you can promise me some dry clothes and some food, I am ready when you are."

Bax looked at Buck and then at both Sheriffs. Buck nodded, and she pulled her handcuffs out of the pouch on her belt.

"Hardy Braxton, you are under arrest. You have the right to remain silent…."

When Bax finished, she asked Hardy to put his hands behind his back, and she applied the cuffs. Sheriff McCabe called over one of his officers and asked him to take Hardy back to Meeker and place him in the holding cell until they could get back to town. He also told him to get him a dry prison jumpsuit and to have someone run over and get him a steak at the Cozy Up.

Sheriff McCabe looked at Buck who looked like he wanted to pass out and he told him to get in the passenger side of his car. He would have one of his deputies drive him to the hospital in Meeker.

Buck asked Bax if she was good and she told him to go on. She would be ok. Buck headed for his car with the help of the deputy. It had been a hell of a day.

Chapter Sixty-Three

Buck woke up in his dark hotel room with a start. He had a headache and ringing in his ears until he realized the ringing was his cell phone, which was sitting on the bedside table. He reached over and picked it up.

"Taylor."

"Hi, Buck. It's Paul Webber. Do you have time to talk?"

Buck, who was now sitting on the side of the bed with his head propped against his hand told him to go ahead. Paul explained that he had continued to research James Robert Galvin and found something he thought might be important. Buck sat up straight and listened carefully to what Paul had to say.

"James Robert Galvin had a son from a previous marriage. I had to scour the country, but I finally found a birth certificate in Enid, Oklahoma that had Galvin listed as the father. I can only assume that Galvin had very little to do with the kid because he was raised by his mother and stepfather and he had the step father's name."

"What's the son's name?" Buck asked.

"His name is Steven Fletcher. The mother's name was Regina Keller. Stepfather is Harold Fletcher."

"Can you background Steven Fletcher?"

Paul explained that he already did. "Fletcher grew up in Enid. In high school, he lettered in football, track, and sharpshooting. He went to the University of Oklahoma and Harvard for law school. Here is where it gets interesting. His current employer is listed as the International Heritage Fund. He is…"

"Mark Richards attorney!" said Buck. "And he was a sharpshooter in high school. Shit Paul, nice work."

Buck hung up and checked his phone. He had four missed calls. He had no idea what time it was, but when he opened the curtains, the sun almost blinded him. He jumped in the shower and was getting dressed when his phone rang.

"Buck, are you ok? I called you four times and no answer."

"I'm good Bax. How long was I out?"

"You've been out about thirty-six hours. You sure you're ok?"

"Yeah, so what's up?"

She told him that Jack Muldoon was awake and on his way to the Rio Blanco Sheriff's office and that Hardy's attorney was requesting a meeting for this afternoon at two.

Buck said he was on his way. He grabbed his gun and badge and clipped them to his belt, grabbed his backpack and ran out the door.

He pulled into the parking lot, grabbed his backpack, walked into the building and presented his ID to the deputy at the desk and headed back to the conference room.

"Looky there," said Sheriff McCabe. "He is alive. You don't look too worse for wear." The Sheriff laughed because Buck looked as bad as he felt. He had assorted cuts and bruises, a black eye, bandages on his knuckles and a concussion. Even with that, Buck was glad to be alive.

Buck smiled and set his backpack down on the desk, grabbed a donut from the box on the desk and a bottle of Coke from the refrigerator. He was starving.

While he ate, he filled everyone in on the phone call, he just had with Paul Webber.

"You think this is the guy who shot at me, but the guy the Sheriff and I talked to was much older than this guy would be?"

"Here's what I'm thinking in my very sore brain. Suppose there was something to Galvin's wife and daughter dying from chemicals that one of Mark Richard's companies dumped near their ranch. Now let's assume for a minute that Fletcher found out Galvin was his real father and then found out he killed himself because of their deaths. He could have decided to get revenge and what better way to do that than from inside the company?"

"Jesus, Buck. That's a lot of assumptions," said Bax. "How would he know he would get a job with Mark Richards? No way that's a coincidence."

Buck wasn't sure how to answer. Bax was right. This was all really slim, and they had no proof of any of this, but the more he thought about, the more he felt he was close. Bax sat down at the table and did an internet search of Steven Fletcher. Buck pulled out his phone and dialed a number.

Tom Whitmore answered on the third ring. "Buck Taylor, twice in one week. To what do I owe the pleasure?"

"Tom, have you ever heard the name, Steven Fletcher?"

"Sure, we all knew Steven."

Tom explained that Steven had contacted Jim Galvin a couple years before his wife and daughter died. Steven had been raised by his mom and stepdad and had no contact with his father until out of the blue he called one day. He wanted to connect. Jim was hesitant at first, but they finally met and really hit it off. He came for a visit and ended up staying for a long time. The family grew very close. Steven was a young attorney and tried to convince Jim to sue, but Jim wasn't interested.

Buck interrupted. "Sue about what?"

"Jim had used a new fertilizer on the ranch, mostly on their vegetables. A few months later, the first signs of the tumors occurred. If I remember right, a couple cows died as well. Jim blamed the fertilizer for the cancer. Jim was a meat eater; his wife was a vegetarian, and that was how they were raising their daughter."

Tom continued, explaining that Steven had tried to get the fertilizer company to cover their medical expenses, and he basically got laughed at, so he tried to get Jim to file a lawsuit. By then it was too late for his wife and daughter. He tried to file a lawsuit after Jim died but the suit was dismissed.

"Steven was heartbroken when Jim killed them. He was back in Oklahoma helping his mom with some legal matter. When he heard the news, he rushed back here and helped with the search for Jim. He took care of all the funeral expenses."

"When Jim killed himself, Steven went off the deep end. Ranting about getting even with those SOBs. Not sure where he is now, but last I heard he went to work at some big financial company his stepdad had worked for. Why you askin?"

Buck didn't answer. Instead, he asked, "Do you remember the name of the fertilizer company and do you know what kind of cars the family drove?"

"Sure. Jim drove an old Chevy pickup truck, and his wife drove an old yellow Ford station wagon. The company was Gardner or something like that. Buck, what's going on?"

"Tom, the car may have been involved in a shooting in Moffat County."

"The one involving one of your agents? Saw the APB but the plate and the description of the driver didn't match their car or anyone I knew."

"Can you have someone run out to the ranch and see if the car is around there someplace and have them take along a fingerprint tech?"

Buck hung up and looked at Bax and the Sheriff. Bax was clicking away on the keys on her laptop, and suddenly she stopped. "Guardian Agricultural Products."

Buck and the Sheriff looked at her, waiting for more.

"Guardian Agricultural Products was started in the nineteen forties. It struggled along until it was purchased by a young entrepreneur in nineteen ninety-eight. The buyer was Mark Richards. The company filed for bankruptcy after allegations came out about one its fertilizer products killing animals. Mark Richards turned the company around. This was the first company he bought after establishing a mutual fund company. Today it is valued at forty billion dollars."

The Sheriff let out a low whistle.

She clicked on another page. "Steven Fletcher, according to everything I could find, has worked for Mark Richard's company for about ten years. Two years ago, he became Mark's personal attorney. I looked up Harold Fletcher, as well. Harold worked as a CPA for the company in the nineties and early two thousands before he retired."

"Would Steven Fletcher try to sue a company that his father worked for?" asked the Sheriff.

"Maybe he didn't know and only found out after his stepdad

retired. It's interesting that he became Mark's personal attorney two years ago and that was about when the fires started," replied Bax.

"I know one thing," said Buck. "We need to talk to Fletcher."

Chapter Sixty-Four

Fletcher would have to wait. Muldoon had been brought into Interrogation One, and Buck needed some answers. Buck opened the door to the interrogation room, walked in and sat down. He looked across the table at a man whose nose was bandaged; he had a split lip, two black eyes, and assorted cuts and bruises. Since Buck didn't look much better, he had no sympathy for the damage he had caused.

Buck laid a file folder on the table and sat back. He wondered how Muldoon would react to questioning? After all, he had been in the military a long time, and when Buck reviewed his file, he noticed that Muldoon had received a great deal of evasion training, as well as, training in how to deal with interrogation. Muldoon had been subjected to some of the most severe interrogation techniques that were in our anti-terrorist playbook. He had been waterboarded, he'd had electrodes connected to his body, and he had been subject to physical and emotional attacks. His record indicated a man who did not crack easily.

"I'm sorry about Margaret Windsong," he said.

Muldoon just shrugged his shoulders, but Buck could see a tear form in the corner of his eye.

"I'll say one thing Jack; may I call you Jack? You are one tough SOB."

"I should have killed you," Muldoon replied unapologetically.

"You certainly tried. I never fought that hard in my life," said Buck. He sat back and looked at Muldoon.

For the next two hours, Buck didn't say a word. So far, he hadn't asked for an attorney, so Buck decided to play it patiently. He needed answers, so he didn't want Muldoon to clam up. So, he sat there quietly.

Buck could see Muldoon was getting anxious. He started fidgeting in his chair, looking around the room and sweating. Muldoon had been subjected to terrible interrogation techniques during his military training. The one thing Buck couldn't find in his file was that he had been tortured with silence and Buck was very good at silence.

Buck finally felt that Muldoon was ready. He opened the file and took out the picture of the charred body of Jimmy Kwon. He looked at it for a minute and slid it across the table. Muldoon tried to stay stone faced, but Buck noticed a small micro reaction in his eyes.

"Why did Jimmy Kwon have to die?" he asked.

Muldoon just stared at the picture. Buck slid another picture out of the folder and looked at. He slid it toward Muldoon, and this one got a definite reaction. Muldoon looked at the picture of Elliot Beech still sitting in the chair in the old pump house. The hole behind his ear was quite visible in the photo.

"Shit," was all he said, but Buck noticed a lot more sweat on his brow and his hands fidgeted enough to jangle the handcuffs.

Buck waited a few more minutes just letting the photos sink in. Then he pulled out another picture and slid it across the table. The image of Margaret Windsong lying in the gulley with her head hanging at a very unnatural angle was more than he could bear, and the tough old fighting guy facade broke in a million pieces. Muldoon hung his head in his hands and cried like a baby. Buck sat back and didn't say another word.

Finally, Muldoon looked up and with tears in his eyes said, "What do you want from me?"

Buck slid several reports out of the folder that he had asked Bax to print off for him from the investigation file. He spread them out on the table. A lot had happened during the thirty-six hours he had been asleep.

"Look Jack, here's the deal. We have you for the murder of Jimmy Kwon and the murder of Elliot Beech. The witnesses and the forensics nail that down. We have the gun you used to kill them both, which we found in your house. We have Kwon's fingerprints in your house and also on the arm of the chair in the pump house. Those two charges alone will get you the death penalty in Colorado. You killed a federal agent, which will get you a federal death sentence and, just so you know, those guys want you bad. We have you for running an illegal prescription drug distribution network. We have you for kidnapping for the town's people you locked in the bunker, flight to avoid prosecution, resisting arrest, assaulting a law enforcement officer and just a whole mess of other crimes, plus the feds want you for the murder and the drug distribution. The list goes on. With all that, if the state or the feds don't kill you, you will spend the rest of your life in jail."

Buck let all that sink in. He only had one question when he walked into the room, and he was holding that for the right moment. Muldoon had turned an interesting pale color and looked like he was going to be sick.

"Oh, I almost forgot about the arson charges for starting the fire at the lodge and causing the wildfire."

He sat back in his chair and waited.

Muldoon sat there, and Buck could see the gears turning in his head. He actually hoped that Muldoon was suffering from the same headache he was right now.

"I may have done all those other things, but I didn't set that fire," Muldoon said.

Buck slid a white pad across the table along with a fine-tipped felt marker and told Muldoon to write his story. Two hours later Muldoon slid the pad back to Buck, sat back and closed his eyes.

Buck read the twenty pages that Muldoon had written. He explained that he had discovered that Kwon was a Fed and that Elliot had been the one to contact him and how he dealt with both of them. He laid out the whole drug distribution set up including the names of some of his principal players. He wrote about finding out that Mark Richards, who had been the one who purchased the ground the town was built on and who had financed the entire operation, had turned on him and was going to ruin him and send him to jail, all because of a stupid lodge.

Buck was no psychologist, but as he read the statement, he could see the paranoia creeping in. Muldoon was probably brilliant when he first put the whole plan together, but some of his decision making was questionable. He finally put down the statement.

"How did you get involved with Mark Richards in the first place?"

The question caught Muldoon off guard, and he glared at Buck.

"You leave her out of this!" he yelled.

"Leave who out of this, Jack. I have no idea who you're talking about."

"Bull shit! All she did was tell me that Richards had sent a Fed into my town. That's it. I will take full blame for everything," he pointed at the pad. "But you stay away from her!" he screamed.

Buck thought he was going to have a heart attack, he was so red in the face as he strained against the handcuffs.

Buck had his answer. "Veronica Richards is your daughter?" he asked.

Muldoon sank into the chair. His face got soft, and his voice got low. "Please, sir. You have my statement. Please don't hurt my little girl. She had nothing to do with any of this, I swear." Tears rolled down his face.

"Ok, Jack. I understand, but I need to know who started the fire at the lodge."

Jack looked up and wiped the tears away. "I have no idea. We put the body in the lodge to embarrass Richards when his first guests arrived. I thought the government started the forest fire to force us out of our town so they could get the drugs. I didn't even know the lodge was the cause until you told me. Thought it was the forest fire that burned the lodge."

Buck thanked him for his candor, gathered up his papers and Jack's statement and left the room. In the hallway, he met the Sheriff and the DA. He handed her the papers and walked away. He needed a handful of aspirin.

Chapter Sixty-Five

They found Buck sitting in the conference room with his head back and his eyes closed.

"Buck, you ok?" asked the Sheriff.

Buck opened his eyes. "Yeah, I'm fine. Just trying to shake this headache."

Muldoon was being processed into the county jail, and the DA was holding a paper in her hand. She handed it to Buck, who read it carefully.

"That's a warrant for Veronica Richards. She is being charged with conspiracy and as an accessory to murder before the fact. From Muldoon's statement, her telling him about the investigation her husband was running on the town directly led to the deaths of Jimmy Kwon and Elliot Beech. She's as responsible as he is," said the DA.

Buck couldn't agree more, and it was the opening he needed to get to Mark Richards and Steven Fletcher. He still wasn't sure how this all would play out, but he had a working theory.

He knew Mark Richards had some shady deals working, and that he had very little direct evidence to convict him. He could use the same charges as they had for Veronica. Mark Richards's investigation into Muldoon also directly led to the deaths of both men. They also had the testimony of Randy Stewart. The picture from the wall in his office was enough to prove a connection between Mark Richards and the illegal dumping.

He knew that Steven Fletcher had set up and executed a very elaborate plan to hurt Mark Richards and had most likely either set the oil well fires or hired someone to do it. He was probably the one who told Veronica about the investigation to ruin Muldoon, not knowing she was his daughter. Logic says he probably had something to do with the fire at the lodge, but Buck still didn't know who actually torched the lodge.

He finished explaining what they knew, and the Sheriff asked, "Why did you believe Muldoon when he said he didn't set the fire?"

One thing Buck knew about career soldiers was that honor was a huge part of their lives. Muldoon had accepted his involvement in all the crimes Buck had listed.

"Accepting the crimes, he had committed was the honorable thing to do, but he was not going to accept being charged for a crime he didn't commit. Call it vanity, call it honor or call it something else, but either way it violated his personal code."

The DA smiled. "Buck, you have an amazing gift for reading people. I am glad you're on our side."

Realizing he had only eaten a donut in the last forty-some hours, Buck decided to walk across the street to the diner and fill up. He pulled out his phone and dialed Pat Sutton at the fire command center.

"Hi, Buck. You doing ok? Heard you got into a hell of a fight."

"Yeah, I'm ok Pat, and you heard correct."

Buck asked him how the fire was doing. He noticed that the

smoke and haze seemed to be gone from the air over Meeker. Pat told him that the fire was about ninety percent contained. He was starting to send some of the firefighters off to other fires around the west. The rain had definitely helped, but Pat had some more to say.

"I owe you a lot, Buck. Getting that heavy equipment and helping lead those townspeople to fight the fire was amazing. At first, I was pissed when we got word what you guys were doing in the town. I figured that against that firestorm, there was no way you could come out ahead and I was worried we would end up burying a lot of people. We understood you had no choice but to stay and fight, but that still took a lot of balls. The wind shift caught us all off guard, and I feared for your safety."

Pat continued. "When we heard that a bunch of the Hotshot teams had to converge on your location because of the wall of flames, we decided it was time to make a stand, so we threw everything we had at that location. It was winner take all and to be honest I had no idea how it was going to turn out. Might have been the biggest mistake of my career, but I had to protect all of you. Once it started raining, I knew we had broken her back. At that point, it was all hands on deck and balls to the walls. I still can't believe how long and hard everyone worked. I owe you one. You ever need anything, you can count on me."

Buck thanked Pat and hung up. He still hadn't heard from Cassie, but he hoped that her team was one of the ones being pulled off the line.

Just before he stepped into the diner, Buck looked down the street. The white pickup truck that had been shadowing him since he arrived was no longer there. He wondered if his visit to Stephanie Street had something to do with his no longer being shadowed. He also wondered if one of the two guys in the truck might have been her brother.

Buck had been toying with the idea that the NETF had targeted the lodge for destruction to make another big statement. He wondered if that was why the gas cans were found outside the building. That thought made him think that something had happened to scare them off.

Could that something have been another fire? That led him back to Steven Fletcher. Did Fletcher set the fire in the lodge to take away one of Richards' prize possessions, without knowing that Muldoon had put a body in the lodge to embarrass Richards? He couldn't wait to get Fletcher and the Richards into an interrogation room.

Buck grabbed a quick lunch at the counter and then headed back to the Sheriff's office. It was almost time to meet with Hardy.

Chapter Sixty-Six

Hardy Braxton and Irv Tuttleman were seated at the table in the conference room opposite Sheriff McCabe, Sheriff Trujillo, and Bax when Buck walked into the room. Bax gave Buck a confused look wondering why they were all there. He just shook his head.

Buck took the seat next to Sheriff McCabe and looked at Hardy. Sheriff McCabe told him that they were waiting for a representative from the US Attorney's office. As they were talking, Bill Unger stepped into the room and took a seat.

Buck was watching Hardy the entire time, and he thought Hardy looked remarkably calm. He also noticed the bags under his eyes. He was betting Hardy hadn't slept much in the past couple days. Jail will do that to a person.

Buck was just about to ask Hardy how he was holding up when a tall, statuesque black woman walked into the conference room followed by a young man with a briefcase and a young woman pulling a small suitcase on wheels.

"Good evening folks don't get up. I am Assistant US Attorney Olivia Rivera." She pointed towards the young man. "This is James Worthington, my associate and the young woman setting up the in the corner is Angie Jackman. Angie is a court reporter and will be making a transcript of everything we say here today. Does anyone have any objection to a written transcript as well as a recorded transcript?" She placed a small digital recorder in the center of the table.

She asked each person around the table to introduce themselves and state the organization they represented. Once that was completed she sat down and opened up a black leather-bound notebook. Buck had never worked with this woman before, so he decided to just listen to what she had to say.

Ms. Rivera looked at Hardy and then at Tuttleman. "Mr. Tuttleman, you pulled a lot of strings to get this meeting, so why don't you tell us why we are all here."

Tuttleman opened a folder he had sitting in front of him and slid a document across the table to Ms. Rivera, who picked it up and read through the three pages. She slid the papers over to Buck, and he, and the Sheriffs each read through the document. He then passed it to Bax and Bill Unger.

"For the record. The document we have just received from Mr. Tuttleman is a statement alleging certain facts as they pertain to the illegal dumping of hazardous chemicals, as well as a proposal for how to remedy those allegations in what Mr. Tuttleman believes is a fair and equitable way. Is that correct Mr. Tuttleman?"

"That is correct."

She waved her hand to indicate that he should continue. Irv Tuttleman explained that his client, Mr. Braxton, had entered into an agreement with Mark Richards to develop several oil fields and that Mark Richards had violated that agreement by getting involved in the dumping of illegal chemicals. He said that Hardy was totally unaware of the dumping. He pulled a piece of paper out of his briefcase and slid it across the table.

"This is a signed and notarized statement from the drilling contractor who was hired at the request of Mark Richards. He states that he falsified the drilling reports and inventory reports at Mark Richards' direction."

He went on to state that even though Hardy was unaware of the situation, he is willing to take responsibility for the dumping since the wells belong to his company, provided he is given complete immunity in exchange for testifying against Mark Richards. He also agrees to deposit five million dollars into an account that would be used to clean up the three well sites under his name and to help anyone in the county impacted by the dumping, as long as they can provide proof that the contamination was a result of the dumping of the chemicals in the wells.

He then reached down and picked up a box off the floor. "This box is one of several that contains information we believe could be used to prosecute Mark Richards for numerous crimes. Mr. Braxton and Mr. Richards are involved in several companies besides energy development, and after a careful review, we are concerned about possible illegal activities that may be taking place at some of those businesses. We will surrender these boxes to agents of the federal government once we have reached an immunity agreement."

Ms. Rivera asked Hardy and his attorney to wait in the hall while they discussed the matter. They rose from their seats and left the room. She then turned her attention to the folks in the room.

"This is a very complicated situation which I am going to make more complicated. The US Justice Department has been running a year-long investigation into Mark Richards' business dealings, and before I ask you to agree with this immunity deal, you need to know that the US Attorney General and the Governor of

Colorado have both signed off on the deal. It seems Mr. Braxton has friends in high places."

Everyone at the table looked surprised, except Buck. He knew that Hardy's political connections ran deep. He was surprised however, that the Director hadn't called him to fill him in, but sometimes that's the way things went. Buck would have been inclined to go along with the deal anyway and not because of family loyalty.

It was unlikely that Hardy would have received jail time, anyway. He was an upstanding member of the community, and he had been taken advantage of by Mark Richards just like everyone else he dealt with, but more importantly, Hardy had come through when they needed him, and he had come through in a big way.

Ms. Rivera went on to explain that several small development companies had come to them with complaints detailing the way Mark Richards did business. She told them that these companies, just like Hardy's company, have been caught in one crime or another and that they have very little in the way of records to implicate Mark Richards.

"A sample of the information Mr. Tuttleman has offered to provide was reviewed by subject matter experts at the Justice Department, last night, and they believe this may be the first time we have a chance to penetrate Mark Richards' world. We have spoken with the District Attorneys in each of your respective counties, and they are willing to go along with whatever decision you make. If you decide to pursue this on your own, we will not interfere, but understand that we can do a lot of things you can't do or don't have the resources to do."

"We have asked you all here because many of the crimes in question are still considered to be local crimes, and we are asking you, on behalf of the United States government, to allow us to take jurisdiction over those crimes. We can now discuss this if you wish."

"It sounds like the decision has already been made, way above us, so why even ask?" asked Bax.

Everyone around the table nodded, except Buck. He looked around the table.

"Bax and I were sent here to help you guys solve a couple, what we thought were unrelated, crimes which we now know are part of what we all believe to be a larger criminal enterprise. I, as much as anyone in this room, would like to get my hands on Mark Richards and his associates and prosecute the shit out of them, but the truth is, the evidence we have against him is mostly conjecture. We all know what he has done, we just can't prove most of it. Ms. Rivera is correct. They have the resources, meaning mostly money, and the infrastructure to run this investigation much better than we can. I believe the information they are offering can be better utilized by the federal government. That said, we will also go along with whatever decision you make."

Both Sheriffs stood up and walked to the back of the conference room. Everyone else watched as they calmly discussed their options. Bax looked like she was ready to explode until he gave her a look that said, "let it go for now."

The Sheriffs stepped back to the table and sat down. Sheriff Trujillo asked the one and only question they had decided on. "We understand that Hardy Braxton gets a pass, but per this agreement Mark Richards, his wife and attorney are completely out of our reach, correct? What happens if you can't prosecute?"

"You are correct. If we fail to prosecute at the federal level, then these people are fair game." Both Sheriffs nodded their agreement.

Chapter Sixty-Seven

Bax was not happy and hadn't been since Ms. Rivera had left, along with copies of all their files. They were sitting on a bench outside the Sheriff's office. Well, Buck was seated, Bax was pacing back and forth.

"It's not fair. We worked our asses off trying to solve these crimes and the Feds are just going the waltz in here and take all of our work. I was shot at, Buck. I want the son of a bitch who did that."

Buck let her get it out of her system, and when she finally calmed down, he said, "You heard what the Director said. The governor is going to be all over the Justice Department to make sure they don't let this drop. You know Governor Kennedy as well as I do, he is not going to let this go."

Bax knew he was right, she just hated to admit it. Prosecuting someone like Richards was going to cost a fortune and the state could not bear that cost all alone, besides the crimes that were being investigated covered violations of federal laws as well as laws in multiple states. This investigation and eventual trial would go on for years.

"Look at it this way," he said. "We stopped a potential environmental crisis here and alerted several other states so that they could begin fixing the problem with the help of the EPA. We broke up a major international prescription drug ring and solved two murders, including the murder of a federal agent and we helped put out a monster forest fire. Not bad for less than a weeks' worth of work."

"But we still don't know who shot at me, and we don't know who burned the lodge down. I hate walking away and leaving the job unfinished."

"Look, Bax, we can't solve them all. All we can do is the best we can do. You did great work on this, and I am proud to have been able to work with you, so go back to the hotel, close out your investigation report and head home tomorrow. We will never run out of crimes to solve."

"Thanks, Buck, it was a real pleasure working with you again."

She gave him a hug and headed for her car. Buck sat there for a few minutes and just enjoyed the silence. He was just about to get up when his phone rang. He looked at the number and smiled.

"Hey, Jason. I thought you fell off the ends of the earth. Where you been?"

His son, Jason, explained that he had gone on a fly-fishing trip to Alaska with some of the guys from his architecture firm. He only got home this afternoon and was stunned with everything that had happened while he was gone. Buck filled him in on some of the events that had unfolded and then suggested they get together the following weekend and he would tell him and his wife the whole story. Jason told him to come to Boulder, and they would do a bar-b-que, and Buck agreed. He hung up the phone just as the rain started. It wasn't heavy, just a nice gentle rain and Buck decided to do something he hadn't done in a long time.

He walked down the street in the rain, to a little mom and pop ice cream parlor. When the kids were younger, and they did a lot of family camping, one of their family traditions was to go out for ice cream. The only stipulation was that it had to be when it was raining. They used to all pile in the car, drive to the nearest place where they could get ice cream and then stand under an overhang of some kind and eat their ice creams and listen to the rain. Even after the kids were grown, Buck and Lucy had continued the tradition. He hadn't done it since Lucy died.

Buck stepped out of the ice cream parlor, walked to the building next door and stood under the awning, his thoughts turning to Lucy and how much he missed her. Tears formed in his eyes and he just stared at the street lost in thought.

At first, he didn't notice that someone had walked up and stood next to him. When he looked over, the first thing he saw was the yellow firefighter shirt and the green suspenders. Cassie stood there eating an ice cream cone. She reached over and wiped a tear from his cheek, then she laid her head against his chest, and he reached around, put his arm around her shoulders and pulled her tighter. With tears in her eyes, she softly said,

"Mom would have loved this."

Epilogue

Steven Fletcher had been told by an anonymous source in the Justice Department that they were all being investigated for various crimes and he filled Mark Richards and his wife in on what he had discovered. He knew Mark and Veronica were safe for now since they were on their private island and had no fear of extradition. He would join them after he cleared up some legal matters and then they would come up with a plan to squash the investigations. A lot of politicians owed their careers to Mark, and his money, so he was confident they could end this before it really got started. At least that was the story he told Mark.

So here they were, Mark and Veronica, on a beautiful white sand beach in a quiet cove on their private island. Veronica was lying naked on a blanket and looked like a Greek goddess with her blond hair and incredible body.

Mark didn't even notice. He was too busy walking up and down the same hundred foot of beach, screaming into his cell phone. Veronica had no idea who he was yelling at, but it was a heated conversation.

Mark had turned and was walking back in her direction when he suddenly stopped and stared out towards the breakwater.

He clicked off his phone, shoved it into the pocket of his shorts, he stepped closer to the water's edge and raised his hand up to shield his eyes.

"Who the fuck does this guy think he is!" he was yelling.

He turned to Veronica and started pointing.

"This is my fucking island, what the fuck? Can't he read the God damn signs?"

Veronica sat up on the blanket and looked towards the end of the secluded bay. A small boat was coming through the channel that cut through the coral reef that protected this little bit of heaven. Mark watched as the boat seemed to slow down. It was almost a half mile across the bay, so he was having trouble making out who was steering it, but he would find out, and this guy was going to have all the trouble he could handle.

He stepped into the water and placed his hands on his hips looking defiantly towards the little boat. The bullet hit him square in the chest, fragmented and blew his spine out through his back. Mark Richards fell over onto the beach. His death had occurred without a sound.

The little boat started moving again and headed for the beach where it plowed into the sand and stopped. An older man with gray hair and a slight beard jumped out of the boat and looked at the body lying in the sand. He still carried his rifle with the unusual looking silencer.

"I really do need to thank the welder. This thing works perfectly," he said to no one in particular.

He looked over at the still naked Veronica sitting on the blanket, and headed in her direction. Veronica, at that very moment, had become the wealthiest woman in the world and that thought made her smile. The guy stopped at the foot of her blanket, and they looked at each other. Steven Fletcher laid the rifle down next to the blanket and pulled off his gray wig and beard. He stripped off his shirt and shorts as Veronica laid back on the blanket and spread her legs.

Steven knelt down on the edge of the blanket and then laid down on top of Veronica. She was lying there listening to his grunts and groans, but she was thinking about the fact that she could have anything or anyone she wanted.

Steven turned his head towards her left shoulder. She slowly put her right hand under the blanket, dug down in the sand a couple of inches and pulled out a six-inch stiletto.

BONUS SHORT STORY

A Very Merry PISmas

A BUCK TAYLOR/CRIME SERIES SHORT STORY

BY

CHUCK MORGAN

Aspen, Colorado has been called the playground of the rich and famous and with good reason. You can find some of the finest stores in the world downtown, and the resort attracts the wealthiest people in the world to ski its slopes. If you stood at the end of the street, you would think you were looking at a Norman Rockwell painting.

The holiday season was in full swing throughout the Roaring Fork Valley, but it was no more impressive than downtown. The shops and restaurants were decked out in their finest holiday decorations and the snow that had been falling for the past couple days, glistened in the sunlight.

Holiday shoppers scurried to and fro, like soldiers on a mission, with shopping lists in hand. It was a race to see who could fulfill their list the fastest. The store windows festively displayed the latest fashions, the newest toys or the most desired electronic games. Yes, the holiday season was in full swing in Aspen for almost everyone.

PIS loved to sit on one of the benches along the pedestrian walkway and just watch the people. Wearing his familiar gray tuxedo pants, faded white shirt, his trademark red cummerbund and ascot, and moccasin boots, he was a familiar sight on Aspen's streets. He had shown up in Aspen twenty years ago and became one of its most interesting and intriguing characters.

He walked the streets and alleys of Aspen every day wearing his black cotton coat and black beret, no matter the temperature. He appeared to be homeless, but no one had ever found him sleeping in the park or in a doorway, and he always had enough money to buy his nightly snifter of brandy at a local watering hole.

Unlike most of the homeless in Aspen, PIS never panhandled for money, and at night he could be seen walking into the woods at the edge of town only to disappear. PIS was truly an enigma.

The storm had dropped over a foot of new snow, but that didn't deter the shoppers as they hurried along the sidewalks with their coffee in one hand and cell phone in the other. There was holiday magic in the air.

*****

PIS spotted the little blond girl from a block away, and he watched her from his spot on the bench. It wasn't unusual to see kids alone on the sidewalks of Aspen and the people rushing by didn't seem to notice her, which PIS thought was odd.

The little girl was wearing pink footy pajamas and a ratty looking sweater that was way too big for her tiny body. The sweater wasn't buttoned and flapped open against the frigid morning air.

PIS stood up and walked towards the little girl who appeared lost and out of place.

"Good morning, young lady. It's a marvelous day for a stroll. Is it not?" His silky-smooth British accent flowed like honey as he knelt next to her.

She stopped and looked up at this strange person, her eyes got large, and she lowered her face. PIS was concerned because her pajama feet were soaking wet and her skin was a shade of gray PIS had seen before amongst hypothermia victims.

He kept his voice low as he leaned closer to her. "Does your mommy know you are out here alone?"

The little girl hesitated at first and then in a voice that was nothing more than a whisper said, "Mommy won't wake up, and I'm hungry."

"Can you show me where you live?"

The little girl remained silent, and PIS could see her body shake. He knew he needed to do something right away, so he picked the little girl up and headed towards the Aspen Police Dept, three blocks away.

****

Aspen Police Chief, Robert Brady, was standing in the lobby talking with two of his officers who were decorating a small Christmas tree when PIS came through the front door carrying the little girl.

"Hey PIS. What have you got there?"

"Not sure, Chief Brady. Found her walking, all by herself, on the pedestrian mall. I think she might be on the edge of hypothermia."

The Chief yelled for his front desk officer to call for paramedics, and he sent an officer to get a couple blankets.

PIS explained what he knew, and the lines on the Chief's face grew deeper when he told him that the little girl said her mommy wouldn't wake up.

While the officer wrapped the little girl in the blankets, the Chief took PIS aside.

"Any thoughts on where she might have come from?"

PIS thought about the question for a minute. "No idea. I haven't seen her around here before today, but if it is ok with you, I would like to see if I can backtrack her from where I found her. Might get lucky if her tracks are still there."

"That's a real longshot," said the Chief. "Might as well give it a try."

PIS was one of the finest trackers in the county. He often worked for the local hunting guides, helping them find game, and on many occasions, he worked with the local police or sheriff to track down criminals or missing persons. No one knew where he had developed his skills, but they were incredible. If anyone could track this little girl, it was him.

PIS buttoned up his old black coat and stepped through the door just as the paramedics pulled up. Nodding to the two techs, he headed back to where he had first encountered the girl.

Standing on the sidewalk, PIS stood and stared at the ground. His eyes focused on the rippled print made by her pajama foot as he memorized every detail of the print. He raised his eyes and scanned ahead. First spotting her near the corner, he headed in that direction, his eyes never leaving the ground.

Several people stopped to watch this tall, odd man as he scanned the ground. Many of the tourists he passed wondered out loud if he was a street performer. Several of the shopkeepers stepped out of their front doors and watched him as he worked. They knew he was on a mission and didn't want to disturb him.

PIS was fortunate that the morning cold kept many people off the sidewalks, so he moved briskly. Each time he lost the prints, he had to backtrack and circle around in ever-widening circles until he spotted them again. Most people found tracking to be tedious, but not PIS. Tracking was where he felt the most at home.

PIS moved beyond downtown and headed into a more residential neighborhood when he looked back and spotted Chief Brady walking a few feet behind him. They were attracting a lot of attention, and the Chief was showing a picture of the girl, on his phone, to people they passed on the street.

****

PIS was amazed at how far they had walked. They were now several blocks from downtown, and he stopped and scratched his three-day-old growth of beard. He had lost the trail, and no matter what he did he couldn't find the track. He was kneeling on the ground staring into the distance when the Chief walked up behind him.

"What do you think, PIS?"

PIS stood up and looked around. "I think she must have started from somewhere around here." The scowl on his face showed the frustration he was feeling.

Just then he spotted a group of people in the park, and he had an idea. Borrowing the Chief's phone, he walked across the street and approached the group of homeless vets who occupied the park. Showing the picture around got a response from several of the group, and he raced back across the street to the Chief.

"She lives with her mother and two younger sisters in the building on the corner. Her father is on active duty somewhere overseas. They haven't seen the mother in a couple days."

PIS and the Chief ran down the street to the small rundown apartment building. The Chief called his dispatcher and requested back up and paramedics as they ran. At the building, the Chief banged on the door of the Manager's apartment until a sleepy voice yelled, "Coming, hold your horses."

The door opened, and a disheveled looking woman wearing a red housecoat and slippers stared at the Chief and PIS. The Chief held up his phone so the woman could see the picture.

"She live here?"

The woman stared at the picture, trying to focus her bloodshot eyes. "Yeah, looks like one of the brats from apartment four, around back. What's this all about?"

By the time she asked the question, PIS and the Chief were tearing around the corner to the back of the building. They could hear the sirens announcing the arrival of the ambulance and the first patrol officer.

Unit four was a basement unit, and they could see newspapers taped to the front window, acting as either insulation or curtains. They walked down the stairs, and the Chief knocked. They could hear tiny footsteps approaching the door which opened revealing another little blond girl in pink footy pajamas who was the spitting image of her older sister.

The first thing PIS noticed as they stepped into the front entry was the temperature. It felt as cold inside as it did outside.

The Chief asked the little girl if her mommy was home and the girl pointed to the one bedroom in the place. Telling PIS to stay back with the little girl he walked over and opened the door. The woman in the bed looked near death as the Chief approached. He could hear shallow, faint breaths as he touched her forehead. She was as cold as ice. As he turned to look at PIS, two little sets of identical eyes looked up at him. The sadness in those eyes was overwhelming.

PIS stepped aside with the two little girls as the paramedics rushed into the apartment followed by a female police officer. The Chief stepped out of the room, looked at PIS and shook his head. PIS looked at the two little girls, a tear rolling down his cheek.

****

The mother had remained in a coma for three days before passing away two days before Christmas. The doctor told the Chief that she had suffered a cerebral hemorrhage. There was nothing they could do for her. The three little girls, Amanda, Jessica and Theresa, were moved in with a foster family until their relatives could be located. The Chief and PIS had looked through the apartment while the female officer found clothes and got the girls dressed. They found several letters from the girls' father.

The father was in the military and was somewhere overseas on assignment. The Pentagon, at the request of the Chief, had been trying to locate him but with the holidays, things were not moving quickly, and the Chief was not hopeful. PIS's eyes showed the sadness he was feeling knowing the three girls, who had just lost their mother, would spend Christmas without their father.

Christmas Eve was cold and clear, and Aspen looked like a winter wonderland, the streets and stores adorned in holiday finery. Frantic shoppers were hurrying from shop to shop, looking for those last-minute gifts or bargains to fill out their lists. The Chief had just stepped through the front doors and was ready to head home when a stretch limo pulled up in front of the police department. The driver stepped out and ran around to the back door and opened it.

The soldier who stepped out of the back looked bewildered as he stood up and looked around. He spotted the Chief and walked towards him.

He introduced himself to the Chief and said he had been told his wife had passed away and he came for his three daughters. The Chief looked dumbfounded.

The last information the Chief had gotten from the Pentagon was that the soldier was at a forward base in the mountains of Afghanistan and they were trying to get word to him. It didn't look good for getting him home by Christmas.

The Chief invited the young Captain into his office, so he could call the foster family and let them know they were on their way. The Captain explained that they were completely isolated until a British commando unit fought their way into the camp and told him that his wife had died and they were there to take him home. He thought they were joking until his commanding officer got word from headquarters that he was to leave with the commandos.

He was taken to Bagram airbase by helicopter, where a General he had never met before, handed him his leave papers and put him on a small civilian jet. The jet came with a British flight crew and a butler, but he was fascinated by the coat of arms emblazoned on the back of the leather seats. The butler noticed him staring and explained that it was a variant of the royal coat of arms of the United Kingdom.

Thirty hours later he landed at the airport in Aspen where a limo was waiting to take him to his daughters. The driver had been told to stop at police headquarters to get the address for the foster family.

The Chief was as stunned by this turn of events as the Captain was. He had no idea who made the travel arrangements for the Captain, but he was glad he was in Aspen and could spend Christmas with his children. He thought it was strange that it was the British who had managed to get him out of Afghanistan and was fascinated when the Captain told him about the plane.

"Was it possible?" he thought. "No way. The only Brit that the Chief knew was PIS, but PIS was just a homeless guy. Right?"

****

At the foster home, the three girls ran down the sidewalk and leaped into the arms of their father. The Chief stood behind them and wiped away the tears from his eyes. As the happy family walked back up the stairs, the oldest girl, Theresa, turned and ran back towards him and wrapped her arms around his legs. In a soft little voice she said, "thank you," and then ran off to join her family.

The Chief climbed into his SUV and headed home. "Maybe there really were Christmas miracles," he thought as he drove away.

****

PIS watched the scene at the foster home from across the street in a small neighborhood park. As the Chief drove off, he smiled, buttoned up his coat and headed downtown. "Christmas truly was a magical time," he thought.

Acknowledgment

A special thank you to my daughter Christina J Morgan, my unofficial editor-in-chief. She devoted a significant amount of time making sure the book was presented as perfectly as possible. Any mistakes the reader may find are solely the responsibility of the author.

Also, I would like to thank my family for all of their encouragement. I have been telling them stories since they were little, and I always told them that someone should be writing this stuff down. I finally decided to write it down myself.

A special thanks to my other daughter Stephanie Morgan for being my Beta reader and offering some great comments as we went through the process.

I want to thank my closest friend, Trish Moakler-Herud. She has been encouraging me for years to write my stories down. I hope this will make her proud.

Finally, a very special thanks to my late wife, Jane. She pushed me for years to become a writer, and my biggest regret is that she didn't live long enough to see it happen. I love her with all my heart and miss her every day. I think she would be pleased.

About The Author

Chuck Morgan attended Seton Hall University and Regis College and spent thirty-five years as a construction project manager. He is an avid outdoorsman, an Eagle Scout, and a licensed private pilot. He enjoys camping, hiking, mountain biking, and especially fly-fishing.

He is the author of the "Crime" series, featuring Colorado Bureau of Investigation agent Buck Taylor. The series includes *Crime Interrupted, Crime Delayed and Crime Unsolved.*

He is also the author of *Her Name Was Jane*, a memoir about his late wife's nine-year battle with breast cancer. He has three children, three grandchildren, and two dogs. He resides in Lone Tree, Colorado.

www.ingramcontent.com/pod-product-compliance
Lightning Source LLC
Chambersburg PA
CBHW071955110726
47910CB00005B/1544